IMPRINT
CLASSICS

The Recollections of
GEOFFRY HAMLYN

HENRY KINGSLEY

Introduced by
Susan K. Martin

Angus&Robertson
An imprint of HarperCollins*Publishers*

An Angus & Robertson Publication

Angus&Robertson, an imprint of
HarperCollins*Publishers*
25 Ryde Road, Pymble, Sydney, NSW 2073, Australia
31 View Road, Glenfield, Auckland 10, New Zealand

First published in 1859 by Macmillan, Cambridge
This Imprint Classics edition published in 1993

National Library of Australia
Cataloguing-in-Publication data:

Kingsley, Henry, 1830–1876
  The recollections of Geoffry Hamlyn.

  ISBN 0 207 17953 0.
  I. Martin, Susan K. II. Title.
A823.1

Cover: Eugene von Guerard, Australia, 1811–1901,
Waterfall, Strath Creek 1862.
Oil on canvas, 83.2 x 65.7 cm. Purchased 1967.
Reproduced with the kind permission of the Art Gallery of New South Wales.
Printed in Australia by Griffin Paperbacks, Adelaide

9 8 7 6 5 4 3 2 1
97 96 95 94 93

CONTENTS

To my father and mother this book,
the fruit of so many weary years of separation,
is dedicated with the deepest love and reverence

~

INTRODUCTION

Commonly regarded in the nineteenth and early twentieth century as the "first" and best colonial Australian novel, Henry Kingsley's 1859 epic, *The Recollections of Geoffry Hamlyn*, looks, in the 1990s, more like a handbook for rebuilding the British class system in Australia. The move of the Buckleys and their friends and acquaintances to Gippsland is not a lonely emigration but the transferral of an entire way of life from England to a place which is depicted as being even more suited to it.

One of the ways in which *Geoffry Hamlyn* sets up an old hierarchy for a new land is by enacting the story of an "ideal" settlement within its own narrative. The novel opens with the patriarchs sitting on the verandah in the successful twilight of a well-spent life, but almost immediately reverts to England and to a setting which at first appears idyllic, but is shown to be partially exhausted and in danger of disintegration. As one of the first to leave, Geoffry Hamlyn's friend

James Stockbridge, says:

> . . . the Old Country . . . is getting too crowded
> for men to live in without a hard push, and
> depend on it, when poor men are afraid to marry
> for fear of having children which they can't sup-
> port, it is time to move somewhere. The hive is too
> hot, and the bees must swarm, so that those that
> go will both better themselves and better those
> they leave behind them, by giving them more
> room to work and succeed. (20)

Thus the solution to overcrowding and lack of land in
Britain is outlined in the conservative utopian vision
of Australia offered by *Geoffry Hamlyn*. If you could,
miraculously, transport a well-ordered English village
to a new place, with plenty of land and sunshine, a
new world order could be established. Not a socialist
new world order such as William Lane outlined in the
1890s in *The Workingman's Paradise*, but a new
world order just like the old one, only with better
weather and more sheep.

This central philosophy of the novel becomes evident in the first view of Australia that we get in its
pages: "A new heaven and a new earth! Tier beyond
tier, height above height, the great wooded ranges go
rolling away west-ward, till on the lofty sky-line they
are crowned with a gleam of everlasting snow . . ."
(135–6) Into this biblical vista is seen advancing a
new party of settlers—a "scene so venerable and
ancient, so seldom seen in the Old World—the patriarchs moving into the desert with all their wealth, to
find a new pasture-ground." Kingsley makes use of
this glorified biblical language throughout *Geoffry
Hamlyn*, and it has the effect of both justifying and
elevating a white invasion into a holy pilgrimage and
a natural progression. The metaphors are rather confused—sometimes it is as bees swarming and some-

times as new Adams and Eves, and sometimes as new children of Noah that the white settlers establish themselves in Australia.

Engaged in a somewhat difficult juggling act Henry Kingsley recounts the settling of the Buckleys and friends into Gippsland during the first half of the nineteenth century. On the one hand this venture must seem new, dangerous and adventurous. On the other hand, if, as I am arguing, Kingsley is laying out a viable Imperial project, a sort of blueprint, it must seem familiar, achievable and not too dangerous.

One of the ways in which the project is made familiar and attractive is by more or less literally transferring an entire Devon village, complete, to Gippsland. The novel works like the disassembly and reassembly of a jigsaw. Somewhat remarkably for a new land 10 000 miles from the old, virtually everyone who turns up in the area occupied by our heroes has previously been sighted living within a twelve mile radius of the protagonists in England. After the arrival of the third or fourth stranger-on-horse-back who turns out to be a long-lost bosom friend of the family, readers are likely to be racking their brains to determine who could possibly be left, ostensibly in Devon but in fact just about to ride up to the door. The use of this sort of coincidence is common in Victorian fiction. In *Geoffry Hamlyn* it feeds the narrative, but also reinforces a picture of the possibility of having your old British lifestyle but having it better; having your cake but eating it too.

The jigsaw construction is not confined to the pattern of transfer—of faithful servants and gentlemanly friends—from England to Australia. The next generation fit together rather neatly as well, luckily for them, and for the continuation of primogeniture and good British stock in the new land. Sam Buckley and Alice Brentwood, destined for one another by good looks, good breeding and geography, not to mention the meaningful glances of all their nearest relatives, fortuitously fall in love at first sight. For the new Eden to work out, though, a few glitches from the old world must be dispensed with, and thus poor Charles Hawker, unfortunate offspring of a bad-tempered mother and a father of bad blood, must be killed off in the narrative, rather than allowed to continue his tainted line. The fact that his father George is a forger and coiner is, of course, significant in the symbolic system of the novel—George has turned out Charles like a false coin or a bad signature in the human economy of the new settlement.

In the long run our protagonists turn out to be too pure a line to actually stay in the new land. The jigsaw is undone and reassembled back in the old country—with the difference that Australian wealth has enabled the settlers to reclaim their hereditary lands and titles, and reinvigorate the English class system. To return to the metaphor used by James Stockbridge at the beginning of the novel—the bees are incited to swarm, but their leaders get to return to the hive, having effectively lured the dross and excess of old England to the new country to follow their example, but presumably not follow them back.

Contradictory projects are laid out here for the 1850s reader. The noble project of setting up as "patriarchs" in a new land is undercut by the somewhat flurried return of the patriarchs to the old land. The stress laid on the high moral fibre and superior standards of the settlers does not quite erase the fact that their noble venture, in retrospect, looks more like a vulgar get-rich-quick scheme of colonial exploitation and land speculation.

It is this "hidden" contradiction which Joseph Furphy satirises 50 years later in the 1904 novel *Such is Life*. In this novel Sam Buckley's noble daughter is

returned to Australia as an evil-tempered and preten-
tious woman working as a housekeeper after three
dubious marriages. Her father Sam has died bankrupt,
"snuffed out by apoplexy" after a life "addicted to
high living and extremely plain thinking".[1] Joseph
Furphy refers scornfully, in the democratic nationalist
fervour of the 1890s, to the "slender-witted, virgin-
souled, overgrown schoolboys who fill Henry
Kingsley's exceedingly trashy and misleading novel
with their insufferable twaddle." (164)

There are two things being colonised in *Geoffry
Hamlyn*—and they're not so far apart—Australia and
women. The discussions of emigration at the beginning of the book are parallel to, and set off by, the
romantic irrationalities of pretty Mary Thornton. The
desire and devotion of Geoffry Hamlyn and James
Stockbridge are transferred from the fickle Mary, who
chooses an unworthy suitor, to Australia, an object of
devotion likely to be a little more forthcoming (and as
a wealthy "woman" who might share her riches
through marriage). In settler cultures the country is
often figured in gendered terms.[2] The critic Kay
Schaffer has pointed out the ways in which Australia
has been viewed as a female in white Australian culture, most commonly as bad mother.[3]

In *Geoffry Hamlyn* Australia is depicted as a welcoming new land, a cure for the broken hearts of
Hamlyn and Stockbridge, and in part this is effected
by setting up Mary as the bad woman—unwelcoming,
not accepting the men who could make her fertile and
happy, who could "cultivate her"—so that Australia
can star as good woman—welcoming, accommodat-
ing, virgin land eagerly awaiting some good British
seed.

The negotiations around the settlement established
by Hamlyn, Stockbridge and the Buckleys are played

out in part through the contrasts of these good and bad females. If you hitch up with the good woman, Australia, and take good care of her, and remain faithful, you will be rewarded by her with prosperity and the fruits of her fertility.

At the same time, however, Mary and Australia are paralleled. Both have their fiery tempers. Note, for instance, the way in which the bushfire is anthropomorphised in *Geoffry Hamlyn* (203–4). Both "females" suffer reverses and must be borne with, cared for and protected. To take the connection to a perhaps unpleasant extent, both women are secretly married to "black men" who must be fought with and destroyed before the rightful British owners can take up occupation.

So Mary is both opposite to Australia in order to show Australia in the most charming light, *and* she is paralleled to it—even difficult women will turn out well in the end if sufficient attention is paid to them. The former, unsuitable, accidental partner, and any associated bad fruit is despatched. Mary and Tom Troubridge, like country and settler, then prepare to spend prosperous years ahead, raising the fruits of an appropriate union between tamed female and good British stock.

One of the problems under consideration in *Geoffry Hamlyn*, with the women, as well as with Australia, is the question of ownership. You can take up occupation with a woman, as Troubridge does with Mary, and you can take up occupation of the land, but real ownership requires more than this. In each case the problem seems to be one of former attachments, though this is more subtly presented in the case of the Aborigines' prior rights in Australia. Australia as already "married" is not stressed, but the necessity of fighting for her, and getting rid of rival claims, is.

A lot of nineteenth-century Australian men's fiction

depicts life on the land and settlement as a series of heroic battles—the bushfire battle, the drought battle, the flood battle, the search for the lost child, the bushranger battle and the battle with the Aborigines. This, I believe, is about an anxiety over ownership. There is a certain wistfulness in early Australian fiction for the battles and treaties of North American settlement. How do you establish ownership and right to a piece of territory without in some sense fighting for it? Some women writers of the period, I would argue, did find other ways of producing an idea of ownership and belonging, but for men's fiction the solution usually lay in rewriting white settlement as a series of fights, with themselves as the winners—each victory establishing or confirming their god-given right to be there.

At the same time, such books are careful not to suggest that the Aborigines have prior rights to the territory under dispute, or legitimate complaints against the "settlers". One of the ways of delegitimising the Aboriginal claims in this fiction, it seems, is by seldom or never having people depicted as defending their own territory. In *Geoffry Hamlyn* "black trouble" arises elsewhere. When a local squatter warns Geoffry and Jim of attacking Aborigines, he tells them: "I don't think they are Macquarrie [that is, local] blacks; I fancy they must have come up from the Darling, through the marshes." (208) In this way their violence can be seen as irrational and unprovoked, as some sort of natural savagery, rather than any concerted programme of guerilla defence. The whole notion of "troublesome" blacks trivialises their actions, and of course the Europeans always win such encounters.

Although Jim Stockbridge is killed by a spear at this point in the narrative, the rest of the Aborigines are frightened off; we only learn about a hundred pages later, and incidentally, that Hamlyn has assuaged his grief with a massacre, fully approved, though not dwelt on: "Ye saved many good lives by that raid of yours after Stockbridge was killed. The devils wanted a lesson, and ye gar'd them read one wi' a vengeance!" (359)

Novels such as *Geoffry Hamlyn* are about the imaginative settling of the country—about naturalising the notion of white ownership and white methods in Australia. The women come in handy again in this context, in that the opposition between Aborigines and whites as belonging on the land is played out through another contrast of women—this time through Alice Brentwood and the old Aboriginal woman called 'old Sally' who comes to visit the Brentwoods at the same time as young Sam Buckley does.

Most of the Aborigines who appear in *Geoffry Hamlyn* seem intended as humorous "types", in the same way that the representation of Aborigines in painting of the period went from the "noble savage" stereotype to caricature. In addition, Aboriginal people are used to highlight the supposedly superior aspects of the white settlers. When young Sam Buckley is sitting on the Brentwood's verandah awaiting Captain Brentwood's as yet unseen daughter he glances at:

The bright green arch which separated the dark verandah from the bright hot garden. The arch was darkened, and looking he saw something which made his heart move strangely . . .

Under the arch between the sunlight and the shade, bareheaded, dressed in white . . . a girl so amazingly beautiful, that Sam wondered for a few moments whether he was asleep or awake. Her hat which she had just taken off, hung on her left arm, and with her delicate right hand she arranged

> *a vagrant tendril of the passion-flower, which in its luxuriant growth had broken bounds and fallen from its place above ...*
>
> *A Norman style of beauty, I believe you would call it. Light hair, deep brilliant blue eyes, and a very fair complexion. Beauty and high-bred grace in every limb and every motion. (246)*

Sam falls immediately in love with her, and awaits her return from seeing to the lunch:

> *Why is she gone so long? He begins to doubt whether he has not after all been asleep and dreaming. There she comes again, however, for the arch under the creepers is darkened again, and he looks up with a pleasant smile upon his face to greet her.*
>
> *God save us! What imp's trick is this? There, in the porch, in the bright sun, where she stood not an hour ago in all her beauty and grace, stands a hideous old savage, black as Tophet, grinning; showing the sharp gap-teeth in her apish jaws, her lean legs shaking with old age and rheumatism:*
>
> *"Can that creature," thinks Sam, "be of the same species as the beautiful Alice Brentwood? Surely not! There seems as much difference between them as between an angel and an ordinary good woman." Hard to believe, truly, Sam; but perhaps, in some of the great European cities, or nearer home, in some of the prison barracks, you may chance to find a white woman or two fallen as low as that poor, starved, ill-treated, filthy old savage! (248–9)*

Ostensibly the alternation of women is a joke upon Sam, the newly smitten lover, and a sober moral comment on the degraded condition of the Aborigines. It also provides an opportunity for the angelic Alice to dispense charity and kindness before the admiring Sam. On a more covert level it asserts the difference between black and white women, by a series of basic oppositions: beautiful/ugly, white/black, young/old. Less obvious oppositions also emerge. The "Norman" beauty Alice, has been imported, like most ladies in nineteenth-century Australian men's novels, as a civilising influence in the wilderness, and she is first encountered engaged in exactly that. She is ordering disorder in nature—rearranging a "vagrant tendril", and she is enforcing boundaries—pushing back "growth" that "had broken its bounds", whereas the old woman is a picture of bestial disorder with her "gap-teeth" in "apish jaws".

This seems a satisfyingly clear set of messages but there is a disturbing element in Sam's first view of the two women—he thinks they are the same. Both appear at that liminal point between verandah and garden, which in nineteenth-century men's novels is far more likely to be a point of division than a zone of blending. Both *darken* the arch. Sam is led by the deception to ask himself whether these women are of the same species. The question is side-stepped, but the answer is present in the text nevertheless. The "savage" and the civilised are both human, but more specifically, they are both female.

At the point of falling in love Sam is struck by a suspicion of the connection which gives such anxiety to many male authors—that the woman they see as wild and the woman they see as civilised are the same woman, that both occupy some imprecise position between nature and culture, and therefore blur dangerously the neatly constructed "civilised" boundaries, and that to marry one is to marry the other. After all, as he immediately discovers, Alice knows the old woman's name, and can understand her speech. The only words that the old woman, Sally, will address to Sam are "Make a light", translated in the foot-note as "See". Sam manages not to see. When Alice re-emerges from the dark interior she is easily translated into the safest stereotype of all, the Madonna "with a look of divine compassion on her beautiful face." (249)

Alice, with her fair "Norman" beauty and refinement is presented as a more fitting replacement for the dark old woman in the land. Indeed, conveniently, "old Sally", whose Koorie identity is erased by the imposed white name, let alone the description, very conveniently believes that when she dies she will come back to earth as "a young white woman with plenty of money". Because the Buckleys and friends are depicted throughout as being on a mission from God this image is a convenient one—heavenly whites replacing the Aborigines.

Nevertheless what so briefly surfaces here is an anxiety about the parallels and oppositions used to make sense of the world in so much Imperial fiction. The old, repulsive, savage, black, feeble woman basically represents the way the bush is portrayed in many novels contemporary with *Geoffry Hamlyn*, but it is a representation that constantly threatens to come undone if it emerges that the golden girl of the civilised is the same species as the black savage of the wilderness.

This moment doesn't just threaten the distinction between Alice and Old Sally, but most of the other distinctions the novel is based on. Can Australia really be a new heaven if all the people from the old earth are there doing the same old things or worse? If it's so good why is it that most of our heroes and heroines don't think twice about bolting back to England at the first opportunity? Indeed the bushrangers and Aboriginal attacks, the murdered shepherds and unhappy working men in Kingsley's novel, despite homilies to the contrary, do seem to suggest that perhaps the new land needed a new society after all. Unfortunately the sort of positive images and lyrical descriptions of the Australian bush and even urban Australia that are plentiful in *The Recollections of Geoffry Hamlyn* get mixed up for later readers with his imperial sentiments and appalling sentimentality, and the whole package is rejected, rather than just some of its parts.

SUSAN K. MARTIN
MELBOURNE, 1993

NOTES

1 Joseph Furphy (The Annotated) *Such is Life* intro & notes, Francis Devlin-Glass, Robin Eaden, Lois Hoffman & G W Turner Melbourne: OUP, 1991. (209)

2 Annette Kolodny, *The Lay of the Land: Metaphor as Experience and History in American Life and Letters*, University of North Carolina Press, Chapel Hill, 1975.

3 Kay Schaffer, *Women and the Bush: Forces of Desire in the Australian Cultural Tradition*, Cambridge University Press, 1988.

CHAPTER I

NEAR the end of February 1857, I think about the 20th or so, though it don't much matter; I only know it was near the latter end of summer, burning hot, with the bushfires raging like volcanoes on the ranges, and the river reduced to a slender stream of water, almost lost upon the broad white flats of quartz shingle. It was the end of February, I said, when Major Buckley, Captain Brentwood (formerly of the Artillery), and I, Geoffry Hamlyn, sat together over our wine in the verandah at Baroona, gazing sleepily on the grey plains that rolled away east and north-east towards the sea.

We had sat silent for some time, too lazy to speak, almost to think. The beautiful flower-garden which lay before us, sloping towards the river, looked rather brown and sere, after the hot winds, although the orange-trees were still green enough, and vast clusters of purple grapes were ripening rapidly among the yellowing vine-leaves. On the whole, however, the garden was but a poor subject of contemplation for one who remembered it in all its full November beauty, and so my eye travelled away to the left, to a broad paddock of yellow grass which bounded the garden on that side, and there I watched an old horse feeding.

A very old horse indeed, a horse which seemed to have reached the utmost bounds of equine existence. And yet such a beautiful beast. Even as I looked some wild young colts were let out of the stock-yard, and came galloping and whinnying towards him, and then it was a sight to see the old fellow as he trotted towards them, with his nose in the air, and his tail arched, throwing his legs out before him with the ease and grace of a four-year-old, and making me regret that he wasn't my property and ten years younger;—altogether, even then, one of the finest horses of his class I had ever seen, and suddenly a thought came over me, and I grew animated.

"Major Buckley," I said, "what horse is that ?"

"What horse is that?" repeated the Major very slowly. "Why, my good fellow, old Widderin, to be sure."

"Bless me!" I said; "You don't mean to say that that old horse is alive still?"

"He looks like it," said the Major. "He'd carry you a mile or two yet."

"I thought he had died while I was in England," I said. "Ah, Major, that horse's history would be worth writing."

"If you began," answered the Major, "to write the history of the horse, you must write also the history of everybody who was concerned in those circumstances which caused Sam to take a certain famous ride upon him. And you would find that the history of the horse would be reduced into very small compass, and that the rest of your book would assume proportions too vast for the human intellect to grasp."

"How so?" I said.

He entered into certain details, which I will not give.

"You would have," he said, "to begin at the end of the last century, and bring one gradually on to the present time. Good heavens! just consider."

"I think you exaggerate," I said.

"Not at all," he answered. "You must begin the histories of the Buckley and Thornton families in the last generation. The Brentwoods also, must not be omitted,—why there's work for several years. What do you say, Brentwood?"

"The work of a lifetime," said the Captain.

"But suppose I were to write a simple narrative of the principal events in the histories of the three families, which no one is more able to do than myself, seeing that nothing important has ever happened without my hearing of it,—how, I say, would you like that?"

"If it amused you to write it, I am sure it would amuse us to read it," said the Major.

"But you are rather old to turn author," said Captain Brentwood; "you'll make a failure of it; in fact, you'll never get through with it."

I replied not, but went into my bedroom, and returning with a thick roll of papers threw it on the floor—as on the stage the honest notary throws down the long-lost will,—and there I stood for a moment with my arms folded, eyeing Brentwood triumphantly.

"It is already done, captain," I said. "There it lies."

The Captain lit a cigar, and said nothing; but the Major said, "Good gracious me! and when was this done?"

"Partly here, and partly in England. I propose to read it aloud to you, if it will not bore you."

"A really excellent idea," said the Major. "My dear!"—this last was addressed to a figure which was now seen approaching us up a long vista of trellised vines. A tall figure dressed in grey. The figure, one could see as she came nearer, of a most beautiful old woman.

Dressed as I said in grey, with a white handkerchief pinned over her grey hair, and a light Indian shawl hanging from her shoulders. As upright as a dart, she came towards us through the burning heat, as calmly and majestically as if the temperature had been delightfully moderate. A hoary old magpie accompanied her, evidently of great age, and from time to time barked like an old bulldog, in a wheezy whisper.

"My dear," said the Major; "Hamlyn is going to read aloud some manuscript to us."

"That will be very delightful, this hot weather," said Mrs. Buckley. "May I ask the subject, old friend?"

"I would rather you did not, my dear madam; you will soon discover, in spite of a change of names, and perhaps somewhat of localities."

"Well, go on," said the Major; and so on I went with the next chapter, which is the first of the story.

The reader will probably ask:

"Now, who on earth is Major Buckley? and who is Captain Brentwood? and last, not least, who the Dickens are you?" If you will have patience, my dear sir, you will find it all out in a very short time—Read on.

CHAPTER II

THE COURTSHIP AND MARRIAGE OF JOHN THORNTON, CLERK, AND THE BIRTH OF SOMEONE WHO TAKES RATHER A CONSPICUOUS PART IN OUR STORY

SOMETIME between the years 1780 and 1790, young John Thornton, then a Servitor at Christ Church, fell in love with pretty Jane Hickman, whose father was a well-to-do farmer, living not far down the river from Oxford and shortly before he took his degree, he called formally upon old Hickman, and asked his daughter's hand.

Hickman was secretly well pleased that his daughter should marry a scholar and a gentleman like John Thornton, and a man too, who could knock over his bird, or kill his trout in the lasher with any one. So after some decent hesitation he told him, that as soon as he got a living good enough to support Jane as she had been accustomed to live, he might take her home with a father's blessing, and a hundred pounds to buy furniture. And you may take my word for it, that there was not much difficulty with the young lady, for in fact the thing had long ago been arranged between them, and she was anxiously waiting in the passage to hear her father's decision, all the time that John was closeted with him.

John came forth from the room well pleased and happy. And that evening when they two were walking together in the twilight by the quiet river, gathering cowslips and fritillaries, he told her of his good prospects, and how a young lord, who made much of him, and treated him as a friend and an equal, though he was but a Servitor—and was used to sit in his room talking with him long after the quadrangle was quiet, and the fast men had reeled off to their drunken slumbers—had only three days before promised him a living of £300 a year, as soon as he should take his priest's orders. And when they parted that night, at the old stile in the meadow, and he saw her go gliding home like a white phantom under the dark elms, he thought joyfully, that in two short years they would be happily settled, never more to part in this world, in his peaceful vicarage in Dorsetshire.

Two short years, he thought. Alas! and alas! Before two years were gone, poor Lord Sandston was lying one foggy November morning on Hampstead Heath, with a bullet through his heart. Shot down at the commencement of a noble and useful career by a brainless gambler—a man who did all things ill, save billiards and pistol-shooting; his beauty and his strength hurried to corruption, and his wealth to the senseless *débauché* who hounded on his murderer to insult him. But I have heard old Thornton tell, with proud tears, how my lord, though outraged and insulted, with no course open to him but to give the villain the power of taking his life, still fired in the air, and went down to the vault of his forefathers without the guilt of blood upon his soul.

So died Lord Sandston, and with him all John's hopes of advancement. A curate now on £50 a year; what hope had he of marrying? And now the tearful couple, walking once more by the river in desolate autumn, among the flying yellow leaves, swore constancy, and agreed to wait till better times should come.

So they waited. John in his parish among his poor people and his school-children, busy always during the day, and sometimes perhaps happy. But in the long winter evenings, when the snow lay piled against the door, and the wind howled in the chimney; or worse, when the wind was still, and the rain was pattering from the eaves, he would sit lonely and miserable by his desolate hearth, and think with a sigh of what might have been had his patron lived. And five-and-twenty years rolled on until James Brown, who was born during the first year of his curateship, came home a broken man, with one arm gone, from the battle of St. Vincent. And the great world roared on, and empires rose and fell, and dull echoes of the great throes without were heard in the peaceful English village, like distant thunder on a summer's afternoon, but still no change for him.

But poor Jane bides her time in the old farmhouse, sitting constant and patient behind the long low latticed window, among the geraniums and roses, watching the old willows by the river. Five-and-twenty times she sees those willows grow green, and the meadow brighten up with flowers, and as often she sees their yellow leaves driven before the strong south wind, and the meadow grow dark and hoar before the breath of autumn. Her father was long since dead, and she was bringing up her brother's children. Her raven hair was streaked with grey, and her step was not so light, nor her laugh so loud, yet still she waited and hoped, long after all hope seemed dead.

But at length a brighter day seemed to dawn for them; for the bishop, who had watched for years John Thornton's patient industry and blameless conversation, gave him, to his great joy and astonishment, the living of Drumston, worth £350 a year. And now, at last, he might marry if he would. True, the morning of his life was gone long since, and its hot noon spent in thankless labour; but the evening, the sober, quiet evening, yet remained, and he and Jane might still render pleasant for one another the downward road towards the churchyard, and hand in hand walk more tranquilly forward to meet that dark tyrant Death, who seemed so terrible to the solitary watcher.

A month or less after John was installed, one soft grey day in March, this patient couple walked slowly arm in arm up the hill, under the lych-gate, past the dark yew that shadowed the peaceful graves, and so through the damp church porch, up to the old stone altar, and there were quietly married, and then walked home again. No feasting or rejoicing was there at that wedding; the very realisation of their long deferred hopes was a disappointment. In March they were married, and before the lanes grew bright with the primroses of another spring, poor Jane was lying in a new-made grave, in the shadow of the old grey tower.

But, though dead, she yet lived to him in the person of a bright-eyed baby, a little girl, born but three months before her mother's death. Who can tell how John watched and prayed over that infant, or how he felt that there was something left for him in this world yet, and thought that if his child would live, he should not go down to the grave a lonely desolate man. Poor John!—who can say whether it would not have been better if the mother's coffin had been made a little larger, and the baby had been carried up the hill, to sleep quietly with its mother, safe from all the evil of this world.

But the child lived and grew, and, at seventeen, I remember her well, a beautiful girl, merry, impetuous, and thoughtless, with black waving hair and dark blue eyes, and all the village loved her and took pride in her. For they said—" She is the handsomest and the best in the parish."

CHAPTER III

THE HISTORY OF (A CERTAIN FAMILY LIVING IN) EUROPE, FROM THE BATTLE OF TRAFALGAR TO THE PEACE OF 1818, CONTAINING FACTS HITHERTO UNPUBLISHED

AMONG all the great old commoner families of the south of England, who have held the lands of their forefathers through every change of dynasty and religion, the Buckleys of Clere stand deservedly high among the brightest and the oldest. All down the stormy page of this great island's history one sees, once in about a hundred years, that name in some place of second-rate honour at least, whether as admiral, general, or statesman; and yet, at the beginning of this present century, the representative of the good old family was living at Clere House, a palace built in the golden times of Elizabeth, on £900 a year, while all the county knew that it took £300 to keep Clere in proper repair.

The two Stuart revolutions had brought them down from county princes to simple wealthy squires, and the frantic efforts made by

Godfrey Buckley, in the "South Sea" scheme to retrieve the family fortunes, had well-nigh broke them. Year by year they saw acre after acre of the broad lands depart, and yet Marmaduke Buckley lived in the home of his ancestors, and the avenue was untouched by axe or saw.

He was a widower, with two sons, John and James. John had been to sea from his earliest youth, and James had joined his regiment a year or more. John had been doing the state good service under his beloved Collingwood; and on the 19th October, 1805, when Nelson and Collingwood made tryst to meet at the gates of hell, John Buckley was one of the immortals on the deck of the *Royal Sovereign.* And when the war fog rolled away to leeward, and Trafalgar was won, and all seas were free, he lay dead in the cockpit, having lived just long enough to comprehend the magnitude of the victory.

Brave old Marmaduke was walking up and down the terrace at Clere uneasy and impatient. Beside him was the good old curate who had educated both the boys, and wearily and oft they turned to watch down the long vista of the ancient avenue for the groom, who had been despatched to Portsmouth to gain some tidings of the lieutenant. They had heard of the victory, and, in their simple way, had praised God for it, drinking a bottle of the rarest old wine to his Majesty's health and the confusion of his enemies, before they knew whether they themselves were among the number of the mourners. And now, as they paced the terrace, every moment they grew more anxious and uneasy for the long-delayed intelligence.

Some trifle took them into the flower-garden, and, when they came back, their hearts leapt up, for the messenger was there dismounted, opening the gate. The curate ran down the steps, and taking a black-edged letter from the sorrowful groom, gave it into the trembling hands of the old man with a choking sob. He opened it and glanced over it, and then, throwing it towards his friend, walked steadily up the steps, and disappeared within the dark porch.

It was just three hasty lines from the great Collingwood himself. That brave heart, in the midst of the din of victory, had found time to scrawl a word to his old schoolmate, and tell him that his boy had died like a hero, and that he regretted him like a son.

The old man sat that evening in the western gallery, tearless and alone, brooding over his grief. Three times the curate had peeped in, and as often had retreated, fearful of disturbing the old man's solemn sorrow. The autumn sun had gone down in

wild and lurid clouds, and the gallery was growing dark and
gloomy, when the white figure of a beautiful girl entering silently
at the lower door came gliding up the darkening vista, past the
light of the windows and the shadow of the piers, to where the
old man sat under the high north window, and knelt at his feet,
weeping bitterly.

It was Agnes Talbot, the daughter of his nearest neighbour and
best friend, whom the curate had slyly sent for, thinking in his
honest heart that she would make a better comforter than he,
and rightly; for the old man, bending over her, lifted up his
voice and wept, speaking for the first time since he heard of his
bereavement, and saying, "Oh, my boy, my boy!"

"He is gone, sir," said Agnes, through her tears; "and gone
the way a man should go. But there is another left you yet; you
remember him."

"Ay, James," said he; "alas, poor James! I wonder if he
knows it. I wish he were here."

"James is here," said she. "He heard of it before you, and
came posting over as fast as he could, and is waiting outside
to know if you can see him."

The door at the lower end of the gallery opened, and a tall and
noble looking young man strode up and took his father's hand.

He was above the ordinary height of man, with a grand broad
forehead and bold blue eyes. Old Marmaduke's heart warmed up
as he parted his curling hair, and he said:

"Thank God, I've got one left still! The old house will not
perish yet, while such a one as you remains to uphold it."

After a time they left him, at his own request, and walked
out together through the dark rooms towards the old hall.

"Agnes, my beloved, my darling!" said James, drawing his arm
round her waist; "I knew I should find you with him like a
ministering angel. Say something to comfort me, my love. You
never could love John as I did; yet I know you felt for him
as your brother, as he soon would have been, if he had lived."

"What can I say to you, my own?" she replied, "save to tell
you that he fell as your brother should fall, amongst the foremost,
fighting for his country's existence. And, James, if you must go
before me, and leave me a widow before I am a bride, it would
render more tolerable the short time that would be left to me
before I followed you, to think that you had fallen like him."

"There will be a chance of it, Agnes," said James, "for Stuart,
they say, is going to Italy, and I go with him. There will be

a long and bloody war, and who knows how it will end? Stay you here quiet with the old man, my love, and pray for me; the end will come some day. I am only eighteen and an ensign; in ten years I may be a colonel."

They parted that night with tears and kisses, and a few days afterwards James went from among them to join his regiment.

From that time Agnes almost lived with old Marmaduke. Her father's castle could be seen over the trees from the windows of Clere, and every morning, wet or dry, the old man posted himself in the great north window of the gallery to watch her coming. All day she would pervade the gloomy old mansion like a ray of sunlight, now reading to him, now leading him into the flower-garden in fine weather, till he grew quite fond of flowers for her sake, and began even to learn the names of some of them. But oftenest of all she would sit working by his side, while he told her stories of times gone by, stories which would have been dull to any but her, but which she could listen to and applaud. Best of all she liked to hear him talk of James, and his exploits by flood and field from his youth up; and so it was that this quiet couple never tired one another, for their hearts were set upon the same object.

Sometimes her two sisters, noble and beautiful girls, would come to see him; but they, indeed, were rather intruders, kind and good as they were. And sometimes old Talbot looked round to see his old friend, and talked of bygone fishing and hunting, which roused the old man up and made him look glad for half a day after. Still, however, Agnes and the old curate were company enough for him, for they were the only two who loved his absent son as well as he. The love which had been divided between the two, seemed now to be concentrated upon the one, and yet this true old Briton never hinted at James's selling out and coming home, for he said that the country had need of every one then, more particularly such a one as James.

Time went on, and he came back to them from Corunna, and spending little more than a month at home, he started away once more; and next they heard of him at Busaco, wounded and promoted. Then they followed him in their hearts along the path of glory, from Talavera by Albuera and Vittoria, across the Pyrenees. And while they were yet reading a long-delayed letter, written from Toulouse at midnight—after having been to the theatre with Lord Wellington, wearing a white cockade—he broke in on them again, to tell them the war was well-nigh over, and that he would soon come and live with them in peace.

Then what delightful reunions were there in the old gallery window, going over all the weary campaigns once more; pleasant rambles, too, down by the riverside in the sweet May evenings, old Marmaduke and the curate discreetly walking in front and James and Agnes loitering far behind. And in the succeeding winter after they were married, what pleasant rides had they to meet the hounds, and merry evenings before the bright wood fire in the hall. Never were four people more happy than they. The war was done, the disturber was confined, and peace had settled down upon the earth.

Peace, yes. But not for long. Spring came on, and with it strange disquieting rumours, growing more certain day by day, till the terrible news broke on them that the faithless tyrant had broke loose again, and that all Europe was to be bathed in blood once more by his insane ambition.

James had sold out of the army, so that when Agnes first heard the intelligence she thanked God that her husband at least would be safe at home during the storm. But she was soon to be undeceived. When the news first came, James had galloped off to Portsmouth, and late in the evening they saw him come riding slowly and sadly up the avenue. She was down at the gate before he could dismount, and to her eager inquiries if the news were true, he replied:

"All too true, my love; and I must leave you this day week."

"My God!" she said; ": leave me again, and not six months married? Surely the king has had you long enough; may not your wife have you for a few short months?"

"Listen to me, dear wife," he replied. "All the Peninsular men are volunteering, and I must not be among the last, for every man is wanted now. Bonaparte is joined by the whole army, and the craven king has fled. If England and Prussia can combine to strike a blow before he gets head, thousands and hundreds of thousands of lives will be spared. But let him once get firmly seated, and then, hey! for ten years' more war. Besides, the thing is done; my name went in this morning."

She said, "God's will be done;" and he left his young bride and his old father once again. The nightingale grew melodious in the midnight woods, the swallows nestled again in the chimneys, and day by day the shadows under the old avenue grew darker and darker till merry June was half gone; and then one Saturday came the rumour of a great defeat.

All the long weary summer Sabbath that followed, Agnes and Marmaduke silently paced the terrace, till the curate—having got through his own services somehow, and broken down in the " prayer during war and tumults,"—came hurrying back to them to give what comfort he could.

Alas! that was but little. He could only speculate whether or not the duke would give up Brussels, and retire for reinforcements. If the two armies could effect a union, they would be near about the strength of the French, but then the Prussians were cut to pieces; so the curate broke down, and became the worst of the three.

Cheer up, good souls! for he you love shall not die yet for many long years. While you are standing there before the porch, dreading the long anxious night, Waterloo has been won, and he—having stood the appointed time in the serried square, watching the angry waves of French cavalry dash in vain against the glittering wall of bayonets—is now leaning against a gun in the French position, alive and well, though fearfully tired, listening to the thunder of the Prussian artillery to the north, and watching the red sun go down across the wild confusion of the battlefield.

But home at Clere none slept that night, but met again next morning weary and harassed. All the long three days none of them spoke much, but wandered about the house uneasily. About ten o'clock on the Wednesday night they went to bed, and the old man slept from sheer weariness.

It was twelve o'clock when there came a clang at the gate, and a sound of horses' feet on the gravel. Agnes was at the window in a moment.

" Who goes there? " she cried.

" An orderly from Colonel Mountford at Portsmouth," said a voice below. " A letter for Mr. Buckley."

She sent a servant to undo the door; and going to the window again, she inquired, trembling :

" Do you know what the news is, orderly? "

" A great victory, my dear," said the man, mistaking her for one of the servants. " Your master is all right. There's a letter from him inside this one."

" And I dare say," Mrs. Buckley used to add, when she would tell this old Waterloo story, as we called it, " that the orderly thought me a most heartless domestic, for when I heard what he said, I burst out laughing so loud, that old Mr. Buckley woke up to see what was the matter, and when he heard, he laughed as loud as I did."

So he came back to them again with fresh laurels, but Agnes never felt safe, till she heard that the powers had determined to chain up her *bête noire*, Bonaparte, on a lonely rock in the Atlantic, that he might disturb the world no more. Then at last she began to believe that peace might be a reality, and a few months after Waterloo, to their delight and exultation, she bore a noble boy.

And as we shall see more of this boy, probably, than of any one else in these following pages, we will, if you please, appoint him hero, with all the honours and emoluments thereunto pertaining. Perhaps when I have finished, you will think him not so much of a hero after all. But at all events you shall see how he is an honest upright gentleman, and in these times, perhaps such a character is preferable to a hero.

Old Marmaduke had been long failing, and two years after this he had taken to his bed, never to leave it again alive. And one day when the son and heir was rolling and crowing on his grandfather's bed, and Agnes was sewing at the window, and James was tying a fly by the bedside, under the old man's directions he drew the child towards him and beckoning Agnes from the window spoke thus:

"My children, I shan't be long with you, and I must be the last of the Buckleys that die at Clere. Nay, I mean it, James; listen carefully to me: when I go, the house and park must go with me. We are very poor, as you well know, and you will be doing injustice to this boy if you hang on here in this useless tumble-down old palace, without money enough to keep up your position in the county. You are still young, and it would be hard for you to break up old associations. It got too hard for me lately, though at one time I meant to do it. The land and the house are the worst investment you can have for your money, and if you sell, a man like you may make money in many ways. Gordon the brewer is dying to have the place, and he has more right to it than we have, for he has ten acres round to our one. Let him have the estate and found a new family; the people will miss us at first, God bless 'em, but they'll soon get used to Gordon, for he's a kindly man, and a just, and I am glad that we shall have so good a successor. Remember your family and your ancestors, and for that reason don't hang on here, as I said before, in the false position of an old county family without money, like the Singletons of Hurst, living in a ruined hall, with a miserable overcropped farm, a corner of the old deer park, under their drawing-room window. No, my boy, I would sooner see you take a farm from my lord, than that. And now I am tired with talking, and so leave me, but after I am gone, remember what I have said."

A few days after this the old man passed peacefully from the world vithout a sigh.

They buried him in the family vault under the chancel windows. And he was the last of the Buckleys that slept in the grave of his forefathers. And the old arch beneath the east window is built up for ever.

Soon after he was gone, the Major, as I shall call him in future, sold the house and park, and the few farms that were left, and found himself with twelve thousand pounds, ready to begin the world again. He funded his money and made up his mind to wait a few years and see what to do; determining that if no other course should open, he would emigrate to Canada—the paradise of half-pay officers. But in the meantime he moved into Devonshire, and took a pretty little cottage which was to let, not a quarter of a mile from Drumston Vicarage.

Such an addition to John Thornton's little circle of acquaintances was very welcome. The Major and he very soon became fast friends, and noble Mrs. Buckley was seldom a day without spending an hour at least with the beautiful, wilful Mary Thornton.

CHAPTER IV

SOME NEW FACES

THE twilight of a winter's evening, succeeding a short and stormy day, was fast fading into night, and old John Thornton sat dozing in his chair before the fire, waiting for candles to resume his reading. He was now but little over sixty, yet his hair was snowy white, and his face looked worn and aged. Anyone who watched his countenance now in the light of the blazing wood might see by the down-drawn brows and uneasy expression that the old man was unhappy and disquieted.

The book that lay in his lap was a volume of Shakespeare, open at the *Merchant of Venice*. Something he had come across in that play had set him thinking. The book had fallen on his knees, and he sat pondering till he had fallen asleep. Yet even in his slumber the uneasy expression stayed upon his face, and now and then he moved uneasily in his chair.

What could there be to vex him? Not poverty at all events, for not a year ago· a relation, whom he had seldom seen, and of late years entirely lost sight of, had left him £5000 and a like sum to his daughter, Mary. And his sister, Miss Thornton, a quiet, good old maid, who had been a governess all her life, had come to live with him, so that he was now comfortably off, with the only two relations he cared about in the world staying with him to make his old age comfortable. Yet notwithstanding all this, John was unhappy.

His daughter, Mary, sat sewing in the window, ostensibly for the purpose of using the last of the daylight. But the piece of white muslin in her hand claimed but a small part of her attention. Sometimes she gave a stitch or two; but then followed a long gaze out of the window, across the damp gravel and plushy lawn, towards the white gate under the leafless larches. Again with an impatient sigh she would address herself to her sewing, but once more her attention would wander to the darkening garden; so at length she rose, and leaning against the window began to watch the white gate once more.

But now she starts, and her face brightens up as the gate swings on its hinges, and a tall man comes with a rapid, eager step up the walk. John moves uneasily in his sleep, but unnoticed by her, for she stands back in the shadow of the curtain, and eagerly watches the new-comer in his approach. Her father sits up in his chair, and after looking sadly at her for a moment, then sinks back with a sigh, as though he would wish to go to sleep again and wake no more.

The maid, bringing in candles, met the new-comer at the door, and, carrying in the lights before him, announced:

"Mr. George Hawker."

I remember his face indistinctly as it was then. I remember it far better as it was twenty years after. Yet I must try to recall it for you as well as I can, for we shall have much to do with this man before the end. As the light from the candles fell upon his figure while he stood in the doorway, any man or woman who saw it would have exclaimed immediately, "What a handsome fellow!" and with justice; for if perfectly regular features, splendid red and brown complexion, faultless white teeth, and the finest head of curling black hair I ever saw, could make him handsome, handsome he was without doubt. And yet the more you looked at him the less you liked him, and the more inclined you felt to pick a quarrel with him. The thin lips, the everlasting smile, the quick suspicious glance, so rapidly shot out from under the overhanging eyebrows, and as quickly withdrawn, were fearfully repulsive, as well as a trick he had of always clearing his throat before he spoke, as if to gain time to frame a lie. But, perhaps, the strangest thing about him was the shape of his head, which, I believe, a child would have observed. The young fellows in those times knew little enough about phrenology. I doubt, indeed, if I had ever heard the word, and yet among the village lads that man went by the name of "flat-headed George." The forehead was both low and narrow, sloping a great way back, while the larger part of the skull lay low down behind the ears. All this was made the more visible by the short curling hair which covered his head.

He was the only son of a small farmer, in one of the distant outlying hamlets of Drumston, called Woodlands. His mother had died when he was very young, and he had had but little education, but had lived shut up with his father in the lonely old farmhouse. And strange stories were in circulation among the villages about that house, not much to the credit of either father or son, which stories John Thornton must in his position as clergyman have heard somewhat of, so that one need hardly wonder at his uneasiness when he saw him enter.

For Mary adored him; the rest of the village disliked and distrusted him; but she, with a strange perversity, loved him as it seldom falls to the lot of man to be loved—with her whole heart and soul.

"I have brought you some snipes, Mr. Thornton," said he, in his most musical tones. "The white frost last night has sent them down off the moor as thick as bees, and this warm rain will soon send them all back again. I only went round through Fernworthy and Combe, and I have killed five couple."

"Thank you, Mr. George, thank you," said John, "they are not so plentiful as they were in old times, and I don't shoot so well either as I used to do. My sight's going, and I can't walk far. It is nearly time for me to go, I think."

"Not yet, sir, I hope; not yet for a long time," said George Hawker, in an offhand sort of way. But Mary slipped round, kissed his forehead, and took his hand quietly in hers.

John looked from her to George, and dropped her hand with a sigh, and soon the lovers were whispering together again in the darkness of the window.

But now there is a fresh footfall on the garden walk, a quick, rapid, decided one. Somebody bursts open the hall door, and, without shutting it, dashes into the parlour, accompanied by a tornado of damp air, and announces in a loud, though not unpleasant voice, with a foreign accent:

"I have got the new Scolopax!"

He was a broad, massive built man, about the middle height, with a square, determined set of features, brightened up by a pair of merry blue eyes. His forehead was, I think, the finest I ever saw; so high, so broad, and so upright; and, altogether, he was the sort of man that in a city one would turn round and look after, wondering who he was.

He stood in the doorway, dripping, and without "Good-even," or salutation of any sort, exclaimed:

"I have got the new Scolopax!"

"No!" cried old John, starting up all alive, "have you though? How did you get him? Are you sure it is not a young Jack? Come in and tell us all about it. Only think."

"The obstinancy and incredulity of you English," replied the new-comer, totally disregarding John's exclamations, and remaining dripping in the doorway, "far exceeds anything I could have conceived, if I had not witnessed it. If I told you once, I told you twenty times, that I had seen the bird on three distinct occasions in the meadow below Reel's mill; and you each time threw your jacksnipe theory in my face. To-day I marked him down in the bare ground outside Haveldon wood, then ran at full speed up to the jager, and offered him five shillings if he would come down and shoot the bird I showed him. He came, killed the bird in a style that I would give a year's tobacco to be master of, and remarked as I paid him his money that he would like to get five shillings for every one of those birds he could shoot in summertime. The jolter-head thought it was a sandpiper, but he wasn't much farther out than you with your jacksnipes. Bah!"

"My dear Dr. Mulhaus," said John mildly, "I confess myself to have been foolishly incredulous, as to our little place being honoured by such a distinguished stranger as the new snipe. But come in to the fire, and smoke your pipe, while you show me your treasure. Mary, you know, likes tobacco, and Mr. George, I am sure," he added, in a slightly altered tone, "will excuse it."

Mr. George would be charmed. But the Doctor, standing staring at him open-eyed for a moment, demanded in an audible whisper:

"Who the deuce is that?"

"Mr. George Hawker, Doctor, from the Woodlands. I should have thought you had met him before."

"Never," replied the Doctor. "And I don't—and I mean I have had the honour of hearing of him from Stockbridge. Excuse me, sir, a moment. I am going to take a liberty. I am a phrenologist." He advanced across the room to where George sat, laid his hand on his forehead, and drawing it lightly and slowly back through his black curls, till he reached the nape of his neck, ejaculated a "Hah!" which might mean anything, and retired to the fire.

He then began filling his pipe, but before it was filled set it suddenly on the table, and drawing from his coat pocket a cardboard box, exhibited to the delighted eyes of the Vicar that beautiful little brown-mottled snipe, which now bears the name of Colonel Sabine, and having lit his pipe, set to work with a tiny penknife, and a pot of arsenical soap, all of which were disinterred from the vast coat pocket before mentioned, to reduce the plump little bird to a loose mass of skin and feathers, fit to begin again his new life in death in a glass case in some collector's museum.

George Hawker had sat very uneasy since the Doctor's phrenological examination, and every now and then cast fierce, angry glances at him from under his lowered eyebrows, talking but little to Mary. But now he grows more uneasy still, for the gate goes again, and still another footfall is heard approaching through the darkness.

That is James Stockbridge. I should know that step among a thousand. Whether brushing through the long grass of an English meadow in May-time, or quietly pacing up and down the orange alley in the New World, between the crimson snow and the blazing west; or treading lightly across the wet ground at black midnight, when the cattle are restless, or the blacks are abroad; or even, I should think, staggering on the slippery deck, when the big grey seas are booming past, and the good ship seems plunging down to destruction.

He had loved Mary dearly since she was almost a child; but she, poor pretty fool, used to turn him to ridicule, and make him fetch and carry for her like a dog. He was handsomer, cleverer, stronger, and better tempered than George Hawker, and yet she had no eyes for him, or his good qualities. She liked him in a sort of way; nay, it might even be said that she was fond of him. But what she liked better than him was to gratify her vanity, by showing her power over the finest young fellow in the village, and to use him as a foil to aggravate George Hawker. My Aunt Betsy (spinster) used to say, that if she were a man, sooner than stand that hussy's airs (meaning Mary's) in the way young Stockbridge did, she'd cut and run to America, which, in the old lady's estimation, was the last resource left to an unfortunate human creature before suicide.

As he entered the parlour, John's face grew bright, and he held out his hand to him. The Doctor, too, shoving his spectacles on his forehead, greeted him with a royal salute, of about twenty-one short words; but he got rather a cool reception from the lovers in the window. Mary gave him a quiet " Good evening," and George hoped, with a sneer, that he was quite well, but directly the pair were whispering together once more in the shadow of the curtain.

So he sat down between the Doctor and the Vicar. James, like all the rest of us, had a profound respect for the Doctor's learning, and old John and he were as father and son; so a better matched trio could hardly be found in the parish as they sat there before the cheerful blaze smoking their pipes.

" A good rain, Jim; a good, warm, kindly rain after the frost," began the Vicar.

" A very good rain, sir," replied Jim.

" Some idiots," said the Doctor, " take the wing bones out first. Now, my method of beginning at the legs and working forward is infinitely superior. Yet that ass at Crediton, after I had condescended to show him, persisted his own way was the best." All this time he was busy skinning his bird.

" How are your Southdowns looking, Jim?" says the Vicar. " Foot-rot, eh?"

" Well, yes, sir," says James, " they always will, you know, in these wet clays. But I prefer 'em to the Leicesters, for all that."

" How is scapegrace Hamlyn?" asked the Vicar.

" He is very well, sir. He and I have been out with the harriers to-day."

" Ah! taking you out with the harriers instead of minding his business; just like him. He'll be leading you astray, James, my boy. Young men like you and he, who have come to be their own masters so young, ought to be more careful than others. Besides, you see, both you and Hamlyn, being squires, have got an example to set to the poorer folks."

" We are neither of us so rich as some of the farmers, sir."

" No; but you are both gentlemen born, you see, and, therefore, ought to be in some way models for those who are not."

"Bosh," said the Doctor. "All this about Hamlyn's going out hare hunting."

"I don't mind it once a week," said the Vicar, ignoring the Doctor's interruption; "but *four times* is rather too much. And Hamlyn has been out four days this week. Twice with Wrefords, and twice with Holes. He can't deny it."

Jim couldn't, so he laughed. "You must catch him, sir," he said, "and give him a real good wigging. He'll mind you. But catch him soon, sir, or you won't get the chance. Doctor, do you know anything about New South Wales?"

"Botany Bay," said the Vicar abstractedly, "convict settlement in South Seas. Jerry Shaw begged the judge to hang him instead of sending him there. Judge wouldn't do it though; Jerry was too bad for that."

"Hamlyn and I are thinking of selling up and going there," said Jim. "Do you know anything about it, Doctor?"

"What!" said the Doctor; "the mysterious hidden land of the great South Sea. Tasman's Land, Nuyt's Land, Leuwin's Land, De Witt's Land, any fool's land who could sail round, and never have the sense to land and make use of it—the new country of Australasia. The land with millions of acres of fertile soil, under a splendid climate, calling aloud for some one to come and cultivate them. The land of the Eucalypti and the Marsupials, the land of deep forests and boundless pastures, which go rolling away westward, plain beyond plain, to none knows where. Yes; I know something about it."

The Vicar was "knocked all of a heap" at James's announcement, and now, slightly recovering himself, said:

"You hear him. He is going to Botany Bay. He is going to sell his estate, 250 acres of the best land in Devon, and go and live among the convicts. And who is going with him? Why, Hamlyn the wise. Oh, dear me. And what is he going for?"

That was a question apparently hard to answer. If there was a reason, Jim was either unwilling or unable to give it. Yet I think that the real cause was standing there in the window with a look of unbounded astonishment on her pretty face.

"Going to leave us, James!" she cried, coming quickly towards him. "Why, whatever shall I do without you?"

"Yes, Miss Mary," said James, somewhat huskily; "I think I may say that we have settled to go. Hamlyn has got a letter from a cousin of his who went from down Plymouth way, and who is making a fortune; and besides, I have got tired of the old place somehow, lately. I have nothing to keep me here now, and there will be a change, and a new life there. In short," said he, in despair of giving a rational reason, " I have made up my mind."

" Oh! " said Mary, while her eyes filled with tears, " I shall be sorry to lose you."

" I, too," said James, " shall be sorry to start away beyond seas and leave all the friends I care about save one behind me. But times are hard for the poor folks here now, and if I, as squire, set the example of going, I know many will follow. The Old Country, Mr. Thornton," he continued, " is getting too crowded for men to live in without a hard push, and depend on it, when poor men are afraid to marry for fear of having children which they can't support, it is time to move somewhere. The hive is too hot, and the bees must swarm, so that those that go will both better themselves and better those they leave behind them, by giving them more room to work and succeed. It's hard to part with the old farm and the old faces now, but perhaps in a few years one will get to like that country just as one does this, from being used to it, and the Old Country will seem only like a pleasant dream after one has awoke."

" Think twice about it, James, my boy," said the Vicar.

" Don't be such an ass as to hesitate," said the Doctor impatiently. " It is the genius of your restless discontented nation to go blundering about the world like buffaloes in search of fresh pasture. You have founded already two or three grand new empires, and you are now going to form another; and men like you ought to have their fingers in the pie."

" Well, God speed you, and Hamlyn, too, wherever you go. Are you going home, Mr. Hawker? "

George, who hated James from the very bottom of his heart, was not ill-pleased to hear there would be a chance of soon getting rid of him. He had been always half jealous of him, though without the slightest cause, and to-night he was more so than ever, for Mary, since she had heard of James's intended departure, had grown very grave and silent. He stood, hat in hand, ready to depart, and, as usual when he meant mischief, spoke in his sweetest tones.

" I am afraid I must be saying good evening, Mr. Thornton. Why, James," he added, " this is something quite new. So you are going to Botany without waiting to be sent there. Ha! ha! Well, I wish you every sort of good luck. My dear friend, Hamlyn, too. What a loss he'll be to our little society, so sociable and affable as he always is to us poor farmers' sons. You'll find it lonely there though. You should get a wife to take with you. Oh, yes, I should certainly get married before I went. Good night."

All this was meant to be as irritating as possible; but as he went out at the door he had the satisfaction to hear James's clear, honest laugh mingling with the Vicar's, for, as George had closed the door the Doctor had said, looking after him:

"Gott in Himmel, that young man has got a skull like a tom-cat."

This complimentary observation was lost on Mary, who had left the room with George. The Vicar looked round for her, and sighed when he missed her.

"Ah!" said he; "I wish he was going instead of you."

"So does the new colony, I'll be bound," added the Doctor.

Soon after this the party separated. When James and the Doctor stood outside the door the latter demanded, "Where are you going?"

"To Sydney, I believe, Doctor."

"Goose. I mean now."

"Home."

"No, you ain't," said the Doctor; "you are going to walk up to Hamlyn's with me, and hear me discourse." Accordingly, about eleven o'clock, these two arrived at my house, and sat before the fire till half-past three in the morning; and in that time the Doctor had given us more information about New South Wales than we had been able to gather from ordinary sources in a month.

CHAPTER V

IN WHICH THE READER IS MADE ACCOMPLICE TO A MISPRISION OF FELONY

THOSE who only know the river Taw as he goes sweeping, clear and full, past orchards and farmhouses, by woods and parks, and through long green meadows, after he has left Dartmoor, have little idea of the magnificent scene which rewards the perseverance of any one who has the curiosity to follow him up to his granite cradle between the two loftiest eminences in the west of England.

On the left, Great Cawsand heaves up, down beyond down, a vast sheet of purple heath and golden whin, while on the right the lofty serrated ridge of Yestor starts boldly up, black against the western sky, throwing a long shadow over the wild waste of barren stone at his feet.

Some Scotchmen, perhaps, may smile at my applying the word "magnificent" to heights of only 2100 feet.   Yet I have been among mountains which double Ben Nevis in height, and with the exception of the Murray Gates in Australia, and a glen in Madeira, whose name I have forgotten, I have never seen among them the equal of some of the northern passes of Dartmoor for gloomy magnificence.   For I consider that scenery depends not so much on height as on abruptness.

It is an evil, depressing place.   Far as the eye can reach up the glen and to the right, it is one horrid waste of grey granite; here and there a streak of yellow grass or a patch of black bog; not a tree nor a shrub within the sky-line.   On a hot summer's day it is wearisome enough for the lonely angler to listen to the river crawling lazily through the rocks that choke his bed, mingled with the clocking of some water-moved boulder, and the chick-chick of the stonechat, or the scream of the golden plover overhead.   But on a wild winter's evening, when day is fast giving place to night, and the mist shrouds the hill, and the wild wind is rushing hoarse through tor and crag, it becomes awful and terrible in the extreme.

On just such a night as that, at that time when it becomes evident that the little light we have had all day is about to leave us, a lonely watcher was standing by the angry swelling river in the most desolate part of the pass, at a place where a vast confusion of formless rocks crosses the stream, torturing it into a hundred boiling pools and hissing cascades.

He stood on the summit of a cairn close to the river, and every now and then, shading his eyes with his hand, he looked eastward through the driving rain, as though expecting someone who came not. But at length, grown tired of watching, he with an oath descended to a sheltered corner among the boulders, where a smouldering peat-fire was giving out more smoke than heat, and, crouching over it, began to fan the embers with his hat.

He was a somewhat short, though powerful man, in age about forty, very dark in complexion, with black whiskers growing half over his chin.   His nose was hooked, his eyes were black and piercing, and his lips thin.   His face was battered like an old sailor's, and every careless, unstudied motion of his body was as wild and reckless as could be.   There was something about his *tout ensemble*, in short, that would have made an Australian policeman swear to him as a convict without the least hesitation.

There were redeeming points in the man's face, too. There was plenty of determination, for instance, in that lower jaw; and as he bent now over the fire, and his thoughts wandered away to other times and places, the whole appearance of the man seemed to change and become milder and kindlier; yet when some slight noise makes him lift his head and look round, there is the old expression back again, and he looks as reckless and desperate as ever; what he is is more apparent, and the ghost of what he might have been has not wholly departed.

I can picture to myself that man scowling behind the bayonet line at Maida, or rapidly and coolly serving his gun at Trafalgar, helping to win the dominion of all seas, or taking his trick at the helm through Arctic ice-blocks with Parry, or toiling on with steadfast Sturt, knee-deep in the sand of the middle desert, patiently yet hopelessly scanning the low, quivering line of the north-west horizon.

In fifty situations where energy and courage are required, I can conceive that man a useful citizen. Yet here he is on the lone moor, on the winter's night, a reckless, cursing, thrice convicted man. His very virtues—his impatient energy and undeniable courage—his greatest stumbling-blocks, leading him into crimes which a lazy man or a coward would have shrunk from. Deserted apparently by God and man, he crouched there over the low fire, among his native rocks, and meditated fresh villainies.

He hâd been transported at eighteen for something, I know not what, which earned transportation in those days, and since then his naturally violent temper, aggravated instead of being broken by penal discipline, had earned him three fresh convictions in the colony. From the last of these sentences he had escaped, with a cunning and address which had baffled the vigilance of the Sydney police, good as they were, and had arrived home, two years before this time, after twenty-one years' absence, at his native village in the moor.

None there knew him, or even guessed who he was. His brother, a small farmer, who would have taken him to his heart had he recognised him, always regarded him as a suspicious stranger; and what cut him deeper still, his mother, his old, half-blind, palsied mother, whose memory he had in some sort cherished through the horrors of the hulk, the convict ship, the chain gang, and the bush, knew him not. Only once, when he was speaking in her presence, she said abruptly:

" The voice of him is like the voice of my boy that was took away. But he was smooth faced, like a girl, and ye're a dark, wrinkled man. 'Sides, he died years agone, over the water."

But the old lady grew thoughtful and silent from that day, and three weeks after she was carried up to her grave:

"By the little grey church on the windy hill."

At the funeral, William Lee, the man whom I have been describing, pushed quietly through the little crowd, and as they threw the first earth on the coffin, stood looking over the shoulder of his brother, who was unconscious of his existence.

Like many men who have been much in great solitudes, and have gone days and weeks sometimes without meeting a fellow creature, he had acquired the habit of thinking aloud, and if any one had been listening they would have heard much such a soliloquy as the following, expletives omitted, or rather softened:

" A brutal cold country this, for a man to camp out in. Never a buck-log to his fire, no, nor a stick thicker than your finger for seven mile round; and if there was, you'd get a month for cutting it. If the young 'un milks free this time, I'll be off to the bay again, I know. But will he? By George, he shall though. The young snob, I know he daren't but come, and yet it's my belief he's late just to keep me soaking out in the rain. Whew! it's cold enough to freeze the tail off a tin possum; and this infernal rubbish won't burn, at least not to warm a man. If it wasn't for the whisky I should be dead. There's a rush of wind; I am glad for one thing there is no dead timber overhead. He'll be drinking at all the places coming along to get his courage up to bounce me, but there ain't a public house on the road six miles from this, so the drink will have pretty much died out of him by the time he gets to me, and if I can get him to sit in this rain, and smoke 'bacca for five minutes, he won't be particular owdacious. I'll hide the grog, too, between the stones. He'll be asking for a drink the minute he comes. I hope Dick is ready; he is pretty sure to be. He's a good little chap, that Dick; he has stuck to me well these five years. I wouldn't like to trust him with another man's horse, though. But this other one is no good; he's got all the inclination to go the whole hog, and none of the pluck necessary. If he ever is lagged he will be a worse one than ever I was, or Dick either. There he is, for a hundred pounds."

A faint " Halloo! " sounded above the war of the weather; and Lee, putting his hand to his mouth, replied with that strange cry, " Coo-ee."

A man was now heard approaching through the darkness, now splashing deep into some treacherous moss hole with a loud curse, now blundering among loose-lying blocks of stone. Lee waited till he was quite close, and then seizing a bunch of gorse lighted it at his fire and held it aloft; the bright blaze fell full upon the face and features of George Hawker.

"A cursed place and a cursed time," he began, "for an appointment. If you had wanted to murder me I could have understood it. But I am pretty safe, I think; your interest don't lie that way."

"Well, well, you see," replied Lee, "I don't want any meetings on the cross up at my place in the village. The whole house ain't mine, and we don't know who may be listening. I am suspected enough already, and it wouldn't look well for you to be seen at my place. Folks would have begun axing what for."

"Don't see it," said George. "Besides, if you did not want to see me at home, why the devil do you bring me out here in the middle of the moor? We might have met on the hill underneath the village, and when we had done business gone up to the public house. Damned if I understand it."

He acquiesced sulkily to the arrangement, however, because he saw it was no use talking about it, but he was far from comfortable. He would have been still less so had he known that Lee's shout had brought up a confederate, who was now peering over the rocks, almost touching his shoulder.

"Well," said Lee, "here we are, so we had better be as comfortable as we can this devil's night."

"Got anything to drink?"

"Deuce a swipe of grog have I. But I have got some real Barret's twist, that never paid duty as I know'd on, so just smoke a pipe before we begin talking, and show you aint vexed."

"I'd sooner have had a drop of grog, such a night as this."

"We must do as the Spaniards do, when they can't get anything," said Lee; "go without."

They both lit their pipes, and smoked in silence for a few minutes, till Lee resumed:

"If the witches weren't all dead there would be some of them abroad to-night; hear that?"

"Only a whimbrel, isn't it?" said George.

"That's something worse than a whimbrel, I'm thinking," said the other. "There's some folks don't believe in witches and the like," he continued; "but a man that's seen a naked old hag of a gin ride away on a myall-bough knows better."

"Lord!" said George. "I shouldn't have thought you'd have believed in the like of that—but I do—that old devil's dam, Dame Parker, that lives alone up in Hatherleigh Wood, got gibbering some infernal nonsense at me the other day for shooting her black cat. I made the cross in the road though, so I suppose it won't come to anything."

"Perhaps not," said Lee; "but I'd sooner kill a man than a black cat."

Another pause. The tobacco, so much stronger than any George had been accustomed to, combined with the cold, made him feel nervous and miserable.

"When I was a boy," resumed Lee, "there were two young brothers made it up to rob the squire's house, down at Gidleigh. They separated in the garden after they cracked the crib, agreeing to meet here in this very place and share the swag, for they had got nigh seventy pound. They met and quarrelled over the sharing up; and the elder one drew out a pistol and shot the younger dead. The poor boy was sitting much where you are sitting now, and that long tuft of grass grew up from his blood."

"I believe that's all a lie," said George; "you want to drive me into the horrors with your humbugging tales."

Lee, seeing that he had gone far enough, if not too far, proposed, somewhat sulkily, that they should begin to talk about what brought them there, and not sit crouching in the wet all night.

"Well," said George, "it's for you to begin. What made you send for me to this infernal place?"

"I want money," said Lee.

"Then you'd better axe about and get some," said George; "you'll get none from me. I am surprised that a man with your knowledge of the world should have sent me such a letter as you did yesterday, I am indeed. What the devil's that?"

He started on his feet. A blaze of sudden light filled the nook where they were sitting, and made it as bright as day, and a voice shouted out:

"Ha, ha, ha! my secret coves, what's going on here? something quiet and sly, eh? something worth a fifty-pound note, eh? Don't you want an arbitrator, eh? Here's one, ready made."

"You're playing a dangerous game, my flashman, whoever you are," said Lee, rising savagely. "I've shot a man down for less than that. So you've been stagging this gentleman and me, and listening, have you? For just half a ha'penny," he added, striding towards him, and drawing out a pistol, "you shouldn't go home this night."

"Don't you be a fool, Bill Lee," said the newcomer. "I saw the light and made towards it, and as I come up I heard some mention made of money. Now then, if my company is disagreeable, why I'll go, and no harm done."

"What! it's you, is it?" said Lee; "well, now you've come, you may stop and hear what it's all about. I don't care, you are not very squeamish, or at least usedn't to be."

George saw that the arrival of this man was pre-concerted, and cursed Lee bitterly in his heart, but he sat still, and thought how he could out-manoeuvre them.

"Now," said Lee, "I ain't altogether sorry that you have come, for I want to tell you a bit of a yarn, and ask your advice about my behaviour. This is about the state of the case: A young gentleman, a great friend of mine, was not very many years ago pretty much given up to fast living, cock fighting, horse racing, and many other little matters which all young fellows worth anything are pretty sure to indulge in, and which are very agreeable for the time, but which cost money, and are apt to bring a man into low society. When I tell you that he and I first met in Exeter, as principals in crossing a fight, you may be sure that these pursuits *had* brought the young gentleman into *very* low company indeed. In fact, he was over head and ears in debt, raising money in every way he could, hook or crook, square or cross, to satisfy certain creditors, who were becoming nasty, impatient, and vexatious. I thought something might be made of this young gentleman, so finding there was no pride about him, I cultivated his acquaintance, examined his affairs, and put him up to the neatest little fakement in the world, just showed him how to raise two hundred pounds, and clear himself with everybody, just by signing his father's name, thereby saving the old gent the trouble of writing it (he is very infirm, is dad), and anticipating by a few years what must be his own at last. Not to mention paying off a lot of poor publicans and horse dealers, who could not afford to wait for their money. Blowed if I don't think it the most honest action he ever did in his life. Well, he committed the—wrote the name I mean—and stood two ten-pound notes for the information, quite handsome. But now this same young gent is going to marry a young lady with five thousand pounds in her own right, and she nearly of age. Her father, I understand, is worth another five thousand, and very old;

so that what he'll get ultimately if he marries into that family, counting his own expectations, won't be much less I should say than twenty thousand pounds. Now I mean to say, under these circumstances, I should be neglecting my own interests most culpably if I didn't demand from him the trifling sum of three hundred pounds for holding my tongue."

"Why, curse you," broke in Hawker, "you said two hundred yesterday."

"Exactly so," said Lee, "but that *was* yesterday. To-morrow, if the job ain't settled, it'll be four, and the day after five. It's no use, George Hawker," he continued; "you are treed, and you can't help yourself. If I give information you swing, and you know it; but I'd rather have the money than see the man hanged. But mind," said he, with a snarl, "if I catch you playing false, by the Lord, I'll hang you for love."

For an instant the wretched George cast a hurried glance around, as if considering what wild chance there was of mastering his two enemies, but that glance showed him that it was hopeless, for they both stood close together, each holding in his hand a cocked pistol, so in despair he dropped his eyes on the fire once more, while Lee chuckled inwardly at his wise foresight in bringing an accomplice.

"By Jove," he said to himself, "it's lucky Dick's here. If I had been alone he'd have been at me then like a tiger. It would have been only man to man, but he would have been as good as me; he'd have fought like a rat in a corner."

George sat looking into the embers for a full half-minute, while the others waited for his answer, determined that he should speak first. At length he raised his head, and said hoarsely, looking at neither of them:

"And where am I to get three hundred pounds?"

"A simple question very easily answered," said Lee. "Do what you did before, with half the difficulty. You manage nearly everything now your father is getting blind, so you need hardly take the trouble of altering the figures in the banker's book, and some slight hint about taking a new farm would naturally account for the old man's drawing out four or five hundred. The thing's easier than ever."

"Take my advice, young man," said Dick, "and take the shortest cut out of the wood. You see my friend here, William, has got tired of these parts, as being, you see, hardly free and easy enough for him, and he wants to get back to a part of the world he was rather anxious to leave a few years ago. If he likes to take me back with him, why he can. I rather fancy the notion myself. Give him the money, and in three months we'll both be fourteen thousand odd miles off. Meanwhile, you marry the young lady, and die in your bed, an honest gentleman, at eighty-four, instead of being walked out some cold morning to a gallows at twenty-two."

"Needs must where the devil drives," replied George. "You shall have the money this day week. And now let me go, for I am nearly froze dead."

"That's the talk," said Lee; "I knew you would be reasonable. If it hadn't been for my necessities, I am sure I never would have bothered you. Well, good night."

George rose and departed eastward, towards the rising moon, while Lee and his companion struck due west across the moor. The rain had ceased, and the sky was clear, so that there was not much difficulty in picking their way through the stones and moss-hags. Suddenly Lee stopped, and said to his comrade, with an oath:

"Dick, my boy, I didn't half like the way that dog left us."

"Nor I either," replied the other. "He has got some new move in his head, you may depend on it. He'll give you the slip if he can."

"Let him try it," said Lee; "Oh, only just let him try it."

And then the pair of worthies walked home.

CHAPTER VI

GEORGE HAWKER GOES TO THE FAIR—WRESTLES, BUT GETS THROWN ON HIS BACK—SHOOTS AT A MARK, BUT MISSES IT

Lee had guessed rightly. When George found himself so thoroughly entrapped, and heard all his most secret relations with Lee so openly discussed before a third man, he was in utter despair, and saw no hope of extrication from his difficulties. But this lasted for a very short time. Even while Lee and Dick were still speaking he was reflecting how to turn the tables on them, and already began to see a sparkle of hope glimmering afar.

Lee was a returned convict, George had very little doubt of that. A thousand queer expressions he had let fall in conversation had shown him that it was so. And now, if he could but prove it, and get Lee sent back out of the way. And yet that would hardly do after all. It would be difficult to identify him. His name gave no clue to who he was. There were a thousand or two of Lees hereabouts, and a hundred William Lees at least. Still it was evident that he was originally from this part of the country; it was odd no one had recognised him.

So George gave up this plan as hopeless. " Still," said he, " there is a week left; surely I can contrive to bowl him out somehow." And then he walked on in deep thought.

He was crossing the highest watershed in the county by an open, low-sided valley on the southern shoulder of Cawsand. To the left lay the mountain, and to the right tors of weathered granite, dim in the changing moonlight. Before him was a small moor-pool, in summer a mere reedy marsh, but now a bleak tarn, standing among dangerous mosses, sending ghostly echoes across the solitude as the water washed wearily against the black peat shores or rustled among the sere skeleton reeds in the shallow bays.

Suddenly he stopped with a jar in his brain and a chill at his heart. His breath came short, and raising one hand he stood beating the ground for half a minute with his foot. He gave a stealthy glance around, and then murmured hoarsely to himself:

" Ay, that would do; that would do well. And I could do it, too, when I was half drunk."

Was that the devil, chuckling joyous to himself across the bog? No, only an innocent little snipe, getting merry over the change of weather, bleating to his companions as though breeding time were come round again.

Crowd close, little snipes, among the cup-moss and wolf's foot, for he who stalks past you over the midnight moor meditates a foul and treacherous murder in his heart.

Yes, it had come to that, and so quickly. He would get this man Lee, who held his life in his hand, and was driving him on from crime to crime, to meet him alone on the moor if he could, and shoot him. What surety had he that Lee would leave him in peace after this next extortion? none but his word—the word of a villain like that. He knew what his own word was worth; what wonder if he set a small value on Lee's? He might be hung as it was; he would be hung for something. Taw Steps was a wild place, and none were likely to miss either Lee or his friend. It would be supposed they had tramped off as they came. There could be no proof against him, none whatever. No one had ever seen them together. They must both go. Well, two men were no worse than one. Hatherleigh had killed four men with his own hand at Waterloo, and they gave him a medal for it. They were likely honest fellows enough, not such scoundrels as these two.

So arguing confusedly with himself, only one thing certain in his mind, that he was committed to the perpetration of this crime, and that the time for drawing back was passed long ago, he walked rapidly onwards towards the little village where he had left his horse in an outhouse, fearing to trust him among the dangerous bogs which he had himself to cross to gain the rendezvous at Taw Steps.

He rapidly cleared the moor and soon gained the little grey street lying calm and peaceful beneath the bright winter moon, which was only now and then obscured for a moment by the last flying clouds of the late storm hurrying after their fellows. The rill which ran brawling loud through the village, swollen by the late rains, at length forced on his perception that he was fearfully thirsty and that his throat was parched and dry.

"This is the way men feel in hell, I think," said he. "Lord! let me get a drink while I can. The rich man old Jack reads about couldn't get one for all his money."

He walked up to a stone horse-trough, a little off the road. He stooped to drink, and started back with an oath. What pale, wild, ghastly face was that looking at him out of the cool, calm water? Not his own, surely? He closed his eyes, and having drunk deep walked on refreshed. He reached the outhouse where his horse was tied, and, as he was leading the impatient animal forth, one of the children within the cottage adjoining woke up and began to cry. He waited still a moment, and heard the mother arise and soothe it; then a window overhead opened, and a woman said:

"Is that you, Mr. Hawker?"

"Ay," said he, "it's me. Come for the horse."

He was startled at the sound of his own voice. It was like another man's. But like the voice of some one he seemed to know, too. A new acquaintance.

"It will be morn soon," resumed the woman. "The child is much worse to-night, and I think he'll go before daybreak. Well, well—much sorrow saved, maybe. I'll go to bed no more to-night, lest my boy should be off while I'm sleeping. Good night, sir. God bless you. May you never know the sorrow of losing a first-born."

Years after he remembered those random words. But now he only thought that if the brat should die there would be only one pauper less in Bickerton. And so thinking, mounted and rode on his way.

He rode fast, and was soon at home. He had put his horse in the stable, and, shoeless, was creeping up to bed when, as he passed his father's door, it opened, and the old man came out, light in hand.

He was a very infirm old man, much bent, though evidently at one time he had been of great stature. His retreating forehead, heavy grey eyebrows, and loose sensual mouth rendered him no pleasing object at any time, and as he stood in the doorway now with a half-drunken satyr-like leer on his face he looked perfectly hideous.

" Where's my pretty boy been?" he piped out. "How pale he looks. Are you drunk, my lad?"

"No! wish I was," replied George. " Give me the keys, dad, and let me get a drink of brandy. I've been vexed, and had nought to drink all night. I shall be getting the horrors if I don't have something before I go to bed."

The old man got him half a tumbler of brandy from his room, where there was always some to be had, and following him into his room sat down on the bed.

" Who's been vexing my handsome son?" said he; " my son that I've been waiting up for all night. Death and gallows to them, whoever they are. Is it that pale-faced little parson's daughter? Or is it her tight-laced hypocrite of a father, that comes whining here with his good advice to me who knows the world so well? Never mind, my boy. Keep a smooth face, and play the humbug till you've got her, and her money, and then break her impudent little heart if you will. Go to sleep, my boy, and dream you are avenged on them all."

" I mean to be, father, on some of them, I tell you," replied George.

" That's right, my man. Good night."

" Good night, old dad," said George. As he watched him out of the room a kinder, softer expression came on his face. His father was the only being he cared for in the world.

He slept a heavy and dreamless sleep that night, and when he woke for the first time the bright winter's sun was shining into his room and morning was far advanced.

He rose, strengthened and refreshed by his sleep, with a light heart. He began whistling as he dressed himself, but suddenly stopped as the recollection of the night before came upon him. Was it a reality, or only a dream? No; it was true enough. He has no need to whistle this morning. He is entangled in a web of crime and guilt from which there is no escape.

He dressed himself and went forth into the fresh morning air for a turn, walking up and down on the broad gravel walk before the dark old porch.

A glorious winter's morning. The dismal old stone house, many gabled, held aloft its tall red chimneys towards the clear blue sky, and looked bright and pleasant in the sunshine. The deep fir and holly wood which hemmed it in on all sides, save in front, were cheerful with sloping gleams of sunlight falling on many a patch of green moss, red fern, and bright brown last year's leaves. In front, far below him, rolled away miles of unbroken woodland, and in the far distance rose the moor, a dim cloud of pearly grey.

A robin sat and sang loud beside him, sole songster left in the wintry woods, but which said, as plain as bird could say, could he have understood it, " See, the birds are not all dead in this dreary winter time. I am still here, a pledge from my brothers. When yon dim grey woods grow green and the brown hollows are yellow with kingcups and primroses the old melody you know so well shall begin again, and the thrush from the oak-top shall answer to the golden-toned blackbird in the copse, saying, 'Our mother is not dead but has been sleeping. She is awake again—let all the land rejoice.' "

Little part had that poor darkened mind in such thoughts as these. If any softening influence were upon him this morning he gave no place to it. The robin ceased, and he only heard the croak of a raven, an old inhabitant of these wild woods, coming from the darkest and tallest of the fir trees. Then he saw his father approaching along the garden walk.

One more chance for thee, unhappy man. Go up to him now and tell him all. He has been a kind father to you, with all his faults. Get him on your side and you may laugh Lee to scorn. Have you not the courage to tell him?

For a moment he hesitated, but the dread of his father's burst of anger kept him silent. He hardened his heart, and, whistling, waited for the old man to come up.

" How is he this morning? " said his father. " What has he got his old clothes on for, and such fine ones as he has in his drawer? "

" Why should I put on my best clothes this day, father? "

" Ain't 'ee going down to revels? "

" True," said George. " I had forgotten all about it. Yes; I shall go down, of course."

" Are you going to play (wrestle)? " asked the father.

" Maybe I may. But come into breakfast. Where's Madge? "

" Indoors," said the father, " waiting breakfast—mortal cross."

" Curse her crossness," said George. " If I were ye, dad, I'd kick her out in the lane next time she got on one of her tantrums."

A tall woman about forty stepped out of the house as he uttered these words. "Ye hear what he says, William Hawker," she said. "Ye hear what ye're own lawful son says. He'd kick me out in the lane. And ye'd stand there and let him, ye old dog; I don't doubt."

"Hush, George," said the old man. "You don't know what you're saying, boy. Go in, Madge, and don't be a fool; you bring it on yourself."

The woman turned in a contemptuous way and walked in. She was a very remarkable looking person—tall and upright, at least six feet high, with swarthy complexion, black eyes, and coal-black hair, looped up loosely in a knot behind. She must have been very beautiful as a young girl, but was now too fierce and hawkish looking, though you would still call her handsome. She was a full-blooded gipsy, of one of the best families, which, however, she totally denied. When I say that she bore the worst of characters morally and had the reputation besides of being a witch of the highest acquirements—a sort of double first at Satan's university—I have said all I need to say about her at present.

These three sat down to breakfast, not before each of them, however, had refreshed themselves with a dram. All the meal through the old man and Madge were quarrelling with one another, till at length the contest grew so fierce that George noticed it, a thing he very seldom took the trouble to do.

"I tell thee," said the old man, "ye'll get no more money this week. What have 'ee done with the last five pounds?"

George knew well enough, she had given it to him. Many a time did she contrive to let him have a pound or two, and blind the old man as to where it was gone. The day before he had applied to her for some money and she had refused, and in revenge George had recommended his father to turn her out, knowing that she could hear every word, and little meaning it in reality.

"Ye *stingy old beast*," she replied, very slowly and distinctly, "I wish ye were dead and out of the way. I'll be doing it myself some of these odd times." And looking at him fixedly and pointing her finger, she began the Hebrew alphabet—Aleph, Beth, etc., from the 119th Psalm.

"I won't have it," screamed the old man. "Stop, or I'll kill you, I will——! George, you won't see your father took before your eyes. Stop her!"

"Come, quiet, oid girl; none of that," said George, taking her round the waist and putting his hand before her mouth. "Be reasonable now." She continued to look at the old man with a smile of triumph for a short time, and then said, with a queer laugh:

"It's lucky you stopped me. Oh, very lucky indeed. Now, are you going to give the money, you old Jew?"

She had carried the day, and the old man sulkily acquiesced. George went upstairs, and having dressed himself to his taste, got on horseback and rode down to the village, which was about three miles.

This was the day of the revels, which corresponds pretty well with what is called in other parts of England a pleasure fair; that is to say, although some business might be done, yet it was only a secondary object to amusement.

The main village of Drumston was about a mile from the church which I have before noticed, and consisted of a narrow street of cobhouses, whitewashed and thatched, crossing at right angles, by a little stone bridge, over a pretty, clear trout-stream. All around the village, immediately behind the backs of the houses, rose the abrupt red hills, divided into fields by broad oak hedges, thickly set with elms. The water of the stream, intercepted at some point higher up, was carried round the crown of the hills for the purposes of irrigation, which, even at this dead season, showed its advantages by the brilliant emerald green of the tender young grass on the hillsides. Drumston, in short, was an excellent specimen of a close, dull, dirty, and, I fear, not very healthy Devonshire village in the red country.

On this day the main street, usually in a state of ankle-deep mud six months in the year, was churned and pounded into an almost knee-deep state, by four or five hundred hobnail shoes in search of amusement. The amusements were various. Drinking (very popular), swearing (ditto), quarrelling, eating pastry, gingerbreads, and nuts (female pastime), and looking at a filthy Italian, leading a still more filthy monkey, who rode on a dog (the only honest one of the three). This all day, till night dropped down on a scene of drunkenness and vice, which we had better not seek to look at further. Surely, if ever man was right, old Joey Bender, the Methodist shoemaker, was right, when he preached against the revels for four Sundays running, and said roundly that he would sooner see all his congregation leave him and go up to the steeple-house (church) in a body, than that they should attend such a crying abomination.

The wrestling, the only honest, sensible amusement to be had, was not in much favour at Drumston. Such wrestling as there was was carried on in a little croft behind the principal of the public-houses, for some trifling prize, given by the publicans. Into this place, James Stockbridge and myself had wandered on the afternoon of the day in question, having come down to the revels to see if we could find someone we wanted.

There was a small ring of men watching the performances, and talking, each and all of them, not to his neighbour, or to himself, but to the ambient air, in the most unintelligible Devonshire jargon, rendered somewhat more barbarous than usual by intoxication. Frequently one of them would address one of the players in language more forcible than choice, as he applauded some piece of finesse, or condemned some clumsiness on the part of the two youths who were struggling about in the centre, under the impression they were wrestling. There were but two moderate wrestlers in the parish, and those two were George Hawker and James Stockbridge. And James and myself had hardly arrived on the ground two minutes, before George, coming up, greeted us.

After a few commonplace civilities, he challenged James to play. " Let us show these muffs what play is," said he; " it's a disgrace to the county to see such work."

James had no objection; so, having put on the jackets, they set to work to the great admiration of the bystanders, one of whom, a drunken tinker, expressed his applause in such remarkable language that I mildly asked him to desist, which of course made him worse.

The two wrestlers made very pretty play of it for some time, till James, feinting at some outlandish manœuvre, put George on his back by a simple trip, akin to scholar's-mate at chess.

George fell heavily, for they were both heavy men. He rose from the ground and walked to where his coat was, sulkily. James, thinking he might have been hurt, went up to speak to him; but the other, greeting him with an oath, turned and walked away through the crowd.

He was in a furious passion, and he went on to the little bridge that crossed the stream. We saw him standing looking into the water below, when a short light-looking man came up to him, and having spoken to him for a few minutes, walked off in the direction of Exeter, at a steady, rapid pace.

That man was Dick, the companion of Lee (I knew all this afterwards). George was standing as I have described on the bridge, when he came up to him, and touching him, said:

" I want to speak to you a moment, Mr. Hawker."

George turned round, and when he saw who it was, asked angrily: " What the devil do you want? "

" No offence, sir. You see, I'm in trouble, there's a warrant out against me, and I must fly. I am as hard up as a poor cove could be; can you give me a trifle to help me along the road? "

Here was a slice of good luck; to get rid of this one so easily. George gave him money, and having wished him farewell, watched him striding steadily up the long hill towards Exeter with great satisfaction; then he went back to the public-house, and sat drinking an hour or more. At last he got out his horse to ride homeward.

The crowd about the public-house door was as thick as ever, and the disturbance greater. Some of the women were trying to get their drunken husbands home, one man had fallen down dead-drunk beside the door in the mud, and his wife was sitting patiently beside him. Several girls were standing wearily about the door, dressed in their best, each with a carefully-folded white pocket-handkerchief in her hand for show, and not for use, waiting for their sweethearts to come forth when it should suit them; while inside the tap all was a wild confusion of talk, quarrelling, oaths, and smoke enough to sicken a scavenger.

These things are changed now, or are changing, year by year. Now we have our rural policeman keeping some sort of order, and some show of decency. And indeed these little fairs, the curse of the country, are gradually becoming extinct by the exertions of a more energetic class of county magistrates; and though there is probably the same amount of vice, public propriety is at all events more respected. I think I may say that I have seen as bad, or even worse, scenes of drunkenness and disorder at an English fair, as ever I have in any Australian mining town.

George Hawker was so hemmed in by the crowd that he was unable to proceed above a foot's pace. He was slowly picking his way through the people, when he felt some one touching him on the. leg, and, looking round, saw Lee standing beside him.

" What, Lee, my boy, you here? " said he; " I have just seen your amiable comrade—he seems to be in trouble."

" Dick's always in trouble, Mr. Hawker," replied he. " He has not care or reason; he isn't a bad fellow, but I'm always glad when he is out of my way; I don't like being seen with him. This is likely to be his last time, though. He is in a serious scrape, and, by way of getting out of it, he is walking into Exeter, along the high-road, as if nothing was the matter. There's a couple of traps in Belston after him now, and I came down here to keep secure. By the bye, have you thought of that little matter we were talking

about the other night? To tell you the truth, I don't care how soon
I am out of this part of the country."

"Oh! ah!" replied George, "I've thought of it, and it's all right.
Can you be at the old place the day after to-morrow?"

"That can I," said Lee, "with much pleasure."

"You'll come alone this time, I suppose," said George. "I
suppose you don't want to share our little matter with the whole
country?"

"No fear, Mr. George; I will be there at eight punctual, and
alone."

"Well, bye-bye," said George, and rode off.

It was getting late in the evening when he started, and ere he
reached home it was nearly dark. For the last mile his road lay
through forest-land: noble oaks, with a plentiful undergrowth of
holly, overshadowed a floor of brown leaves and red fern; and at the
end of the wood nearest home, where the oaks joined his own fir
plantations, one mighty gnarled tree, broader and older than all the
rest, held aloft its withered boughs against the frosty sky.

This oak was one of the bogy haunts of the neighbourhood. All
sorts of stories were told about it, all of which George, of course,
believed; so that when his horse started and refused to move
forward, and when he saw a dark figure sitting on the twisted roots
of the tree, he grew suddenly cold, and believed he had seen a ghost.

The figure rose, and stalked towards him through the gathering
gloom; he saw that it held a baby in its arms, and that it was tall
and noble-looking. Then a new fear took possession of him, not
supernatural; and he said in a low voice, "Ellen!"

"That was my name once, George Hawker," replied she, standing
beside him, and laying her hand upon his horse's shoulder. "I
don't know what my name is now, I'm sure; it surely can't remain
the same, and me so altered."

"What on earth brings you back just at this time, in God's
name?" asked George.

"Hunger, cold, misery, drunkenness, disease. Those are the merry
companions that lead me back to my old sweetheart. Look here,
George, should you know him again?"

She held up a noble child about a year old, for him to look at.
The child, disturbed from her warm bosom, began to wail.

"What! cry to see your father, child?" she exclaimed. "See
what a bonnie gentleman he is, and what a pretty horse he rides,
while we tread along through the mire."

"What have you come to me for, Ellen?" asked George. "Do

you know that if you are seen about here just now you may do me a great injury?"

"I don't want to hurt you, George," she replied; "but I must have money. I cannot work, and I dare not show my face here. Can't you take me in to-night, George, only just to-night, and let me lie by the fire? I'll go in the morning; but I know it's going to freeze, and I do dread the long cold hours so. I have lain out two nights, now, and had naught to eat all day. Do'ee take me in, George; for old love's sake, do!"

She was his own cousin, an orphan, brought up in the same house with him by his father. Never very strong in her mind, though exceedingly pretty, she had been early brought to ruin by George. On the birth of a boy, about a year before, the old man's eyes were opened to what was going on, and in a furious rage he turned her out of doors, and refused ever to see her again. George, to do him justice, would have married her, but his father told him, if he did so, he should leave the house with her. So the poor thing had gone away and tried to get needlework in Exeter, but her health failing, and George having ceased to answer all applications from her, she had walked over, and lurked about in the woods to gain an interview with him.

She laid her hand on his, and he felt it was deadly cold. "Put my coat over your shoulders, Nelly, and wait an instant while I go and speak to Madge. I had better let her know you are coming; then we shan't have any trouble."

He rode quickly through the plantation, and gave his horse to a boy who waited in front of the door. In the kitchen he found Madge brooding over the fire, with her elbows on her knees, and without raising her head or turning round, she said:

"Home early, and sober! what new mischief are you up to?"

"None, Madge, none! but here's the devil to pay. Ellen's come back. She's been lying out these two nights, and is awful hard up. It's not my fault, I have sent her money enough, in all conscience."

"Where is she?" inquired Madge curtly.

"Outside, in the plantation."

"Why don't you bring her in, you treacherous young wolf?" replied she. "What did you bring her to shame for, if you are going to starve her?"

"I was going to fetch her in," said George indignantly; "only I wanted to find out what your temper was like, you vicious old cow. How did I know but what you would begin some of your tantrums, and miscall her?"

"No fear o' that! no fear of pots and kettles with me! Lead her in, lad, before she's frozen!"

George went back for her, and finding her still in the same place; brought her in. Madge was standing erect before the fire, and, walking up to the unfortunate Ellen, took her baby from her, and made her sit before the fire.

"Better not face the old man," said she; "he's away to the revels, and he'll come home drunk. Make yourself happy for to-night, at all events."

The poor thing began to cry, which brought on such a terrible fit of coughing that Madge feared she would rupture a blood-vessel. She went to get her a glass of wine, and returned with a candle, and then, for the first time, they saw what a fearful object she was.

"Oh!" she said to George, "you see what I am now. I ain't long for this world. Only keep me from worse, George, while I am alive, and do something for the boy afterwards, and I am content. You're going to get married, I know, and I wish you well. But don't forget this poor little thing when it's motherless; if you do, and let him fall into vice, you'll never be lucky, George."

"Oh!" she said to George, "you see what I am now. I ain't long many years yet. You're pulled down, and thin, but you'll pick up again with the spring. Now, old girl, get some supper out before he comes home."

They gave her supper, and put her to bed. In the morning, very early, George heard the sound of wheels below his bedroom window; and looking out, saw that Madge was driving out of the yard in a light cart, and, watching her closely, saw her pick up Ellen and the child just outside the gate. Then he went to bed again, and, when he awoke, he heard Madge's voice below, and knew she was back.

He went down, and spoke to her. "Is she gone?" he asked.

"In course she is," replied Madge. "Do you think I was going to let her stay till the old man was about?"

"How much money did you give her, besides what she had from me?"

"I made it five pounds in all; that will keep her for some time, and then you must send her some more. If you let that wench starve, you ought to be burnt alive. A *man* would have married her in spite of his father."

"A likely story," said George, "that I was to disinherit myself for her. However, she shan't want at present, or we shall have her back again. And that won't do, you know."

"George," said Madge, "you promise to be as great a rascal as your father."

The old man had, as Madge prophesied, come home very drunk the night before, and had lain in bed later than usual, so that, when he came to breakfast, he found George, gun in hand, ready to go out.

"Going shooting, my lad?" said the father. "Where be going?"

"Down through the hollies for a woodcock. I'll get one this morning, it's near full moon."

All the morning they heard him firing in the bottom below the house, and at one o'clock he came home, empty handed.

"Why, George!" said his father, "what has thee been shooting at? I thought 'ee was getting good sport."

"I've been shooting at a mark," he replied.

"Who be going to shoot now, eh, George?" asked the old man.

"No one as I know of," he replied.

"Going over to Eggesford, eh, Georgey? This nice full moon is about the right thing for thee. They Fellowes be good fellows to keep a fat haunch for their neighbours."

George laughed, as he admitted the soft impeachment of deer-stealing, but soon after grew sullen, and all the afternoon sat over the fire brooding and drinking. He went to bed early, and had just got off his boots, when the door opened, and Madge came in.

"What's up to now, old girl?" said George.

"What are you going to be up to, eh?" she asked, "with your gun?"

"Only going to get an outlying deer," said he.

"That's folly enough, but there's a worse folly than that. It's worse folly to wipe out money-scores in blood. It's a worse folly if you are in a difficulty to put yourself in a harder one to get out of the first. It's a worse——"

"Why, you're mad," broke in George. "Do you think I am fool enough to make away with one of the keepers?"

"I don't know what you are fool enough to do. Only mind my words before it's too late."

She went out, and left him sitting moodily on the bed. "What a clever woman she is," he mused. "How she hits a thing off. She's been a good friend to me. I've a good mind to ask her advice. I'll think about it to-morrow morning."

But on the morrow they quarrelled about something or another, and her advice was never asked. George was moody and captious all day; and at evening, having drunk hard, he slipped off, and, gun in hand, rode away through the darkening woods towards the moor.

It was dark before he had got clear of the labyrinth of lanes through which he took his way. His horse he turned out in a small croft close to where the heather began; and, having hid the saddle and bridle in a hedge, strode away over the moor with his gun on his shoulder.

He would not think; he would sooner whistle; distance seemed like nothing to him; and he was surprised and frightened to find himself already looking over the deep black gulf through which the river ran before he thought he was half-way there.

He paused to look before he began to descend. A faint light still lingered in the frosty sky to the south-west, and majestic Yestor rose bold and black against it. Down far, far beneath his feet was the river, dimly heard, but not seen; and, as he looked to where it should be, he saw a little flickering star, which arrested his attention. That must be Lee's fire—there he began to descend.

Boldly at first, but afterwards more stealthily, and now more silently still, for the fire is close by, and it were well to give him no notice. It is in the old place, and he can see it now, not ten yards before him, between two rocks.

Nearer yet a little, with catlike tread. There is Lee, close to the fire, sitting on the ground, dimly visible, yet clearly enough for his purpose. He rests the gun on a rock, and takes his aim.

He is pinioned from behind by a vigorous hand, and a voice he knows cries in his ear, " Help, Bill, or you'll be shot! "

The gun goes off in the scuffle, but hurts nobody, and Lee running up, George finds the tables completely turned, and himself lying, after a few desperate struggles, helplessly pinioned on the ground.

Dick had merely blinded him by appearing to go to Exeter. They both thought it likely that he would attack Lee, but neither supposed he would have stolen on him so treacherously. Dick had just noticed him in time, and sprung upon him, or Lee's troubles would have been over for ever.

" You treacherous young sweep, you shall hang for this," were Lee's first words. " Ten thousand pounds would not save you now. Dick, you're a jewel. If I had listened to you, I shouldn't have trusted my life to the murdering vagabond. I'll remember to-night, my boy, as long as I live."

Although it appeared at first that ten thousand pounds would not prevent Lee handing George over to justice, yet, after a long and stormy argument, it appeared that the lesser sum of five hundred would be amply sufficient to stay any ulterior proceedings, provided the money was forthcoming in a week. So that ultimately George found himself at liberty again, and, to his great astonishment, in higher spirits than he could have expected.

"At all events," said he to himself, as he limped back, lame and bruised, "I have not got *that* on my mind. Even if this other thing was found out, there is a chance of getting off. Surely my own father wouldn't prosecute—though I wouldn't like to trust to it, unless I got Madge on my side."

His father, I think I have mentioned, was too blind to read, and George used to keep all his accounts; so that nothing would seem at first to look more easy than to imitate his father's signature, and obtain what money he wished. But George knew well that the old man was often in the habit of looking through his banker's book, with the assistance of Madge, so that he was quite unsafe without her. His former embezzlement he had kept secret, by altering some figures in the banker's book; but this next one, of a much larger amount, he felt somewhat anxious about. He, however, knew his woman well, and took his measures accordingly.

On the day mentioned, he met Lee, and gave him the money agreed on; and having received his assurances that he valued his life too much to trouble him any more, saw him depart, fully expecting that he should have another application at an early date; under which circumstances, he thought he would take certain precautions which should be conclusive.

But he saw Lee no more. No more for many, many years. But how and when they met again, and who came off best in the end, this tale will truly and sufficiently set forth hereafter.

CHAPTER VII

MAJOR BUCKLEY GIVES HIS OPINION ON TROUT FISHING, ON EMIGRATION, AND ON GEORGE HAWKER

SPRING had come again, after a long wet winter, and every orchard-hollow blushed once more with apple-blossoms. In warm, sheltered southern valleys hedges were already green, and even the tall hedgerow-elms began, day after day, to grow more shady and dense.

It was a bright April morning, about ten o'clock, when Mary Thornton, throwing up her father's study window from the outside, challenged him to come out and take a walk; and John, getting his hat and stick, immediately joined her in front of the house.

"Where is your aunt, my love?" said John.

"She is upstairs," said Mary. "I will call her."

She began throwing gravel at one of the upper windows, and crying out, "Auntie! Auntie!"

The sash was immediately thrown (no, that is too violent a word —say lifted) up, and a beautiful old lady's face appeared at the window.

"My love," it said, in a small, soft voice, "pray be careful of the windows. Did you want anything, my dear?"

"I want you out for a walk, Auntie; so come along."

"Certainly, my love. Brother, have you got your thick kerchief in your pocket?"

"No," said the Vicar, "I have not, and I don't mean to have."

Commencement of a sore-throat lecture from the window, cut short by the Vicar, who says:

"My dear, I shall be late if you don't come." (Jesuitically on his part, for he was going nowhere.)

So she comes accordingly, as sweet-looking an old maid as ever you saw in your life. People have no right to use up such beautiful women as governesses. It's a sheer waste of material. Miss Thornton had been a governess all her life; and now, at the age of five-and-forty, had come to keep her brother's house for him, add her savings to his, and put the finishing touch on Mary's somewhat rough education.

"My love," said she, "I have brought you your gloves."

"Oh, indeed, Auntie, I won't wear them," said Mary. "I couldn't be plagued with gloves. Nobody wears them here."

"Mrs. Buckley wears them, and it would relieve my mind if you were to put them on, my dear. I fear my lady's end was accelerated by, unfortunately, in her last illness, catching sight of Lady Kate's hands after she had been assisting her brother to pick green walnuts."

Mary was always on the eve of laughing at these aristocratic recollections of her aunt; and to her credit be it said, she always restrained herself, though with great difficulty. She, so wildly brought up, without rule or guidance in feminine matters, could not be brought to comprehend that prim line-and-rule life, of which her aunt was the very personification. Nevertheless, she heard what

Miss Thornton had to say with respect; and if ever she committd an extreme gaucherie, calculated to set her aunt's teeth on edge, she always discovered what was the matter, and mended it as far as she was able.

They stood on the lawn while the glove controversy was going on, and a glorious prospect there was that bright spring morning. In one direction the eye was carried down a long, broad, and rich vale, intersected by a gleaming river, and all the way down set thick with hamlet, farm, and church. In the dim soft distance rose the two massive towers of a cathedral, now filling all the country-side with the gentle melody of their golden-toned bells, while beyond them, in the misty south, there was a gleam in the horizon, showing where the sky

" Dipped down to sea and sands."

" It's as soft and quiet as a Sunday," said the Vicar, " and what a fishing day! I have half a mind—— Hallo! look here."

The exclamation was caused by the appearance on the walk of a very tall and noble-looking man, about thirty, leading a grey pony, on which sat a beautiful woman with a child in her arms. Our party immediately moved forward to meet them, and a most friendly greeting took place on both sides, Mary at once taking possession of the child.

This was Major Buckley and his wife Agnes. I mentioned before that, after Clere was sold, the Major had taken a cottage in Drumston, and was a constant visitor on the Vicar; generally calling for the old gentleman to come fishing or shooting, and leaving his wife and his little son Samuel in the company of Mary and Miss Thornton.

" I have come, Vicar, to take you out fishing," said he. " Get your rod and come. A capital day. Why, here's the Doctor."

So there was, standing among them before any one had noticed him.

" I announce," said he, " that I shall accept the most agreeable invitation that any one will give me. What are you going to do, Major?"

" Going fishing."

" Ah! and you, madam?" turning to Miss Thornton.

" I am going to see Mrs. Lee, who has a low fever, poor thing."

" Which Mrs. Lee, madam?"

" Mrs. Lee of Eyford."

" And which Mrs. Lee of Eyford, madam?"

" Mrs. James Lee."

" Junior or senior ? " persevered the Doctor.

" Junior," replied Miss Thornton, laughing.

" Ah ! " said the Doctor, " now we have it. I would suggest that all the Mrs. Lees in the parish should have a ticket with a number on it, like the *voituriers*. Buckley, lay it before the quarter-sessions. If you say the idea came from a foreigner, they will adopt it immediately. Miss Thornton, I will do myself the honour of accompanying you, and examine the case."

So the ladies went off with the Doctor, while the Vicar and Major Buckley turned to go fishing.

" I shall watch you, Major, instead of fishing myself," said the Vicar. " Where do you propose going ? "

" To the red water," said the Major. Accordingly they turn down a long, deep lane, which looks certainly as if it would lead one to a red brook, for the road and banks are of a brick colour. And so it does, for presently before them they discern a red mill, and a broad, pleasant ford, where a crystal brook dimples and sparkles over a bed of reddish-purple pebbles.

" It is very clear," says the Major. " What's the fly to be, Vicar ? "

" That's a very hard question to answer," says the Vicar. " Your Scotchman, eh ? or a small blue dun ? "

" We'll try both," says the Major; and in a very short time it becomes apparent that the small dun is the man, for the trout seem to think that it is the very thing they have been looking for all day, and rise at it two at a time.

They fish downwards; and after killing half a dozen half-pound fish, come to a place where another stream joins the first, making it double its original size, and here there is a great oak-root jutting into a large deep pool.

The Vicar stands back, intensely excited. This is a sure place for a big fish. The Major, eager but cool, stoops down and puts his flies in just above the root at once; not as a greenhorn would, taking a few wide casts over the pool first, thereby standing a chance of hooking a little fish, and ruining his chance for a big one; and at the second trial a deep-bodied brown fellow, about two pounds, dashes at the treacherous little blue, and gulps him down.

Then what a to-do is there. The Vicar jumping about on the grass, giving all sorts of contradictory advice. The Major, utterly despairing of ever getting his fish ashore, fighting a losing battle with infinite courage, determined that the trout shall remember him, at all events, if he does get away. And the trout, furious and indignant, but not in the least frightened, trying vainly to get back to the old root. Was there ever such a fish?

But the Major is the best man, for after ten minutes troutie is towed up on his side to a convenient shallow, and the Vicar puts on his spectacles to see him brought ashore. He scientifically pokes him in the flank, and spans him across the back, and pronounces *ex cathedra*:

"You'll find, sir, there won't be a finer fish, take him all in all, killed in the parish this season."

"Ah, it's a noble sport," says the Major. "I shan't get much more of it, I'm afraid."

"Why shouldn't you?"

"Well, I'll tell you," says the Major. "Do you know how much property I have got?"

"No, indeed."

"I have only ten thousand pounds; and how am I to bring up a family on the interest of that?"

"I should fancy it was quite enough for you," said the Vicar; "you have only one son."

"How many more am I likely to have, eh? And how should I look to find myself at sixty with five boys grown up, and only £300 a year?"

"That is rather an extreme case," said the Vicar; "you would be poor then, certainly."

"Just what I don't want to be. Besides wanting to make some money, I am leading an idle life here, and am getting very tired of it. And so——" he hesitated.

"And so?" said the Vicar.

"I am thinking of emigrating. To New South Wales. To go into the sheep-farming line. There."

"There indeed," said the Vicar. "And what has put you up to it?"

"Why, my wife and I have been thinking of going to Canada for some time, and so the idea is not altogether new. The other day Hamlyn (you know him) showed me a letter from a cousin of his who is making a good deal of money there. Having seen that letter, I was much struck with it, and having made a great many other inquiries, I laid the whole information before my wife, and begged her to give me her opinion."

"And she recommended you to stay at home in peace and comfort," interposed the Vicar.

"On the contrary, she said she thought we ought by all means to go," returned the Major.

"Wonderful, indeed. And when shall you go?"

"Not for some time, I think. Not for a year."

"I hope not. What a lonely old man I shall be when you are all gone."

"Nay, Vicar, I hope not," said the Major. "You will stay behind to see your daughter happily married, and your grandchildren about your knees."

The Vicar sighed heavily, and the Major continued.

"By the bye, Miss Thornton seems to have made a conquest already. Young Hawker seems desperately smitten; did it ever strike you?"

"Yes, it has struck me; very deep indeed," said the Vicar; "but what can I do?"

"You surely would not allow her to marry him?"

"How can I prevent it? She is her own mistress, and I never could control her yet. How can I control her when her whole heart and soul is set on him?"

"Good God!" said the Major, "do you really think she cares for him?"

"Oh, she loves him with her whole heart. I have seen it a long while."

"My dear friend, you should take her away for a short time, and see if she will forget him. Anything sooner than let her marry him."

"Why should she not marry him?" said the Vicar. "She is only a farmer's granddaughter. We are nobody, you know."

"But he is not of good character."

"Oh, there is nothing more against him than there is against most young fellows. He will reform and be steady. Do you know anything special against him?" asked the Vicar.

"Not actually against him; but just conceive, my dear friend, what a family to marry into! His father—I speak the plain truth—is a most disreputable, drunken old man, living in open sin with a gipsy woman of the worst character, by whom George Hawker has been brought up. What an atmosphere of vice! The young fellow himself is universally disliked, and distrusted too, all over the village. Can you forgive me for speaking so plain?"

"There is no forgiveness necessary, my good friend," said the Vicar. "I know how kind your intentions are. But I cannot bring myself to have a useless quarrel with my daughter merely because I happen to dislike the object of her choice. It would be quite a useless quarrel. She has always had her own way, and always will."

"What does Miss Thornton say?" asked the Major.

"Nothing; she never does say anything. She regards Hawker as Mary's accepted suitor; and though she may think him vulgar, she would sooner die than commit herself so far as to say so. She has been so long under others, and without an opinion save theirs, that she cannot form an opinion at all."

They had turned and were walking home, when the Vicar, sticking his walking-cane upright in the grass, began again.

"It is the most miserable and lamentable thing that ever took place in this world. Look at my sister again : what a delicate old maid she is ! used to move and be respected, more than most governesses are, in the highest society in the land. There'll be a home for her when I die! Think of her living in the house with any of the Hawkers; and yet, so, that woman's sense of duty is such that she'd die sooner than leave her niece. Sooner be burnt at the stake than go óne inch out of the line of conduct she has marked out for herself."

The Vicar judged his sister most rightly : we shall see that hereafter.

"A man of determination and strength of character could have prevented it at the beginning, you would say. I dare say he might have; but I am not a man of determination and strength of character. I never was, and I never shall be."

"Do you consider it in the light of a settled question, then," said the Major, "that your daughter should marry young Hawker?"

"God knows. She will please herself. I spoke to her at first about encouraging him, and she began by laughing at me, and ended by making a scene whenever I spoke against him. I was at one time in hopes that she would have taken a fancy to young Stockbridge; but I fear I must have set her against him by praising him too much. It wants a woman, you know, to manage those sort of things."

"It does, indeed."

"You see, as I said before, I have no actual reason to urge against Hawker, and he will be very rich. I shall raise my voice against her living in the house with that woman Madge—in fact, I won't have it; but take it all in all, I fear I shall have to make the best of it."

Major Buckley said no more, and soon after they got home.

There was Mrs. Buckley, queenly and beautiful, waiting for her husband; and there was Mary, pretty, and full of fun; there also was the Doctor, smoking and contemplating a new fern; and Miss Thornton, with her gloved hands folded, calculating uneasily what amount of detriment Mary's complexion would sustain in consequence of walking about without her bonnet in an April sun.

One and all cried out to know what sport; and little Sam tottered forward demanding a fish for himself, which, having got, he at once put into his mouth head foremost. The Doctor, taking off his spectacles, examined the contents of the fish-basket, and then demanded:

"Now, my good friend, why do you give yourself the trouble to catch trout in that roundabout way, requiring so much skill and patience? In Germany we catch them with a net—a far superior way, I assure you. Get any one of the idle young fellows about the village to go down to the stream with a net, and they will get more trout in a day than you would in a week."

"What!" said the Major indignantly; "put a net in my rented water?—If I caught any audacious scoundrel carrying a net within half a mile of it, I'd break his neck. You can't appreciate the delights of fly-fishing, Doctor—you are no sportsman."

"No, I ain't," said the Doctor; "you never said anything truer than that, James Buckley. I am nothing of the sort. When I was a young man, I had a sort of brute instinct, which made me take the same sort of pleasure in killing a boar that a cat does in killing a mouse; but I have outlived such barbarism."

"Ha, ha!" said the Vicar; "and yet he gave five shillings for a snipe. And he's hand and glove with every poacher in the parish."

"The snipe was a new species, sir," said the Doctor indignantly; "and if I do employ the hunters to collect for me, I see no inconsistency in that. But I consider this fly-fishing mania just of a piece with your *idiotic,* I repeat it, *idiotic* institution of fox-hunting. Why, if you laid baits poisoned with nux vomica about the haunts of those animals, you would get rid of them in two years."

The Doctor used to delight in aggravating the Major by attacking English sports; but he had a great admiration for them nevertheless.

The Major got out his wife's pony; and setting her on it, and handing up the son and heir, departed home to dinner. They were hardly inside the gate when Mrs. Buckley began:

"My dear husband, did you bring him to speak of the subject we were talking about?"

" He went into it himself, wife, tooth and nail."

" Well ? "

" Well! indeed, my dear Agnes, do you know that, although I love the old man dearly, I must say I think he is rather weak."

" So I fear," said Mrs. Buckley; " but he is surely not so weak as to allow that young fellow to haunt the house, after he has had a hint that he is making love to Mary ? "

" My dear, he accepts him as her suitor. He says he has been aware of it for some time, and that he has spoken to Mary about it, and made no impression; so that now he considers it a settled thing."

" What culpable weakness! So Mary encourages him, then ? "

" She adores him, and won't hear a word against him."

" Unfortunate girl! " said Mrs. Buckley, " and with such a noble young fellow as Stockbridge ready to cut off his head for her! It is perfectly inconceivable."

" Young Hawker is very handsome, my dear, you must remember."

" Is he ? " said Mrs. Buckley. " *I* call him one of the most evil-looking men I ever saw."

" My dear Agnes, I think if you were to speak boldly to her, you might do some good. You might begin to undermine this unlucky infatuation of hers! and I am sure, if her eyes were once opened, that the more she saw him, the less she would like him."

" I think, James," said Mrs. Buckley, " that it becomes the duty of us, who have been so happy in our marriage, to prevent our good old Vicar's last days from being rendered miserable by such a *mésalliance* as this. I am very fond of Mary; but the old Vicar, my dear, has taken the place of your father to me."

" He is like a second father to me too," said the Major; " but he wants a good many qualities that my own father had. He hasn't his energy or determination. Why, if my father had been in his place, and such an ill-looking young dog as that came hanging about the premises, my father would have laid his stick about his back. And it would be a good thing if somebody would do it now."

Such was Major Buckley's opinion.

CHAPTER VIII

THE VICAR HEARS SOMETHING TO HIS ADVANTAGE

" MY dear," said old Miss Thornton, that evening, " I have consulted Mrs. Buckley on the sleeves, and she is of opinion that they should be pointed."

" Do you think," said Mary, " that she thought much about the matter?"

" She promised to give the matter her earnest attention," said Miss Thornton; " so I suppose she did. Mrs. Buckley would never speak at random, if she once promised to give her real opinion."

" No, I don't think she would, Auntie, but she is not very particular in her own dress."

" She always looks like a thorough lady, my dear: Mrs. Buckley is a woman whom I could set before you as a model for imitation far sooner than myself."

" She is a duck, at all events," said Mary; " and her husband is a darling."

Miss Thornton was too much shocked to say anything. To hear a young lady speak of a handsome military man as a " darling," went quite beyond her experience. She was considering how much bread and water and blackboard she would have felt it her duty to give Lady Kate, or Lady Fanny, in old times, for such an expression, when the Vicar, who had been dozing, woke up and said :

" Bless us, what a night! The equinoctial gales come back again. This rain will make up for the dry March with a vengeance; I am glad I am safely housed before a good fire."

Unlucky words! he drew nearer to the fire, and began rubbing his knees; he had given them about three rubs, when the door opened and the maid's voice was heard ominous of evil.

" Thomas Jewel is worse, sir, and if you please his missis don't expect he'll last the night; and could you just step up?"

" Just stepping up " was a pretty little euphemism for walking three long miles dead in the teeth of a gale of wind, with a fierce rushing tropical rain. One of the numerous tenders of the ship Jewel (74), had just arrived before the wind under bare poles, an attempt to set a rag of umbrella having ended in its being blown out of the bolt-ropes, and the aforesaid tender Jewel was now in the vicarage harbour of refuge, reflecting what an awful job it would have in beating back against the monsoon.

" Who has come with this message ? " said the Vicar, entering the kitchen followed by Miss Thornton and Mary.

" Me, sir," says a voice from the doorway.

" Oh, come in, will you," said the Vicar; " it's a terrible night, is it not ? "

" Oh Lord ! " said the voice in reply—intending that ejaculation for a very strong affirmative. And advancing towards the light, displayed a figure in a long brown greatcoat reaching to the ankles, and topped by some sort of head-dress, resembling very closely a small black carpet-bag, tied on with a red cotton handkerchief. This was all that was visible, and the good Vicar stood doubting whether it was male or female, till catching sight of an immense pair of hob-nail boots peeping from the lower extremity of the coat, he made up his mind at once, and began :

" My good boy——"

There was a cackling laugh from under the carpet-bag, and a harsh grating voice replied :

" I be a gurl."

" Dear me," said the Vicar, " then what do you dress yourself in that style for ?—So old Jewel is worse."

" Us don't think a'll live the night."

" Is the Doctor with him ? " said the Vicar.

" The 'Talian's with 'un."

By which he understood her to mean Dr. Mulhaus, all foreigners being considered to be Italians in Drumston. An idea they got, I take it, from the wandering organ men being of that nation.

" Well," said the Vicar, " I will start at once, and come. It's a terrible night."

The owner of the greatcoat assented with a fiendish cackle, and departed. The Vicar, having been well wrapped up by his sister and daughter, departed also, with a last injunction from Miss Thornton to take care of himself.

Easier said than done, such a night as this. A regular south-westerly gale, accompanied by a stinging, cutting rain, which made it almost impossible to look to windward. Earth and sky seemed mixed together, and each twig and bough sent a separate plaint upon the gale, indignant at seeing their fresh-acquired honours torn from them and scattered before the blast.

The Vicar put his head down and sturdily walked against it. It was well for him that he knew every inch of the road, for his knowledge was needed now. There was no turn in the road after he had passed the church, but it took straight away over the high ground up to Hawker's farm on the woodlands.

Old Jewel, whom he was going to see, had been a hind of Hawker's for many years; but about a twelve-month before the present time he had left his service, partly on account of increasing infirmity, and partly in consequence of a violent quarrel with Madge. He was a man of indifferent character. He had been married once in his life, but his wife only lived a year, and left him with one son, who had likewise married and given to the world seven as barbarous, neglected young savages as any in the parish. The old man, who was now lying on his deathbed, had been a sort of confidential man to old Hawker, retained in that capacity on account, the old man said once in his drink, of not having any wife to worm family affairs out of him. So it was generally believed by the village folks that old Jewel was in possession of some fearful secrets (such as a murder or two, for instance, or a brace of forgeries), and that the Hawkers daren't turn him out of the cottage where he lived for their lives.

Perhaps some of these idle rumours may have floated through the Vicar's brain as he fought forwards against the storm; but if any did, they were soon dismissed again, and the good man's thoughts carried into a fresh channel. And he was thinking what a fearful night this would be at sea, and how any ship could live against such a storm, when he came to a white gate, which led into the deep woods surrounding Hawker's house, and in a recess of which lived old Jewel and his family.

Now began the most difficult part of his journey. The broader road that led from the gate up to the Hawker's house was plainly perceptible, but the little path which turned up to the cottage was not so easily found, and when found, not easily kept on such a black wild night as this. But, at length, having hit it, he began to follow it with some difficulty, and soon beginning to descend rapidly, he caught sight of a light, and, at the same moment, heard the rushing of water.

" Oh," said he to himself, " the water is come down, and I shall have a nice job to get across it. Any people but the Jewels would have made some sort of a bridge by now; but they have been content with a fallen tree ever since the old bridge was carried away."

He scrambled down the steep hillside with great difficulty, and not without one or two nasty slips, which, to a man of his age, was no trifle, but at length stood trembling with exertion before a flooded brook, across which lay a fallen tree, dimly seen in the dark against the gleam of the rushing water.

"I must stand and steady my nerves a bit after that tumble," he said, "before I venture over there. That's the 'Brig of Dread' with a vengeance. However, I never came to harm yet when I was after duty, so I'll chance it."

The cottage stood just across the brook, and he hallooed aloud for some one to come. After a short time the door opened, and a man appeared with a lantern.

"Who is there?" demanded Dr. Mulhaus's well-known voice. "Is it you, Vicar?"

"Ay," rejoined the other, "it's me at present; but it won't be me long if I slip coming over that log. Here goes," he said, as he steadied himself and crossed rapidly, while the Doctor held the light. "Ah," he added, when he was safe across, "I knew I should get over all right."

"You did not seem very certain about it just now," said the Doctor. "However, I am sincerely glad you are come. I knew no weather would stop you."

"Thank you, old friend," said the Vicar; "and how is the patient?"

"Going fast. More in your line than mine. The man believes himself bewitched."

"Not uncommon," said the Vicar, "in these parts; they are always bothering me with some of that sort of nonsense."

They went in. Only an ordinary scene of poverty, dirt, and vice, such as exists to some extent in every parish, in every country on the globe. Nothing more than that, and yet a sickening sight enough.

A squalid, damp, close room, with the earthen floor sunk in many places and holding pools of water. The mother smoking in the chimney-corner, the eldest daughter nursing an illegitimate child, and quarrelling with her mother in a coarse, angry tone. The children, ragged and hungry, fighting for the fireside. The father away, at some unlawful occupation probably, or sitting drinking his wages in an alehouse. That was what they saw, and what any man may see to-day for himself in his own village, whether in England or Australia, that working man's paradise. Drink, dirt, and sloth, my friends of the working orders, will produce the same effects all over the world.

As they came in the woman of the house rose and curtseyed to the Vicar, but the eldest girl sat still and turned away her head.

The Vicar, after saluting her mother, went gently up to her, and patting the baby's cheek, asked her kindly how she did. The girl tried to answer him, but could only sob. She bent down her head again over the child, and began rocking it to and fro.

"You must bring it to be christened," said the Vicar kindly. "Can you come on Wednesday?"

"Yes, I'll come," she said with a sort of choke. And now the woman having lit a fresh candle, ushered them into the sick man's room.

"Typhus and scarlatina!" said the Doctor. "How this place smells after being in the air. He is sensible again, I think."

"Quite sensible," the sick man answered aloud. "So you've come, Mr. Thornton; I'm glad of it; I've got a sad story to tell you; but I'll have vengeance if you do your duty. You see the state I am in!"

"Ague!" said the Vicar.

"And who gave it to me?"

"Why, God sent it to you," said the Vicar. "All people living in a narrow wet valley among woodlands like this, must expect ague."

"I tell you she gave it to me. I tell you she has overlooked me; and all this doctor's stuff is no use, unless you can say a charm as will undo her devil's work."

"My good friend," said the Vicar, "you should banish such fancies from your mind, for you are in a serious position, and ought not to die in enmity with any one."

"Not die in enmity with her? I'd never forgive her till she took off the spell."

"Whom do you mean?" asked the Vicar.

"Why, that infernal witch, Madge, that lives with old Hawker," said the old man excitedly. "That's who I mean!"

"Why, what injury has she done you?"

"Bewitched me, I tell you! Given me these shaking fits. She told me she would, when I left; and so she has, to prevent my speaking. I might a spoke out anytime this year, only the old man kept me quiet with money; but now it's nigh too late!"

"What might you have spoken about?" asked the Vicar.

"Well, I'll just relate the matter to you," said the man, speaking fast and thick, "and I'll speak the truth. A twelvemonth agone, this Madge and me had a fierce quarrel, and I miscalled her awful, and told her of some things she wasn't aware I knew of; and then she said, 'If ever a word of that escapes your lips, I'll put such a spell on ye that your bones shall shake apart.' Then I says, ' If you do, your bastard son shall swing.' "

" Who do you mean by her bastard son? "

" Young George Hawker. He is not the son of old Mrs. Hawker! Madge was brought to bed of him a fortnight before her mistress; and when she bore a still-born child, old Hawker and I buried it in the wood, and we gave Madge's child to Mrs. Hawker, who never knew the difference before she died."

" On the word of a dying man, is that true? " demanded the Vicar.

" On the word of a dying man that's true, and this also. I says to Madge, ' Your boy shall swing, for I know enough to hang him.' And she said, ' Where are your proofs? ' and I—— O Lord! O Lord! she's at me again."

He sank down again in a paroxysm of shivering, and they got no more from him. Enough there was, however, to make the Vicar a very silent and thoughtful man, as he sat watching the sick man in the close stifling room.

" You had better go home, Vicar," said the Doctor; " you will make yourself ill staying here. I do not expect another lucid interval."

" No," said the Vicar, " I feel it my duty to stay longer. For my own sake too. What he has let out bears fearfully on my happiness, Doctor."

" Yes, I can understand that, my friend, from what I have heard of the relations that exist between your daughter and that young man. You have been saved from a terrible misfortune, though at the cost, perhaps, of a few tears, and a little temporary uneasiness."

" I hope it may be as you say," said the Vicar. " Strange, only to-day Major Buckley was urging me to stop that acquaintance."

" I should have ventured to do so too, Vicar, had I been as old a friend of yours as Major Buckley."

" He is not such a very old friend," said the Vicar, " only of two years' standing, yet I seem to have known him ten."

At daybreak the man died, and made no sign. So as soon as they had satisfied themselves of the fact, they departed, and came out together into the clear morning air. The rain-clouds had broken, though when they had scrambled up out of the narrow little valley where the cottage stood, they found that the wind was still high and fierce, and that the sun was rising dimly through a yellow haze of driving scud.

They stepped out briskly, revived by the freshness of all around, and had made about half the distance home, when they descried a horseman coming slowly towards them. It seemed an early time for any one to be abroad, and their surprise was increased at seeing that it was George Hawker returning home.

"Where can he have been so early?" said the Doctor.

"So late, you mean," said the Vicar; "he has not been home all night. Now I shall brace up my nerves and speak to him."

"My good wishes go with you, Vicar," said the Doctor, and walked on, while the other stopped to speak with George Hawker.

"Good-morning, Mr. Thornton. You are early afoot, sir."

"Yes, I have been sitting up all night with old Jewel. He is dead."

"Is he indeed, sir?" said Hawker. "He won't be much loss, sir, to the parish. A sort of happy release, one may say, for every one but himself."

"Can I have the pleasure of a few words with you, Mr. Hawker?"

"Surely, sir," said he, dismounting. "Allow me to walk a little on the way back with you?"

"What I have to say, Mr. Hawker," said the Vicar, "is very short, and, I fear, also very disagreeable to all parties. I am going to request you to discontinue your visits to my house altogether, and, in fact, drop our acquaintance."

"This is very sudden, sir," said Hawker. "Am I to understand, sir, that you cannot be induced by any conduct of mine to reconsider this decision?"

"You are to understand that such is the case, sir."

"And this is final, Mr. Thornton?"

"Quite final, I assure you," said the Vicar; "nothing on earth should make me flinch from my decision."

"This is very unfortunate, sir," said George. "For I had reason to believe that you rather encouraged my visits than otherwise."

"I never encouraged them. It is true I permitted them. But since then circumstances have come to my ears which render it imperative that you should drop all communication with the members of my family, more especially, to speak plainly, with my daughter."

"At least, sir," said George, "let me know what charge you bring against me."

"I make no charges of any sort," replied the Vicar. "All I say is, that I wish the intercourse between you and my daughter to cease; and I consider, sir, that when I say that, it ought to be sufficient. I conceive that I have the right to say so much without question."

" I think you are unjust, sir; I do, indeed," said George.

" 1 may have been unjust, and I may have been weak, in allowing an intimacy (which I do not deny, mind you) to spring up between my daughter and yourself. But I am not unjust now, when 1 require that it should cease. I begin to be just."

" Do you forbid me your house, sir ? "

" I forbid you my house, sir. Most distinctly. And I wish you good-day."

There was no more to be said on either side. George stood beside his horse, after the Vicar had left him, till he was fairly out of earshot. And then, with a fierce oath, he said :

" You puritanical old humbug, I'll do you yet. You've heard about Nell and her cursed brat. But the daughter ain't always the same way of thinking with the father, old man."

The Vicar walked on, glad enough to have got the interview over, till he overtook the Doctor, who was walking slowly till he came up. He felt as though the battle was gained already, though he still rather dreaded a scene with Mary.

" How have you sped, friend ? " asked the Doctor. " Have you given the young gentleman his *congé* ? "

" I have," he replied. " Doctor, now half the work is done, I feel what a culpable coward I have been not to do it before. I have been deeply to blame. I never should have allowed him to come near us. Surely the girl will not be such a fool as to regret the loss of such a man. I shall tell her all I know about him, and after that I can do no more. No more ? I never had her confidence. She has always had a life apart from mine. The people in the village, all so far below us in every way, have been to me acquaintances, and only that; but they have been her world, and she has seen no other. She is a kind, affectionate daughter, but she would be as good a daughter to any of the farmers round as she is to me. She is not a lady. That is the truth. God help the man who brings up a daughter without a wife."

" You do her injustice, my friend," said the Doctor. " I understand what you mean, but you do her injustice. All the female society she has ever seen, before Mrs. Buckley and your sister came here, was of a rank inferior to herself, and she has taken her impressions from that society to a great extent. But still she is a lady; compare her to any of the other girls in the parish, and you will see the difference."

"Yes, yes, that is true," said the Vicar. "You must think me a strange man to speak so plainly about my own daughter, Doctor, and to you, too, whom I have known so short a time. But one must confide in somebody, and I have seen your discretion manifested so often that I trust you."

They had arrived opposite the Vicar's gate, but the Doctor, resisting all the Vicar's offers of breakfast, declined to go in. He walked homeward toward his cottage lodgings, and as he went he mused to himself somewhat in this style:

"What a good old man that is. And yet how weak. I used to say to myself when I first knew him, what a pity that a man with such a noble intellect should be buried in a country village, a pastor to a lot of ignorant hinds. And yet he is fit for nothing else, with all his intelligence, and all his learning. He has no go in him—no back to his head. Contrast him with Buckley, and see the difference. Now Buckley, without being a particularly clever man, sees the right thing, and goes at it through fire and water. But our old Vicar sees the right, and leaves it to take care of itself. He can't manage his own family even. That girl is a fine girl, a very fine girl. A good deal of character about her. But her animal passions are so strong that she would be a Tartar for any one to manage. She will be too much for the Vicar. She will marry that man in the end. And if he don't use her properly, she'll hate him as much as she loves him now. She is more like an Italian than an English girl. Hi! there's a noble Rhamnea!"

The Vicar went into his house, and found no one up but the maids, who were keeping that saturnalia among the household gods, which, I am given to understand, goes on in every well-regulated household before the lords of the creation rise from their downy beds. I have never seen this process myself, but I am informed, by the friend of my heart, who looked on it once for five minutes, and then fled, horror-struck, that the first act consists in turning all the furniture upside down, and beating it with brooms. Further than this, I have no information. If any male eye has penetrated these awful secrets beyond that, let the owner of that eye preserve a decent silence. There are some things that it is better not to know. Only let us hope, brother, that you and I may always find ourselves in a position to lie in bed till it is all over. In Australia, it may be worth while to remark, this custom, with many other religious observances, has fallen into entire desuetude.

The Vicar was very cross this morning. He had been sitting up all night, which was bad, and he had been thinking these last few minutes that he had made a fool of himself, by talking so freely to the Doctor about his private affairs, which was worse. Nothing irritated the Vicar's temper more than the feeling of having been too free and communicative with people who did not care about him, a thing he was very apt to do. And, on this occasion, he could not disguise from himself that he had been led into talking about his daughter to the Doctor, in a way which he characterised in his own mind as being " indecent."

As I said, he was cross. And anything in the way of clearing up or disturbance always irritated him, though he generally concealed it. But there was a point at which his vexation always took the form of a protest, more or less violent. And that point was determined by any one meddling with his manuscript sermons.

So, on this unlucky morning, in spite of fresh-lit fires smoking in his face, and fenders in dark passages throwing him headlong into lurking coal-scuttles, he kept his temper like a man, until coming into his study, he found his favourite discourse on the sixth seal lying on the floor by the window, his lectures on the 119th Psalm on the hearth-rug, and the maid fanning the fire with his *chef d'œuvre,* the Waterloo thanksgiving.

Then, I am sorry to say, he lost his temper. Instead of calling the girl by her proper name, he addressed her as a distinguished Jewish lady, a near relation of King Ahab, and, snatching the sermon from her hand, told her to go and call Miss Mary, or he'd lay a stick about her back.

The girl was frightened—she had never seen her master in this state of mind before. So she ran out of the room, and, having fetched Mary, ensconced herself outside the door to hear what was the matter.

Mary tripped into the room looking pretty and fresh. " Why, father," she said, " you have been up all night. I have ordered you a cup of coffee. How is old Jewel? "

" Dead," said the Vicar. " Never mind him. Mary, I want to speak to you, seriously, about something that concerns the happiness of your whole life."

" Father," she said, " you frighten me. Let me get you your coffee before you begin, at all events."

" Stay where you are, I order you," said the father. " I will have no temporising until the matter grows cold. I will speak now; do you hear? Now, listen."

She was subdued, and knew what was coming. She sat down, and waited. Had he looked in her face, instead of in the fire, he would have seen an expression there which he would little have liked—a smile of obstinacy and self-will.

"I am not going to mince matters, and beat about the bush, Mary," he began. "What I say I mean, and will have it attended to. You are very intimate with young Hawker, and that intimacy is very displeasing to me."

"Well?" she said.

"Well," he answered. "I say it is not well. I will not have him here."

"You are rather late, father," she said. "He has had the run of this house these six months. You should have spoken before."

"I speak now, miss," said the Vicar, succeeding in working himself into a passion, "and that is enough. I forbid him the house, now!"

"You had better tell him so, father. I won't."

"I dare say you won't," said the Vicar. "But I have told him so already this morning."

"You have!" she cried. "Father, you had no right to do that. You encouraged him here. And now my love is given, you turn round and try to break my heart."

"I never encouraged him. You all throw that in my face. You have no natural affection, girl. I always hated the man. And now I have heard things about him sufficient to bar him from any honest man's house."

"Unjust!" she said. "I will never believe it."

"I dare say you won't," said the Vicar. "Because you don't want to. You are determined to make my life miserable. There was Jim Stockbridge. Such a noble, handsome, gentlemanly young fellow, and nothing would please you but to drive him wild, till he left the country. Now, go away, and mind what I have said. You mean to break my heart, I see."

She turned as she was going out. "Father," she said, "is James Stockbridge gone?"

"Yes; gone. Sailed a fortnight ago. And all your doing. Poor boy, I wonder where he is now."

Where is he now? Under the cliffs of Madeira. Standing on the deck of a brave ship, beneath a rustling cloud of canvas, watching awe-struck that noble island, like an aerial temple, brown in the lights, blue in the shadows, floating between a sapphire sea and an azure sky. Far aloft in the air is Ruivo, five thousand feet overhead, father of the great ridges and sierras that run down jagged and abrupt, till they end in wild surf-washed promontories. He is watching a mighty glen that pierces the mountain, dark with misty shadows. He is watching the waterfalls that stream from among the vineyards into the sea below, and one long white monastery, perched up among the crags above the highway of the world.

Borne upon the full north wind, the manhood and intelligence of Europe goes past, day by day, in white-winged ships. And above all, unheeding, century after century, the old monks have vegetated there, saying their masses, and ringing their chapel bells, high on the windy cliff.

CHAPTER IX

WHEN THE KYE CAME HAME

And when Mary had left the room, the Vicar sat down musing before the fire in his study. " Well," said he to himself, " she took it quieter than I thought she would. Now I can't blame myself. I think I have shown her that I am determined, and she seems inclined to be dutiful. Poor dear girl, I am sorry for her. There is no doubt she has taken a fancy to this handsome young scamp. But she must get over it. It can't be so very serious as yet. At all events I have done my duty, though I can't help saying that I wish I had spoken before things went so far."

The maid looked in timidly, and told him that breakfast was ready. He went into the front parlour, and there he found his sister making tea. She looked rather disturbed, and, as the Vicar kissed her, he asked her " where was Mary ? "

" She is not well, brother," she answered. " She is going to stay upstairs; I fear something has gone wrong with her."

" She and I had some words this morning," answered he, " and that happens so seldom, that she is a little upset, that is all."

" I hope there is nothing serious, brother," said Miss Thornton.

" No; I have only been telling her that she must give up receiving George Hawker here. And she seems to have taken a sort of fancy to his society, which might have grown to something more serious. So I am glad I spoke in time."

" My dear brother, do you think you have spoken in time ? I have always imagined that you had determined, for some reason which I was not master of, that she should look on Mr. Hawker as her future husband. I am afraid you will have trouble. Mary is self-willed."

Mary was very self-willed. She refused to come downstairs all day, and, when he was sitting down to dinner, he sent up for her. She sent him for an answer, that she did not want any dinner, and that she was going to stay where she was.

The Vicar ate his dinner notwithstanding. He was vexed, but, on the whole, felt satisfied with himself. This sort of thing, he said to himself, was to be expected. She would get over it in time. He hoped that the poor girl would not neglect her meals, and get thin. He might have made himself comfortable if he had seen her at the cold chicken in the back kitchen.

She could not quite make the matter out. She rather fancied that her father and Hawker had had some quarrel, the effects of which would wear off, and that all would come back to its old course. She thought it strange too that her father should be so different from his usual self, and this made her uneasy. One thing she was determined on, not to give up her lover, come what would. So far in life she had always had her own way, and she would have it now. All things considered, she thought that sulks would be her game. So sulks it was. To be carried on until the Vicar relented.

She sat up in her room till it was evening. Twice during the day her aunt had come up, and the first time she had got rid of her under pretence of headache, but the second time she was forced in decency to admit her, and listen entirely unedified to a long discourse, proving, beyond power of contradiction, that it was the duty of every young Englishwoman to be guided entirely by her parents in the choice of a partner for life. And how that Lady Kate, as a fearful judgment on her for marrying a captain of artillery against the wishes of her noble relatives, was now expiating her crimes on £400 a year, and when she might have married a duke.

Lady Kate was Miss Thornton's "awful example," her "naughty girl." She served to point many a moral of the old lady's. But Lady Fanny, her sister, was always represented as the pattern of all Christian virtues—who had crowned the hopes of her family and well-wishers by marrying a gouty marquis of sixty-three, with fifty thousand a year. On this occasion, Mary struck the old lady dumb —"knocked her cold," our American cousins would say—by announcing that she considered Lady Fanny to be a fool, but that Lady Kate seemed to be a girl of some spirit. So Miss Thornton left her to her own evil thoughts, and, as evening began to fall, Mary put on her bonnet, and went out for a walk.

Out by the back door, and round through the shrubbery, so that she gained the front gate unperceived from the windows; but ere she reached it she heard the latch go, and found herself face to face with a man.

He was an immensely tall man, six foot at least. His long heavy limbs loosely hung together, and his immense broad shoulders slightly rounded. In features he was hardly handsome, but a kindly pleasant-looking face made ample atonement for want of beauty. He was dressed in knee breeches, and a great blue coat, with brass buttons, too large even for him, was topped by a broad-brimmed beaver hat, with fur on it half an inch long. In age, this man was about five-and-twenty, and well known he was to all the young fellows round there for skill in all sporting matters, as well as for his kind-heartedness and generosity.

When he saw Mary pop out of the little sidewalk right upon him, he leaned back against the gate and burst out laughing. No, hardly " burst out." His laughter seemed to begin internally and silently, till, after one or two rounds, it shook the vast fabric of his chest beyond endurance, and broke out into so loud and joyous a peal that the blackbird fled, screeching indignantly, from the ivy-tree behind him.

" What! Thomas Troubridge," said Mary. " My dear cousin, how are you? Now, don't stand laughing there like a great gaby, but come and shake hands. What on earth do you see to laugh at in me? "

" Nothing, my cousin Poll, nothing," he replied. " You know that is my way of expressing approval. And you look so pretty standing there in the shade, that I would break any man's neck who didn't applaud. Shake hands, says you, I'll shake hands with a vengeance." So saying, he caught her in his arms, and covered her with kisses.

" You audacious," she exclaimed, when she writhed herself free. " I'll never come within arm's-length of you again. How dare you? "

" Only cousinly affection, I assure you, Poll. Rather more violent than usual at finding myself back in Drumston. But entirely cousinly."

" Where have you been, then, Tom? " she asked.

" Why, to London, to be sure. Give us ano——"

" You keep off, sir, or you'll catch it. What took you there? "

" Went to see Stockbridge and Hamlyn off."

" Then, they are gone? " she asked.

" Gone, sure enough. I was the last friend they'll see for many a long year."

"How did Stockbridge look? was he pretty brave?"

"Pretty well. Braver than I was. Mary, my girl, why didn't ye marry him?"

"What—you are at me with the rest, are you?" she answered. "Why, because he was a gaby, and you're another; and I wouldn't marry either of you to save your lives—now then!"

"Do you mean to say you would not have me, if I asked you? Pooh! pooh! I know better than that, you know." And again the shrubbery rang with his laughter.

"Now, go in, Tom, and let me get out," said Mary. "I say Tom, dear, don't say you saw me. I am going out for a turn, and I don't want them to know it."

Tom twisted up his great face into a mixture of mystery, admiration, wonder, and acquiescence, and, having opened the gate for her, went in.

But Mary walked quickly down a deep narrow lane, over-arched with oak, and melodious with the full rich notes of the thrush, till she saw down the long vista, growing now momentarily darker, the gleaming of a ford where the road crossed a brook.

Not the brook where the Vicar and the Major went fishing. Quite a different sort of stream, although they were scarcely half a mile apart, and joined just below. Here all the soil was yellow clay, and, being less fertile, was far more densely wooded than any of the red country. The hills were very abrupt, and the fields but sparely scattered among the forest land. The stream itself, where it crossed the road, flowed murmuring over a bed of loose blue slate pebbles, but both above and below this place forced its way, almost invisible, through a dense oak wood, deeply tangled with undergrowth.

A stone foot-bridge spanned the stream, and having reached this, it seemed as if she had come to her journey's end. For leaning on the rail she began looking into the water below, though starting and looking round at every sound.

She was waiting for someone. A pleasant place this to wait in. So dark, so hemmed in with trees, and the road so little used; spring was early here, and the boughs were getting quite dense already. How pleasant to see the broad red moon go up behind the feathery branches, and listen to the evensong of the thrush, just departing to roost, and leaving the field clear for the woodlark all night. There were a few sounds from the village, a lowing of cows, and the noise of the boys at play; but they were so tempered down by the distance, that they only added to the evening harmony.

There is another sound now. Horse's feet approaching rapidly from the side opposite to that by which she has come; and soon a horseman comes in sight, coming quickly down the hill. When he sees her he breaks into a gallop, and only pulls up when he is at the side of the brook below her.

This is the man she was expecting—George Hawker. Ah, Vicar! how useless is your authority when lovers have such intelligence as this. It were better they should meet in your parlour, under your own eye, than here, in the budding spring-time, in this quiet spot under the darkening oaks.

Hawker spoke first. "I guessed," he said, "that it was just possible you might come out to-night. Come down off the bridge, my love, and let us talk together while I hang up the horse."

So as he tied the horse to a gate, she came down off the bridge. He took her in his arms, and kissed her. "Now, my Poll," said he, "I know what you are going to begin talking about."

"I dare say you do, George," she answered. "You and my father have quarrelled."

"The quarrel has been all on one side, my love," he said; "he has got some nonsense into his head, and he told me when I met him this morning, that he would never see me in his house again."

"What has he heard, George? It must be something very shocking to change him like that. Do you know what it is?"

"Perhaps I do," he said; "but he has no right to visit my father's sins on me. He hates me, and he always did; and he has been racking his brains to find out something against me. That rascally German doctor has found him an excuse, and so he throws in my teeth, as fresh discovered, what he must have known years ago."

"I don't think that, George. I don't think he would be so deceitful."

"Not naturally he wouldn't, I know; but he is under the thumb of that doctor; and you know how *he* hates me—if you don't I do."

"I don't know why Dr. Mulhaus should hate you, George."

"I do, though; that sleeky dog Stockbridge, who is such a favourite with him, has poisoned his mind, and all because he wanted you and your money, and because you took up with me instead of him."

"Well now," said Mary; "don't go on about him—he is gone, at all events; but you must tell me what this is that my father has got against you."

"I don't like to. I tell you it is against my father, not me."

"Well!" she answered; "if it was any one but me, perhaps, you ought not to tell it; but you ought to have no secrets from me, George—I have kept none from you."

"Well, my darling, I will tell you then: you know Madge, at our place?"

"Yes; I have seen her."

"Well, it's about her. She and my father live together like man and wife, though they ain't married; and the Vicar must have known that these years, and yet now he makes it an excuse for getting rid of me."

"I always thought she was a bad woman," said Mary; "but you are wrong about my father. He never knew it till now I am certain; and of course, you know, he naturally won't have me go and live in the house with a bad woman."

"Does he think then, or do you think," replied George, with virtuous indignation, "that I would have thought of taking you there? No, I'd sooner have taken you to America!"

"Well, so I believe, George."

"This won't make any difference in you, Mary? No, I needn't ask it, you wouldn't have come here to meet me to-night if that had been the case."

"It ought to make a difference, George," she replied; "I am afraid I oughtn't to come out here and see you, when my father don't approve of it."

"But you will come, my little darling, for all that," he said. "Not here though—the devil only knows who may be loitering round here. Half a dozen pair of lovers a night perhaps—no, meet me up in the croft of a night. I am often in at Gosford's of an evening, and I can see your window from there; you put a candle in the right-hand corner when you want to see me, and I'll be down in a very few minutes. I shall come every evening and watch."

"Indeed," she said, "I won't do anything of the sort; at least, unless I have something very particular to say. Then, indeed, I might do such a thing. Now I must go home or they will be missing me."

"Stay a minute, Mary," said he; "you just listen to me. They will, some of them, be trying to take my character away. You won't throw me off without hearing my defence, dear Mary, I know you won't. Let me hear what lies they tell of me, and don't you condemn me unheard because I come from a bad house. Tell me that you'll give me a chance of clearing myself with you, my girl, and I'll go home in peace and wait."

What girl could resist the man she loved so truly, when he pleaded so well? With his arm about her waist, and his handsome face bent over her, lit up with what she took to be love. Not she, at all events. She drew the handsome face down towards her, and as she kissed him fervently, said:

"I will never believe what they say of you, love. I should die if I lost you. I will stay by you through evil report and good report. What is all the world to me without you?"

And she felt what she said, and meant it. What though the words in which she spoke were borrowed from the trashy novels she was always reading—they were true enough for all that. George saw that they were true, and saw also that now was the time to speak about what he had been pondering over all day.

"And suppose, my own love," he said, "that your father should stay in his present mind, and not come round?"

"Well!" she said.

"What are we to do?" he asked; "are we to be always content with meeting here and there, when we dare? Is there nothing further?"

"What do you mean?" she said in a whisper. "What shall we do?"

"Can't you answer that?" he said softly. "Try."

"No, I can't answer. You tell me what."

"Fly!" he said in her ear. "Fly, and get married, that's what I mean."

"Oh! that's what you mean," she replied. "Oh, George, I should not have courage for that."

"I think you will, my darling, when the time comes. Go home and think about it."

He kissed her once more, and then she ran away homeward through the dark. But she did not run far before she began to walk slower and think.

"Fly with him," she thought. "Run away and get married." What a delightfully wild idea. Not to be entertained for a moment, of course, but still what a pleasant notion. She meant to marry George in the end; why not that way as well as any other? She thought about it again and again, and the idea grew more familiar. At all events, if her father should continue obstinate, here was a way out of the difficulty. He would be angry at first, but when he found he could not help himself he would come round, and then they would all be happy. She would shut her ears to anything they said against George. She could not believe it. She would not. He should be her husband, come what might. She would dissemble,

and keep her father's suspicions quiet. More, she would speak
lightly of George, and make them believe she did not care for him.
But most of all, she would worm from her father everything she
could about him. Her curiosity was aroused, and she fancied,
perhaps, George had not told her all the truth. Perhaps he might
be entangled with some other woman. She would find it all out if
she could.

So confusedly thinking she reached home, and approaching the
door, heard the noise of many voices in the parlour. There was
evidently company, and in her present excited state nothing would
suit her better; so gaining her room, and changing her dress
a little, she came down and entered the parlour.

"Behold," cried the Doctor, as she entered the room, "the evening
star has arisen at last. My dear young lady, we have been loudly
lamenting your absence and indisposition."

"I have been listening to your lamentations, Doctor," she replied.
"They were certainly loud, and from the frequent bursts of laughter,
I judged they were getting hysterical, so I came down."

There was quite a party assembled. The Vicar and Major Buckley
were talking earnestly together. Troubridge and the Doctor were
side by side, while next the fire was Mrs. Buckley, with young Sam
asleep on her lap, and Miss Thornton siting quietly beside her.

Having saluted them all, Mary sat down by Mrs. Buckley, and
began talking to her. Then the conversation flowed back into the
channel it had been following before her arrival.

"I mean to say, Vicar," said the Major, "that it would be better
to throw the four packs into two. Then you would have less
squabbling and bickering about the different boundaries, and you
would kill the same number of hares with half the dogs."

"And you would throw a dozen men out of work, sir," replied
the Vicar, "in this parish and the next, and that is to be considered;
and about half the quantity of meat and horseflesh would be
consumed, which is another consideration. I tell you I believe things
are better as they are."

"I hear they got a large stern-cabin; did they, Mr. Troubridge?"
said the Doctor. "I hope they'll be comfortable. They should have
got more amidships if they could. They will be sick the longer in
their position."

"Poor boys!" said Troubridge; "they'll be more heart-sick than
stomach-sick, I expect. They'd half repented before they sailed."

Mary sat down by Mrs. Buckley, and had half an hour's agreeable
conversation with her, till they all rose to go. Mrs. Buckley was

surprised at her sprightliness and good spirits, for she had expected
to find her in tears. The Doctor had met the Major in the morning,
and told him what had passed the night before, so Mrs. Buckley
had come in to cheer Mary up for the loss of her lover, and to her
surprise found her rather more merry than usual. This made the
good lady suspect at once that Mary did not treat the matter very
seriously, or else was determined to defy her father, which, as Mrs.
Buckley reflected, she was perfectly able to do, being rich in her
own right, and of age. So when she was putting on her shawl to
go home, she kissed Mary, and said kindly :

" My love, I hope you will always honour and obey your father,
and I am sure you will always, under all circumstances, remember
that I am your true friend. Good night."

And having bidden her good night, Mary went in. The Doctor
was gone with the Major, but Tom Troubridge sat still before the
fire, and as she came in was just finishing off one of his thundering
fits of laughter at something that the Vicar had said.

" My love," said the Vicar, " I am so sorry you have been poorly,
though you look better to-night. Your dear aunt has seen to Tom's
room, so there is nothing to do, but to sit down and talk to us."

" Why, cousin Tom," she said, laughing, " I had quite forgot
you; at least, quite forgot you were going to stay here. Why, what
a time it is since I saw you."

" Isn't it ? " he replied; " such a very long time. If I remember
right, we met last out at the gate. Let's see. How long was that
ago ? "

" You ought to remember," she replied; " you're big enough. Well,
good-night. I'm going to bed."

She went to her room, but not to bed. She sat in the window,
looking at the stars, pale in the full moonlight, wondering. Wondering what George was doing. Wondering whether she would listen
to his audacious proposal. And wondering, lastly, what on earth
her father would say if she did.

CHAPTER X

IN WHICH WE SEE A GOOD DEAL OF MISCHIEF BREWING

A MONTH went on, and May was well advanced. The lanes had
grown dark and shadowy with their summer bravery; the banks were
a rich mass of verdure once more, starred with wild-rose and

eglantine; and on the lesser woodland stream the king fern was again concealing the channel with brilliant golden fronds; while brown bare thorn thickets, through which the wind had whistled savagely all winter, were now changed into pleasant bowers, where birds might build and sing.

A busy month this had been for the Major. Fishing every day, and pretty near all day, determined, as he said, to make the most of it, for fear it should be his last year. There was a beaten path worn through the growing grass all down the side of the stream by his sole exertions; and now the may-fly was coming, and there would be no more fishing in another week, so he worked harder than ever. Mrs. Buckley used to bring down her son and heir and sit under an oak by the riverside sewing. Pleasant, long days they were when dinner would be brought down to the old tree, and she would spend the day there, among the long meadow-grass, purple and yellow with flowers, bending under the soft west wind. Pleasant to hear the corncrake by the hedge side, or the moorhen in the water. But pleasantest of all was the time when her husband, tired of fishing, would come and sit beside her, and the boy, throwing his lately-petted flowers to the wind, would run crowing to the spotted beauties which his father had laid out for him on the grass.

The Vicar was busy in his garden, and the Doctor was often helping him, although the most of his time was spent in natural history, to which he seemed entirely devoted. One evening they had been employed rather later than usual, and the Doctor was just gone, when the Vicar turned round and saw that his sister was come out, with her basket and scissors, to gather a fresh bouquet for the drawing-room.

So he went to join her, and as he approached her he admired her with an affectionate admiration. Such a neat, trim figure, with the snow-white handkerchief over her head, and her white garden gloves; what a contrast to Mary, he thought; " Both good of their sort, though," he added.

" Good evening, brother," began Miss Thornton. " Was not that Dr. Mulhaus went from you just now? "

" Yes, my dear."

" You had letters of introduction to Dr. Mulhaus when he came to reside in this village? " asked Miss Thornton.

" Yes; Lord C——, whom I knew at Oxford, recommended me to him."

" His real name, I dare say, is not Mulhaus. Do you know what his real name is, brother? "

How very awkward plain, plump questions of this kind are. The Vicar would have liked to answer " No," but he could not tell a lie. He was also a very bad hand at prevaricating; so with a stammer he said " Yes! "

" So do I! " said Miss Thornton.

" Good Lord, my dear, how did you find it out? "

" I recognised him the first instant I saw him, and was struck dumb. I was very discreet, and have never said a word even to you till now; and, lately, I have been thinking that you might know, and so I thought I would sound you."

" I suppose you saw him when you were with her Ladyship in Paris, in '14? "

" Yes; often," said Miss Thornton. " He came to the house several times. How well I remember the last. The dear girls and I were in the conservatory in the morning, and all of a sudden we heard the door thrown open, and two men coming towards us talking from the breakfast-room. We could not see them for the plants, but when we heard the voice of one of them the girls got into a terrible flutter, and I was very much frightened myself. However, there was no escape, so we came round the corner on them as bold as we could, and there was this Dr. Mulhaus, as we call him, walking with him."

" With him?—with who? "

" The Emperor Alexander, my dear, whose voice we had recognised; I thought you would have known whom I meant."

" My dear love," said the Vicar, " I hope you reflect how sacred that is, and what a good friend I should lose if the slightest hint as to who he was were to get among the gentry round. You don't think he has recognised you? "

" How is it likely, brother, that he would remember an English governess, whom he never saw but three times, and never looked at once? I have often wondered whether the Major recognised him."

" No; Buckley is a Peninsular man, and although at Waterloo, never went to Paris. Lans—Mulhaus, I mean, was not present at Waterloo. So they never could have met. My dear discreet old sister, what tact you have! I have often said to myself, when I have seen you and he together, ' If she only knew who he was;'—and to think of your knowing all the time. Ha! ha! ha! That's very good."

" I have lived long where tact is required, my dear brother. See, there goes young Mr. Hawker! "

" I'd sooner see him going home than coming here. Now, I'd go out for a turn in the lanes, but I know I should meet half a dozen couples courting, as they call it. Bah! So I'll stay in the garden."

The Vicar was right about the lanes being full of lovers. Never a vista that you looked down but what you saw a ghostly pair, walking along side by side. Not arm in arm, you know. The man has his hands in his pockets, and walks a few feet off the woman. They never speak to one another—I think I don't go too far in saying that. I have met them and overtaken them, and come round sharp round corners on to them, but I never heard them speak to one another. I have asked the young men themselves whether they ever said anything to their sweethearts, and those young men have answered, " No; that they didn't know as they did." So that I am inclined to believe that they are contented with that silent utterance of the heart which is so superior to the silly whisperings one hears on dark ottomans in drawing-rooms.

But the Vicar had a strong dislike to lovers' walks. He was a practical man, and had studied parish statistics for some years, so that his opinion is entitled to respect. He used to ask why an honest girl should not receive her lover at her father's house, or in broad daylight, and many other impertinent questions which we won't go into, but which many a west-country parson has asked before, and never got an answer to.

Of all pleasant places in the parish, surely one of the pleasantest for a meeting of this kind was the old oak at the end of Hawker's plantation, where George met Nelly a night we know of. So quiet and lonely, and such pleasant glimpses down long oaken glades, with a bright carpet of springing fern. Surely there will be a couple here this sweet May evening.

So there is! Walking this way, too! George Hawker is one of them; but we can't see who the other is. Who should it be but Mary, though, with whom he should walk, with his arm round her waist talking so affectionately. But see, she raises her head. Why! that is not Mary. That is old Jewel's dowdy, handsome, brazen-faced granddaughter.

" Now I'm going home to supper, Miss Jenny," he says. " So you pack off, or you'll have your amiable mother asking after you. By the by, your sister's going to be married, ain't she? "

He referred to her elder sister—the one that the Vicar and the Doctor saw nursing a baby the night that old Jewel died.

" Yes," replied the girl. " Her man's going to have her at last;

that's his baby she's got, you know; and it seems he'll sooner make her work for keeping it than pay for it hisself. So they're going to be married; better late than never."

George left her and went in; into the gloomy old kitchen, now darkening rapidly. There sat Madge before the fire, in her favourite attitude, with her chin on her hand and her elbow on her knee.

"Well, old woman," said he, "where's the old man?"

"Away to Colyton fair," she answered.

"I hope he'll have the sense to stay there to-night, then," said George. "He'll fall off his horse in a fit coming home drunk some of these nights, and be found dead in a ditch!"

"Good thing for you if he was!"

"Maybe," said George; "but I'd be sorry for him, too!"

"You would," she said, laughing. "Why, you young fool, you'd be better off in fifty ways!"

"Why, you unnatural old vixen," said he indignantly, "do you miscall a man for caring for his own father? Ay, and not such a bad 'un either; and that's a thing I'm best judge of!"

"He's been a good father to you, George, and I like you the better, lad, for speaking up for him. He's an awful old rascal, my boy, but you'll be a worse if you live!"

"Now, stop that talk of yours, Madge, and don't go on like a madwoman, or else we shall quarrel; and that I don't want, for I've got something to tell you. I want your help, old girl!"

"Ay, and you'll get it, my pretty boy; though you never tell me aught till you are forced."

"Well, I'm going to tell you something now; so keep your ears open. Madge, where is the girl?"

"Upstairs."

"Where's the man?"

"Outside, in the stable, doing down your horse. Bend over the fire, and whisper in my ear, lad!"

"Madge, old girl," he whispered, as they bent their heads together—"I've wrote the old man's name where I oughtn't to have done."

"What! again!" she answered. "Three times! For God's sake, mind what you are at, George."

"Why," said he, astonished, "did you know I'd done it before?"

"Twice I know of," she said. "Once last year, and once last month. How do you think he'd have been so long without finding it out if it hadn't been for me? And what a fool you were not to tell me before. Why, you must be mad. I as near let the cat out of the bag coming over that last business in the book without being ready for it as anything could be. However, it's all right at present. But what's this last?"

"Why, the five hundred. I only did it twice."

"You mustn't do it again, George. You were a fool ever to do it without me. We are hardly safe now, if he should get talking to the bank people. However, he never goes there, and you must take care he don't."

"I say, Madge," said George, "what would he do if he found it out?"

"I couldn't answer for him," said she. "He likes you best of anything next his money; and sometimes I am afraid he wouldn't spare even you if he knew he had been robbed. You might make yourself safe for any storm, if you liked."

"How?"

"Marry that little doll Thornton, and get her money. Then, if it came to a row, you could square it up."

"Well," said George, "I am pushing that on. The old man won't come round, and I want her to go off with me, but she can't get her courage up yet."

"Well, at all events," said Madge, "you should look sharp. There's a regular tight-laced mob about her, and they all hate you. There's that Mrs. Buckley. Her conversation will be very different from yours, and she'll see the difference, and get too proud for the like of you. That woman's a real lady, and that's very dangerous, for she treats her like an equal. Just let that girl get over her first fancy for you, and she'll care no more about you than nothing. Get hold of her before she's got tired of you."

"And there's another thing," said George. "That Tom Troubridge is staying there again."

"That's very bad," said Madge. "She is very likely to take a fancy to him. He's a fine young fellow. You get her to go off with you. I'll find the money, somehow. Here comes the old man."

Old Hawker came in half drunk and sulky.

"Why, George," he said; "you at home. I thought you'd have been down hanging about the parson's. You don't get on very fast with that girl, lad. I though you'd have had her by now. You're a fool, boy."

He reeled up to bed, and left the other two in the kitchen.

"George," said Madge, "tell us what you did with that last money."

"I ain't going to tell you," he answered.

"Ha, ha!" she said; "you hadn't need to hid anything from me now."

"Well, I like to tell you this least of all," he said. "That last money went to hush up the first matter."

"Did anyone know of the first matter, then?" said Madge, aghast.

"Yes; the man who put me up to it."

"Who was that?"

"No one you know. William Lee of Belston."

"No one I know," she answered sarcastically. "Not know my old sweetheart, Bill Lee of Belston. And I the only one that knew him when he came back. Well, I've kept that to myself, because no good was to be got by peaching on him, and a secret's always worth money. Why, lad, I could have sent that man abroad again quicker than he come, if I had a-wanted. Why hadn't you trusted me at first? You'd a-saved five hundred pound. You'll have him back as soon as that's gone."

"He'd better mind himself, then," said George vindictively.

"None o' that now," said Madge; "that's what you were after the other night with your gun. But nothing came of it; I saw that in your face when you came home. Now get off to bed; and if Bill Lee gives you any more trouble, send him to me."

He went to bed, but instead of sleeping lay thinking.

"It would be a fine thing," he thought, "to get her and her money. I am very fond of her for her own sake, but then the money would be the making of me. I ought to strike while the iron is hot. Who knows but what Nell might come gandering back in one of her tantrums and spoil everything. And this cursed cheque, too; that ought to be provided against. What a fool I was not to tell Madge about it before. I wonder whether she is game to come, though I think she is; she has been very tender lately. It don't look as if she was getting tired of me, though she might take a fancy into her head about Troubridge. I dare say her father is putting him up to it; though, indeed, that would be sure to set her against him. If he hadn't done that with Stockbridge she'd have married him, I believe. Well, I'll see her to-morrow night, and carry on like mad. Terribly awkward it will be, though, if she won't. However, we'll see. There's a way to make her;" and so he fell asleep.

As Somebody would have it, the very next day the Vicar and Mary had a serious quarrel. Whether his digestion was out of order; whether the sight of so many love couples passing his gate the night before had ruffled him and made him bilious; or whether some one was behindhand with his tithe, we shall never know. Only we know that shortly after dinner they disagreed about some trifle, and Mary remained sulky all the afternoon; and that at tea-time, driven on by pitiless fate, little thinking what was hanging over him, he made some harsh remark, which brought down a flood of tears. Whereat, getting into a passion, he told Mary, somewhat unjustly, that she was always sulking, and was making his life miserable. That it was time that she was married. That Tom Troubridge was an excellent young fellow, and that he considered it was her duty to turn her attention immediately to gaining his affections.

Mary said, with tearful indignation, that it was notorious that he was making love to Miss Burrit, of Paiskow. And that if he wasn't she'd never, never think of him, for that he was a great, lumbering, stupid, stupid fool. There now.

Then the Vicar got into an unholy frame of mind, and maddened by Mary's tears, and the sight of his sister wiping her frightened face with her handkerchief, said, with something like an asseveration, that she was always at it. That she was moping about, and colloguing with that infamous young scoundrel, Hawker. That he would not have it. That if he found him lurking about his premises he'd either break his neck himself or find someone who could; and a great deal more frantic nonsense such as weak men generally indulge in when they get in a passion; much better left unsaid at any time, but which on this occasion, as the reader knows, was calculated to be ruinous.

Mary left the room, and went to her own. She was in a furious passion against her father, against all the world. She sat on the bed for a time and cried herself quiet. It grew dark, and she lit a candle, and put it in the right-hand corner of the window, and soon after, wrapping a shawl around her, she slipped down the back stairs and went into the croft.

Not long before she heard a low whistle, to which she replied, and in a very few minutes felt George's arm round her waist and his cheek against hers.

"I knew you would not disappoint me to-night, my love," he began. "I have got something particular to say to you. You seem out of sorts to-night, my dear. It's not my fault, is it?"

"Not yours, George. Oh, no," she said. "My father has been very cruel and unjust to me, and I have been in a great passion and very miserable. I am so glad you came to-night that I might tell you how very unhappy I was."

" Tell me everything, my love. Don't keep back any secrets from me."

" I won't, indeed, George. I'll tell you everything. Though some of it will make you very angry. My father broke out about you at tea-time, and said that you were hanging about the place, and that he wouldn't have it. And then he said that I ought to marry Tom Troubridge, and that I said I'd never do. And then he went on worse again. He's quite changed lately, George. I ain't at all happy with him."

" The cure is in your own hands, Mary. Come off with me. I can get a licence, and we could be married in a week or so, or two. Then, what follows? Why, your father is very angry. He is that at present. But he'll, of course, make believe he is in a terrible way. Well, in a few weeks he'd see it was no use carrying on. That his daughter had married a young man of property, who was very fond of her, and as she was very fond of. And that matters might be a deal worse. That a bird in hand is worth two in the bush. And so he'll write a kind, affectionate letter to his only child, and say that he forgives her husband for her sake. That's how the matter will end, depend upon it."

" Oh, George, George! if I could only think so."

" Can you doubt it? Use your reason, my dear, and ask yourself what he would gain by holding out. You say he's so fond of you."

" Oh, I know he is."

" Well, my darling, he wouldn't show it much if he was angry very long. You don't know what a change it will make when the thing's once done. When I am his son-in-law he'll be as anxious to find out that I'm a saint as he is now to make me out a sinner. Say yes, my girl."

" I am afraid, George."

" Of nothing. Come, you are going to say yes, now."

" But when, George? Not yet?"

" To-morrow night."

" Impossible! Sunday evening?"

" The better the day the better the deed. Come, no refusal now, it is too late, my darling. At ten o'clock I shall be here, under your window. One kiss more, my own, and good night."

CHAPTER XI

IN WHICH THE VICAR PREACHES A FAREWELL SERMON

WHO has not seen the misery and despair often caused in a family by the senseless selfishness of one of its members? Who has not felt enraged at such times, to think that a man or woman should presume on the affection and kind-heartedness of their relatives, and yet act as if they were wholly without those affections themselves? And, lastly, who of us all is guiltless of doing this? Let him that is without sin among us cast the first stone.

The spring sun rose on the Sabbath morning, as if no trouble were in store for any mortal that day. The Vicar rose with the sun, for he had certain arrears of the day's sermons to get through, and he was in the habit of saying that his best and clearest passages were written with his window open, in the brisk morning air.

But although the air was brisk and pleasant this morning, and all nature was in full glory, the inspiration did not come to the Vicar quite so readily as usual. In fact, he could not write at all, and at one time was thinking of pleading ill-health and not preaching, but afterwards changed his mind, and patched the sermons up somehow, making both morning and afternoon five minutes shorter than usual.

He felt queer and dull in the head this morning. And, after breakfast, he walked to church with his sister and daughter, not speaking a word. Miss Thornton was rather alarmed, he looked so dull and stupid. But Mary set it all down to his displeasure at her.

She was so busy with far other thoughts at church that she did not notice the strange halting way in which her father read the service—sometimes lisping, sometimes trying twice before he could pronounce a word at all. But, after church, Miss Thornton noticed it to her; and she also noticed, as they stood waiting for him under the lychgate, that he passed through the crowd of neighbours, who stood as usual round the porch to receive him, without a word, merely raising his hat in salutation. Conduct so strange that Miss Thornton began to cry, and said she was sure her brother was very ill. But Mary said it was because he was still angry with her that he spoke to no one, and that when he had forgotten his cause of offence he would be the same again.

At lunch the Vicar drank several glasses of wine, which seemed to do him good; and by the time he had, to Miss Thornton's great astonishment, drunk half a bottle, he was quite himself again. Mary was all this time in her room, and the Vicar asked for her. But Miss Thornton said she was not very well.

"Oh, I remember," said the Vicar, "I quarrelled with her last night. I was quite in the wrong, but, my dear sister, all yesterday and to-day I have been so nervous, I have not known what I said or did. I shall keep myself up to the afternoon service with wine, and to-morrow we will see the Doctor. Don't tell Mary I'm ill. She will think she is the cause, poor girl."

Afternoon service went off well enough. When Mary heard his old familiar voice, strong, clear, and harmonious, filling the aisles and chapels of the beautiful old church she was quite reassured. He seemed stronger than usual even, and never did the congregation listen to a nobler or better sermon from his lips than the one they heard that spring afternoon; the last, alas, they ever had from their kind old Vicar.

Mary could not listen to it. The old innocent interest she used to have in her father's success in preaching was gone. As of old, sitting beneath the carved oak screen, she heard the sweet simple harmony of the evening hymn roll up and die in pleasant echoes among the lofty arches overhead. As of old, she could see through the rich traceried windows the moor sloping far away, calm and peaceful, bathed in a misty halo of afternoon sunshine. All these familiar sights and sounds were the same, but she herself was different. She was about to break rudely through from the old world of simple routine and homely pleasure and to cast herself unthinking into a new world of passion and chance, and take the consequences of such a step, let them be what they might. She felt as if she was the possessor of some guilty secret, and felt sometimes as if someone would rise in church and denounce her. How would all these quiet folks talk of her to-morrow morning? That was not to be thought of. She must harden her heart and think of nothing. Only that to-morrow she would be far away with her lover.

Poor Mary! many a woman, and many a man, who sat so quiet and calm in the old church that afternoon had far guiltier secrets than any you ever had to trouble them, and yet they all drank, slept, and died, as quietly as many honest and good men. Poor girl! let us judge as kindly of her as we can, for she paid a fearful penalty for her self-will. She did but break through the prejudices of her education, we may say; and if she was undutiful, what girls are not, under the influence of passion? If such poor excuses as these will cause us to think more kindly of her, let us make them, and leave the rest to God. Perhaps, brother, you and I may stand in a position to have excuses made for us one day; therefore, we will be charitable.

My Lord was at church that afternoon, a very rare circumstance, for he was mostly at his great property in the north, and had lately been much abroad for his health. So when Miss Thornton and Mary joined the Vicar in the main aisle, and the three went forth into the churchyard, they found the villagers drawn respectfully back upon the graves and his Lordship waiting in close confabulation with farmer Wreford to receive the Vicar as he came out.

A tall, courtly, grizzled-looking man he was, with clear grey eyes and a modulated harmonious voice. Well did their lordships of the Upper House know that voice when after a long sleepy debate it aroused them from ambrosial slumbers, with biting sarcasm and most disagreeably told truths. And most heartily did a certain proportion of their lordships curse the owner of that voice, for a talented, eloquent, meddlesome innovator. But on all his great estates he was adored by the labourers and townsfolk, though hated by the farmers and country squires; for he was the earliest and fiercest of the reform and free-trade warriors.

He came up to the Vicar with a pleasant smile. "I have to thank you, Mr. Thornton, for a most charming sermon, though having the fault common to all good things, of being too short. Miss Thornton, I hope you are quite well; I saw Lady D—— the other day, and she begged that when I came down here I would convey her kindest love to you. I think she mentioned that she was about to write to you."

"I received a letter from her Ladyship last week," said Miss Thornton; "informing me that dear Lady Fanny had got a son and heir."

"Happy boy," said my Lord; "fifty thousand a year, and nothing to do for it, unless he likes. Besides a minority of at least ten years; for L—— is getting very shaky, Miss Thornton, and is still devotedly given to stewed mushrooms. Nay, my dear lady, don't look distressed, she will make a noble young dowager. This must be your daughter, Mr. Thornton—pray introduce me."

Mary was introduced, and his Lordship addressed a few kindly commonplaces to her, to which she replied with graceful modesty. Then he demanded of the Vicar, "Where is Dr. Mulhaus, has he been at church this afternoon?"

At that moment the Doctor, attended by the old clerk, was head and shoulders into the old oak chest that contained the parish registers, looking for the book of burials for sixteen hundred and something. Not being able to get to the bottom, he got bodily in, as into a bath, and after several dives succeeded in fishing it up from the bottom, and standing there absorbed for a few minutes, up to his middle in dusty parchments and angry moths, he got his finger on a particular date, and dashed out of church, book in hand, and hatless, crying, "Vicar, Vicar!" just as the villagers had cleared off, and my Lord was moving away with the Vicar to the parsonage to take dinner.

When his Lordship saw the wild, dusty figure come running out of the church porch. with the parish register in his hand and no hat on his head he understood the position immediately. He sat down on a tombstone and laughed till he could laugh no longer.

"No need to tell me," he said through his laughter, "that he is unchanged; just as mad and energetic as ever at whatever he takes in hand, whether getting together impossible ministries or searching the parish register of an English village. How do you do, my dear old friend?"

"And how do you do, old democrat?" answered the Doctor. "Politics seem to agree with you; I believe you would die without vexation—just excuse me a moment. Look you here, you infidel," to the Vicar, showing him the register; "there's his name plain— 'Burrows, Curate of this parish, 1698.'—Now what do you say?"

The Vicar acquiesced with a sleepy laugh, and proposed moving homewards. Miss Thornton hoped that the Doctor would join them at dinner as usual. The Doctor said of course, and went back to fetch his hat, my Lord following him into the church. When the others had gone down the hill, and were waiting for the noble-man and the Doctor at the gate, Miss Thornton watched the two coming down the hill. My Lord stopped the Doctor, and eagerly demonstrated something to him with his forefinger on the palm of his hand; but the Doctor only shook his head, and then the pair moved on.

My Lord made himself thoroughly agreeable at dinner, as did also the Doctor. Mary was surprised, too, at the calm high-bred bearing of her aunt, the way she understood and spoke of every subject of conversation, and the deference with which they listened to her. It was a side of her aunt's character she had never seen before, and she felt it hard to believe that that intellectual, dignified lady, referred to on all subjects, was the old maid she had been used to laugh at, and began to feel that she was in an atmosphere far above what she was accustomed to.

"All this is above me," she said to herself; "let them live in this sphere who are accustomed to it, I have chosen wiser, out of the rank in which I have been brought up. I would sooner be George Hawker's wife than sit there crushed and bored by their highflown talk."

Soon after dinner she retired with her aunt; they did not talk much when they were alone, so Mary soon retired to her room, and having made a few very slight preparations, sat down at the window. The time was soon to come, but it was very cold; the maids were out, as they always were on Sunday evening, and there was a fire in the kitchen—she would go and sit there—so down she went.

She wished to be alone, so when she saw a candle burning in the kitchen she was disappointed, but went in nevertheless. My Lord's groom, who had been sitting before the fire, rose up and saluted her. A handsome young man, rather square and prominent about the jaws, but nevertheless foolish and amiable looking. The sort of man one would suppose who, if his lord were to tell him to jump into the pit Tophet, would pursue one of two courses, either jump in himself without further to-do or throw his own brother in with profuse apologies. From the top of his sleek, round head to the sole of his perfect topboot the model and living exponent of what a servant should be—fit to be put into a case and ticketed as such.

He saluted her as she came in, and drawing a letter from his hat put it into her astonished hands. "My orders were, miss, that I was not to give it to you unless I saw you personally."

She thanked him and withdrew to read it. It was a scrawl from George Hawker, the first letter she had ever received from him, and ran as follows:

My Heart's Darling,—

I shall be in the croft to-night, according to promise, ready to make you the happiest woman in England, so I know you won't fail. My Lord is coming to church this afternoon, and will be sure to dine with you. So I send this present by his groom, Sam, a good young chap, which I have known since he was so high, and like well, only that he is soft, which is not to his disadvantage.   G.H.

She was standing under the lamp reading this when she heard the dining-room door open, and the men coming out from their wine. She slipped into the room opposite, and stood listening in the dark. She could see them as they came out. There was my Lord and the Doctor first and behind came Major Buckley, who had dropped in, as his custom was on Sunday evening, and who must have arrived while she was upstairs. As they passed the door inside which she stood his Lordship turned round and said:

"I tell you what, my dear Major, if that old Hawker was a tenant of mine I'd take away his lease and, if I could, force him to leave the parish. One man of that kind does incalculable harm in a village by lowering the tone of the morality of the place. That's the use of a great landlord if he does his duty. He can punish evildoers whom the law does not reach."

"Don't say anything more about him," said the Doctor in a low voice. "It's a tender subject in this house."

"It is, eh!" said my Lord; "thanks for the hint, good—bah!— Mulhaus. Let us go up and have half an hour with Miss Thornton before I go!"

They went up, and then her father followed. He seemed flushed, and she thought he must have been drinking too much wine. After they were in the drawing-room she crept upstairs and listened. They were all talking except her father. It was half-past nine, and she wished they would go. So she went into her bedroom and waited. The maids had come home, and she heard them talking to the groom in the kitchen. At ten o'clock the bell was rung, and my Lord's horse ordered. Soon he went, and not long afterwards the Major and the Doctor followed. Then she saw Miss Thornton go to her room and her father walk slowly to his; and all was still throughout the house.

She took her hat and shawl and slipped downstairs shoeless into her father's study. She laid a note on his chimney-piece, which she had written in the morning, and opening the back door fled swiftly forth, not daring to look behind her. Quickly, under the blinking stars, under the blooming apple trees, out to the croft gate, and there was George waiting for her, according to promise.

"I began to fear you were not coming, my dear. Quick, jump!"

She scrambled over the gate, and jumped into his arms; he hurried her down the lane about a hundred yards, and then became aware of a dark object in the middle of the road.

"That's my gig, my dear. Once in that and we are soon in Exeter. All right, Bob?"

"All right!" replied a strange voice in the dark, and she was lifted into the gig quickly; in another moment George was beside her, and they were flying through the dark, steep lanes at a dangerous speed.

The horse was a noble beast—the finest in the countryside—and, like his driver, knew every stick and stone on the road; so that ere poor Mary had recovered her first flurry they had crossed the red ford and were four miles on the road towards the capital, and began to feel a little more cheerful, for she had been crying bitterly.

" Don't give way, Polly," said George.

" No fear of my giving way now, George. If I had been going to do that I'd have done it before. Now tell us what you are going to do? I have left everything to you."

" I think we had better go straight on to London, my dear," he replied, " and get married by licence. We could never stop in Exeter; and if you feel up to it, I should like to get off by early coach to-morrow morning. What do you say?"

" By all means! Shall we be there in time?"

" Yes, two hours before the coach starts."

" Have you money enough, George?" she asked.

" Plenty!" he replied.

" If you go short you must come to me, you know," she said.

They rattled through the broad streets of a small country town just as the moon rose. The noble minster, which had for many years been used as the parish church, slept quietly among the yews and gravestones; all the town was still; only they two were awake, flying, she thought, from the fellowship of all quiet men. Was her father asleep now? she wondered. What would Miss Thornton say in the morning, and many other things she was asking herself when she was interrupted by George saying, " Only eight miles to Exeter; we shall be in by daybreak."

So they left Crediton Minster behind them and rolled away along the broad road by the river beneath the whispering poplars.

As Miss Thornton was dressing herself next morning she heard the Vicar go down into his study as usual. She congratulated herself that he was better, from being up thus early, but determined, nevertheless, that he should see a doctor that day, who might meet and consult with Dr. Mulhaus.

Then she wondered why Mary had not been in. She generally came into her aunt's room to hook-and-eye her, as she called it; but not having come this morning, Miss Thornton determined to go to her, and accordingly went and rapped at her door.

No answer. "Could the girl have been fool enough?" thought Miss Thornton. "Nonsense! no! She must be asleep!"

She opened the door and went in. Everything tidy. The bed had not been slept in. Miss Thornton had been in at an elopement, and a famous one, before; so she knew the symptoms in a moment. Well she remembered the dreadful morning when Lady Kate went off with Captain Brentwood, of the Artillery. Well she remembered the Countess going into hysterics. But this was worse than that; this touched her nearer home.

"Oh, you naughty girl! Oh, you wicked, ungrateful girl; to go and do such a thing at a time like this, when I've been watching the paralysis creeping over him day by day! How shall I tell him? How shall I ever tell him? He will have a stroke as sure as fate. He was going to have one without this. I dare not tell him till breakfast, and yet I ought to tell him at once. I was brought into the world to be driven mad by girls. Oh dear, I wish they were all boys, and we might send them to Eton and wash our hands of them. Well, I must leave crying, and prepare for telling him."

She went into his study, and at first could not see him; but he was there—a heap of black clothes lay on the hearthrug, and Miss Thornton running up, saw that it was her brother, speechless, senseless, clasping a letter in his hand.

She saw that the worst was come, and nerved herself for work, like a valiant soul as she was. She got him carried to his bed by two sturdy maids, and sent an express for Dr. Mulhaus, and another for the professional surgeon. Then she took from her pocket the letter which she had found in the poor Vicar's hand, and, going to the window, read as follows:

When you get this, father, I shall be many miles away. I have started to London with George Hawker, and God only knows whether you will see me again. Try to forgive me, father, and if not, forget that you ever had a daughter who was only born to give you trouble.
                    —Your erring but affectionate Mary.

It will be seen by the reader that this unlucky letter, written in agitation and hurry, contained no allusion whatever to marriage, but rather left one to infer that she was gone with Hawker as his mistress. So the Vicar read it again and again, each time more mistily, till sense and feeling departed, and he lay before his hearth a hopeless paralytic.

At that moment Mary, beside George, was rolling through the

fresh morning air, up the beautiful Exe valley. Her fears were gone with daylight and sunshine, and as he put his arm about her waist, she said:

" I am glad we came outside."

" Are you quite happy now ? " he asked.

" Quite happy ! "

CHAPTER XII

IN WHICH A NEW FACE IS INTRODUCED, BY MEANS OF A RAT AND TERRIER

FOR the first four weeks that the Vicar lay paralysed the neighbouring clergymen had done his duty; but now arose a new difficulty at Drumston. Who was to do the duty while the poor Vicar lay there on his back speechless ?

" How," asked Miss Thornton of Tom Troubridge, " are we to make head against the dissenters now ? Let the duty lapse but one single week, my dear friend, and you will see the chapels overflowing once more. My brother has always had a hard fight to keep them to church, for they have a natural tendency to dissent here. And a great number don't care what the denominations are so long as there is noise enough."

" If that is the case," answered Tom, " old Mark Hook's place of worship should pay best. I'd back them against Bedlam any day."

" They certainly make the loudest noise at a Revival," said Miss Thornton. " But what are we to do ? "

" That I am sure I don't know, my dearest Auntie," said Troubridge, " but I am here, and my horse too, ready to go any amount of errands."

" I see no way," said Miss Thornton, " but to write to the Bishop."

" And I see no way else," said Tom, " unless you like to dress me up as a parson and see if I would do."

Miss Thornton wrote to the Bishop, with whom she had some acquaintance, and told him how her brother had been struck down with paralysis, and that the parish was unprovided for: that if he would send any gentleman he approved of she would gladly receive him at Drumston.

Armed with this letter, Tom found himself, for the first time in his life, in an episcopal palace. A sleek servant in black opened the door with cat-like tread, and admitted him into a dark, warm hall; and on Tom's saying, in a hoarse whisper, as if he was in church, that he had brought a note of importance, and would wait for an answer, the man glided away and disappeared through a spring-door, which swung to behind him. Tom thought it would have banged, but it didn't. Bishops' doors never bang.

Tom had a great awe for your peers spiritual. He could get on well enough with a peer temporal, particularly if the proud aristocrat happened to be in want of a horse; but a bishop was quite another matter.

So he sat rather uncomfortable in the dark, warm hall, listening to such dull sounds as could be heard in the gloomy mansion. A broad oak staircase led up from the hall into lighter regions, and there stood, on a landing above, a lean, wheezy old clock, all over brass knobs, which, as he looked on it, choked, and sneezed four.

But now there was a new sound in the house. An indecent, secular sound. A door near the top of the house was burst violently open, and there was a scuffle. A loud voice shouted twice unmistakably and distinctly, " So-o, good bitch! " And then the astounded Tom heard the worrying of a terrier and the squeak of a dying rat. There was no mistake about it; he heard the bones crack. Then he made out that a dog was induced to go into a room on false pretences and deftly shut up there, and then he heard a heavy step descending the stairs towards him.

But before there was time for the perpetrator of these sacrileges to come in sight a side door opened and the Bishop himself came forth with a letter in his hand (a mild, clever, gentlemanly-looking man he was, too, Tom remarked) and said:

" Pray is there not a messenger from Drumston here? "

Tom replied that he had brought a letter from his cousin, the Vicar. He had rather expected to hear it demanded, " Where is the audacious man who has dared to penetrate these sacred shades? " and was agreeably relieved to find that the Bishop wasn't angry with him.

" Dear me," said the Bishop; " I beg a thousand pardons for keeping you in the hall; pray walk into my study."

So in he went and sat down. The Bishop resumed:

" You are Mr. Thornton's cousin, sir? "

Tom bowed. " I am about the nearest relation he has besides his sister, my Lord."

" Indeed," said the Bishop. " I have written to Miss Thornton to say that there is a gentleman, a relation of my own, now living in the house with me, who will undertake Mr. Thornton's duties, and I dare say, also, without remuneration. He has nothing to do at present. Oh, here is the gentleman I spoke of!"

Here was the gentleman he spoke of, holding a dead rat by the tail and crying out:

"Look here, uncle; what did I tell you? I might have been devoured alive had it not been for my faithful Fly, your enemy."

He was about six feet or nearly so in height, with a highly intellectual though not a handsome face. His brown hair, carelessly brushed, fell over a forehead both broad and lofty, beneath which shone a pair of bold, clear grey eyes. The moment Troubridge saw him he set him down in his own mind as a "goer," by which he meant a man who had go, or energy, in him. A man, he thought, who was thrown away as a parson.

The Bishop, ringing the bell, began again, "This is my nephew, Mr. Frank Maberly."

The sleek servant entered.

"My dear Frank, pray give the rat to Sanders, and let him take it away. I don't like such things in the study."

"I only brought it to convince you, uncle," said the other. "Here you are, Sanders!"

But Sanders would have as soon shaken hands with the Pope. He rather thought the rat was alive; and taking the tongs he received the beast at a safe distance, while Tom saw a smile of contempt pass over the young curate's features.

"You'd make a good missionary, Sanders," said he; and turning to Troubridge, continued, "Pray excuse this interlude, sir. You don't look as if you would refuse to shake me by my ratty hand."

Tom thought he would sooner shake hands with him than fight him, and was so won by Maberly's manner that he was just going to say so when he recollected the presence he was in and blushed scarlet.

"My dear Frank," resumed his uncle, "Mr. Thornton of Drumston is taken suddenly ill, and I want you to go over and do his duties for him till he is better."

"Most certainly, my dear lord; and when shall I go?"

"Say to-morrow; will that suit your household, sir?" said the Bishop.

Tom replied, "Yes, certainly," and took his leave. Then the Bishop, turning to Frank, said:

"The living of Drumston, nephew, is in my gift; and if Mr. Thornton does not recover, as is very possible, I shall give it to you.

I wish you, therefore, to go to Drumston, and become acquainted with your future parishioners. You will find Miss Thornton a most charming old lady."

Frank Maberly was the second son of a country gentleman of good property, and was a very remarkable character. His uncle had always said of him, that whatever he chose to take up he would be first in; and his uncle was right. At Eton he was not only the best cricketer and runner but decidedly the best scholar of his time. At Cambridge for the first year he was probably the noisiest man in his college, though he never lived what is called "hard"; but in the second year he took up his books once more, and came forth third wrangler and first-class, and the second day after the class-list came out made a very long score in the match with Oxford. Few men were more popular, though the fast men used to call him crotchety; and on some subjects, indeed, he was very impatient of contradiction. And most of his friends were a little disappointed when they heard of his intention of going into the Church. His father went so far as to say:

"My dear Frank, I always thought you would have been a lawyer."

"I'd sooner be a——well, never mind what."

"But you might have gone into the army, Frank," said his father.

"I am going into the army, sir," he said; "into the army of Christ."

Old Mr. Maberly was at first shocked by this last expression from a son who rarely or never talked on religious matters, and told his wife so that night.

"But," he added, "since I've been thinking of it, I'm sure Frank meant neither *blague* nor irreverence. He is in earnest. I never knew him tell a lie; and since he was six years old he has known how to call a spade a spade."

"He'll make a good parson," said the mother.

"He'll be first in that, as he is in everything else," said the father.

"But he'll never be a bishop," said Mrs. Maberly.

"Why not?" said the husband indignantly.

"Because, as you say yourself, husband, he will call a spade a spade."

"Bah! you are a radical," said the father. "Go to sleep."

At the time of John Thornton's illness he had been ordained about a year and a half. He had got a title for orders as a curate in a remote part of Devon, but had left it in consequence of a violent disagreement with his rector, in which he had been most fully borne out by his uncle, who, by the by, was not the sort of man who would have supported his own brother had he been in the wrong. Since then Frank Maberly had been staying with his uncle, and, as he expressed it, "working the slums" at Exeter.

Miss Thornton sat in the drawing-room at Drumston the day after Tom's visit to the Bishop, waiting dinner for the new curate. Tom and she had been wondering how he would come. Miss Thornton said, probably in the Bishop's carriage; but Tom was inclined to think he would ride over. The dinner-time was past some ten minutes when they saw a man in black put his hand on the garden gate, vault over, and run breathless up to the hall door. Tom had recognised him, and dashed out to receive him, but ere he had time to say " Good day " even, the newcomer pulled out his watch, and having looked at it, said in a tone of vexation :

" Twenty-one minutes, as near as possible; nay, a little over. By Jove! how pursy a fellow gets mewed up in town! How far do you call it, now, from the Buller Arms ? "

" It is close upon four miles," said Tom, highly amused.

" So they told me," replied Frank Maberly. " I left my portmanteau there, and the landlord fellow had the audacity to say in conversation that I couldn't run the four miles in twenty minutes. It's lucky a parson can't bet or I should have lost my money. But the last mile is very much uphill, as you must allow."

" I'll tell you what, sir," said Tom; " there isn't a man in this parish would go that four mile under twenty minutes. If any man could I ought to know of it."

Miss Thornton had listened to this conversation with wonder not unmixed with amusement. At first she had concluded that the Bishop's carriage was upset, and that Frank was the breathless messenger sent forward to chronicle the mishap. But her tact soon showed the sort of person she had to deal with, for she was not unacquainted with the performances of public schoolboys. She laughed when she called to mind the *bouleversement* that used to take place when Lord Charles and Lord Frederick came home from Harrow, and invaded her quiet schoolroom. So she advanced into the passage to meet the newcomer with one of her pleasantest smiles.

" I must claim an old woman's privilege of introducing myself, Mr. Maberly," she said. " Your uncle was tutor to the B——s when I was governess to the D——s; so we are old acquaintances."

" Can you forgive me, Miss Thornton ? " he said, " for running up to the house in this lunatic sort of way? I am still half a schoolboy, you know." "What an old jewel she is!" he added to himself.

Tom said: "May I show you your room, Mr. Maberly?"

"If you please, do," said Frank; and added, "Get out, Fly; what are you doing here?"

But Miss Thornton interceded for the dog, a beautiful little black and tan terrier, whose points Tom was examining with profound admiration.

"That's a brave little thing, Mr. Maberly," said he, as he showed him to his room. "I should like to put in my name for a pup."

They stood face to face in the bedroom as he said this, and Frank, not answering him, said abruptly:

"By Jove! what a splendid man you are! What do you weigh, now?"

"Close upon eighteen stone, just now, I should think;" said Tom.

"Ah, but you are carrying a little flesh," said Frank.

"Why, yes," said Tom. "I've been to London for a fortnight."

"That accounts for it," said Frank. "Many dissenters in this parish?"

"A sight of all sorts," said Tom. "They want attracting to church here; they don't go naturally, as they do in some parts."

"I see," said Frank; "I suppose they'll come next Sunday though, to see the new parson; my best plan will be to give them a stinger, so that they'll come again."

"Why, you see," said Tom, "it's got about that there'll be no service next Sunday, so they'll make an excuse for going to Meeting. Our best plan will be for you and I to go about and let them know that there's a new minister. Then you'll get them together, and after that I leave it to you to keep them. Shall we go down to dinner?"

They came together going out of the door, and Frank turned and said:

"Will you shake hands with me? I think we shall suit one another."

"Ay! that we shall," said Tom heartily; "you're a man's parson; that's about what you are. But," he added seriously; "you wouldn't do among the old women, you know."

At dinner Miss Thornton said, "I hope, Mr. Maberly, you are none the worse after your run? Are you not afraid of such violent exercise bringing on palpitation of the heart?"

"Not I, my dear madam," he said. "Let me make my defence for what, otherwise, you might consider mere boyish folly. I am passionately fond of athletic sports of all kinds, and indulge in them as a pleasure. No real man is without some sort of pleasure, more or less harmless. Nay, even your fanatic is a man who makes a pleasure and an excitement of religion. My pleasures are very harmless; what can be more harmless than keeping this shell of ours in the highest state of capacity for noble deeds? I know," he said, turning to Tom, "what the great temptation is that such men as you or I have to contend against. It is 'the pride of life'; but if we know that and fight against it how can it prevail against us? It is easier conquered than the lust of the flesh or the lust of the eye, though some will tell you that I can't construe my Greek Testament, and that the 'pride of life' means something very different. I hold my opinion, however, in spite of them. Then, again, although I have taken a good degree (not so good as I might, though), I consider that I have only just begun to study. Consequently, I read hard still, and shall continue to do so the next twenty years, please God. I find my head the clearer and my intellect more powerful in consequence of the good digestion produced by exercise; so I mean to use it till I get too fat, which will be a long while first."

"Ain't you afraid," said Tom, laughing, "of offending some of your weaker brothers' consciences by running four miles because a publican said you couldn't?"

"Disputing with a publican might be an error of judgment," said Frank. "Bah! *might* be—it *was*; but with regard to running four miles—no. It is natural and right that a man at five-and-twenty should be both able and willing to run four miles, a parson above all others, as a protest against effeminacy. With regard to consciences, those very tender-conscienced men oughtn't to want a parson at all."

Miss Thornton had barely left the room to go up to the Vicar, leaving Tom and Frank Maberly over their wine, when the hall door was thrown open and the well-known voice of the Doctor was heard exclaiming in angry tones:

"If! sir, if! always at if's. 'If Blücher had destroyed the bridge,' say you, as if he ever meant to be such a vandal. And if he had meant to do it, do you think that fifty Wellesleys in one would have stayed him? No, sir; and if he had destroyed every bridge on the Seine, sir, he would have done better than to be overruled by the counsels of Wellington (glory go with him, however! He was a good man). And why, forsooth?—because the English bore the brunt at Waterloo, in consequence of the Prussians being delayed by muddy roads."

"And Ligny," said the laughing voice of Major Buckley. "Oh, Doctor, dear! I like to make you angry, because then your logic is so very outrageous. You are like the man who pleaded not guilty of murder: first, because he hadn't done it; second, that he was drunk when he did it; and third, that it was a case of mistaken identity."

"Ha, ha!" laughed the Doctor merrily, recovering his good humour in a moment. "That's an Irish story for a thousand pounds. There's nothing English about that. Ha! ha!"

Frank was presented to them as the new curate. The Doctor, after a courteous salutation, put on his spectacles and examined him carefully. Frank looked at him all the time with a quiet smile, and in the end the Doctor said:

"Allow me the privilege of shaking hands with you, sir. Shall I be considered rude if I say that I seldom or never saw a finer head than yours on a man's shoulders? And judging by the face, it is well lined."

"Like a buck-basket," said Frank, "full of dirty linen. Plenty of it, and of some quality, but not in a state fit for use yet. I will have it washed up, and wear such of it as is worth soon."

The Doctor saw he had found a man after his own heart, and it was not long before Frank and he were in the seventh heaven of discussion. Meanwhile, the Major had drawn up alongside of Tom, and said:

"Any news of the poor little dove that has left the nest, old friend?"

"Yes," said Tom eagerly; "we have got a letter. Good news, too."

"Thank God for that," said the Major. "And where are they?"

"They are now at Brighton."

"What's that?" said the Doctor, turning round. "Any news?"

They told him, and then it became necessary to tell Frank Maberly what he had not known before, that the Vicar had a daughter who had "gone off."

"One of the prettiest, sweetest creatures, Mr. Maberly," said the Major, "that you ever saw in your life. None of us, I believe, knew how well we loved her till she was gone."

"And a very remarkable character, besides," said the Doctor. "Such a force of will as you see in few women of her age.

Obscured by passion and girlish folly, it seemed more like obstinancy to us. But she has a noble heart, and, when she has outlived her youthful fancies I should not be surprised if she turned out a very remarkable woman."

CHAPTER XIII

THE DISCOVERY

ONE morning the man who went once a week from old Hawker's, at the Woodlands, down to the post, brought back a letter, which he delivered to Madge at the door. She turned it over and examined it more carefully than she generally did the old man's letters, for it was directed in a clerk-like hand, and was sealed with a big and important-looking seal, and when she came to examine this seal she saw that it bore the words " B. and F. Bank." " So, they are at it again, are they?" she said. " The deuce take 'em, I say: though for that matter I can't exactly blame the folks for looking after their own. Well, there's no mistake about one thing, he must see this letter, else some of 'em will be coming over and blowing the whole thing. He will ask me to read it for him, and I'll do so, right an-end. Lord, what a breeze there'll be! I hope I shall be able to pull my lad through, though it very much depends on the old 'un's temper. However, I shall soon know."

Old Hawker was nearly blind, and although an avaricious, suspicious old man, as a general rule, trusted implicitly on ordinary occasions to George and Madge in the management of his accounts, reflecting, with some reason, that it could not be their interest to cheat him. Of late, however, he had been uneasy in his mind. Madge, there was no denying, had got through a great deal more money than usual, and he was not satisfied with her account of where it had gone. She, we know, was in the habit of supplying George's extravagances in a way which tried all her ingenuity to hide from him, and he, mistrusting her statements, had determined as far as he could to watch her.

On this occasion she laid the letter on the breakfast table, and waited his coming down, hoping that he might be in a good humour, so that there might be some chance of averting the storm from George. Madge was much terrified for the consequences, but was quite calm and firm.

Not long before she heard his heavy step coming down the stairs, and soon he came into the room, evidently in no favourable state of mind.

"If you don't kill or poison that black tom-cat," was his first speech, "by the Lord I will. I suppose you keep him for some of your witchwork. But if he's the devil himself, as I believe he is, I'll shoot him. I won't be kept out of my natural sleep by such a devil's brat as that. He's been keeping up such a growling and a scrowling on the hen-house roof all night that I thought it was Old Scratch come for you, and getting impatient. If you must keep an imp of Satan in the house, get a mole, or a rat, or some quiet beast of that sort and not such a vicious toad as him."

"Shoot him after breakfast if you like," she said. "He's no friend of mine. Get your breakfast, and don't be a fool. There's a letter for you; take and read it."

"Yah! Read it, she says, and knows I'm blind," said Hawker. "You artful minx, you want to read it yourself."

He took the letter up and turned it over and over. He knew the seal, and shot a suspicious glance at her. Then, looking at her fixedly, he put it in his breast pocket and buttoned up his coat.

"There!" he said. "I'll read it. Oh, yes, believe me, I'll read it. You Jezebel!"

"You'd better eat your meat like a Christian man," she answered, "and not make such faces as them."

"Where's the man?" he asked.

"Outside, I suppose."

"Tell him I want the gig. I'm going out for a drive. A pleasure drive, you know. All down the lane, and back again. Cut along and tell him before I do you a mischief."

She saw he was in one of his evil humours, when nothing was to be done with him, and felt very uneasy. She went and ordered the gig, and when he had finished breakfast he came out to the door.

"You'd best take your big coat," she said, "else you'll be getting cold, and be in a worse temper than you are—and that's bad enough, Lord knows, for a poor woman to put up with."

"How careful she is!" said Hawker. "What care she takes of the old man! I've left you ten thousand pounds in my will, ducky. Good-bye."

He drove off and left her standing in the porch. What a wild, tall figure she was, standing so stern and steadfast there in the morning sun!—a woman one would rather have for a friend than an enemy.

Hawker was full of other thoughts than these. Coupling his other suspicions of Madge with the receipt of this letter from the bank, he was growing very apprehensive of something being wrong. He wanted this letter read to him, but whom could he trust? Who better than his old companion Burrows, who lived in the valley below the Vicarage? So, whipping up his horse, he drove there, but found he was out. He turned back again, puzzled, going slowly, and as he came to the bottom of the hill below the Vicarage he saw a tall man leaning against the gate and smoking.

"He'll do for want of a better," he said to himself. "He's an honest-going fellow, and we've always been good friends, and done good business together, though he is one of the cursed Vicarage lot."

So he drew up when he came to the gate. "I beg your pardon, Mr. Troubridge," he said, with a very different tone and manner to what we have been accustomed to hear him use, "but could you do a kindness for a blind old man? I have no one about me that I can trust since my son is gone away. I have reason to believe that this letter is of importance; could you be so good as to read it to me?"

"I shall be happy to oblige you, Mr. Hawker," said Tom. "I am sorry to hear that your sight is so bad."

"Yes; I'm breaking fast," said Hawker. "However, I shan't be much missed. I don't inquire how the Vicar is, because I know already, and because I don't think he would care much for my inquiries after the injury my son has done him. I will break the seal. Now may I trouble you?"

Tom Troubridge read aloud:

B. and F. Bank [Such a date.]

Sir,—May I request that you will favour me personally with a call, at the earliest possible opportunity, at my private office, 166 Broad Street? I have reason to fear that two forged cheques, bearing your signature, have been inadvertently cashed by us. The amount, I am sorry to inform you, is considerable. I need not further urge your immediate attention. This is the third communication we have made to you on the subject, and are much surprised at receiving no answer. I hope that you will be so good as to call at once.—Yours, sir, etc.,

P. Rollox, Manager.

"I thank you, Mr. Troubridge," said the old man, quietly and politely. "You see I was not wrong when I thought that this letter was of importance. May I beg as a favour that you would not mention this to anyone?"

"Certainly, Mr. Hawker. I will respect your wish. I hope your loss may not be heavy."

"The loss will not be mine though, will it?" said old Hawker. "I anticipate that it will fall on the bank. It is surely at their risk to cash cheques. Why, a man might sign for all the money I have in their hands, and surely they would be answerable for it?"

"I am not aware how the law stands, Mr. Hawker," said Troubridge. "Fortunately, no one has ever thought it worth while to forge my name."

"Well, I wish you a good day, sir, with many thanks," said Hawker. "Can I do anything for you in Exeter?"

Old Hawker drove away rapidly in the direction of Exeter; his horse, a fine black, clearing the ground in splendid style. Although a cunning man, he was not quick in following a train of reasoning, and he was half-way to Exeter before he had thoroughly comprehended his situation. And then all he saw was that somebody had forged his name, and he believed that Madge knew something about it.

"I wish my boy George was at home," he said. "He'd save me getting a lawyer now. I am altogether in the hands of those bank folks if they like to cheat me, though it's not likely they'd do that. At all events I will take Dickson with me."

Dickson was an attorney of good enough repute. A very clever quiet man, and a good deal employed by old Hawker, when his business was not too disreputable. Some years before, Hawker had brought some such excessively dirty work to his office, that the lawyer politely declined having anything to do with it, but recommended him to an attorney who he thought would undertake it. And from that time the old fellow treated him with marked respect, and spoke everywhere of him as a man to be trusted: such an effect had the fact of a lawyer refusing business had on him!

He reached Exeter by two o'clock, so rapidly had he driven. He went at once to Dickson's, and found him at home, busy swinging the poker, in deep thought, before the fireplace in his inner office. He was a small man, with an impenetrable, expressionless face, who never was known to unbend himself to a human being. Only two facts were known about him. One was, that he was the best swimmer in Exeter, and had saved several lives from drowning; and the other was, that he gave away (for him) large sums in private charity.

Such was the man who now received old Hawker, with quiet politeness; and having sent his horse round to the inn stable by a clerk, sat down once more by the fire, and began swinging the poker, and waiting for the other to begin the conversation.

"If you are not engaged, Mr. Dickson," said Hawker, "I would be much obliged to you if you could step round to the B. and F. Bank with me. I want you to witness what passes, and to read any letters or papers for me that I shall require."

The attorney put down the poker, got his hat, and stood waiting, all without a word.

"You won't find it necessary to remark on anything that occurs, Mr. Dickson, unless I ask your opinion."

The attorney nodded, and whistled a tune. And then they started together through the crowded street.

The bank was not far, and Hawker pushed his way in among the crowd of customers. It was some time before he could get hold of a clerk, there was so much business going on. When, at last, he did so, he said, "I want to see Mr. Rollox; he told me to call on him at once."

"He is engaged at present," said the clerk. "It is quite impossible you can see him."

"You don't know what you are talking about, man," said Hawker. "Send in and tell him Mr. Hawker, of Drumston, is here."

"Oh, I beg your pardon, Mr. Hawker. I have only just come here, and did not know you. Porter, show Mr. Hawker in."

They went into the formal bank parlour. There was the leather writing-table, the sheet almanac, the iron safe, and all the weapons by which bankers war against mankind, as in all other sanctuaries of the kind. Moreover, there was the commander-in-chief himself, sitting at the table. A bald, clever, gentlemanly-looking man, who bowed when they came in. "Good day, Mr. Hawker. I am obliged to you for calling at last. We thought something was wrong. Mr. Dickson, I hope you are well. Are you attending with Mr. Hawker, or are you come on private business?"

The attorney said, "I'm come at his request," and relapsed into silence.

"Ah!" said the manager. "I am, on the whole, glad that Mr. Hawker has brought a professional adviser with him. Though," he added, laughing, "it is putting me rather at a disadvantage, you know. Two to one—eh?"

"Now, gentlemen, if you will be so good as to close the door carefully, and be seated, I will proceed to business, hoping that you will give me your best attention. About six or eight months ago—let me be particular, though," said he, referring to some papers —" that is rather a loose way of beginning. Here it is. The fourth of September last year—yes. On that day, Mr. Hawker, a cheque was presented at this bank, drawn 'in favour of bearer,' and signed in your name, for two hundred pounds, and cashed, the person who presented it being well known here."

"Who?" interrupted Hawker.

"Excuse me, sir," said the manager; "allow me to come to that hereafter. You were about to say, I anticipate, that you never drew a cheque 'on bearer' in your life. Quite true. That ought to have excited attention, but it did not until a very few weeks ago; our head clerk, casting his eyes down your account, remarked on the peculiarity, and, on examining the cheque, was inclined to believe that it was not in your usual handwriting. He intended communicating with me, but was prevented for some days by my absence; and, in the meantime, another cheque, similar, but better imitated, was presented by the same person, and cashed, without the knowledge of the head clerk. On the cheque coming into his hands, he reprimanded the cashier, and he and I, having more closely examined them, came to the conclusion that they were both forgeries. We immediately communicated with you, and, to our great surprise, received no answer either to our first or second application. We, however, were not idle. We ascertained that we could lay our hands on the utterer of the cheques at any moment, and tried a third letter to you, which has been successful."

"The two letters you speak of have never reached me, Mr. Rollox," said Hawker. "I started off on the receipt of yours this morning—the first I saw. I am sorry, sir, that the bank should lose money through me; but, by your own showing, sir, the fault lay with your own clerks."

"I have never attempted to deny it, Mr. Hawker," said the manager. "But there are other matters to be considered. Before I go on, I wish to give you an opportunity of sending away your professional adviser, and continuing this conversation with me alone."

They both turned and looked at the lawyer. He was sitting with his hands in his pockets, and one would have thought he was whistling, only no sound came. His face showed no signs of intelligence in any feature save his eyes, and they were expressive of the wildest and most unbounded astonishment.

"I have nothing to do in this matter, sir," said Hawker, "that I should not wish Mr. Dickson to hear. He is an honourable man, and I confide in him thoroughly."

"So be it, then, Mr. Hawker," said the manager. "I have as high an opinion of my friend Mr. Dickson as you have; but I warn you, that some part of what will follow will touch you very unpleasantly."

"I don't see how," said Hawker; "go on, if you please."

"Will you be good enough to examine these two cheques, and say whether they are genuine or not?"

"I have only to look at the amount of this large one, to pronounce it an impudent forgery," said Hawker. "I have not signed so large a cheque for many years. There was one last January twelve-month of £400, for the land at Highcot, and that is the largest, I believe, I ever gave in my life."

"There can be no doubt they are forgeries. Your sight, I believe, is too bad to swear easily to your own signature; but that is quite enough. Now, I have laid this case before our governor, Lord C——, and he went so far as to say that, under the painful circumstances of the case, if you were to refund the money, the bank might let the matter drop; but that, otherwise, it would be their most painful duty to prosecute."

"*I* refund the money!" laughed Hawker; "you are playing with me, sir. Prosecute the dog; I will come and see him hung! Ha! ha!"

"It will be a terrible thing if we prosecute the utterer of these cheques," said the manager.

"Why?" said Hawker. "By the by, you know who he is, don't you? Tell me who it is?"

"Your own son, Mr. Hawker," said the manager, almost in a whisper.

Hawker rose and glared at them with such a look of deadly rage that they shrank from him appalled. Then he tottered to the mantel-piece, and leant against it, trying to untie his neckcloth with feeble, trembling fingers.

"Open your confounded window there, Rollox," cried the lawyer, starting up. "Where's the wine? Look sharp, man!"

Hawker waved to him impatiently to sit down, and then said, at first gasping for breath, but afterwards more quietly:

"Are you sure it was he that brought those cheques?"

"Certainly, sir," said the manager. "You may be sure it was he.

Had it been any one else, they would not have been cashed without more examination; and on the last occasion he accounted rather elaborately for your drawing such a large sum."

Hawker recovered himself and sat down.

"Don't be frightened, gentlemen," he said. "Not this time. I've something to do before that comes. It won't be long, the doctor says, but I must transact some business first. O Lord! I see it all now. That cursed, cursed woman and her boy have been hoodwinking me and playing with me all this time, have they? Oh, but I'll have my vengeance on 'em—one to the stocks, and another to the gallows. I, unfortunately, can't give you any information where that man is that has the audacity to bear my name, sir," said he to the manager. "His mother at one time persuaded me that he was a child of mine; but such infernal gipsy drabs as that can't be depended on, you know. I have the honour to wish you a very good afternoon, sir, thanking you for your information, and hoping your counsel will secure a speedy conviction. I shall probably trouble you to meet me at a magistrate's to-morrow morning, where I will take my oath in his presence that those cheques are forgeries. You will find alterations in my banker's book, too, I expect. We'll look into it all to-morrow. Come along, Dickson, my sly little weasel; I've a gay night's work for you; I'm going to leave all my property to my cousin Nick, my bitterest enemy, and a lawsuit with it that'll break his heart. There's fun for the lawyers—eh, my boy!"

So talking, the old man strode firmly forth, with a bitter, malignant scowl on his flushed face. The lawyer followed him, and, when they were in the street, Hawker again asked him to come to the inn and make his will for him.

"I'll stay by you, Hawker, and see that you don't make a fool of yourself. I wish you would not be so vindictive. It's indecent; you'll be ashamed of it to-morrow; but, in the meantime, it's indecent."

"Ha, ha!" laughed Hawker; "how quietly he talks! One can see that he hasn't had a bastard child fathered on him by a gipsy hag. Come along, old fellow; there's fifty pounds' worth of work for you this week, if I only live through it!"

He took the lawyer to the inn, and they got dinner. Hawker ate but little, for him, but drank a good deal. Dickson thought he was getting drunk; but when dinner was over, and Hawker had ordered in spirits-and-water, he seemed sober enough again.

"Now, Mr. Dickson," said he, "I am going to make a fresh will to-morrow morning, and I shall want you to draw it up for me.

After that I want you to come home with me and transact business. You will do a good day's work, I promise you. You seem to me now to be the only man in the world I can trust. ·I pray you don't desert me."

"As I said before," replied the lawyer, "I won't desert you; but listen to me. I don't half like the sudden way you have turned against your own son. Why don't you pay this money, and save the disgrace of that unhappy young man? I don't say anything about your disinheriting him—that's no business of mine—but don't be witness against him. The bank, or rather my Lord C——, has been very kind about it. Take advantage of their kindness and hush the matter up."

"I know you ain't in the pay of the bank," said Hawker, "so I won't charge you with it. I know you better than to think you'd lend yourself to anything so mean; but your conduct looks suspicious. If you hadn't done me a few disinterested kindnesses lately, I should say that they paid you to persuade me to stop this, so as they might get their money back, and save the cost of a prosecution. But I ain't so far gone as to believe that; and so I tell you, as one man to another, that if you'd come suddenly on such a mine of treason and conspiracy as I have this afternoon, and found a lad that you have treated as, and tried to believe was, your own son, you'd be as bad as me. Every moment I think of it, it comes out clearer. That woman that lives with me has palmed that brat of hers on me as my child; and he and she have been plundering me these years past. The money that woman has made away with would build a ship, sir. What she's done with it, her master, the devil, only knows; and I've said nought about it, because she's a witch, and I was afraid of her. But now I've found her out. She has stopped the letters that they wrote to me about this boy's forgery, and that shows she was in it. She shall pack. I won't prosecute her; no. I've reasons against that; but I'll turn her out in the world without a sixpence. You see I'm quiet enough now!"

"You're quiet enough," said the lawyer, "and you've stated your case very well. But are you sure this lad is not your son?"

"If I was sure that he was," said Hawker, "it wouldn't make any difference, as I know on. Ah, man, you don't know what a rage I'm in. If I chose, I could put myself into such an infernal passion at this moment as would bring on a 'plectic fit, and lay me dead on the floor. But I won't do it, not yet. I'll have another drop of brandy, and sing you a song. Shall I give 'ee 'Roger a-Maying,' or what'll ye have?"

"I'll have you go to bed, and not take any more brandy," said the lawyer. "If you sing, get in one of the waiters, and sing to him; he'd enjoy it. I'm going home, but I shall come to breakfast to-morrow morning, and find you in a different humour."

"Good night, old mole," said Hawker; "good night, old bat, old parchment skin, old sixty per cent. Ha, ha! If a wench brings a brat to thee, old lad, chuck it out o' window, and her after it. Thou can only get hung for it, man. They can only hang thee once, and that is better than to keep it and foster it, and have it turn against thee when it grows up. Good night."

Dickson came to him in the morning, and found him in the same mind. They settled down to business, and Hawker made a new will. He left all his property to his cousin (a man he had had a bitter quarrel with for years), except £100 to his groom, and £200 to Tom Troubridge, "for an act of civility" (so the words ran), "in reading a letter for a man who ought to have been his enemy." And when the will (a very short one) was finished, and the lawyer proposed getting two of his clerks as witnesses, Hawker told him to fold it up and keep it; that he would get it witnessed by and by.

"You're coming home with me," he said, "and we'll get it witnessed there. You'll see why, when it's done."

Then they went to the manager of the bank, and got him to go before a magistrate with him, whilst he deposed on oath that the two cheques, before mentioned, were forgeries, alleging that his life was so uncertain that the criminal might escape justice by his sudden death. Then he and Dickson went back to the inn, and after dinner started together to drive to Drumston.

They had been so engaged with business that they had taken no notice of the weather. But when they were clear of the northern suburbs of the town, and were flying rapidly along the noble turnpike-road that turning eastward skirts the broad Exe for a couple of miles before turning north again, they remarked that a dense black cloud hung before them, and that everything foreboded a violent thunderstorm.

"We shall get a drowning before we reach your place, Hawker," said the lawyer. "I'm glad I brought my coat."

"Lawyers never get drowned," said Hawker, "though I believe you have tried it often enough."

When they crossed the bridge, and turned to the north, along the pretty banks of the Creedy, they began to hope that they would leave it on the right; but ere they reached Newton St. Cyres they saw that it was creeping up overhead, and, stopping a few minutes in that village, perceived that the folks were all out at their doors talking to one another, as people do for company's sake when a storm is coming on.

Before they got to Crediton they could distinguish, above the sound of the wheels, the thunder groaning and muttering perpetually, and as they rattled quickly past the grand old minster a few drops of rain began to fall.

The boys were coming out of the Grammar School in shoals, laughing, running, whooping, as the manner of boys is. Hawker drove slowly as he passed through the crowd, and the lawyer took that opportunity to put on his greatcoat.

"We've been lucky so far," he said, "and now we are going to pay for our good luck. Before it is too late, Hawker, pull up and stay here. If we have to stop all night, I'll pay expenses; I will indeed. It will be dark before we are home. Do stop."

"Not for a thousand pound," said Hawker. "I wouldn't baulk myself now for a thousand pound. Hey! fancy turning her out such a night as this without sixpence in her pocket. Why, a man like you, that all the county knows, a man who has got two gold medals for bravery, ain't surely afraid of a thunderstorm?"

"I ain't afraid of the thunderstorm, but I am of the rheumatism," said the other. "As for a thunderstorm, you're as safe out of doors as in; some say safer. But you're mistaken if you suppose I don't fear death, Hawker. I fear it as much as any man."

"It didn't look like it that time you soused in over the weir after the groom lad," said Hawker.

"Bah! man," said the lawyer; "I'm the best swimmer in Devon. That was proved by my living in that weir in flood time. So I have less to fear than any one else. Why, if that boy hadn't been as quiet and plucky as he was, I knew I could kick him off any minute, and get ashore. Hallo, that's nearer."

The storm burst on them in full fury, and soon after it grew dark. The good horse, however, stepped out gallantly, though they made but little way; for, having left the high-road and taken to the narrow lanes, their course was always either up hill or down, and every bottom they passed grew more angry with the flooding waters as they proceeded. Still, through darkness, rain, and storm, they held their way till they saw the lights of Drumston below them.

"How far is it to your house, Hawker?" said the lawyer. "This storm seems to hang about still. It is as bad as ever. You must be very wet."

" It's three miles to my place, but a level road, at least all uphill,
gently rising. Cheer up! We won't be long."

They passed through the village rapidly, lighted by the lightning.
The last three miles were done as quickly as any part of the
journey, and the lawyer rejoiced to find himself before the white
gate that led up to Hawker's house.

It was not long before they drew up to the door. The storm
seemed worse than ever. There was a light in the kitchen, and
when Hawker had hallooed once or twice, a young man ran out to
take the horse.

" Is that you, my boy?" said Hawker. " Rub the horse down,
and come in to get something. This ain't a night fit for a dog to
be out in; is it?"

" No, indeed, sir," said the man. " I hope none's out in it but what
likes to be."

They went in. Madge looked up from arranging the table for
supper, and stared at Hawker keenly. He laughed aloud, and
said:

" So you didn't expect me to-night, deary, eh?"

" You've chose a bad night to come home in, old man," she
answered.

" A terrible night, ain't it? Wouldn't she have been anxious if
she'd a' known I'd been out?"

" Don't know as I should," she said. " That gentleman had better
get dried, and have his supper."

" I've got a bit of business first, deary. Where's the girl?"

" In the other kitchen."

" Call her.—Lord! listen to that."

A crash of thunder shook the house, heard loud above the rain
which beat furiously against the windows. Madge immediately
returned with the servant girl, a modest, quiet-looking creature,
evidently in terror at the storm.

" Get out that paper, Dickson, and we'll get it signed."

The lawyer produced the will, and Madge and the servant girl
were made to witness it. Dickson, having dried the signatures, took
charge of it again; and then Hawker turned round fiercely to
Madge.

" That's my new will," he said; " my new will, old woman. Oh,
you cat! I've found you out."

Madge saw a storm was coming, worse than the one which raged
and rattled outside, and she braced her nerves to meet it.

" What have you found out, old man?" she said quietly.

"I've found out that you and that young scoundrel have been robbing and cheating me in a way that would bring me to the workhouse in another year. I have found out that he has forged my name for nearly a thousand pounds, and that you've helped him. I find that you yourself have robbed me of hundreds of pounds, and that I have been blinded, and cozened, and hoodwinked, by two that I kept from the workhouse, and treated as well as I treated myself. That's what I have found out, gipsy."

"Well?" was all Madge said, standing before him with her arms folded.

"So I say," said Hawker; "it is very well. The mother to the streets, and the boy to the gallows."

"You wouldn't prosecute him, William; your own son?"

"No, I shan't," he replied;—"but the bank will."

"And couldn't you stop it?"

"I could. But if holding up my little finger would save him, I wouldn't do it."

"Oh, William," she cried, throwing herself on her knees; "don't look like that. I confess everything; visit it on me, but spare the boy."

"You confess, do you?" he said. "Get up. Get out of my house; you shan't stay here."

But she would not go, but hanging round him, kept saying, "Spare the boy, William, spare the boy!" over and again, till he struck her in his fury, and pulled her towards the door.

"Get out and herd with the gipsies you belong to," he said. "You witch, you can't cry now."

"But," she moaned, "oh, not such a night as this, William; not to-night. I am frightened of the storm. Let me stay to-night. I am frightened of the lightning. Oh, I wouldn't turn out your dog such a night as this."

"Out, out, you devil!"

"Oh, William, only one——"

"Out, you Jezebel, before I do you a mischief."

He had got the heavy door open, and she passed out, moaning low to herself. Out into the fierce rain and the black darkness; and the old man held open the door for a minute, to see if she were gone.

No. A broad, flickering riband of light ineffable wavered for an instant of time before his eyes, lighting up the country far and wide; but plainly visible between him and the blaze was a tall, dark, bareheaded woman, wildly raising her hands above her head, as if imploring vengeance upon him, and, ere the terrible explosion which followed had ceased to shake the old house to its foundations, he shut the door, and went muttering alone up to his solitary chamber.

The next morning the groom came into the lawyer's room, and informed him that when he went to call his master in the morning, he had found the bed untouched, and Hawker sitting half undressed in his arm-chair, dead and cold.

CHAPTER XIV

THE MAJOR'S VISIT TO THE NAG'S HEAD

MAJOR BUCKLEY and his wife stood together in the veranda of their cottage, watching the storm. All the afternoon they had seen it creeping higher and higher, blacker and more threatening up the eastern heavens, until it grew painful to wait any longer for its approach. But now that it had burst on them, and night had come on dark as pitch, they felt the pleasant change in the atmosphere, and, in spite of the continuous gleam of the lightning, and the eternal roll and crackle of the thunder, they had come out to see the beauty and majesty of the tempest.

They stood with their arms entwined for some time, in silence; but after a crash louder than any of those which had preceded it, Major Buckley said:

" My dearest Agnes, you are very courageous in a thunderstorm."

" Why not, James? " she said; " you cannot avoid the lightning and the thunder won't harm you. Most women fear the sound of the thunder more than anything, but I suspect that Ciudad Rodrigo made more noise than this, husband? "

" It did indeed, my dear. More noise than I ever heard in any storm yet. It is coming nearer."

" I am afraid it will shake the poor old Vicar very much," said Mrs. Buckley. " Ah, there is Sam crying."

They both went into the sitting-room; little Sam had petitioned to go to bed on the sofa till the storm was over, and now, awakened by the thunder, was sitting up in his bed, crying out for his mother.

The Major went in and lay down by the child on the sofa, to quiet him. " What! " said he, " Sammy, you're not afraid of thunder, are you? "

"Yes! I am," said the child; "very much indeed. I am glad you are come, father."

"Lightning never strikes good boys, Sam," said the Major.

"Are you sure of that, father?" said the little one.

That was a poser; so the Major thought it best to counterfeit sleep; but he overdid it, and snored so loud, that the boy began to laugh, and his father had to practise his deception with less noise. And by degrees, the little hand that held his moustache dropped feebly on the bed-clothes, and the Major, ascertaining by the child's regular breathing that his son was asleep, gently raised his vast length, and proposed to his wife to come into the veranda again.

"The storm is breaking, my love," said he; "and the air is deliciously cool out there. Put your shawl on and come out."

They went out again; the lightning was still vivid, but the thunder less loud. Straight down the garden from them stretched a broad gravel walk, which now, cut up by the rain into a hundred water channels, showed at each flash like rivers of glittering silver. Looking down this path toward the black wood during one of the longest continued illuminations of the lightning, they saw for an instant a dark, tall figure, apparently advancing towards them. Then all the prospect was wrapped again in tenfold gloom.

Mrs. Buckley uttered an exclamation, and held tighter to her husband's arm. Every time the garden was lit up, they saw the figure nearer and nearer, till they knew it was standing before them in the darkness; the Major was about to speak, when a hoarse voice, heard indistinctly above the rushing of the rain, demanded:

"Is that Major Buckley?"

At the same minute the storm-light blazed up once more, and fell upon an object so fearful and startling that they both fell back amazed. A woman was standing before them, tall, upright, and bareheaded; her long black hair falling over a face as white and ghastly as a three days' corpse; her wild countenance rendered more terrible by the blue glare of the lightning shining on the rain that streamed from every lock of her hair and every shred of her garments. She looked like some wild daughter of the storm, who had lost her way, and came wandering to them for shelter.

"I am Major Buckley," was the answer. "What do you want? But in God's name come in out of the rain."

"Come in and get your things dried, my good woman," said Mrs. Buckley. "What do you want with my husband such a night as this?"

"Before I dry my things, or come in, I will state my business," said the woman, coming under the veranda. "After that I will accept your hospitality. This is a night when polecats and rabbits would shelter together in peace; and yet such a night as this, a man turns out of his house the woman who has lain beside him twenty years."

"Who are you, my good soul?" said the Major.

"They call me Madge the Witch," she said; "I lived with old Hawker, at the Woodlands, till to-night, and he has turned me out. I want to put you in possession of some intelligence that may save much misery to some that you love."

"I can readily believe that you can do it," said the Major, "but pray don't stand there; come in with my wife, and get your things dried."

"Wait till you hear what I have to say: George Hawker, my son——"

"Your son—good God!"

"I thought you would have known that. The Vicar does. Well, this son of mine has run off with the Vicar's daughter."

"Well?"

"Well, he has committed forgery. It'll be known all over the country to-morrow, and even now I fear the runners are after him. If he is taken before he marries that girl, things will be only worse than they are. But never mind whether he does or not, perhaps you differ with me; perhaps you think that, if you could find the girl now, you could stop her and bring her home; but you don't know where she is. I do, and if you will give me your solemn word of honour as a gentleman to give him warning that his forgery for five hundred pounds is discovered, I will give you his direction."

The Major hesitated for a moment, thinking.

"If you reflect a moment, you must see how straightforward my story is. What possible cause can I have to mislead you? I know which way you will decide, so I wait patiently."

"I think I ought to say yes, my love," said the Major to his wife; "if it turned out afterwards that I neglected any opportunity of saving this poor girl (particularly if this tale of the forgery be true), I should never forgive myself."

"I agree with you, my dear," said Mrs. Buckley. "Give your promise, and go to seek her."

"Well, then," said the Major; "I give you my word of honour that I will give Hawker due warning of his forgery being discovered, if you will give me his direction. I anticipate that they are in

London, and I shall start to-night, to be in time for the morning coach. Now, will you give me the address?"

"Yes!" said Madge. "They are at the Nag's Head, Buckingham Street, Strand, London; can you remember that?"

"I know where the street is," said the Major; "now will you go into the kitchen, and make yourself comfortable? My dear, you will see my valise packed? Ellen, get this person's clothes dried, and get her some hot wine. By the by," said he, following her into the kitchen, "you must have had a terrible quarrel with Hawker, for him to send you out such a night as this?"

"It was about this matter," she said; "the boy forged on his father, and I knew it, and tried to screen him. My own son, you know."

"It was natural enough," said the Major. "You are not deceiving me, are you? I don't see why you should, though."

"Before God, I am not. I only want the boy to get warning."

"You must sleep here to-night," said the Major; "and to-morrow you can go on your way, though, if you cannot conveniently get away in the morning, don't hurry, you know. My house is never shut against unfortunate people. I have heard a great deal of you, but I never saw you before; you must be aware, however, that the character you have held in the place is not such as warrants me in asking you to stay here for any time."

The Major left the kitchen, and crossed the yard. In a bedroom above the stable slept his groom, a man who had been through his campaigns with him from first to last. It was to waken him that the Major took his way up the narrow stairs towards the loft.

"Jim," he said, "I want my horse in an hour."

The man was out of bed in a moment, and while he was dressing the Major continued:

"You know Buckingham Street, Strand, Jim, don't you? When you were recruiting you used to hang out at a public-house there, unless I am mistaken."

"Exactly so, sir! We did; and a many good chaps we picked up there, gents and all sorts. Why, it was in that werry place, Major, as we 'listed Lundon; him as was afterwards made sergeant for being the first man into Sebastian, and arterwards married Skettles: her as fell out of eighteen stories at Brussels looking after the Duke, and she swore at them as came to pick her up, she did; and walked in at the front door as bold as brass."

"There, my good lad," said the Major; "what's the good of telling such stories as that? Nobody believes them, you know. Do you know the Nag's Head there? It's a terribly low place, is it not?"

"It's a much changed if it ain't, sir," said Jim, putting on his breeches. "I was in there not eighteen months since. It's a fighting-house; and there used to be a dog show there, and a reunion of vocal talent, and all sorts of villainies."

"Well, see to the horse, Jim, and I'll sing out when I'm ready," said the Major, and went back into the house.

He came back through the kitchen, and saw that Madge was being treated by the maids with that respect that a reputed witch never fails to command; then, having sat for some time talking to his wife, and finding that the storm was cleared off, he kissed his sleeping child and its mother, and mounting his horse in the stable-yard, rode off towards Exeter.

In the morning, when Mrs. Buckley came downstairs, she inquired for Madge. They told her she had been up some time, and, having got some breakfast, was walking up and down in front of the house. Going there, Mrs. Buckley found her. Her dress was rearranged with picturesque neatness, and a red handkerchief pinned over her rich dark hair, that last night had streamed wild and wet in the tempest. Altogether, she looked an utterly different being from the strange, storm-beaten creature who had craved their hospitality the night before. Mrs. Buckley admired the bold, upright, handsome figure before her, and gave her a cheery "good morning."

"I only stayed," said Madge, "to wish you good-bye, and thank you for your kindness. When they who should have had some pity on me turned me out, you took me in!"

"You are heartily welcome," said Mrs. Buckley. "Cannot I do more for you? Do you want money? I fear you must!"

"None, I thank you kindly," she replied; "that would break the spell. Good-bye!"

"Good-bye!" said Mrs. Buckley.

Madge stood in front of the door and raised her hand.

"The blessing of God," she said, "shall be upon the house of the Buckleys, and more especially upon you and your husband, and the boy that is sleeping inside. He shall be a brave and a good man, and his wife shall be the fairest and best in the country-side. Your kine shall cover the plains until no man can number them, and your sheep shall be like the sands of the sea. When misfortune and death and murder fall upon your neighbours, you shall stand between the dead and the living, and the troubles that pass over your heads shall be like the shadows of the light clouds that fly across the moor on a sunny day. And when in your ripe and honoured old age you shall sit with your husband, in a garden of your own planting, in the lands far away, and see your grandchildren playing around you, you shall think of the words of the wild, lost gipsy woman, who gave you her best blessing before she went away and was seen no more."

Mrs. Buckley tried to say " Amen," but found herself crying. Something there was in that poor creature, homeless, penniless, friendless, that made her heart like wax. She watched her as she strode down the path, and afterwards looked for her reappearing on a high exposed part of the road, a quarter of a mile off, thinking she would take that way. But she waited long, and never again saw that stern, tall figure, save in her dreams.

She turned at last, and one of the maids stood beside her.

" Oh, missis," she said, " you're a lucky woman to-day. There's some in this parish would have paid a hundred pounds for such a fortune as that from her. It'll come true—you will see! "

" I hope it may, you silly girl," said Mrs. Buckley, and then she went in and knelt beside her sleeping boy, and prayed that the blessing of the gipsy woman might be fulfilled.

It was quite late on the evening of his second day's journey that the Major, occupying the box-seat of the " Exterminator," dashed with comet-like speed through so much of the pomps and vanities of this wicked world as showed itself in Piccadilly at half-past seven on a spring afternoon.

" Hah! " he soliloquised, passing Hyde Park Corner, " these should be the folks going out to dinner. They dine later and later every year. At this rate they'll dine at half-past one in twenty years' time. That's the Duke's new house; eh, coachman? By George, there's his Grace himself, on his brown cob; God bless him! There are a pair of good-stepping horses, and old Lady E—— behind 'em, by Jove!—in her war-paint and feathers—pinker than ever. She hasn't got tired of it yet. She'd dance at her own funeral if she could. And there's Charley Bridgenorth in the club balcony —I wonder what he finds to do in peace time?—and old B—— talking to him. What does Charley mean by letting himself be seen in the same balcony with that disreputable old fellow? I hope he won't get his morals corrupted! Ah! So here we are! eh? "

He dismounted at the White Horse Cellar, and took a hasty dinner. His great object was speed; and so he hardly allowed

himself ten minutes to finish his pint of port before he started into
the street, to pursue the errand on which he had come.

It was nearly nine o'clock, and he thought he would be able to
reach his destination in ten minutes. But it was otherwise ordered.
His evil genius took him down St. James's Street. He tried to
persuade himself that it was the shortest way, though he knew
all the time that it wasn't. And so he was punished in this way:
he had got no farther than Crockford's, when, in the glare of light
opposite the door of that establishment, he saw three men standing,
one of whom was talking and laughing in a tone perhaps a little
louder than it is customary to use in the streets nowadays. Buckley
knew that voice well (better, perhaps, among the crackle of musketry than in the streets of London), and, as the broad-shouldered
owner of it turned his jolly, handsome face towards him, he could
not suppress a low laugh of satisfaction. At the same moment the
before-mentioned man recognised him, and shouted out his name.

" Busaco Buckley, by the Lord," he said, " revisiting once more
the glimpses of the gas-lamps ! My dear old fellow, how are you,
and where do you come from? "

The Major found himself quickly placed under a lamp for
inspection, and surrounded by three old and well-beloved fellow-
campaigners. What could a man do under the circumstances?
Nothing, if human and infallible, I should say, but what the Major
did—stay there, laughing and joking, and talking of old times, and
freshen up his honest heart, and shake his honest sides with many
an old half-forgotten tale of fun and mischief.

" Now," he said at last, " you must let me go. You Barton " (to
the first man he recognised), " you are a married man; what are
you doing at Crockford's? "

" The same as you are," said the other—" standing outside the
door. The pavement's free, I suppose. I haven't been in such a
place these five years. Where are you staying, old boy? "

The Major told them, and they agreed to meet at breakfast next
morning. Then, after many farewells, and callings back, he pursued
his way towards the Strand, finding to his disgust that it was nearly
ten o'clock.

He, nevertheless, held on his way undiscouraged, and turning by
degrees into narrower and narrower streets, came at last on one
quieter than the others, which ended abruptly at the river.

It was a quiet street, save at one point, and that was where a
blaze of gas (then recently introduced, and a great object of
curiosity to the Major) was thrown across the street, from the broad

ornamented windows of a flash public-house. Here there was noise enough. Two men fighting, and three or four more encouraging, while a half-drunken woman tried to separate them. From the inside, too, came a noise of singing, quarrelling, and swearing, such as made the Major cross the road, and take his way on the darker side of the street.

But when he got opposite the aforesaid public-house, he saw that it was called the Nag's Head and that it was kept by one J. Trotter. "What an awful place to take that girl to!" said the Major. "But there may be some private entrance, and a quiet part of the house set by for a hotel." Nevertheless, having looked well about him, he could see nothing of the sort, and perceived that he must storm the bar.

But he stood irresolute for a moment. It looked such a very low place, clean and handsome enough, but still the company about the door looked so very disreputable. "J. Trotter!" he reflected. "Why, that must be Trotter the fighting-man. I hope it may be; he will remember me."

So he crossed. When he came within the sphere of the gas-lamps, those who were assisting at the fight grew silent, and gazed upon him with open eyes. As he reached the door one of them remarked, with a little flourish of oaths as a margin or garland round his remark, that "of all the swells he'd ever seen, that 'un was the biggest, at all events."

Similarly, when they in the bar saw that giant form, the blue coat and brass buttons, and, above all, the moustache (sure sign of a military man in those days), conversation ceased, and the Major then and there became the event of the evening. He looked round as he came in, and, through a door leading inwards, he saw George Hawker himself, standing talking to a man with a dog under each arm.

The Major was not deceived as to the identity of J. Trotter. J. Trotter, the hero of a hundred fights, stood himself behind his own bar, a spectacle for the gods. A chest like a bull, a red neck, straight up and down with the back of his head, and a fist like a seal's flipper, proclaimed him the prize-fighter; and his bright grey eye, and ugly laughing face, proclaimed him the merry, good-humoured varlet that he was.

What a wild state of amazement he was in when he realized the fact that Major Buckley of the —th was actually towering aloft under the chandelier, and looking round for some one to address! With what elephantine politeness and respect did he show the Major into a private parlour, sweeping off at one round nearly a dozen pint-pots that covered the table, and then, shutting the door, stand bowing and smiling before his old pupil!

"And so you are gone into business, John, are you?" said the Major. "I'm glad to see it. I hope you are doing as well as you deserve."

"Much better than that," said the prize-fighter. "Much better than *that,* sir, I assure you."

"Well, I'm going to get you to do something for me," said the Major. "Do you know, John, that you are terribly fat?"

"The business allus does make flesh, sir. More especially to coves as has trained much."

"Yes, yes, John, I am going from the point. There is a young man of the name of Hawker here?"

The prize-fighter remained silent, but a grin gathered on his face. "I never contradicts a gentleman," he said. "And if you say he's here, why, in course, he is here. But I don't say he's here; you mind that, sir."

"My good fellow, I saw him as I came in," said the Major.

"Oh, indeed," said the other; "then that absolves me from any responsibility. He told me to deny him to anybody but one, and you ain't she. He spends a deal of money with me, sir; so, in course, I don't want to offend him. By the by, sir, excuse me a moment."

The Major saw that he had got hold of the right man, and waited willingly. The fighting-man went to the door, and called out, "My dear." A tall, good-looking woman came to the bar, who made a low curtsey on being presented to the Major. "My dear," repeated Trotter, "the south side." "The particular, I suppose," she said. "In course," said he. So she soon appeared with a bottle of Madeira, which was of such quality that the Major, having tasted it, winked at the prize-fighter, and the latter laughed, and rubbed his hands.

"Now," said the Major, "do you mind telling me whether this Hawker is here alone?"

"He don't live here. He only comes here of a day, and some-times stays till late. This evening a pretty young lady—yes, a *lady* —come and inquired for him in my bar, and I was struck all of a heap to see such a creature in such a place, all frightened out of her wits. So I showed her through in a minute, and upstairs to where my wife sits, and she waited there till he come in. And she hadn't been gone ten minutes when you come."

The Major swore aloud, without equivocation or disguise. "Ah," he said, "if I had not met Barton! Pray, Trotter, have you any idea where Hawker lives?"

"Not the least in the world, further than it's somewhere Hampstead way. That's a thing he evidently don't want known."

"Do you think it likely that he and that young lady live in the same house? I need not disguise from you that I am come after her, to endeavour to get her back to her family."

"I know they don't live in the same house," said Trotter, "because I heard her say to-night, before she went away, 'Do look round, George,' she says, 'at my house for ten minutes before you go home.'"

"You have done me a great kindness," said the Major, "in what you have told me. I don't know how to thank you."

"It's only one," said the prize-fighter, "in return for a many you done me; and you are welcome to it, sir. Now, I expect you'd like to see this young gent; so follow me, if you please."

Through many passages, past many doors, he followed him, until they left the noise of the revelry behind, and at last, at the end of a long dark passage, the prize-fighter suddenly threw open a door, and announced—"Major Buckley!"

There were four men playing at cards, and the one opposite to him was George Hawker. The Major saw at a glance, almost before any one had time to speak, that George was losing money, and that the other three were confederates.

The prize-fighter went up to the table and seized the cards; then, after a momentary examination, threw both packs in the fire.

"When gents play cards in my house, I expect them to use the cards I provides at the bar, and not private packs, whether marked or not. Mr. Hawker, I warned you before about this; you'll lose every sixpence you're worth, and then you will say it was done at my house, quite forgetting to mention that I warned you of it repeatedly."

But George took no notice of him. "Really, Major Buckley," he began, "this is rather——"

"Rather an intrusion, you would say—eh, Mr. Hawker?" said the Major; "so it is, but the urgency of my business must be my apology. Can you give me a few words alone?"

George rose and came out with them. The prize-fighter showed them into another room, and the Major asked him to stand in the passage, and see that no one was listening; "you see, John," he added, "we are very anxious not to be overheard."

"I am not at all particular myself," said George Hawker. "I have nothing to conceal."

"You will alter your mind before I have done, sir," said the Major.

George didn't like the look of affairs.—How came it that the Major and the prize-fighter knew one another so well? What did the former mean by all this secrecy? He determined to put a bold face on the matter.

"Miss Thornton is living with you, sir, I believe?" began the Major.

"Not at all, sir; Miss Thornton is in lodgings of her own. I have the privilege of seeing her for a few hours every day. In fact, I may go as far as to say that I am engaged to be married to her, and that that auspicious event is to come off on Thursday week."

"May I ask you to favour me with her direction?" said the Major.

"I am sorry to disoblige you, Major Buckley, but I must really decline," answered George. "I am not unaware how disinclined her family are to the connection; and, as I cannot but believe that you come on their behalf, I cannot think that an interview would be anything but prejudicial to my interest. I must remind you, too, that Miss Thornton is of age, and her own mistress in every way."

While George had been speaking, it passed through the Major's mind: "What a checkmate it would be, if I were to withhold the information I have, and set the runners on him here! I might save the girl, and further the ends of justice; but my hands are tied by the promise I gave that woman—how unfortunate!"

"Then, Mr. Hawker," he said aloud, "I am to understand that you refuse me this address?"

"I am necessitated to refuse it most positively, sir."

"I am sorry for it. I leave it to your conscience. Now, I have got a piece of intelligence to give you, which I fear will be somewhat unpalatable—I got your address at this place from a woman of the name of Madge——"

"You did!" exclaimed George.

"Who was turned out of doors by your father, the night before last, in consequence, I understood, of some misdeeds of hers having come to light. She came immediately to my house, and offered to give me your direction, on condition of my passing my word of honour to deliver you this message: 'that the forgery (£500 was the sum mentioned, I think) was discovered, and that the bank was going to prosecute.' I of course form no judgment as to the truth or falsehood of this: I leave you to take your own measures about it—only I once again ask you whether you will give me an interview with Miss Thornton?"

George had courage enough left to say hoarsely and firmly, " No ! "

" Then," replied the Major, " I must call you to witness that I have performed my errand to you faithfully. I beg, also, that you will carry all our kindest remembrances to Miss Thornton, and tell her that her poor father was struck with paralysis when he missed her, and that he is not expected to live many weeks. And I wish you good night."

He passed out, and down the stairs; as he passed the public parlour-door, he heard a man bawling out a song, two or three lines of which he heard, and which made him blush to the tips of his ears, old soldier as he was.

As he walked up the street, he soliloquised: " A pretty mess I've made of it—done him all the service I could, and not helped her a bit—I see there is no chance of seeing her, though I shall try. I will go round Hampstead to-morrow, though that is a poor chance. In Paris, now, or Vienna, one could find her directly. What a pity we have no police ! "

CHAPTER XV

THE BRIGHTON RACES AND WHAT HAPPENED THEREAT

GEORGE HAWKER just waited till he heard the retiring footsteps of the Major, and then, leaving the house, held his way rapidly towards Mary's lodgings, which were in Hampstead; but finding he would be too late to gain admittance, altered his course when he was close to the house, and went to his own house, which was not more than a few hundred yards distant. In the morning he went to her, and she ran down the garden to meet him before the servant had time to open the door, looking so pretty and bright. " Ah, George! " said she, " you never came last night, after all your promises. I shall be glad when it's all over, George, and we are together for good."

" It won't be long; first, my dear," he answered, " we must manage to get through that time as well as we can, and then we'll begin to sound the old folks. You see I am come to breakfast."

" I expected you," she said; " come in and we will have such a pleasant chat, and after that you must take me down the town, George, and we will see the carriages."

"Now, my love," said George, "I've got to tell you something that will vex you; but you must not be down-hearted about it, you know. The fact is, that your friends, as they call themselves, moving heaven and earth to get you back, by getting me out of the way, have hit on the expedient of spreading false reports about me, and issuing scandals against me. They found out my address at the Nag's Head, and came there after me not half an hour after you were gone, and I only got out of their way by good luck. You ought to give me credit for not giving any living soul the secret of our whereabouts, so that all I have got to do is to keep quiet here until our little business is settled, and then I shall be able to face them boldly again, and set everything straight."

"How cruel!" she said; "how unjust! I will never believe anything against you, George."

"I am sure of that, my darling," he said, kissing her. "But now, there is another matter I must speak about, though I don't like to—I am getting short of money, love."

"I have got nearly a hundred pounds, George," she said; "and, as I told you, I have five thousand pounds in the funds, which I can sell out at any time I like."

"We shall do well, then, my Polly. Now let us go for a walk."

All that week George stayed with her quietly, till the time of residence necessary before they could be married was expired. He knew that he was treading on a mine, which at any time might burst and blow his clumsy schemes to the wind. But circumstances were in his favour, and the time came to an end at last. He drank hard all the time without letting Mary suspect it, but afterwards, when it was all over, wondered at his nerve and self-possession through all those trying days, when he was forced eternally to have a smile or a laugh ready, and could not hear a step behind him without thinking of an officer, or look over his head without thinking he saw a gallows in the air.

It was during this time that he nursed in his heart a feeling of desperate hatred and revenge against William Lee, which almost became the leading passion of his life. He saw, or thought he saw, that this man was the author of all the troubles that were gathering so thick around his head, and vowed, if chance threw the man in his way again, that he would take ample and fearful vengeance, let it cost what it might. And though this feeling may have sometimes grown cold, yet he never (as we shall see) to the last day forgot or forgave the injuries this man had done him.

Mary was as innocent of business as a child, and George found little difficulty in persuading her, that the best thing she could do under present circumstances, was to sell out the money she had in the funds, and place it in a bank, to be drawn on as occasion should require; saying that they should be so long, perhaps, before they had any other fund to depend on, that they might find it necessary to undertake some business for a living, in which case, it would be as well to have their money under command at a moment's notice.

There was, not far from the bank, an old stockbroker, who had known her father and herself for many years, and was well acquainted with all their affairs, though they had but little intercourse by letter. To him she repaired, and, merely informing him that she was going to marry without her father's consent, begged him to manage the business for her; which he, complimenting her upon her good fortune in choosing a time when the funds were so high, immediately undertook; at the same time recommending her to a banker, where she might open an account.

On the same day that this business was concluded, a licence was procured, and their wedding fixed for the next day. " Now," thought George, as he leapt into bed on that night, " let only to-morrow get over safely, and I can begin to see my way out of the wood again."

And in the morning they were married in Hampstead church. Parson, clerk, pew-opener, and beadle, all remarked what a handsome young couple they were, and how happy they ought to be; and the parson departed, and the beadle shut up the church, and the mice came out again, and ate the Bibles, and the happy pair walked away down the road, bound together by a strong chain, which nothing could loose but death. They went to Brighton. Mary had said she would so like to see the sea; and the morning after they arrived there—the morning after their wedding—Mary wrote an affectionate penitential letter to her father, telling him that she was married, and praying his forgiveness.

They were quite gay at Brighton, and she recovered her spirits wonderfully at first. George soon made acquaintances, who soon got very familiar, after the manner of their kind—greasy, tawdry, bedizened bucks—never asleep, always proposing a game of cards, always carrying off her husband. Mary hated them, while she at times was proud to see her husband in such fine company.

Such were the eagles that gathered round the carcass of George Hawker; and at last these eagles began to bring the hen-birds with them, who frightened our poor little dove with the amplitude and splendour of their feathers, and their harsh, strange notes. George knew the character of those women well enough; but already he cared little enough about his wife, even before they had been a month married, going on the principle that the sooner she learned to take care of herself, the better for her; and after they had been married little more than a month, Mary thought she began to see a change in her husband's behaviour to her.

He grew sullen and morose, even to her. Every day almost he would come to her with a scowl upon his face; and when she asked if he was angry with her, would say, " No, that he wasn't angry with her; but that things were going wrong—altogether wrong; and if they didn't mind, he couldn't see his way out of it at all."

But one night he came home cheerful and hilarious, though rather the worse for liquor. He showed her a roll of notes which he had won at roulette—over a hundred pounds—and added, " That shall be the game for me in future, Polly; all square and above-board there."

" My dear George, I wish you'd give up gambling."

" So I will, some of these fine days, my dear. I only do it to pass the time. It's cursed dull having nothing to do."

" To-morrow is the great day at the races, George. I wish you would take me; I never saw a horse-race."

" Ay, to be sure," said he; " we'll go, and, what's more, we'll go alone. I won't have you seen in public with those dowdy drabs."

So they went alone. Such a glorious day as it was—the last happy day she spent for very long! How delightful it was, all this rush and crush, and shouting and hubbub around, while you were seated in a phaeton, secure above the turmoil! What delight to see all the beautiful women in the carriages, and, grandest sight of all, which struck awe and admiration into Mary's heart, was the great Prince himself, that noble gentleman, in a gutter-sided hat, and a wig so fearfully natural that Mary secretly longed to pull his hair.

But princes and duchesses were alike forgotten when the course was cleared for the great event of the day, and, one by one, the sleek beauties came floating along, above the crowd, towards the starting-post. Then George, leaving Mary in the phaeton to the care of their landlady, pushed his way among the crowd, and, by dint of hard squeezing, got against the rail. He had never seen such horses as these; he had never known what first-class horse-racing was. Here was a new passion for him, which, like all his others, should only by its perversion end in his ruin.

He had got some money on one of the horses, though he, of course, had never seen it. There was a cheer all along the line, and a dark bay fled past towards the starting-post, seeming rather to belong to the air than the ground. "By George," he said aloud, as the blood mounted to his face, and tingled in his ears, "I never saw such a sight as that before."

He was ashamed of having spoken aloud in his excitement, but a groom who stood by said, for his consolation:

"I don't suppose you ever did, sir, nor no man else. That's young Velocipede, and that's Chiffney a-ridin' him. You'll see that horse walk over for everything next year.

But now the horses came down, five of them abreast, at a walk, amid a dead silence from the crowd, three of them steady old stagers, but two jumping and pulling. "Back, Velocipede; back, Lara!" says the starter; down goes the flag, they dart away, and then there is a low hum of conversation, until a murmur is heard down the course, which swells into a roar as you notice it. The horses are coming. One of the royal huntsmen gallops by, and then, as the noise comes up towards you, you can hear the maddening rush of the horses' feet upon the turf, and, at the same time, a bay and a chestnut rush past in the last fierce struggle, and no man knows yet who has won.

Then the crowd poured once more over the turf, and surged and cheered round the winning horses. Soon it came out that Velocipede had won, and George, turning round delighted, stood face to face with a gipsy woman.

She had her hood low on her head, so that he could not see her face, but she said, in a low voice, "Let me tell your fortune."

"It is told already, mother," said George. "Velocipede has won; you won't tell me any better news than that this day, I know."

"No, George Hawker, I shan't," replied the gipsy, and, raising her hood for an instant, he discovered to his utter amazement the familiar countenance of Madge.

"Will you let me tell your fortune now, my boy?" she said.

"What, Madge, old girl! By jove, you shall. Well, who'd a' thought of seeing you here?"

"I've been following you, and looking for you ever so long," she said. "They at the Nag's Head didn't know where you were gone, and if I hadn't been a gipsy, and o' good family, I'd never have found you."

"You're a good old woman," he said. "I suppose you've some news for me?"

"I have," she answered; "come away after me."

He followed her into a booth, and they sat down. She began the conversation.

"Are you married?" she asked.

"Ay; a month since."

"And you've got her money?"

"Yes," he said; "but I've been walking into it."

"Make the most of it," said Madge. "Your father's dead."

"Dead!'

"Ay, dead. And what's worse, lad, he lived long enough to alter his will."

"O Lord! What do you mean?"

"I mean," she said, "that he has left all his money to your cousin. He found out everything, all in a minute, as it were; and he brought a new will home from Exeter, and I witnessed it. And he turned me out of doors, and, next morning, after I was gone, he was found dead in his bed. I got to London, and found no trace of you there, till, by an accident, I heard that you had been seen down here, so I came on. I've got my living by casting fortins, and begging, and cadging, and such-like. Sometime I've slept in a barn, and sometime in a hedge, but I've fought my way to you, true and faithful, through it all, you see."

"So he's gone," said George, between his teeth, "and his money with him. That's awful. What an unnatural old villain!"

"He got it into his head at last, George, that you weren't his son at all."

"The lunatic!—and what put that into his head?"

"He knew you weren't his wife's son, you see, and he had heard some stories about me before I came to live with him, and so, at the last, he took to saying he'd nought to do with you."

"Then you mean to say——"

"That you are my boy," she said, "my own boy. Why, lad, who but thy own mother would a' done for thee what I have? And thou never thinking of it all these years! Blind lad!"

"Good God!" said George. "And if I had only known that before, how differently I'd have gone on. How I'd have sneaked and truckled, and fetched and carried for him! Bah, it's enough to drive one mad. All this hide-and-seek work don't pay, old woman. You and I are bowled out with it. How easy for you to have given me a hint of this years ago, to make me careful! But you delight in mystery and conglomeration, and you always will. There—I ain't ungrateful, but when I think of what we've lost, no wonder I get wild. And what the devil am I to do now?"

"You've got the girl's money to go on with," she said.

"Not so very much of it," he replied. "I tell you I've been playing like—never mind what, this last month, and I've lost every night. Then I've got another woman in tow, that costs—oh, curse her, what don't she cost, what with money and bother?—In short, if I don't get something from somewhere, in a few months I shall be in Queer Street. What chance is there of the parson's dying?"

"It don't matter much to you when he dies, I expect," said she, "for you may depend that those that's got hold of him won't let his money come into your hands. He's altered his will, you may depend on it."

"Do you really think so?"

"I should think it more probable than not. You see that old matter with the bank is known all over the country, although they don't seem inclined to push it against you, for some reason. Yet it's hardly likely that the Vicar would let his money go to a man who couldn't be seen for fear of a rope."

"You're a raven, old woman," he said. "What am I to do?"

"Give up play, to begin with."

"Well?"

"Start some business with what's left."

"Ha, ha! Well, I'll think of it. You must want some money, old girl! Here's a fipunnote."

"I don't want money, my boy; I'm all right," she said.

"Oh, nonsense; take it."

"I won't," she answered. "Give me a kiss, George."

He kissed her forehead, and bent down his head reflecting. When he looked up she was gone.

He ran out of the booth and looked right and left, but saw her nowhere. Then he went sulkily back to his wife. He hardly noticed her, but said it was time to go home. All the way back, and after they had reached their lodgings, he kept the same moody silence, and she, frightened at some unheard-of calamity, forbore to question him. But when she was going to bed she could withhold her anxiety no longer, and said to him:

"Oh, George, you have got some bad news; let me share it with you. If it is anything about my father, I implore you to tell me.

How is it I have got no answer to the letter I wrote a month ago?"

He answered her savagely, "I don't know anything about your father, and I don't care. I've got bad news, damned bad news, if that will make you sleep the sounder. And, once for all, you'll find it best, when you see me sulky, not to give me any of your tantrums in addition. Mind that."

He had never spoken to her like that before. She went to her bed crushed and miserable, and spent the night in crying, while he went forth and spent the night with some of his new companions, playing wildly and losing recklessly, till the summer morning sun streamed through the shutters, and shone upon him desperate and nigh penniless, ripe for a fall lower than any he had had as yet.

CHAPTER XVI

THE END OF MARY'S EXPEDITION

LET us hurry over what is to follow. I who knew her so well can have no pleasure in dwelling over her misery and degradation. And he who reads these pages will, I hope, have little sympathy with the minor details of the life of such a man as George Hawker.

Some may think she has been punished enough already, for leaving her quiet happy home to go away with such a man. "She must have learnt already," such would say, "that he cares nothing for her. Let her leave her money behind, and go back to her father to make such amends as she may for the misery she has caused him." Alas, my dear madam, who would rejoice in such a termination of her troubles more than myself? But it is not for me to mete out degrees of punishment. I am trying with the best of my poor abilities to write a true history of certain people whom I knew. And I, no more than any other human creature, can see the consequences that will follow on any one act of folly or selfishness, such as this poor foolish girl has committed. We must wait and watch, judging with all charity. Let you and me go on with her even to the very end.

Good men draw together very slowly. Yet it is one of the greatest happinesses one is capable of, to introduce two such to one another, and see how soon they become friends. But bad men congregate like crows or jackals, and when a new one appears, he is received into the pack without question, as soon as he has given proof sufficient of being a rascal.

This was the case with George Hawker. His facility for making acquaintance with rogues and blacklegs was perfectly marvellous. Any gentleman of this class seemed to recognise him instinctively, and became familiar immediately. So that soon he had round him such a circle of friends as would have gone hard to send to the dogs the most honourable and virtuous young man in the three kingdoms.

When a new boy goes to school, his way is smoothed very much at first by the cakes and pocket-money he brings with him. Till these are gone he must be a weak boy indeed who cannot (at a small school) find someone to fight his battles and fetch and carry for him. Thackeray has thought of this (what does he not think of?) in his little book, *Dr. Birch,* where a young sycophant is represented saying to his friend, who has just received a hamper, " Hurrah, old fellow, *I'll lend you my knife.*" This was considered so true to nature, on board a ship in which I once made a long voyage, that it passed into a proverb with us, and if anyone was seen indulging in a luxury out of the way at dinner—say an extra bottle of wine out of his private store—half a dozen would cry out at once, " Hurrah, old fellow, I'll lend you my knife "; a modest way of requesting to be asked to take a glass of wine better than that supplied by the steward.

In the same way, George Hawker was treated by the men he had got round him as a man who had a little property that he had not got rid of, and as one who was to be used with some civility, until his money was gone, and he sank down to the level of the rest of them—to the level of living by his wits, if they were sharp enough to make a card or billiard sharper; or otherwise to find his level among the proscribed of society, let that be what it might.

And George's wits were not of the first order, or the second; and his manners and education were certainly not those of a gentleman, or likely to be useful in attracting such unwary persons as these Arabs of the metropolis preyed upon. So it happened that when all his money was played away, which came to pass in a month or two, the higher and cleverer class of rascals began to look uncommonly cold upon him.

At first poor crushed Mary used to entertain of an evening some of the *élite* among the card-sharpers of London—men who actually could have spoken to a gentleman in a public place, and not have got kicked. These men were polite, and rather agreeable, and one of them, a Captain Saxon, was so deferential to her, and seemed so entirely to understand her position, that she grew very fond of him, and was always pleased to see him at her house.

Though, indeed, she saw but little of any men who came there, soon after any of them arrived, she used to receive a signal from George, which she dared not disobey, to go to bed. And when she lay there, lonely and sleepless, she could detect, from the absence of conversation, save now and then a low, fierce oath, that they were playing desperately, and at such times she would lie trembling and crying. Once or twice, during the time she remembered these meetings, they were rudely broken upon by oaths and blows, and on one particular occasion, she heard one of the gamesters, when infuriated, call her husband " a damned swindling dog of a forger."

In these times, which lasted but a few months, she began to reflect what a fool she had been, and how to gratify her fancy she had thrown from her everything solid and worth keeping in the world. She had brought herself to confess, in bitterness and anguish, that he did not love her, and never had, and that she was a miserable unhappy dupe. But, notwithstanding, she loved him still, though she dreaded the sight of him, for she got little from him now but oaths and taunts.

It was soon after their return from Brighton that he broke out, first on some trivial occasion, and cursed her aloud. He said he hated the sight of her pale face, for it always reminded him of ruin and misery; that he had the greatest satisfaction in telling her that he was utterly ruined; that his father was dead, and had left his money elsewhere, and that her father was little better; that she would soon be in the workhouse; and, in fine, said everything that his fierce, wild, brutal temper could suggest.

She never tempted another outbreak of the kind; that one was too horrible for her, and crushed her spirit at once. She only tried by mildness and submission to deprecate his rage. But every day he came home looking fiercer and wilder; as time went on her heart sank within her, and she dreaded something more fearful than she had experienced yet.

As I said, after a month or two, his first companions began to drop off, or only came, bullying and swearing, to demand money. And now another class of men began to take their place, the sight of whom made her blood cold—worse dressed than the others, and worse mannered, with strange, foul oaths on their lips. And then, after a time, two ruffians, worse looking than any of the others, began to come there, of whom the one she dreaded most was called Maitland.

He was always very civil to her; but there was something about him, his lowering, evil face, and wild looks, which made him a living nightmare to her. She knew he was flying from justice, by the way he came and went, and by the precautions always taken when he was there. But when he came to live in the room over theirs, and when, by listening at odd times, she found that he and her husband were engaged in some great villainy, the nature of which she could not understand, then she saw that there was nothing to do, but in sheer desperation to sit down and wait the catastrophe.

About this time she made another discovery, that she was penniless, and had been so some time. George had given her money from time to time to carry on household expenses, and she contrived to make these sums answer well enough. But one day, determined to know the worst, she asked him, at the risk of another explosion, how their account stood at the bank? He replied in the best of his humours, apparently, "that the five thousand they had had there had been overdrawn some six weeks, and that, if it hadn't been for his exertions in various ways, she'd have been starved out before now."

"All gone!" she said; "and where to?"

"To the devil," he answered. "And you may go after it."

"And what are we to do now, George?"

"The best we can."

"But the baby, George? I shall lie-in in three months."

"You must take your chance, and the baby too. As long as there's any money going you'll get some of it. If you wrote to your father you might get some."

"I'll never do that," she said.

"Won't you?" said he; "I'll starve you into it when money gets scarce."

Things remained like this till it came to be nearly ten months from their marriage. Mary had never written home but once, from Brighton, and then, as we know, the answer had miscarried; so she, conceiving she was cast off by her father, had never attempted to communicate with him again. The time drew nigh that she should be confined, and she got very sick and ill, and still the man Maitland lived in the house, and he and George spent much of their time away together at night.

Yet poor Mary had a friend who stayed by her through it all—Captain Saxon, the great billiard-sharper. Many a weary hour, when she was watching up anxious and ill, for her husband, this man would come up and sit with her, talking agreeably and well about many things, but chiefly about the life he used to lead before he fell so low as he was then.

He used to say, " Mrs. Hawker, you cannot tell what a relief and pleasure it is to me to have a *lady* to talk to again. You must conceive how a man brought up like myself misses it."

" Surely, Captain Saxon," she would say, "you have some relations left. Why not go back to them ? "

" They wouldn't own me," he said. " I smashed everything, a fine fortune amongst other things, by my goings-on; and they very properly cast me off. I never got beyond the law, though. Many well-known men speak to me now, but they won't play with me, though; I am too good. And so you see I play dark to win from young fellows, and I am mixed up with a lot of scoundrels. A man brought an action against me the other day to recover two hundred pounds I won of him, but he couldn't do anything. And the judge said, that though the law couldn't touch me, yet I was mixed up notoriously with a gang of sharpers. That was a pleasant thing to hear in court, wasn't it ?—but true."

" It has often surprised me to see how temperate you are, Captain Saxon," she said.

" I am forced to be," he said; " I must keep my hand steady. See there; it's as firm as a rock. No; the consolation of drink is denied me; I have something to live for still. I'll tell you a secret. I've insured my life very high in favour of my little sister whom I ruined, and who is out as a governess. If I don't pay up to the last, you see, or if I commit suicide, she'll lose the money. 1 pay very high, I assure you. On one occasion not a year ago, I played for the money to pay the premium only two nights before it would have been too late. There was touch and go for you! But my hand was as steady as a rock, and after the last game was over I fainted."

" Good Lord," she said, " what a terrible life! But suppose you fall into sickness and poverty. Then you may fall into arrear, and she will lose everything after all."

He laughed aloud. A strange wild laugh. " No," said he; " I am safe there, if physicians are to be believed. Sometimes, when I am falling asleep, my heart begins to flutter and whirl, and I sit up in bed, breathless and perspiring till it grows still again. Then I laugh to myself, and say, ' Not this time then, but it can't be long now.' Those palpitations, Mrs. Hawker, are growing worse and worse each month. I have got a desperate incurable heart complaint, that will carry me off, sudden and sure, without warning, I hope to a better sort of world than this."

"I am sorry for you, Captain Saxon," she said, sobbing, "so very, very sorry for you!"

"I thank you kindly, my good friend," he replied. "It's long since I had so good a friend as you. Now change the subject. I want to talk to you about yourself. You are going to be confined."

"In a few days, I fear," she said.

"Have you money?"

"My husband seems to have money enough at present, but we have none to fall back upon."

"What friends have you?"

"None that I can apply to."

"H'm," he said. "Well, you must make use of me, and as far as I can manage it, of my purse, too, in case of an emergency. I mean, you know, Mrs. Hawker," he added, looking full at her, "to make this offer to you as I would to my own sister. Don't in God's name refuse my protection, such as it is, from any mistaken motives of jealousy. Now tell me, as honestly as you dare, how do you believe your husband gets his living?"

"I have not the least idea, but I fear the worst."

"You do right," he said. "Forewarned is forearmed, and, at the risk of frightening you, I must bid you prepare for the worst. Although I know nothing about what he is engaged in, yet I know that the man Maitland, who lives above, and who you say is your husband's constant companion, is a desperate man. If anything happens, apply to me straightway, and I will do all I can. My principal hope is in putting you in communication with your friends. Could you not trust me with your story, that we might take advice together?"

She told him all from beginning to the end, and at the last she said, "If the worst should come, whatever that may be, I would write for help to Major Buckley, for the sake of the child that is to come."

"Major Buckley!"—he asked eagerly—"do you mean James Buckley of the —th?"

"The same man," she replied, "my kindest friend."

"O Lord!" he said, growing pale, "I've got one of these spasms coming on. A glass of water, my dear lady, in God's name!"

He held both hands on his heart, and lay back in his chair a little, with livid lips, gasping for breath. By degrees his white hands dropped upon his lap, and he said with a sigh, "Nearer still, old friend, nearer than ever. Not far off now."

But he soon recovered and said, "Mrs. Hawker, if you ever see that man Buckley again, tell him that you saw Charley Biddulph, who was once his friend, fallen to be the consort of rogues and thieves, cast off by every one, and dying of a heart complaint; but tell him he could not die without sending a tender love to his good old comrade, and that he remembered him and loved him to the very end."

"And I shall say too," said Mary, "when all neglected me, and forgot me, this Charles Biddulph helped and cheered me; and when I was fallen to the lowest, that he was still to me a courteous gentleman, and a faithful adviser; and that but for him and his goodness I should have sunk into desperation long ago. Be sure that I will say this, too."

The door opened, and George Hawker came in.

"Good evening, Captain Saxon," said he. "My wife seems to make herself more agreeable to you than she does to me. I hope you are pleased with her. However, you are welcome to be. I thank God I ain't jealous. Where's Maitland?"

"He has not been here to-night, George," she said timidly.

"Curse him, then. Give me a candle; I'm going upstairs. Don't go on my account, Captain Saxon. Well, if you will, good night."

Saxon bade him good night, and went. George went up into Maitland's room, where Mary was never admitted; and soon she heard him hammer, hammering at metal, overhead. She was too used to that sound to take notice of it; so she went to bed, but lay long awake, thinking of poor Captain Saxon.

Less than a week after that she was confined. She had a boy, and that gave her new life. Poorly provided for as the child was, he could not have been more tenderly nursed or more prized and loved, if he had been born in the palace, with his Majesty's right honourable Ministers in the anteroom, drinking dry Sillery in honour of the event.

Now she could endure what was to come better. And less than a month after, just as she was getting well again, all her strength and courage were needed. The end came.

She was sitting before the fire, about ten o'clock at night, nursing her baby, when she heard the street-door opened by a key; and the next moment her husband and Maitland were in the room.

"Sit quiet, now, or I'll knock your brains out with the poker," said George; and, seizing a china ornament from the chimney-piece, he thrust it into the fire, and heaped the coals over it.

"We're caught like rats, you fool, if they have tracked us," said Maitland; "and nothing but your consummate folly to thank for it. I deserve hanging for mixing myself up with such a man in a thing like this. Now, are you coming; or do you want half an hour to wish your wife good-bye?"

George never answered that question. There was a noise of breaking glass downstairs, and a moment after a sound of several feet on the stair.

"Make a fight for it," said Maitland, "if you can do nothing else. Make for the back-door."

But George stood aghast, while Mary trembled in every limb. The door was burst open, and a tall man coming in said, "In the King's name, I arrest you, George Hawker and William Maitland, for coining."

Maitland threw himself upon the man, and they fell crashing over the table. George dashed at the door, but was met by two others. For a minute there was a wild scene of confusion and struggling, while Mary crouched against the wall with the child, shut her eyes, and tried to pray. When she looked round again she saw her husband and Maitland securely handcuffed, and the tall man, who first came in, wiping the blood from a deep cut in his forehead, said:

"There is nothing against this woman, is there, Sanders?"

"Nothing, sir, except that she is the prisoner Hawker's wife."

"Poor woman!" said the tall man. "She has been lately confined, too. I don't think it will be necessary to take her into custody. Take away the prisoners; I shall stay here and search."

He began his search by taking the tongs and pulling the fire to pieces. Soon he came to the remanants of the china ornament which George had thrown in; and, after a little more raking, two or three round pieces of metal fell out of the grate.

"A very green trick," he remarked. "Well, they must stay there to cool before I can touch them"; and turning to Mary said, "Could you oblige me with some sticking-plaster? Your husband's confederate has given me an ugly blow."

She got some, and put it on for him. "Oh, sir!" she said, "can you tell me what this is all about?"

"Easy, ma'am," said he. "Maitland is one of the most notorious coiners in England, and your husband is his confederate and assistant. We've been watching, just to get a case that there would be no trouble about, and we've got it."

"And if it is proved?" she asked, trembling.

He looked very serious. "Mrs. Hawker, I know your history, as well as your husband's, the same as if you told it to me. So I am sorry to give a lady who is in misfortune more pain than I can help; but you know coining is a hanging matter."

She rocked herself wildly to and fro, and the chair where she sat, squeezing the child against her bosom till he cried. She soothed him again without a word, and then said to the officer, who was searching every nook and cranny in the room:

"Shall you be obliged to turn me out of here, or may I stay a few nights?"

"You can stay as long as you please, madam," he said; "that's a matter with your landlady, not me. But if I was you I'd communicate with my friends, and get some money to have my husband defended."

"They'd sooner pay for the rope to hang him," she said. "You seem a kind and pitiful sort of man; tell me honestly, is there any chance for him?"

"Honestly, none. There may be some chance of his life; but there is evidence enough on this one charge, leave alone others, mind you, to convict twenty men. Why, we've evidence of two forgeries committed on his father before ever he married you; so that, if he is acquitted on this charge, he'll be arrested for another outside the court."

All night long she sat up nursing the child before the fire, which from time to time she replenished. The officers in possession slept on sofas, and dozed in chairs; but when the day broke she was still there, pale and thoughtful, sitting much in the same place and attitude as she did before all this happened, the night before, which seemed to her like a year ago, so great was the change since then. "So," thought she, "he was nothing but a villain after all. He had merely gained her heart for money's sake, and cast her off when it was gone. What a miserable fool she had been, and how rightly served now, to be left penniless in the world!"

Penniless, but not friendless. She remembered Captain Saxon, and determined to go to him and ask his advice. So when the strange weird morning had crept on, to such time as the accustomed crowd began to surge through the street, she put on her bonnet, and went away for the first time to seek him at his lodgings, in a small street, leading off Piccadilly.

An old woman answered the door. "The Captain was gone," she said, "to Boulogne, and wouldn't be back yet for a fortnight. Would she leave any name?"

She hardly thought it worth while. All the world seemed to have deserted her now; but she said, more in absence of mind than for any other reason, "Tell him that Mrs. Hawker called, if you please."

"Mrs. Hawker!" the old woman said; "there's a letter for you, ma'am, I believe; and something particular, too, 'cause he told me to keep it in my desk till you called. Just step in, if you please."

Mary followed her in, and she produced a letter directed to Mrs. Hawker. When Mary opened it, which she did in the street, after the door was shut, the first thing she saw was a banknote for five pounds, and behind it was the following note:

I am forced to go to Boulogne, at a moment's notice, with a man whom I must not lose sight of. Should you have occasion to apply to me during my absence (which is fearfully probable), I have left this, begging your acceptance of it, in the same spirit as that in which it was offered; and I pray you to accept this piece of advice at the same time:

Apply instantly to your friends, and go back to them at once. Don't stop about London on any excuse. You have never known what it is to be without money yet; take care you never do. When a man or a woman is poor and hungry, there is a troop of devils who always follow such, whispering all sorts of things to them. They are all, or nearly all, known to me: take care you do not make their acquaintance.

Yours most affectionately,

CHARLES BIDDULPH.

What a strange letter, she thought. He must be mad. Yet there was method in his madness, too. Devils such as he spoke of had leant over her chair and whispered to her before now, plain to be heard. But that was in the old times, when she sat brooding alone over the fire at night. She was no longer alone now, and they had fled—fled, scared at the face of a baby.

She went home and spoke to the landlady. But little was owing, and that she had money enough to pay without the five pounds that the kind gambler had given her. However, when she asked the landlady whether she could stay there a week or two longer, the woman prayed her with tears to begone; that she and her husband had brought trouble enough on them already.

But there was still a week left of their old tenancy, so she held possession in spite of the landlady; and from the police-officers, who were still about the place, she heard that the two prisoners had been committed for trial, and that that trial would take place early in the week at the Old Bailey.

Three days before the trial she had to leave the lodgings, with but little more than two pounds in the world. For those three days she got lodging as she could in coffee-houses and such places, always meeting, however, with that sort of kindness and sympathy from the women belonging to them which could not be bought for money. She was in such a dull state of despair, that she was happily insensible to all smaller discomforts, and on the day of the trial she endeavoured to push into the court with her child in her arms.

The crowd was too dense, and the heat was too great for her, so she came outside and sat on some steps on one side of a passage. Once she had to move as a great personage came up, and then one of the officers said:

"Come, my good woman, you mustn't sit there, you know. That's the judges' private door."

"I beg pardon," she said, "and I will move, if you wish me. But they are trying my husband for coining, and the court is too hot for the child. If you will let me sit there, I will be sure to get out of the way when my Lord comes past."

The man looked at her as if it was a case somewhat out of his experience, and went away. Soon, however, he came back again, and after staring at her a short time, said:

"Do you want anything, missis? Anything I can get?"

"I am much obliged to you, nothing," she said; "but if you can tell me how the trial is going on, I shall be obliged to you."

He shook his head and went away, and when he returned, telling her that the judge was summing up, he bade her follow him, and found her a place in a quiet part of the court. She could see her husband and Maitland standing in the dock, quite close to her, and before them the judge was calmly, slowly, and distinctly giving the jury the history of the case from beginning to end. She was too much bewildered and desperate to listen to it, but she was attracted by the buzz of conversation which arose when the jury retired. They seemed gone a bare minute to her, when she heard and understood that the prisoners were found guilty. Then she heard Maitland sentenced to death, and George Hawker condemned to be transported beyond the seas for the term of his natural life.

in consideration of his youth; so she brought herself to understand that the game was played out, and turned to go.

The officer who had been kind to her stopped her, and asked her " where she was going ? " She answered, " To Devonshire," and passed on, but almost immediately pushed back to him through the crowd, which was pouring out of the doors, and thanked him for his kindness to her. Then she went out with the crowd into the street, and almost instinctively struck westward.

Through the western streets, roaring with carriages, crowded with foot passengers, like one in a dream; past the theatres, and the arches, and all the great, rich world, busy seeking its afternoon pleasure: through the long suburbs, getting more scattered as she went on, and so out on to the dusty broad western highway: a lonely wanderer, with only one thought in her throbbing head, to reach such home as was left her before she died.

At the first quiet spot she came to she sat down and forced herself to think. Two hundred miles to go, and fifteen shillings to keep her. Never mind, she could beg; she had heard that some made a trade of begging, and did well; hard if she should die on the road. So she pushed on through the evening toward the sinking sun, till the milestones passed slower and slower, and then she found shelter in a tramps' lodging-house, and got what rest she could. In a week she was at Taunton. Then the weather, which had hitherto been fair and pleasant, broke up, and still she held on (with the rain beating from the westward in her face, as though to stay her from her refuge), dizzy and confused, but determined still, along the miry high-road.

She had learnt from a gipsy woman, with whom she had walked in company for some hours, how to carry her child across her back, slung in her shawl. So, with her breast bare to the storm, she fought her way over the high bleak downs, glad and happy when the boy ceased his wailing, and lay warm and sheltered behind her, swathed in every poor rag she could spare from her numbed and dripping body.

Late on a wild rainy night she reached Exeter, utterly penniless, and wet to the skin. She had had nothing to eat since noon, and her breast was failing for want of nourishment and over-exertion. Still it was only twenty miles farther. Surely, she thought, God had not saved her through two hundred such miles, to perish at last. The child was dry and warm, and fast asleep, and if she could get some rest in one of the doorways in the lower part of the town, till she was stronger, she could fight her way on to

Drumston; so she held on to St. Thomas's, and finding an archway drier than the others, sat down, and took the child upon her lap.

Rest!—rest was a fiction; she was better walking—such aches, and cramps, and pains in every joint! She would get up and push on, and yet minute after minute went by, and she could not summon courage.

She was sitting with her beautiful face in the light of a lamp. A woman well and handsomely dressed was passing rapidly through the rain, but on seeing her stopped and said:

"My poor girl, why do you sit there in the damp entry such a night as this?"

"I am cold, hungry, ruined; that's why I sit under the arch," replied Mary, rising up.

"Come home with me," said the woman: "I will take care of you."

"I am going to my friends," replied she.

"Are you sure they will be glad to see you, my dear," said the woman, "with that pretty little pledge at your bosom?"

"I care not," said Mary, "I told you I was desperate."

"Desperate, my pretty love," said the woman; "a girl with beauty like yours should never be desperate; come with me."

Mary stepped forward and struck her, so full and true that the woman reeled backwards, and stood whimpering and astonished.

"Out! you false jade," said Mary; "you are one of those devils that Saxon told me of, who come whispering, and peering, and crowding behind those who are penniless and deserted; but I have faced you, and struck you, and I tell you to go back to your master, and say that I am not for him."

The woman went crying and frightened down the street, thinking that she had been plying her infamous trade on a lunatic; but Mary sat down again and nursed the child.

But the wind changed a little, and the rain began to beat in on her shelter; she rose, and went down the street to seek a new one.

She found a deep arch, well sheltered, and, what was better, a lamp inside, so that she could sit on the stone step and see her baby's face. Dainty quarters, truly! She went to take possession, and started back with a scream.

What delusion was this? There, under the lamp, on the step, sat a woman, her own image, nursing a baby so like her own that she looked down at her bosom to see if it was safe. It must be a fancy of her own disordered brain; but no—for when she gathered up her courage, and walked towards it, a woman she knew well started up, and, laughing wildly, cried out:

"Ha! ha! Mary Thornton."

"Ellen Lee?" said Mary, aghast.

"That's me, dear," replied the other; "you're welcome, my love, welcome to the cold stones, and wet streets, and to hunger and drunkenness, and evil words, and the abomination of desolation. That's what we all come to, my dear. Is that his child?"

"Whose?" said Mary. "This is George Hawker's child."

"Hush, my dear!" said the other; "we never mention his name in our society, you know. This is his, too—a far finer one than yours. Cis Jewell had one of his, too, a poor little rat of a thing that died, and now the minx is flaunting about the High Street every night, in her silks and her feathers as bold as brass. I hope you'll have nothing to say to her; you and I will keep house together. They are looking after me to put me in the madhouse. You'll come, too, of course."

"God have mercy on you, poor Nelly!" said Mary.

"Exactly so, my dear," the poor lunatic replied. "Of course He will. But about him you know. You heard the terms of his bargain?"

"What do you mean?" asked Mary.

"Why, about him you know, G—— H——, Madge the Witch's son. He sold himself to the deuce, my dear, on condition of ruining a poor girl every year. And he has kept his contract hitherto. If he don't, you know—— Come here, I want to whisper to you."

The poor girl whispered rapidly in her ear; but Mary broke away from her and fled rapidly down the street, poor Ellen shouting after her, "Ha, ha! the parson's daughter, too—ha, ha!"

"Let me get out of this town, O Lord!" she prayed most earnestly, "if I die in the fields." And so she sped on, and paused not till she was full two miles out of the town towards home, leaning on the parapet of the noble bridge that even then crossed the river Exe.

The night had cleared up, and a soft and gentle westerly breeze was ruffling the broad waters of the river, where they slept deep, dark, and full above the weir. Just below where they broke over the low rocky barrier, the rising moon showed a hundred silver spangles among the broken eddies.

The cool breeze and the calm scene quieted and soothed her, and, for the first time for many days, she began to think.

She was going back, but to what? To a desolated home, to a heart-broken father, to the jeers and taunts of her neighbours. The wife of a convicted felon, what hope was left for her in this world? None. And that child that was sleeping so quietly on her bosom, what a mark was set on him from this time forward!—the son of Hawker the coiner! Would it not be better if they both were lying below there in the cold, still water, at rest?

But she laughed aloud. "This is the last of the devils he talked of," she said. "I have fought the others and beat them. I won't yield to this one."

She paused abashed, for a man on horseback was standing before her as she turned. Had she not been so deeply engaged in her own thoughts she might have heard him merrily whistling as he approached from the town, but she heard him not, and was first aware of his presence when he stood silently regarding her, not two yards off.

"My girl," he said, "I fear you're in a bad way. I don't like to see a young woman, pretty as I can see you are even now, standing on a bridge, with a baby, talking to herself."

"You mistake me," she said, "I was not going to do that; I was resting and thinking."

"Where are you going?" he asked.

"To Crediton," she replied. "Once there, I should almost fancy myself safe."

"See here," he said; "my wagon is coming up behind. I can give you a lift as far as there. Are you hungry?"

"Ah," she said, "if you knew. If you only knew!"

They waited for the wagon's coming up, for they could hear the horses' bells chiming cheerily across the valley. "I had an only daughter went away once," he said. "But, glory to God! I got her back again, though she brought a child with her. And I've grown to be fonder of that poor little base-born one than anything in this world. So cheer up."

"I am married," she said; "this is my lawful boy, though it were better, perhaps, he had never been born."

"Don't say that, my girl," said the old farmer, for such she took him to be, "but thank God you haven't been deceived like so many are."

The wagon came up and was stopped. He made her take such refreshment as was to be got, and then get in and lie quiet among the straw till in the grey morning they reached Crediton. The weather had grown bad again, and long before sunrise, after thanking and blessing her benefactor, poor Mary struck off once more, with what strength she had left, along the deep red lanes, through the driving rain.

CHAPTER XVII

EXODUS

BUT let us turn and see what has been going forward in the old parsonage this long, weary year. Not much that is noteworthy, I fear. The chronicle of a year's sickness and unhappiness would be rather uninteresting, so I must get on as quick as I can.

The Vicar only slowly revived from the fit in which he fell on the morning of Mary's departure to find himself hopelessly paralytic, unable to walk without support, and barely able to articulate distinctly. It was when he was in this state, being led up and down the garden by the Doctor and Frank Maberly, the former of whom was trying to attract his attention to some of their old favourites, the flowers, that Miss Thornton came to him with the letter which Mary had written from Brighton, immediately after their marriage.

It was, on the whole, a great relief for the Vicar. He had dreaded to hear worse than this. They had kept from him all knowledge of Hawker's forgery on his father, which had been communicated to them by Major Buckley. So that he began to prepare his mind for the reception of George Hawker as a son-in-law, and to force himself to like him. So with shaking palsied hand he wrote:

> Dear Girl,—In sickness or sorrow, remember that I am still your father. I hope you will not stop long in London, but come back and stay near me. We must forget all that has passed, and make the best of it.—JOHN THORNTON.

Miss Thornton wrote:

> My dearest, foolish Mary,—How could you leave us like that, my love! Oh, if you had only let us know what was going on, I could have told you such things, my dear. But now you will never know them, I hope. I hope Mr. Hawker will use you kindly. Your father hopes that you and he may come down and live near him, but we know that is impossible. If your father were to know of your husband's fearful delinquencies it

would kill him at once. But when trouble comes on you, my love, as it must in the end, remember that there is still a happy home left you here.

These letters she never received. George burnt them without giving them to her, so that for a year she remained under the impression that they had cast her off. So only at the last did she, as the sole hope of warding off poverty and misery from her child, determine to cast herself upon their mercy.

The year had nearly passed when the Vicar had another stroke, a stroke that rendered him childish and helpless, and precluded all possibility of his leaving his bed again. Miss Thornton found that it was necessary to have a man-servant in the house now, to move him, and so on. So one evening, when Major and Mrs. Buckley and the Doctor had come down to sit with her, she asked, " Did you know a man who could undertake the business ? "

" I do," said the Doctor. " I know a man who would suit you exactly. A strong knave enough. An old soldier."

" I don't think we should like a soldier in the house, Doctor," said Miss Thornton. " They use such very odd language sometimes, you know."

" This man never swears," said the Doctor.

" But soldiers are apt to drink sometimes, you know, Doctor," said Miss Thornton. " And that wouldn't do in this case."

" I've known the man all my life," said the Doctor with animation. " And I never saw him drunk."

" He seems faultless, Doctor," said the Major, smiling.

" No, he is not faultless, but he has his qualifications for the office, nevertheless. He can read passably, and might amuse our poor old friend in that way. He is not evil tempered, though hasty, and I think he would be tender and kindly to the old man. He had a father once himself, this man, and he nursed him to his latest day, as well as he was able, after his mother had left them and gone on the road to destruction. And my man has picked up some knowledge of medicine, too, and might be a useful ally to the physician."

" A paragon ! " said Mrs. Buckley, laughing. " Now let us hear his faults, dear Doctor."

" They are many," he replied, " I don't deny. But not such as to make him an ineligible person in this matter. To begin with, he is a fool—a dreaming fool, who once mixed himself up with politics, and went on the assumption that truth would prevail against humbug. And when he found his mistake, this fellow, instead of staying at his post, as a man should, he got disgusted, and beat a cowardly retreat, leaving his duty unfulfilled. When I look at one side of this man's life I wonder why such useless fellows as he were born into the world. But I opine that every man is of some use, and that my friend may still have manhood enough left in him to move an old paralytic man in his bed."

"And his name, Doctor? You must tell us that," said Mrs. Buckley, looking sadly at him.

"I am that man," said the Doctor, rising. "Dear Miss Thornton, you will allow me to come down and stay with you. I shall be so glad to be of any use to my old friend, and I am so utterly useless now."

What could she say but "Yes," with a thousand thanks, far more than she could express? So he took up his quarters at the Vicarage, and helped her in the labour of love.

The Sunday morning after he came to stay there he was going downstairs, shortly after daybreak, to take a walk in the fresh morning air when on the staircase he met Miss Thornton, and she, putting sixpence into his hand, said:

"My dear Doctor, I looked out of window just now, and saw a tramper woman sitting on the doorstep. She has black hair and a baby, like a gipsy. And I am so nervous about gipsies, you know. Would you give her that and tell her to go away?"

The Doctor stepped down with the sixpence in his hand to do as he was bid. Miss Thornton followed him. He opened the front door, and there sure enough sat a woman, her hair, wet with the last night's rain, knotted loosely up behind her hatless head. She sat upon the doorstep rocking herself to and fro, partly it would seem from disquietude and partly to soothe the baby which was lying on her lap crying. Her back was towards him, and the Doctor only had time to notice that she was young, when he began:

"My good soul, you mustn't sit there, you know. It's Sunday morning, and——"

No more. He had time to say no more. Mary rose from the step and looked at him.

"You are right, sir, I have no business here. But if you will tell him that I only came back for the child's sake he will hear me. I couldn't leave it in the workhouse, you know."

Miss Thornton ran forward, laughing wildly, and hugged her to her honest heart. "My darling!" she said, "my own darling! I knew she would find her home at last. In trouble and in sorrow

I told her where she was to come. O happy trouble, that has brought our darling back to us!"

"Aunt! aunt!" said Mary, "don't kill me. Scold me a little, aunt dear, only a little."

"Scold you, my darling! Never, never! Scold you on this happy Sabbath morn! Oh! never, my love."

And the foolishness of these two women was so great that the Doctor had to go for a walk. Right down the garden, round the cow-yard, and in by the back way to the kitchen, where he met Frank, and told him what had happened. And there they were at it again. Miss Thornton kneeling, wiping poor Mary's blistered feet before the fire; while the maid, foolishly giggling, had got possession of the baby, and was talking more affectionate nonsense to it than ever baby heard in this world before.

Mary held out her hand to him, and when he gave her his vast brown paw, what does she do, but put it to her lips and kiss it?—as if there was not enough without that. And, to make matters worse, she quoted Scripture, and said, "For as much as ye have done it unto the least of these, ye have done it unto me." So our good Doctor had nothing left but to break through that cloak of cynicism which he delighted to wear (Lord knows why!), and to kiss her on the cheek, and to tell her how happy she had made them by coming back, let circumstances be what they might.

Then she told them, with bursts of wild weeping, what those circumstances were. And at last, when they were all quieted, Miss Thornton boldly volunteered to go up and tell the Vicar that his darling was returned.

So she went up, and Mary and the Doctor waited at the bedroom door and listened. The poor old man was far gone beyond feeling joy or grief to any great extent. When Miss Thornton raised him in his bed and told him that he must brace up his nerves to hear some good news, he smiled a weary smile, and Mary looking in saw that he was so altered that she hardly knew him.

"I know," he said, lisping and hesitating painfully, "what you are going to tell me, sister. She is come home. I knew she would come at last. Please tell her to come to me at once; but I can't see *him* yet. I must get stronger first." So Mary went into him, and Miss Thornton came out and closed the door. And when Mary came downstairs soon afterwards she could not talk to them, but remained a long time silent, crying bitterly.

The good news soon got up to Major Buckley's, and so after church they saw him striding up the path, leading the pony carrying his wife and baby. And while they were still busy welcoming her back, came a ring at the door, and a loud voice, asking if the owner of it might come in.

Who but Tom Troubridge! Who else was there to raise her four good feet off the ground, and kiss her on both cheeks, and call her his darling little sister! Who else was there who could have changed their tears into laughter so quick that their merriment was wafted up to the Vicar's room, and made him ring his bell, and tell them to send Tom up to him! And who but Tom could have lit the old man's face up with a smile, with the history of a new colt, that my Lord's mare, Thetis, had dropped last week!

That was her welcome home. To the home she had dreaded coming to, expecting to be received with scorn and reproaches. To the home she had meant to come to only as a penitent, to leave her child there and go forth into the world to die. And here she found herself the honoured guest—treated as one who had been away on a journey, whom they had been waiting and praying for all the time, and who came back to them sooner than expected. None hold the force of domestic affection so cheap as those who violate it most rudely. How many proud, unhappy souls are there at this moment voluntarily absenting themselves from all that love them in the world because they dread sneers and cold looks at home! And how many of these, going back, would find only tears of joy to welcome them, and hear that ever since their absence they had been spoken of with kindness and tenderness, and loved, perhaps, above all the others!

After dinner, when the women were alone together, Mrs. Buckley began:

" Now, my dear Mary, you must hear all the news. My husband has had a letter from Stockbridge."

" Ah, dear old Jim!" said Mary; "and how is he?"

" He and Hamlyn are quite well," said Mrs. Buckley, "and settled. He has written such an account of that country to Major Buckley that he, half persuaded before, is now wholly determined to go there himself."

" I heard of this before," said Mary. "Am I to lose you, then, at once?"

" We shall see," said Mrs. Buckley; "I have my ideas. Now, who do you think is going beside?"

" Half Devonshire, I should think," said Mary; "at least, all whom I care about."

"It would seem so, indeed, my good girl," said Mrs. Buckley; "for your cousin, Troubridge, has made up his mind to come."

"There was a time when I could have stopped him," she thought; "but that is gone by now." And she answered Mrs. Buckley:

"Aunt and I will stay here, and think of you all. Shall we ever hear from you? It is the other side of the world, is it not?"

"It is a long way; but we must wait and see how things turn out. We may not have to separate after all. See, my dear; are you fully aware of your father's state? I fear you have only come home to see the last of him. He probably will be gone before this month is out. You see the state he is in. And when he is gone, have you reflected what to do?"

Mary, weeping bitterly, said, "No;" only that she could never live in Drumston, or anywhere where she was known.

"That is wise, my love," said Mrs. Buckley, "under the circumstances. Have you made up your mind where to go, Miss Thornton, when you have to leave the Vicarage for a new incumbent?"

"I have made up my mind," answered Miss Thornton, "to go wherever Mary goes, if it be to the other end of the earth. We will be Ruth and Naomi, my dear. You would never get on without me."

"That is what I say," said Mrs. Buckley. "Never leave her. Why not come away out of all unhappy associations, and from the scorn and pity of your neighbours, to live safe and happy with all the best friends you have in the world?"

"What do you mean?" said Mary. "Ah, if we could only do so!"

"Come away with us," said Mrs. Buckley, with animation; "come away with us, and begin a new life. There is Troubridge looking high and low for a partner with five thousand pounds. Why should not Miss Thornton and yourself be his partners?"

"Ah, me!" said Miss Thornton. "And think of the voyage! But I shall not decide on anything; Mary shall decide."

Scarcely more than a week elapsed from the day that Mary came home when there came a third messenger for old John Thornton, and one so peremptory that he arose and followed it in the dead of night. So, when they came to his bedside in the morning, they found his body there, laid as it was when he wished them good-night, but cold and dead. He himself was gone, and nothing remained but to bury his body decently beside his wife's, in the old church-yard, and to shed some tears at the thought never, by the fireside, or in the solemn old church, they should hear that kindly voice again.

And then came the disturbance of household gods, and the rupture of life-old associations. And although they were begged by the newcomer not to hurry or incommode themselves, yet they, too, wished to be gone from the house whence everything they loved had departed.

Their kind, true friend, Frank, was presented with the living, and they accepted Mrs. Buckley's invitation to stay at their house till they should have decided what to do. It was two months yet before the Major intended to sail, and long before those two months were past Mary and Miss Thornton had determined that they would not rend asunder the last ties they had this side of the grave, but would cast in their lot with the others, and cross the weary sea with them towards a more hopeful land.

One more scene, and we have done with the Old World for many a year. Some of these our friends will never see it more, and those who do will come back with new thoughts and associations, as strangers to a strange land. Only those who have done so know how much effort it takes to say, " I will go away to a land where none know me or care for me, and leave for ever all that I know and love." And few know the feeling which comes upon all men after it is done—the feeling of isolation, almost of terror, at having gone so far out of the bounds of ordinary life; the feeling of self-distrust and cowardice at being alone and friendless in the world, like a child in the dark.

A golden summer's evening is fading into a soft, cloudless summer's night, and Dr. Mulhaus stands upon Mount Edgecombe, looking across the trees, across the glassy harbour, over the tall men-of-war, out beyond the silver line of surf on the breakwater, to where a tall ship is rapidly spreading her white wings, and speeding away each moment more rapidly before a fair wind, towards the south-west. He watches it growing more dim, minute by minute, in distance and in darkness, till he can see no longer; then brushing a tear from his eye he says aloud:

" There goes my English microcosm. All my new English friends with whom I was going to pass the rest of my life, peaceful and contented, as a village surgeon. Pretty dream, two years long!

Truly man hath no sure abiding-place here. I will go back to Prussia, and see if they are all dead, or only sleeping."

So he turned down the steep path under the darkening trees, towards where he could see the town lights along the quays, among the crowded masts.

CHAPTER XVIII

THE FIRST PUFF OF THE SOUTH WIND

A NEW heaven and a new earth! Tier beyond tier, height above height, the great wooded ranges go rolling away westward, till on the lofty skyline they are crowned with a gleam of everlasting snow. To the eastward they sink down, breaking into isolated forest-fringed peaks, and rock-crowned eminences, till with rapidly straightening lines they fade into the broad grey plains, beyond which the Southern Ocean is visible by the white sea-haze upon the sky.

All creation is new and strange. The trees, surpassing in size the largest English oaks, are of a species we have never seen before. The graceful shrubs, the bright-coloured flowers, ay, the very grass itself, are of species unknown in Europe; while flaming lories and brilliant parroquets fly whistling, not unmusically, through the gloomy forest, and overhead in the higher fields of air, still lit up by the last rays of the sun, countless cockatoos wheel and scream in noisy joy, as we may see the gulls do about an English headland.

To the northward a great glen, sinking suddenly from the saddle on which we stand, stretches away in long vista, until it joins a broader valley, through which we can dimly see a full-fed river winding along in gleaming reaches, through level meadow land, interspersed with clumps of timber.

We are in Australia. Three hundred and fifty miles south of Sydney, on the great watershed which divides the Belloury from the Maryburnong, since better known as the Snowy River of Gippsland.

As the sun was going down on the scene I have been describing, James Stockbridge and I, Geoffry Hamlyn, reined up our horses on the ridge abovementioned, and gazed down the long gully which lay stretched at our feet. Only the tallest trees stood with their higher boughs glowing with the gold of the departing day, and we stood undetermined which route to pursue, and half inclined to camp at the next waterhole we should see We had lost some cattle, and among others a valuable imported bull, which we were very anxious to recover. For five days we had been passing on from run to run, making inquiries without success, and were now fifty long miles from home in a southerly direction. We were beyond the bounds of all settlement; the last station we had been at was twenty miles to the north of us, and the occupiers of it, as they had told us the night before, had only taken up their country about ten weeks, and were as yet the furthest pioneers to the southward.

At this time Stockbridge and I had been settled in our new home about two years, and were beginning to get comfortable and contented. We had had but little trouble with the blacks, and having taken possession of a fine piece of country, were flourishing and well-to-do.

We had never heard from home but once, and that was from Tom Troubridge, soon after our departure, telling us that if we succeeded he should follow, for that the old place seemed changed now we were gone. We had neither of us left any near relations behind us, and already we began to think that we were cut off for ever from old acquaintances and associations, and were beginning to be resigned to it.

Let us return to where he and I were standing alone in the forest. I dismounted to set right some strap or another, and, instead of getting on my horse again at once, stood leaning against him, looking at the prospect, glad to ease my legs for a time, for they were cramped with many hours' riding.

Stockbridge sat in his saddle immovable and silent as a statue, and when I loked in his face I saw that his heart had travelled farther than his eye could reach, and that he was looking far beyond the horizon that bounded his earthly vision, away to the pleasant old home which was home to us no longer.

" Jim," said I, " I wonder what is going on at Drumston now ? "

" I wonder," he said softly.

A pause.

Below us, in the valley, a mob of jackasses were shouting and laughing uproariously, and a magpie was chanting his noble vesper hymn from a lofty tree.

" Jim," I began again, " do you ever think of poor little Mary now ? "

" Yes, old boy, I do," he replied; " I can't help it; I was thinking of her then—I am always thinking of her, and, what's more, I always shall be. Don't think me a fool, old friend, but I love that girl as well now as ever I did. I wonder if she has married that fellow Hawker?"

"I fear there is but little doubt of it," I said; "try to forget her, James. Get in a rage with her, and be proud about it; you'll make all your life unhappy if you don't."

He laughed. "That's all very well, Jeff, but it's easier said than done. Do you hear that? There are cattle down the gully."

There was some noise in the air beside the evening rustle of the south wind among the tree-tops. Now it sounded like a far-off hubbub of waters, now swelled up harmonious, like the booming of cathedral bells across some rich old English valley on a still summer's afternoon.

"There are cattle down there, certainly," I said, "and a very large number of them; they are not ours, depend upon it: there are men with them, too, or they would not make so much noise. Can it be the blacks driving them off from the strangers we stayed with last night, do you think? If so, we had best look out for ourselves."

"Blacks could hardly manage such a large mob as there are there," said James. "I'll tell you what I think it is, old Jeff; it's some new chums going to cross the watershed and look for new country to the south. If so, let us go down and meet them: they will camp down by the river yonder."

James was right. All doubt about what the newcomers were was solved before we reached the river, for we could hear the rapid detonation of the stockwhips loud above the lowing of the cattle; so we sat and watched them debouche from the forest into the broad river meadows in the gathering gloom: saw the scene so venerable and ancient, so seldom seen in the Old World—the patriarchs moving into the desert with all their wealth, to find a new pasture ground. A simple primitive action, the first and simplest act of colonisation, yet producing such great results on the history of the world as did the parting of Lot and Abraham in times gone by.

First came the cattle lowing loudly, some trying to stop and graze on the rich pasture after their long day's travel, some heading noisily towards the river, now beginning to steam with the rising evening mist. Now a lordly bull, followed closely by two favourite heifers, tries to take matters into his own hands, and cut out a route for himself, but is soon driven ignominiously back in a lumbering gallop by a quick-eyed stockman. Now a silly calf takes it into his head to go for a small excursion up the range, followed, of course, by his doting mother, and has to be headed in again, not without muttered wrath and lowerings of the head from madame. Behind the cattle come horsemen, some six or seven in number, and last, four drays, bearing the household goods, come crawling up the pass.

We had time to notice that there were women on the foremost dray, when it became evident that the party intended camping in a turn of the river just below. One man kicked his feet out of the stirrups, and sitting loosely in his saddle, prepared to watch the cattle for the first few hours till he was relieved. Another lit a fire against a fallen tree, and while the bullock-drivers were busy unyoking their beasts, and the women were clambering from the dray, two of the horsemen separated from the others and came forward to meet us.

Both of them I saw were men of vast stature. One rode upright, with military seat, while his companion had his feet out of his stirrups, and rode loosely, as if tired with his journey. Further than this, I could distinguish nothing in the darkening twilight; but, looking at James, I saw that he was eagerly scanning the strangers, with elevated eyebrow and opened lips. Ere I could speak to him he had dashed forward with a shout, and when I came up with him, wondering, I found myself shaking hands, talking and laughing, everything in fact short of crying, with Major Buckley and Thomas Troubridge.

"Range up alongside here, Jeff, you rascal," said Tom, "and let me get a fair hug at you. What do you think of this for a lark; eh?—to meet you out here, all promiscuous, in the forest, like Prince Arthur! We could not go out of our way to see you, though we knew where you were located, for we must hurry on and get a piece of country we have been told of on the next river. We are going to settle down close by you, you see. We'll make a new Drumston in the wilderness."

"This is a happy meeting, indeed, old Tom," I said, as we rode towards the drays, after the Major and James. "We shall have happy times, now we have got some of our old friends round us. Who is come with you? How is Mrs. Buckley?"

"Mrs. Buckley is as well as ever, and as handsome. My pretty little cousin, Mary Hawker, and old Miss Thornton are with us; the poor old Vicar is dead."

"Mary Hawker with you?" I said. "And her husband, Tom?"

"Hardly, old friend. We travel in better company," said he. "George Hawker is transported for life."

"Alas, poor Mary!" I answered. "And what for?"

" Coining," he answered. " I'll tell you the story another time. To-night let us rejoice."

I could not but watch James, who was riding before us, to see how he would take this news. The Major, I saw, was telling him all about it, but James seemed to take it quite quietly, only nodding his head as the other went on. I knew how he would feel for his old love, and I turned and said to Troubridge:

" Jim will be very sorry to hear of this. I wish she had married him."

" That's what we all say," said Tom. " I am sorry for poor Jim. He is about the best man I know, take him all in all. If that fellow were to die, she might have him yet, Hamlyn."

We reached the drays. There sat Mrs. Buckley on a log, a noble, happy matron, laughing at her son as he toddled about, busy gathering sticks for the fire. Beside her was Mary, paler and older-looking than when we had seen her last, with her child upon her lap, looking sad and worn. But a sadder sight for me was old Miss Thornton, silent and frightened, glancing uneasily round, as though expecting some new horror. No child for her to cling to and strive for. No husband to watch for and anticipate every wish. A poor, timid, nervous old maid, thrown adrift in her old age upon a strange sea of anomalous wonders. Every old favourite prejudice torn up by the roots. All old formulas of life scattered to the winds!

She told me in confidence that evening that she had been in sad trouble all day. At dinner-time some naked blacks had come up to the dray, and had frightened and shocked her. Then the dray had been nearly upset, and her hat crushed among the trees. A favourite and precious bag, which never left her, had been dropped in the water; and her Prayer-book, a parting gift from Lady Kate, had been utterly spoiled. A hundred petty annoyances and griefs, which Mary barely remarked, and which brave Mrs. Buckley, in her strong determination of following her lord to the ends of the earth, and of being as much help and as little encumbrance to him as she could, had laughed at, were to her great misfortunes. Why, the very fact, as she told me, of sitting on the top of a swinging, jolting dray was enough to keep her in a continual state of agony and terror, so that when she alit at night and sat down she could not help weeping silently, dreading lest anyone should see her.

Suddenly, Mary was by her side, kneeling down.

" Aunt," she said, " dearest aunt, don't break down. It is all my wicked fault. You will break my heart, auntie dear, if you cry like that. Why did ever I bring you on this hideous journey?"

"How could I leave you in your trouble, my love?" said Miss Thornton. "You did right to come, my love. We are among old friends. We have come too far for trouble to reach us. We shall soon have a happy home again now, and all will be well."

So she, who needed so much comforting herself, courageously dried her tears and comforted Mary. And when we reached the drays she was sitting with her hands folded before her in serene misery.

"Mary," said the Major, "here are two old friends."

He had no time to say more, for she, recognising Jim, sprang up, and, running to him, burst into hysterical weeping.

"Oh, my good old friend!" she cried; "oh, my dear old friend! Oh, to meet you here in this lonely wilderness! Oh, James, my kind old brother!"

I saw how his big heart yearned to comfort his old sweetheart in her distress. Not a selfish thought found place with him. He could only see his old love injured and abandoned, and nought more.

"Mary," he said, "what happiness to see you among all your old friends come to live among us again! It is almost too good to believe in. Believe me, you will get to like this country as well as old Devon soon, though it looks so strange just now. And what a noble boy, too! We will make him the best bushman in the country when he is old enough."

So he took the child of his rival to his bosom, and when the innocent little face looked into his he would see no likeness to George Hawker there. He only saw the mother's countenance as he knew her as a child in years gone by.

"Is nobody going to notice me or my boy, I wonder?" said Mrs. Buckley. "Come here immediately, Mr. Stockbridge, before we quarrel."

In a very short time all our party were restored to their equanimity, and were laying down plans for pleasant meetings hereafter. And long after the women had gone to bed in the drays, and the moon was riding high in the heavens, James and myself, Troubridge and the Major, sat before the fire; and we heard, for the first time, of all that had gone on since we left England, and of all poor Mary's troubles. Then each man rolled himself in his blanket and slept soundly under the rustling forest boughs.

In the bright, cool morning, ere the sun was up, and the belated

opossum had run back to his home in the hollow log, James and
I were afoot looking after our horses. We walked silently side by
side for a few minutes, until he turned and said:

"Jeff, old fellow, of course you will go on with them, and stay
until they are settled?"

"Jim, old fellow," I replied, "of course you will go on with
them, and stay till they are settled?"

He pondered a few moments, and then said, "Well, why not?
I suppose she can be still to me what she always was? Yes, I
will go with them."

When we returned to the dray we found them all astir, preparing
for a start. Mrs. Buckley, with her gown tucked up, was preparing
breakfast, as if she had been used to the thing all her life. She
had an imperial sort of way of manoeuvring a frying-pan, which
did one good to see. It is my belief that if that woman had been
called upon to groom a horse she'd have done it in a ladylike way.

While James went among the party to announce his intention of
going on with them, I had an opportunity of looking at the son
and heir of all the Buckleys. He was a sturdy, handsome child,
about five years old, and was now standing apart from the others,
watching a bullock-driver yoking-up his beast. I am very fond of
children, and take great interest in studying their characters; so I
stood, not unamused, behind this youngster as he stood looking
with awe and astonishment at the man as he managed the great,
formidable beasts, and brought each one into his place; not,
however, without more oaths than one would care to repeat.
Suddenly the child, turning and seeing me behind him, came back,
and took my hand.

"Why is he so angry with them?" the child asked at once. "Why
does he talk to them like that?"

"He is swearing at them," I said, "to make them stand in their
places."

"But they don't understand him," said the boy. "That black
and white one would have gone where he wanted it in a minute;
but it couldn't understand, you know; so he hit it over the nose.
Why don't he find out how they talk to one another? Then he'd
manage them much better. He is very cruel."

"He does not know any better," I said. "Come with me and
get some flowers."

"Will you take me up?" he said. "I mustn't run about, for fear
of snakes."

I took him up, and we went to gather flowers.

" Your name is Samuel Buckley, I think," said I.

" How did you know that ? "

" I remember you when you were a baby," I said. " I hope you may grow to be as good a man as your father, my lad. See, there is mamma calling for us."

" And how far south are you going, Major ? " I asked at breakfast.

" No farther than we can help," said the Major. " I stayed a night with my old friend Captain Brentwood, by the way; and there I found a man who knew of some unoccupied country down here, which he had seen in some bush expedition. We found the ground he mentioned taken up; but he says there is equally good on the next river. I have bought him and his information."

" We saw good country away to the south yesterday," I said. " But are you wise to trust this man ? Do you know anything about him ? "

" Brentwood has known him these ten years, and trusts him entirely; though, I believe, he has been a convict. If you are determined to come with us, Stockbridge, I will call him up, and examine him about the route. William Lee, just step here a moment."

A swarthy and very powerfully built man came up. No other than the man I have spoken of under that name before. He was quite unknown either to James or myself, although, as he told us afterwards, he had recognised us at once, but kept out of our sight as much as possible, till by the Major's summons he was forced to come forward.

" What route to-day, William ? " asked the Major.

" South and by east across the range. We ought to get down to the river by night, if we're lucky."

So, while the drays were getting under way, the Major, Tom, James, and myself rode up to the saddle where we had stood the night before, and gazed south-east across the broad prospect, in the direction that the wanderers were to go.

" That," said the Major, " to the right there, must be the great glen out of which the river comes; and there, please God, we will rest our weary bodies and build our house. Odd, isn't it, that I should have been saved from shot and shell when so many better men were put away in the trench, to come and end my days in a place like this ? Well, I think we shall have a pleasant life of it, watching the cattle spread farther across the plains year after year, and seeing the boy grow up to be a good man. At all events, for weal or woe, I have said good-bye to old England, for ever and a day."

The cattle were past, and the drays had arrived at where we stood. With many a hearty farewell, having given a promise to come over and spend Christmas Day with them, I turned my horse's head homewards and went on my solitary way.

CHAPTER XIX

I HIRE A NEW HORSE-BREAKER

I MUST leave them to go their way towards their new home, and follow my own fortunes a little, for that afternoon I met with an adventure quite trifling indeed, but which is not altogether without interest in this story.

I rode on till high noon, till having crossed the valley of the Belloury, and followed up one of its tributary creeks, I had come on to the water system of another main river, and the rapid widening of the gully whose course I was pursuing assured me that I could not be far from the main stream itself. At length I entered a broad flat intersected by a deep and tortuous creek, and here I determined to camp till the noonday heat was past before I continued my journey, calculating that I could easily reach home the next day.

Having watered my horse, I turned him loose for a graze, and, making such a dinner as was possible under the circumstances, I lit a pipe and lay down on the long grass, under the flowering wattle-trees, smoking, and watching the manœuvres of a little tortoise, who was disporting himself in the watérhole before me. Getting tired of that I lay back on the grass and watched the green leaves waving and shivering against the clear blue sky, given up entirely to the greatest of human enjoyments—the after-dinner pipe, the pipe of peace.

Which is the pleasantest pipe in the day? We used to say at home that a man should smoke but four pipes a day: the matutinal, another I don't specify, the post-prandial, and the symposial or convivial, which last may be infinitely subdivided, according to the quantity of drink taken. But in Australia this division won't obtain, particularly when you are on the tramp. Just when you wake from a dreamless sleep beneath the forest boughs, as the east begins to blaze and the magpie gets musical, you dash to the embers of last night's fire, and after blowing many fire-sticks find one which is alight, and proceed to send abroad on the morning breeze the scent of last night's dottle. Then, when breakfast is over and the horses are caught up and saddled, and you are jogging across the plain, with the friend of your heart beside you, the burnt incense once more goes up, and conversation is unnecessary. At ten o'clock when you cross the creek (you always cross a creek about ten if you are in a good country), you halt and smoke. So after dinner in the lazy noontide, one or perhaps two pipes are necessary, with, perhaps, another about four in the afternoon, and last, and perhaps best of all, are the three or four you smoke before the fire at night, when the day is dying and the opossums are beginning to chatter in the twilight. So that you find that a fig of Barret's twist, seventeen to the pound, is gone in the mere hours of daylight, without counting such a casualty as waking up cold in the night, and going at it again.

So I lay on my back dreaming, wondering why a locust who was in full screech close by took the trouble to make that terrible row when it was so hot, and hoping that his sides might be sore with the exertion, when to my great astonishment I heard the sound of feet brushing through the grass towards me. "Blackfellow," I said to myself; but no, those were shodden feet that swept along so wearily. I raised myself on my elbow, with my hand on my pistol, and reconnoitred.

There approached me from down the creek a man, hardly reaching the middle size, lean and active-looking, narrow in the flanks, thin in the jaws, his knees well apart; with a keen bright eye in his head. His clothes looked as if they had belonged to ten different men; and his gait was heavy, and his face red, as if from a long, hurried walk; but I said at once, "Here comes a riding man, at all events, be it for peace or war."

"Good day, lad," said I.

"Good day, sir."

"You're rather off the tracks for a foot-man," said I. "Are you looking for your horse?"

"Deuce a horse have I got to my name, sir—have you got a feed of anything? I'm nigh starved."

"Ay, surely: the tea's cold; put it on the embers and warm it a bit; here's beef, and damper, too, plenty."

I lit another pipe and watched his meal. I like feeding a real hungry man; it's almost as good as eating oneself—sometimes better.

When the edge of his appetite was taken off he began to talk; he said first:

"Got a station anywheres about here, sir?"

"No, I'm Hamlyn of the Durnongs, away by Maneroo."

"Oh! ay; I know you, sir; which way have you come this morning?"

"Southward; I crossed the Belloury about seven o'clock."

"That, indeed! You haven't seen anything of three bullock drays and a mob of cattle going south?"

"Yes! I camped with such a lot last night!"

"Not Major Buckley's lot?"

"The same."

"And how far were they on?"

"They crossed the range at daylight this morning—they're thirty miles away by now."

He threw his hat on the ground with an oath: "I shall never catch them up. I daren't cross that range on foot into the new country, and those black devils lurking round. He shouldn't have left me like that—all my own fault, though, for staying behind! No, no, he's true enough—all my own fault. But I wouldn't have left him so, neither; but, perhaps, he don't think I'm so far behind."

I saw that the man was in earnest, for his eyes were swimming— he was too dry for tears; but though he looked a desperate scamp, I couldn't help pitying him and saying:

"You seem vexed you couldn't catch them up; were you going along with the Major, then?"

"No, sir; I wasn't hired with him; but an old mate of mine, Bill Lee, is gone along with him to show him some country, and I was going to stick to him and see if the Major would take me; we haven't been parted for many years, not Bill and I haven't; and the worst of it is that he'll think I've slipped away from him instead of following him fifty mile on foot to catch him. Well! it can't be helped now; I must look round and get a job somewhere till I get a chance to join him. Were you travelling with them, sir?"

"No, I'm after some cattle I've lost; a fine imported bull, too— worse luck! We'll never see him again, I'm afraid, and if I do find them, how I am to get them home single-handed I don't know."

"Do you mean a short-horned Durham bull with a key brand? Why, if that's him, I can lay you on to him at once; he's up at Jamieson's here to the west. I was staying at Watson's last night, and one of Jamieson's men stayed in the hut—a young hand; and, talking about beasts, he said that there was a fine short-horned bull come on to their run with a mob of heifers and cows, and they couldn't make out who they belonged to; they were all different brands."

"That's our lot for a thousand," says I; "a lot of store cattle we bought this year from the Hunter and haven't branded yet—more shame to us."

"If you could get a horse and saddle from Jamieson's, sir," said he, "I could give you a hand home with them: I'd like to get a job somehow, and I am well used to cattle."

"Done with you," said I; "Jamieson's isn't ten miles from here, and we can do that to-night if we look sharp. Come along, my lad."

So I caught up the horse, and away we went. Starting at right angles with the sun, which was nearly overhead, and keeping to the left of him—holding such a course, as he got lower, that an hour and half, or thereabouts, before setting he should be in my face, and at sundown a little to the left; which is the best direction I can give you for going about due west in November without a compass—which, by the way, you always ought to have.

My companion was foot-sore, so I went slowly; he, however, shambled along bravely when his feet got warm. He was a talkative, lively man, and chattered continually.

"You've got a nice place up at the Durnongs, sir," said he; "I stayed in your huts one night. It's the comfortablest bachelor station on this side. You've got a smart few sheep, I expect?"

"Twenty-five thousand. Do you know these parts well?"

"I knew that country of yours long before any of it was took up."

"You've been a long while in the country, then?"

"I was sent out when I was eighteen; spared, as the old judge said, on account of my youth: that's eleven years ago."

"Spared, eh? It was something serious, then."

"Trifling enough: only for having a rope in my hand."

"They wouldn't lag a man for that," said I.

"Ay, but," he replied, "there was a horse at the end of the rope. I was brought up in a training stable, and somehow there's something in the smell of a stable is sure to send a man wrong if he don't take care. I got betting and drinking, too, as young chaps will, and lost my place, and got from bad to worse till I shook a nag, and got bowled out and lagged. That's about my history, sir; will you give me a job now?" And he looked up, laughing.

"Ay, why not?" said I. "Because you tried hard to go to the

devil when you were young and foolish, it don't follow that you should pursue that line of conduct all your life. You've been in a training stable, eh? If you can break horses I may find you something to do."

" I'll break horses against any man in this country—though that's not saying much, for I ain't seen not what I call a breaker since I've been here; as for riding, I'd ridden seven great winners before I was eighteen; and that's what ne'er a man alive can say. Ah, those were the rosy times! Ah for old Newmarket!"

" Are you a Cambridgeshire man, then?"

" Me? Oh, no; I'm a Devonshire man. I come near from where Major Buckley lived some years. Did you notice a pale, pretty-looking woman was with him—Mrs. Hawker?"

I grew all attention. " Yes," I said, " I noticed her."

" I knew her husband well," he said, " and an awful rascal he was: he was lagged for coining, though he might have been for half a dozen things besides."

" Indeed!" said I; " and is he in the colony?"

" No; he's over the water, I expect."

" In Van Diemen's Land, you mean?"

" Just so," he said; " he had better not show Bill Lee much of his face, or there'll be mischief."

" Lee owes him a grudge, then?"

"Not exactly that," said my communicative friend, " but I don't think that Hawker will show much where Lee is."

" I am very glad to hear it," I thought to myself. " I hope Mary may not have some trouble with her husband still."

" What is the name of the place Major Buckley comes from?" I inquired.

" Drumston."

" And you belong there, too?" I knew very well, however, that he did not, or I must have known him.

" No," he answered; " Okehampton is my native place. But you talk a little Devon yourself, sir."

The conversation came to a close, for we heard the barking of dogs, and saw the station where we were to spend the night. In the morning I went home, and my new acquaintance, who called himself Dick, came along with me. Finding that he was a first-rate rider, and gentle and handy among horses, I took him into my service permanently, and soon got to like him very well.

CHAPTER XX

A WARM CHRISTMAS DAY

ALL through November and part of December, I and our Scotch overseer, George Kyle, were busy as bees among the sheep. Shearers were very scarce, and the poor sheep got fearfully "tomahawked" by the new hands, who had been a very short time from the barracks. Dick, however, my new acquaintance, turned out a valuable ally, getting through more sheep and taking off his fleece better than any man in the shed. The prisoners, of course, would not work effectually without extra wages, and thus gave a deal of trouble; knowing that there was no fear of my sending them to the magistrate (fifty miles off) during such a busy time. However, all evils must come to an end some time or another, and so did shearing, though it was nearly Christmas before our wool was pressed and ready for the drays.

Then came a breathing time. So I determined, having heard nothing of James, to go over and spend my Christmas with the Buckleys, and see how they were getting on at their new station; and about noon on the day before Boxing Day, having followed the track made by their drays from the place I had last parted with them, I reined up on the cliffs above a noble river, and could see their new huts, scarce a quarter of a mile off, on the other side of the stream.

They say that Christmas Day is the hottest day in the year in those countries, but some days in January are, I think, generally hotter. To-day, however, was as hot as a salamander could wish. All the vast extent of yellow plain to the eastward quivered beneath a fiery sky, and every little eminence stood like an island in a lake of mirage. Used as I had got to this phenomenon, I was often tempted that morning to turn a few hundred yards from my route, and give my horse a drink at one of the broad, glassy pools that seemed to lie right and left. Once the faint track I was following headed straight towards one of these apparent sheets of water, and I was even meditating a bathe, but, lo! when I was a hundred yards or so off, it began to dwindle and disappear, and I found nothing but the same endless stretch of grass, burnt up by the midsummer sun.

For many miles I had distinguished the new huts, placed at the apex of a great cape at the continent of timber which ran down from the mountains into the plains. I thought they had chosen a strange place for their habitation, as there appeared no signs of a watercourse near it. It was not till I pulled up within a quarter of a mile of my destination that I heard a hoarse roar as if from the bowels of the earth, and found that I was standing on the edge of a glen about four hundred feet deep, through which a magnificent snow-fed river poured ceaselessly, here flashing bright among bars of rock, there lying in dark, deep reaches, under tall, white-stemmed trees.

The scene was so beautiful and novel that I paused and gazed at it. Across the glen, behind the houses, rose up a dark mass of timbered ranges, getting higher and steeper as far as the eye could reach, while to the north-east the river's course might be traced through the plains by the timber that fringed the water's edge, and sometimes feathered some tributary gully almost to the level of the flat lofty tableland. On either side of it, down behind down folded one over the other, and, bordered by great forests, led the eye towards the river's source, till the course of the deep valley could no longer be distinguished, lost among the distant ranges; but above where it had disappeared, rose a tall blue peak with streaks of snow.

I rode down a steep pathway, and crossed a broad gravelly ford. As my horse stopped to drink I looked delighted up the vista which opened on my sight. The river, partly overshadowed by tall trees, was hurrying and spouting through upright columns of basalt, which stood in groups everywhere like the pillars of a ruined city; in some places solitary, in others, clustered together like fantastic buildings; while a hundred yards above was an island, dividing the stream, on which, towering above the variety of low green shrubs which covered it, three noble fern trees held their plumes aloft, shaking with the concussion of falling water.

I crossed the river. A gully, deep at first, but getting rapidly shallower, led up by a steep ascent to the tableland above, and as I reached the summit I found myself at Major Buckley's front door. They had, with good taste, left such trees as stood near the house— a few deep-shadowed light-woods and black wattles, which formed pretty groups in what I could see was marked out for a garden. Behind, the land began to rise, at first, in park-like timbered forest glades, and farther back, closing into dense deep woodlands.

"What a lovely place they will make of this in time!" I said to myself; but I had not much time for cogitation. A loud, cheerful voice shouted: "Hamlyn, you are welcome to Baroona!" and close to me I saw the Major, carrying his son and heir in his arms, advancing to meet me from the house-door.

"You are welcome to Baroona!" echoed the boy; "and a merry Christmas and a happy New Year to you!"

I went into the house and was delighted to find what a change a few weeks of quiet, and *home* had made in the somewhat draggle-tailed and disconsolate troop that I had parted with on their road. Miss Thornton, with her black mittens, white apron, and spectacles, had found herself a cool corner by the empty fireplace, and was stitching away happily at baby linen. Mrs. Buckley, in the character of a duchess, was picking raisins, and Mary was helping her; and, as I entered, laughing loudly, they greeted me kindly with all the old sacred good wishes of the season.

"I very much pity you, Mr. Hamlyn," said Mrs. Buckley, "at having outlived the novelty of being scorched to death on Christmas Day. My dear husband, please refresh me with reading the thermometer!"

"One hundred and nine in the shade," replied the Major, with a chuckle.

"Ah, dear!" said Mrs. Buckley. "If the dear old rheumatic creatures from the almshouse at Clere could only spend to-morrow with us, how it would warm their old bones! Fancy how they are crouching before their little pinched grate just now!"

"Hardly that, Mrs. Buckley," I said, laughing; "they are all snug in bed now. It is three o'clock in the morning, or thereabouts, at home, you must remember. Miss Thornton, I hope you have got over your journey."

"Yes, and I can laugh at all my mishaps now," she replied; "I have just got homely and comfortable here, but we must make one more move, and that will be the last for me. Mary and Mr. Troubridge have taken up their country to the south-west, and as soon as he has got our house built, we are going to live there."

"It is not far, I hope," said I.

"A trifle: not more than ten miles," said Miss Thornton; "they call the place Toonarbin. Mary's run joins the Major's on two sides, and beyond again, we already have neighbours, the Mayfords. They are on the river again; but we are on a small creek towards the ranges. I should like to have been on the river, but they say we are very lucky."

"I am so glad to see you," said Mary; "James Stockbridge said you would be sure to come; otherwise, we should have sent over for you. What do you think of my boy?"

She produced him from an inner room. He was certainly a beautiful child, though very small, and with a certain painful likeness to his father, which even I could see, and I could not help comparing him unfavourably, in my own mind, with that noble six-year-old Sam Buckley, who had come to my knee where I sat, and was looking in my face as if to make a request.

"What is it, my prince?" I asked.

He blushed, and turned his handsome grey eyes to a silver-handled riding-whip that I held in my hand. "I'll take such care of it," he whispered, and, having got it, was soon astride of a stick, full gallop for Banbury Cross.

James and Troubridge came in. To the former I had much to tell that was highly satisfactory about our shearing; and from the latter I had much to hear about the state of both the new stations, and the adventures of a journey he had had back towards Sydney to fetch up his sheep. But these particulars will be but little interesting to an English reader, and perhaps still less so to an Australian. I am writing a history of the people themselves, not of their property. I will only say, once for all, that the Major's run contained very little short of 60,000 acres of splendidly grassed plain-land, which he took up originally with merely a few cattle, and about 3000 sheep; but which, in a few years, carried 28,000 sheep comfortably. Mrs. Hawker and Troubridge had quite as large a run; but a great deal of it was rather worthless forest, badly grassed; which Tom, in his wisdom, like a great many other new chums, had thought superior to the bleak plains on account of the shelter. Yet, notwithstanding this disadvantage, they were never, after a year or two, with less than 15,000 sheep, and a tolerable head of cattle. In short, in a very few years, both the Major and Troubridge, by mere power of accumulation, became very wealthy people.

Christmas morn rose bright; but ere the sun had time to wreak his fury upon us, every soul in the household was abroad, under the shade of the light-wood trees, to hear the Major read the Litany.

A strange group we were. The Major stood with his back against a tree-stem, and all his congregation were ranged around him. To his right stood Miss Thornton, her arms folded placidly before her; and with her, Mary and Mrs. Buckley, in front of whom sat the two boys; Sam, the elder, trying to keep Charles, the younger, quiet. Next, going round the circle, stood the old housekeeper, servant of the Buckleys for thirty years; who now looked askance off her

Prayer-book to see that the two convict-women under her charge were behaving with decorum. Next, and exactly opposite the Major, were two free servants: one a broad, brawny, athletic-looking man, with, I thought, not a bad countenance; and the other a tall, handsome, foolish-looking Devonshire lad. The round was completed by five convict man-servants, standing vacantly looking about them; and Tom, James, and myself, who were next the Major.

The service, which he read in a clear manly voice, was soon over, and we returned to the house in groups. I threw myself in the way of the two free servants, and asked:

"Pray, which of you is William Lee?"—for I had forgotten him.

The short thick-set man I had noticed before touched his hat and said that he was. That touching of the hat is a very rare piece of courtesy from working men in Australia. The convicts were forced to do it, and so the free men made it a point of honour not to do so.

"Oh!" said I, "I have got a groom who calls himself Dick. I found him sorefooted in the bush the day I met the Major. He was trying to pick you up. He asked me to tell you that he was afraid to cross the range alone on account of the blacks, or he would have come up with you. He seemed anxious lest you should think it was his fault."

"Poor chap!" said Lee. "What a faithful little fellow it is! Would it be asking a liberty if you would take back a letter for me, sir?"

I said, "No; certainly not."

"I am much obliged to you, sir," he said. "I am glad Dick has got with a *gentleman*."

That letter was of some importance to me, though I did not know it till after, but I may as well say why now. Lee had been a favourite servant of my father's, and when he got into trouble my father had paid a counsel to defend him. Lee never forgot this, and this letter to Dick was, shortly, to the effect that I was one of the *right sort*, and was to be taken care of, which injunction Dick obeyed to the very letter, doing me services for pure goodwill, which could not have been bought for a thousand a year.

After breakfast arose the question, "What is to be done?" Which Troubridge replied to by saying: "What could any sensible man do such weather as this, but get into the water and stop there?"

"Shall it be, 'All hands to bathe,' then?" said the Major.

"You won't be without company," said Mrs. Buckley, "for the

blackfellows are camped in the bend, and they spend most of their time in the water such a day as this."

So James and Troubridge started for the river with their towels, the Major and I promising to follow them immediately, for I wanted to look at my horse, and the Major had also something to do in the paddock. So we walked together.

"Major," said I, when we had gone a little way, "do you never feel anxious about Mary Hawker's husband appearing and giving trouble?"

"Oh, no!" said he. "The man is safe in Van Diemen's Land. Besides, what could he gain? I, for one, without consulting her, should find means to pack him off again. There is no fear."

"By the by, Major," I said, "have you heard from our friend Dr. Mulhaus since your arrival? I suppose he is at Drumston still?"

"Oh dear, no!" said he. "He is gone back to Germany. He is going to settle there again. He was so sickened of England when all his friends left, that he determined to go home. I understood that he had some sort of patrimony there, on which he will end his days. Wherever he goes, God go with him, for he is a noble fellow!"

"Amen," I answered. And soon after, having got towels, we proceeded to the river; making for a long reach a little below where I had crossed the night before.

"Look there!" said the Major. "There's a bit for one of your painters! I wish Wilkie or Martin were here."

I agreed with him. Had Etty been on the spot he would have got a hint for one of his finest pictures; and though I can give but little idea of it in writing, let me try. Before us was a long reach of deep, still water, unbroken by a ripple, so hemmed in on all sides by walls of deep green black wattle, tea-tree, and delicate silver acacia, that the water seemed to flow in a deep shoreless rift of the forest, above which the taller forest trees towered up two hundred feet, hiding the lofty cliffs, which had here receded a little back from the river.

The picture had a centre, and a strange one. A little ledge of rock ran out into deep water, and upon it, rising from a heap of light-coloured clothing, like a white pillar, in the midst of the sombre green foliage, rose the naked carcase of Thomas Troubridge, Esq., preparing for a header, while at his feet were grouped three or four blackfellows, one of whom as we watched slid off the rock like an otter. The reach was covered with black heads belonging to the savages, who were swimming in all directions, while groups of all ages and both sexes stood about on the rock bank in Mother Nature's full dress.

We had a glorious bathe, and then sat on the rock, smoking, talking, and watching the various manœuvres of the blacks. An old lady, apparently about eighty, with a head as white as snow, topping her black body (a flourbag cobbler, as her tribe would call her), was punting a canoe along in the shallow water on the opposite side of the river. She was entirely without clothes, and in spite of her decrepitude stood upright in the cockle-shell, handling it with great dexterity. When she was a little above us, she made way on her barque, and shot into the deep water in the middle of the stream, evidently with the intention of speaking to us. As, however, she was just half-way across, floating helplessly, unable to reach the bottom with the spear she had used as a punt-pole in the shallower water, a mischievous black imp canted her over, and souse she went into the river. It was amazing to see how boldly and well the old woman struck out for the shore, keeping her white head well out of the water; and having reached dry land once more, sat down on her haunches, and began scolding with a volubility and power which would soon have silenced the loudest tongue in old Billingsgate.

Her anger, so far from wearing out, grew on what fed it; so that her long-drawn yells, which seemed like parentheses in her jabbering discourse, were getting each minute more and more acute, and we were just thinking about moving homewards, when a voice behind us sang out:

"Hallo, Major! Having a little music, eh? What a sweet song that old girl is singing! I must write it down from dictation, and translate it, as Walter Scott used to do with the old wives' ballads in Scotland."

"I have no doubt it would be quite Ossianic—equal to any of the abusive scenes in Homer. But, my dear Harding, how are you? You are come to eat your Christmas dinner with us, I hope?"

"That same thing, Major," answered the newcomer. "Troubridge and Stockbridge, how are you? This, I presume, is your partner, Hamlyn?"

We went back to the house. Harding, I found, was half-owner of a station to the north-east, an Oxford man, a great hand at sky-larking, and an inveterate writer of songs. He was good-looking, too, and gentleman-like, in fact, a very pleasant companion in every way.

Dinner was to be at six o'clock, in imitation of home hours; but we did not find the day hang heavy on our hands, there was so much to be spoken of by all of us. And when that important meal was over we gathered in the open air in front of the house, bent upon making Christmas cheer.

"What is your last new song, eh, Harding?" said the Major; "now is the time to ventilate it."

"I've been too busy shearing for song-writing, Major."

Soon after this we went in, and there we sat till nearly ten o'clock, laughing, joking, singing, and drinking punch. Mary sat between James Stockbridge and Tom, and they three spoke together so exclusively and so low, that the rest of us were quite forgotten. Mary was smiling and laughing, first at one and then at the other, in her old way, and now and then as I glanced at her I could hardly help sighing. But I soon remembered certain resolutions I had made, and tried not to notice the trio, but to make myself agreeable to the others. Still my eyes wandered towards them again intuitively. I thought Mary had never looked so beautiful before. Her complexion was very full, as though she were blushing at something one of them had said to her, and while I watched I saw James rise and go to a jug of flowers, and bring back a wreath of scarlet Kennedia, saying:

"Do us a favour on Christmas night, Mary; twine this in your hair."

She blushed deeper than before, but she did it, and Tom helped her. There was no harm in that, you say, for was he not her cousin? But still I could not help saying to myself, "Oh, Mary, Mary, if you were a widow, how long would you stay so?"

"What a gathering it is, to be sure!" said Mrs. Buckley, "all the old Drumstonians who are alive collected under one roof."

"Except the Doctor," said the Major.

"Ah, yes, dear Dr. Mulhaus. I am so sad sometimes to think that we shall never see him again."

"I miss him more than anyone," said the Major. "I have no one to contradict me now."

"I shall have to take that duty upon me, then," said his wife.

"Hark! there is Lee come back from the sheep station. Yes, that must be his horse. Call him in and give him a glass of grog. I was sorry to send him out to-day."

"He is coming to make his report," said Mrs. Buckley; "there is his heavy tramp outside the door."

The door was opened, and the newcomer advanced to where the glare of the candles fell upon his face.

Had the Gentleman in Black himself advanced out of the darkness at that moment, with his blue bag on his arm and his bundles of documents in his hand, we should not have leapt to our feet and cried out more suddenly than we did then. For Dr. Mulhaus stood in the middle of the room, looking around him with a bland smile.

CHAPTER XXI

JIM STOCKBRIDGE BEGINS TO TAKE ANOTHER VIEW OF MATTERS

HE stood in the candle-light, smiling blandly, while we all stayed for an instant, after our first exclamation, speechless with astonishment.

The Major was the first who showed signs of consciousness, for I verily believe that one half of the company at least believed him to be a ghost. " You are the man," said the Major, " who in the flesh called himself Maximilian Mulhaus ! Why are you come to trouble us, O spirit ?—not that we shouldn't be glad to see you if you were alive, you know, but—my dear old friend, how are you ? "

Then we crowded round him, all speaking at once and trying to shake hands with him. Still he remained silent, and smiled. I, looking into his eyes, saw that they were swimming, and divined why he would not trust himself to speak. No one hated a show of emotion more than the Doctor, and yet his brave warm heart would often flood his eyes in spite of himself.

He walked round to the fireplace, and, leaning against the board that answered for a chimney-piece, stood looking at us with beaming eyes, while we anxiously waited for him to speak.

" Ah ! " he said at length, with a deep sigh, " this does me good. I have not made my journey in vain. A man who tries to live in this world without love must, if he is not a fool, commit suicide in a year. I went to my own home, and my own dogs barked at me. Those I had raised out of the gutter, and set on horseback, splashed mud on me as I walked. I will go back, I said, to the little English family who loved and respected me for my own sake, though they be at the ends of the earth. So I left those who should have loved me with an ill-concealed smile on their faces, and when I come here I am welcomed with tears of joy from those I have known five years. Bah ! Here is my home, Buckley : let me live and die with you."

"Live!" said the Major—"ay, while there's a place to live in; don't talk about dying yet, though—we'll think of that presently. I can't find words enough to give him welcome. Wife, can you?"

"Not I, indeed," she said; "and what need? He can see a warmer welcome in our faces than an hour's clumsy talk could give him. I say, Doctor, you are welcome, now and forever. Will that serve you, husband?"

I could not help looking at Miss Thornton. She sat silently staring at him through it all, with her hands clasped together, beating upon her knee. Now, when all was quiet, and Mrs. Buckley and Mary had run off to the kitchen to order the Doctor some supper, he seemed to see her for the first time, and bowed profoundly. She rose, and, looking at him intently, sat down again.

The Doctor had eaten his supper, and Mrs. Buckley had made him something to drink with her own hands; the Doctor had lit his pipe, and we had gathered round the empty fireplace, when the Major said:

"Now, Doctor, do tell us your adventures, and how you have managed to drop upon us from the skies on Christmas Day."

"Soon told, my friend," he answered. "See here. I went back to Germany because all ties in England were broken. I went to Lord C——: I said, 'I will go back and see the palingenesis of my country; I will see what they are doing, now the French are in the dust.' He said, 'Go, and God speed you!' I went. What did I find? Beggars on horseback everywhere, riding post-haste to the devil—not as good horsemen, either, but as tailors of Brentford, and crowding one another into the mud to see who would be there first. 'Let me get out of this before they ride over me,' said I. So I came forth to England, took ship, and here I am."

"A most lucid and entirely satisfactory explanation of what you have been about, I must say," answered the Major; "however, I must be content."

At this moment, little Sam, who had made his escape in the confusion, came running in, breathless. "Papa! Papa!" said he, "Lee has come home with a snake seven feet long." Lee was at the door with the reptile in his hand—a black snake, with a deep salmon-coloured belly, deadly venomous, as I knew. All the party went out to look at it, except the Doctor and Miss Thornton, who stayed at the fireplace.

"Mind your hands, Lee!" I heard James say; "though the brute is dead, you might prick your fingers with him."

I was behind all the others, waiting to look at the snake, which was somewhat of a large one, and worth seeing, so I could not help overhearing the conversation of Miss Thornton and the Doctor, and having heard the first of it my ears grew so unnaturally quickened, that I could not for the life of me avoid hearing the whole, though I was ashamed of playing eavesdropper.

"My God, sir!" I heard her say, "what new madness is this? Why do you persist in separating yourself from your family in this manner?"

"No madness at all, my dear madam," he answered; "you would have done the samé under the circumstances. My brother was civil, but I saw he would rather have me away and continue his stewardship. And so I let him."

Miss Thornton put another question which I did not catch, and the sense of which I could not supply, but I heard his answer plainly: it was:

"Of course I did, my dear lady, and, just as you may suppose, when I walked up the Ritter Saal, there was a buzz and a giggle, and not one held out his hand save noble Von H——; long life to him!"

"But——?" said Miss Thornton, mentioning somebody, whose name I could not catch.

"I saw him bend over to M—— as I came up to the Presence, and they both laughed. I saw a slight was intended, made my devoirs, and backed off. The next day he sent for me, but I was off and away. I heard of it before I left England."

"And will you never go back?" she said.

"When I can with honour, not before; and that will never be till he is dead, I fear; and his life is as good as mine. So, hey for natural history, and quiet domestic life, and happiness with my English friends! Now, am I wise or not?"

"I fear not," she said.

The Doctor laughed, and taking her hand, kissed it gallantly; by this time we had all turned round, and were coming in.

"Now, Doctor," said the Major, "if you have done flirting with Miss Thornton, look at this snake."

"A noble beast, indeed," said the Doctor. "Friend," he added to Lee, "if you don't want him, I will take him off your hands for a sum of money. He shall be pickled, as I live."

"He is very venomous, sir," said Lee. "The blacks eat 'em, it's true, but they always cut the head off first. I'd take the head off, sir, before I ventured to taste him."

We all laughed at Lee's supposing that the Doctor meant to make a meal of the deadly serpent, and Lee laughed as loudly as anybody.

"You see, sir," he said, "I've always heard that you French gents ate frogs, so I didn't know as snakes would come amiss."

"Pray don't take me for a Frenchman, my good lad," said the Doctor; "and as for frogs, they are as good as chickens."

"Well, I've eaten guaners myself," said Lee, "though I can't say much for them. They're uglier than snakes anyway."

Lee was made to sit down and take a glass of grog. So, very shortly, the conversation flowed on into its old channel, and, after spending a long and pleasant evening, we all went to bed.

James and I slept in the same room; and, when we were going to bed, I said:

"James, if that fellow were to die, there would be a chance for you yet."

"With regard to what?" he asked.

"You know well enough, you old humbug," I said; "with regard to Mary Hawker—*née* Thornton!"

"I doubt it, my lad," he said. "I very much doubt it indeed; and, perhaps, you have heard that there must be two parties to a bargain, so that even if she were willing to take me, I very much doubt if I would ask her."

"No one could blame you for that," I said, "after what has happened. There are but few men who would like to marry the widow of a coiner."

"You mistake me, Jeff. You mistake me altogether," he answered, walking up and down the room with one boot off. "That would make but little difference to me. I've no relations to sing out about a *mésalliance,* you know. No, my dear old fellow, not that; but—Jeff, Jeff! you are the dearest friend I have in the world."

"Jim, my boy," I answered, "I love you like a brother. What is it?"

"I have no secrets from you, Jeff," he said; "so I don't mind telling you." Another hesitation! I grew rather anxious. "What the deuce is coming?" I thought. "What can she have been up to? Go on, old fellow," I added aloud; "let's hear all about it."

He stood at the end of the room, looking rather sheepish. "Why, the fact is, old fellow, that I begin to suspect that I have outlived any little attachment I had in that quarter. I've been staying in the house two months with her, you see: and, in fact!—in fact!"— here he brought up short again.

"James Stockbridge," I said, sitting up in bed, "you atrocious humbug; two months ago you informed me, with a sigh like a groggy pair of bellows, that her image could only be effaced from your heart by death. You have seduced me, whose only fault was loving you too well to part with you, into coming sixteen thousand miles to a barbarous land, far from kindred and country, on the plea that your blighted affections made England less endurable than— France, I'll say for argument;—and now, having had two months' opportunity of studying the character of the beloved one, you coolly inform me that the whole thing was a mistake. I repeat that you are a humbug."

"If you don't hold your tongue, and that quick," he replied, "I'll send this boot at your ugly head. Now, then!"

I ducked, fully expecting it was coming, and laughed silently under the bed-clothes. I was very happy to hear this—I was very happy to hear that a man, whom I really liked so well, had got the better of a passion for a woman who I knew was utterly incapable of being to him what his romantic high-flown notions required a wife to be. "If this happy result," I said to myself, "can be rendered the more sure by ridicule, that shall not be wanting. Meanwhile, I will sue for peace, and see how it came about."

I rose again and saw he had got his other boot half off, and was watching for me. "Jim," said I, "you ain't angry because I laughed at you, are you?"

"Angry!" he answered. "I am never angry with you, and you know it. I've been a fool, and I ought to be laughed at."

"Pooh!" said I, "no more a fool than other men have been before you, from father Adam downwards."

"And he was a most con——"

"There," I interrupted: "don't abuse your ancestors. Tell me why you have changed your mind so quick?"

"That's a precious hard thing to do, mind you," he answered. "A thousand trifling circumstances, which taken apart are as worthless straws, when they are bound up together become a respectable truss, which is marketable, and ponderable. So it is with little traits in Mary's character, which I have only noticed lately, nothing separately; yet, when taken together, are, to say the least, different to what I had imagined while my eyes were blinded. To take one instance among fifty; there's her cousin Tom, one of the finest fellows that ever stepped; but still I don't like to see her, a married woman, allowing him to pull her hair about, and twist flowers in it."

This was very true, but I thought that if James instead of Tom had been allowed the privilege of decorating her hair, he might have looked on it with different eyes. James, I saw, cared too little about her to be very jealous, and so I saw that there was no fear of any coolness between him and Troubridge, which was a thing to be rejoiced at, as a quarrel would have been a terrible blow on our little society.

"Jim," said I, "I have got something to tell you. Do you know, I believe there is some mystery about Dr. Mulhaus."

"He is a walking mystery," said Jim: "but he is a noble good fellow, though unhappily a frog-eater."

"Ah! but I believe Miss Thornton knows it."

"Very likely," said Jim, yawning.

I told him all the conversation I overheard that evening.

"Are you sure she said 'the king'?" he asked.

"Quite sure," I said; "now, what do you make of it?"

"I make this of it," he said: "that it is no earthly business of ours, or we should have been informed of it; and if I were you, I wouldn't breathe a word of it to any mortal soul, or let the Doctor suspect that you overheard anything. Secrets where kings are concerned are precious sacred things, old Jeff. Good night!"

CHAPTER XXII

SAM BUCKLEY'S EDUCATION

THIS narrative which I am now writing is neither more nor less than an account of what befell certain of my acquaintances during a period extending over nearly, or quite, twenty years, interspersed, and let us hope embellished, with descriptions of the country in which these circumstances took place, and illustrated by conversations well known to me by frequent repetition, selected as throwing light upon the characters of the persons concerned. Episodes there are, too, which I have thought it worth while to introduce, as being more or less interesting, as bearing on the manners of a country but little known, out of which materials it is difficult to select those most proper to make my tale coherent; yet it has been my object, neither to dwell on the one hand unnecessarily on the more unimportant passages, nor on the other hand to omit anything which may be supposed to bear on the general course of events.

Now, during all the time above mentioned, I, Geoffry Hamlyn, have happened to lead a most uninteresting, and with few exceptions prosperous existence. I was but little concerned, save as a hearer, in the catalogue of exciting accidents and offences which I chronicle. I have looked on with the deepest interest at the love-making, and ended a bachelor; I have witnessed the fighting afar off, only joining the battle when I could not help it, yet I am a steady old fogey, with a mortal horror of a disturbance of any sort. I have sat drinking with the wine-bibbers, and yet at sixty my hand is as steady as a rock. Money has come to me by mere accumulation; I have taken more pains to spend it than to make it; in short, all through my life's dream, I have been a spectator and not an actor, and so in this story I shall keep myself as much as possible in the background, only appearing personally when I cannot help it.

Acting on this resolve I must now make my *congé,* and bid you farewell for a few years, and go back to those few sheep which James Stockbridge and I own in the wilderness, and continue the history of those who are more important than myself. I must push on, too, for there is a long period of dull, stupid prosperity coming to our friends at Baroona and Toonarbin which we must get over as quickly as is decent. Little Sam Buckley also, though at present a most delightful child, will soon be a mere uninteresting boy. We must teach him to read and write, and ride, and what not, as soon as possible, and see if we can't find a young lady—well, I won't anticipate, but go on. Go on, did I say? Jump on, rather—two whole years at once.

See Baroona now. Would you know it? I think not. That hut where we spent the pleasant Christmas Day you know of is degraded into the kitchen, and seems moved backward, although it stands in the same place, for a new house is built nearer the river, quite overwhelming the old slab hut in its grandeur—a long, low wooden house, with deep, cool verandas all round, already festooned with passion flowers, and young grapevines, and fronted by a flower garden all ablaze with petunias and geraniums.

It was a summer evening, and all the French windows reaching to the ground were open to admit the cool south wind, which had just come up, deliciously icily cold after a scorching day. In the veranda sat the Major and the Doctor over their claret (for the Major had taken to dining late again now, to his great comfort), and in the garden were Mrs. Buckley and Sam watering the flowers, attended by a man who drew water from a new-made reservoir near the house.

"I think, Doctor," said the Major, "that the habit of dining in the middle of the day is a gross abuse of the gifts of Providence, and I'll prove it to you. What does a man dine for? Answer me that."

"To satisfy his hunger, *I* should say," answered the Doctor.

"Pooh! pooh! stuff and nonsense, my good friend," said the Major; "you are speaking at random. I suppose you will say, then, that a blackfellow is capable of dining?"

"Highly capable, as far as I can judge from what I have seen," replied the Doctor. "A full-grown fighting black would be ashamed if he couldn't eat a leg of mutton at a sitting."

"And you call that *dining*?" said the Major. "I call it gorging. Why, those fellows are more uncomfortable after food than before. I have seen them sitting close before the fire and rubbing their stomachs with mutton fat to reduce the swelling. Ha! ha! ha!— dining, eh? Oh Lord!"

"Then if you don't dine to satisfy your hunger, what the deuce do you eat dinners for at all?" asked the Doctor.

"Why," said the Major, spreading his legs out before him with a benign smile, and leaning back in his chair, "I eat my dinner, not so much for the sake of the dinner itself as for the after-dinnerish feeling which follows: a feeling that you have nothing to do, and that if you had you'd be shot if you'd do it. That, to return to where I started from, is why I won't dine in the middle of the day."

"If that is the way you feel after dinner, I certainly wouldn't."

"All the most amiable feelings in the human breast," continued the Major, "are brought out in their full perfection by dinner. If a fellow were to come to me now and ask me to lend him ten pounds, I'd do it, provided, you know, that he would fetch out the cheque-book and pen and ink."

"Laziness is nothing," said the Doctor, "unless well carried out. I only contradicted you, however, to draw you out; I agree entirely. Do you know, my friend, I am getting marvellously fond of this climate."

"So am I. But then you know, Doctor, that we are sheltered from the north wind here by the snow ranges. The summer in Sydney, now, is perfectly infernal. The dust is so thick you can't see your hand before you."

"So I believe," said the Doctor. "By the by, I got a new butterfly to-day: rather an event, mind you, here, where there are so few."

"What is he?"

" An Hipparchia," said the Doctor. " Sam saw him first and gave chase."

" You seem to be making quite a naturalist of my boy, Doctor. I am sincerely obliged to you. If we can make him take to that sort of thing it may keep him out of much mischief."

" He will never get into much," said the Doctor, " unless I am mistaken; he is the most docile child I ever came across. It is a pleasure to be with him. What are you going to do with him? "

" He must go to school, I am afraid," said the Major, with a sigh; " I can't bring my heart to part with him; but his mother has taught him all she knows, so I suppose he must go to school and fight, and get flogged, and come home with a pipe in his mouth, and an oath on his lips, with his education completed. I don't fancy his staying here among these convict servants when he is old enough to learn mischief."

" He'll learn as much mischief at a colonial school, I expect," said the Doctor, " and more, too. All the evil he hears from these fellows will be like the water on a duck's back; whereas, if you send him to school in a town he'll learn a dozen vices he'll never hear of here. Get him a tutor."

" That is easier said than done, Doctor. It is very hard to get a respectable tutor in the colony."

" Here is one at your hand," said the Doctor. " Take me."

" My dear friend," said the Major, jumping up, " I would not have dared to ask such a thing. If you would undertake him for a short time? "

" I will undertake the boy's education altogether. Potztausend, and why not! It will be a labour of love, and therefore the more thoroughly done. What shall he learn, now? "

" That I must leave to you."

" A weighty responsibility," said the Doctor. " No Latin or Greek, I suppose? They will be no use to him here."

" Well—no; I suppose not. But I should like him to learn his Latin grammar. You may depend upon it there's something in the Latin grammar."

" What use has it been to you, Major? "

" Why, the least advantage it has been to me is to give me an insight into the construction of languages, which is some use. But while I was learning the Latin grammar, I learnt other things besides, of more use than the construction of any languages, living or dead. First, I learnt that there were certain things in this world that *must* be done. Next, that there were people in this world, of whom the Masters of Eton were a sample, whose orders must be obeyed without question. Third, I found that it was pleasanter in all ways to do one's duty than to leave it undone. And last, I found out how to bear a moderate amount of birching without any indecent outcry."

"All very useful things," said the Doctor. "Teach a boy one thing well and you show him how to learn others. History, I suppose?"

"As much as you like, Doctor. His mother has taught him his catechism, and all that sort of thing, and she is the fit person, you know. With the exception of that and the Latin grammar, I trust everything to your discretion."

"There is one thing I leave to you, Major, if you please, and that is corporal chastisement. I am not at all sure that I could bring myself to flog Sam, and, if I did, it would be very inefficiently done."

"Oh, I'll undertake it," said the Major, "though I believe I shall have an easy task. He won't want much flogging."

At this moment Mrs. Buckley approached with a basketful of fresh-gathered flowers. "The roses don't flower well here, Doctor," she said, "but the geraniums run mad. Here is a salmon-coloured one for your button-hole."

"He has earned. it well, Agnes," said her husband. "He has decided the discussion we had last night by offering to undertake Sam's education himself."

"And God's blessing on him for it!" said Mrs. Buckley warmly. "You have taken a great load off my mind, Doctor. I should never have been happy if that boy had gone to school. Come here, Sam."

Sam came bounding into the veranda, and clambered up on his father, as if he had been a tree. He was now eleven years old, and very tall and well-formed for his age. He was a good-looking boy, with regular features, and curly chestnut hair. He had, too, the large grey-blue eye of his father, an eye that never lost for a moment its staring expression of kindly honesty, and the lad's whole countenance was one which, without being particularly handsome, or even very intelligent, won an honest man's regard at first sight.

"My dear Sam," said his mother, "leave off playing with your father's hair, and listen to me, for I have something serious to say to you. Last night your father and I were debating about sending you to school, but Dr. Mulhaus has himself offered to be your tutor, thereby giving you advantages, for love, which you never could have secured for money. Now, the least we can expect of you, my dear boy, is that you will be docile and attentive to him."

"I will try, Doctor dear," said Sam. "But I am very stupid sometimes, you know."

So the good Doctor, whose head was stored with nearly as much of human knowledge as mortal head could hold, took simple, guileless little Sam by the hand, and led him into the garden of knowledge. Unless I am mistaken, these two will pick more flowers than they will dig potatoes in the aforesaid garden, but I don't think that two such honest souls will gather much unwholesome fruit. The danger is that they will waste their time, which is no danger at all, but a certainty.

I believe that such an education as our Sam got from the Doctor would have made a slattern and a *fainéant* out of half the boys in England. If Sam had been a clever boy, or a conceited boy, he would have ended with a superficial knowledge of things in general, imagining he knew everything when he knew nothing, and would have been left in the end, without a faith either religious or political, a useless, careless man.

This danger the Doctor foresaw in the first month, and going to the Major abruptly, as he walked up and down the garden, took his arm, and said:

"See here, Buckley; I have undertaken to educate that boy of yours, and every day I like the task better, and yet every day I see that I have undertaken something beyond me. His appetite for knowledge is unsatiable, but he is not an intellectual boy; he makes no deductions of his own, but takes mine for granted. He has no commentary on what he learns, but that of a dissatisfied idealist like me, a man who has been thrown among circumstances sufficiently favourable to make a prime minister out of some men, and yet who has ended by doing nothing. Another thing: this is my first attempt at education, and I have not the schoolmaster's art to keep him to details. Every day I make new resolutions, and every day I break them. The boy turns his great eyes upon me in the middle of some humdrum work and asks me a question. In answering, I get off the turnpike road, and away we go from lane to lane, from one subject to another, until lesson-time is over, and nothing done. And, if it were merely time wasted, it could be made up, but he remembers every word I say, and believes in it like gospel, when I myself couldn't remember half of it to save my life. Now, my dear fellow, I consider your boy to be a very sacred trust to me, and so I have mentioned all this to you, to give you an opportunity of removing him to where he might be under a stricter discipline, if you thought fit. If he was like some boys, now, I should resign my post at once; but, as it is, I shall wait till you turn me out, for two reasons. The first is that I take such delight in my task that I do not care to relinquish it; and the other is that the lad is naturally so orderly and gentle that he does not need discipline, like most boys."

"My dear Doctor," replied Major Buckley, "listen to me. If we were in England and Sam could go to Eton, which, I take it you know, is the best school in the world, I would still earnestly ask you to continue your work. He will probably inherit a great deal of money, and will not have to push his way in the world by his brains; so that close scholarship will be rather unnecessary. I should like him to know history well and thoroughly; for he may mix in the political life of this little colony by and by. Latin grammar, you know," he said, laughing, " is indispensable. Doctor, I trust my boy with you because I know that you will make him a gentleman, as his mother, with God's blessing, will make him a Christian."

So, the Doctor buckled to his task again, with renewed energy; to Euclid, Latin grammar, and fractions. Sam's good memory enabled him to make light of the grammar, and the fractions, too, were no great difficulty, but the Euclid was an awful trial. He couldn't make out what it was all about. He got on very well until he came nearly to the end of the first book, and then getting among the parallelogram "props," as we used to call them (may their fathers' graves be defiled!), he stuck dead. For a whole evening did he pore patiently over one of them till A B, setting to C D, crossed hands, poussetted, and whirled round " in Sahara Waltz " through his throbbing head. Bedtime, but no rest! Whether he slept or not he could not tell. Who could sleep with the long-bodied, ill-tempered-looking parallelogram A H standing on the bed clothes, and crying out in tones loud enough to waken the house, that it never had been, nor ever would be equal to the fat jolly square C K? So, in the morning, Sam woke to the consciousness that he was further off from the solution than ever, but, having had a good cry, went into the study and tackled to it again.

No good! Breakfast-time, and matters much worse! That long, peak-nose vixen of a triangle A H C, which yesterday Sam had made out was equal to half the parallelogram and half the square, now had the audacity to declare that she had nothing to do with either of them; so what was to be done now?

After breakfast Sam took his book and went out to his father, who was sitting smoking in the veranda. He clambered up on to his knee, and then began:

"Father, dear, see here; can you understand this? You've got to prove, you know—oh, dear! I've forgot that now."

"Let's see," said the Major. "I'm afraid this is a little above me. There's Brentwood, now, could do it; he was in the Artillery, you know, and learnt fortification, and that sort of thing. I don't think I can make much hand of it, Sam."

But Sam had put his head upon his father's shoulder, and was crying bitterly.

"Come, come, my old man," said the Major, "don't give way, you know; don't be beat."

"I can't make it out at all," said Sam, sobbing. "I've got such a buzzing in my head with it! and if I can't do it I must stop; because I can't go on to the next till I understand this. Oh, dear me!"

"Lay your head there a little, my boy, till it gets clearer: then perhaps you will be able to make it out. You may depend on it that you ought to learn it, or the good Doctor wouldn't have set it to you; never let a thing beat you, my son."

So Sam cried on his father's shoulder a little, and then went in with his book; and not long after, the Doctor looked in unperceived and saw the boy with his elbows on the table and the book before him. Even while he looked a big tear fell plump into the middle of A H; so the Doctor came quietly in and said:

"Can't you manage it, Sam?"

Sam shook his head.

"Just give me hold of the book; will you, Sam?"

Sam complied without word or comment; the Doctor sent it flying through the open window, halfway down the garden. "There!" said he, nodding his head, "that's the fit place for him this day: you've had enough of him at present; go and tell one of the blacks to dig some worms, and we'll make holiday and go a-fishing."

Sam looked at the Doctor, and then through the window at his old enemy lying in the middle of the flower-bed. He did not like to see the poor book, so lately his master, crumpled and helpless, fallen from its high estate so suddenly. He would have gone to its assistance and picked it up and smoothed it, the more so as he felt that he had been beaten.

The Doctor seemed to see everything. "Let it lie there, my

child," he said; "you are not in a position to assist a fallen enemy; you are still the vanquished party. Go and get the worms."

He went, and when he came back he found the Doctor sitting beside his father in the veranda, with a penknife in one hand and the ace of spades in the other. He cut the card into squares, triangles, and parallelograms, while Sam looked on, and, demonstrating as he went, fitted them one into the other, till the boy saw his bugbear of a proposition made as clear as day before his eyes.

"Why," said Sam, "that's as clear as need be. I understand it. Now may I pick the book up, Doctor?"

History was the pleasantest part of all Sam's tasks, for they would sit in the little room given up for a study, with the French windows open looking on the flower garden, Sam reading aloud and the Doctor making discursive commentaries. At last, one day, the Doctor said:

"My boy, we are making too much of a pleasure of this: you must really learn your dates. Now tell me the date of the accession of Edward the Sixth."

No returns.

"Ah! I thought so: we must not be so discursive. We'll learn the dates of the Grecian History, as being an effort of memory, you not having read it yet."

But this plan was rather worse than the other; for one morning, Sam having innocently asked, at half-past eleven, what the battle of Thermopylæ was, Mrs. Buckley coming in, at one, to call them to lunch, found the Doctor, who had begun the account of that glorious fight in English, and then gone on to German, walking up and down the room in a state of excitement, reciting to Sam, who did not know delta from psi, the soul-moving account of it from Herodotus in good sonorous Greek. She asked, laughing, "What language are you talking now, my dear Doctor?"

"Greek, madam, Greek! and the very best of Greek!"

"And what does Sam think of it? I should like you to learn Greek, my boy, if you can."

"I thought he was singing, mother," said Sam; but after that the lad used to sit delighted, by the riverside, when they were fishing, while the Doctor, with his musical voice, repeated some melodious ode of Pindar's.

And so the intellectual education proceeded, with more or less energy; and meanwhile the physical and moral part was not forgotten, though the two latter, like the former, were not very closely attended to, and left a good deal to Providence. (And, having done your best for a boy, in what better hands can you leave him?) But the Major, as an old soldier, had gained a certain faith in the usefulness of physical training; so, when Sam was about twelve, you might have seen him any afternoon on the lawn, with his father, the Major, patiently teaching him singlestick, and Sam as patiently learning, until the boy came to be so marvellously active on his legs, and to show such rapidity of eye and hand, that the Major, on one occasion, having received a more than usually agonising cut on the forearm, remarked that he thought he was not quite so active on his pins as formerly, and that he must hand the boy over to the Doctor.

"Doctor," said he that day, "I have taught my boy ordinary sword play till, by Jove, sir, he is getting quicker than I am. I wish you would take him in hand and give him a little fencing."

"Who told you I could fence?" said the Doctor.

"Why, I don't know; no one, I think. I have judged, I fancy, more by seeing you flourish your walking-stick than anything else. You are a fencer, are you not?"

The Doctor laughed. He was in fact a consummate *maitre d'armes*; and Captain Brentwood, before spoken of, no mean fencer, coming to Baroona on a visit, found that our friend could do exactly as he liked with him, to the Captain's great astonishment. And Sam soon improved under his tuition, not indeed to the extent of being a master of the weapon; he was too large and loosely built for that; but, at all events, so far as to gain an upright and elastic carriage, and to learn the use of his limbs.

The Major issued an edict, giving the most positive orders against its infringement, that Sam should never mount a horse without his special leave and licence. He taught him to ride, indeed, but would not give him much opportunity for practising it. Once or twice a week he would take him out, but seldom oftener. Sam, who never dreamt of questioning the wisdom and excellence of any of his father's decisions, rather wondered at this; pondering in his own mind how it was that, while all the lads he knew around, now getting pretty numerous, lived, as it were, on horseback, never walking a quarter of a mile on any occasion, he alone should be discouraged from it. "Perhaps," he said to himself one day, "he doesn't want me to make many acquaintances. It is true, Charley Delisle smokes and swears, which is very ungentlemanly; but Cecil Mayford, dad says, is a perfect little gentleman, and I ought to see as much of him as possible, and yet he wouldn't give me a horse to go to their muster. Well, I suppose he has some reason for it."

One holiday the Doctor and the Major were sitting in the veranda after breakfast, when Sam entered to them, and, clambering on to his father as his wont was, said:

"See here, father! Harry is getting in some young beasts at the stockyard-hut, and Cecil Mayford is coming over to see if any of theirs are among them; may I go out and meet him?"

"To be sure, my boy; why not?"

"May I have Bronsewing, father? He is in the stable."

"It is a nice cool day, and only four miles; why not walk out, my boy?"

Sam looked disappointed, but said nothing.

"I know all about it, my child," said the Major; "Cecil will be there on Blackboy, and you would like to show him that Bronsewing is the superior pony of the two. That's all very natural; but still I say, get your hat, Sam, and trot through the forest on your own two legs, and bring Cecil home to dinner."

Sam still looked disappointed, though he tried not to show it. He went and got his hat, and, meeting the dogs, got such a wild welcome from them that he forgot all about Bronsewing. Soon his father saw him merrily crossing the paddock with the whole kennel of the establishment, kangaroo dogs, cattle dogs, and collies, barking joyously around him.

"There's a good lesson manfully learnt, Doctor," said the Major; "he has learnt to sacrifice his will to mine without argument, because he knows I have always a reason for things. I want that boy to ride as little as possible, but he has earned an exception in his favour to-day. Jerry!" (After a few calls the stableman appeared.) "Put Mr. Samuel's saddle on Bronsewing, and mine on Ricochette, and bring them round."

So Sam, walking cheerily forward singing, under the light and shadow of the old forest, surrounded by his dogs, hears horses' feet behind him, and looking back sees his father riding and leading Bronsewing saddled.

"Jump up, my boy," said the Major; "Cecil shall see what Bronsewing is like, and how well you can sit him. The reason I altered my mind was that I might reward you for acting like a man, and not arguing. Now, I don't want you to ride much yet for a few years. I don't want my lad to grow up with a pair of bow legs like a groom, and probably something worse, from living on horseback before his bones are set. You see I have good reason for what I do."

But I think that the lessons Sam liked best of all were the

swimming lessons, and at a very early age he could swim and dive like a black, and once when disporting himself in the water, when not more than thirteen, poor Sam nearly had a stop put to his bathing for ever, and that in a very frightful manner.

His father and he had gone down to bathe one hot noon; the Major had swum out and was standing on the rock wiping himself, while Sam was still disporting in the mid-river; as he watched the boy he saw what seemed a stick upon the water, and then, as he perceived the ripple around it, the horrible truth burst on the affrighted father: it was a large black snake crossing the river, and poor little Sam was swimming straight towards it, all unconscious of his danger.

The Major cried out and waved his hand; the boy seeing something was wrong, turned and made for the shore, and the next moment his father, bending his body back, hurled himself through the air and alighted in the water alongside of him, clutching him round the body, and heading down the river with furious strokes.

"Don't cling, Sam, or get frightened; make for the shore."

The lad, although terribly frightened at he knew not what, with infinite courage seconded his father's efforts although he felt sinking. In a few minutes they were safe on the bank, in time for them to see the reptile land, and crawling up the bank disappear among the rocks.

"God has been very good to us, my son. You have been saved from a terrible death. Mind you don't breathe a word to your mother about this."

That night Sam dreamt that he was in the coils of a snake, but waking up found that his father was laid beside him in his clothes with one arm round his neck, so he went to sleep again and thought no more of the snake.

"My son, if sinners entice thee, consent thou not"—a saying which it is just possible you have heard before. I can tell you where it comes from: it is one of the apothegms of the king of a little eastern nation who at one time were settled in Syria, and whose writings are not much read nowadays, in consequence of the vast mass of literature of a superior kind which this happy century has produced. I can recommend the book, however, as containing some original remarks, and being generally worth reading. The meaning of the above quotation (and the man who said it, mind you, had at one time a reputation for shrewdness), is, as I take it, that a man's morals are very much influenced by the society he is thrown among; and although in these parliamentary times we know that kings must of necessity be fools, yet in this instance I think that the man shows some glimmerings of reason, for his remark tallies singularly with my own personal observation; so, acting on this, while I am giving you the history of this little wild boy of the bush, I cannot do better than give some account of the companions with whom he chiefly associated out of school hours.

With broad, intelligent forehead, with large loving hazel eyes, with a frill like Queen Elizabeth, with a brush like a fox; deep in the brisket, perfect in markings of black, white, and tan; in sagacity a Pitt, in courage an Anglesey, Rover stands first on my list, and claims to be king of collie dogs. In politics I should say Conservative of the high Protectionist sort. Let us have no strange dogs about the place to grub up sacred bones, or we will shake out our frills and tumble them in the dust. Domestic cats may mioul in the garden at night to a certain extent, but a line must be drawn; after that they must be chased up trees and barked at, if necessary, all night. Opossums and native cats are unfit to cumber the earth, and must be hunted into holes, wherever possible. Cows and other horned animals must not come into the yard, or even look over the garden fence, under penalties. Blackfellows must be barked at, and their dogs chased to the uttermost limits of the habitable globe. Such were the chief points of the creed subscribed to by Sam's dog, Rover.

All the love that may be between dog and man, and man and dog, existed between Sam and Rover. Never a fresh, cheery morning when the boy arose with the consciousness of another happy day before him but that the dog was waiting for him as he stepped from his window into clear, morning air. Never a walk in the forest but that Rover was his merry companion. And what would lessons have been without Rover looking in now and then with his head on one side and his ears cocked, to know when he would be finished and come out to play?

Oh, memorable day, when Sam got separated from his father in Yass, and, looking back, saw a cloud of dust in the road, and dimly descried Rover, fighting valiantly against fearful odds, with all the dogs in the township upon him! He rode back, and prayed for assistance from the men lounging in front of the public-house; who, pitying his distress, pulled off all the dogs till there were only left Rover and a great white bulldog to do battle. The fight seemed going against Sam's dog; for the bulldog had him by the neck, and held him firm, so that he could do nothing. Nevertheless, mind yourself, master bulldog; you've only got a mouthful of long hair there; and when you do let go, I think, there is danger for you in those fierce, gleaming eyes, and terrible grinning fangs.

Sam was crying; and the men round were saying, " Oh! take the bulldog off; the collie's no good to him," when a man suddenly appeared at Sam's side and called out:

" I'll back the collie for five pounds, and here's my money! "

Half a dozen five-pound notes were ready for him at once; and he had barely got the stakes posted before the event proved he was right. In an evil moment for him the bulldog loosed his hold, and, ere he had time to turn round, Rover had seized him below the eye, and was dragging him about the road, worrying him as he would an opossum: so the discomfitted owner had to remove his bulldog to save his life. Rover, after showing his teeth and shaking himself, came to Sam as fresh as a daisy; and the newcomer pocketed his five pounds.

" I am so much obliged to you," said Sam, turning to him, " for taking my dog's part! They were all against me."

" I'm much obliged to your dog, sir, for winning me five pounds so easy. But there ain't a many bad dogs or bad men either, about Major Buckley's house."

" Then you know us? " said Sam.

" Ought to it, sir. An old Devonshire man. Mr. Hamlyn's stud groom, sir—Dick."

Well, I won't any further entrench on my subject matter, save to say that, while on the subject of Sam's education, I could not well omit a notice of the aforesaid Rover. For I think all a man can learn from a dog, Sam learnt from him; and that is something. Now let us go on to the next of his noble acquaintances.

Who is this glorious, blue-eyed, curly-headed boy, who bursts into the house like a whirlwind, making it ring again with merry laughter? This is Jim Brentwood, of whom we shall see much anon.

At Waterloo, when the French cavalry were coming up the hill, and our artillerymen were running for the squares, deftly trundling their gun-wheels before them, it happened that there came running towards the square where Major Buckley stood like a tower of strength (the tallest man in the regiment), an artillery officer, begrimed with mud and gunpowder, and dragging a youth by the collar, or rather, what seemed to be the body of a youth. Some cried out to him to let go; but he looked back, seeming to measure the distance between the cavalry and the square, and then, never loosing his hold, held on against hope. Everyone thought he would

be too late; when someone ran out of the square (men said it was
Buckley), and, throwing the wounded lad over his shoulder, ran
with him into safety; and a cheer ran along the line from those who
saw him do it. Small time for cheering then; for neither could
recover his breath before there came a volley of musketry, and all
around them, outside the bayonets, was a wild sea of fierce men's
faces, horses' heads, gleaming steel, and French blasphemy.   A
strange scene for the commencement of an acquaintance! And yet
it throve; for that same evening, Buckley, talking to his Colonel,
saw the artillery officer coming towards them, and asked who he
might be?

"That," said the Colonel, "is Brentwood of the Artillery, who
ran away with Lady Kate Bingley, and they haven't a rap to bless
themselves with, sir. It was her brother that you and he fetched
into the square to-day."

And so began a friendship which lasted the lives of both men;
and, I doubt not, will last their sons' lives, too. For Brentwood
lived within thirty miles of the Major, and their sons spent much
of their time together, having such a friendship for one another as
only boys can have.

Captain Brentwood's son, Jim, was a very different boy to Sam,
though a very fine fellow, too. Mischief and laughter were the
apparent objects of his life; and when the Doctor saw him
approaching the house he used to put away Sam's lesson-books
with a sigh and wait for better times. The Captain had himself
undertaken his son's education, and, being a somewhat dreamy man,
excessively attached to mathematics, Jim had got, altogether, a very
remarkable education indeed; which, however, is hardly to our
purpose just now. Brentwood, I must say, was a widower, and a
kind-hearted, easy-going man; he had, besides, a daughter, who was
away at school. Enough of them at present.

The next of Sam's companions who takes an important part in
this history is Cecil Mayford—a delicate, clever little dandy, and
courageous withal; with more brains in his head, I should say, than
Sam and Jim could muster between them. His mother was a widow,
who owned the station next down the river from the Buckleys,
distant about five miles, and which, since the death of her husband,
Dr. Mayford, she had managed with the assistance of an overseer.
She had, besides Cecil, a little daughter of great beauty.

Also, I must here mention that the next station below Mrs.
Mayford's, on the river, distant by the windings of the valley
fifteen miles, and yet, in consequence of a bend, scarcely ten from

Major Buckley's at Baroona, was owned and inhabited by Yahoos (by name Donovan), with whom we had nothing to do. But this aforesaid station, which is called Garoopna, will shortly fall into other hands, when you will see that many events of deep importance will take place there, and many pleasant hours spent there by all our friends, more particularly one—by name, Sam.

There is one other left of whom I must say something here, and more immediately. The poor, puling little babe, born in misery and disaster, Mary Hawker's boy, Charles!

Toonarbin was but a short ten miles from Baroona, and, of course, the two families were as one. There was always a hostage from the one house staying as a visitor in the other; and, under such circumstances, of course, Charles and Sam were much together, and, as time went on, got to be firm friends.

Charles was two years younger than Sam; the smallest of all the lads, and perhaps the most unhappy. For the truth must be told: he was morose and uncertain in his temper; and although all the other boys bore with him most generously, as one of whom they had heard that he was born under some great misfortune, yet he was hardly a favourite amongst them; and the poor boy, sometimes perceiving this, would withdraw from his play, and sulk alone, resisting all the sober, kind inducements of Sam, and the merry, impetuous persuasions of Jim, to return.

But he was a kind, good-hearted boy, nevertheless. His temper was not under control; but, after one of his fierce, volcanic bursts of ill-humour, he would be acutely miserable and angry with himself for days, particularly if the object of it had been Jim or Sam, his two especial favourites. On one occasion, after a causeless fit of anger with Jim, while the three were at Major Buckley's together, he got his pony and rode away home secretly, speaking to no one. The other two lamented all the afternoon that he had taken the matter so seriously, and were debating even next morning going after him to propitiate him, when Charles reappeared, having apparently quite recovered his temper, but evidently bent upon something.

He had a bird, a white corrella, which could talk and whistle surprisingly, probably, in fact, the most precious thing he owned. This prodigy he had now brought back in his basket as a peace-offering, and refused to be comforted, unless Jim accepted it as a present.

"But see, Charley," said Jim, "I was as much in the wrong as you were" (which was not fact, for Jim was perfectly innocent). "I wouldn't take your bird for the world."

But Charles said that his mother approved of it, and if Jim didn't take it he'd let it fly.

"Well, if you will, old fellow," said Jim, "I'll tell you what I would rather have. Give me Fly's dun pup instead, and take the bird home."

So this was negotiated after a time, and the corella was taken back to Toonarbin, wildly excited by the journey, and calling for strong liquor all the way home.

Those who knew the sad circumstances of poor Charles's birth (the Major, the Doctor, and Mrs. Buckley) treated him with such kindness and consideration that they won his confidence and love. In any of his berserk fits, if his mother were not at hand, he would go to Mrs. Buckley and open his griefs; and her motherly tact and kindness seldom failed to still the wild beatings of that poor, sensitive, silly little heart, so that in time he grew to love her as only second to his mother.

Such is my brief and imperfect, and I fear tedious account of Sam's education, and of the companions with whom he lived, until the boy had grown into a young man, and his sixteenth birthday came round, on which day, as had been arranged, he was considered to have finished his education, and stand up, young as he was, as a man.

Happy morning, and memorable for one thing at least—that his father, coming into his bedroom and kissing his forehead, led him out to the front door, where was a groom holding a horse handsomer than any Sam had seen before, which pawed the gravel impatient to be ridden, and ere Sam had exhausted half his expressions of wonder and admiration—that his father told him the horse was his, a birthday present from his mother.

CHAPTER XXIII

TOONARBIN

"BUT," I think I hear you say, "what has become of Mary Hawker all this time? You raised our interest about her somewhat, at first, as a young and beautiful woman, villain-beguiled, who seemed, too, to have a temper of her own, and promised, under circumstances, to turn out a bit of a b—mst—ne. What is she doing all this time? Has she got fat, or had the small-pox, that you neglect her like this? We had rather more than we wanted of her and her villainous husband in the first part of this volume; and now nothing. Let us, at all events, hear if she is dead or alive. And her husband, too—although we hope, under Providence, that he has left this wicked world, yet we should be glad to hear of it for certain. Make inquiries, and let us know the result. Likewise, be so good as inform us, how is Miss Thornton?"

To all this I answer humbly, that I will do my best. If you will bring a dull chapter on you, duller even than all the rest, at least read it, and exonerate me. The fact is, my dear sir, that women like Mary Hawker are not particularly interesting in the piping times of peace. In volcanic and explosive times they, with their wild animal passions, become tragical and remarkable, like baronesses of old. But in tranquil times, as I said, they fall into the background, and show us the value and excellence of such placid, noble helpmates as the serene, high-bred Mrs. Buckley.

A creek joined the river about a mile below the Buckleys' station, falling into the main stream with rather a pretty cascade, which even at the end of the hottest summer poured a tiny silver thread across the black rocks. Above the cascade the creek cut deep into the tableland, making a charming glen, with precipitous bluestone walls, some eighty or ninety feet in height, fringed with black wattle and lightwood, and here and there, among the fallen rocks nearest the water, a fern tree or so, which last I may say are no longer there, Dr. Mulhaus having cut the hearts out of them and eaten them for cabbage. Should you wander up this little gully on a hot summer's day, you would be charmed with the beauty of the scenery, and the shady coolness of the spot; till coming upon a black snake coiled away among the rocks, like a rope on the deck of a man-of-war, you would probably withdraw, not without a strong inclination to "shy" at every black stick you saw for the rest of the day. For this lower part of the Moira Creek was, I am sorry to say, the most troubled locality for snakes—diamond, black, carpet, and other—which I ever happened to see.

But following this creek you would find that the banks got rapidly less precipitous, and at length it swept in long curves through open forest glades, spreading, too, into deep dark water-holes, only connected by gravelly fords, with a slender stream of clear water running across the yellow pebbles. These water-holes were the haunts of the platypus and the tortoise. Here, too, were flocks of black duck and teal, and as you rode past, the merry little snipe would rise from the water's edge, and whisk away like lightning through the trees. Altogether, a pleasant woodland creek, alongside of which, under the mighty box trees, ran a sandy road, bordered with deep beds of bracken fern, which led from Baroona of the Buckleys to Toonarbin of the Hawkers.

A pleasant road, indeed, winding through the old forest straight towards the mountains, shifting its course so often that every minute some new vista opened upon you, till at length you came suddenly upon a clear space, beyond which rose a picturesque little granite cap, at the foot of which you saw a charming house, covered with green creepers, and backed by huts, sheep-yards, a wool-shed, and the usual concomitants of a flourishing Australian sheep station. Behind all again towered lofty, dark hanging woods, closing the prospect.

This is Toonarbin, where Mary Hawker, with her leal and trusty cousin, Tom Troubridge, for partner, has pitched her tent, after all her spasmodic, tragical troubles, and here she is leading as happy, and by consequence as uninteresting, an existence as ever fell to the lot of a handsome woman yet.

Mary and Miss Thornton had stayed with the Buckleys until good cousin Tom had got a house ready to receive them, and then they moved up and took possession. Mary and Tom were from the first co-partners, and, latterly, Miss Thornton had invested her money, about £2000, in the station. Matters were very prosperous, and, after a few years, Tom began to get weighty and didactic in his speech, and to think of turning his attention to politics.

To Mary the past seemed like a dream—as an old dream, well-nigh forgotten. The scene was so changed that at times she could hardly believe that all those dark old days were real. Could she, now so busy and happy, be the same woman who sat worn and frightened over the dying fire with poor Captain Saxon? Is she the same woman whose husband was hurried off one wild night and transported for coining? Or is all that a hideous imagination?

No. Here is the pledge and proof that it is all too terribly real. This boy, whom she loves so wildly and fiercely, is that man's son, and his father, for aught she knows, is alive, and only a few poor hundred miles off. Never mind; let it be forgotten as though it never was. So she forgot it, and was happy.

But not always. Sometimes she could not but remember what she was, in spite of the many kind friends who surrounded her, and the new and busy life she led. Then would come a fit of despondency, almost of despair, but the natural elasticity of her temper soon dispersed these clouds, and she was her old self again.

Her very old self, indeed. That delicate-minded, intellectual old maid, Miss Thornton, used to remark with silent horror on what she called Mary's levity of behaviour with men, but more especially with honest Tom Troubridge. Many a time, when the old lady was sitting darning (she was always darning; she used to begin darning the things before they were a week out of the draper's shop), would her tears fall upon her work, as she saw Mary sitting with her child in her lap, smiling, while the audacious Tom twisted a flower in her hair, in the way that pleased him best. To see anything wrong, and to say nothing, was a thing impossible. She knew that speaking to Mary would only raise a storm, and so, knowing the man she had to deal with, she determined to speak to Tom.

She was not long without her opportunity. Duly darning one evening, while Mary was away putting her boy to bed, Tom entered from his wine. Him, with a combination of valour and judgment, she immediately attacked, acting upon a rule once laid down to Mary—"My dear, if you want to manage a man, speak to him after dinner."

"Mr. Troubridge," said Miss Thornton. "May I speak a few words to you on private affairs?"

"Madam," said Tom, drawing up a chair, "I am at your service night or day."

"A younger woman," said Miss Thornton, "might feel some delicacy in saying what I am going to say. But old age has its privileges, and so I hope to be forgiven."

"Dear Miss Thornton," said Tom, "you must be going to say something very extraordinary if it requires forgiveness from me."

"Nay, my dear kinsman," said Miss Thornton; "if we begin exchanging compliments we shall talk all night, and never get to the gist of the matter after all. Here is what I want to say. It seems to me that your attentions to our poor Mary are somewhat more than cousinly, and it behoves me to remind you that she is still a married woman. Is that too blunt? Have I offended you?"

"Nay—no," said Tom; "you could never offend me. I think you are right, too. It shall be amended, madam."

And after this Mary missed many delicate little attentions that Tom had been used to pay her. She thought he was sulky on some account at first, but soon her good sense showed her that, if they two were to live together, she must be more circumspect, or mischief would come.

For, after all, Tom had but small place in her heart. Heart filled almost exclusively with this poor sulky little lad of hers, who seemed born to trouble as the sparks went upward. In teething even, aggravating beyond experience, and afterwards suffering from the whole list of juvenile evils in such a way as boy never did before; coming out of these troubles, too, with a captious, disagreeable temper, jealous in the extreme—not a member who, on the whole, adds much to the pleasure of the little household—yet with, the blindest love towards some folks. Instance his mother, Thomas Troubridge, and Sam Buckley.

For these three the lad had a wild hysterical affection, and yet none of them had much power over him. Once by one unconsidered word arouse the boy's obstinacy and all chance of controlling him was gone. Then your only chance was to call in Miss Thornton, who had a way of managing the boy, more potent than Mary's hysterics, and Tom's indignant remonstrances, or Sam's quiet persuasions.

For instance: Once, when he was about ten years old, his mother set him to learn some lesson or another, when he had been petitioning to go off somewhere with the men. He was furiously naughty, and threw the book to the other end of the room, all the threats and scoldings of his mother proving insufficient to make him pick it up again. So that at last she went out, leaving him alone, triumphant, with Miss Thornton, who said not a word, but only raised her eyes off her work, from time to time, to look reproachfully on the rebellious boy. He could stand his mother's anger, but he could not stand those steady wondering looks that came from under the old lady's spectacles. So that, when Mary came in again, she found the book picked up and the lesson learned. Moreover, it was a fortnight before the lad misbehaved himself again.

In sickness and in health, in summer and in winter, for ten long years after they settled at Toonarbin did this noble old lady stand beside Mary as a rock of refuge in all troubles, great or small. Always serene, patient, and sensible, even to the last; for the time came when this true and faithful servant was removed from among them to receive her reward.

One morning she confessed herself unable to leave her bed; that was the first notice they had. Dr. Mayford, sent for secretly, visited her. " Break up of the constitution," said he—" no organic disease " —but shook his head. " She will go," he added, " with the first frost. I can do nothing." And Dr. Mulhaus, being consulted, said he was but an amateur doctor, but concurred with Dr. Mayford. So there was nothing to do but to wait for the end as patiently as might be.

During the summer she got out of bed and sat in a chair, which Tom used to lift dexterously into the veranda. There she would sit very quietly; sometimes getting Mrs. Buckley, who came and lived at Toonarbin that summer, to read a hymn for her; and, during this time, she told them where she would like to be buried.

On a little knoll, she said, which lay to the right of the house, barely two hundred yards from the window. Here the grass grew shorter and closer than elsewhere, and here freshened more rapidly beneath the autumn rains. Here, on winter's evenings, the slanting sunbeams lingered longest, and here, at such times, she had been accustomed to saunter, listening to the sighing of the wind in the dark funeral she-oaks and cypresses, like the far-off sea upon a sandy shore. Here, too, came oftener than elsewhere a flock of lories, making the dark, low trees gay with flying living blossoms. And here she would lie with her feet towards the east, her sightless eyes towards that dreary ocean which she would never cross again.

One fresh spring morning she sat up and talked serenely to Mrs. Buckley about matters far higher and more sacred than one likes to deal with in a tale of this kind, and, after a time, expressed a wish for a blossom of a great amaryllis which grew just in front of her window.

Mrs. Buckley got the flower for her; and so, holding the crimson-striped lily in her delicate, wasted fingers, the good old lady passed from this world without a struggle, as decently and as quietly as she had always lived in it.

This happened when Charles was about ten years old, and, for some time, the lad was subdued and sad. He used to look out of the window at night towards the grave, and wonder why they had put her they all loved so well to lie out there under the wild, sweeping winter rain. But, by degrees, he got used to the little square white railing on the she-oak knoll, and, ere half a year was gone the memory of his aunt had become very dim and indistinct.

Poor Mary, too, though a long while prepared for it, was very deeply and sincerely grieved at Miss Thornton's death; but she soon recovered from it. It came in the course of nature, and, although the house looked blank and dull for a time, yet there was too much life all around her, too much youthful happy life, to make it possible to dwell very long on the death of one who had left them full of years and honour. But Lord Frederick (before spoken of incidentally in this narrative), playing billiards at Gibraltar, about a year after this, had put into his hand a letter, from which, when opened, there fell a lock of silver-grey hair on the green cloth, which he carefully picked up, and, leaving his game, went home to his quarters. His comrades thought it was his father who was dead, and when they heard it was only his sister's old governess they wondered exceedingly; " for Fred," said they, " is not given to be sentimental."

And now, in a year or two, it began to be very difficult to keep Master Charley in order. When he was about thirteen there was a regular guerilla-war between him and his mother on the subject of learning, which ended, ultimately, in the boy flatly refusing to learn anything. His natural capacities were but small, and, under any circumstances, knowledge would only have been acquired by him with infinite pains. But, as it was, with his selfishness fostered so excessively by his mother's indulgence, and Tom's good-humoured carelessness, it became totally impossible to teach him anything. In vain his mother scolded and wept, in vain Tom represented to him the beauties and excellences of learning—learn the boy would not; so that at fourteen he was given up in despair by his mother, having learnt nearly enough of reading, writing, and ciphering to carry on the most ordinary business of life—a most lamentable state of things for a lad who, in after life, would be a rich man, and who, in a young and rapidly-rising country, might become, by the help of education, politically influential.

I think that when Samuel Buckley and James Brentwood were grown to be young men of eighteen or nineteen, and he was about seventeen or so, a stranger would have seen a great deal of difference between the two former and the latter, and would, probably, have remarked that James and Sam spoke and behaved like two gentlemen but that Charles did not, but seemed as though he had come from a lower grade in society—with some truth, too, for there was a circumstance in his bringing-up which brought him more harm than all his neglect of learning and all his mother's foolish indulgences.

Both Major Buckley and Captain Brentwood made it a law of the Medes and Persians that neither of their sons should hold any conversation with the convict servants, save in the presence of competent authorities; and, indeed, they both, as soon as increased emigration enabled them, removed their old household servants and replaced them by free men, newly arrived : a lazy independent class, certainly, with exaggerated notions of their own importance in this new phase of their life, but without the worse vices of the convicts. This rule, even in such well-regulated households, was a very hard one to get observed, even under flogging penalties; and, indeed, formed the staple affliction of poor, thoughtless Jim's early life, as this little anecdote will show:

One day, going to see Captain Brentwood, when Jim was about ten years old, I met that young gentleman (looking, I thought, a little out of sorts) about two hundred yards from the house. He turned with me to go back, and, after the first salutations, I said:

"Well, Jim, my boy, I hope you've been good since I saw you last?"

"Oh dear, no," was the answer, with a shake of the head that meant volumes.

"I'm sorry to hear that; what is the matter?"

"I've been *catching* it," said Jim, in a whisper, coming close alongside of me. "A tea-stick as thick as my forefinger all over." Here he entered into particulars, which, however, harmless in themselves, were not of a sort usually written in books.

"That's a bad job," I said; "what was it for?"

"Why, I slipped off with Jerry to look after some colts on the black swamp, and was gone all the afternoon; and so dad missed me; and when I got home didn't I *catch it*! O Lord, I'm all over blue weals; but that ain't the worst."

"What's the next misfortune?" I inquired.

"Why, when he got hold of me he said, 'Is this the first time you have been away with Jerry, sir?' and I said 'Yes' (which was the awfullest lie ever you heard, for I went over to Barker's with him two days before); then he said, 'Well, I must believe you if you say so. I shall not disgrace you by making inquiries among the men'; and then he gave it me for going that time, and since then I've felt like Cain and Abel for telling him such a lie. What would you do—eh?"

"I should tell him all about it," I said.

"Ah, but then I shall catch it again, don't you see! Hadn't I better wait till these weals are gone down?"

"I wouldn't, if I were you," I answered; "I'd tell him at once."

"I wonder why he is so particular," said Jim; "the Delisles and the Donovans spend as much of their time in the huts as they do in the house."

"And fine young blackguards they'll turn out," I said; in which I was right in those two instances. And although I have seen young fellows brought up among convicts who have turned out respectable in the end, yet it is not a promising school for good citizens.

But at Toonarbin no such precautions as these were taken with

regard to Charles. Tom was too careless, and Mary too indulgent.
It was hard enough to restrain the boy during the lesson hours,
falsely so called. And after that he was allowed to go where he
liked, and even his mother sometimes felt relieved by his absence;
so that he was continually in the men's huts, listening to their yarns
—sometimes harmless bush adventures, sometimes, perhaps, ribald
stories which he could not understand; but one day Tom Troubridge
coming by the hut looked in quietly, and saw master Charles
smoking a black pipe (he was not more than fourteen) and heard
such a conversation going on that he advanced suddenly upon them
and ordered the boy home in a sterner tone than he had ever used
to him before, and looked out of the door till he had disappeared.
Then he turned round to the men.

There were three of them, all convicts, one of whom, the one he
had heard talking when he came in, was a large, desperate-looking
fellow. When these men mean to deprecate your anger, I have
remarked they always look you blankly in the face; but if they
mean to defy you and be impudent they never look at you but
always begin fumbling and fidgeting with something. So when Tom
saw that the big man before mentioned (Daniel Harvey by name)
was stooping down before the fire, he knew he was going to have
a row, and waited.

"So, boss," began the ruffian, not looking at him, "we ain't fit
company for the likes of that kinchin—eh?"

"You're not fit company for any man except the hangman," said
Tom, looking more like six-foot-six than six-foot-three.

"Oh, my —— colonial oath!" said the other; "oh my ——
'cabbage tree!' So there's going to be a coil about that scrubby
little myrnonger, eh? Don't you fret your bingy, boss; he'll be as
good a man as his father yet."

For an instant a dark shadow passed over Tom's face.

"So," he thought," "these fellows know all about George Hawker,
eh? Well, never mind; what odds if they do?" And then he
said aloud, turning round on Harvey, "Look you here, you dog;
if I ever hear of your talking in that style before that boy, or
any other boy, by George I'll twist your head off!"

He advanced towards him, as if to perform that feat on the
spot; in a moment the convict had snatched his knife from his
belt and rushed upon him.

Very suddenly indeed; but not quite quick enough to take the
champion of Devon by surprise. Ere he was well within reach Tom
had seized the hand that held the knife, and with a backward kick

of his left foot sent the embryo assassin sprawling on his back on the top of the fire, whence Tom dragged him by his heels, far more astonished than burnt. The other two men had, meanwhile, sat taking no notice, or seeming to take none, of the disturbance. Now, however, one of them spoke, and said:

"I'm sure, sir, you didn't hear me say nothing wrong to the young gent," and so on, in a whining tone, till Tom cut him short by saying that "if he had any more nonsense among them, he would send 'em all three over to Captain Desborough, to the tune of fifty (lashes) a-piece."

After this little *émeute* Charles did not dare to go into the huts, and soon after these three men were exchanged. But there remained one man whose conversation and teaching, though not, perhaps, so openly outrageously villainous as that of the worthy Harvey, still had a very unfortunate effect on his character.

This was a rather small, wiry, active man, by name Jackson, a native, colonially convicted, very clever among horses, a capital lightweight boxer, and in running superb, a pupil and protege of the immortal "flying pieman" (may his shadow never be less!), a capital cricketer, and a supreme humbug. This man, by his various accomplishments and great tact had won a high place in Tom Troubridge's estimation, and was put in a place of trust among the horses; consequently having continual access to Charles, to whom he made himself highly agreeable, as being heir to the property; giving him such insights into the worst side of sporting life, and such truthful accounts of low life in Sydney, as would have gone far to corrupt a lad of far stronger moral principle than he.

And so, between this teaching of evil and neglect of good, Mary Hawker's boy did not grow up all that might be desired. And at seventeen, I am sorry to say, he got into a most disreputable connexion with a Highland girl, at one of the Donovans' out-station huts; which caused his kindly guardian, Tom Troubridge, a great deal of vexation, and his mother the deepest grief, which was much increased at the same time by something I will relate in the next chapter.

So sixteen years rolled peacefully away, chequered by such trifling lights and shadows as I have spoken of. The new generation, the children of those whom we knew at first, are now ready to take their places, and bear themselves with more or less credit in what may be going on. And now comes a period which in the memory of all those whom I have introduced to you ranks as the most important of their lives. To me, looking back upon nearly sixty years of memory, the events which are coming stand out from the rest of my quiet life, well defined and remarkable, above all others. As looking on our western moors, one sees the long, straight sky-line, broken only once in many miles by some fantastic Tor.

CHAPTER XXIV

IN WHICH MARY HAWKER LOSES ONE OF HER OLDEST SWEETHEARTS

SIXTEEN years of peace and plenty had rolled over the heads of James Stockbridge and myself, and we had grown to be rich. Our agent used to rub his hands and bow whenever our high mightinesses visited town. There was money in the bank, there was claret in the cellar, there were racehorses in the paddock; in short, we were wealthy, prosperous men—James a magistrate.

November set in burning hot, and by the tenth the grass was as dry as stubble; still we hoped for a thunderstorm and a few days' rain, but none came. December wore wearily on, and by Christmas the smaller creeks, except those which were snow-fed, were reduced to a few muddy pools, and vast quantities of cattle were congregated within easy reach of the river, from other people's runs, miles away.

Of course, feed began to get very scarce, yet we were hardly so bad off yet as our neighbours, for we had just parted with every beast we could spare, at high prices, to Port Phillip, and were only waiting for the first rains to start after store cattle, which were somewhat hard to get near the new colony.

No rain yet, and we were in the end of January; the fountains of heaven were dried up, but now all round the northern horizon the bush-fires burnt continually, a pillar of smoke by day, and a pillar of fire by night.

Nearer, by night, like an enemy creeping up to a beleagured town. The weather had been very still for some time, and we took precaution to burn great strips of grass all round the paddocks to the north, but, in spite of all our precautions, I knew that, should a strong wind come on from that quarter, nothing short of a miracle would save us.

But as yet the weather was very still, not very bright, but rather cloudy, and a dense haze of smoke was over everything, making the distances look ten times as far as they really were, and rendering the whole landscape as grey and melancholy as you can conceive. There was nothing much to be done but to sit in the veranda, drinking claret-and-water, and watching and hoping for a thunderstorm.

On the third of February the heat was worse than ever, but there was no wind; and as the sun went down among the lurid smoke, red as blood, I thought I made out a few white brush-shaped clouds rising in the north.

Jim and I sat there late, not talking much. We knew that if we were to be burnt out our loss would be very heavy; but we thanked God that even were we to lose everything it would not be irreparable, and that we should still be wealthy. Our brood mares and racing stock were our greatest anxiety. We had a good stock of hay, by which we might keep them alive for another month, supposing all the grass was burnt; but if we lost that our horses would probably die. I said at last:

" Jim, we may make up our minds to have the run swept. The fire is burning up now."

" Yes, it is brightening," said he, " but it must be twenty miles off still, and if it comes down with a gentle wind we shall save the paddocks and hay. There is a good deal of grass in the lower paddock. I am glad we had the forethought not to feed it down. Well, fire or no fire, I shall go to bed."

We went to bed, and, in spite of anxiety, mosquitoes, and heat, I fell asleep. In the grey morning I was awakened, nearly suffocated, by a dull continuous roar. It was the wind in the chimney. The north wind, so long imprisoned, had broke loose, and the boughs were crashing, and the trees were falling, before the majesty of his wrath.

I ran out, and met James in the veranda. " It's all up," I said. " Get the women and children into the river, and let the men go up to windward with the sheep-skins.* I'll get on horseback, and go out and see how the Morgans get on. That obstinate fellow will wish he had come in now."

Morgan was a stockman of ours, who lived, with a wife and two children, about eight miles to the northward. We always thought it would have been better for him to move in, but he had put it off, and now the fire had taken us by surprise.

I rode away, dead up-wind.   Our station had a few large trees about it, and then all was clear plain and short grass for two miles;

---

*Sheep-skins, on sticks, used for beating out the fire when in short grass.

after that came scrubby ranges, in an open glade of which the Morgans' hut stood. I feared, from the density of the smoke, that the fire had reached them already, but I thought it my duty to go and see, for I might meet them fleeing, and help them with the children.

I had seen many bush-fires, but never such a one as this. The wind was blowing a hurricane, and, when I had ridden about two miles into scrub, high enough to brush my horse's belly, I began to get frightened. Still I persevered, against hope; the heat grew more fearful every moment; but I reflected that I had often ridden up close to a bush-fire, turned when I began to see the flame through the smoke, and cantered away from it easily.

Then it struck me that I had never yet seen a bush-fire in such a hurricane as this. Then I remembered stories of men riding for their lives, and others of burnt horses and men found in the bush. And, now, I saw a sight which made me turn in good earnest.

I was in lofty timber, and, as I paused, I heard the mighty crackling of fire coming through the wood. At the same instant the blinding smoke burst into a million tongues of flickering flame, and I saw the fire—not where I had ever seen it before—not creeping along among the scrub—but up aloft, a hundred and fifty feet overhead. It had caught the dry bituminous tops of the higher boughs, and was flying along from tree-top to tree-top like lightning. Below, the wind was comparatively moderate, but, up there, it was travelling twenty miles an hour. I saw one tree ignite like gun-cotton, and then my heart grew small, and I turned and fled.

I rode as I never rode before. There were three miles to go ere I cleared the forest, and got among the short grass, where I could save myself—three miles! Ten minutes nearly of intolerable heat, blinding smoke, and mortal terror. Any death but this! Drowning were pleasant, glorious to sink down into the cool sparkling water. But, to be burnt alive! Fool that I was to venture so far! I would give all my money now to be naked and penniless, rolling about in a cool pleasant river.

The maddened, terrified horse went like the wind, but not like the hurricane—that was too swift for us. The fire had outstripped us overhead, and I could see it dimly through the infernal choking reek, leaping and blazing a hundred yards before us, among the feathery foliage, devouring it, as the south wind devours the thunder-clouds. Then I could see nothing. Was I clear of the forest? Thank the Lord, yes—I was riding over grass.

I managed to pull up the horse, and as I did so, a mob of kangaroos blundered by, blinded, almost against me, noticing me no more in their terror than if I had been a stump or a stone. Soon the fire came hissing along through the grass scarcely six inches high, and I walked my horse through it; then I tumbled off on the blackened ground, and felt as if I should die.

I lay there on the hot black ground. My head felt like a block of stone, and my neck was stiff so that I could not move my head. My throat was swelled and dry as a sand-hill, and there was a roaring in my ears like a cataract. I thought of the cool water-falls among the rocks far away in Devon. I thought of everything that was cold and pleasant, and then came into my head about Dives praying for a drop of water. I tried to get up, but could not, so lay down again with my head upon my arm.

It grew cooler, and the atmosphere was clearer. I got up, and, mounting my horse, turned homeward. Now I began to think about the station. Could it have escaped? Impossible! The fire would fly a hundred yards or more such a day as this even in low plain. No, it must be gone! There was a great roll in the plain between me and home, so that I could see nothing of our place—all around the country was black, without a trace of vegetation. Behind me were the smoking ruins of the forest I had escaped from, where now the burnt-out trees began to thunder down rapidly, and before, to the south, I could see the fire raging miles away.

So the station is burnt, then? No! For as I top the ridge, there it is before me, standing as of old—a bright oasis in the desert of burnt country round! Ay! the very haystack is safe! And the paddocks?—all right!—glory be to God!

I got home, and James came running to meet me.

"I was getting terribly frightened, old man," said he. "I thought you were caught. Lord save us, you look ten years older than you did this morning!"

I tried to answer, but could not speak for drought. He ran and got me a great tumbler of claret-and-water; and, in the evening, having drunk about an imperial gallon of water, and taken after-wards some claret, I felt pretty well revived.

Men were sent out at once to see after the Morgans, and found them perfectly safe, but very much frightened; they had, however, saved their hut, for the fire had passed before the wind had got to its full strength.

So we were delivered from the fire; but still no rain. All day, for the next month, the hot north wind would blow till five o'clock, and then a cool southerly breeze would come up and revive us; but still the heavens were dry, and our cattle died by hundreds.

On the eighteenth of March, we sat in the veranda looking still over the blackened unlovely prospect, but now cheerfully and with hope; for the eastern sky was piled up range beyond range with the scarlet and purple splendour of cloudland, and, as darkness gathered, we saw the lightning, not twinkling and glimmering harmlessly about the horizon, as it had been all the summer, but falling sheer in violet-coloured rivers behind the dark curtain of rain that hung from the black edge of a teeming thunder-cloud.

We had asked our overseer in that night, being Saturday, to drink with us; he sat very still, and talked but little, as was his wont. I slapped him on the back, and said:

"Do you remember, Geordie, that muff in Thalaba who chose the wrong cloud? He should have got you or me to choose for him; we wouldn't have made a mistake, I know. We would have chosen such a one as yon glorious big-bellied fellow. See how grandly he comes growling up!"

"It's just come," said he, "without the praying for. When the fire came over the hill the other day, I just put up a bit prayer to the Lord, that He'd spare the haystack, and He spared it. (I didna stop working, ye ken; I worked the harder; if ye dinna mean to work, ye should na pray.) But I never prayed for rain—I didna, ye see, like to ask the Lord to upset all His gran' laws of electricity and evaporation, just because it would suit us. I thocht He'd likely ken better than mysel. Hech, sirs, but that chiel's riding hard!"

A horseman appeared making for the station at full speed; when he was quite close, Jim called out, "By Jove, it is Dr. Mulhaus!" and we ran out into the yard to meet him.

Before any one had time to speak, he shouted out: "My dear boys, I'm so glad I am in time: we are going to see one of the grandest electrical disturbances it has ever been my lot to witness. I reined up just now to look, and I calculated that the southern point of explosion alone is discharging nine times in the minute. How is your barometer?"

"Haven't looked, Doctor."

"Careless fellow," he replied, "you don't deserve to have one."

"Never mind, sir, we have got you safe and snug out of the thunderstorm. It is going to be very heavy, I think. I only hope we will have plenty of rain."

"Not much doubt of it," said he. "Now, come into the veranda and let us watch the storm."

We went and sat there; the highest peaks of the great cloud alps, lately brilliant red, were now cold silver-grey, harshly defined against a faint crimson background, and we began to hear the thunder rolling and muttering. All else was deadly still and heavy.

"Mark the lightning!" said the Doctor; "that which is before the rain-wall is white, and that behind violet-coloured. Here comes the thunder-gust."

A fierce blast of wind came hurrying on, carrying a cloud of dust and leaves before it. It shook the four corners of the house and passed away. And now it was a fearful sight to see the rain-spouts pouring from the black edge of the lower cloud as from a pitcher, nearly overhead, and lit up by a continuous blaze of lightning. Another blast of wind, now a few drops, and in ten minutes you could barely distinguish the thunder above the rattle of the rain on the shingles.

It warred and banked around us for an hour, so that we could hardly hear one another speak. At length the Doctor bawled:

"We shall have a crack closer than any yet, you'll see; we always have one particular one—our atmosphere is not restored to its balance yet—there!"

The curtains were drawn, and yet, for an instant, the room was as bright as day. Simultaneously there came a crack and an explosion, so loud and terrifying, that, used as I was to such an event, I involuntarily jumped up from my seat.

"Are you all right here?" said the Doctor; and, running out into the kitchen, shouted, "Anyone hurt?"

The kitchen girl said that the lightning had run all down her back like cold water, and the housekeeper averred that she thought the thunder had taken the roof of the house off. So we soon perceived that nothing was the matter, and sat down again to our discourse, and our supper. "Well," began I, "here's the rain come at last. In a fortnight there will be good grass again. We ought to start and get some store-cattle."

"But where?" replied James. "We shall have to go a long way for them; every one will be wanting the same thing now. We must push a long way north, and make a depot somewhere westward. Then we can pick them up by sixes and sevens at a time. When shall we go?"

"The sooner the better."

"I think I will come with you," said the Doctor. "I have not been a journey for some time."

"Your conversation, sir," I said, "will shorten the journey by one-half"—which was sincerely said.

Away we went northward, with the mountains on our left, leaving snow-streaked Kosciusko nearly behind us, till a great pass, through the granite walls, opened to the westward, up which we turned, Mount Murray towering up the south. Soon we were on the Murrumbidgee, sweeping from side to side of his mountain valley in broad curves, sometimes rushing hoarse, swollen by the late rains, under beds of high timber, and sometimes dividing broad meadows of rich grass, growing green once more under the invigorating hand of autumn. All nature had awakened from her deep summer sleep, the air was brisk and nimble, and seldom did three happier men ride on their way that James, the Doctor, and I.

Good Doctor! How he beguiled the way with his learning—in ecstasies all the time, enjoying everything, animate or inanimate, as you or I would enjoy a new play or a new opera. How I envied him! He was like a man always reading a new and pleasant book. At first the stockmen rode behind, talking about beasts, and horses, and what not—often talking about nothing at all, but riding along utterly without thought, if such a thing could be. But soon I noticed they would draw up closer, and regard the Doctor with some sort of attention, till towards the evening of the second day, one of them, our old acquaintance Dick, asked the Doctor a question, as to why, if I remember right, certain trees should grow in certain localities, and there only. The Doctor reined up alongside him directly, and in plain forcible language explained the matter: how that some plants required more of one sort of substance than another, and how they get it out of particular soils; and how, in the lapse of years, they had come to thrive best on the soil that suited them, and had got stunted and died out in other parts. "See," said he, "how the turkey holds to the plains, and the lyre-bird to the scrub, because each one finds its food there. Trees cannot move; but by time, and by positively refusing to grow on unkindly soils, they arrange themselves in the localities which suit them best."

So after this they rode with the Doctor always, both hearing him and asking him questions, and at last, won by his blunt kindliness, they grew to like and respect him in their way, even as we did.

So we fared on through bad weather and rough country, enjoying a journey which, but for him, would have been a mere trial of patience. Northward ever, through forest and plain, over mountain and swamp, across sandstone, limestone, granite, and rich volcanic land, each marked distinctly by a varying vegetation. Sometimes we would camp out, but oftener managed to reach a station at night. We got well across the dry country between the Murrumbidgee and the Lachlan, now abounding with pools of water; and, having crossed the latter river, held on our course towards Croker's Range, which we skirted; and, after having been about a fortnight out, arrived at the lowest station on the Macquarie late in the afternoon.

This was our present destination. The owner was a friend of ours, who gave us a hearty welcome, and, on our inquiries as to store cattle, thought that we might pick up a good mob of them from one station or another. "We might," said he, "make a depot for them, as we collected them, on some unoccupied land down the river. It was poor country, but there was grass enough to keep them alive. He would show us a good place, in a fork, where it was impossible to cross on two sides, and where they would be easily kept together; that was, if we liked to risk it."

"Risk what?" we asked.

"Blacks," said he. "They are mortal troublesome just now down the river. I thought we had quieted them, but they have been up to their old games lately, spearing cattle, and so on. I don't like, in fact, to go to far down there alone. I don't think they are Macquarie blacks; I fancy they must have come up from the Darling, through the marshes."

We thought we should have no reason to be afraid with such a strong party as ours; and Owen, our host, having some spare cattle, we were employed for the next three days in getting them in. We got nearly a hundred head from him.

The first morning we got there the Doctor had vanished; but the third evening, as we were sitting down to supper, in he came, dead beat, with a great bag full of stones. When we had drawn round the fire, I said:

"Have you got any new fossils for us to see?"

"Not one," said he; "only some minerals."

"Do not you think, sir," said Owen, our host, "that there are some ores of metals round this country? The reason I ask you is, we so often pick up curious-coloured stones, like those we get from the miners at home, in Wales, where I come from."

"I think you will find some rich mines near here soon. Stay; it can do you no harm. I will tell you something: three days ago

I followed up the river, and about twenty miles above this spot I became attracted by the conformation of the country, and remarked it as being very similar to some very famous spots in South America. 'Here,' I said to myself, 'Maximilian, you have your volcanic disturbance, your granite, your clay, slate, and sandstone upheaved, and seamed with quartz—why should you not discover here, what is certainly here, more or less?'—I looked patiently for two days, and I will show you what I found."

He went to his bag and fetched an angular stone about as big as one's fist. It was white, stained on one side with rust-colour, but in the heart veined with a bright yellow metallic substance, in some places running in delicate veins into the stone, in others breaking out in large shining lumps.

"That's iron-pyrites," said I, as pat as you please.

"Goose!" said the Doctor; "look again."

I looked again, it was certainly different to iron-pyrites; it was brighter, it ran in veins into the stone; it was lumpy, solid, and clean. I said, "It is very beautiful; tell us what it is?"

"Gold!" said he triumphantly, getting up and walking about the room in an excited way; "that little stone is worth a pound; there is a quarter of an ounce in it. Give me ten tons, only ten cartloads such stone as that, and I would buy a principality."

Every one crowded round the stone open-mouthed, and James said:

"Are you sure it is gold, Doctor?"

"He asks me if I know gold when I see it—me, you understand, who has scientifically examined all the best mines in Peru, not to mention the Minas Geraés in the Brazils! My dear fellow, to a man who has once seen it, native gold is unmistakable, utterly so; there is nothing at all like it."

"But this is a remarkable discovery, sir," said Owen. "What are you going to do?"

"I shall go to the Government," said he, "and make the best bargain I can."

I had better mention here that he afterwards did go to the Government, and announce his discovery. Rather to the Doctor's disgust, however, though he acknowledged the wisdom of the thing, the courteous and able gentleman who then represented his Majesty, informed him that he was perfectly aware of the existence of gold, but that he for one should assert the prerogative of the Crown, and prevent anyone mining on Crown-lands; as he considered that, were the gold abundant, the effects on the convict population would be eminently disastrous. To which obvious piece of good sense the Doctor bowed his head, and the whole thing passed into oblivion—so much so, that when I heard of Hargraves's discovery in 1851, I had nearly forgotten the Doctor's gold adventure; and I may here state my belief that the knowledge of its existence was confined to very few, and those well-educated men, who never guessed (how could they without considerable workings?) how abundant it was. As for the stories of shepherds finding gold and selling it to the Jews in Sydney, they are very mythical, and I for one entirely disbelieved them.

In time we had collected about 250 head of cattle from various points into the fork of the river, which lay farther down, some seven miles, than his house. As yet we had not been troubled by the blackfellows. Those we had seen seemed pretty civil, and we had not allowed them to get familiar; but this pleasant state of things was not to last. James and the Doctor, with one man, were away for the very last mob, and I was sitting before the fire at the camp, when Dick, who was left behind with me, asked for my gun to go and shoot a duck. I lent it him, and away he went, while I mounted my horse and rode slowly about, heading back such of the cattle as appeared to be wandering too far.

I heard a shot, and almost immediately another; then I heard a queer sort of scream, which puzzled me extremely. I grew frightened and rode towards the quarter where the shots came from, and almost immediately heard a loud coo-ee. I replied, and then I saw Dick limping along through the bushes, peering about him and holding his gun as one does when expecting a bird to rise. Suddenly he raised his gun and fired. Out dashed a blackfellow from his hiding-place, running across the open, and with his second barrel Dick rolled him over. Then I saw half a dozen others rise, shaking their spears; but seeing me riding up, and supposing I was armed, they made off.

" How did this come about, Dick, my lad?" said I. " This is a bad job."

" Well," he said, " I just fired at a duck, and the moment my gun was gone off, up jumped half a dozen of them, and sent a shower of spears at me, and one has gone into my leg. They must a' thought that I had a single-barrel gun and waited till I'd fired it; but they found their mistake, the devils; for I gave one of them a charge of shot in his stomach at twenty yards, and dropped him; they threw a couple more spears, but both missed, and I hobbled out as well as I could, loading as I went with a couple of tallow cartridges. I saw this other beast skulking, and missed him first time, but he has got something to remember me by now."

"Do you think you can ride to the station and get some help?" said I. "I wish the others were back."

"Yes," he replied, "I will manage it, but I don't like to leave you alone."

"One must stay," I said, "and better the sound man than the wounded one. Come, start off, and let me get to the camp, or they will be plundering that next."

I started him off and ran back to the camp. Everything was safe as yet, and the ground round being clear, and having a double-barrel gun and two pistols, I was not so very much frightened. It is no use to say I was perfectly comfortable, because I wasn't. A Frenchman writing this, would represent himself as smoking a cigar, and singing with the greatest nonchalance. I did neither. Being an Englishman, I may be allowed to confess that I did not like it.

I had fully made up my mind to fire on the first black who showed himself, but I did not get the opportunity. In about two hours I heard a noise of men shouting and whips cracking, and the Doctor and James rode up with a fresh lot of cattle.

I told them what had happened, and we agreed to wait and watch till news should come from the station, and then to start. There was, as we thought, but little danger while there were four or five together; but the worst of it was, that we were but poorly armed. However, at nightfall, Owen and one of his men came down, reporting that Dick, who had been speared, was getting all right, and bringing also three swords, and a brace of pistols.

James and I took a couple of swords, and began fencing, in play.

"I see," said the Doctor, "that you know the use of a sword, you two."

"Lord bless you!" I said, "we were in the Yeomanry (Land-wehr you call it); weren't we, Jim? I was a corporal."

"I wish," said Owen, "that, now we are together, five of us, you would come and give these fellows a lesson; they want it badly."

"Indeed," I said, "I think they have had lesson enough for the present. Dick has put down two of them. Beside, we could not leave the cattle."

"I am sorry," said James, "that any of our party has had this collision with them. I cannot bear shooting the poor brutes. Let us move out of this, homeward, to-morrow morning."

Just before dark, who should come riding down from the station but Dick!—evidently in pain, but making believe that he was quite comfortable.

"Why, Dick, my boy," I said, "I thought you were in bed; you ought to be, at any rate."

"Oh, there's nothing much the matter with me, Mr. Hamlyn," he said. "You will have some trouble with these fellows, unless I am mistaken. *I was told to look after you once,* and I mean to do it."

(He referred to the letter that Lee had sent him years before.)

That night Owen stayed with us at the camp. We set a watch, and he took the morning spell. Everything passed off quietly; but when we came to examine our cattle in the morning, the lot that James had brought in the night before were gone.

The river, flooded when we first came, had now lowered considerably, so that the cattle could cross if they really tried. These last, being wild and restless, had gone over, and we soon found the marks of them across the river.

The Doctor, James, Dick, and I started off after them, having armed ourselves for security. We took a sword a-piece, and each had a pistol. The ground was moist, and the beasts easily tracked; so we thought an easy job was before us, but we soon changed our minds.

Following on the trail of the cattle, we very soon came on the footsteps of a blackfellow, evidently more recent than the hoof-marks; then another footstep joined in, and another, and at last we made out that above a dozen blacks were tracking our cattle, and were between us and them.

Still we followed the trail as fast as we could. I was uneasy for we were insufficiently armed, but I found time to point out to the Doctor, what he had never remarked before, the wonderful difference between the naked footprint of a white man and a savage. The white man leaves the impression of his whole sole, every toe being distinctly marked, while your blackfellow leaves scarce any toe-marks, but seems merely to spurn the ground with the ball of his foot.

I felt very ill at ease. The morning was raw, and a dense fog was over everything. One always feels wretched on such a morning, but on that one I felt miserable. There was an indefinable horror over me, and I talked more than anyone, glad to hear the sound of my own voice.

Once the Doctor turned round and looked at me fixedly from under his dark eyebrows. "Hamlyn," he said, "I don't think you are well; you talk fast, and are evidently nervous. We are in no danger, I think, but you seem as if you were frightened."

"So I am, Doctor, but I don't know what at."

Jim was riding first, and he turned and said, "I have lost the blackfellows' tracks entirely: here are the hoof-marks, safe enough but no footprints, and the ground seems to be rising."

The fog was very thick, so that we could see nothing above a hundred yards from us. We had come through forest all the way, and were wet with pushing through low shrubs. As we paused came a puff of air, and in five minutes the fog had rolled away, and a clear blue sky and a bright sun were overhead.

Now we could see where we were. We were in the lower end of a precipitous mountain-gully, narrow where we were, and growing rapidly narrower, as we advanced. In the fog we had followed the cattle-track right into it, passing, unobserved, two great heaps of tumbled rocks which walled the glen; they were thickly fringed with scrub, and it immediately struck me that they stood just in the place where we had lost the track of the blackfellows.

I should have mentioned this, but, at this moment, James caught sight of the lost cattle, and galloped off after them; we followed, and very quickly we had headed them down the glen, and were posting homeward as hard as we could go.

I remember well there was a young bull among them that took the lead. As he came nearly opposite the two piles of rock which I have mentioned, I saw a blackfellow leap on a boulder, and send a spear into him.

He headed back, and the other beasts came against him. Before we could pull up we were against the cattle, and then all was confusion and disaster. Two hundred blackfellows were on us at once, shouting like devils, and sending down their spears upon us like rain. I heard the Doctor's voice, above all the infernal din, crying "Viva! Swords, my boys; take your swords!" I heard two pistol shots, and then, with deadly wrath in my heart, I charged at a crowd of them, who were huddled together, throwing their spears wildly, and laid about me with my cutlass like a madman.

I saw them scrambling up over the rocks in wild confusion; then I heard the Doctor calling me to come on. He had reined up, and a few of the discomfited savages were throwing spears at him from a long distance. When he saw me turn to come, he turned also, and rode after James, who was two hundred yards ahead, reeling in his saddle like a drunken man, grinding his teeth, and making fierce clutches at a spear which was buried deep in his side, and which at last he succeeded in tearing out. He went a few yards farther, and then fell off his horse on the ground.

We were both off in a moment, but when I got his head on my lap, I saw he was dying. The Doctor looked at the wound, and shook his head. I took his right hand in mine, and the other I held upon his true and faithful heart, until I felt it flutter, and stop for ever.

Then I broke down altogether. "Oh! good old friend! Oh! dear old friend, could you not wait for me? Shall I never see you again?"

Yes! I think that I shall see him again. When I have crossed the dark river which we must all cross, I think he will be one of those who come down to meet me from the gates of the Everlasting City.

"A man," said the Doctor to me, two days after, when we were sitting together in the station parlour, "who approached as nearly the model which our Great Master has left us as any man I know. I studied and admired him for many years, and now I cannot tell you not to mourn. I can give you no comfort for the loss of such a man, save it be to say that you and I may hope to meet him again, and learn new lessons from him, in a better place than this."

CHAPTER XXV

IN WHICH THE NEW DEAN OF B—— MAKES HIS APPEARANCE, AND ASTONISHES THE MAJOR OUT OF HIS PROPRIETY

ONE evening towards the end of that winter Mrs. Buckley and Sam sat alone before the fire, in the quickly-gathering darkness. The candles were yet unlighted, but the cheerful flickering light produced by the combustion of three or four logs of she-oak, topped by one of dead gum, shone most pleasantly on the well-ordered dining-room, on the close-drawn curtains, on the nicely-polished furniture, on the dinner-table, laid with fair array of white linen, silver, and glass, but, above all, on the honest, quiet face of Sam, who sat before his mother in an easy-chair, with his head back, fast asleep.

While she is alternately casting glances of pride and affection towards her sleeping son, and keen looks on the gum log, in search of centipedes, let us take a look at her ourselves, and see how sixteen years have behaved to that handsome face. There is change here, but no deterioration. It is a little rounder perhaps, and also a little fuller in colour, but there are no lines there yet. " Happiness and ceaseless good temper don't make many wrinkles, even in a warmer climate than old England," says the Major, and says also, confidentially, to Brentwood, " Put a red camellia in her hair, and send her to the opera even now, and see what a sensation she would make, though she is nearer fifty than forty "—which was strictly true, although said by her husband, for the raven hair is as black as it was when decorated with the moss-roses of Clere, and the eye is as brilliant as ever it was.

Now, the beautiful profile is turned again towards the sleeper as he moves. " Poor boy! " she said. " He is quite knocked up. He must have been twenty-four hours in the saddle. However, he had better be after cattle than in a billiard-room. I wonder if his father will be home to-night."

Suddenly Sam awoke. " Heigho! " said he. " I'm nice company, mother. Have I been asleep? "

" Only for an hour or so, my boy," said she. " See; I've been defending you while you slumbered. I have killed three centipedes, which came out of that old gum log. I cut this big one in half with the fire-shovel, and the head part walked away as if nothing had happened. I must tell the man not to give us rotten wood, or some of us will be getting a nip. It's a long fifty miles from Captain Brentwood's," said Mrs. Buckley, after a time. " And that's a very good day's work for little Bronsewing, carrying your father."

" And what has been the news since I have been away—eh, mother? "

" Why, the greatest news is that the Donovans have sold their station, and are off to Port Phillip."

" All the world is moving there," said Sam. " Who has he sold it to? "

" That I can't find out.—There's your father, my love."

There was the noise of horses' feet and merry voices in the little gravelled yard behind the house, heard above a joyous barking of dogs. Sam ran out to hold his father's horse, and soon after came into the room again, accompanied by his father and Captain Brentwood.

After the first greetings were over, candles were lighted, and the three men stood on the hearth-rug together—a very remarkable group, as you would have said, had you seen them. You might go a long while in any country without seeing three such men in company.

Captain Brentwood, of artillery renown, was a square, powerfully built man, say five-foot-ten in height. His face, at first sight, appeared rather a stupid one beside the Major's, expressing rather determination than intelligence; but once engage him in a conversation which interested him, and you would be surprised to see how animated it would become. Then the man, usually so silent, would open up the store-house of his mind, speaking with an eloquence and a force which would surprise one who did not know him, and which made the Doctor often take the losing side of an argument for the purpose of making him speak. Add to this that he was a thoroughly amiable man, and, as Jim would tell you (in spite of a certain severe whipping you wot of), a most indulgent and excellent father.

Major Buckley's shadow had grown no less—nay, rather greater, since first we knew him. In other respects, there was very little alteration, except that his curling brown hair had grown thinner about the temples, and was receding a little from his forehead. But what cared he for that! He was not the last of the Buckleys.

One remarks now, as the two stand together, that Sam, though but nineteen, is very nearly as tall as his father, and promises to be as broad across the shoulders, some day, being an exception to colonially-bred men in general, who are long and narrow. He is standing and talking to his father.

"Well, Sam," said the Major, "so you're back safe—eh, my boy! A rough time, I don't doubt. Strange store-cattle are queer to drive at any time, particularly such weather as you have had."

"And such a lot, too!" said Sam. "Tell you what, father, it's lucky you got them cheap, for the half of them are off the ranges."

"Scrubbers, eh?" said the Major; "well, we must take what we can catch, with this Port Phillip rush. Let's sit down to dinner; I've got some news that will please you, Fish, eh? See there, Brentwood! What do you think of that for a black-fish? What was his weight, my dear?"

"Seven pounds and a half, as the blackfellows brought him in," said Mrs. Buckley.

"A very pretty fish," said the Major. "My dear, what is the news?"

"Why, the Donovans have sold their station."

"Ha! ha!" laughed the Major. "Why, we have come from there to-day. Why, we were there last night at a grand party. All the

Irishmen in the country-side. Such a turmoil I haven't seen since I was quartered at Cove. So that's your news—eh?"

"And so you stepped on there without calling at home, did you," said Mrs. Buckley. "And perhaps you know who the purchaser is?"

"Don't you know, my love?"

"No, indeed!" said Mrs. Buckley. "I have been trying to find out these two days. It would be very pleasant to have a good neighbour there—not that I wish to speak evil of the Donovans; but really they did go on in such terrible style, you know, that one could not go there. Now, tell me who has bought Garoopna."

"One Brentwood, captain of artillery."

"Nonsense!" said Mrs. Buckley. "Is he not joking now, Captain Brentwood? That is far too good news to be true."

"It is true, nevertheless, madam," said Captain Brentwood. "I thought it would meet with your approval, and I can see by Sam's face that it meets with his. You see, my dear, Buckley has got to be rather necessary to me. I miss him when he is absent, and I want to be more with him. Again, I am very fond of my son Jim, and my son Jim is very fond of your son Sam, and is always coming here after him when he ought to be at home. So I think I shall see more of him when we are ten miles apart than when we are fifty. And, once more, my daughter Alice, now completing her education in Sydney, comes home to keep house for me in a few months, and I wish her to have the advantage of the society of the lady whom I honour and respect above all others. So I have bought Garoopna."

"If that courtly bow is intended for me, my dear Captain," said Mrs. Buckley, "as I cannot but think it is, believe me that your daughter shall be as my daughter."

"Teach her to be in some slight degree like yourself, Mrs. Buckley," said the Captain, "and you will put me under obligations which I can never repay."

"Altogether, wife," said the Major, "it is the most glorious arrangement that ever was come to. Let us take a glass of sherry all round on it. Sam, my lad, your hand! Brentwood, we have none of us ever seen your daughter. She should be handsome."

"You remember her mother?" said the Captain.

"Who could ever forget Lady Kate who had once seen her?" said the Major.

"Well, Alice is more beautiful than her mother ever was."

There went across the table a bright electric spark out of Mrs.

Buckley's eye into her husband's, as rapid as those which move the quivering telegraph needles, and yet not unobserved, I think, by Captain Brentwood, for there grew upon his face a pleasant smile, which, rapidly broadening, ended in a low laugh, by no means disagreeable to hear, though Sam wondered what the joke could be until the Captain said:

"An altogether comical party that last night at the Donovans', Buckley; the most comical I ever was at."

Nevertheless, I don't believe that it was that which made him laugh at all.

"A capital party!" said the Major, laughing. "Do you know, Brentwood, I always liked those Donovans, under the rose, and last night I liked them better than ever. They were not such very bad neighbours, although old Donovan wanted to fight a duel with me once. At all events, the welcome I got last night will make me remember them kindly in future."

"I must go down and call there before they go," said Mrs. Buckley. "People who have been our neighbours for so many years must not go away without a kind farewell. Was Desborough there?"

"Indeed, he was. Don't you know he is related to the Donovans?"

"Impossible!"

"Fact, my dear, I assure you, according to Mrs. Donovan, who told me that the De Novans and the Desboroughs were cognate Norman families, who settled in Ireland together, and have since frequently intermarried."

"I suppose," said Mrs. Buckley, laughing, "that Desborough did not deny it."

"Not at all, my dear: as he said to me privately, 'Buckley, never deny a relationship with a man worth forty thousand pounds, the least penny, though your ancestors' bones should move in their graves.'"

"I suppose," said Mrs. Buckley, "that he made himself as agreeable as usual."

"As usual, my dear. He made even Brentwood laugh; he danced all the evening with that giddy girl Lesbia Burke, who let slip that she remembered me at Naples, in 1805, when she was there with that sad old set, and who consequently must be nearly as old as myself."

"I hope you danced with her," said Mrs. Buckley.

"Indeed I did, my dear. And she wore a wreath of yellow chrysanthemum, no other flowers being obtainable. I assure you we 'kept the flure' in splendid style."

They were all laughing at the idea of the Major dancing, when Sam exclaimed, "Good Lord!"

"What's the matter, my boy?" said the Major.

"I must cry *peccavi*," said Sam. "Father, you will never forgive me! I forgot till this moment a most important message. I was rather knocked up, you see, and went to sleep, and that sent it out of my head."

"You are forgiven, my boy, be it what it may. I hope it is nothing very serious."

"Well, it is very serious," said Sam. "As I was coming by Hanging Rock, I rode up to the door a minute, to see if Cecil was at home—and Mrs. Mayford came out and wanted me to get off and come in, but I hadn't time; and she said, 'The Dean is coming here to-night, and he'll be with you to-morrow night, I expect. So don't forget to tell your mother.'"

"To-morrow night!" said Mrs. Buckley, aghast. "Why, my dear boy, that is to-night! What shall I do?"

"Nothing at all, my love," said the Major, "but make them get some supper ready. He can't have expected us to wait dinner till this time."

"I thought," said Captain Brentwood, "that the Dean was gone back to England."

"So he is," said the Major. "But this is a new one. The good old Dean has resigned."

"What is the new one's name?" said the Captain.

"I don't know," said the Major. "Desborough said it was a Dr. Maypole, and that he was very like one in appearance. But you can't trust Desborough, you know; he never remembers names. I hope he may be as good a man as his predecessor."

"I hope he may be no worse," said Captain Brentwood; "but I hope, in addition, that he may be better able to travel, and look after his outlying clergy a little more."

"It looks like it," said the Major, "to be down as far as this, before he has been three months installed."

Mrs. Buckley went out to the kitchen to give orders; and after that they sat for an hour or more over their wine, till at length the Major said:

"We must give him up in another hour."

Then, as if they had heard him, the dogs began to bark. Rover, who had, against rules, sneaked into the house, and lain *perdu* under the sofa, discovered his retreat by low growling, as though determined to do his duty, let the consequences be what they might. Every now and then, too, when his feelings overpowered him, he would discharge a "Woof," like a minute-gun at sea.

"That must be him, father," said Sam. "You'll catch it, Mr. Rover!"

He ran out; a tall black figure was sitting on horseback before the door, and a pleasant cheery voice said, "Pray, is this Major Buckley's?"

"Yes, sir," said Sam; "we have been expecting you."

He called for the groom, and held the stranger's horse while he dismounted. Then he assisted him to unstrap his valise, and carried it in after him.

The Major, Mrs. Buckley, and the Captain had risen, and were standing ready to greet the Church dignitary as he came in, in the most respectful manner. But when the Major had looked for a moment on the tall figure in black which advanced towards the fire, instead of saying, "Sir, I am highly honoured by your visit," or "Sir, I bid you most heartily welcome," he dashed forward in the most undignified fashion, upsetting a chair, and seizing the reverend Dean by both hands, exclaimed, "God bless my heart and soul! Frank Maberly!"

It was he: the mad curate, now grown into a colonial dean—sobered, apparently, but unchanged in any material point: still elastic and upright, looking as if for twopence he would take off the black cut-away coat and the broad-brimmed hat, and row seven in the University eight, at a moment's notice. There seemed something the matter with him though, as he held the Major's two hands in his, and looked on his broad handsome face. Something like a shortness of breath prevented his speech, and, strange, the Major seemed troubled with the same complaint; but Frank got over it first, and said:

"My dear old friend, I am so glad to see you!"

And Mrs. Buckley said, laying her hand upon his arm, "It seems as if all things were arranged to make my husband and myself the happiest couple in the world. If we had been asked to-night, whom of all people in the world we should have been most glad to see as the new Dean, we should have answered at once, Frank Maberly; and here he is!"

"Then, you did not know whom to expect?" said Frank.

"Not we, indeed," said the Major. "Desborough said the new Dean was a Dr. Maypole; and I pictured to myself an old schoolmaster with a birch rod in his coat-tail pocket. And we have been in such a stew all the evening about giving the great man a proper reception. Ha! ha! ha!"

"And will you introduce me to this gentleman?" said the Dean, moving towards Sam, who stood behind his mother.

"This," said the Major, with a radiant smile, "is my son Samuel, whom, I believe, you have seen before."

"So, the pretty boy that I knew at Drumston," said the Dean, laying his hands on Sam's shoulders, "has grown into this noble gentleman! It makes me feel old, but I am glad to feel old under such circumstances. Let me turn your face to the light and see if I can recognise the little lad whom I used to carry pick-a-back across Hatherleigh Water."

Sam looked in his face—such a kindly good placid face, that it seemed beautiful, though by some rules it was irregular and ugly enough. The Dean laid his hand on Sam's curly head, and said, "God bless you, Samuel Buckley," and won Sam's heart for ever.

All this time Captain Brentwood had stood with his back against the chimney-piece, perfectly silent, having banished all expression from his countenance; now, however, Major Buckley brought up the Dean and introduced him:

"My dear Brentwood, the Dean of B——; not Dean to us though, so much as our dear old friend Frank Maberly."

"Involved grammar," said the Captain to himself, but added aloud: "A Churchman of your position, sir, will do me an honour by using my house; but the Mr. Maberly of whom I have so often heard from my friend Buckley, will do me a still higher honour if he will allow me to enrol him among the number of my friends."

Frank the Dean thought that Captain Brentwood's speech would have made a good piece to turn into Greek prose, in the style of Demosthenes; but he didn't say so. He looked at the Captain's stolid face for a moment, and said, as Sam thought, a little abruptly:

"I think, sir, that you and I shall get on very well together when we understand one another."

The Captain made no reply in articulate speech, but laughed internally, till his sides shook, and held out his hand. The Dean laughed too, as he took it, and said:

"I met a young lady at the Bishop's the other day, a Miss Brentwood."

"My daughter, sir," said the Captain.

"So I guessed—partly from the name, and partly from a certain look about the eyes, rather unmistakable. Allow me to say, sir, that I never remember to have seen such remarkable beauty in my life."

They sat Frank down to supper, and when he had done, the conversation was resumed.

"By the by, Major Buckley," said he, "I miss an old friend, who I heard was living with you—a very dear old friend—where is Dr. Mulhaus?"

"Dear Doctor," said Mrs. Buckley, "this is his home indeed, but he is away at present on an expedition with two old Devon friends, Hamlyn and Stockbridge."

"Oh!" said Frank, "I have heard of those men; they came out here the year before the Vicar died. I never knew either of them, but I well remember how kindly Stockbridge used to be spoken of by every one in Drumston. I must make his acquaintance."

"You will make the acquaintance of one of the finest fellows in the world, Dean," said the Major; "I know no worthier man than Stockbridge. I wish Mary Thornton had married him."

"And I hear," said Frank, "that the pretty Mary is your next-door neighbour, in partnership with that excellent giant Troubridge. I must go and see them to-morrow. I will produce one of those great roaring laughs of his, by reminding him of our first introduction at the Palace, through a rat."

"I am sorry to say," said the Major, "that Tom is away at Port Phillip, with cattle."

"Port Phillip again," said Frank; "I have heard of nothing else throughout my journey. I am getting bored with it. Will you tell me what you know about it for certain?"

"Well," said the Major, "it lies about 250 miles south of this, though we cannot get at it without crossing the mountains, in consequence of some terribly dense scrub on some low ranges close to it, which they call, I believe, the Dandenong. It appears, however, when you are there, that there is a great harbour, about forty miles long, surrounded with splendid pastures, which stretch west farther than any man has been yet. Take it all in all, I should say it was the best watered and most available piece of country yet discovered in New Holland."

"Any good rivers?" asked the Dean.

"Plenty of small ones, only one of any size, apparently, which seems to rise somewhere in this direction, and goes in at the head of the bay. They tried years ago to form a settlement on this bay, but Collins, the man entrusted with it, could find no fresh water, which seems strange, as there is, according to all accounts, a fine full-flowing river running by the town."

"They have formed a town there, then?" said the Dean.

" There are a few wooden houses gone up by the riverside.   I
believe they are going to make a town there, and call it Melbourne;
we may live to see it a thriving place."

The Major has lived to see his words fulfilled—fulfilled in such
marvellous sort, that bald bare statistics read like the wildest
romance.   At the time he spoke, twenty-two years ago from this
present year 1858, the Yarra rolled its clear waters to the sea
through the unbroken solitude of a primeval forest, as yet unseen
by the eye of a white man.   Now there stands there a noble city,
with crowded wharves, containing with its suburbs not less than
120,000 inhabitants.   A thousand vessels have lain at one time side
by side, off the mouth of that little river; and through the low sandy
heads that close the great port towards the sea, thirteen millions
sterling of exports is carried away each year by the finest ships in
the world.   Here, too, are waterworks constructed at fabulous
expense, a service of steamships, between this and the other great
cities of Australia, vieing in speed and accommodation with the
coastal steamers of Great Britain; noble churches, handsome theatres.
In short, a great city, which, in its amazing rapidity of growth,
utterly surpasses all human experience.

I never stood in Venice contemplating the decay of the grand
palaces of her old merchant princes, whose time has gone by for
ever.   I never watched the slow downfall of a great commercial
city; but I have seen what to him who thinks aright is an equally
grand subject of contemplation—the rapid rise of one.   I have seen
what but a small moiety of the world, even in these days, has seen,
and what, save in this generation, has never been seen before, and
will, I think, never be seen again.   I have seen Melbourne.   Five
years in succession did I visit that city, and watch each year how it
spread and grew until it was beyond recognition.   Every year the
press became denser, and the roar of the congregated thousands grew
louder, till at last the scream of the flying engine rose above the
hubbub of the streets, and two thousand miles of electric wire began
to move the clicking needles with ceaseless intelligence.

Unromantic enough, but beyond all conception wonderful.   I stood
at the east end of Bourke Street, not a year ago, looking at the black
swarming masses, which thronged the broad thoroughfare below.
All the town lay at my feet, and the sun was going down beyond
the distant mountains; I had just crossed from the front of the new
Houses of Legislature, and had nearly been run over by a great
omnibus.   Partly to recover my breath, and partly, being not used
to large cities, to enjoy the really fine scene before me, I stood at

the corner of the street in contemplative mood. I felt a hand on my shoulder, and looked round—it was Major Buckley.

" This is a wonderful sight, Hamlyn," said he.

" When you think of it," I said, " really think of it, you know, how wonderful it is! "

" Brentwood," said the Major, " has calculated by his mathematics that the progress of the species is forty-seven, decimal eight, more rapid than it was thirty-five years ago."

" So I should be prepared to believe," I said; " where will it all end? Will it be a grand universal republic, think you, in which war is unknown, and universal prosperity has banished crime? I may be too sanguine, but such a state of things is possible. This is a sight which makes a man look far into the future."

" Prosperity," said the Major, " has not done much towards abolishing crime in this town, at all events; and it would not take much to send all this back into its primeval state."

" How so, Major? " said I; " I see here the cradle of a new and mighty empire."

" Two rattling good thumps of an earthquake," said the Major, " would pitch Melbourne into the middle of Port Phillip, and bury all the gold far beyond the reach even of the Ballarat deep-sinkers. The world is very, very young, my dear Hamlyn. Come down and dine with me at the club."

CHAPTER XXVI

WHITE HEATHENS

CAPTAIN BRENTWOOD went back to Garoopna next morning; but Frank Maberly kept to his resolution of going over to see Mary; and, soon after breakfast, they were all equipped ready to accompany him, standing in front of the door, waiting for the horses. Frank was remarking how handsome Mrs. Buckley looked in her hat and habit, when she turned and said to him:

" My dear Dean, I suppose you never jump over five-barred gates nowadays? Do you remember how you used to come over the white gate at the Vicarage? I suppose you are getting too dignified for any such thing? "

There was a three-railed fence dividing the lower end of the yard from the paddock. He rammed his hat on tight, and took it flying, with his black coat-tails fluttering like wings; and, coming back laughing, said:

"There's a bit of the old Adam for you, Mrs. Buckley! Be careful how you defy me again."

The sun was bright overhead, and the land in its full winter verdure, as they rode along the banks of the creek that led to Toonarbin. Frank Maberly was as humorous as ever, and many a merry laugh went ringing through the woodland solitudes, sending the watchman cockatoo screaming aloft to alarm the flock, or startling the brilliant thick-clustered lories (richest coloured of all parrots in the world), as they hung chattering on some silver-leaved acacia, bending with their weight the fragile boughs down towards the clear still water, lighting up the dark pool with strange, bright reflections of crimson and blue; startling, too, the feeding doe-kangaroo, who skipped slowly away, followed by her young one— so slowly that the watching travellers expected her to stop each moment, and could scarcely believe she was in full flight till she topped a low ridge and disappeared.

"That is a strange sight to a European, Mrs. Buckley," said Frank; "a real wild animal. It seems so strange to me, now, to think that I could go and shoot that beast, and account to no man for it. That is, you know, supposing I had a gun, and powder and shot, and, also, that the kangaroo would be fool enough to wait till I was near enough; which, you see, is presupposing a great deal. Are they easily approached?"

"Easily enough, on horseback," said Sam, "but very difficult to come near on foot, which is also the case with all wild animals and birds worth shooting in this country. A footman, you see, they all mistake for their hereditary enemy, the blackfellow; but, as yet, they have not come to distinguish a man on horseback from a four-footed beast. And this seems to show that animals have their traditions like men."

"Pray, Sam, are not these pretty beasts, these kangaroos, becoming extinct?"

"On sheep-runs, very nearly so. Sheep drive them off directly: but on cattle-runs, so far from becoming extinct, they are becoming so numerous as to be a nuisance; consuming a most valuable quantity of grass."

"How can you account for that?"

"Very easily," said Sam; "their enemies are all removed. The settlers have poisoned, in well-settled districts, the native dogs and eagle-hawks which formerly kept down their numbers. The blacks prefer the beef of the settlers to bad and hard-earned kangaroo venison; and, lastly, the settlers never go after them, but leave them to their own inventions. So that the kangaroo has better times of it than ever."

"That is rather contrary to what one has heard, though," said Frank.

"But Sam is right, Dean," said the Major. "People judge from seeing none of them on the plains, from which they have been driven by the sheep; but there are as many in the forest as ever."

"The emu, now," said Frank, "are they getting scarce?"

"They will soon be among the things of the past," said the Major; "and I am sorry for it, for they are a beautiful and harmless bird."

"Major," said Frank, "how many outlying huts have you?"

"Five," said the Major. "Four shepherds' huts, and one store-keeper's in the range, which we call the heifer station."

"You have no church here, I know," said Frank; "but do these men get any sort of religious instruction?"

"None whatever," said the Major. "I have service in my house on Sunday, but I cannot ask them to come to it, though sometimes the stockmen do come. The shepherds, you know, are employed on Sunday as on any other day. Sheep must eat!"

"Are any of these men convicts?"

"All the shepherds," said the Major. "The stockman and his assistant are free men, but their hut-keeper is bond."

"Are any of them married?"

"Two of the shepherds; the rest single; but I must tell you that on our run we keep up a regular circulation of books among the huts, and my wife sticks them full of religious tracts, which is really about all that we can do without a clergyman."

"Do you find they read your tracts, Mrs. Buckley?" asked Frank.

"No," said Mrs. Buckley, "with the exception, perhaps of 'Black Giles the Poacher,' which always comes home very dirty. Narrative tracts they will read when there is nothing more lively at hand; but such treatises as 'Are You Ready?' and 'The Sinner's Friend,' fall dead. One copy lasts for years."

"One copy of either of them," said Frank, "would last me some time. Then these fellows, Major, are entirely godless, I suppose?"

"Well, I'll tell you, Dean," said the Major, stopping short, "it's about as bad as bad can be! it can't be worse, sir. If by any means you could make it worse, it would be by sending such men round here as the one who was sent here last. He served as a standing joke to the hands for a year or more; and I believe he was sincere enough, too."

"I must invade some of these huts, and see what is to be done," said Frank. "I have had a hard spell of work in London since old times; but I have seen enough already to tell me that that work was not so hopeless as this will be. I think, however, that there is more chance here than among the little farmers in the settled districts. Here, at all events, I shan't have the rum-bottle eternally standing between me and my man. What a glorious, independent, happy set of men are those said small freeholders, Major! What a happy exchange an English peasant makes when he leaves an old, well-ordered society, the ordinances of religion, the various give-and-take relations between rank and rank, which make up the sum of English life, for independence, godlessness, and rum! He gains, say you! yes, he gains meat for his dinner every day, and *voilà tout*! Contrast an English workhouse schoolboy—I take the lowest class for example, a class which should not exist—with a small farmer's son in one of the settled districts. Which will make the most useful citizen? Give me the workhouse lad!"

"Oh, but you are overstating the case, you know, Dean," said the Major. "You must have a class of small farmers! Wherever the land is fit for cultivation it must be sold to agriculturists; or, otherwise, in case of a war, we shall be dependent on Europe and America for the bread we eat. I know some excellent and exemplary men who are farmers, I assure you."

"Of course! of course!" said Frank. "I did not mean quite all I said; but I am angry and disappointed. I pictured to myself the labourer, English, Scotch, or Irish—a man whom I know, and have lived with and worked for some years, emigrating, and, after a few years of honest toil, which, compared to his old hard drudgery, was child's play, saving money enough to buy a farm. I pictured to myself this man accumulating wealth, happy, honest, godly, bringing up a family of brave boys and good girls, in a country where, theoretically, the temptations to crime are all but removed: this is what I imagined. I come out here, and what do I find? My friend the labourer has got his farm, and is prospering, after a sort. He has turned to be a drunken, godless, impudent fellow, and his wife little better than himself; his daughters dowdy hussies; his sons lanky, lean, pasty-faced, blaspheming blackguards, drinking rum before breakfast, and living by cheating one another out of horses. Can you deny this picture?"

"Yes," said the Major, "I can disprove it by many happy

instances, and yet, to say the truth, it is fearfully true in as many more. There is no social influence in the settled districts; there are too many men without masters. Let us wait and hope."

"This is not to the purpose at present, though," said Mrs. Buckley. "See what you can do for us in the bush, my dear Dean. You have a very hopeless task before you, I fear."

"The more hopeless, the greater glory, madam," said Frank, taking off his hat and waving it. Called, Chosen, and Faithful. "There is a beautiful house!"

"That is Toonarbin," said the Major; "and there's Mary Hawker in the veranda."

"Let us see," said Mrs. Buckley, "if she will know him. If she does not recognise him, let no one speak before me."

When they had ridden up and dismounted, Mrs. Buckley presented Frank. "My dear," said she, "the Dean is honouring us by staying at Baroona for a week, and proposes to visit round at the various stations. To-morrow we go to the Mayfords, and next day to Garoopna."

Mary bowed respectfully to Frank, and said, "that she felt highly honoured," and so forth. "My partner is gone on a journey, and my son is away on the run, or they would have joined with me in bidding you welcome, sir."

Frank would have been highly honoured at making their acquaintance.

Mary started, and looked at him again. "Mr. Maberly! Mr. Maberly!" she said, "your face is changed, but your voice is unchangeable. You are discovered, sir!"

"And are you glad to see me?"

"No!" said Mary plainly.

"Now," said Mrs. Buckley to herself, "she is going to give us one of her tantrums. I wish she would behave like a reasonable being. She is always bent on making a scene"; but she kept this to herself, and only said aloud: "Mary, my dear! Mary!"

"I am sorry to hear you say so, Mrs. Hawker," said Frank; "but it is just and natural."

"Natural," said Mary, "and just. You are connected in my mind with the most unhappy and most degraded period of my life. Can you expect that I should be glad to see you? You were kind to me then, as is your nature to be, kind and good above all men whom I know. I thought of you always with love and admiration, as one whom I deeply honoured, but would not care to look upon again. As the one of all whom I would have forget me in my disgrace. And now, to-day of all days, just when I have found the father's vices confirmed in the son, you come before me, as if from the bowels of the earth, to remind me of what I was."

Mrs. Buckley was very much shocked and provoked by this, but held her tongue magnanimously. And what do you think, my dear reader, was the cause of all this hysteric tragic nonsense on the part of Mary? Simply this. The poor soul had been put out of temper. Her son Charles, as I mentioned before, had had a scandalous *liaison* with one Meg Macdonald, daughter of one of the Donovans' (now Brentwoods') shepherds. That morning, this brazen hussy, as Mary very properly called her, had come coolly up to the station and asked for Charles. And on Mary's shaking her fist at her, and bidding her be gone, she had then and there rated poor Mary in the best of Gaelic for a quarter of an hour; and Mary, instead ot venting her anger on the proper people, had taken her old plan of making herself disagreeable to those who had nothing to do with it, which naturally made Mrs. Buckley very angry, and even ruffled the placid Major a little, so that he was not sorry when he saw in his wife's face, from the expression he knew so well, that Mary was going to " catch it."

" I wish, Mary Hawker," said Mrs. Buckley, " that you would remember that the Dean is our guest, and that on our account alone there is due to him some better welcome than what you have given him."

" Now, you are angry with me for speaking the truth too abruptly," said Mary, crying.

" Well, I am angry with you," said Mrs. Buckley. " If that was the truth, you should not have spoken it now. You have no right to receive an old friend like this."

" You are very unkind to me," said Mary. " Just when after so many years' peace and quietness my troubles are beginning again, you are all turning against me." And so she laid down her head and wept.

" Dear Mrs. Hawker," said Frank, coming up and taking her hand, " if you are in trouble, I know well that my visit is well timed. Where trouble and sorrow are, there is my place, there lies my work. In prosperity my friends sometimes forget me, but my hope and prayer is, that when affliction and disaster come, I may be with them. You do not want me now; but when you do, God grant I may be with you! Remember my words."

She remembered them well.

Frank made an excuse to go out, and Mary, crying bitterly, went into her bedroom. When she was gone, the Major, who had been standing by the window, said:

"My dear wife, that boy of hers is aggravating her. Don't be too hard upon her."

"My dear husband," said Mrs. Buckley, "I have no patience with her, to welcome an old friend, whom she has not seen for nearly twenty years, in that manner! It is too provoking."

"You see, my love," said the Major, "that her nerves have been very much shaken by misfortune, and at times she is really not herself."

"And I tell you what, mother dear," said Sam, "Charles Hawker is going on very badly. I tell you, in the strictest confidence, mind, that he has not behaved in a very gentlemanlike way in one particular, and if he was any one else but who he is, I should have very little to say to him."

"Well, my dear husband and son," said Mrs. Buckley, "I will go in and make the *amende* to her. Sam, go and see after the Dean."

Sam went out, and saw Frank across the yard playing with the dogs. He was going towards him, when a man entering the yard suddenly came up and spoke to him.

It was William Lee—grown older, and less wild-looking, since we saw him first at midnight on Dartmoor, but a striking person still. His hair had become grizzled, but that was the only sign of age he showed. There was still the same vigour of motion, the same expression of enormous strength about him as formerly; the principal change was in his face. Eighteen years of honest work, among people who in time, finding his real value, had got to treat him more as a friend than a servant, had softened the old expression of reckless ferocity into one of good-humoured independence. And Tom Troubridge, no careless observer of men, had said once to Major Buckley, that he thought his face grew each year more like what it must have been when a boy. A bold flight of fancy for Tom, but, like all else he said, true.

Such was William Lee, as he stopped Sam in the yard, and, with a bold, honest look of admiration, said:

"It makes me feel young to look at you, Mr. Buckley. You are a great stranger here lately. Some young lady to run after, I suppose? Well, never mind; I hope it ain't Miss Blake."

"A man may not marry his grandmother, Lee," said Sam, laughing.

" True for you, sir," said Lee. " That was wrote up in Drumston church, I mind, and some other things alongside of it, which I could say by heart once on a time—all on black boards, with yellow letters. And also, I remember a spick and span new board, about how Anthony Hamlyn (that's Mr. Geoffry Hamlyn's father) ' repaired and beautified this church '; which meant that he built a handsome new pew for himself in the chancel. Lord, I think I see him asleep in it now. But never mind that—I've kept a pup of Fly's for you, sir, and got it through the distemper. Fly's pup, by Rollicker, you know."

" Oh, thank you," said Sam. " I am really much obliged to you. But you must let me know the price, you know, Lee. The dog should be a good one."

" Well, Mr. Buckley," said Lee, " I have been cosseting this little beast up in the hopes you'd accept it as a present. And then, says I to myself, when he takes a new chum out to see some sport, and the dog pulls down a flying doe, and the dust goes up like smoke, and the dead sticks come flying about his ears, he will say to his friends, ' That's the dog Lee gave me. Where's his equal?' So don't be too proud to take a present from an old friend."

" Not I, indeed, Lee," said Sam. " I thank you most heartily."

" Who is this long gent in black, sir?" said Lee (looking towards Frank, who was standing and talking with the Major). " A parson, I reckon."

" The Dean of B——," answered Sam.

" Ah! so,"—said Lee—" come to give us some good advice? Well, we want it bad enough, I hope some on us may foller it. Seems a man, too, and not a monkey."

" My father says," said Sam, " that he was formerly one of the best boxers he ever saw."

Any further discussion of Frank's physical powers was cut short by his coming up to Sam and saying:

" I was thinking of riding out to one of the outlying huts, to have a little conversation with the men. Will you come with me?"

" If you will allow me, I shall be delighted beyond all measure."

" I beg your pardon, sir," said Lee, " but I understood you to say that you were going to one of our huts to give the men a discourse. Would you let me take you out to one of them? I'd like well to hear what you'd got to say myself, sir, and I promise you the lads I'll show you want good advice as well as any."

" You will do me infinite service," said Frank. " Sam, if you will excuse me, let me ask you to stay behind. I have a fancy for going up alone. Let me take these men in the rough, and see what I can do unassisted."

"You will be apt to find them uncivil, sir," said Sam. "I am known, and my presence would ensure you outward respect, at all events."

"Just what I thought," said Frank. "But I want to see what I can do alone and unassisted. No; stay, and let me storm the place single-handed."

So Lee and he started towards the ranges, riding side by side.

"You will find, sir," said Lee, "that these men, in this here hut, are a rougher lot than you think for. Very like they'll be cheeky. I would almost have wished you'd a' let Mr. Buckley come. He's a favourite round here, you see, and you'd have gone in as his friend."

"You see," said Frank, turning confidentially to Lee, "I am not an ordinary parson. I am above the others. And what I want is not so much to see what I can do myself, but what sort of a reception any parson coming haphazard among these men will get. That is why I left Mr. Buckley behind. Do you understand me?"

"I understand you, sir," said Lee. "But I'm afear'd."

"What are you afraid of?" said Frank, laughing.

"Why, if you'll excuse me, sir, that you'll only get laughed at."

"That all!" said Frank. "Laughter breaks no bones. What are these men that we are going to see?"

"Why, one," said Lee, "is a young Jimmy (I beg your pardon, sir, an emigrant), the other two are old prisoners. Now see here. These prisoners hate the sight of a parson above all mortal men. And for why? Because when they're in prison, all their indulgences, and half their hopes of liberty depend on how far they can manage to humbug the chaplain with false piety. And so, when they are free again, they hate him worse than any man. I am an old prisoner myself, and I know it."

"Have you been a prisoner, then?" said Frank, surprised.

"I was transported, sir, for poaching."

"That all!" said Frank. "Then you were the victim of a villainous old law. Do you know," he added, laughing, "that I rather believe I have earned transportation myself? I have a horrible schoolboy recollection of a hare who would squeak in my pocket, and of a keeper passing within ten yards of where I lay hidden. If that is all, give me your hand."

Lee shook his head. "That is what I was sent out for," said he, "but since then there are precious few villainies I have not committed. You hadn't ought to shake hands with me, sir."

Frank laid his hand kindly on his shoulder. "I am not a judge," he said. "I am a priest. We must talk together again. Now, we have no time, for, if I mistake not, there is our destination."

They had been riding through splendid open forest, growing denser as they approached the ranges. They had followed a creek all the way, or nearly so, and now came somewhat suddenly on a large reedy waterhole, walled on all sides by dense-stringy-bark timber, thickly undergrown with scrub. Behind them opened a long vista formed by the gully, through which they had been approaching, down which the black burnt stems of the stringy-bark were agreeably relieved by the white stems of the red and blue gum, growing in the moister and more open space near the creek. In front of them was a slab hut of rich mahogany colour, by no means an unpleasing object among the dull unbroken green of the forest. In front of it was a trodden space littered with the chips of fire-wood. A pile of the last article lay a few yards in front of the door. And against the walls of the tenement was a long bench, on which stood a calabash, with a lump of soap and a coarse towel; a camp oven, and a pair of black top-boots, and underneath which lay a noble cattle dog, who, as soon as he saw them, burst out into furious barking, and prepared to give battle.

"Will you take my horse for me," said Frank to Lee, "while I go inside?"

"Certainly, sir," said Lee. "But mind the dog."

Frank laughed and jumped off. The dog was unprepared for this. It was irregular. The proper and usual mode of proceedings would have been for the stranger to have stayed on horseback, and for him (the dog) to have barked himself hoarse, till some one came out of the hut and pacified him by throwing billets of wood at him; no conversation possible till his barking was turned into mourning. He was not up to the emergency. He had never seen a man clothed in black from head to foot before. He probably thought it was the Devil. His sense of duty not being strong enough to outweigh considerations of personal safety, he fled round the house, and being undecided whether to bark or to howl, did both, while Frank opened the door and went in.

The hut was like most other bush huts, consisting of one undivided apartment, formed of split logs, called slabs, set upright in the ground. The roof was of bark, and the whole interior was stained by the smoke into a rich dark brown, such as Teniers or our own beloved Cattermole would delight in. You entered by a door in one of the long sides, and saw that the whole of the end on your right was taken up by a large fireplace, on which blazed a pile of timber. Round the falls were four bed places, like the bunks on board ship, each filled with a heap of frowzy blankets, and in the centre stood a rough table, surrounded by logs of wood, sawed square off, which served for seats.

The living occupants of the hut were scarcely less rude than the hut itself. One of the bed places was occupied by a sleepy, black-haired, not bad-looking young fellow, clad in greasy red shirt, greasy breeches and boots, and whose shabby plated spurs were tangled in the dirty blankets. He was lying on his back, playing with a beautiful little parrot. Opposite him, sitting up in his bunk, was another young fellow, with a singularly coarse, repulsive countenance, long yellow hair, half-way down his back, clothed like the other in greasy breeches. This last one was puffing at a short black pipe, in an affected way, making far more noise than was necessary in that operation, and seemed to be thinking of something insolent to say to the last speaker, whoever he may have been.

Another man was sitting on the end of the bench before the fire, with his legs stretched out before it. At the first glance Frank saw that this was a superior person to the others. He was dressed like the others in black top-boots, but, unlike the others, he was clean and neat. In fact the whole man was clean and neat, and had a clean-shaved face, and looked respectable, so far as outward appearances were concerned. The fourth man was the hut-keeper, a wicked-looking old villain, who was baking bread.

Frank looked at the sleepy young man with the parrot, and said to himself, " There's a bad case." He looked at the flash, yellow-haired young snob who was smoking, and said, " There's a worse." He looked at the villainous grey-headed old hut-keeper, and said, " There's a hopeless case altogether." But when he looked at the neatly dressed man, who sat in front of the fire, he said, " That seems a more likely person. There is some sense of order in him, at all events. See what I can do with him."

He stood with his towering tall black figure in the doorway. The sleepy young man with the black hair sat up and looked at him in wonder, while his parrot whistled and chattered loudly. The yellow-haired young man looked round to see if he could get the others to join him in a laugh. The hut-keeper said, " Oh, hell! " and attended once more to the cooking; but the neat-looking man rose up, and gave Frank courteously " Good day."

"I am a clergyman," said Frank, "come to pay you a visit, if you will allow me."

Black-hair looks as if astonishment were a new sensation to him, and he was determined to have the most of it. Meanwhile, little parrot taking advantage of his absence of mind, clambers up his breast and nips off a shirt-button, which he holds in his claw, pretending it is immensely good to eat. Hut-keeper clatters pots and pans, while Yellow-hair lies down whistling insolently. These last two seemed inclined to constitute themselves his Majesty's Opposition in the present matter, while Black-hair and the neat man are evidently inclined towards Frank. There lay a boot in front of the fire, which the neat man, without warning, seized and hurled at Yellow-hair, with such skill and precision that the young fellow started upright in bed and demanded, with many verbs and adjectives, what he meant by that?

"I'll teach you to whistle when a gentleman comes into the hut—you Possumguts! Lie down now, will you?"

Yellow-hair lay down, and there was no more trouble with him. Hut-keeper, too, seeing how matters were going, left off clattering his pots, and Frank was master of the field.

"Very glad to see you, sir," says the neat man; "very seldom we get a visit from a gentleman in a black coat, I assure you."

Frank shook hands with him and thanked him, and then, turning suddenly upon Black-hair, who was sitting with his bird on his knee, one leg out of his bunk, and his great black vacant eyes fixed on Frank, said:

"What an exceedingly beautiful bird you have got there! Pray, what do you call it?"

Now it so happened that Black-hair had been vacantly wondering to himself whether Frank's black coat would meet across his stomach, or whether the lower buttons and button-holes were "dummies." So that when Frank turned suddenly upon him he was, as it were, caught in the act, and could only reply in a guilty whisper, "Mountain blue."

"Will he talk?" asked Frank.

"Whistle," says Black-hair, still in a whisper, and then, clearing his throat, continued in his natural tone, "Whistle beautiful. Black-fellows gets 'em young out of the dead trees. I'll give you this one if you've a mind."

Frank couldn't think of it; but could Black-hair get him a young cockatoo, and leave it with Mr. Sam Buckley for transmission?—would be exceedingly obliged.

Yes, Black-hair could. Thinks, too, what a pleasant sort of chap this parson was. "Will get him a cockatoo certainly."

Then Frank asks, may he read them a bit out of the Bible, and neat man says they will be highly honoured. And Black-hair gets out of his bunk and sits listening in a decently respectful way. Opposition are by no means won over. The old hut-keeper sits sulkily smoking, and the yellow-haired man lies in his bunk with his back towards them. Lee had meanwhile come in, and, after recognitions from those inside, sat quietly down close to the door. Frank took for a text, "Servants, obey your masters," and preached them a sermon about the relations of master and servant, homely, plain, sensible and interesting, and had succeeded in awakening the whole attention and interest of the three who were listening, when the door was opened and a man looked in.

Lee was next the door, and cast his eyes upon the new-comer. No sooner had their eyes met than he uttered a loud oath, and, going out with the stranger, shut the door after him.

"What can be the matter with our friend, I wonder?" asked Frank. "He seems much disturbed."

The neat man went to the door and opened it. Lee and the man who had opened the door were standing with their backs turned towards them, talking earnestly. Lee soon came back without a word, and, having caught and saddled his horse, rode away with the stranger, who was on foot. He was a large, shabbily-dressed man, with black curly hair; this was all they could see of him, for his back was always towards them.

"Never saw Bill take on like that before," said the neat man. "That's one of his old pals, I reckon. He ain't very fond of meeting any of 'em, you see, since he has been on the square. The best friends in prison, sir, are the worst friends out."

"Were you ever in prison, then?" said Frank.

"Lord bless you!" said the other, laughing, "I was lagged for forgery."

"I will make you another visit if I can," said Frank. "I am much obliged to you for the patience with which you heard me."

The other ran out to get his horse for him, and had it saddled in no time. "If you will send a parson round," he said, when Frank was mounted, "I will ensure him a hearing, and good-bye, sir."

"And God speed you," says Frank. But, lo! as he turned to ride away, Black-hair the sleepy-headed comes to the hut-door, looking important, and says, "Hi!" Frank is glad of this, for he likes the stupid-looking young fellow better than he fancied he would have done at first, and says to himself, "There's the making of a man in that fellow, unless I am mistaken." So he turns politely to meet him, and, as he comes towards him, remarks what a fine, good-humoured young fellow he is. Black-hair ranges alongside, and, putting his hand on the horse's neck, says mysteriously:

"Would you like a native companion?"

"Too big to carry, isn't it?" says Frank.

"I'll tie his wings together, and send him down on the ration dray," says Black-hair. "You'll come round and see us again, will you?"

So Frank fares back to Toonarbin, wondering where Lee has gone. But Black-hair goes back into the hut, and taking his parrot from the bed-place, puts it on his shoulder, and sits rubbing his knees before the fire. Yellow-hair and the hut-keeper are now in loud conversation, and the former is asking, in a loud authoritative tone (the neat man being outside), "whether a chap is to be hunted and badgered out of his bed by a parcel of —— parsons?" To which Hut-keeper says, "No, by ——! A man might as well be in barracks again." Yellow-hair, morally comforted and sustained by this opinion, is proceeding to say, that, for his part, a parson is a useless sort of animal in general, who gets his living by frightening old women, but that this particular parson is an unusually offensive specimen, and that there is nothing in this world that he (Yellow-hair) would like better than to have him out in front of the house for five minutes, and see who was best man—when Black-hair, usually a taciturn, peaceable fellow, astonishes the pair by turning his black eyes on the other, and saying, with lowering eyebrows:

"You damned humbug! Talk about fighting him! Always talk about fighting a chap when he's out of the way, when you know you've no more fight in you than a bronsewing. Why, he'd kill you, if you only waited for him to hit you! And see here: if you don't stop your jaw about him, you'll have to fight me, and that's a little more than you're game for, I'm thinking."

This last was told me by the man distinguished above as "the neat man," who was standing outside, and heard the whole.

But Frank arrived in due time at Toonarbin, and found all there much as he had left it, save that Mary Hawker had recovered her serenity, and was standing expecting him, with Charles by her side. Sam asked him, "Where was Lee?" and Frank, thinking more of other things, said he had left him at the hut, not thinking it worth while to mention the circumstance of his having been called out—a circumstance which became of great significance hereafter; for, though we never found out for certain who the man was, we came in the end to have strong suspicions.

However, as I said, all clouds had cleared from the Toonarbin atmosphere, and, after a pleasant meal, Frank, Major and Mrs. Buckley, Sam, and Charles Hawker, rode home to Baroona under the forest arches, and reached the house in the gathering twilight.

The boys were staying behind at the stable as the three elders entered the darkened drawing-room. A figure was in one of the easy-chairs by the fire—a figure which seemed familiar there, though the Major could not make out who it was until a well-known voice said:

" Is that you, Buckley? "

It was the Doctor. They both welcomed him warmly home, and waited in the gloom for him to speak, but only saw that he had bent down his head over the fire.

" Are you ill, Doctor? " said Mrs. Buckley.

" Sound in wind and limb, my dear madam, but rather sad at heart. We have had some very severe black fighting, and we have lost a kind old friend—James Stockbridge."

" Is he wounded, then? " said Mrs. Buckley.

" Dead."

" Dead! "

" Speared in the side. Rolled off his horse, and was gone in five minutes."

" Oh, poor James! " cried Mrs. Buckley. " He, of all men! The man who was their champion. To think that he, of all men, should end in that way! "

Charles Hawker rode home that night, and went into the room where his mother was. She was sitting sewing by the fire, and looked up to welcome him home.

" Mother," said he, " there is bad news to tell. We have lost a good friend. James Stockbridge is killed by the blacks on the Macquarie."

She answered not a word, but buried her face in her hands, and very shortly rose and left the room. When she was alone, she began moaning to herself, and saying:

" Some more fruit of the old cursed tree! If he had never seen me, he would have died at home, among his old friends, in a ripe, honoured old age."

CHAPTER XXVII

THE GOLDEN VINEYARD

On a summer's morning, almost before the dew had left the grass on the north side of the forest, or the belated opossum had gone to his nest, in fact just as the east was blazing with its brightest fire, Sam started off for a pleasant canter through the forest, to visit one of their out-station huts, which lay away among the ranges, and which was called, from some old arrangement, now fallen into disuse, "the heifer station."

There was the hut, seen suddenly down a beautiful green vista in the forest, the chimney smoking cheerily. " What a pretty contrast of colours! " says Sam, in a humour for enjoying everything. " Dark brown hut among the green shrubs, and blue smoke rising above all; prettily, too, that smoke hangs about the foliage this still morning, quite in festoons. There's Matt at the door! "

A lean, long-legged, clever-looking fellow, rather wide at the knees, with a brown complexion, and not unpleasant expression of face, stood before the door plaiting a cracker for his stock-whip. He looked pleased when he saw Sam, and indeed it must be a surly fellow indeed who did not greet Sam's honest face with a smile. Never a dog but wagged his tail when he caught Sam's eye.

" You're abroad early this morning, sir," said the man; " nothing the matter, is there, sir? "

" Nothing," said Sam, " save that one of Captain Brentwood's bulls is missing, and I came out to tell you to have an extra look round."

" I'll attend to it, sir."

" Hi! Matt," said Sam, " you look uncommonly smart."

Matt bent down his head, and laughed in a rather sheepish sort of way.

" Well, you see sir, I was coming in to the home station to see if the Major could spare me for a few days."

" What, going a-courting, eh? Well, I'll make that all right for you. Who is the lady—eh? "

" Why, it's Elsy Macdonald, I believe."

" Elsy Macdonald! " said Sam.

" Ay, yes, sir. I know what you mean, but she ain't like her sister; and that was more Mr. Charles Hawker's fault than her own. No; Elsy is good enough for me, and I'm not very badly off, and begin to fancy I would like some better sort of welcome in the evening than what a cranky old brute of a hut-keeper can give me. So I think I shall bring her home."

" I wish you well, Matt," said Sam; " I hope you are not going to leave us, though."

" No fear, sir; Major Buckley is too good a master for that! "

" Well, I'll get the hut coopered up a bit for you, and you shall be as comfortable as circumstances will permit. Good morning."

" Good morning, sir; I hope I may see you happily married yourself some of these days."

Sam laughed; " That would be a fine joke," he thought, " but why shouldn't it be, eh? I suppose it must come some time or another. I shall begin to look out; I don't expect I shall be very easily suited. Heigh ho! "

I expect, however, Mr. Sam, that you are just in the state of mind to fall headlong in love with the first girl you meet with a nose on her face; let us hope, therefore, that she may be eligible.

But here is home again, and here is the father standing majestic and broad in the veranda, and the mother with her arm round his neck, both waiting to give him a hearty morning's welcome. And there is Dr. Mulhaus kneeling in spectacles before his new Grevillea Victoriæ, the first bud of which is bursting into life; and the dogs catch sight of him and dash forward, barking joyfully; and as the ready groom takes his horse, and the fat housekeeper looks out all smiles, and retreats to send in breakfast, Sam thinks to himself, that he could not leave his home and people, not for the best wife in broad Australia; but then, you see, he knew no better.

" What makes my boy look so happy this morning? " asked his mother. " Has the bay mare foaled, or have you negotiated James Brentwood's young dog? Tell us, that we may participate."

" None of these things have happened, mother; but I feel in rather a holiday humour, and I'm thinking of going down to Garoopna this morning, and spending a day or two with Jim."

" I will throw a shoe after you for luck," said his mother. " See, the Doctor is calling you."

Sam went to the Doctor, who was intent on his flower. " Look here, my boy; here is something new: the handsomest of the Grevilleas, as I live. It has opened since I was here."

" Ah! " said Sam, " this is the one that came from the Quartz Ranges, last year, is it not? It has not flowered with you before."

" If Linnæus wept and prayed over the first piece of English furze which he saw," said the Doctor, " what everlasting smelling-bottle hysterics he would have gone into in this country! I don't sympathise with his tears much, though, myself; though a new flower is a source of the greatest pleasure to me."

"And so you are going to Garoopna, Sam?" said his father, at breakfast. "Have you heard, my dear, when the young lady is to come home?"

"Next month, I understand, my dear," said Mrs. Buckley. "When she does come I shall go over and make her a visit."

"What is her name, by the by?" asked the Doctor.

"Alice."

So, behold Sam starting for his visit. The very Brummell of bush-dandies. Hunt might have made his well-fitting cord breeches, Hoby might have made those black top-boots, and Chifney might have worn them before royalty, and not been ashamed. It is too hot for coat or waistcoat; so he wears his snow-white shirt, topped by a blue "bird's-eye handkerchief," and keeps his coat in his valise, to be used as occasion shall require. His costume is completed with a cabbage-tree hat, neither too new nor too old; light, shady, well ventilated, and three pounds ten, the production, after months of labour, of a private in her Majesty's Fortieth Regiment of Foot: not with long streaming ribands down his back, like a Pitt Street bully, but with short and modest ones as becomes a gentleman—altogether as fine a looking young fellow, as well dressed, and as well mounted too, as you will find on the country-side.

Let me say a word about his horse, too; horse Widderin. None ever knew what that horse had cost Sam. The Major even had a delicacy about asking. I can only discover by inquiry that, at one time about a year before this, there came to the Major's a traveller, an Irishman by nation, who bored them all by talking about a certain Arcturus colt, which had been dropped to a happy proprietor by his mare Larkspur, among the Shoalhaven gullies; described by him as a colt the like of which was never seen before; as indeed he should be, for his sire Arcturus, as all the world knows, was bought up by a great Hunter-river horse-breeder from the Duke of C——; while his dam, Larkspur, had for grandsire, the great Bombshell himself. What more would you have than that, unless you would like to drive Veno in our dog-cart? However, it so happened that, soon after the Irishman's visit, Sam went away on a journey, and came back riding a new horse; which when the Major saw, he whistled, but discreetly said nothing. A very large colt he was, with a neck like a rainbow, set into a splendid shoulder, and a marvellous way of throwing his legs out—

very dark chestnut in colour, almost black, with longish ears, and an eye so full, honest, and impudent, that it made you laugh in his face. Widderin, Sam said was his name, price and history being suppressed; called after Mount Widderin, to the northward there, whose loftiest sublime summit bends over like a horse's neck, with two peaked crags for ears. And the Major comes somehow to connect this horse with the Arcturus colt mentioned by our Irish friend, and observes that Sam takes to wearing his old clothes for a twelvemonth, and never seems to have any ready money. We shall see some day whether or no this horse will carry Sam ten miles, if required, on such direful emergency as falls to the lot of few men. However, this is all to come. Now in holiday clothes and in holiday mind, the two noble animals cross the paddock, and so down by the fence towards the river; towards the old gravel ford you may remember years ago. Here is the old flood, spouting and streaming as of yore, through the basalt pillars. There stand the three fern trees, too, above the dark scrub on the island. Now up the rock bank, and away across the breezy plains due north.

Brushing through the long grass tussocks, he goes his way singing, his dog Rover careering joyously before him. The horse is clearly for a gallop, but it is too hot to-day. The tall flat-topped volcanic hill which hung before him like a grey afint cloud when he started, now rears its fluted columns overhead, and now is getting dim again behind him. But ere noon is high he once more hears the brawling river beneath his feet, ard Garoopna is before him on the opposite bank.

The river, as it left Major Buckley's at Baroona, made a sudden bend to the west, a great arc, including with its minor windings nearly twenty-five miles, over the chord of which arc Sam had now been riding, making, from point to point, ten miles or thereabouts. The Mayfords' station, also, lay to the left of him, being on the curved side of the arc, about five miles from Baroona. The reader may, if he please, remember this.

Garoopna is an exceedingly pretty station; in fact, one of the most beautiful I have ever seen. It stands at a point where the vast forests, which surround the mountains in a belt, from ten to twenty miles broad, run down into the plains and touch the river. As at Baroona, the stream runs in through a deep cleft in the tableland, which here, though precipitous on the eastern bank, on the western breaks away into a small natural amphitheatre bordered by fine hanging woods, just in advance of which, about two hundred yards from the river, stands the house, a long, low building densely covered with creepers of all sorts, and fronted by a beautiful garden. Right and left of it are the wool-sheds, sheep-yards, stock-yards, men's huts, etc.; giving it almost the appearance of a little village; and behind the wooded ranges begin to rise, in some places broken beautifully by sheer scraps of grey rock. The forest crosses the river a little way; so that Sam, gradually descending from the plains to cross, went the last quarter of a mile through a shady sandy forest tract, fringed with bracken, which led down to a broad crossing-place, where the river sparkled under tall over-arching red gums and box-trees; and then following the garden fence, found himself before a deep cool-looking porch, in a broad neatly-kept courtyard behind the house.

A groom came out and took his horse. Rover has enough to do; for there are three or four sheep-dogs in the yard, who walk round him on tiptoe, slowly, with their frills out and their tails arched, growling. Rover, also, walks about on tiptoe, arches his tail, and growls with the best of them. He knows that the slightest mistake would be disastrous, and so manœuvres till he gets to the porch, where, a deal of gravel having been kicked backwards, in the same way as the ancients poured out their wine when they drank a toast, or else (as I think is more probable) as a symbol that animosities were to be buried, Rover is admitted as a guest, and Sam feels it safe to enter the house.

A cool, shady hall, hung round with coats, hats, stock-whips; a gun in the corner, and on a slab, the most beautiful nosegay you can imagine. Remarkable that for a bachelor's establishment—but there is no time to think about it, for a tall, comfortable-looking housekeeper, whom Sam has never seen before, comes in from the kitchen and curtseys.

" Captain Brentwood not at home, is he ? " said Sam.

" No, sir! Away on the run with Mr. James."

" Oh! very well," says Sam; " I am going to say a few days."

" Very well, sir; will you take anything before lunch ? "

" Nothing, thank you."

" Miss Alice is somewhere about, sir. I expect her in every minute."

" Miss Alice! " says Sam, astonished. " Is she come home ? "

" Came home last week, sir. Will you walk in and sit down ? "

Sam got his coat out of his valise, and went in. He wished that he had put on his plain blue necktie, instead of the blue one with white spots. He would have liked to have worn his new yellow riding-trousers, instead of breeches and boots. He hoped his hair was in order, and tried to arrange his handsome brown curls without a glass, but, in the end, concluded that things could not be mended now, so he looked round the room.

What a charming room it was! A couple of good pictures, and several fine prints on the walls. Over the chimney-piece, a sword, and an old gold-laced cap, on which Sam looked with reverence. Three French windows opened on to a dark cool veranda, beyond which was a beautiful flower-garden. The floor of the room, uncarpeted, shone dark and smooth, and the air was perfumed by vases of magnificent flowers, a hundred pounds' worth of them, I should say, if you could have taken them to Covent-garden that December morning. But what took Sam's attention more than anything was an open piano, in a shady recess, and on the keys a little fairy white glove.

"White kid gloves, eh, my lady?" says Sam; "that don't look well." So he looked through the book-shelves, and, having lighted on Boswell's *Johnson,* proceeded into the veranda. A collie she-dog was lying at one end, who banged her tail against the floor in welcome, but was too utterly prostrated by the heat and the persecution of her puppy to get up and make friends. The pup, however, a ball of curly black wool, with a brown-striped face, who was sitting on the top of her with his head on one side, seemed to conclude that a game of play was to be got out of Sam, and came blundering towards him; but Sam was, by this time, deep in a luxurious rocking-chair, so the puppy stopped half-way, and did battle with a great black tarantula spider who happened to be abroad on business.

Sam went to the club with his immortal namesake, bullied Bennet Langton, argued with Beauclerk, put down Goldsmith, and extinguished Boswell. But it was too hot to read; so he let the book fall on his lap, and lay a-dreaming.

What a delicious veranda is this to dream in! Through the tangled passion-flowers, jessamines, and magnolias, what a soft gleam of bright hazy distance, over the plains and far away! The deep river-glen cleaves the tableland, which, here and there, swells into breezy downs. Beyond, miles away to the north, is a great forest-barrier, above which there is a blaze of late snow, sending strange light aloft into the burning haze. All this is seen through an arch in the dark mass of verdure which clothes the trellis-work, only broken through in this one place, as though to make a frame for the picture. He leans back, and gives himself up to watching trifles.

See here. A magpie comes furtively out of the house with a key in his mouth, and, seeing Sam, stops to consider if he is likely to betray him. On the whole, he thinks not; so he hides the key in a crevice, and whistles a tune.

Now enters a cockatoo, waddling along comfortably and talking to himself. He tries to enter into conversation with the magpie, who, however, cuts him dead, and walks off to look at the prospect.

Flop! flop! A great foolish-looking kangaroo comes through the house and peers round him. The cockatoo addresses a few remarks to him, which he takes no notice of, but goes blundering out into the garden, right over the contemplative magpie, who gives him two or three indignant pecks on his clumsy feet, and sends him flying down the gravel walk.

Two bright-eyed little kangaroo rats come out of their box peering and blinking. The cockatoo finds an audience in them, for they sit listening to him, now and then catching a flea, or rubbing the backs of their heads with their fore-paws. But a buck 'possum, who stealthily descends by a pillar from unknown realms of mischief on the top of the house, evidently discredits cockey's stories, and departs down the garden to see if he can find something to eat.

An old cat comes up the garden walk, accompanied by a wicked kitten, who ambushes round the corner of the flower-bed, and pounces on her mother, knocking her down and severely maltreating her. But the old lady picks herself up without a murmur, and comes into the veranda followed by her unnatural offspring, ready for any mischief. The kangaroo rats retire into their box, and the cockatoo, rather nervous, lays himself out to be agreeable.

But the puppy, born under an unlucky star, who has been watching all these things from behind his mother, thinks at last, " Here is some one to play with," so he comes staggering forth and challenges the kitten to a lark.

She receives him with every symptom of disgust and abhorrence; but he, regardless of all spitting and tail-swelling, rolls her over, spurring and swearing, and makes believe he will worry her to death. Her scratching and biting tell but little on his woolly hide, and he seems to have the best of it out and out, till a new ally appears unexpectedly, and quite turns the tables. The magpie hops up, ranges alongside of the combatants, and catches the puppy such a dig over the tail as sends him howling to his mother with a flea in his ear.

Sam lay sleepily amused by this little drama; then he looked at the bright green arch which separated the dark verandah from the bright hot garden. The arch was darkened, and looking he saw something which made his heart move strangely, something that he has not forgotten yet, and never will.

Under the arch between the sunlight and the shade, bareheaded, dressed in white, stood a girl, so amazingly beautiful, that Sam wondered for a few moments whether he was asleep or awake. Her hat, which she had just taken off, hung on her left arm, and with her delicate right hand she arranged a vagrant tendril of the passion-flower, which in its luxuriant growth had broken bounds and fallen from its place above.—A girl so beautiful that I in all my life never saw her superior. They showed me the other day, in a carriage in the Park, one they said was the most beautiful girl in England, a descendant of I know not how many noblemen. But, looking back to the times I am speaking of now, I said at once and decidedly, " Alice Brentwood twenty years ago was more beautiful than she."

A Norman style of beauty, I believe you would call it. Light hair, deep brilliant blue eyes, and a very fair complexion. Beauty and high-bred grace in every limb and every motion. She stood there an instant on tiptoe, with the sunlight full upon her, while Sam, buried in gloom, had time for a delighted look, before she stepped into the veranda and saw him.

She floated towards him through the deep shadow. " I think," she said in the sweetest, most musical little voice, " that you are Mr. Buckley. If so, you are a very old friend of mine by report." So she held out her little hand, and with one bold kind look from the happy eyes, finished Sam for life.

Father and mother, retire into the chimney-corner and watch. Your day is done. Dr. Mulhaus, put your good advice into your pocket and smoke your pipe. Here is one who can exert a greater power for good or evil than all of you put together. It was written of old—" A man shall leave his father and mother and cleave unto his——" Hallo! I am getting on rather fast, I am afraid.

He had risen to meet her. " And you, Miss Brentwood," he said, " are tolerably well known to me. Do you know now that I believe by an exertion of memory I could tell you the year and the month when you began to learn the harp? My dear old friend Jim has kept me quite *au fait* with all your accomplishments."

" I hope you are not disappointed in me," said Alice, laughing.

" No," said Sam. " I think rather the contrary. Are you? "

" I have not had time to tell yet," she said. " I will see how you behave at lunch, which we shall have in half an hour *tête à tête*. You have been often here before, I believe? Do you see much change?"

"Not much. I noticed a new piano, and a little glove that I had never seen before. Jim's menagerie of wild beasts is as numerous as ever, I see. He would have liked to be in Noah's Ark."

"And so would you and I, Mr. Buckley," she answered, laughing, "if we had been caught in the flood."

Good gracious! Think of being in Noah's Ark with her!

"You find them a little troublesome, don't you, Miss Brentwood?"

"Well, it requires a good deal of administrative faculty to keep the kitten and the puppy from open collision, and to prevent the magpie from pecking out the cockatoo's eye and hiding it in the flower-bed. Last Sunday morning he (the magpie) got into my father's room, and stole thirty-one shillings and sixpence. We got it all back but half a sovereign, and that we shall never see."

The bird thus alluded to broke into a gush of melody, so rich, full, and metallic, that they both turned to look at him. Having attracted attention, he began dancing, crooning a little song to himself, as though he would say, "I know where it is." And lastly he puffed out his breast, put back his bill, and swore two or three oaths that would have disgraced a London scavenger, with such remarkable distinctness too, that there was no misunderstanding him; so Sam's affectation of not having caught what the bird said, was a dead failure.

"Mr. Buckley," said she, "if you will excuse me I will go and see about lunch. Can you amuse yourself there for half an hour?" Well, he would try. So he retired again to the rocking-chair, about ten years older than when he rose from it. For he had grown from a boy into a man.

He had fallen over head and ears in love, and all in five minutes. Fallen deeply, seriously in love, to the exclusion of all other sublunary matters, before he had well had time to notice whether she spoke with an Irish brogue or a Scotch (happily she did neither). Sudden, you say: well, yes; but, in lat. 34°, and lower, whether in the southern or northern atmosphere, these sort of affairs come on with a rapidity and violence only equalled by the thunderstorms of those regions, and utterly surprising to you who perhaps read this book in 52° north, or perhaps higher. I once went to a ball with as free-and-easy, heart-whole a young fellow as any I know, and agreed with him to stay half an hour, and then come away and play pool. In twenty-five minutes by my watch, which keeps time

like a ship's chronometer, that man was in the tragic or cut-throat
stage of the passion with a pretty little thing of forty, a cattle-
dealer's widow, who stopped *his* pool-playing for a time, until she
married the great ironmonger in George Street. Romeo and Juliet's
little matter was just as sudden, and very Australian in many points.
Only mind, that Romeo, had he lived in Australia, instead of taking
poison, would probably have

"Took to drinking ratafia, and thought of poor Miss Baily,"

for full twenty-four hours after the catastrophe.

At least such would have been the case in many instances, but not
in all. With some men these suddenly-conceived passions last their
lives, and then I should be inclined to say longer, were there not
strong authority against it.

But Sam? He saw the last twinkle of her white gown disappear,
and then leant back and tried to think. He could only say to
himself, "By Jove, I wonder if I can ever bring her to like me.
I wish I had known she was here; I'd have dressed myself better.
She is a precious superior girl. She might come to like me in
time. Heigh ho!"

The idea of his having a rival, or of any third person stepping
in between him and the young lady to whom he had thrown his
handkerchief, never entered into his Sultanship's head. Also, when
he came to think about it, he really saw no reason why she should
not be brought to think well of him. "As well me as another," said
he to himself; "that's where it is. She must marry somebody, you
know!"

Why is she gone so long? He begins to doubt whether he has not
after all been asleep and dreaming. There she comes again, however,
for the arch under the creepers is darkened again, and he looks
up with a pleasant smile upon his face to greet her.

God save us! What imp's trick is this? There, in the porch,
in the bright sun, where she stood not an hour ago in all her
beauty and grace, stands a hideous old savage, black as Tophet,
grinning; showing the sharp gap-teeth in her apish jaws, her lean
legs shaking with old age and rheumatism.

The collie shakes out her frill, and, raising the hair all down her
back, stands grinning and snarling, while her puppy barks pot-
valiantly between her legs. The little kangaroo rats ensconce themselves once more in their box, and gaze out amazed from their bright
little eyes. The cockatoo hooks and clambers up to a safe place in
the trellis, and Sam, after standing thunder-struck for a moment,
asks what she wants.

" Make a light," * says the old girl, in a pathetic squeak. Further answers she makes none, but squats down outside, and begins a petulant whine: sure sign that she has a tale of woe to unfold, and is going to ask for something.

" Can that creature," thinks Sam, " be of the same species as the beautiful Alice Brentwood? Surely not! There seems as much difference between them as between an angel and an ordinary good woman." Hard to believe, truly, Sam; but perhaps, in some of the great European cities, or even nearer home, in some of the prison barracks, you may chance to find a white woman or two fallen as low as that poor, starved, ill-treated, filthy old savage!

Alice comes out once more, and brings sunshine with her. She goes up to the old lubra with a look of divine compassion on her beautiful face; the old woman's whine grows louder as she rocks herself to and fro. " Yah marah, Yah boorah, Oh boora Yah! Yah Ma!"

" What! old Sally!" says the beautiful girl. " What is the matter? Have you been getting waddy again?"

" Baal!" says she, with a petulant burst of grief.

" What is it, then?" says Alice. " Where is the gown I gave you?"

Alice had evidently vibrated the right chord. The " Yarah Moorah " coronach was begun again; and then suddenly, as if her indignation had burst bounds, she started off with a shrillness and rapidity astonishing to one not accustomed to blackfellows, into something like the following: " Oh Yah (very loud), oh Mah! Barkmaburrawurrah, Barmamurrahwurrah Oh Ya Barkmanurrawah Yee (in a scream. Then a pause). Oh Mooroo (pause). O hinaray (pause). Oh Barknamurrwurrah Yee!"

Alice looked as if she understood every word of it, and waited till the poor old soul had " blown off the steam," and then asked again:

" And what has become of the gown, Sally?"

" Oh dear! Young lubra, Betty (big thief that one) tear it up and stick it along a fire. Oh, plenty cold this old woman. Oh, plenty hungry this old woman. Oh, Yarah Moorah," etc.

" There! go round to the kitchen," said Alice, " and get something to eat. Is it not abominable, Mr. Buckley? I cannot give anything to this old woman but the young lubras take it from her. However, I will ' put the screw on them.' They shall have nothing from me

---

* " Make a light " means simply " See."

till they treat her better. It goes to my heart to see a woman of that age, with nothing to look forward to but kicks and blows. I have tried hard to make her understand something of the next world: but I can't get it out of her head that when she dies she will go across the water and come back a young white woman with plenty of money. Mr. Sandford, the missionary, says he has never found one who could be made to comprehend the existence of God. However, I came to call you to lunch; will you give me your arm?"

Such a self-possessed, intrepid little maiden, not a bit afraid of him, but seeming to understand and trust him so thoroughly. Not all the mock-modesty and blushing in the world would have won him half so surely, as did her bold, quiet, honest look. Although a very young man, and an inexperienced, Sam could see what a candid, honest, gentle soul looked at him from those kind blue eyes; and she, too, saw something in Sam's broad noble face which attracted her marvellously, and in all innocence she told him so, plump and plain, as they were going into the house.

"I fancy I shall like you very much, Mr. Buckley. We ought to be good friends, you know; your father saved the lives of my father and uncle."

"I never heard of that before," said Sam.

"I dare say not," said Alice. "Your father is not the man to speak of his own noble deeds; yet he ran out of his square and pulled my father and uncle almost from under the hoofs of the French cavalry at Waterloo. It makes my cheeks tingle to tell of it now."

Indeed it did. Sam thought that if it brought such a beautiful flush to her face, and such a flash from her eyes, whenever she told it, that he would get her to tell it again more than once.

But lunch! Don't let us starve our new pair of turtle-doves, in the outset. Sam is but a growing lad, and needs carbon for his muscles, lime for his bones, and all that sort of thing; a glass of wine won't do him any harm either, and let us hope that his new passion is not of such lamentable sort as to prevent his using a knife and fork with credit and satisfaction to himself.

Here, in the dark, cool parlour, stands a banquet for the gods, white damask, pretty bright china, and clean silver. In the corner of the table is a frosted claret-jug, standing, with freezing polite-ness, upright, his hand on his hip, waiting to be poured out. In the centre, the grandfather of water-melons, half hidden by peaches and pomegranates, the whole heaped over by a confusion of ruby cherries (oh, for Lance to paint it!). Are you hungry, though? If so, here is a mould of potted-head and a cold wild duck, while, on the sideboard, I see a bottle of pale ale. My brother, let us breakfast in Scotland, lunch in Australia, and dine in France, till our lives' end.

And the banquet being over, she said, as pleasantly as possible, "Now, I know you want to smoke in the veranda. For my part, I should like to bring my work there and sit with you, but, if you had rather not have me, you have only to say that 'you could not think,' etc., etc., and I will obediently take myself off."

But Sam didn't say that. He said that he couldn't conceive anything more delightful, if she was quite sure she didn't mind.

Not she, indeed! So she brought her work out, and they sat together. A cool wind came up, bending the flowers, swinging the creepers to and fro, and raising a rushing sound, like the sea, from the distant forest. The magpie having been down the garden when the wind came on, and having been blown over, soon joined them in a very captious frame of mind; and when Alice dropped a ball of red worsted, he seized it as lawful prize, and away in the house with a hop and a flutter. So both Sam and Alice had to go after him, and hunt him under the sofa, and the bird, finding that he must yield, dropped the ball suddenly, and gave Sam two vicious digs on the fingers to remember him by. But when Alice just touched his hand in taking it from him, he wished it had been a whip-snake instead of a magpie.

So the ball of worsted was recovered, and they sat down again. He watched her nimble fingers on the delicate embroidery; he glanced at her quiet face and down-turned eyelids, wondering who she was thinking of. Suddenly she raised her eyes and caught him in the act. You could not swear she blushed; it might only be a trifling reflection from one of the red China roses that hung between her and the sun; yet, when she spoke, it was not quite with her usual self-possession; a little hurriedly perhaps.

"Are you going to be a soldier, as your father was?"

Sam had thought for an instant of saying "yes," and then to prove his words true of going to Sydney, and enlisting in the "Half Hundred." Truth, however, prompting him to say "no," he compromised the matter by saying he had not thought of it.

"I am rather glad of that, do you know," she said. "Unless in India, now, a man had better be anything than a soldier. I am afraid my brother Jim will be begging for a commission, some day. I wish he would stay quietly at home."

That was comforting. He gave up all thoughts of enlisting at once. But now the afternoon shadows were beginning to slant longer and longer, and it was nearly time that the Captain and Jim should make their appearance. So Alice proposed to walk out to meet them, and as Sam did not say no, they went forth together.

Down the garden, faint with the afternoon scents of the flowers before the western sun, among petunias and roses, oleander and magnolia; here a towering Indian lily, there a thicket of scarlet geranium and fuchsia. By shady young orange-trees, covered with fruit and blossom, between rows of trellised vines, bearing rich promise of a purple vintage. Among fig-trees and pomegranates, and so leaving the garden, along the dry slippery grass, towards the hoarse rushing river, both silent till they reached it. There is a silence that is golden.

They stood gazing on the foaming tide an instant, and then Alice said:

"My father and Jim will come home by the track across there. Shall we cross and meet them? We can get over just below."

A little lower down, all the river was collected into one headlong race; and a giant tree, undermined by winter floods, had fallen from one bank to the other, offering a giddy footway across the foaming water.

"Now," said Alice, "if you will go over, I will follow you."

So he ran across, and then looked back to see the beautiful figure tripping fearlessly over, with outstretched arms, and held out his great brown hand to take her tiny fingers as she stepped down from the upturned roots, on to the soft white sand. He would like to have taken them again, to help her up the bank, but she sprang up like a deer, and would not give him the opportunity. Then they had a merry laugh at the magpie, who had fluttered down all this way before them, to see if they were on a foraging expedition, and if there were any plunder going, and now could not summon courage to cross the river, but stood crooning and cursing by the brink. Then they sauntered away through the forest, side by side, along the sandy track, among the knolls of bracken, with the sunlit boughs overhead whispering knowingly to one another in the evening breeze, as they passed beneath.—An evening walk long remembered by both of them.

> "Oh see ye not that pleasant road,
>   That winds along the ferny brae?
> Oh that's the road to fairy land,
>   Where thou and I this e'en must gae."

"And so you cannot remember England, Mr. Buckley?" says Alice.

" Oh dear, no. Stay though, I am speaking too fast. I can remember some few places. I remember a steep, red road, that led up to the church, and have some dim recollection of a vast grey building, with a dark porch, which must have been the church itself. I can see, too, at this moment, a broad green flat, beside a creek, which was covered with yellow and purple flowers, which mother and I made into nosegays. That must be the place my father speaks of as the Hatherleigh Meadows, where he used to go fishing, and, although I must have been there often, yet I can only remember it on one occasion, when he emptied out a basket of fish on the grass for me to look at. My impression of England is, that everything was of a brighter colour than here; and they tell me I am right."

" A glorious country," said Alice; " what would I give to see it?— so ancient and venerable, and yet so amazingly young and vigorous. It seems like a waste of experience for a man to stay here tending sheep, when his birthright is that of an Englishman: the right to move among his peers, and find his fit place in the greatest empire in the world. Never had any woman such a noble destiny before her as this young lady who has just ascended the throne."

But the conversation changed here, and her Majesty escaped criticism for the time. They came to an open space in the forest, thickly grown with thickets of bracken fern, prickly acacia, and here and there a solitary dark-foliaged lightwood. In the centre rose a few blackened posts, the supports of what had once been a hut, and as you looked, you were surprised to see an English rose or two, flowering among the dull-coloured prickly shrubs, which were growing around. A place, as any casual traveller would have guessed, which had a history, and Sam, seeing Alice pause, asked her, " what old hut was this? "

" This," she said, " is the Donovans' old station, where they were burnt out by the blacks."

Sam knew the story well enough, but he would like to hear her tell it; so he made believe to have heard some faint reports of the occurrence, and what could she do, but give him the particulars?

" They had not been here a year," she said; " and Mrs. Donovan had been confined only three days; there was not a soul on the station but herself, her son Murtagh, and Miss Burke. All day the blackfellows were prowling about, and getting more and more insolent, and at night, just as Murtagh shut the door, they raised their yell, and rushed against it. Murtagh Donovan and Miss Burke had guessed what was coming all day, but had kept it from the sick woman, and now, when the time came, they were cool and prepared. They had two double-barrelled guns loaded with slugs, and with these they did such fearful execution from two loop-holes they had made in the slabs, that the savages quickly retired; but poor Miss Burke, incautiously looking out to get a shot, received a spear wound in her shoulder, which she bears the mark of to this day. But the worst was to come. The blackfellows mounted on the roof, tried to take off the bark, and throw their spears into the hut, but here they were foiled again. Wherever a sheet of bark was seen to move they watched, and on the first appearance of an enemy, a charge of shot at a few yards' distance told with deadly effect. Mrs. Donovan, who lay in bed and saw the whole, told my father that Lesbia Burke loaded and fired with greater rapidity and precision than did her cousin. A noble woman, I say."

"Good old Lesbia!" said Sam; "and how did it end?"

"Why, the foolish blacks fired the woolshed, and brought the Delisles upon them; they tried to fire the roof of the hut, but it was raining too hard: otherwise it would have gone hard with poor Miss Burke. See, here is a peach-tree they planted, covered with fruit; let us gather some; it is pretty good, for the Donovans have kept it pruned in memory of their escape."

"But the hut was not burnt," said Sam, "where did it stand?"

"That pile of earth there, is the remains of the old turf chimney. They moved across the river after it happened."

But peaches, when they grow on a high tree, must be climbed for, particularly if a young and pretty girl expresses a wish for them. And so it fell out, that Sam was soon astride of one of the lower boughs, throwing the fruit down to Alice, who put them one by one into the neatest conceivable little basket that hung on her arm.

And so they were employed, busy and merry, when they heard a loud cheery voice, which made both of them start.

"Quite a scene from *Paradise Lost,* I declare; only Eve ought to be up the tree handing down the apples to Adam, and not *vice versa.* I miss a carpet snake, too, who would represent the Deuce, and make the thing complete—Sam Buckley, how are you?"

It was Captain Brentwood who had come on them so inaudibly along the sandy track, on horseback, and beside him was his son Jim, looking rather mischievously at Sam, who did not show to the best of advantage up in the peach-tree; but, having descended, and greetings being exchanged, father and son rode on to dress for dinner, the hour for which was now approaching, leaving Sam and Alice to follow at leisure, which they did; for Captain Brentwood and Jim had time to dress and meet in the veranda, before they saw the pair come sauntering up the garden.

"Father," said Jim, taking the Captain's hand, "how would that do?"

"Marvellous well, I should say," replied the Captain.

"And so I think, too," said Jim. "Hallo! you two; dinner is ready, so look sharp."

After dinner the Captain retired silently to the chimney-corner, and read his book, leaving the three young people to amuse themselves as they would. Nothing the Captain liked so much as quiet, while he read some abstruse work on gunnery, or some scientific voyage; but I am sorry to say he had got very little quiet of an evening since Alice came home, and Jim had got someone to chatter to. This evening, however, seemed to promise well, for Alice brought out a great book of coloured prints, and the three sat down to turn them over, Jim, of course, you know, being in the middle.

The book was *Wild Sports of the East,* a great volume of coloured lithographs, worth some five-and-twenty guineas. One never sees such books as that nowadays, somehow; people, I fancy, would not pay that price for them. What modern travels have such plates as the old editions of *Cook's Voyages?* The number of illustrated books is increased tenfold, but they are hardly improved in quality.

But Sam, I think, would have considered any book beautiful in such company. "This," said Alice, "is what we call the 'Tiger Book'—why, you will see directly—you turn over, Jim, and don't crease the pages."

So Jim turned over, and kept them laughing by his simple remarks, more often affected than real, I suspect. Now they went through the tangled jungle, and seemed to hear the last mad howl of the dying tiger, as the elephant knelt and pinned him to the ground with his tusks. Now they chased a lordly buffalo from his damp lair in the swamp; now they saw the English officers flying along on their Arabs through the high grass with well-poised spears after the snorting hog. They have come unexpectedly on a terrible old tiger; one of the horses swerves, and a handsome young man, losing his seat, seems just falling into the monster's jaws, while the pariah dogs scud away terrified through the grass.

"That chap will be eaten immediately," says Jim.

"He has been in that position ever since I can remember," says Alice; "so I think he is pretty safe."

Now they are with the British army on the march. A scarlet bar stretches across the plain, of which the further end is lost in the white mirage—all in order; walking irresistibly on to the conquest of an empire greater than Haroun Al Raschid's. So naturally done too, that as you look, you think you see the columns swing as they advance, and hear the heavy, weary tramp of the troops above the din and shouting of the crowd of camp-followers, on camels and elephants, which surrounds them. Beyond the plain the faint blue hills pierce the grey air, barred with a few long white clouds, and far away a gleaming river winds through a golden country spanned with long bridges, and fringed with many a fantastic minaret.

"How should I like to see that!" said Alice.

"Would you like to be a countess," said Jim, "and ride on an elephant in a howitzer?"

"Howdah, you goose!" said Alice. "Besides, that is not a countess; that is one of the soldiers' wives. Countesses don't go to India: they stay at home to mind the Queen's clothes."

"What a pleasant job for them," said Jim, "when her Most Gracious Majesty has got the toothache! I wonder whether she wears her crown under her bonnet or over it?"

Captain Brentwood looked up. "My dear boy," he said, "does it not strike you that you are talking nonsense?"

"Did you ever see the old King, father?" said Jim.

"I saw King George the Third many times."

"Ah, but I mean to speak to him."

"Once only, and then he was mad. He was sitting up with her Majesty, waiting for intelligence which I brought. His Royal Highness took the dispatches from me, but the King insisted on seeing me."

"And what did he say, father? Do tell us," said Alice eagerly.

"Little enough, my love," said the Captain, leaning back. "He asked, 'Is this the officer who brought the dispatches, York?' And his Royal Highness said 'Yes.' Then the King said, 'You bring good news, sir: I was going to ask you some questions, but they are all gone out of my head. Go and get your supper; get your supper, sir.' Poor old gentleman. He was a kindly old man, and I had a great respect for him. Alice, sing us a song, my love."

She sang them "The Burial of Sir John Moore" with such perfect taste and pathos that Sam felt as if the candle had gone out when she finished. Then she turned round and said to him, "You ought to like that song; your father was one of the actors in it."

" He has often told me the story," said Sam, " but I never knew what a beautiful one it was till I heard you sing it."

All pleasant evenings must end, and at last she rose to go to bed. But Sam, before he went off to the land of happy dreams, saw that the little white glove which he had noticed in the morning was lying neglected on the floor; so he quietly secured and kept it. And, last year, opening his family Bible to refer to certain entries, now pretty numerous, in the beginning, I found a little white glove pinned to the fly-leaf, which I believe to be the same glove here spoken of.

CHAPTER XXVIII

A GENTLEMAN FROM THE WARS

I NEED hardly say that Sam was sorry when the two days which he had allowed himself for his visit were over. But that evening, when he mentioned the fact that he was going away in the morning, the Captain, Alice, and Jim, all pressed him so eagerly to stay another week, that he consented; the more as there was no earthly reason he knew of why he should go home.

And the second morning from that on which he should have been at home, going out to the stable before breakfast, he saw his father come riding over the plain, and, going to meet him, found that he, too, meditated a visit to the Captain.

" I thought you were come after me, father," said Sam. " By the by, do you know that the Captain's daughter, Miss Alice, is come home ? "

" Indeed ! " said the Major; " and what sort of a body is she ? "

" Oh, she is well enough. Something like Jim. Plays very well on the piano, and all that sort of thing, you know. Sings too."

" Is she pretty ? " asked the Major.

" Oh, well, I suppose she is," said Sam. " Yes; I should say that a great many people would consider her pretty."

They had arrived at the door, and the groom had taken the Major's horse, when Alice suddenly stepped out and confronted them.

The Major had been prepared to see a pretty girl, but he was by no means prepared for such a radiant, lovely, blushing creature as stepped out of the darkness into the fresh morning to greet him, clothed in white, bareheaded, with

" A single rose in her hair."

As he told his wife, a few days after, he was struck "all of a heap"; and Sam heard him whisper to himself, "By Jove!" before he went up to Alice and spoke.

"My dear young lady, you and I ought not to be strangers, for I recognise you from my recollections of your mother. Can you guess who I am?"

"I recognise you from my recollections of your son, sir," said Alice, with a sly look at Sam; "I should say that you were Major Buckley."

The Major laughed, and, taking her hand, carried it to his lips; a piece of old-fashioned courtesy she had never experienced before, and which won her heart amazingly.

"Come, come, Buckley!" said the quiet voice of Captain Brentwood from the dark passage; "what are you at there with my daughter? I shall have to call out and fight some of you young fellows yet, I see."

Alice went in past her father, stopping to give him a kiss, and disappeared into the breakfast-room. The Captain came out, and shook hands warmly with the Major, and said:

"What do you think of her—eh?"

"I never saw such beauty before," answered the Major; "never, by Jove! I tell you what, Brentwood, I wish she could come out this season in London. Why, she might marry a duke."

"Let us get her a rouge-pot and a French governess, and send her home by the next ship; eh, Buckley?" said the Captain, with his most sardonic smile. "She would be the better for a little polishing; wouldn't she, eh? Too hoydenish and forward, I am afraid; too fond of speaking the truth. Let's have her taught to amble, and mince, and—— Bah, come to breakfast!"

The Major laughed heartily at this tirade of the Captain's. He was fond of teasing him, and I believe the Captain liked to be teased by him.

"And what are you three going to do with yourselves to-day, eh?" asked the Captain at breakfast. "It is a matter of total indifference to me, so long as you take yourselves off somewhere, and leave me in peace."

Alice was spokesman: "We are going up to the Limestone Gates; Mr. Samuel Buckley has expressed a desire to see them, and so Jim and I thought of taking him there."

This was rather a jesuitical speech. The expedition to the Limestone Gates involved a long ride through very pretty scenery, which she herself had proposed. As for Sam, bless you; he didn't care whether they rode east, west, north, or south, so long as he rode beside her; however, having got his cue, he expressed a strong wish to examine, geologically, the great band of limestone which alternated with the slate towards the mountains, the more particularly as he knew that the Captain and the Major intended to ride out in another direction, to examine some new netting for sheep-yards which the Captain had imported.

If Major Buckley thought Alice beautiful as he had seen her in the morning, he did not think her less so when she was seated on a beautiful little horse, which she rode gracefully and courageously, in a blue riding-habit, and a sweet little grey hat with a plume of companion's feathers hanging down on one side. The cockatoo was on the door-step to see her start, and talked so incessantly in his excitement, that even when the magpie (who wanted, you know, to see the thing quietly and form his opinion, not to have everybody talking at once) assaulted him and pulled a feather out of his tail, he could not be quiet. Sam's horse Widderin capered with delight, and Sam's dog Rover coursed far and wide before them, with joyful bark. So they three went off through the summer's day as happy as though all life were one great summer's holiday, and there were no storms below the horizon to rise and overwhelm them; through the grassy flat, where the quail whirred before them, and dropped again as if shot; across the low rolling forest land, where a million parrots fled whistling to and fro, like jewels in the sun; past the old stock-yard, past the sheep-wash hut, and then through forest which grew each moment more dense and lofty, along the faint and narrow track which led into one of the most abrupt and romantic gullies which pierce the Australian Alps.

All this became classic ground to them afterwards, and the causes which made it so were now gathering to their fulfilment, even now, while these three were making happy holiday together, little dreaming of what was to come. Afterwards, years after, they three came and looked on this valley again; not as now, with laughter and jokes, but silently, speaking in whispers, as though they feared to wake the dead.

The road they followed, suddenly rising from the forest, took over the shoulder of a rocky hill, and then, plunging down again, followed a little running creek, up to where a great ridge of slate, crossing the valley, hemmed them in on either side, leaving only room for the creek and the road. Following it further, the glen opened out, sweeping away right and left in broad curves, while straight before them, a quarter of a mile distant, there rose out of the low scrub and fern a mighty wall of limestone, utterly barring all further progress save in a single spot to the left, where the vast grey wall was split, giving a glimpse of another glen beyond. This great natural cleft was the limestone gate which they had come to see, and which was rendered the more wonderful by a tall pinnacle of rock, which stood in the centre of the gap about 300 feet in height, not unlike one of the same kind in Dovedale.

"I don't think I ever saw anything so beautiful," said Alice. "How fine that spire of rock is, shooting up from the feathered shrubs at the base! I will come here some day and try to draw it."

"Wait a minute," said Jim; "you have not seen half yet."

He led them through the narrow pass, among the great boulders which lined the creek. The instant they came beyond, a wind, icy cold, struck upon their cheeks, and Alice, dropping her reins, uttered a cry of awe and wonder, and Sam too exclaimed aloud; for before them, partly seen through crowded tree stems, and partly towering above the forest, lay a vast level wall of snow, flecked here and there by the purple shadow of some flying summer cloud.

A sight so vast and magnificent held them silent for a little; then suddenly, Jim, looking at Alice, saw that she was shivering.

"What is the matter, Alice, my dear?" he said; "let us come away: the snow-wind is too much for you."

"Oh! it is not that!" she said. "Somebody is walking over my grave."

"Oh, that's all!" said Jim; "they are always at it with me, in cold weather. Let 'em. It won't hurt, that I know of."

But they turned homeward, nevertheless; and coming through the rock walls again, Jim said:

"Sam, what was that battle the Doctor and you were reading about one day, and you told me all about it afterwards, you know?"

"Malplaquet?"

"No; something like that, though. Where they got bailed up among the rocks, you know, and fought till they were all killed."

"Thermopylæ?"

"Ah! This must be just such another place, I should think."

"Thermopylæ was by the seashore," said Alice.

"Now, I should imagine," said Sam, pointing to the natural glacis formed by the decay of the great wall which they had seen fronting them as they came up, "that a few determined men with rifles, posted among those fern-trees, could make a stand against almost any force."

"But, Sam," said Jim, "they might be cut up by cavalry. Horses could travel right up the face of the slope there. Now, suppose a gang of bushrangers in that fern-scrub; do you think an equal number of police could not turn them out of it? Why, I have seen the place where Moppy's gang turned and fought Desborough on the Macquarie. It was stronger than this, and yet—you know what he did with them, only kept one small one for hanging, as he elegantly expressed it."

"But I ain't talking of bushrangers," said Sam. "I mean such fellows as the Americans in the War of Independence. See what a dance they led our troops with their bush-fighting."

"I wonder if ever there will be a War of Independence here," said Alice.

"I know which side I should be on, if there was," said Sam.

"Which would that be?" asked Jim.

"My dear friend," said Sam testily, "how can you, an officer's son, ask me, an officer's son, such a question? The King's (I beg pardon, the Queen's) side, of course."

"And so would I," said Jim, "if it came to that, you know."

"You would never have the honour of speaking to your sweet sister again, if you were not," said Alice.

"But I don't think those Americans were in the wrong; do you, Miss Brentwood?" said Sam.

"Why no; I don't suppose that such a man as General Washington, for instance, would have had much to do with them, if they had been."

"However," said Sam, "we are talking of what will never occur here. To begin with, we could never stand alone against a great naval power. They would shut us up here to starve. We have everything to lose, and nothing to gain by a separation. I would hardly like, myself, for the sake of a few extra pounds taxes, to sell my birthright as an Englishman."

"Conceive," said Alice, "being in some great European city, and being asked if you were British, having to say, No!"

They were coming through the lower pass, and turned to look back on the beautiful rock-walled amphitheatre, sleeping peaceful and still under the afternoon sun. The next time (so it happened) that Sam and Jim looked at that scene together, was under very different circumstances. Now the fronds of the fern-trees were scarce moved in the summer's breeze, and all was silent as the grave. They saw it again—when every fern tuft blazed with musketry, and the ancient cliffs echoed with the shouts of fighting, and the screams of dying men and horses.

"It is very early," said Alice. "Let us ride to the left, and see the great waterfall you speak of, Jim."

It was agreed. Instead of going home they turned through the forest, and debouched on the plains about two miles above Garoopna, and, holding their course to the river, came to it at a place where a great trap dike, crossing, formed a waterfall, over which the river, now full with melting snow, fell in magnificent confusion. They stood watching the grand scene with delight for a short time, and then, crossing the river by a broad, shallow ford, held their way homeward, along the eastern and more level bank, sometimes reining up their horses to gaze into the tremendous glen below them, and watch the river crawling on through many impediments, and beginning to show a golden light in its larger pools beneath the sloping, westering sun.

Just as they sighted home, on the opposite side of the river, they perceived two horsemen before them, evidently on the track between Major Buckley's and Garoopna. They pushed on to overhaul them, and found that it was Dr. Mulhaus, whom they received with boisterous welcome, and a tall, handsome young gentleman, a stranger.

"A young gentleman, Sam," said the Doctor, "Mr. Halbert by name, who arrived during your father's absence with letters of introduction. I begged him to follow your father over here, and, as his own horse was knocked up, I mounted him at his own request on Jezebel, he preferring her to all the horses in the paddock on account of her beauty, after having been duly warned of her wickedness. But Mr. Halbert seems of the Centaur species, and rather to enjoy an extra chance of getting his neck broke."

Politeness to strangers was one of the first articles of faith in the Buckley and Brentwood families : so the young folks were soon on the best of terms.

"Are you from Sydney way, Mr. Halbert?" said Sam.

"Indeed," said the young man, "I have only landed in the country six weeks. I have got three years' leave of absence from my regiment in India, and, if I can see a chance, I shall cut the army and settle here."

"Oh!" said Alice, "are you a soldier, Mr. Halbert?"

"I have that honour, Miss Brentwood. I am a lieutenant in the Bengal Horse Artillery."

"That is delightful. I am a soldier's daughter, and Mr. Buckley here also, as you know, I suppose."

"A soldier's daughter, is he?" said impudent Jim. "A very fine girl, too!"

Sam, and Jim too, had some disrespectful ideas about soldiers' riding qualities; Sam could not help saying:

"I hope you will be careful with that mare, Mr. Halbert; I should not like a guest of ours to be damaged. She's a desperate brute—I'm afraid of her myself."

"I think I know the length of her ladyship's foot," said Halbert, laughing good-naturedly.

As they were speaking, they were passing through a narrow way in a wattle scrub. Suddenly a blundering kangaroo, with Rover in full chase, dashed right under the mare's nose and set her plunging furiously. She tried to wheel round, but, finding herself checked, reared up three or four times, and at last seemed to stand on her hind legs, almost overbalancing herself.

Halbert sat like a statue till he saw there was a real chance of her falling back on him; then he slipped his right foot quickly out of the stirrup, and stood with his left toe in the iron, balancing himself till she was quieter; then he once more threw his legs across the saddle, and regained his seat, laughing.

Jim clapped his hands; "By Jove, Sam, we must get some of these army men to teach us to ride, after all!"

"We must do so," said Sam. "If that had been you or I, Jim, with our rough clumsy hands, we should have had the mare back atop of us."

"Indeed," said Alice, "you are a splendid rider, Mr. Halbert; but don't suppose, from Mr. Buckley's account of himself, that he can't ride well; I assure you we are all very proud of him. He can sit some bucking horses which very few men will attempt to mount."

"And that same bucking, Miss Brentwood," said Halbert, "is just what puzzles me utterly. I got on a bucking horse in Sydney the other day, and had an ignominious tumble in the sale-yard, to everybody's great amusement."

"We must give one another lessons, then, Mr. Halbert," said Sam; "but I can see already, that you have a much finer hand than I."

Soon after they got home, where the rest of the party were watching for them, wondering at their late absence. Halbert was introduced to the Major by the Doctor, who said, "I deliver over to you a guest, a young conqueror from the Himalayas, and son of an old brother warrior. If he now breaks his neck horse-riding, his death will not be at my door; I can now eat my dinner in peace."

After dinner the three young ones, Sam, Alice, and Jim, gathered round the fire, leaving Halbert with the Major and the Captain talking military, and the Doctor looking over an abstruse mathematical calculation, with which Captain Brentwood was not altogether satisfied. Alice and Sam sat in chairs side by side, like Christians, but Jim lay on the floor, between the two, like a blackfellow; they talked in a low voice about the stranger.

"I say," said Jim, "ain't he a handsome chap, and can't he ride? I dare say he's a devil to fight, too—hear him tell how they pounded away at those Indians in that battle. I expect they'd have made a general of him before now, only he's too young. Dad says he's a very distinguished young officer. Alice, my dear, you should see the wound he's got, a great seam all down his side. I saw it when he was changing his shirt in my room before dinner."

"Poor fellow!" said Alice; "I like him very much. Don't you, Mr. Buckley?"

"I like him exceedingly; I hope he'll stop with us," continued Jim.

"And I also," said Sam, "but what shall we do to-morrow?"

"Let's have a hunt," said Jim. "Halbert, have you ever been kangaroo hunting?"

"Never!—I want to go!"

"Well, we can have a capital hunt to-morrow: Sam has got his dog Fly here, and I'll take one of my best dogs, and we'll have a good run, I dare say."

"I shall come, too," said Alice: "that is," added she, looking shyly at Sam, "if you would be kind enough to take care of me, and let Mr. Halbert and Jim do the riding. But I'm afraid I shall be sadly in your way."

"If you don't go," said Sam, "I shall stay at home: now then!"

At this minute, the housekeeper came in bearing jugs and glasses. "Eleanor," said Jim, "Is Jerry round?"

"Yes, sir; he's coiled somewhere in the woodhouse," said she.

"Just rouse him out and send him in."

"Who is this Jerry who coils in wood-houses?" said Halbert.

"A tame black belonging to us. He is great at all sorts of hunting; I want to see if he can find us a flying doe for to-morrow."

Jerry entered, and advanced with perfect self-possession towards the fire. He was a tall savage, with a big black beard, and wavy hair like a Cornishman. He was dressed in an old pair of dandy riding breeches of Jim's, which reached a short way below the knees, fitting closely, and a blue check shirt rolled up above the elbows showing his lean wiry forearm, seamed and scarred with spear wounds and bruises. He addressed nobody, but kept his eyes wandering all over the room; at length he said, looking at the ceiling:

"Cobbon thirsty this fellow: you got a drop of brandy?"

"Jerry," said Jim, having produced the brandy, "you make a light kangaroo."

"All about plenty kangaroo," said Jerry.

"Yowi; but mine want it big one flying doe."

"Ah-h-h! Mine make a light flying doe along a stock-yard this morning; close by, along a fent, you see!"

"That'll do," says Jim. "We'll be up round the old stock-yard after breakfast to-morrow. You, Jerry, come with us."

It was a fresh breezy autumn morning in April, when the four sallied forth, about nine o'clock, for their hunt. The old stock-yard stood in the bush, a hundred yards from the corner of the big paddock fence, and among low rolling ranges and gullies, thickly timbered with gum, cherry, and she-oak: a thousand parrots flew swiftly in flocks, whistling and screaming from tree to tree, while wattled-birds and numerous other honey-eaters clustered on the flowering banksias. The spur-winged plover and the curlew ran swiftly among the grass, and on a tall dead tree white cockatoos and blue cranes watched the intruders curiously.

Alice and Sam rode together soberly, and before them were Halbert and Jim, girt up, ready for the chase. Before them, again, was the active blackfellow, holding the dogs in leash—two tall hounds, bred of foxhound and greyhound, with a dash of collie.

A mob of kangaroos crosses their path, but they are all small; so the dogs, though struggling fiercely, are still held tight by Jerry: now he crosses a little ridge before them and looks down into the gully beyond, holding up his hand.

The two young men gather up their reins and settle themselves in their seats. "Now, Halbert," says Jim, "sit fast and mind the trees."

They ride up to the blackfellow; through the low wattles, they can see what is in the gully before them, though the dogs cannot.

"Baal, flying doe this one," says Jerry in a whisper. "Old man this fellow, cobbon matong (very strong), mine think it."

A great six-foot kangaroo was standing about two hundred yards from them, staring stupidly about him.

"Let go, Jerry," said Jim. The dogs released, sprang forward, and, in an instant, saw their quarry, which, with a loud puff of alarm, bounded away up the opposite slope at full speed, taking twenty feet at each spring.

Halbert and Jim dashed off after the dogs, who had got a good start of them, and were laying themselves out to their work right gallantly; Sam's dog, Fly, slightly leading. Both dogs were close on the game, and Halbert said:

"We are going to have a short run, I'm afraid."

"Talk about that twenty minutes hence," said Jim, settling to his work.

Over range after range they hold their headlong course. Now a bandicoot scuttles away from under their feet to hide in his hollow log; now a mob of terrified cattle huddle together as they sweep by; now they are flying past a shepherd's hut, and the mother runs out to snatch up a child, and bear him out of harm's way, after they are safe past. A puppy, three weeks old, joins the chase with heart and soul, but "caves in" at about fifty yards, and sits him down to bark. Now they are rushing on through a broad flat, with another great range before them. Still always the grey bounding figure holds on, through sunlight and shadow, with the dogs grim and steadfast close in his wake.

The work begins to tell on the horses. Fat Jezebel, who could hardly be held at first, now is none the worse for a little spur; and Jim's lean, long-legged horse, seems to consider that the entertainment ought to conclude shortly. "Well done, Fly!" he shouts; "bravely tried, my girl!" She had drawn herself ahead, and made a bold strike at the kangaroo, but missed him. Now the other dog, Bolt, tries it, but without luck; and now they have both dropped a little back, and seem in for another mile or so.

Well done, lass!—there she goes again! With a furious effort she pushes ahead, and seizes the flying beast by the hock—this time with some luck, for down he goes in a cloud of dust and broken sticks, and both the dogs are on him at once. Now he is up again and running, but feebly. And see, what is the matter with the young dog? He runs on, but keeps turning, snapping fiercely at his side, and his footsteps are marked with blood. Poor lad! he has got a bad wound in that last tumble—the kangaroo has ripped up his flank with a kick from his hind foot. But now the chase is over— the hunted beast has turned, and is at bay against a tree, Fly standing before him, waiting for assistance, snarling fiercely.

They pulled up. Jim took out a pistol and presented it to Halbert.

"Thank you," said he. "Hair trigger?"

"Yes."

He balanced it for a second, and in another the kangaroo was lying quivering on the ground, shot through the heart.

"Well done!" said Jim. "Now I must look to this dog."

All his flank along the ribs was laid open, and Jim, producing a needle and thread, proceeded to sew it up.

"Will you let me do that for you?" said Halbert.

"I wish you would. I'm fond of the poor thing, and my hand shakes. You've seen the surgeons at work, I expect."

"Yes, indeed." And he tenderly and carefully stitched up the dog's side, while Jim held him.

"What do we do with the game?" said he.

"Oh, Jerry will be along on our tracks presently," said Jim. "He brings me the tail, and does what he likes with the rest. I wonder where Sam and Alice are?"

"Oh, they are right enough," said Halbert, laughing. "I dare say they are not very anxious about the kangaroo, or anything else. That's 'a case,' I suppose?"

"Well, I hope it is," said Jim; "but you see I don't know. Girls are so odd."

"Perhaps he has never asked her."

"No; I don't think he has. I wish he would. You are not married, are you?"

"My God—no!" said Halbert, "nor ever shall be."

"Never?"

"Never, Jim. Let me tell you a story as we ride home. You and I shall be good friends, I know. I like you already, though we have only known one another two days. I can see well what you are made of. They say it eases a man's mind to tell his grief. I wish it would mine. Well; before I left England I had secretly engaged myself to marry a beautiful girl, very much like your sister, a governess in my brother-in-law's family. I went off to join my regiment, and left here there with my sister and her husband, Lord Carstone, who treated her as if she was already one of the family—God bless them! Two years ago my father died, and I came into twenty thousand pounds; not much, but enough to get married on in India, particularly as I was getting on in my profession. So I wrote to her to come out to me. She sailed in the *Assam* for Calcutta, but the ship never arrived. She was spoken off the Mauritius, but never seen after. The underwriters have paid up her insurance, and every one knows now that the *Assam* went down in a typhoon, with all hands."

"God bless you!" said Jim, "I am very sorry for that."

"Thank you. I have come here for a change of scene more than anything, but I think I shall go back soon."

"I shall come with you," said Jim. "I have determined to be a soldier, and I know the governor has interest enough to get me into some regiment in India." (I don't believe he had ever thought of it before that morning.)

"If you are determined, he might. His services in India were too splendid to have been forgotten yet."

"I wonder," said Jim, "if he will let me go? I'd like to see Alice married first."

They jogged on in silence for a little, and slowly, on account of the wounded dogs. Then Jim said:

"Well, and how did you like your sport?

"Very much indeed; but I thought bush-riding was harder work. We have only had one or two leaps over fallen logs altogether."

"There ain't much leaping, that's a fact. I suppose you have been fox-hunting?"

"My father was a master of hounds," replied Halbert. "On the first day of the season, when the hounds met at home, there would be two hundred horsemen on our terrace, fifty of them, at least, in pink. It was a regular holiday for all the country round. Such horses, too. My father's horse, the Elk, was worth £300, and there were better horses than him to be seen in the field, I promise you."

"And all after a poor little fox!"

"You don't know Charley, I can see," said Halbert. "Poor little fox, indeed! Why, it's as fair a match between the best-tried pack of hounds in England, and an old dog-fox, as one would wish to see. And as hard work as it is to ride up to them, even without a stiff fence at every two hundred yards, to roll you over on your head, if your horse is blown or clumsy. Just consider how many are run, and how few are killed. I consider a fox to be the noblest quarry in the world. His speed, courage, and cunning are wonderful. I have seen a fox run fifteen miles as the crow flies, and only three of us in at the death. That's what I call sport."

"So do I, by Jove!" said Jim. "You have some good sport in India, too?"

"Yes. Pig-sticking is pretty—very pretty, I may say, if you have two or three of the right sort with you. All the Griffins ought to hunt together, though. There was a young fellow, a King's-officer, and a nobleman, too, came out with us the other day, and rode well forward, but as the pig turned he contrived to spear my horse through the pastern. He was full of apologies, and I was outwardly highly polite and indifferent, but internally cursing him up hill and down dale. I went home and had the horse shot; but when I got up next morning, there was a Syce leading up and down a magnificent Australian, a far finer beast than the one which I had lost, which my Lord had sent up to replace my unfortunate nag. I went down to his quarters and refused to accept it; but he forced me in the end, and it gave me a good lesson about keeping my temper over an unavoidable accident, which I don't mean to forget. Don't you think it was prettily done?"

"Yes, I do," said Jim; "but you see these noblemen are so rich that they can afford to do that sort of thing, where you or I couldn't. But I expect they are very good fellows on the whole."

"There are just as large a proportion of good noblemen as there are of any other class—more than that you have no right to expect. I'm a liberal, as my father was before me, and a pretty strong one too; but I think that a man with sixty thousand acres, and a seat in the House of Lords, is entitled to a certain sort of respect. A Grand Seigneur is a very capital institution if he will only stay on his estates some part of the year."

"Ay!" said Jim; who was a shrewd fellow in his way. "They know that here, well enough; look at our Macarthurs and Wentworths—but then they must be men, and not snobs, as the governor says."

When they got home, they found Sam and Alice sitting in the veranda as comfortable as you please.

"Well," said Jim, "you are a nice lot! This is what you call kangaroo-hunting!"

"Oh, you went too fast for us. Have you killed?"

"Yes! out by the big swamp."

"You have taken your time to get home then."

"Poor Bolt is cut up, and we couldn't go out of a walk. Now give us something to eat, will you, Alice?"

"Well, ring the bell and we will have lunch."

But just as Jim rang the bell, there was a loud voice outside, and the three young men went out to see who it was, and found two horsemen in front of the door.

One, who was still sitting on his horse, was a dark-haired slight young man, Charles Hawker in fact, whom we know already, but the other, who had dismounted, and was leaning against his horse, was a high-bred, delicate little fellow, to whom we have yet to be introduced.

He was a slight lad, perhaps not more than eighteen, with one of the pleasantest, handsomest faces of his own that you could wish to see, and also a very intellectual look about him, which impressed you at once with the idea that if he lived he would have made some sort of figure in life. He was one of the greatest dandies, also, in those parts, and after the longest ride used to look as if he had been turned out of a bandbox. On the present occasion he had on two articles of dress which attracted Jim's attention amazingly. The first was a new white hat, which was a sufficiently remarkable thing in those parts at that time; and the second, a pair of yellow leather riding-trousers.

"Why, Cecil Mayford!" said Sam, "how do you do? Charley, how are you? Just in time for lunch. Come in."

Jim was walking round and round Cecil without speaking a word. At last the latter said, "How do *you* do, James Brentwood?"

"How do your breeches do, Cecil?" answered Jim; "that is a much more important question. By the by, let me introduce you to Mr. Halbert. Also, allow me to have the honour to inform you that my sister Alice is come home from school."

"I am aware of that, and am come over to pay my respects. Sam, leave me alone. If I were to disarrange my dress before I was presented to Miss Brentwood, I would put a period to my existence. Jim, my dear soul, come in and present me. Don't all you fellows come mobbing in, you know."

So Jim took Cecil in, and the other young fellows lounged about the door in the sun. "Where have you come from, Charley?" asked Sam.

"I have been staying at the Mayfords'; and this morning, hearing that you and your father were here, we thought we would come over and stay a bit."

"By the by," said Sam, "Ellen Mayford was to have come home from Sydney the same time as Alice Brentwood, or thereabouts. Pray, is she come?"

"Oh, yes!" said Charles; "she is come this fortnight, or more."

"What sort of a girl has she grown to be?"

"Well, *I* call her an uncommonly pretty girl. A very nice girl indeed, I should say. Have you heard the news from the north?"

"No!"

"Bushrangers! Nine or ten devils, loose on the upper Macquarie, caught the publican at Marryong alone in the bush; he had been an overlooker, or some such thing, in old times, so they stripped him, tied him up, gave him four dozen, and left him to the tender mercies of the blowflies, in consequence of which he was found dead next day, with the cords at his wrists cutting down to the bone with the struggles he made in his agony."

" Whew! " said Sam. " We are going to have some of the old-fashioned work over again. Let us hope Desborough will get hold of them before they come this way."

" Some of our fellow-countrymen," said Halbert, " are, it seems to me, more detestably ferocious than savages, when they once get loose."

" Much of a muchness—no better, and perhaps no worse," said Sam. " All men who act entirely without any law in their actions arrive at much the same degree, whether white or black."

" And will this Captain Desborough, whom you speak of, have much chance of catching these fellows? " asked Halbert.

" They will most likely disperse on his approach if he takes any force against them," said Sam. " I heard him say, myself, that the best way was to tempt them to stay and show fight, by taking a small force against them, as our admirals used to do to the French, in the war. By the by, how is Tom Troubridge? He is quite a stranger to me. I have only seen him twice since he was back from Port Phillip."

" He is off again now, after some rams, up to the north."

" I hope he won't fall in with the bushrangers. Anybody with him? "

" William Lee," answered Charles.

" A good escort. There is lunch going in—come along."

CHAPTER XXIX

SAM MEETS WITH A RIVAL, AND HOW HE TREATED HIM

THAT week one of those runs upon the Captain's hospitality took place which are common enough in the bush, and, although causing a temporary inconvenience, are generally as much enjoyed by the entertainer as entertained. Everybody during this next week came to see them, and nobody went back again. So by the end of the week there were a dozen or fourteen guests assembled, all uninvited, and apparently bent on making a good long stay of it.

Alice, who had expected to be rather put out, conducted everything with such tact and dignity that Mrs. Buckley remarked to Mrs. Mayford, when they were alone together, " that she had never seen such beauty and such charming domestic grace combined, and that he would be a lucky young fellow who got her for a wife."

"Well, yes, I should be inclined to say so too," answered Mrs. Mayford. "Rather much of the boarding-school as yet, but that will wear off, I dare say. I don't think the young lady will go very long without an offer. Pray, have you remarked anything, my dear madam?"

Yes, Mrs. Buckley had remarked something on her arrival the day before yesterday. She had remarked Sam and Alice come riding over the paddock, and Sam, by way of giving a riding-lesson, holding the little white hand in his, teaching it (the dog!) to hold the reins properly. And on seeing Alice she had said to herself, " That will do." But all this was not what Mrs. Mayford meant—in fact, these two good ladies were at cross-purposes.

"Well, I thought I did," replied Mrs. Buckley, referring to Sam. " But one must not be premature. They are both very young, and may not know their own minds."

"They seem as if they did," said Mrs. Mayford. "Look there!" Outside the window they saw something which gave Mrs. Buckley a sort of pang, and made Mrs. Mayford laugh.

There was no one in the garden visible but Cecil Mayford and Alice, and she was at that moment busily engaged in pinning a rose into his button-hole. "The audacious girl!" thought Mrs. Buckley; " I am afraid she will be a daughter of debate among us. I wish she had not come home." While Mrs. Mayford continued:

"I am far from saying, mind you, my dear Mrs. Buckley, that I don't consider Cecil might do far better for himself. The girl is pretty, very pretty, and will have money. But she is too decided, my dear. Fancy a girl of her age expressing opinions! Why, if I had ventured to express opinions at her age, I—I don't know what my father would have said."

"Depend very much on what sort of opinions they were; wouldn't it?" said Mrs. Buckley.

"No; I mean any opinions. Girls ought to have no opinions at all. There, last night when the young men were talking all together, she must needs get red in the face and bridle up, and say, ' She thought an Englishman who wasn't proud of Oliver Cromwell was unworthy of the name of an Englishman.' Her very words, I assure you. Why, if my daughter Ellen had dared to express herself in that way about a murderous Papist, I'd have slapped her face!"

"I don't think Cromwell was a Papist; was he?" said Mrs. Buckley.

"A Dissenter, then, or something of that sort," said Mrs. Mayford. "But that don't alter the matter. What I don't like to see is a young girl thrusting her oar in in that way. However, I shall make no opposition, I can assure you. Cecil is old enough to choose for himself, and a mother's place is to submit. Oh, no, I assure you, whatever my opinions may be, I shall offer no opposition."

"I shouldn't think you would," said Mrs. Buckley, as the other left the room: "rather a piece of luck for your boy to marry the handsomest and richest girl in the country. However, madam, if you think I am going to play a game of chess with you for that girl, or any other girl, why, you are mistaken."

And yet it was very provoking. Ever since she had begun to hear from various sources how handsome and clever Alice was, she had made up her mind that Sam should marry her, and now to be put out like this by people whom they had actually introduced into the house! It would be a great blow to Sam too. She wished he had never seen her. She would sooner have lost a limb than caused his honest heart one single pang. But, after all, it might be only a little flirtation between her and Cecil. Girls would flirt; but then there would be Mrs. Mayford manœuvring and scheming her heart out, while she, Agnes Buckley, was constrained by her principles only to look on and let things take their natural course.

Now, there arose a coolness between Agnes Buckley and the Mayfords, mother and son, which was never made up—never, oh, never! Not very many months after this she would have given ten thousand pounds to have been reconciled to the kind-hearted old busybody; but then it was too late.

But now, going out into the garden, she found the Doctor busy planting some weeds he had found in the bush, in a quiet corner, with an air of stealth, intending to privately ask the gardener to see after them till he could fetch them away. The magpie, having seen from the window a process of digging and burying going on, had attended in his official capacity, standing behind the Doctor, and encouraging him every now and then with a dance, or a few flute-like notes of music. I need hardly mention that the moment the Doctor's back was turned the bird rooted up every one of the plants, and buried them in some secret spot of his own, where they lie, I believe, till this day.

To the Doctor she told the whole matter, omitting nothing, and then asked his advice. " I suppose," she said, " you will only echo my own determination of doing nothing at all ? "

" Quite so, my dear madam. If she loves Sam, she will marry him; if she don't, he is better without her."

" That is true," said Mrs. Buckley. " I hope she will have good taste enough to choose my boy."

" I hope so too, I am sure," said the Doctor. " But we must not be very furious if she don't. Little Cecil Mayford is both handsomer and cleverer than Sam. We must not forget that, you know."

That evening was the first thoroughly unhappy evening, I think, that Sam ever passed in his life. I am inclined to imagine that his digestion was out of order. If any of my readers ever find themselves in the same state of mind that he was in that night, let them be comforted by considering that there is always a remedy at hand, before which evil thoughts and evil tempers of all kinds fly like mist before the morning sun. How many serious family quarrels, marriages out of spite, and alterations of wills might have been prevented by a gentle dose of blue pill! What awful instances of chronic dyspepsia are presented to our view by the immortal bard in the characters of Hamlet and Othello! I look with awe on the digestion of such a man as the present King of Naples. Banish dyspepsia and spirituous liquors from society, and you would have no crime, or at least so little that you would not consider it worth mentioning.

However, to return to Sam. He, Halbert, Charles Hawker, and Jim had been away riding down an emu, and had stayed out all day. But Cecil Mayford, having made excuse to stay at home, had been making himself in many ways agreeable to Alice, and at last had attended her on a ride, and on his return had been rewarded with a rose, as we saw. The first thing Sam caught sight of when he came home was Alice and Cecil walking up and down the garden very comfortably together, talking and laughing. He did not like to see this. He dreaded Cecil's powers of entertainment too much, and it made him angry to hear how he was making Alice laugh. Then, when the four came into the house, this offending couple took no notice of them at all, but continued walking up and down in the garden, till Jim, who, not being in love, didn't care twopence whether his sister came in or not, went out to the veranda, and called out " Hi! "

" What now? " said Alice, turning round.

" Why, we're come home," said Jim, " and I want you."

" Then you won't get me, impudence," said Alice, and began walking up and down again. But not long after, having to come in, she just said, " How do, Mr. Halbert? " and passed on, never speaking to Sam. Now there was no reason why she should have spoken to him, but " Good evening, Mr. Buckley," would not have hurt anybody. And now in came Cecil, with that unlucky rose, and Jim immediately began:

" Hallo, Cis, where did you get your flower? "

" Ah, that's a secret," said Cecil, with an affected look.

" No secret at all," said Alice, coming back. " I gave it to him. He had the civility to stay and take me out for a ride, instead of going to run down those poor pretty emus. And that is his reward. I pinned it into his coat for him." And out she went again.

Sam was very sulky, but he couldn't exactly say with whom. With himself more than anybody, I believe.

" Like Cecil's consummate impudence! " was his first thought; but after he had gone to his room to dress, his better nature came to him, and before dinner came on he was his old self again, unhappy still, but not sulky, and determined to be just.

" What right have I to be angry, even suppose she does come to care more for him than for me? What can be more likely? he is more courtly, amusing, better-looking, they say, and certainly cleverer; oh, decidedly cleverer. He might as well make me his enemy as I make him mine. No; dash it all! He has been like a brother to me ever since he was so high, and I'll be damned if there shan't be fair play between us two, though I should go into the army through it. But I'll watch, and see how things go."

So he watched at dinner and afterwards, but saw little to comfort him. Saw one thing, nay, two things, most clearly. One was, that Cecil Mayford was madly in love with Alice; and the other was, that poor Cecil was madly jealous of Sam. He treated him differently to what he had ever done before, as though on that evening he had first found his rival. Nay, he became almost rude, so that once Jim looked suddenly up, casting his shrewd blue eyes first on one and then on the other, as though to ask what the matter was. But Sam only said to himself, " Let him go on. Let him say what he will. He is beside himself now, and some day he will be sorry. He shall have fair play, come what will."

But it was hard for our lad to keep his temper sometimes. It was hard to see another man sitting alongside of her all the evening, paying her all those nameless little attentions which somehow, however unreasonably, he had brought himself to think were his right, and no one else's, to pay. Hard to wonder and wonder whether or no he had angered her, and if so, how? Halbert, good heart, saw it all, and sitting all the evening by Sam, made himself so agreeable, that for a time even Alice herself was forgotten. But then, when he looked up, and saw Cecil still beside her, and her laughing and talking so pleasantly, while he was miserable and unhappy, the old chill came on his heart again, and he thought—was the last happy week only a deceitful gleam of sunshine, and should he ever take his old place beside her again?

Once or twice more during the evening Cecil was almost insolent to him, but still his resolution was strong.

"If he is a fool, why should I be a fool? I will wait and see if he can win her. If he does, why there is India for me. If he does not, I will try again. Only I will not quarrel with Cecil, because he is blinded. Little Cecil, who used to bathe with me, and ride pick-a-back round the garden! No; he shall have fair play. By Jove, he shall have fair play, if I die for it."

And he had some little comfort in the evening. When they had all risen to go to bed, and were standing about in confusion lighting candles, he suddenly found Alice by his side, who said in a sweet, low, musical tone:

"Can you forgive me?"

"What have I to forgive, my dear young lady?" he said softly. "I was thinking of asking your forgiveness for some unknown fault."

"I have behaved so ill to you to-day," she said, "the first of my new friends! I was angry at your going out after our poor emus, and I was cross to you when you came home. Do let us be friends again."

There was a chance for a reconciliation! But here was Cecil Mayford thrusting between them with a lit candle just at the wrong moment; and she gave him such a sweet smile, and such kind thanks, that Sam felt nearly as miserable as ever.

And next morning everything went wrong again. Whether it was merely coquetry, or whether she was angry at their hunting emus, or whether she for a time preferred Cecil's company, I know not; but she, during the next week, neglected Sam altogether, and refused to sit beside him, making a most tiresome show of being unable to get on without Cecil Mayford, who squired her here, there, and everywhere, in the most provoking fashion.

But it so happened that the Doctor and the Major sat up later than the others that night, taking a glass of punch together before the fire, and the Major said, abruptly:

"There will be mischief among the young fellows about that girl. It is a long while since I saw one man look at another as young Mayford did at our Sam to-night. I wish she were out of the way. Sam and Mayford are both desperately in love with her, and one must go to the wall. I wish that boy of mine was keener; he stayed aloof from her all to-night."

"Don't you see his intention?" said the Doctor. "I am very much mistaken if I do not. He is determined to leave the field clear for all comers, unless she herself makes some sort of advances to him. 'If she prefers Mayford,' says Sam to himself, 'in the way she appears to, why, she is welcome to him, and I can go home as soon as I am assured of it.' And go home he would, too, and never say one word of complaint to any living soul."

"What a clear, brave, honest soul that lad has!" said the Major.

"Truly," said the Doctor, "I only know one man who is his equal."

"And who is he?"

"His father. Good night: good dreams!"

So Sam kept to his resolution of finding out whether or no Alice was likely to prefer Cecil to him. And, for all his watching and puzzling, he couldn't. He had never confided one word of all this to his mother, and yet she knew it all as well as he.

Meanwhile, Cecil was quite changed. He almost hated Sam, and seldom spoke to him, and at the same time hated himself for it. He grew pale, too, and never could be persuaded to join any sport whatever; while Sam, being content to receive only a few words in the day from My Lady, worked harder than ever, both in the yards and riding. All day he and Jim would be working like horses, with Halbert for their constant companion, and, half an hour before dinner, would run whooping down to the river for their bathe, and then come in clean, happy, hungry—so full of life and youth, that in these sad days of deficient grinders, indigestion, and liver, I can hardly realise that once I myself was as full of blood and as active and hearty as any of them.

There was much to do the week that Alice and Sam had their little tiff. The Captain was getting in the "scrubbers," cattle which had been left, under the not very careful rule of the Donovans, to run wild in the mountains. These beasts had now to be got in, and put through such processes as cattle are born to undergo. The Captain and the Major were both fully stiff for working in the yards, but their places were well supplied by Sam and Jim. The two fathers, with the assistance of the stock-man, and sometimes of the sons, used to get them into the yards, and then the two young men would go to work in a style I have never seen surpassed by any two of the same age. Halbert would sometimes go into the yard and assist, or rather hinder; but he had to give up just when he was beginning to be of some use, as the exertion was too violent for an old wound he had.

Meanwhile Cecil despised all these things, and, though a capital hand among cattle, was now grown completely effeminate, hanging about the house all day, making, in fact, "rather a fool of himself about that girl," as Halbert thought, and thought, besides, "What a confounded fool she will make of herself if she takes that little dandy!—not that he isn't a very gentleman-like little fellow, but that Sam is worth five hundred of him."

One day, it so happened that every one was out but Cecil and Alice; and Alice, who had been listening to the noises at the stock-yard a long while, suddenly proposed to go there.

"I have never been," she said; "I should so like to go! I know I am not allowed, but you need not betray me, and I am sure the others won't. I should so like to see what they are about!"

"I assure you, Miss Brentwood, that it is not a fit place for a lady."

"Why not?"

Cecil blushed scarlet. If women only knew what awkward questions they ask sometimes! In this instance he made an ass of himself, for he hesitated and stammered.

"Come along!" said she; "you are going to say that it is dangerous" (nothing was further from his thoughts); "I must learn to face a little danger, you know. Come along."

"I am afraid," said Cecil, "that Jim will be very angry with me;" which was undoubtedly very likely.

"Never mind Jim," she said; "come along."

So they went, and in the rush and confusion of the beasts' feet got to the yard unnoticed. Sam and Jim were inside, and Halbert was perched upon the rails; she came close behind him and peeped through.

She was frightened. Close before her was Sam, hatless, in shirt and breeches only, almost unrecognisable, grimed with sweat, dust, and filth beyond description. He had been nearly horned that

morning, and his shirt was torn from his armpit downwards, showing rather more of a lean muscular flank than would have been
desirable in a drawing-room. He stood there with his legs wide
apart, and a stick about eight feet long and as thick as one's wrist
in his hand; while before him, crowded into a corner of the yard,
were a mob of infuriated, terrified cattle. As she watched, one
tried to push past him and get out of the yard; he stepped aside
and let it go. The next instant a lordly young bull tried the same
game, but he was "wanted"; so, just as he came nearly abreast
of Sam, he received a frightful blow on the nose from the stick,
which turned him.

But only for a moment. The maddened beast shaking his head
with a roar rushed upon Sam like a thunderbolt, driving him
towards the side of the yard. He stepped on one side rapidly, and
then tumbled himself bodily through the rails, and fell with his fine
brown curls in the dust, right at the feet of poor Alice, who would
have screamed, but could not find the voice.

Jim and Halbert roared with laughter, and Sam, picking himself
up, was beginning to join as loud as anybody, when he saw Alice,
looking very white and pale, and went towards her.

"I hope you haven't been frightened by that evil-disposed bull,
Miss Brentwood," he said pleasantly; "you must get used to that
sort of work."

"Hallo, sister!" shouted Jim; "what the deuce brings you here?
I thought you were at home with your worsted work. You should
have seen what we were at, Cecil, before you brought her up. Now,
miss, just mount that rail alongside of Halbert, and keep quiet."

"Oh, do let me go home, Jim dear; I am so frightened!"

"Then you must learn not to be frightened," he said. "Jump
up now!"

But meanwhile the bull had the best of it, and had got out of
the yard. A long lithe lad, stationed outside on horseback, was in
full chase, and Jim, leaping on one of the horses tied to the rails,
started off to his assistance. The two chased the unhappy bull
as a pair of greyhounds chase a hare, with their whips cracking
as rapidly and as loudly as you would fire a revolver. After an
excursion of about a mile into the forest, the beast was turned
and brought towards the yard. Twice he turned and charged the
lad, with the same success. The cunning old stock-horse wheeled
round or sprang aside, and the bull went blundering into empty
space with two fourteen-foot stock-whips playing on his unlucky hide

like rain. At length he was brought in again, and one by one those entitled to freedom were passed out by Sam, and others reserved unto a day of wrath—all but one cow with her calf.

All this time Alice had sat by Halbert. Cecil had given no assistance, for Jim would have done anything rather than press a guest into the service. Halbert asked her, what she thought of the sport?

"Oh, it is horrible," she said. "I should like to go home. I hope it is all over."

"Nearly," said Halbert; "that cow and calf have got to go out. Don't get frightened now; watch your brother and Buckley."

It was a sight worth watching; Sam and Jim advanced towards the maddened beasts to try and get the cow to bolt. The cattle were huddled up at the other end of the yard, and having been so long in hand, were getting dangerous. Once or twice young beasts had tried to pass, but had been driven back by the young men, with a courage and dexterity which the boldest matador in Spain could not have surpassed. Cecil Mayford saw, with his well-accustomed eye, that matters were getting perilous, and placed himself at the rails, holding one ready to slip if the beasts should break. In a moment, how or why none could tell, they made a sudden rush: Jim was borne back, dealing blows about him like a paladin, and Sam was down, rolled over and over in the dust, just at Alice's feet.

Half a dozen passed right over him as he lay. Jim had made good his retreat from the yard, and Cecil had quietly done just the right thing: put up the rail he held, and saved the day's work. The cattle were still safe, but Sam lay there in the dust, motionless.

Before any of them had appreciated what had happened, Alice was down, and, seizing Sam by the shoulders, had dragged him to the fence. Halbert, horrified to see her actually in the presence of the cattle, leaped after her, put Sam through the rails, and lifted her up to her old post on the top. In another instant the beasts swept furiously round the yard, just over the place where they had been standing.

They gathered round Sam, and for an instant thought he was dead; but just as Jim hurriedly knelt down, and raising his head began to untie his handkerchief, Sam uprose, and, shaking himself and dusting his clothes, said:

"If it had been any other beast which knocked me down but that poley heifer, I should have been hurt!" and then said that "it was bathing-time, and they must look sharp to be in time for dinner:" three undeniable facts, showing that, although he was a little unsteady on his legs, his intellect had in nowise suffered.

And Halbert, glancing at Alice, saw something in her face that made him laugh; and dressing for dinner in Jim's room, he said to that young gentleman:

"Unless there are family reasons against it, Jim, which of course I can't speak about, you know, I should say you would have Sam for your brother-in-law in a very short time."

"Do you really think so, now?" said Jim; "I rather fancied she had taken up with Cecil. I like Sam's fist, mind you, better than Cecil's whole body, though he is a good little fellow, too."

"She has been doing that, I think, rather to put Sam on his mettle; for I think he was taking things too easy with her at first; but now, if Cecil has any false hopes, he may give them up; the sooner the better. No woman who was fancy free could stand seeing that noble head of Sam's come rolling down in the dust at her feet; and what courage and skill he exhibited, too! Talk of bull-fights! I have seen one. Bah! it is like this nail-brush to a gold watch, to what I saw to-day. Sam, sir, has won a wife by cattle-drafting."

"If that is the case," said Jim, pensively brushing his hair, "I am very glad that Cecil's care for his fine clothes prevented his coming into the yard; for he is one of the bravest, coolest hands among cattle, I know; he beats me."

"Then he beats a precious good fellow, Jim. A man who could make such play as you did to-day, with a stick, ought to have nothing but a big three-foot of blue steel in his hand, and her Majesty's commission to use it against her enemies."

"That will come," said Jim, "the day after Sam has got the right to look after Alice; not before; the governor is too fond of his logarithms."

When Sam came to dress for dinner he found that he was bruised all over, and had to go to the Captain for "shin plaster," as he called it.

Captain Brentwood had lately been trying homœopathy, which in his case, there being nothing the matter with him, was a decided success. He doctored Sam with arnica externally, and gave him the five-hundredth of a grain of something to swallow; but what made Sam forget his bruises quicker than these dangerous and violent remedies, was the delightful change in Alice's behaviour. She was so agreeable that evening, that he was in the seventh heaven; the only drawback to his happiness being poor Cecil

Mayford's utter distraction and misery. Next morning, too, after a swim in the river, he handled such a singularly good knife and fork, that Halbert told Jim privately, that if he, Sam, continued to sport such a confoundedly good appetite, he would have to be carried half a mile on a heifer's horns and left for dead, to keep up the romantic effect of his tumble the day before.

They were sitting at breakfast, when the door opened, and there appeared before the assembled company the lithe lad I spoke of yesterday, who said:

"Beg pardon, sir; child lost, sir."

They all started up. "Whose child?" asked the Captain.

"James Grewer's child, sir, at the wattle hut."

"Oh!" said Alice, turning to Sam, "it is that pretty little boy up the river that we were admiring so last week."

"When was he lost?" asked Major Buckley.

"Two days now, sir," said the lad.

"But the hut is on the plain side of the river," said the Major; "he can't be lost on the plains."

"The river is very low, sir," said the lad; "hardly ankle-deep just there. He may have crossed."

"The blackfellows may have found him," suggested Mrs. Buckley.

"They would have been here before now to tell us, if they had, I am afraid," said Captain Brentwood. "Let us hope they may have got him; however, we had better start at once. Two of us may search the river between this and the hut, and two may follow it towards the Mayfords'. Sam, you have the best horse; go down to the hut, and see if you can find any trace across the river, on this side, and follow it up to the ranges. Take some one with you, and, by the by, take your dog Rover."

They were all quickly on the alert. Sam was going to ask Jim to come with him; but as he was putting the saddle on Widderin he felt a hand on his arm, and, turning, saw Cecil Mayford.

"Sam Buckley," said Cecil, "let me ride with you; will you?"

"Who sooner, old friend?" answered Sam heartily: "let us come together by all means, and if we are to go to the ranges, we had better take a blanket apiece, and a wedge of damper. So if you will get them from the house, I will saddle your horse."

CHAPTER XXX

HOW THE CHILD WAS LOST, AND HOW HE GOT FOUND AGAIN—WHAT
CECIL SAID TO SAM WHEN THEY FOUND HIM—AND HOW IN CASTING
LOTS, ALTHOUGH CECIL WON THE LOT, HE LOST THE PRIZE

FOUR or five miles up the river from Garoopna stood a solitary hut, snug—sheltered by a lofty bare knoll, round which the great river chafed among the boulders. Across the stream was the forest sloping down in pleasant glades from the mountain; and behind the hut rose the plain four or five hundred feet overhead, seeming to be held aloft by the blue-stone columns which rose from the riverside.

In this cottage resided a shepherd, his wife, and one little boy, their son, about eight years old. A strange, wild little bush child, able to speak articulately, but utterly without knowledge or experience of human creatures, save of his father and mother; unable to read a line; without religion of any sort or kind; as entire a little savage, in fact, as you could find in the worst den in your city, morally speaking, and yet beautiful to look on; as active as a roe, and, with regard to natural objects, as fearless as a lion.

As yet unfit to begin labour. All the long summer he would wander about the river-bank, up and down the beautiful rock-walled paradise where he was confined, sometimes looking eagerly across the water at the waving forest boughs, and fancying he could see other children far up the vistas beckoning to him to cross and play in that merry land of shifting lights and shadows.

It grew quite into a passion with the poor little man to get across and play there; and one day when his mother was shifting the hurdles, and he was handing her the strips of green hide which bound them together, he said to her:

"Mother, what country is that across the river?"

"The forest, child."

"There's plenty of quantongs over there, eh, mother, and raspberries? Why mayn't I get across and play there?"

"The river is too deep, child, and the Bunyip lives in the water under the stones."

"Who are the children that play across there?"

"Black children, likely."

"No white children?"

"Pixies; don't go near 'em, child; they'll lure you on, Lord knows where. Don't get trying to cross the river, now, or you'll be drowned."

But next day the passion was stronger on him than ever. Quite early on the glorious cloudless midsummer day he was down by the riverside, sitting on a rock, with his shoes and stockings off, paddling his feet in the clear tepid water, and watching the million fish in the shallows—black fish and grayling—leaping and flashing in the sun.

There is no pleasure that I have ever experienced like a child's midsummer holiday. The time, I mean, when two or three of us used to go away up the brook, and take our dinners with us, and come home at night tired, dirty, happy, scratched beyond recognition, with a great nosegay, three little trout, and one shoe, the other one having been used for a boat till it had gone down with all hands out of soundings. How poor our Derby days, our Greenwich dinners, our evening parties, where there are plenty of nice girls, are after that! Depend on it, a man never experiences such pleasure or grief after fourteen as he does before: unless in some cases in his first love-making, when the sensation is new to him.

But, meanwhile, there sat our child, barelegged, watching the forbidden ground beyond the river. A fresh breeze was moving the trees, and making the whole a dazzling mass of shifting light and shadow. He sat so still that a glorious violet and red kingfisher perched quite close, and, dashing into the water, came forth with a fish, and fled like a ray of light along the winding of the river. A colony of little shell parrots, too, crowded on a bough, and twittered and ran to and fro quite busily, as though they said to him, " We don't mind you, my dear; you are quite one of us."

Never was the river so low. He stepped in; it scarcely reached his ankle. Now surely he might get across. He stripped himself, and, carrying his clothes, waded through, the water never reaching his middle all across the long, yellow, gravelly shallow. And there he stood naked and free in the forbidden ground.

He quickly dressed himself, and began examining his new kingdom, rich beyond his utmost hopes. Such quantongs, such raspberries, surpassing imagination; and when he tired of them, such fern boughs, six or eight feet long! He would penetrate this region, and see how far it extended.

What tales he would have for his father to-night. He would bring him here, and show him all the wonders, and perhaps he would build a new hut over here, and come and live in it? Perhaps the pretty young lady, with the feathers in her hat, lived somewhere here, too?

There! There is one of those children he has seen before across the river. Ah! ah! it is not a child at all, but a pretty grey beast, with big ears. A kangaroo, my lad; he won't play with you, but skips away slowly, and leaves you alone.

There is something like the gleam of water on that rock. A snake! Now a sounding rush through the wood, and a passing shadow. An eagle! He brushes so close to the child, that he strikes at the bird with a stick, and then watches him as he shoots up like a rocket, and, measuring the fields of air in ever-widening circles, hangs like a motionless speck upon the sky; though, measure his wings across, and you will find he is nearer fifteen feet than fourteen.

Here is a prize, though! A wee little native bear, barely eight inches long—a little grey beast, comical beyond expression, with broad flapped ears, sits on a tree within reach. He makes no resistance, but cuddles into the child's bosom, and eats a leaf as they go along; while his mother sits aloft, and grunts indignant at the abstraction of her offspring, but, on the whole, takes it pretty comfortably, and goes on with her dinner of peppermint leaves.

What a short day it has been! Here is the sun getting low, and the magpies and jackasses beginning to tune up before roosting.

He would turn and go back to the river. Alas! which way?

He was lost in the bush. He turned back and went, as he thought, the way he had come, but soon arrived at a tall, precipitous cliff, which, by some infernal magic, seemed to have got between him and the river. Then he broke down, and that strange madness came on him which comes even on strong men when lost in the forest: a despair, a confusion of intellect, which has cost many a man his life. Think what it must be with a child!

He was fully persuaded that the cliff was between him and the home, and that he must climb it. Alas! every step he took aloft carried him farther from the river and the hope of safety; and when he came to the top, just at dark, he saw nothing but cliff after cliff, range after range, all around him. He had been wandering through steep gullies all day unconsciously, and had penetrated far into the mountains. Night was coming down, still and crystal-clear, and the poor little lad was far away from help or hope, going his last long journey alone.

Partly perhaps walking, and partly sitting down and weeping, he got through the night; and when the solemn morning came up again he was still tottering along the leading range, bewildered; crying, from time to time, " Mother, mother! " still nursing his little bear, his only companion, to his bosom, and holding still in his hand a few poor flowers he had gathered the day before. Up and on all day, and at evening, passing out of the great zone of timber, he came on the bald, thunder-smitten summit ridge, where one ruined tree held up its skeleton arms against the sunset, and the wind came keen and frosty. So, with failing, feeble legs, upward still, towards the region of the granite and the snow; towards the eyrie of the kite and the eagle.

Brisk as they all were at Garoopna, none were so brisk as Cecil and Sam. Charles Hawker wanted to come with them, but Sam asked him to go with Jim; and, long before the others were ready, our two had strapped their blankets to their saddles, and, followed by Sam's dog Rover, now getting a little grey about the nose, cantered off up the river.

Neither spoke at first. They knew what a solemn task they had before them; and, while acting as though everything depended on speed, guessed well that their search was only for a little corpse, which, if they had luck, they would find stiff and cold under some tree or crag.

Cecil began: " Sam, depend on it that child has crossed the river to this side. If he had been on the plains he would have been seen from a distance in a few hours."

" I quite agree," said Sam. " Let us go down this side till we are opposite the hut, and search for marks by the riverside."

So they agreed; and in half an hour were opposite the hut, and, riding across it to ask a few questions, found the poor mother sitting on the door-step, with her apron over her head, rocking herself to and fro.

" We have come to help you, mistress," said Sam. " How do you think he is gone? "

She said, with frequent bursts of grief, that " some days before he had mentioned having seen white children across the water, who beckoned him to cross and play; that she, knowing well that they were fairies, or perhaps worse, had warned him solemnly not to mind them; but that she had very little doubt that they had helped him over and carried him away to the forest; and that her husband would not believe in his having crossed the river."

" Why, it is not knee-deep across the shallow," said Cecil.

" Let us cross again," said Sam: " he *may* be drowned, but I don't think it."

In a quarter of an hour from starting they found, slightly up the stream, one of the child's socks, which in his hurry to dress he had forgotten. Here brave Rover took up the trail like a bloodhound, and before evening stopped at the foot of a lofty cliff.

" Can he have gone up here ? " said Sam, as they were brought up by the rock.

" Most likely," said Cecil. " Lost children always climb from height to height. I have heard it often remarked by old bush hands. Why they do so, God, who leads them, only knows; but the fact is beyond denial. Ask Rover what he thinks ? "

The brave old dog was half-way up, looking back for them. It took them nearly till dark to get their horses up; and, as there was no moon, and the way was getting perilous, they determined to camp, and start again in the morning.

They spread their blankets and lay down side by side. Sam had thought, from Cecil's proposing to come with him in preference to the others, that he would speak of a subject nearly concerning them both; but Cecil went off to sleep and made no sign; and Sam, ere he dozed, said to himself, " By Jove, if he don't speak this journey, I will. It is unbearable that we should not come to some understanding. Poor Cecil ! "

At early dawn they caught up their horses, which had been hobbled with the stirrup leathers, and started afresh. Both were more silent than ever, and the dog, with his nose to the ground, led them slowly along the rocky rib of the mountain, ever going higher and higher.

" It is inconceivable," said Sam, " that the poor child can have come up here. There is Tuckerimbid close to our right, five thousand feet above the river. Don't you think we must be mistaken ? "

" The dog disagrees with you," said Cecil. " He has something before him not very far off. Watch him."

The trees had become dwarfed and scattered; they were getting out of the region of trees; the real forest zone was now below them, and they saw they were emerging towards a bald elevated down, and that a few hundred yards before them was a dead tree, on the highest branch of which sat an eagle.

" The dog has stopped," said Cecil; " the end is near."

" See," said Sam, " there is a handkerchief under the tree."

" That is the boy himself," said Cecil.

They were up to him and off in a moment. There he lay, dead and stiff, one hand still grasping the flowers he had gathered on his last happy play-day, and the other laid as a pillow, between the soft cold cheek and the rough cold stone. His midsummer holiday was over, his long journey was ended. He had found out at last what lay beyond the shining river he had watched so long.

Both the young men knelt beside him for a moment in silence. They had found only what they had expected to find, and yet, now that they had found it, they were far more touched and softened than they could have thought possible. They stayed in silence a few moments, and then Cecil, lifting up his head, said suddenly:

" Sam Buckley! there can be no debate between us two, with this lying here between us. Let us speak now."

" There has never been any debate, Cecil," said he, " and there never would be, though this little corpse was buried fathoms deep. It takes two to make a quarrel, Cecil, and I will not be one."

" Sam," said Cecil, " I love Alice Brentwood better than all the world besides."

" I know it."

" And you love her too, as well, were it possible, as I do."

" I know that too."

" Why," resumed Cecil hurriedly, " has this come to pass? Why has it been my unlucky destiny, that the man I love and honour above all others should become my rival? Are there no other women in the world? Tell me, Sam, why is it forced on me to choose between my best friend and the woman I love dearer than life? Why has this terrible emergency come between us?"

" I will tell you why," said Sam, speaking very quietly, as though fearing to awaken the dead: " to teach us to behave like men of honour and gentlemen, though our hearts break. That is why, Cecil."

" What shall we do?" said Cecil.

" Easily answered," said Sam. " Let her decide for herself. It may be, mind you, that she will have neither of us. There has been one living in the house with her lately, far superior in every point to you or I. How if she thought fit to prefer him?"

" Halbert!"

" Yes, Halbert! What more likely? Let you and I find out the truth, Cecil, like men, and abide by it. Let each one ask her in his turn what chance he has."

" Who first?"

" See here," said Sam; " draw one of these pieces of grass out of my hand. If you draw the longest piece ask her at once. Will you abide by this?"

He said " Yes," and drew—the longest piece.

" That is well," said Sam. " And now no more of this at

present. I will sling this poor little fellow in my blanket and carry him home to his mother. See, Cecil, what is Rover at?"

Rover was on his hind legs against the tree, smelling at something. When they came to look, there was a wee little grey bear perched in the hollow of the tree.

"What a very strange place for a young bear!" said Cecil.

"Depend on it," said Sam, "that the child had caught it from its dam, and brought it up here. Take it home with you, Cecil, and give it to Alice."

Cecil took the little thing home, and in time it grew to be between three and four feet high, a grandfather of bears. The magpie protested against his introduction to the establishment, and used to pluck billfuls of hair from his stomach under pretence of lining a nest, which was never made. But in spite of this, the good gentle beast lived nigh as long as the magpie—long enough to be caressed by the waxen fingers of little children, who would afterwards gather round their father, and hear how the bear had been carried to the mountains in the bosom of the little boy who lost his way on the granite ranges, and went to heaven, in the year that the bushrangers came down.

Sam carried the little corpse back in his blanket, and that evening helped the father to bury it by the riverside. Under some fern-trees they buried him, on a knoll which looked across the river, into the treacherous beautiful forest which had lured him to his destruction.

Alice was very sad for a day or two, and thought and talked much about this sad accident, but soon she recovered her spirits again. And it fell out that a bare week after this, the party being all out in one direction or another, that Cecil saw Alice alone in the garden, tending her flowers, and knew that the time was come for him to keep his bargain with Sam and speak to her. He felt like a man who was being led to execution; but screwed his courage to the highest point, and went down to where she was tying up a rose-tree.

"Miss Brentwood," he said, "I am come to petition for a flower."

"You shall have a dozen, if you will," she answered. "Help yourself; will you have a peony or a sunflower? If you have not made up your mind, let me recommend a good large yellow sunflower."

Here was a pretty beginning!

"Miss Brentwood, don't laugh at me, but listen to me a moment. I love you above all earthly things besides. I worship the ground you walk on. I loved you from the first moment I saw you. I shall love you as well, ay, better, if that could be, on the day my heart is still, and my hand is cold for ever: can you tell me to hope? Don't drive me, by one hasty half-considered word, to despair and misery for the rest of my life. Say only one syllable of encouragement, and I will bide your time for years and years."

Alice was shocked and stunned. She saw he was in earnest by his looks, and by his hurried, confused way of speaking. She feared she might have been to blame, and have encouraged him, in her thoughtlessness, more than she ought. "I will make him angry with me," she said to herself. "I will treat him to ridicule. It is the only chance, poor fellow!"

"Mr. Mayford," she said, "if I thought you were in jest, I should feel it necessary to tell my father and brother that you had been impertinent. I can only believe that you are in earnest, and I deeply regret that your personal vanity should have urged you to take such an unwarrantable liberty with a girl you have not yet known for ten days."

He turned and left her without a word, and she remained standing where she was, half inclined to cry, and wondering if she had acted right on the spur of the moment—sometimes half inclined to believe that she had been unladylike and rude. When a thing of this kind takes place, both parties generally put themselves in immediate correspondence with a confidant. Miss Smith totters into the apartments of her dearest friend, and falls weeping on the sofa, while Jones rushes madly into Brown's rooms in the Temple, and shying his best hat into the coal-scuttle, announces that there is nothing now left for him but to drown the past in debauchery. Whereupon Brown, if he is a good fellow, as all the Browns are, produces the whisky and hears all about it.

So in the present instance two people were informed of what had taken place before they went to bed that night; and those two were Jim and Dr. Mulhaus. Alice had stood where Cecil had left her, thinking, could she confide it to Mrs. Buckley, and ask for advice? But Mrs. Buckley had been a little cross to her that week for some reason, and so she was afraid: and, not knowing anybody else well enough, began to cry.

There was a noise of horses' feet just beyond the fence, and a voice calling to her to come. It was Jim, and, drying her eyes, she went out, and he, dismounting, put his arm round her waist and kissed her.

"Why, my beauty," he said, "who has been making you cry?"

She put her head on his shoulder and began sobbing louder than ever. "Cecil Mayford," she said, in a whisper.

"Well, and what the devil has he been at?" said Jim, in a rather startling tone.

"Wants to marry me," she answered, in a whisper, and hid her face in his coat.

"The deuce doubt he does," said Jim; "who does not? What did you tell him?"

"I told him that I wondered at his audacity."

"Sent him off with a flea in his ear, in fact," said Jim. "Well, quite right. I suppose you would do the same for any man?"

"Certainly I should," she said, looking up.

"If Dr. Mulhaus, now—eh?"

"I'd box his ears, Jim," she said, laughing: "I would, indeed."

"Or Sam Buckley; would you box his ears, if he were to—you know?"

"Yes," she said. But there spread over her face a sudden crimson blush, like the rosy arch which heralds the tropical sun, which made Jim laugh aloud.

"If you dared to say a word, Jim," she said, "I would never, never——"

Poor Cecil had taken his horse and had meant to ride home, but came back again at night, "just," he thought, "to have one more look at her; before he entered on some line of life which would take him far away from Garoopna and its temptations."

The Doctor (who has been rather thrust aside lately in the midst of all this love-making and so on) saw that something had gone very wrong with Cecil, who was a great friend of his, and, as he could never bear to see a man in distress without helping him, he encouraged Cecil to stroll down the garden with him, and then kindly and gently asked him what was wrong.

Cecil told him all, from beginning to end, and added that life was over for him, as far as all pleasure and excitement went; and, in short, said what we have all said, or had said to us, in our time, after a great disappointment in love; which the Doctor took for exactly what it was worth, although poor little Cecil's distress was very keen; and, remembering some old bygone day when he had suffered so himself, he cast about to find some comfort for him.

"You will get over this, my boy," said he, "if you would only believe it."

"Never, never!" said Cecil.

"Let me tell you a story as we walk up and down. If it does not

comfort you, it will amuse you. How sweet the orange bloom smells!
Listen: Had not the war broke out so suddenly, I should have
been married, two months to a day, before the battle of Saarbruck.
Catherine was a distant cousin, beautiful and talented, about ten
years my junior. Before Heaven, sir, on the word of a gentleman,
I never persecuted her with my addresses, and if either of them
say I did, tell them from me, sir, that they lie, and I will prove
it on their bodies. Bah! I was forgetting. I, as head of the family,
was her guardian, and, although my younger brother was nearer
her age, I courted her, in all honour and humility proposed to her,
and was accepted with even more willingness than most women
condescend to show on such occasions, and received the hearty
congratulations of my brother. Few women were ever loved better
than I loved Catherine. Conceive, Cecil, that I loved her as well
as you love Miss Brentwood, and listen to what follows.

"The war-cloud burst so suddenly that, leaving my bride that was
to be, to the care of my brother, and putting him in charge over
my property, I hurried off to join the Landsturm, two regiments
of which I had put into a state of efficiency by my sole exertions.

"You know partly what followed—in one day an army of 150,000
men destroyed, the King in flight to Königsberg, and Prussia a
province of France.

"I fled, wounded badly, desperate and penniless, from that field.
I learnt from the peasants, that what I had thought to be merely
a serious defeat was an irretrievable disaster; and, in spite of
wounds, hunger, and want of clothes, I held on my way towards
home.

"The enemy were in possession of the country, so I had to travel
by night alone, and beg from such poor cottages as I dared to
approach. Sometimes I got a night's rest, but generally lay abroad
in the fields. But at length, after every sort of danger and hard-
ship, I stood above the broad, sweeping Maine, and saw the towers
of my own beloved castle across the river, perched as of old above
the vineyards, looking protectingly down upon the little town which
was clustered on the river-bank below, and which owned me for its
master.

"I crossed at dusk. I had to act with great caution, for I did
not know whether the French were there or no. I did not make
myself known to the peasant who ferried me over, further than as
one from the war, which my appearance was sufficient to prove.
I landed just below a long high wall which separated the town
from the river, and, ere I had time to decide what I should do first,

a figure coming out of an archway caught me by the hand, and I
recognised my own major-domo, my foster-brother.

"'I knew you would come back to me,' he said, 'if it was only as
a pale ghost: though I never believed you dead, and have watched
here for you night and day to stop you.'

"'Are the French in my castle, then?'

"'There are worse than the French there,' he said; 'worse than
the devil Bonaparte himself. Treason, treachery, adultery!'

"'Who has proved false?' I cried.

"'Your brother! False to his king, to his word, to yourself.
He was in correspondence with the French for six months past,
and, now that he believes you dead, he is living in sin with her who
was to have been your wife.'

"I did not cry out or faint, or anything of that sort. I only
said, 'I am going to the castle, Fritz,' and he came with me. My
brother had turned him out of the house when he usurped my
property, but by a still faithful domestic we were admitted, and I,
knowing every secret passage in my house, came shoeless from
behind some arras, and stood before them as they sat at supper.
I was a ghastly sight. I had not shaved for a fortnight, and my
uniform hung in tatters from my body; round my head was the
same bloody white handkerchief with which I had bound up my
head at Jena. I was deadly pale from hunger, too; and from my
entering so silently they believed they had seen a ghost. My brother
rose, and stood pale and horrified, and Catherine fell fainting on
the floor. This was all my revenge, and ere my brother could
speak, I was gone—away to England, where I had money in the
funds, accompanied by my faithful Fritz, whom Mary Hawker's
father buried in Drumston churchyard.

"So in one day I lost a brother, a mistress, a castle, a king, and
a fatherland. I was a ruined, desperate man. And yet I lived
to see old Blücher with his dirty boots on the silken sofas at the
Tuileries, and to become as stout and merry a middle-aged man as
any Prussian subject in her young Majesty's dominions."

CHAPTER XXXI

HOW TOM TROUBRIDGE KEPT WATCH FOR THE FIRST TIME

HUMAN affairs are subject to such an infinite variety of changes and complications, that any attempt to lay down particular rules for individual action, under peculiar circumstances, must prove a failure. Hence I consider proverbs, generally speaking, to be a failure, only used by weak-minded men, who have no opinion of their own. Thus, if you have a chance of selling your station at fifteen shillings, and buying in, close to a new gold-field on the same terms, where fat sheep are going to the butcher at from eighteen shillings to a pound, butter, eggs, and garden produce at famine prices, some dolt unsettles you, and renders you uncertain and miserable by saying that "rolling stone gathers no moss;" as if you wanted moss! Again, having worked harder than the Colonial Secretary all the week, and wishing to lie in bed till eleven o'clock on Sunday, a man comes into your room at half-past seven, on a hot morning, when your only chance is to sleep out an hour or so of the heat, and informs you that the "early bird gets the worm." I had a partner, who bought in after Jim Stockbridge was killed, who was always flying this early bird, when he couldn't sleep for mosquitoes. I have got rid of him now; but for the two years he was with me, the dearest wish of my heart was that my tame magpie Joshua could have had a quiet two minutes with that early bird before any one was up to separate them. I rather fancy he would have been spoken of as "the late early bird" after that. In short, I consider proverbs as the refuge of weak minds.

The infinite sagacity of the above remarks cannot be questioned; their application may. I will proceed to give it. I have written down the above tirade, in order to call down the wrath of all wise men, if any such have done me the honour of getting so far in this volume, on the most trashy and false proverb of the whole: "Coming events cast their shadows before."

Now, they don't, you know. They never did, and never will. I myself used to be a strong believer in presentiments; until I found by experience that, although I was always having presentiments, nothing ever came of them. Sometimes somebody would walk over my grave, and give me a creeping in the back, which, as far as I can find out, proceeded from not having my braces properly buttoned behind. Sometimes I have heard the death-watch, produced by a small spider (may the deuce confound him!), not to mention many other presentiments and depressions of spirit, which I am now firmly persuaded proceed from indigestion. I am far from denying the possibility of a coincidence in point of time between a fit of indigestion and a domestic misfortune. I am far from denying the possibility of more remarkable coincidences than that. I have read in books, novels by the very best French authors, how a man, not heard of for twenty years, having, in point of fact, been absent during that time in the interior of Africa, may appear at Paris at a given moment, only in time to save a young lady from dishonour, and rescue a property of ten million francs. But these great writers of fiction don't give us any warning whatever. The door is thrown heavily open, and he stalks up to the table where the will is lying, quite unexpectedly; stalks up always, or else strides. (How would it be, my dear author, if, in your next novel, he were to walk in, or run in, or hop in, or, say, come in on all-fours like a dog?—anything for a change, you know.) And these masters of fiction are right—" Coming events do not cast their shadows before."

If they did, how could it happen that Mary Hawker sat there in her veranda at Toonarbin singing so pleasantly over her work? And why did her handsome, kindly face light up with such a radiant smile when she saw her son Charles come riding along under the shadow of the great trees only two days after Cecil Mayford had proposed to Alice, and had been refused?

He came out of the forest shadow with the westering sunlight upon his face, riding slowly. She, as she looked, was proud to see what a fine seat he had on his horse, and how healthy and handsome he looked.

He rode round to the back of the house, and she went through to meet him. There was a square court behind, round which the house, huts, and store formed a quadrangle, neat and bright, with white quartz gravel. By the by, there was a prospecting party who sank two or three shafts in the flat before the house last year; and I saw about eighteen pennyweights of gold which they took out. But it did not pay, and is abandoned. (This in passing, apropos of the quartz.)

" Is Tom Troubridge come home, mother? " said he, as he leaned out of the saddle to kiss her.

" Not yet, my boy," she said. " I am all alone. I should have had a dull week, but I knew you were enjoying yourself with your old friend at Garoopna. A great party there, I believe? "

" I am glad to get home, mother," he said. " We were jolly at first, but latterly Sam Buckley and Cecil Mayford have been looking at one another like cat and dog. Stay, though; let me be just; the fierce looks were all on Cecil Mayford's side."

" What was the matter?"

" Alice Brentwood was the matter, I rather suspect," he said, getting off his horse. " Hold him for me, mother, while I take the saddle off."

She did as requested. " And so they two are at loggerheads, eh, about Miss Brentwood? Of course. And what sort of a girl is she?"

" Oh, very pretty; deuced pretty, in fact. But there is one there takes my fancy better."

" Who is she?"

" Ellen Mayford; the sweetest little mouse—— Dash it all: look at this horse's back. That comes of that infernal flash military groom of Jim's putting on the saddle without rubbing his back down. Where is the bluestone?"

She went in and got it for him as naturally as if it was her place to obey, and his to command. She always waited on him, as a matter of course, save when Tom Troubridge was with them, who was apt to rap out something awkward about Charles being a lazy young hound, and about his waiting on himself, whenever he saw Mary yielding to that sort of thing.

" I wonder when Tom will be back?" resumed Charles.

" I have been expecting him this last week; he may come any night. I hope he will not meet any of those horrid bushrangers."

" Hope not either," said Charles; " they would have to go a hundred or two of miles out of their way to make it likely. Driving rams is slow work; they may not be here for a week."

" A nice price he has paid!"

" It will pay in the end, in the quality of the wool," said Charles.

They sat in silence. A little after, Charles had turned his horse out, when at once, without preparation, he said to her:

" Mother, how long is it since my father died?"

She was very much startled. He had scarcely ever alluded to his father before; but she made shift to answer him quietly.

" How old are you?"

" Eighteen," he said.

" Then he has been dead eighteen years. He died just as you were born. Never mention him, lad. He was a bad man, and by God's mercy you are delivered from him."

She rose and went into the house quite cheerfully. Why should she not? Why should not a handsome, still young, wealthy widow be cheerful? For she was a widow. For years after settling at Toonarbin, she had contrived, once in two or three years, to hear some news of her husband. After about ten years, she heard that he had been reconvicted, and sentenced to the chain-gang for life; and lastly, that he was dead. About his being sentenced for life, there was no doubt, for she had a piece of newspaper which told of his crime—and a frightful piece of villainy it was—and after that, the report of his death was so probable that no one for an instant doubted its truth. Men did not live long in the chain-gang, in Van Diemen's Land, in those days, brother. Men would knock out one another's brains in order to get hung, and escape it. Men would cry aloud to the judge to hang them out of the way! It was the most terrible punishment known, for it was hopeless. Penal servitude for life, as it is now, gives the very faintest idea of what it used to be in old times. With a little trouble I could tell you the weight of iron carried by each man. I cannot exactly remember, but it would strike you as being incredible. They were chained two and two together (a horrible association), to lessen the chances of escape; there was no chance of mitigation for good conduct; there was hard mechanical, uninteresting work, out of doors in an inclement climate, in all weathers: what wonder if men died off like rotten sheep? And what wonder, too, if sometimes the slightest accident—such as a blow from an overseer, returned by a prisoner, produced a sudden rising, unpreconcerted, objectless, the result of which were half a dozen murdered men, as many lunatic women, and five or six stations lighting up the hillside, night after night, while the whole available force of the colony was unable to stop the ruin for months?

But to the point. Mary was a widow. When she heard of her husband's death, she said to herself, " Thank God! " But when she had gone to her room, and was sat a-thinking, she seemed to have had another husband before she was bound up with that desperate, coining, forging George Hawker—another husband bearing the same name; but surely that handsome curly-headed young fellow, who used to wait for her so patiently in the orchard at Drumston, was not the same George Hawker as this desperate convict? She was glad the convict was dead and out of the way; there was no doubt of that; but she could still find a corner in her heart to be sorry for her poor old lover—her handsome old lover—ah me!

But that even was passed now, and George Hawker was as one who had never lived. Now on this evening we speak of, his memory came back just an instant, as she heard the boy speak of the father, but it was gone again directly. She called her servants, and was telling them to bring supper, when Charles looked suddenly in, and said—" Here they are! "

There they were, sure enough, putting the rams into the sheep-yard. Tom Troubridge, as upright, brave-looking a man as ever, and, thanks to bushwork, none the fatter. William Lee, one of our oldest acquaintances, was getting a little grizzled, but otherwise looked as broad and as strong as ever.

They rode into the yard, and Lee took the horses.

" Well, cousin," said Tom; " I am glad to see you again."

" You are welcome home, Tom; you have made good speed."

Tom and Charles went into the house, and Mary was about following them, when Lee said, in so low a tone, that it did not reach the others—" Mrs. Hawker! "

She turned round and looked at him; she had welcomed him kindly when he came into the yard with Tom, and yet he stood still on horseback, holding Tom's horse by the bridle. A stern, square-looking figure he was; and when she looked at his face, she was much troubled, at—she knew not what.

" Mrs. Hawker," he said, " can you give me the favour of ten minutes' conversation alone, this evening? "

" Surely, William, now! "

" Not now—my story is pretty long, and, what is more, ma'am, somebody may be listening, and what I have got to tell you must be told in no ear but your own."

" You frighten me, Lee! You frighten me to death."

" Don't get frightened, Mrs. Hawker. Remember if anything comes about, that you have good friends about you; and that I, William Lee, am not the worst of them."

Lee went off with the horses, and Mary returned to the house. What mystery had this man to tell her, " that no one might hear but she "?—very strange and alarming! Was he drunk?—no, he was evidently quite sober; as she looked out once more, she could see him at the stable, cool and self-possessed, ordering the lads about: something very strange and terrifying to one who had such a dark blot in her life.

But she went in, and as she came near the parlour, she heard Charles and Tom roaring with laughter. As she opened the door she heard Tom saying: " And, by Jove, I sat there like a great snipe, face to face with him, as cool and unconcerned as you like. I took him for a flash overseer, sporting his salary, and I was as thick as you like with him. And, 'Matey,' says I (you see I was familiar, he seemed such a jolly sort of bird), 'Matey, what station are you on?' 'Maraganoa,' says he. 'So,' says I, 'you're rather young there, ain't you. I was by there a fortnight ago.' He saw he'd made a wrong move, and made it worse. 'I mean,' says he, 'Maraganoa on the Clarence side.' 'Ah,' says I, 'in the Cedar country?' 'Precisely,' says he. And there we sat drinking together, and I had no more notion of its being him than you would have had."

She sat still listening to him, eating nothing. Lee's words outside had, she knew not why, struck a chill into her heart, and as she listened to Tom's story, although she could make nothing of it, she felt as though getting colder and colder. She shivered, although the night was hot. Through the open window she could hear all those thousand commingled indistinguishable sounds that make the night-life of the bush, with painful distinctness. She arose and went to the window.

The night was dark and profoundly still. The stars were overhead, though faintly seen through a haze; and beyond the narrow enclosures in front of the house, the great forest arose like a black wall. Tom and Charles went on talking inside, and yet, though their voices were loud, she was hardly conscious of hearing them, but found herself watching the high dark wood and listening to the sound of the frogs in the creek, and the rustle of a million crawling things, heard only in the deep stillness of night.

Deep in the forest somewhere, a bough cracked, and fell crashing, then all was silent again. Soon arose a wind, a partial wandering wind, which came slowly up, and, rousing the quivering leaves to life for a moment, passed away; then again a silence, deeper than ever, so that she could hear the cattle and horses feeding in the lower paddock, a quarter of a mile off; then a low wail in the wood, then two or three wild weird yells, as of a devil in torment, and a pretty white curlew skirled over the house-top to settle on the sheep-wash dam.

The stillness was awful; it boded a storm, for behind the forest blazed up a sheet of lightning, showing the shape of each fantastic elevated bough. Then she turned round to the light, and said:

"My dear partner, I had a headache, and went to the window. What was the story you were telling Charles just now? Who was the man you met in the public-house, who seems to have frightened you so?"

"No less a man that Captain Touan, my dear cousin!" said

Tom, leaning back with the air of a man who has made a point, and would be glad to hear " what you have to say to that, sir."

" Touan? " repeated Mary. " Why, that's the great bushranger, that is out to the north; is it not? "

" The same man, cousin! And there I sat hob and nob with him for half an hour in the Lake George public-house. If Desborough had come in, he'd have hung me for being found in bad company. Ha! ha! ha! "

" My dear partner," she said, " what a terrible escape! Supposing he had risen on you? "

" Why I'd have broken his back, cousin," said Tom, " unless my right hand had forgot her cunning. He is a fine man of his weight: but, Lord, in a struggle for life or death, I could break his neck, and have one more claim on heaven for doing so; for he is the most damnable villain that ever disgraced God's earth, and that is the truth. That man, cousin, in one of his devil's raids, tore a baby from its mother's breast by the leg, dashed its brains out against a tree, and then—I daren't tell a woman what happened." *

" Tom! Tom! " said Mary, " how can you talk of such things? "

" To show you what we have to expect if he comes this way, cousin; that is all."

" And is there any possibility of such a thing? " asked Mary.

" Why not? Why should he not pay us the compliment of looking round this way? "

" Why do they call him Touan, Tom? " asked Charles.

" Can't you see? " said Tom; " the Touan, the little grey flying squirrel, only begins to fly about at night, and slides down from his bough sudden and sharp. This fellow has made some of his most terrible raids at night, and so he got the name of Touan."

" God deliver us from such monsters! " said Mary, and left the room.

She went into the kitchen. Lee sat there smoking. When she came in he rose, and, knocking the ashes out of his pipe, touched his forehead and stood looking at her.

" Now then, old friend," she said, " come here."

He followed her out. She led the way swiftly, through the silent night, across the yard, over a small paddock, up to the sheep-yard beside the wool-shed. There she turned shortly round, and, leaning on the fence, said abruptly:

---

* Tom was confusing Touan with Michael Howe. The latter actually did commit this frightful atrocity; but I never heard that the former actually combined the two crimes in this way.

"No one can hear us here, William Lee. Now, what have you to say?"

He seemed to hesitate a moment, and then began: "Mrs. Hawker, have I been a good servant to you?"

"Honest, faithful, kindly, active; who could have been a better servant than you, William Lee! A friend, and not a servant; God is my witness; now then?"

"I am glad to hear you say so," he answered. "I did you a terrible injury once; I have often been sorry for it since I knew you, but it cannot be mended now."

"Since you knew me?" she said. "Why, you have known me ever since I have been in the country, and you have never injured me since then, surely."

"Ay, but at home," he said. "In England. In Devonshire."

"My God!"

"I was your husband's companion in all his earlier villainies. I suggested them to him, and egged him on. And now, mind you, after twenty years, my punishment is coming."

She could only say still, "My God!" while her throat was as dry as a kiln.

"Listen to what I have got to tell you now. Hear it all in order, and try to bear up, and use your common sense and courage. As I said before, you have good friends around you, and you at least are innocent."

"Guilty! guilty!" she cried. "Guilty of my father's death! Read me this horrible riddle, Lee."

"Wait and listen," said Lee, unable to forego, even in her terror, the great pleasure that all his class have of spinning a yarn, and using as many words as possible. "See here. We came by Lake George, you know, and heard everywhere accounts of a great gang of bushrangers being out. So we didn't feel exactly comfortable, you see. We came by a bush public-house, and Mr. Troubridge stops, and says he, 'Well, lad, suppose we yard these rams an hour, and take drink in the parlour?' 'All right,' I says, with a wink, 'but the tap for me, if you please. That's my place, and I'd like to see if I can get any news of the whereabouts of the lads as are sticking up all round, because, if they're one way, I'd as lief be another.' 'All right,' says he. So in I goes, and sits down. There was nobody there but one man, drunk under the bench. And I has two nobblers of brandy, and one of Old Tom; no, two Old Toms it was, and a brandy; when in comes an old chap as I knew for a lag in a minute. Well, he and I cottoned together, and found out that we had been prisoners together five-and-twenty years agone. And so I shouted for him, and he for me, and at last I says, 'Butty,' says I, 'who are these chaps round here on the lay?' And he says, 'Young 'uns—no one as we know.' And I says, 'Not likely, matey; I've been on the square this twenty year.' 'Same here,' says the old chap; 'give us your flipper. And now,' says he, 'what sort of a cove is your boss' (meaning Mr. Troubridge)? 'One of the *real right sort*,' says I. 'Then see here,' says he, 'I'll tell you something: the head man of that there gang is at this minute a-sitting yarning with your boss in the parlour.' 'The devil!' says I. 'Is so,' says he, 'and no flies.' So I sings out, 'Mr. Troubridge, those sheep will be out'; and out he came running, and I whispers to him, 'Mind the man you're sitting with, and leave me to pay the score.' So he goes back, and presently he sings out, 'Will, have you got any money?' And I says, 'Yes, thirty shillings.' 'Then,' says he, 'pay for this, and come along.' And thinks I, I'll go in and have a look at this great new captain of bushrangers; so I goes to the parlour door, and now who do you think I saw?"

"I know," she said. "It was that horrid villain they call Touan."

"The same man," he answered. "Do you know who he is?"

She found somehow breath to say, "How can I? How is it possible?"

"I will tell you," said Lee. "There, sitting in front of Mr. Troubridge, hardly altered in all these long years, sat George Hawker, formerly of Drumston—your husband!"

She gave a low cry, and beat the hard rail with her head till it bled. Then, turning fiercely round, she said, in a voice hoarse and strangely altered:

"Have you anything more to tell me, you croaking raven?"

He had something more to tell, but he dared not speak now. So he said, "Nothing at present, but if laying down my life——"

She did not wait to hear him, but, with her hands clasped above her head, she turned and walked swiftly towards the house. She could not cry, or sob, or rave; she could only say, "Let it fall on me, O God, on me!" over and over again.

Also, she was far too crushed and stunned to think precisely what it was she dreaded so. It seemed afterwards, as Frank Maberly told me, that she had an indefinable horror of Charles meeting his father, and of their coming to know one another. She half feared that her husband would appear and carry away her son with him, and even if he did not, the lad was reckless enough as it was, without being known and pointed at through the country as the son of Hawker the bushranger.

These were after-thoughts, however; at present she leaned giddily against the house-side, trying, in the wild hurrying night-rack of her thoughts, to distinguish some tiny star of hope, or even some glimmer of reason. Impossible! Nothing but swift, confused clouds everywhere, driving wildly on—whither?

But a desire came upon her to see her boy again, and compare his face to his father's. So she slid quietly into the room where Tom and Charles were still talking together of Tom's adventure, and sat looking at the boy, pretending to work. As she came in, he was laughing loudly at something, and his face was alive and merry. "He is not like what his father was at his age," she said.

But they continued their conversation. "And now, what sort of man was he, Tom?" said Charles. "Was he like any one you ever saw?"

"Why, no. Stay, let's see. Do you know, he was something like you in the face."

"Thank you!" said Charles, laughing. "Wait till I get a chance of paying you a compliment, old fellow. A powerful fellow—eh?"

"Why, yes—a tough-looking subject," said Tom.

"I shouldn't have much chance with him, I suppose?"

"No; he'd be too powerful for you, Charley."

A change came over his face, a dark, fierce look. Mary could see the likeness *now* plain enough, and even Tom looked at him for an instant with a puzzled look.

"Nevertheless," continued Charles, "I would have a turn with him if I met him. I'd try what six inches of cold steel between——"

"Forbear, boy! Would you have the roof fall in and crush you dead?" said Mary, in a voice that appalled both of them. "Stop such foolish talk, and pray that we may be delivered from the very sight of these men, and suffered to get away to our graves in peace, without any more of these horrors and surprises. I would sooner," she said, increasing in rapidity as she went on, "I would far sooner live like some one I have heard of, with a sword above his head, than thus. If he comes and looks on me, I shall die."

She had risen and stood in the firelight, deadly pale. Somehow one of the bands of her long black hair had fallen down, and half covered her face. She looked so unearthly that, coupling her appearance with the wild, senseless words she had been uttering, Tom had a horrible suspicion that she was gone mad.

"Cousin," he said, "let me beseech you to go to bed. Charles, run for Mrs. Barker. Mary," he added, as soon as he was gone, "come away, or you'll be saying something before that boy you'll be sorry for. You're hysterical; that's what is the matter with you. I am afraid we have frightened you by our talk about bushrangers."

"Yes, that is it! that is it!" she said; and then, suddenly, "Oh! my dear old friend, you will not desert me?"

"Never, Mary; but why ask such a question now?"

"Ask Lee," she said, and the next moment Mrs. Barker, the housekeeper, came bustling in with smelling-salts, and so on, to minister to a mind diseased. And Mary was taken off to bed.

"What on earth can be the matter with her, cousin Tom?" said Charles, when she was gone.

"She is out of sorts, and got hysterical: that's what it is," said Tom.

"What odd things she said!"

"Women do when they are hysterical. It's nothing more than that."

But Mrs. Barker came in with a different opinion. She said that Mary was very hot and restless, and had very little doubt that a fever was coming on. "Terribly shaken she had been," said Mrs. Barker, "hoped nothing was wrong."

"There's something decidedly wrong, if your mistress is going to have a fever," said Tom. "Charley, do you think Dr. Mulhaus is at Baroona or Garoopna?"

"Up at the Major's," said Charles. "Shall I ride over for him? There will be a good moon in an hour."

"Yes," said Tom, "and fetch him over at once. Tell him we think it's a fever, and he will know what to bring. Ride like hell, Charley."

As soon as he was alone, he began thinking. "What the *doose* is the matter?" was his first exclamation, and, after half an hour's cogitation, only had arrived at the same point, "What the *doose* is the matter?" Then it flashed across him, what did she mean by "ask Lee"? Had she any meaning in it, or was it nonsense? There was an easy solution for it; namely, *to* ask Lee. And so arising he went across the yard to the kitchen.

Lee was bending low over the fire, smoking. "William," said Tom, "I want to see you in the parlour."

"I was thinking of coming across myself," said Lee. "In fact I should have come when I had finished my pipe."

" Bring your pipe across, then," said Tom. " Girl, take in some hot water and tumblers."

" Now, Lee," said Tom, as soon as Lee had gone through the ceremony of " Well, here's my respex, sir,"—" now, Lee, you have heard how ill the mistress is."

" I have indeed, sir," said he; " and very sorry I am, as I am partly the cause of it."

" All that simplifies matters, Will, considerably," said Tom. " I must tell you that when I asked her what put her in that state, she said, ' Ask Lee.' "

" Shows her sense, sir. What she means is, that you ought to hear what she and I have heard; and I mean to tell you more than I have her. If she knew everything, I am afraid it would kill her."

" Ay! I know nothing as yet, you know."

Lee in the first place put him in possession of what we already know—the fact of Hawker's reappearance, and his identity with " The Touan "; then he paused.

" This is very astonishing, and very terrible, Lee," said he. " Is there anything further ? "

" Yes, the worst. That man has followed us home ! "

Tom had exhausted all his expression of astonishment and dismay before this; so now he could only give a long whistle, and say, " Followed us home ? "

" Followed us home " said Lee. " As we were passing the black swamp, not two miles from here, this very morning, I saw that man riding parallel with us through the bush."

" Why did not you tell me before ? "

" Because I had not made up my mind how to act. First I resolved to tell the mistress; that I did. Then after I had smoked a pipe, I resolved to tell you, and that I did, and now here we are, you see."

That was undeniable. There they were, with about as pretty a complication of mischief to unravel as two men could wish to have. Tom felt so foolish and nonplussed, that he felt inclined to laugh at Lee, when he said, " Here we are." It so exactly expressed the state of the case; as if he had said, " All so and so has happened, and a deuce of a job it is, and here sit you and I, to deliberate what's to be done with regard to so and so."

He did not laugh, however; he bit his lip, and stopped it. Then he rose, and, leaning his great shoulders against the mantelpiece, stood before the fireless grate, and looked at Lee. Lee also looked at him, and I think that each one thought what a splendid specimen of his style the other was. If they did not think so, "they ought to it," as the Londoners say. But neither spoke a few minutes; then Tom said:

"Lee, Will Lee, though you came to me a free man, and have served me twenty years, or thereabouts, as free man, I don't conceal from myself the fact, that you have been a convict. Pish, man! don't let us mince matters now—a lag."

Lee looked him full in the face, without changing countenance, and nodded.

"Convicted more than once, too," continued Tom.

"Three times," said Lee.

"Ah!" said Tom. "And if a piece of work was set before me to do, which required pluck, honesty, courage, and cunning, and one were to say to me, 'Who will you have to help you?' I would answer out boldly, 'Give me Will Lee, the lag; my old friend, who has served me so true and hearty these twenty years.'"

"And you'd do right, sir," said Lee quietly. And rising up, he stood beside Tom, with one foot on the fender, bending down and looking into the empty grate.

"Now, Will," said Tom, turning round and laying his hand on his shoulder, "this fellow has followed us home, having found out who we were. Why has he done so?"

"Evident," said Lee, "to work on the fears of the mistress, and get some money from her."

"Good!" said Tom. "Well answered. We shall get to the bottom of our difficulty like this. Only answer the next question as well, and I will call you a Poly—, Poly—; damn the Greek."

"Not such a bad name as that, I hope, sir," said Lee, smiling. "Who might she have been? A bad 'un, I expect. You don't happen to refer to Hobarttown Polly, did you, sir?"

"Hold your tongue, you villain," said Tom, "or you'll make me laugh; and these are not laughing times."

"Well, what is your question, sir?" asked Lee.

"Why, simply this: What are we to do?"

"I'll tell you," said Lee, speaking in an animated whisper. "Watch, watch, and watch again, till you catch him. Tie him tight, and hand him over to Captain Desborough. He may be about the place to-night: he will be sure to be. Let us watch to-night, you and I, and for many nights, till we catch him."

"But," whispered Tom, "he will be hung."

"He has earned it," said Lee. "Let him be hung."

"But he is her husband," urged Tom, in a whisper. "He is that boy's father. I cannot do it. Can't we buy him off?"

"Yes," answered Lee in the same tone, "till his money is gone. Then you will have a chance of doing it again, and again, all your life."

"This is a terrible dilemma," said Tom; and added in a perplexity almost comical, "Drat the girl! Why didn't she marry poor old Jim Stockbridge, or sleepy Hamlyn, or even your humble servant? Though, in all honour, I must confess I never asked her, as those two others did. No! I'll tell you what, Lee: we will watch for him, and catch him if we can. After that we will think what is to be done. By the by, I have been going to ask you: do you think he recognised you at the public-house there?"

"That puzzles me," said Lee. "He looked me in the face, but I could not see that he did. I wonder if he recognised you?"

"I never saw him in my life before," said Tom. "It is very likely that he knew me, though. I was champion of Devon and Cornwall, you know, before little Abraham Cann kicked my legs from under me that unlucky Easter Monday. (The deuce curl his hair for doing it!) I never forgave him till I heard of that fine bit of play with Polkinghorn. Yes! he must have known me."

Lee lit the fire, while Tom, blowing out the candles, drew the curtains, so that any one outside could not see into the room. Nevertheless, he left the French window open, and then went outside, and secured all the dogs in the dog-house.

The night was wonderfully still and dark. As he paused before entering the house, he could hear the bark falling from the trees a quarter of a mile off, and the opossums scratching and snapping little twigs as they passed from bough to bough. Somewhere, apparently at an immense distance, a morepork was chanting his monotonous cry. The frogs in the creek were silent even, so hot was the night. "A good night for watching," said he to Lee when he came in. "Lie you down; I'll take the first watch."

They blew out the candle, and Lee was in the act of lying down, when he arrested himself, and held up his finger to Tom.

They both listened, motionless and in silence, until they could hear the spiders creeping on the ceiling. There it was again; a stealthy step on the gravel.

Troubridge and Lee crouched down breathless. One minute, two, five, but it did not come again. At length they both moved, as if by concert, and Lee said, "'Possum."

"Not a bit," said Troubridge; and then Lee lay down again, and slept in the light of the flickering fire. One giant arm was thrown around his head, and the other hung down in careless grace; the great chest was heaved up, and the head thrown back; the seamed and rugged features seemed more stern and marked than ever in the chiaroscuro; and the whole man was a picture of reckless strength such as one seldom sees. Tom had dozed and had awoke again, and now sat thinking, "What a terrible tough customer that fellow would be!" when suddenly he crouched on the floor, and, reaching out his hand, touched Lee, who woke, and silently rolled over with his face towards the window.

There was no mistake this time—that was no opossum. There came the stealthy step again; and now, as they lay silent, the glass door was pushed gently open, showing the landscape beyond. The gibbous moon was just rising over the forest, all blurred with streaky clouds, and between them and her light they could see the figure of a man, standing inside the room.

Tom could wait no longer. He started up, and fell headlong with a crash over a little table that stood in his way. They both dashed into the garden, but only in time to hear flying footsteps, and immediately after the gallop of a horse, the echoes of which soon died away, and all was still.

"Missed him, by George!" said Lee. "It was a precious close thing, though. What could he mean by coming into the house—eh?"

"Just as I expected; trying to get an interview with the mistress. He will be more cautious in future, I take it."

"I wonder if he will try again?"

"Don't know," said Troubridge; "he might: not to-night, however."

They went in and lay down again, and Troubridge was soon asleep; and very soon that sleep was disturbed by dreadful dreams. At one time he thought he was riding madly through the bush for his bare life; spurring on a tired horse, which was failing every moment more and more. But always through the tree-stems on his right he saw glancing, a ghost on a white horse, which kept pace with him, do what he would. Now he was among the precipices on the ranges. On his left, a lofty inaccessible cliff; on the right, a frightful blue abyss; while the slaty soil kept sliding from beneath his horse's feet. Behind him came the phantom, always gaining on him, and driving him along the giddiest wallaby tracks. If he could only turn and face it, he might conquer, but he dare not. At length the path grew narrower and narrower, and he turned in desperation and awoke—woke to see in the dim morning light a dark figure bending over him. He sprang up, and clutched it by the throat.

"A most excellent fellow this!" said the voice of Dr. Mulhaus. "He sends a frantic midnight message for his friend to come to him, regardless of personal convenience and horseflesh; and when this friend comes quietly in, and tries to wake him without disturbing the sick folks, he seizes him by the throat and nearly throttles him."

"I beg a thousand pardons, Doctor," said Tom; "I had been dreaming, and I took you for the devil. I am glad to find my mistake."

"You have good reason," said the Doctor; "but now, how is the patient?"

"Asleep at present, I believe; the housekeeper is with her."

"What is the matter with her?"

"She has had a great blow. It has shaken her intellect, I am afraid."

"What sort of a blow?" asked the Doctor.

Tom hesitated. He did not know whether to tell him or not.

"Nay," said the Doctor, "you had better let me know. I can help you then, you know. Now, for instance, has she heard of her husband?"

"She has, Doctor. How on earth came you to guess that?"

"A mere guess, though I have always thought it quite possible, as the accounts of his death were very uncertain."

Tom then set to work, and told the Doctor all that we know. He looked very grave. "This is far worse than I had thought," he said, and remained thoughtful.

Mary awoke in a fever and delirious. They kept Charles as much from her as possible, lest she should let drop some hint of the matter to the boy; but even in her delirium she kept her secret well; and towards the evening the Doctor, finding her quieter, saddled his horse, and rode away ten miles to a township, where resided a drunken surgeon, one of the greatest blackguards in the country.

The surgeon was at home. He was drunk, of course; he always was, but hardly more so to-day than usual. So the Doctor hoped for success in his object, which was to procure a certain drug which was neither in the medicine-chest at the Buckleys nor at Toonarbin; and putting on his sweetest smile when the surgeon came to the door, he made a remark about the beauty of the weather, to which the other very gruffly responded.

"I come to beg a favour," said Mulhaus. "Can you let me have a little—so and so?"

"See you damned first," was the polite reply. "A man comes a matter of fourteen thousand miles, makes a pretty little practice, and then gets it cut into by a parcel of ignorant foreigners, whose own country is too hot to hold them. And not content with this, they have the brass to ask for the loan of a man's drugs. As I said before, I'll see you damned first, AND THEN I WON'T." And so saying, he slammed the door.

Dr. Mulhaus was beside himself with rage. For the first and last time since I have known him he forgot his discretion, and instead of going away quietly, and treating the man with contempt, he began kicking at the door, calling the man a scoundrel, etc., and between the intervals of kicking, roaring through the keyhole, "Bring out your diploma; do you hear, you impostor?" and then fell to work kicking again. "Bring out your forged diploma, will you, you villain?"

This soon attracted the idlers from the public-house: a couple of sawyers, a shepherd or two, all tipsy of course, except one of the sawyers, who was drunk. The drunken sawyer at length made out to his own complete satisfaction that Dr. Mulhaus's wife was in labour, and that he was come for the surgeon, who was probably drunk and asleep inside. So, being able to sympathise, he prepared to assist, and for this purpose took a stone about half a hundred-weight, and coming behind the Doctor, when he was in full kick, he balanced himself with difficulty, and sent it at the lock with all the force of his arm, and of course broke the door in. In throwing the stone, he lost his balance, came full butt against Dr. Mulhaus, propelled him into the passage, into the arms of the surgeon, who was rushing out infuriated to defend his property, and down went the three in the passage together, the two doctors beneath, and the drunken sawyer on the top of them.

The drunken surgeon, if, to use parliamentary language, he will allow me to call him so, was of course underneath the others; but, being a Londoner, and consequently knowing the use of his fists, ere he went down delivered a " one, two," straight from the shoulder in our poor dear Doctor's face, and gave him a most disreputable black eye, besides cutting his upper lip open. This our Doctor, being, you must remember, a foreigner, and not having the rules of the British ring before his eyes, resented by getting on the top of him, taking him round the throat, and banging the back of his head against the brick floor of the passage, until he began to goggle his eyes and choke. Meanwhile the sawyer, exhilarated beyond measure in his drunken mind at having raised a real good promising row, having turned on his back, lay procumbent upon the twain, and kicking everything soft and human he came across with his heels, struck up "The Bay of Biscay, Oh," until he was dragged forth by two of his friends; and being in a state of wild excitement, ready to fight the world, hit his own mate a violent blow in the eye, and was only quieted by receiving a sound thrashing, and being placed in a sitting posture in the veranda of the public-house, from which he saw Dr. Mulhaus come forth from the surgeon's with rumpled feathers, but triumphant.

I am deeply grieved to have recorded the above scene, but I could not omit it. Having undertaken to place the character of that very noble gentleman, Dr. Mulhaus, before my readers, I was forced not to omit this. As a general rule, he was as self-contained, as calm, and as frigid as the best Englishman among us. But under all this there was, to speak in carefully-selected scientific language, a substratum of pepper-box, which has been apparent to me on more than one occasion. I have noticed the above occasion per force. Let the others rest in oblivion. A man so true, so wise, so courteous, and so kindly, needs not my poor excuses for having once in a way made a fool of himself. He will read this, and he will be angry with me for a time, but he knows well that I, like all who knew him, say heartily, God bless you, old Doctor.

But the consequences of the above were, I am sorry to say, eminently disastrous. The surgeon got a warrant against Dr. Mulhaus for burglary with violence, and our Doctor got a warrant against him for assault with intent to rob. So there was the deuce to pay. The affair got out of the hands of the Bench. In fact they sent *both* parties for trial in order to get rid of the matter, and at sessions, the surgeon swore positively that Dr. Mulhaus had, assisted by a convict, battered his door down with stones in open day, and nearly murdered him. Then in defence Dr. Mulhaus called the sawyer, who, as it happened, had just completed a contract for fencing for Mrs. Mayford, the proceeds of which bargain he was spending at the public-house when the thing happened, and had just undertaken another for one of the magistrates; having also a large family dependent on him; being, too, a man who prided himself in keeping an eye to windward, and being slightly confused by a trifling attack of delirium tremens (diddleums, he called it): he, I say, to our Doctor's confusion and horror, swore positively that he never took a stone in his hand on the day in question; that he never saw a stone for a week before or after that date: that he did not deny having rushed into the passage to assist the complainant (drunken surgeon), seeing him being murdered by defendant; and lastly, that he was never near the place on the day specified. So it would have gone hard with our Doctor, had not his Honour called the jury's attention to the discrepancies in this witness's evidence; and when Dr. Mulhaus was acquitted, delivered a stinging reproof to the magistrates for wasting public time by sending such a trumpery case to a jury. But, on the other hand, Dr. Mulhaus's charge of assault with intent, fell dead; so that neither party had much to boast of.

The night or so after the trial was over, the Doctor came back to Toonarbin, in what he intended for a furious rage. But, having told Tom Troubridge the whole affair, and having unluckily caught Tom's eye, they two went off into such hearty fits of laughter that poor Mary, now convalescent, but still in bed, knocked at the wall to know what the matter was.

CHAPTER XXXII

IN WHICH TOM AND MARY HEAR OF AN ESCAPE

THE state of terror and dismay into which poor Mary Hawker was thrown on finding that her husband, now for many years the *bête noire* of her existence, was not only alive, but promising fairly to cause her more trouble than ever he did before, superadded, let me say, for mere truth's sake, to a slight bilious attack, brought on by good living and want of exercise, threw her into a fever, from which, after several days' delirium, she rose much shattered, and looking suddenly older. All this time the Doctor, like a trusty dog, had kept his watch, and done more, and with a better will than any paid doctor would have been likely to do. He was called away a good deal by the prosecution arising out of that unhappy affair with the other doctor, and afterwards with a prosecution for perjury, which he brought against the sawyer; but he was generally back at night, and was so kind, so attentive, and so skilful that Mary took it into her head, and always affirmed afterwards, that she owed her life to him.

She was not one to receive any permanent impression from anything. So now, as day by day she grew stronger, she tried to undervalue the mischief which had at first so terrified her, and caused her illness—tried, and with success, in broad daylight; but, in the silent dark nights, as she lay on her lonely bed, she would fully appreciate the terrible cloud that hung over her, and would weep and beat her pillow, and pray in her wild fantastic way to be delivered from this frightful monster, cut off from communion with all honest men by his unutterable crimes, but who, nevertheless, she was bound to love, honour, and obey, till death should part her from him.

Mrs. Buckley, on the first news of her illness, had come up and taken her quarters at Toonarbin, acting as gentle a nurse as man or woman could desire to have. She took possession of the house, and managed everything. Mrs. Barker, the housekeeper, the only one who did not submit at once to her kindly rule, protested, obstructed, protocolled, presented an ultimatum, and, at last, was so ill advised as to take up arms. There was a short campaign, lasting only one morning—a decisive battle—and Mrs. Barker was compelled to sue for peace. "Had Mr. Troubridge been true to himself," she said, "she would never have submitted;" but, having given Tom warning, and Tom, in a moment of irritation, having told her, without hesitation or disguise, to go to the devil (no less), she bowed to the circumstances, and yielded.

Agnes Buckley encouraged Dr. Mulhaus, too, in his legal affairs, and, I fear, was the first person who proposed the prosecution for perjury against the sawyer: a prosecution, however, which failed, in consequence of his mate and another friend, who was present at the affair, coming forward to the sawyer's rescue, and getting into such a labyrinth and mist of perjury, that the Bench (this happened just after quarter sessions) positively refused to hear anything more on either side. Altogether, Agnes Buckley made herself so agreeable, and kept them all so alive, that Tom wondered how he had got on so long without her.

At the end of three weeks Mary was convalescent; and one day, when she was moved into the veranda, Mrs. Buckley beside her, Tom and the Doctor sitting on the step smoking, and Charles sleepily reading aloud *Hamlet,* with a degree of listlessness and want of appreciation unequalled, I should say, by any reader before; at such time, I say, there entered suddenly to them a little cattle-dealer, as brimful of news as an egg of meat. Little Burnside it was: a man about eight stone nothing, who always wore top-boots and other people's clothes. As he came in, Charles recognised on his legs a pair of cord breeches of his own, with a particular grease patch on the thigh: a pair of breeches he had lent Burnside and which Burnside had immediately got altered to his own size. A good singer was Burnside. A man who could finish his bottle of brandy, and not go to bed in his boots. A man universally liked and trusted. An honest, hearty little fellow, yet one who always lent or spent his money as fast as he got it, and was as poor as Job. The greatest vehicle of news in the district, too. " Snowy River Times," he used to be called.

After the usual greetings, Tom, seeing he was bursting with something, asked him, " What's the news? "

Burnside was in the habit of saying that he was like the Lord Mayor's fool—fond of everything that was good. But his greatest pleasure, the one to which he would sacrifice everything, was retailing a piece of news. This was so great an enjoyment with him that he gloried in dwelling on it, and making the most of it. He used to retail a piece of news, as a perfect novel, in three volumes. In his first he would take care to ascertain that you were acquainted with the parties under discussion; and, if you were not, make you so, throwing in a few anecdotes illustrative of their characters. In his second, he would grow discursive, giving an episode or two, and dealing in moral reflections and knowledge of human nature rather largely. And in his third he would come smash, crash down on you with the news itself, and leave you gasping.

He followed this plan on the present occasion. He answered Tom's question by asking:

" Do you know Desborough? "

" Of course I do," said Tom; " and a noble good fellow he is."

" Exactly," said Burnside; " super of police; distinguished in Indian wars; nephew of my Lord Covetown. An Irishman is Desborough, but far from objectionable."

This by way of first volume: now comes his second:

" Now, sir, I, although a Scotchman born, and naturally proud of being so, consider that until these wretched national distinctions between the three great nations are obliterated we shall never get on, sir; never. That the Scotch, sir, are physically and intellectually superior——"

" Physically and intellectually the devil," burst in Tom. " Pick out any dozen Scotchmen, and I'll find you a dozen Londoners who will fight them, or deal with them till they'd be glad to get over the borders again. As for the Devon and Cornish lads, find me a Scotchman who will put me on my back, and I'll write you a cheque for a hundred pounds, my boy. We English opened the trade of the world to your little two millions and a half up in the north there; and you, being pretty well starved out at home, have had the shrewdness to take advantage of it; and now, by Jove, you try to speak small of the bridge that carried you over. What did you do towards licking the Spaniards, eh? And where would you be now, if they had not been licked in 1588, eh? Not in Australia, my boy! A Frenchman is conceited enough, but, by George, he can't hold a candle to a Scotchman."

Tom spoke in a regular passion; but there was some truth in what he said, I think. Burnside didn't like it, and merely saying, " You interrupt me, sir," went on to his third volume without a struggle.

" You are aware, ladies, that there has been a gang of bushrangers out to the north, headed by a miscreant, whom his companions call Touan, but whose real name is a mystery."

Mrs. Buckley said, " Yes; " and Tom glanced at Mary. She had grown as pale as death, and Tom said, " Courage, cousin; don't be frightened at a name."

" Well, sir," continued Burnside, putting the forefinger and thumb of each hand together, as if he was making " windows " with soapsuds, " Captain Desborough has surprised that gang in a gully, sir, and," spreading his hands out right and left, " obliterated them."

" The devil! " said Tom, while the Doctor got up and stood beside Mary.

" Smashed them, sir," continued Burnside; " extinguished them utterly. He had six of his picked troopers with him, and they came on them suddenly and brought them to bay. You see, two troopers have been murdered lately, and so our men, when they got face to face with the cowardly hounds, broke discipline and wouldn't be held. They hardly fired a shot, but drew their sabres, and cut the dogs down almost to a man. Three only out of twelve have been captured alive, and one of them is dying of a wound in the neck." And, having finishd, little Burnside folded his arms and stood in a military attitude, with the air of a man who had done the thing himself, and was prepared to receive his meed of praise with modesty.

" Courage, Mary," said Tom; " don't be frightened at shadows." He felt something sticking in his throat, but spoke out nevertheless.

"And their redoubted captain," he asked; "what has become of him?"

"What, Touan himself?" said Burnside. "Well, I am sorry to say that that chivalrous and high-minded gentleman was found neither among the dead nor the living. Not to mince matters, sir, he has escaped."

The Doctor saw Mary's face quiver, but she bore up bravely, and listened.

"Escaped, has he?" said Tom. "And do they know anything about him?"

"Desborough, who told me himself," said Burnside, "says no, that he is utterly puzzled. He had made sure of the arch-rascal himself; but, with that remarkable faculty of saving his own skin which he has exhibited on more than one occasion, he has got off for the time, with one companion."

"A companion; eh?"

"Yes," said Burnside, "whereby hangs a bit of romance, if I may profane the word in speaking of such men. His companion is a young fellow, described as being more like a beautiful woman than a man, and bearing the most singular likeness in features to the great Captain Touan himself, who, as you have heard, is a handsome dog. In short, there is very little doubt that they are father and son."

Tom thought to himself, "Who on earth can this be? What son can George Hawker have, and we not know of it?" He turned to Burnside.

"What age is the young man you speak of?" he asked.

"Twenty, or thereabouts, by all description," said the other.

Tom thought again: "This gets very strange. He could have no son of that age got in Van Diemen's Land: it was eight years before he was free. It must be someone we know of. He had some by-blows in Devon, by all accounts. If this is one of them, how the deuce did he get here?"

But he could not think. We shall see presently who it was. Now we must leave these good folks for a time, and just step over to Garoopna, and see how affairs go there.

CHAPTER XXXIII

IN WHICH JAMES BRENTWOOD AND SAMUEL BUCKLEY, ESQUIRES, COMBINE TO DISTURB THE REST OF CAPTAIN BRENTWOOD, R.A., AND SUCCEED IN DOING SO

THE morning after Cecil Mayford had made his unlucky offer to Alice, he appeared at Sam's bedside very early, as if he had come to draw Priam's curtains; and told him shortly, that he had spoken, and had been received with contempt; that he was a miserable brute, and that he was going back home to attend to his business— under the circumstances, the best thing he could possibly do.

So the field was clear for Sam, but he let matters stay as they were, being far too pleasant to disturb lightly; being also, to tell the truth, a little uncertain of his ground, after poor Cecil had suffered so severely in the encounter. The next day, too, his father and mother went home, and he thought it would be only proper for him to go with them, but, on proposing it, Jim quietly told him he must stay where he was and work hard for another week, and Halbert, although a guest of the Buckleys, was constrained to remain still at the Brentwood's, in company with Sam.

But at the end of a week they departed, and Jim went back with them, leaving poor Alice behind, alone with her father. Sam turned when they had gone a little way, and saw her white figure still in the porch, leaning in rather a melancholy attitude against the door-post. The audacious magpie had perched himself on the top of her head, from which proud elevation he hurled wrath, scorn, and mortal defiance against them as they rode away. Sam took off his hat, and as he went on kept wondering whether she was thinking of him at all, and hoping that she might be sorry that he was gone. "Probably, however," he thought, "she is only sorry for her brother."

They three stayed at Baroona a week or more, one of them riding up every day to ask after Mary Hawker. Otherwise they spent their time shooting and fishing, and speculating how soon the rains would come, for it was now March, and autumn was fairly due.

But at the end of this week, as the three were sitting together, one of those long-legged, slab-sided, lean, sunburnt, cabbage-tree-hatted lads, of whom Captain Brentwood kept always, say half a dozen, and the Major four or five (I should fancy, no relation to one another, and yet so exactly alike, that Captain Brentwood never called them by their right names by any chance); lads who were employed about the stable and the paddock, always in some way with the horses; one of those representatives of the rising Australian generation, I say, looked in, and without announcing himself came up to Jim across the drawing-room, as quiet and self-possessed as if he was quite used to good society, and, putting a letter in his hand, said merely, " Miss Alice," and relapsed into silence, amusing himself by looking round Mrs. Buckley's drawing-room, the like of which he had never seen before.

Sam envied Jim the receipt of that little three-cornered note. He wondered whether there was anything about him in it. Jim read it, and then folded it up again, and said " Hallo! "

The lad—I always call that sort of individual a lad; there is no other word for them, though they are of all ages, from sixteen to twenty—the lad, I say, was so taken up with the contemplation of a blown-glass *presse-papiers* on the table, that Jim had to say, " Hallo there, John! "

The lad turned round, and asked in a perfectly easy manner, " What the deuce is this thing for, now? "

" That," said Jim, " is the button of a Chinese mandarin's hat, who was killed at the battle of Waterloo in the United States by Major Buckley."

" Is it now? " said the lad, quite contented. " It's very pretty; may I take it up? "

" Of course you may," said Jim. " Now, what's the foal like? "

" Rather leggy, *I* should say," he returned. " Is there any answer? "

Jim wrote a few lines with a pencil on half his sister's note, and gave it him. He put it in the lining of his hat, and had got as far as the door, when he turned again. He looked wistfully towards the table where the *presse-papiers* was lying. It was too much for him. He came back and took it up again. What he wanted with it, or what he would have done with it if he had got it, I cannot conceive, but it had taken his simple fancy more, probably, than an emerald of the same size would have done. At last he put it to his eye.

" Why, darn my cabbage-tree," he said, " if you can't see through it! He wouldn't sell it, I suppose, now? "

Jim pursed his lips and shook his head, as though to say that such an idea was not to be entertained, and the lad, with a sigh, laid it down and departed. Then Jim with a laugh threw his sister's note over to Sam. I discovered this very same note only last week, while searching the Buckley papers for information about the family at this period. I have reason to believe that it has never been printed before, and, as far as I know, there is no other copy extant, so I proceed to give it in full.

What a dear, disagreeable old Jim you are (it begins) to stay away there at Baroona, leaving me moping here with our daddy, who is calculating the explosive power of shells under water at various temperatures. I have a good mind to learn the Differential Calculus myself, only on purpose to bore you with it when you come home.

By the by, Corella has got a foal. Such a dear little duck of a thing, with a soft brown nose, and sweet long ears, like leaves! Do come back and see it; I am so very, very lonely!

I hope Mr. Halbert is pretty well, and that his wound is getting quite right again. Don't let him undertake cattle-drafting or anything violent. I wish you could bring him back with you, he is such a nice, agreeable creature.

Your magpie has attacked cocky, and pulled a yellow feather out of his crest, which he has planted in the flower-bed, either as a trophy, or to see if it will grow.

Now this letter is historically important, when taken in connection with certain dates in my possession. It was written on a Monday, and Halbert, Jim, and Sam started back to Garoopna the next day, rather a memorable day for Sam, as you will see directly. Now I wish to call attention to the fact, that Sam, far from being invited, is never once mentioned in the whole letter. Therefore what does Miss Burke mean by her audacious calumnies? What does she mean by saying that Alice made love to Sam, and never gave the " poor boy " a chance of escape? Can she, Lesbia, put her hand on her heart and say that she wasn't dying to marry Sam herself, though she was (and is still, very likely) thirty years his senior? The fact is, Lesbia gave herself the airs, and received the privileges of being, the handsomest woman in those parts, till Alice came, and put her nose out of joint, for which she never forgave her.

However, to return to this letter. I wonder now, as I am looking at the age-stained paper and faded writing, whether she who wrote it contemplated the possibility of its meeting Sam's eye. I rather imagine that she did, from her provoking silence about him. At any rate, Jim was quite justified in showing him the letter, " for you know," he said, " as there is nothing at all about you in it, there can be no breach of confidence."

" Well! " said Sam, when he had read it.

"Well!" said Jim. "Let us all three ride over and look at the foal."

So they went, and were strictly to be home at dinner-time; whereas not one of them came home for a week.

When they came to the door at Garoopna, there was Alice, most bewitchingly beautiful. Papa was away on the run, and Dr. Mulhaus with him; so the three came in. Alice was very glad to see Halbert—was glad also to see Sam; but not so glad, or, at all events, did not say so much about it.

"Alice, have you seen the newspaper?" said Jim.

"No; why?"

"There is a great steamer gone down at sea, and three hundred persons drowned."

"What a horrible thing! I should never have courage to cross the sea."

"You would soon get accustomed to it, I think," said Halbert.

"I have never even seen it as yet," she said, "save at a distance."

"Strange, neither have I," said Sam. "I have dim recollections of our voyage here, but I never stood upon the shore in my life."

"I have beat you there," said Jim. "I have been down to Cape Chatham, and seen the great ocean itself: a very different thing from Sydney Harbour, I promise you. You see the great Cape running out a mile into the sea, and the southern rollers tumbling in over the reefs like cascades."

"Let us go and see it!—how far is it?" said Alice.

"About thirty miles. The Barkers' station is about half a mile from the Cape, and we could sleep there, you know."

"It strikes me as being a most brilliant idea," said Sam.

And so the arrangement was agreed to, and the afternoon went on pleasantly. Alice walked up and down with Sam among the flowers, while Jim and Halbert lay beneath a mulberry tree and smoked.

They talked on a subject which had engaged their attention a good deal lately. Jim's whim for going soldiering had grown and struck root, and become a determination. He would go back to India when Halbert did, supposing that his father could be tempted to buy him a commission. Surely he might manage to join some regiment in India, he thought: India was the only place worth living in just now.

"I hope, Halbert," he said, "that the governor will consent. I wouldn't care when I went; the sooner the better. I am tired of being a cattle-dealer on a large scale; I want to get at some *man's* work. If one thing were settled I would go to-morrow."

" And what is that? " said Halbert.

Jim said nothing, but looked at the couple among the flower-beds.

"Is that all?" said Halbert. "What will you bet me that that affair is not concluded to-night? "

" I'll bet you five pounds to one it ain't," said Jim; " nor any time this twelvemonth. They'll go on shilly-shallying half their lives, I believe."

" Nevertheless I'll bet with you. Five to one it comes off to-night! Now! There goes your sister into the house; just go in after her."

Jim sauntered off, and Sam came and laid his great length down by the side of Halbert.

They talked on indifferent matters for a few minutes, till the latter said:

" You are a lucky fellow, Sam."

" With regard to what? " said Sam.

" With regard to Miss Brentwood, I mean."

" What makes you think so? "

" Are you blind, Sam? Can't you see that she loves you better than any man in the world? "

He answered nothing, but turning his eyes upon Halbert, gazed at him a moment to see whether he was jesting or no. No, he was in earnest. So he looked down on the grass again, and, tearing ittle tufts up, said:

" What earthly reason have you for thinking that? "

" What reason!—fifty thousand reasons. Can you see nothing in her eyes when she speaks to you, which is not there at other times; hey, Bat?—I can, if you can't."

" If I could think so! " said Sam. " If I could find out? "

" When I want to find out anything, I generally ask," said Halbert.

Sam gave him the full particulars of Cecil's defeat.

" All the better for you," said Halbert; " depend upon it. I don't know much about women, it is true, but I know more than you do."

" I wish I knew as much as you do," said Sam.

" And I wish I knew as little as you do," said Halbert.

Dinner-time came, but the Captain and the Doctor were not to the fore. After some speculations as to what had become of them, and having waited an hour, Jim said, that, in the unexplained absence of the crowned head, he felt it his duty to the country, to assume the reins of government, and order dinner. Prime Minister Alice, having entered a protest, offered no further opposition, and dinner was brought in.

Young folks don't make so much of dinner as old ones at any time, and this dinner was an unusually dull one. Sam was silent and thoughtful, and talked little; Alice, too, was not quite herself. Jim, as usual, ate like a hero, but talked little; so the conversation was principally carried on by Halbert, in the narrative style, who really made himself very useful and agreeable, and I am afraid they would have been a very " slow " party without him.

Soon after the serious business of eating was over, Jim said:

" Alice, I wonder what the governor will say ? "

" About what, brother ? "

" About my going soldiering."

" Save us! What new crotchet is this ? "

" Only that I'm going to bother the governor till he gets me a commission in the army."

" Are you really serious, Jim ? "

" I never was more so in my life."

" So, Mr. Halbert," said Alice, looking round at him, " you are only come to take my brother away from me ! "

" I assure you, Miss Brentwood, that I have only aided and abetted : the idea was his own."

" Well, well, I see how it is—we were too happy, I suppose."

" But, Alice," said Jim, " won't you be proud to see your brothe a good soldier ? "

" Proud ! I was always proud of you. But I wish the idea had never come into your head. If it was in war time I would say nothing, but now it is very different. Well, gentlemen, I shall leave you to your wine. Mr. Halbert, I like you very much, but I wish you hadn't turned Jim's head."

She left them, and walked down the garden; through the twilight among the vines, which were dropping their yellow leaves lightly on the turf before the breath of the autumn evening. So Jim was going—going to be killed probably, or only coming back after ten years' absence, " full of strange oaths and bearded like a pard ! " She knew well how her father would jump at his first hint of being a soldier, and would move heaven and earth to get him a commission—yes, he would go—her own darling, funny, handsome Jim, and she would be left all alone.

No, not quite ! There is a step on the path behind her that she knows; there is an arm round her waist which was never there before, and yet she starts not as a low voice in her ear says:

"Alice, my love, my darling, I have come after you to tell you that you are dearer to me than my life, and all the world besides. Can you love me half as well as I love you? Alice, will you be my wife?"

What answer? Her hands pressed to her face, with a flood of happy tears, she only says:

"Oh! I'm so happy, Sam! So glad, so glad!"

Pipe up there, golden-voiced magpie; give us one song more before you go to roost. Laugh out, old jackass, till you fetch an echo back from the foggy hollow. Up on your bare boughs, it is dripping, dreary autumn: but down here in the vineyard are bursting the first green buds of an immortal spring.

There are some scenes which should only be undertaken by the hand of a master, and which, attempted by an apprentice like myself, would only end in disastrous failure, calling down the wrath of all honest men and true critics upon my devoted head—not undeservedly. Three men in a century, or thereabouts, could write with sufficient delicacy and purity, to tell you what two such young lovers as Sam Buckley and Alice Brentwood said to one another in the garden that evening, walking up and down between the yellow vines. I am not one of those three. Where Charles Dickens has failed, I may be excused from being diffident. I am an old bachelor, too—further excuse. But no one can prevent my guessing, and I guess accordingly—that they talked in a very low tone, and when, after an hour, Alice said it was time to come in that Sam was quite astonished to find how little had been said, and what very long pauses there had been.

They came in through the window into the sitting-room, and there was Dr. Mulhaus, Captain Brentwood, and also, of all people, Major Buckley, whom the other two had picked up in their ride and brought home. My information about this period of my history is very full and complete. It has come to my knowledge on the best authority, that when Sam came forward to the light, Halbert kicked Jim's shins under the table, and whispered, "You have lost your money, old fellow!" and that Jim answered, "I wish it was ten pounds instead of five."

But old folks are astonishingly obtuse. Neither of the three seniors saw what had happened; but entered *con amore* into the proposed expedition to Cape Chatham, and when bedtime came, Captain Brentwood, honest gentleman, went off to rest, and having said his prayers and wound up his watch, prepared for a comfortable night's rest, as if nothing was the matter.

He soon found his mistake. He had got his boots off, and was sitting pensively at his bedside, meditating further disrobements, when Jim entered mysteriously, and quietly announced that his whole life in future would be a weary burden if he didn't get a commission in the army, or at least a cadetship in the East India Company's service. Jim the Captain settled by telling, that if he didn't change his mind in a month he'd see about it, and so packed him off to bed. Secondly, as he was taking off his coat, wondering exceedingly at Jim's communication, Sam appeared, and humbly and respectfully informed him that he had that day proposed to his daughter and been accepted—provisionally; hoping that the Captain would not disapprove of him as a son-in-law. He was also rapidly packed off to bed, by the assurance that he (Brentwood) had never felt so happy in his life, and had been sincerely hoping that the young folks would fall in love with one another for a year past.

So, Sam dismissed, the Captain got into bed; but as soon as the light was blown out two native cats began grunting under the washing-stand, and he had to get out, and expel them in his shirt; and finally he lost his temper and began swearing. "Is a man never to get to sleep?" said he. "The devil must be abroad to-night, if ever he was in his life."

No sleep that night for Captain Brentwood. His son, asking for a commission in the army, and his daughter going to be married! Both desirable enough in their way, but not the sort of facts to go to sleep over, particularly when fired off in his ear just as he was lying down. So he lay tossing about, more or less uncomfortable all night, but dozed off just as the daylight began to show more decidedly in the window. He appeared to have slept from thirty to thirty-five seconds, when Jim woke him with:

"It's time to get up, father, if you are going to Cape Chatham to-day."

"Damn Cape Chatham," was his irreverent reply when Jim was gone, which sentiment has been often re-echoed by various coasting skippers in later times. "Why, I haven't been to sleep ten minutes —and a frosty morning, too. I wish it would rain. I am not vindictive, but I do indeed. Can't the young fools go alone, I wonder? No; hang it, I'll make myself agreeable to-day, at all events!"

CHAPTER XXXIV

HOW THEY ALL WENT HUNTING FOR SEA-ANEMONES AT CAPE CHATHAM —AND HOW THE DOCTOR GOT A TERRIBLE FRIGHT—AND HOW CAPTAIN BLOCKSTROP SHOWED THAT THERE WAS GOOD REASON FOR IT

AND presently, the Captain, half dressed, working away at his hair with two very stiff brushes, betook himself to Major Buckley's room, whom he found shaving. " I'll wait till you're done," said he; " I don't want you to cut yourself."

And then he resumed: " Buckley, your son wants to marry my daughter."

" Shows his good taste," said the Major. " What do you think of it ? "

" I am very much delighted," said the Captain.

" And what does she say to it ? "

" She is very much delighted."

" And I am very much delighted, and I suppose Sam is too. So there we are, you see: all agreed."

And that was the way the marriage negotiations proceeded; indeed, it was nearly all that was ever said on the subject. But one day the Major brought two papers over to the Captain (who signed them), which were supposed to refer to settlements, and after that all the arrangements were left to Alice and Mrs. Buckley.

They started for Cape Chatham about nine o'clock in the day; Halbert and Jim first, then Sam and Alice, and lastly the three elders. This arrangement did not last long, however; for very soon Sam and Alice called aloud to Halbert and Jim to come and ride with them, for that they were boring one another to death. This they did, and now the discreet and sober conversation of the oldsters was much disturbed by the loud laughter of the younger folks, in which, however, they could not help joining. It was a glorious crystal clear day in autumn; all nature, aroused from her summer's rest, had put off her suit of hodden grey, and was flaunting in gaudiest green. The atmosphere was so amazingly pure, that miles away across the plains the travellers could distinguish the herds of turkeys (bustards) stalking to and fro, while before them, that noble maritime mountain Cape Chatham towered up, sharply defined above the gleaming haze which marked the distant sea.

For a time their way lay straight across the broad well-grassed plains, marked with ripples as though the retiring sea had but just left it. Then a green swamp; through the tall reeds the native companion, king of cranes, waded majestic; the brilliant porphyry water hen, with scarlet bill and legs, flashed like a sapphire among the emerald-green water-sedge. A shallow lake, dotted with wild ducks, here and there a group of wild swan, black with red bills, floating calmly on its bosom.—A long stretch of grass as smooth as a bowling-green.—A sudden rocky rise, clothed with native cypress (Exocarpus—O my botanical readers!), honeysuckle (Banksia), she-oak (Casuarina), and here and there a stunted gum. Cape Chatham began to show grander and nearer, topping all; and soon they saw the broad belt of brown sandy heath that lay along the shore.

"Here," said the Doctor, riding up, "we leave the last limit of the lava streams for Mirngish and the Organ-hill. Immediately you shall see how we pass from the richly-grassed volcanic plains, into the barren sandstone heaths; from a productive pasture-land into a useless flower-garden. Nature here is economical, as she always is: she makes her choicest ornamental efforts on spots otherwise useless. You will see a greater variety of vegetation on one acre of your sandy heath than on two square miles of the thickly-grassed country we have been passing over."

It was as he said. They came soon on to the heath; a dark dreary expanse, dull to look upon after so long a journey upon the bright green grass. It stretched away right and left interminably, only broken here and there with islands of dull-coloured trees; as melancholy a piece of country as one could conceive: yet far more thickly peopled with animal, as well as vegetable life, than the rich pastoral downs farther inland. Now they began to see the little red brush kangaroo, and the grey forester, skipping away in all directions; and had it been summer they would have been startled more than once by the brown snake, and the copper snake, deadliest of their tribe. The painted quail, and the brush quail (the largest of Australian game birds, I believe), whirred away from beneath their horses' feet; and the ground parrot, green, with mottlings of gold and black, rose like a partridge from the heather, and flew low. Here, too, the Doctor flushed a "White's thrush," close to an outlying belt of forest, and got into a great state of excitement about it. "The only known bird," he said, "which is found in Europe, America, and Australia alike." Then he pointed out the emu wren, a little tiny brown fellow, with long hairy tail-feathers, flitting from bush to bush; and then, leaving ornithology, he called their attention to the wonderful variety of low vegetation that they were riding through; Hakeas, Acacias, Grevilleas, and what not.

In spring this brown heath would have been a brilliant mass of flowers; but now, nothing was to be seen save a few tall crimson spikes of Epacris, and here and there a bunch of lemon-coloured Correas. Altogether, he kept them so well amused, that they were astonished to come so quickly upon the station, placed in a snug cove of the forest, where it bordered on the heath beside a sluggish creek. Then, seeing the mountain towering up close to them, and hearing, as they stayed at the door, a low continuous thunder behind a high roll in the heath which lay before them, they knew that the old ocean was close at hand, and that their journey was done.

The people at the station were very glad to see them, of course, Barker, the paterfamilias, was an old friend of both the Major and the Captain, and they found so much to talk about, that after a heavy midday meal, excellent in kind, though that kind was coarse, and certain libations of pale ale and cold claret-and-water, the older of the party, with the exception of Dr. Mulhaus, refused to go any farther; so the young people started forth to the Cape, under the guidance of George Barker, the fourth or fifth son, who happened to be at home.

"Doctor," said Alice, as they were starting, " do you remark what beautiful smooth grass covers the Cape itself, while here we have nothing but this scrubby heath? The mountain is, I suppose, some different formation?"

"Granite, my dear young lady," said the Doctor. "A cap of granite rising through and partly overlying this sandstone."

"You can always tell one exactly what one wants to know," said Alice; and, as they walked forwards, somehow got talking to Halbert, which I believe most firmly had been arranged beforehand with Sam. For he, falling back, ranged alongside of the Doctor, and, managing to draw him behind the others, turned to him and said suddenly:

"My dear old friend! my good old tutor!"

The Doctor stopped short, pulled out a pair of spectacles, wiped them, put them on, and looked at Sam through them for nearly a minute, and then said:

"My dear boy, you don't mean to say——"

"I do, Doctor.—Last night.—And, oh! if you could only tell how happy I am at this moment! If you could but guess at it!——"

"Pooh, pooh!" said the Doctor; "I am not so old as that, my dear boy. Why, I am a marrying man myself. Sam, I am so very, very glad! You have won her, and now wear her, like a pearl beyond all price. I think that she is worthy of you: more than that she could not be."

They shook hands, and soon Sam was at her side again, toiling up the steep ascent. They soon distanced the others, and went forwards by themselves.

There was such a rise in the ground seawards, that the broad ocean was invisible till they were half-way up the grassy down. Then right and left they began to see the nether firmament, stretching away infinitely. But the happy lovers paused not till they stood upon the loftiest breezy knoll, and seemed alone together between the blue cloudless heaven and another azure-sphere which lay beneath their feet.

A cloudless sky and a sailless sea. Far beneath them they heard but saw not the eternal surges gnawing at the mountain. A few white albatrosses skimmed and sailed below, and before, seaward, the sheets of turf, falling away, stretched into a shoreless headland, fringed with black rock and snow-white surf.

She stood there flushed and excited with the exercise, her bright hair dishevelled, waving in the free sea-breeze, the most beautiful object in that glorious landscape, her noble mate beside her. Awe, wonder, and admiration kept both of them silent for a few moments, and then she spoke.

" Do you know any of the choruses in the *Messiah*? " asked she.

" No, I do not," said Sam.

" I am rather sorry for it," she said, " because this is so very like some of them."

" I can quite imagine that," said Sam. " I can quite imagine music which expresses what we see now. Something infinitely *broad* I should say. Is that nonsense now? "

" Not to me," said Alice.

" I imagined," said Sam, " that the sea would be much rougher than this. In spite of the ceaseless thunder below there, it is very calm."

" Calm, eh? " said the Doctor's voice behind them. " God help the ship that should touch that reef this day, though a nautilus might float in safety! See how the ground-swell is tearing away at those rocks; you can just distinguish the long heave of the water, before it breaks. There is the most dangerous ground-swell in the world off this coast. Should this country ever have a large coast-trade, they will find it out, in calm weather with no anchorage."

A great coasting trade has arisen; and the Doctor's remark has proved terribly true. Let the *Monumental City*, and the *Schomberg*, the *Duncan Dunbar* and the *Catherine Adamson,* bear witness to it. Let the drowning cries of hundreds of good sailors, who have been missed and never more heard of, bear witness that this is the most pitiless and unprotected, and, even in calm weather, the most dangerous coast in the world.

But Jim came panting up, and throwing himself on the short turf, said:

" So this is the great Southern Ocean; eh! How far can one see, now, Halbert? "

" About thirty miles."

" And how far to India; eh? "

" About seven thousand."

" A long way," said Jim. " However, not so far as to England."

" Fancy," said Halbert, " one of those old Dutch voyagers driving on this unknown coast on a dark night. What a sudden end to their voyage! Yet that must have happened to many ships which have never come home. Perhaps when they come to explore this coast a little more they may find some old ship's ribs jammed on a reef; the ribs of some ship whose name and memory has perished."

" The very thing you mention is the case," said the Doctor. " Down the coast here, under a hopeless, black basaltic cliff, is to be seen the wreck of a very, very old ship, now covered with coral and seaweed. I waited down there for a spring tide, to examine her, but could determine nothing, save that she was very old; whether Dutch or Spanish I know not. You English should never sneer at those two nations; they were before you everywhere."

" If you will just come here," said Alice, " where those black rocks are hid by the bend of the hill, you get only three colours in your landscape; blue sky, grey grass, and purple sea. But look, there is a man standing on the promontory. He makes quite an eyesore there. I wish he would go away."

" I suppose he has as good a right there as any of us," answered the Doctor. " But he certainly does not harmonise very well with the rest of the colouring. What a strange place he has chosen to stand in, looking out over the sea, as though he were a ship-wrecked mariner—the last of the crew."

" A shipwrecked mariner would hardly wear breeches and boots, my dear Doctor," said Jim. " That man is a stockman."

" Not one of ours, however," said George Barker; " even at this distance I can see that. See, he's gone! Strange! I know of no way down the cliff thereabouts. Would you like to come down to the shore? "

So they began their descent to the shore by a winding path of turf, among tumbled heaps of granite; down towards the rock-walled cove; a horseshoe of smooth white sand lying between two long black reefs, among whose isolated pinnacles the ground-swell leapt and spouted ceaselessly.

Halbert remarked, "This granite coast is hardly so remarkable as our Cornish one. There are none of those queer pinnacles and tors one sees there, just ready to topple down into the sea. This granite is not half so fantastic."

"Earthquakes, of which you have none in Cornwall," said the Doctor, "will just account for the difference. I have felt one near here quite as strong as your famous lieutenant, who capsized the Logan stone."

But now, getting on the level sands, they fell to gathering shells and seaweeds like children. Jim, trying to see how near he could get to a wave without being caught, got washed up like jetsam. Alice took Sam's pocket-handkerchief, and filled it indiscriminately with flotsam, and everything she could lay her hand on, principally, however, lagend. Trochuses, as big as one's fist, and "Venus-ears," scarlet outside. And after an hour, wetfooted and happy, dragging a yard or so of sea-tang behind her, she looked round for the Doctor, and saw him far out on the reef, lying flat on his stomach, and closely examining a large still pool of salt water, contained in the crevices of the rocks.

He held up his hand and beckoned. Sam and Alice advanced towards him over the slippery beds of seaweed, Sam bravely burying his feet in the wet clefts, and holding out his hand to help her along. Once there was a break in the reef, too broad to be jumped, and then for the first time he had her fairly in his arms and swung her across, which was undoubtedly very delightful, but unfortunately soon over. At length, however, they reached the Doctor, who was seated like a cormorant on a wet rock, lighting a pipe.

"What you have collected?" he asked. "Show me."

Alice proudly displayed the inestimable treasures contained in Sam's handkerchief.

"Rubbish! Rubbish!" said the Doctor. "Do you believe in mermaidens?"

"Of course I do, if you wish it," said Alice. "Have you seen one?"

"No, but here is one of their flower-gardens. Bend down and look into this pool."

She bent and looked. The first thing that she saw was her own exquisite face, and Sam's brown phiz peering over her shoulder. A golden tress of hair, loosened by the sea-breeze, fell down into the water, and had to be looped up again. Then gazing down once more, she saw beneath the crystal water a bed of flowers; dahlias, ranunculuses, carnations, chrysanthemums, of every colour in the rainbow save blue. She gave a cry of pleasure: " What are they, Doctor? What do you call them? "

" Sea-anemones, in English, I believe," said the Doctor, " actinias, serpulas, and sabellas. You may see something like that on the European coasts, on a small scale, but there is nothing I ever have seen like that great crimson fellow with cream-coloured tentacles. I do not know his name. I suspect he has never been described. The common European anemone they call ' crassicornis ' is something like him, but not half as fine."

" Is there any means of gathering and keeping them, Doctor? " asked Sam. " We have no flowers in the garden like them."

" No possible means," said the Doctor. " They are but lumps of jelly. Let us come away and get round the headland before the tide comes in."

They wandered on from cove to cove, under the dark cliffs, till rounding a little headland the Doctor called out:

" Here is something in your Cornish style, Halbert."

A thin wall of granite, like a vast buttress, ran into the sea, pierced by a great arch, some sixty feet high. Aloft all sharp grey stone: below, wherever the salt water had reached, a mass of dark, clinging weed: while beyond, as though set in a dark frame, was a soft glimpse of a blue sky and snow-white sea-birds.

" There is nothing so grand as that in Cornwall, Doctor," said Halbert.

" Can we pass under it, Mr. Barker? " said Alice. " I should like to go through; we have been into none of the caves yet."

" Oh, yes! " said George Barker. " You may go through for the next two hours. The tide has not turned yet."

" I'll volunteer first," said the Doctor, " and if there's anything worth seeing beyond, I'll come for you."

It was, as I said, a thin wall of granite, which ran out from the rest of the hill, seaward, and was pierced by a tall arch; the blocks which had formerly filled the void now lay, weed-grown, half buried in sand, forming a slippery threshold. Over these the Doctor climbed and looked beyond.

A little sandy cove, reef-bound, like those they had seen before, lay under the dark cliffs; and on a water-washed rock, not a hundred yards from him, stood the man they had seen on the downs above, looking steadily seaward.

The Doctor slipped over the rocks like an otter, and approached the man across the smooth sand, unheard in the thunder of the surf. When he was close upon him, the stranger turned, and the Doctor uttered a low cry of wonder and alarm.

It was George Hawker! The Doctor knew him in a moment: but whether the recognition was mutual, he never found out, for Hawker, stepping rapidly from stone to stone, disappeared round the headland, and the thunderstruck Doctor retraced his steps to the arch.

There were all the young people gathered, wondering and delighted. But Alice came to meet him, and said:

" Who was that with you just now?"

" A mermaid! " replied he.

" That, indeed! " said Alice. " And what did she say?"

" She said, ' Go home to your supper; you have seen quite enough; go home in good time.' "

" Doctor, there is something wrong! " said Alice. " I see it in your face. Can you trust me, and tell me what it is?"

" I can trust you so far as to tell you that you are right. I don't like the look of things at all. I fear there are evil times coming for some of our friends! Further than this I can say nothing. Say your prayers, and trust God! Don't tell Sam anything about this: to-morrow I shall speak to him. We won't spoil a pleasant holiday on mere suspicion."

They rejoined the others, and the Doctor said, " Come away home now; we have seen enough. Some future time we will come here again: you might see this fifty times, and never get tired of it."

After a good scramble they stood once more on the down above, and turned to take a last look at the broad blue sea before they descended inland; at the first glance seaward, Halbert exclaimed:

" See there, Doctor; see there! A boat!"

" It's only a whale, I think," said George Barker.

There was a black speck far out at sea, but no whale; it was too steady for that. All day the air had been calm; if anything, the breeze was from the north, but now a strong wind was coming up from the south-east, freshening every moment, and bringing with it a pent bank of dark clouds; and, as they watched, the mysterious black speck was topped with white, and soon they saw that it was indeed a boat driving before the wind under a sprit-sail, which had just been set.

"That is very strange!" said George Barker. "Can it be a shipwrecked party?"

"More likely a mob of escaped convicts from Van Diemen's Land," said Jim. "If so, look out for squalls, you George, and keep your guns loaded."

"I don't think it can be that, Jim," said Sam. "What could bring them so far north? They would have landed, more likely, somewhere in the Straits, about the big lakes."

"There may have been driven off shore by these westerly winds which have been blowing the last few days," replied Jim, "and kept their boat's head northward, to get nearer the settlements. They will be terribly hungry when they do land, for certain. What's your opinion, Doctor?"

"I think that wise men should be always prepared. We should communicate with Captain Desborough, and set the police on the alert."

"I wonder," said Sam, "if that mysterious man we saw to-day, watching on the cliff, could have had any connection with this equally mysterious boat. Not likely, though. However, if they are going to land to-night, they had better look sharp, for it is coming on to blow."

The great bank of cloud which they had been watching, away to the south-east, was growing and spreading rapidly, sending out little black avant-couriers of scud, which were hurrying fanlike across the heavens, telling the news of the coming storm. Landward, in the west, the sun was going down in purple and scarlet splendour, but seaward, all looked dark and ominous.

The young folks stood together in the veranda before they went in to dinner, listening to the wind which was beginning to scream angrily round the corners of the house. The rain had not yet gathered strength to fall steadily, but was whisked hither and thither by the blast, in a few uncertain drops. They saw that a great gale was coming up, and knew that, in a few hours, earth and sky would be mingled in furious war.

"How comfortable it is to think that all the animals are under shelter to-night!" said Sam. "Jim, my boy, I am glad you and I are not camped out with cattle this evening. We have been out on nights as bad as this though; eh? O Lord! fancy sitting the saddle all to-night, under the breaking boughs, wet through!"

"No more of that for me, old Sam. No more jolly gallops after cattle or horses for me. But I was always a good hand at anything of that sort, and I mean to be a good soldier now. You'll see."

At dark, while they were sitting at dinner, the storm was raging round the house in full fury; but there in the well-lighted room, before a good fire, they cared little for it. When dinner was over, the Doctor called the Captain and the Major aside, and told them in what manner he had seen and recognised George Hawker on the beach that day; and raised their fears still more by telling them of that mysterious boat which the Doctor thought Hawker had been watching for. None of them could understand it, but all agreed that these things boded no good; and so, having called their host into their confidence, with regard to the boat, they quietly loaded all the firearms in the place, and put them together in the hall. This done, they returned to the sitting-room, and, having taken their grog, retired to bed.

It must be remembered that hitherto Major Buckley knew nothing of George Hawker's previous appearance, but the Doctor now let him into the secret. The Major's astonishment and wrath may be conceived, at finding that his old protégée Mary, instead of being a comfortable widow, was the persecuted wife of one of the greatest bushrangers known. At first he was stunned and confused, but, ere he slept, his clear straightforward mind had come to a determination that the first evil was the worst, and that, God give him grace, he would hand the scoundrel over to justice on the first opportunity, sure that he was serving Mary best by doing so.

That night Jim and Sam lay together in a little room to the windward of the house. They were soon fast asleep, but, in the middle of the night, Jim was awoke by a shake on the shoulder, and, rousing himself, saw that Sam was sitting up in the bed.

" My God, Jim! " said he—" I have had such an awful dream! I dreamed that those fellows in the boat were carrying off Alice, and I stood by and saw it, and could not move hand or foot. I am terribly frightened. That was something more than a dream, Jim."

" You ate too much of that pie at dinner," said Jim, " and you've had the nightmare—that's what is the matter with you. Lord bless you, I often have the nightmare when I have eaten too much at supper, and lie on my back. Why, I dreamed the other night that the devil had got me under the wool-press, screwing me down as hard as he could, and singing the Hundredth Psalm all the time. That was a much worse dream than yours."

Sam was obliged to confess that it was. " But still," said he, " I think mine was something more than a dream. I'm frightened still."

" Oh, nonsense; lie down again. You are pulling all the clothes off me."

They lay down, and Jim was soon asleep, but not so Sam. His dream had taken such hold of his imagination, that he lay awake, listening to the storm howling around the house. Now and then he could hear the unearthly scream of some curlew piercing the din, and, above all, he could hear the continuous earth-shaking thunder of the surf upon the beach. Soon after daylight, getting Halbert to accompany him, he went out to have a look at the shore, and, forcing their way against the driving, cutting rain, they looked over the low cliff at the furious waste of waters beneath them, and saw mountain after mountain of water hurl itself, in a cloud of spray, upon the shore.

" What terrible waves, now!" said Sam.

" Yes," replied Halbert; " there's no land to windward for six thousand miles or more. I never saw heavier seas than those. I enjoy this, Sam. It reminds me of a good roaring winter's day in old Cornwall."

" I like it, too," said Sam. " It freshens you up. How calm the water is to the leeward of the Cape!"

" Yes; a capital harbour of refuge that. Let us go home to breakfast."

He turned to go, but was recalled by a wild shout from Sam.

" A ship! A ship!"

He ran back and looked over into the seething hell of waters below. Was it only a thicker spot in the driving mist, or was it really a ship? If so, God help her.

Small time to deliberate. Ere he could think twice about it, a full-rigged ship, about five hundred tons, with a close-reefed topsail, and a rag of a foresail upon her, came rushing, rolling, diving, and plunging on, apparently heading for the deadly white line of breakers which stretched into the sea at the end of the promontory.

" A Queen's ship, Sam! A Queen's ship! The *Tartar,* for a thousand pounds! Oh, what a pity; what a terrible pity!"

" Only a merchant ship, surely," said Sam.

" Did you ever see a merchant ship with six such guns as those on her upper deck, and a hundred blue-jackets at quarters? That is the *Tartar,* Sam, and in three minutes there will be no *Tartar.*"

They had run in their excitement out to the very end of the Cape, and now the ship was almost under their feet, an awful sight to see. She was rolling fearfully, going dead before the wind. Now and then she would slop tons of water on her deck, and her mainyard would almost touch the water. But still the dark clusters of men along her bulwarks held steadfast, and the ship's head never veered half a point. Now it became apparent that she would clear the reef by a hundred yards or more, and Halbert, waving his hat, cried out:

"Well done, Blockstrop! Bravely done, indeed! He is running under the lee of the Cape for shelter. Her Majesty has one more ship-of-war than I thought she would have had, five minutes ago."

As he spoke, she had passed the reef. The yards, as if by magic, swung round, and, for a moment, she was broadside on to the sea. One wave broke over her, and nought but her masts appeared above a sheet of white foam; but, ere the water had well done pouring from her open deck ports, she was in smooth water, her anchor was down, and the topsail yard was black with men.

"Let us come down, Sam," said Halbert: "very likely they will send a boat ashore."

As they were scrambling down the leeward side of the cliff, they saw a boat put off from the ship, and gained the beach in time to meet a midshipman coming towards them. He, seeing two well-dressed gentlemen before him, bowed, and said:

"Good morning; very rough weather."

"Very, indeed," said Halbert. "Is that the *Tartar*, pray?"

"That is the *Tartar*; yes. We were caught in the gale last night, and we lay-to. This morning, as soon as we recognised the Cape, we determined to run for this cove, where we have been before. We had an anxious night last night, I assure you. We have been terribly lucky. If the wind had veered a few more points to the east, we should have been done for. We never could have beaten off in such a sea as this."

"Are you going to Sydney?"

"No; we are in chase of a boat full of escaped convicts from Launceston. Cunning dogs; they would not land in the Straits. We missed them and got across to Port Phillip, and put Captain D—— and his black police on the alert; and the convicts have got a scent of it, and coasted up north. We have examined the coast all along, but I am afraid they have given us the slip; there is such a system of intelligence among them. However, if they had not landed before last night, they have saved us all trouble; and if they are ashore we wash our hands of them, and leave them to the police."

Halbert and Sam looked at one another. Then the former said:

"Last night, about an hour before it came on to blow, we saw a boat making for this very headland, which puzzled us exceedingly; and, what was stranger still, we saw a man on the Cape, who seemed to be on the lookout."

"That is quite possible," replied the midshipman; "these fellows have a queer system of communication. The boat you saw must certainly have been them; and if they landed at all they must have landed here."

I must change the scene here, if you please, my dear reader, and get you to come with me on board his (I beg pardon, her) Majesty's ship *Tartar,* for a few minutes, for on the quarter-deck of that noble sloop there are at this moment two men worth rescuing from oblivion.

The first is a stoutish, upright, middle-aged man, in a naval uniform, with a brick-dust complexion, and very light scanty whiskers; the jolliest, cheeriest-looking fellow you are likely to meet in a year's journey. Such a bright merry blue eye as he has, too! This is Captain Blockstrop, now, I am happy to say, C.B.; a right valiant officer, as the despatches of Lyons and Peel will testify.

The other is a very different sort of man—a long, wiry, brown-faced man, with a big forehead, and a comical expression about his eyes. This is no less a person than the Colonial Secretary of one of our three great colonies: of which I decline to mention. Those who know the Honourable Abiram Pollifex do not need to be told; and those who do not must find out for themselves. I may mention that he has been known to retain office seven years in succession, and yet he seldom threatens to resign his office and throw himself upon the country fewer than three times, and sometimes four, per annum. Latterly I am sorry to say, a miserable faction, taking advantage of one of his numerous resignations, have assumed the reins of government, and, in spite of three votes of want of confidence, persist in retaining the seals of office. Let me add to this, that he is considered the best hand at quiet "chaff" in the House, and is allowed, both by his supporters and opponents, to be an honourable man, and a right good fellow.

Such were the two men who now stood side by side on the quarter-deck, looking eagerly at Sam and Halbert through a pair of telescopes.

"Pollifex," said the Captain, "what do you make of these?"

"Gentlemen," said the Secretary curtly.

"So I make out," said the Captain: "and apparently in good condition, too. A very well-fed man that biggest, I should say."

"Ye-es; well, ye-es," said the Secretary; "he does look well-fed enough. He must be a stranger to these parts; probably from the Maneroo plains, or thereabout."

"What makes you think so?"

"Dear me," said the Secretary; "have you been stationed nearly three years on this coast, and ask how a man could possibly be in good condition living in those scrubby heaths?"

"Bad-looking country; eh?" said the Captain.

"Small cattle-stations, sir," said the Secretary, "I can see at a glance. Salt beef, very tough, and very little of it. I shall run a bill through the House for the abolition of small cattle-stations next session."

"Better get your estimates through first, old fellow. The bagpipes will play quite loud enough over them to last for some time."

"I know it, but tremble not," replied the undaunted Secretary; "I have got used to it. I fancy I hear Callaghan beginning now: 'The unbridled prodigality, sir, and the reckless profligacy, sir, of those individuals who have so long, under the name of government——'"

"That'll do now," said the Captain; "you are worse than the reality. I shall go ashore, and take my chance of getting breakfast. Will you come?"

"Not if I know it, sir, with pork chops for breakfast in the cabin. Blockstrop, have you duly reflected what you are about to do? You are about to land alone, unarmed, unprovisioned, among the offscourings of white society, scarcely superior in their habits of life to the nomadic savages they have unjustly displaced. Pause and reflect, my dear fellow. What guarantee have you that they will not propose to feed you on damper, or some other nameless abomination of the same sort?"

"It was only the other day in the House," said the Captain, "that you said the small squatters and freehold farmers represented the greater part of the intelligence and education of the colony, and now——"

"Sir! sir!" said the Secretary, "you don't know what you are talking about. Sir, we are not in the House now. Are you determined, then?"

The Captain was quite determined, and they went down to the waist. They were raising a bag of potatoes from somewhere, and the Colonial Secretary, seizing two handfuls of them, presented them to the Captain.

"If you will go," he said, "take these with you, and teach the poor benighted white savages to plant them. So if you fall a victim to indigestion, we will vote a monument to you on the summit of the Cape, and write: 'He did not live in vain. He introduced the potato among the small cattle-stations around Cape Chatham.'"

He held out his potatoes towards the retiring Captain with the air of Burke producing the dagger. His humour, I perceive, reads poor enough when written down, but when assisted by his comical impassible face, and solemn drawling delivery, I never heard anything much better.

Good old Pollifex! my heart warms towards him now. When I think what the men were whose clamour put him out of office in 184—, I have the conviction forced upon me, that the best among them was not worth his little finger. He left the colony in a most prosperous state, and, retiring honourably to one of his stations, set to work, as he said, to begin life again on a new principle. He is wealthy, honoured, and happy, as he deserves to be.

I cannot help, although somewhat in the wrong place, telling the reader under what circumstances I saw him last. Only two years ago, fifteen after he had left office, I happened to be standing with him, at the door of a certain club, in a certain capital, just after lunch time, when we saw the then Colonial Secretary, the man who had succeeded Pollifex, come scurrying round the corner of the street, fresh from his office. His face was flushed and perspiring, his hat was on the wrong-side before, with his veil hanging down his back. In the one hand he held papers, in the other he supported over his fevered brow his white cotton umbrella; altogether he looked harassed beyond the bounds of human endurance, but when he caught sight of the open club-doors, he freshened a bit, and mended his pace. His troubles were not over, for ere he reached his haven, two Irishmen, with two different requests, rose as if from the earth, and confronted him. We saw him make two promises, contradictory to each other, and impossible of fulfilment, and as he came up the steps, I looked into the face of Ex-Secretary Pollifex, and saw there an expression which is beyond description. Say that of the ghost of a man who has been hanged, attending an execution. Or say the expression of a Catholic, converted by torture, watching the action of the thumb-screws upon another heretic. The air, in short, of a man who had been through it all before. And as the then Secretary came madly rushing up the steps, Pollifex confronted him, and said:

"Don't you wish you were me, T——?"

"Sir!" said the Secretary, "dipping" his umbrella and dropping his papers, for the purpose of rhetorically pointing with his left hand at nothing; "Sir! flesh and blood can't stand it. I resign to-morrow." And so he went in to his lunch, and is in office at this present moment.

I must apologise most heartily for this long digression. The Captain's gig, impelled by the "might of England's pride," was cleverly beached alongside of the other boat, and the Captain stepped out and confronted the midshipman.

"Got any news, Mr. Vang?"

"Yes, sir," said the midshipman. "These gentlemen saw the boat yesterday afternoon."

Sam and Halbert, who were standing behind him, came forward. The Captain bowed, and looked with admiration at the two highbred-looking men, that this unpromising desert had produced. They told him what they had told the midshipman, and the Captain said, "It will be a very serious thing for this countryside, if these dogs have succeeded in landing. Let us hope that the sea has done good service in swallowing fourteen of the vilest wretches that ever disgraced humanity. Pray, are either of you gentlemen magistrates?"

"My father, Major Buckley, is a magistrate," said Sam. "This gentleman is Lieutenant Halbert, of the Bengal Artillery."

The Captain bowed to Halbert, and turning to Sam, said, "So you are the son of my old friend Major Buckley! I was midshipman in the *Phlegethon* when she took him and part of his regiment to Portugal, in 1811. I met him at dinner in Sydney, the other day. Is he in the neighbourhood?"

"He is waiting breakfast for us not a quarter of a mile off," said Sam. "Will you join us?"

"I shall be delighted; but duty first. If these fellows have succeeded in landing, you will have to arm and prepare for the worst. Now, unless they were caught by the gale and drowned, which I believe to be the case, they must have come ashore in this very bay, about five o'clock last night. There is no other place where they could have beached their boat for many miles. Consequently, the thing lies in a nutshell: if we find the boat, prepare yourselves—if not, make yourselves easy. Let us use our wits a little. They would round the headland as soon as possible, and probably run ashore in that farthest cove to our right, just inside the reef. I have examined the bay through a telescope, and could make out nothing of her. Let us come and examine carefully. Downhaul!" (to his coxswain). "Come with me."

They passed three or four indentations in the bay, examining as they went, finding nothing, but when they scrambled over the rocks which bounded the cove the Captain had indicated, he waved his hat, and laughing said:

"Ha, ha! just as I thought. There she is."

"Where, Captain Blockstrop?" said Halbert. "I don't see her."

"Nor I either," said the Captain. "But I see the heap of sea-weed that the cunning dogs have raked over her. Downhaul; heave away at this weed, and show these gentlemen what is below it."

The coxswain began throwing away a pile of sea-tang heaped against a rock. Bit by bit was disclosed the clear run of a beautiful white whale-boat, which when turned over discovered her oars laid neatly side by side, with a small spritsail. The Captain stood by with the air of a man who had made a hit, while Sam and Halbert stared at one another with looks of blank discomfiture and alarm.

CHAPTER XXXV

A COUNCIL OF WAR

"THIS is a very serious matter for us, Captain Blockstrop," said Sam, as they were walking back to the boats. "An exceedingly serious matter."

"I have only one advice to give you, Mr. Buckley," said the Captain; "which is unnecessary, as it is just what your father will do. Fight, sir!—hunt 'em down. Shoot 'em! they will give you no quarter: be sure you don't give them any."

A wild discordant bellow was here heard from the ship, on which the Captain slapped his leg and said:

"Dash my buttons, if he hasn't got hold of my speaking-trumpet."

The midshipman came up with a solemn face, and, touching his cap, "reported":

"Colonial Secretary hailing, sir."

"Bless my soul, Mr. Vang, I can hear that," said the Captain. "I don't suppose any of my officers would dare to make such an inarticulate, no sailor-like bellow as that on her Majesty's quarter-deck. Can you make out what he says? That would be more to the purpose."

Again the unearthly bellow came floating over the water, happily deadened by the wind, which was roaring a thousand feet overhead.

"*Can* you make out anything, Mr. Vang?" said the Captain.

"I make out 'pork chops!' sir," said the midshipman.

"Take one of the boats on board, Mr. Vang. My compliments. and will be much obliged if he will come ashore immediately! on important business, say. Tell him the convicts have landed, will you? Also, tell the lieutenant of the watch that I want either Mr. Tacks, or Mr. Sheets: either will do."

The boat was soon seen coming back with the Colonial Secretary in a statesmanlike attitude in the stern sheets, and beside him that important officer Mr. Tacks, a wee little dot of a naval cadet, apparently about ten years old.

"What were you bellowing about pork chops, Pollifex?" asked the Captain, the moment the boat touched the shore.

"A failure, sir," said the Colonial Secretary; "burnt, sir; disgracefully burnt up to a cinder, sir. I have been consulting the honourable member for the Cross-jack-yard (I allude to Mr. Tacks, N.C., my honourable friend, if he will allow me to call him so) as to the propriety of calling a court-martial on the cook's mate. He informs me that such a course is not usual in naval jurisprudence. I am, however, of opinion that in one of the civil courts of the colony an action for damages would lie. Surely I have the pleasure of seeing Mr. Buckley, of Baroona?"

Sam and he had met before, and the Secretary, finding himself on shore, and where he was known, dropped his King Cambyses's vein, and appeared in his real character of a shrewd, experienced man. They walked up together, and when they arrived at the summit of the ridge, and saw the magnificent plains stretching away inland, beyond the narrow belt of heath along the shore, the Secretary whispered to the Captain:

"I have been deceived. We shall get some breakfast, after all. As fine a country as I ever saw in my life!"

The party who were just sitting down to breakfast at the station were sufficiently astonished to see Captain Blockstrop come rolling up the garden walk, with that small ship-of-war Tacks sailing in his wake, convoying the three civilians; but on going in and explaining matters, and room having been made for them at the table, Sam was also astonished on looking round to see that a new arrival had taken place since that morning.

It was that of a handsome singular-looking man. His hair was light, his whiskers a little darker, and his blonde moustache curled up towards his eyes like corkscrews or ram's horns (congratulate me on my simile). A very merry laughing eye he had, too, blue of course, with that coloured hair; altogether a very pleasant-looking man, and yet whose face gave one the idea that it was not at all times pleasant, but on occasions might look terribly tigerish and fierce. A man who won you at once, and yet one with whom one would hardly like to quarrel. Add to this, also, that when he opened his mouth to speak, he disclosed a splendid set of white teeth, and the moment he'd uttered a word, a stranger would remark to himself, " That is an Irishman."

Sam, who had ensconced himself beside Alice, looked up the long table towards him with astonishment. " Why, good gracious, Captain Desborough," he said, " can that be you? "

" I have been waiting," said Desborough, " with the greatest patience, to see how long you would have the audacity to ignore my presence. How do you do, my small child? Sam, my dear, if ever I get cashiered for being too handsome to remain in the Service, I'll carry you about and exhibit you, as the biggest and ugliest boy in the Australian colonies."

Captain Desborough has been mentioned before in these pages. He was an officer in the army, at the present time holding the situation of Inspector of Police in this district. He was a very famous hunter-down of bushrangers, and was heartily popular with everyone he was thrown against, except the aforesaid bushrangers. Sam and he were very old friends, and were very fond of one another.

Desborough was sitting now at the upper end of the table, with the Colonial Secretary, Major Buckley, Captain Blockstrop, Captain Brentwood, and Dr. Mulhaus. They looked very serious indeed.

" It was a very lucky thing, Desborough," said the Major, " that you happened to meet Captain Blockstrop. He has now, you perceive, handed over the care of these rascals to you. It is rather strange that they should have landed here."

" I believe that they were expected," said the Doctor. " I believe that there is a desperate scheme of villainy afloat, and that some of us are the objects of it."

" If you mean," said Desborough, " that that man you saw on the Cape last night was watching for the boat, I don't believe it possible. It was, possibly, some stockman or shepherd, having a look at the weather."

The Doctor had it on the tip of his tongue to speak, and astound them by disclosing that the lonely watcher was none other than the ruffian Touan, alias George Hawker; but the Major pressed his foot beneath the table, and he was silent.

"Well," said Desborough, "and that's about all that's to be said at present, except that the settlers must arm and watch, and if necessary fight."

"If they will only do that," said the Colonial Secretary; "if they will only act boldly in protecting their property and lives, the evil is reduced by one-half; but when Brallagan was out, nothing that I or the Governor could do would induce the majority of them to behave like men."

"Look here, now," said Barker, the host, "I was over the water when Brallagan was out, and when Howe was out too. And what could a lonely squatter do against half a dozen of 'em? Answer me that!"

"I don't mean that," said the Colonial Secretary; "what I refer to is the cowardly way in which the settlers allowed themselves to be prevented by threats from giving information. I speak the more boldly, Mr. Barker, because you were not one of those who did so."

Barker was appeased. "There's five long guns in my hall, and there's five long lads can use 'em," he said. "By the by, Captain Desborough, let me congratulate you on the short work you made with that gang to the north, the other day. I am sorry to hear that the principal rascal of the lot, Captain Touan, gave you the slip."

The Doctor had been pondering, and had made up his mind to a certain course; he bent over the table, and said:

"I think, on the whole, that it is better to let you all know the worst. That man whom we saw on the cliff last night I met afterwards, alone, down on the shore, and that man is no other than the one you speak of, Captain Touan."

Anyone watching Desborough's face as the Doctor spoke would have seen his eyebrows contract heavily, and a fierce scowl settle on his face. The name the Doctor mentioned was a very unwelcome one. He had been taunted and laughed at, at Government-house, for having allowed Hawker to outwit him. His hot Irish blood couldn't stand that, and he had vowed to have the fellow somehow. Here he had missed him, again, and by so little, too! He renewed his vow to himself, and in an instant the cloud was gone, and the merry Irishman was there again.

"My dear Doctor," he said, "I am aware that you never speak at random, or I should ask you, were you sure of the man? Are you not mistaken?"

"Mistaken in *him*—eh?" said the Doctor. "No, I was not mistaken."

"You seem to know too much of a very suspicious character,

Doctor!" said Desborough. "I shall have to keep my eye on you, I see!"

Meanwhile, at the other end of the table, more agreeable subjects were being talked of. There sat our young coterie, laughing loudly, grouping themselves round some exceedingly minute object, which apparently was between Sam and Alice, and which, on close examination, turned out to be little Tacks, who was evidently making himself agreeable in a way hardly to be expected in one of his tender years. And this is the way he got there:

When Captain Blockstrop came in, Alice was duly impressed by the appearance of that warrior. But when she saw little Tacks slip in behind him, and sit meekly down by the door; and when she saw how his character was appreciated by the cattle-dogs, one of whom had his head in the lad's lap, while the other was licking his face—when she saw, I say, the little blue and gold apparition, her heart grew pitiful, and, turning to Halbert, she said:

"Why, good gracious me! You don't mean to tell me that they take such a child as that to sea; do you?"

"Oh dear, yes!" said Halbert, "and younger, too. Don't you remember the story about Collingwood offering his cake to the first lieutenant? He became, remember, a greater man that Nelson, in all except worldly honour."

"Would you ask him to come and sit by me, if you please?" said Alice.

So Halbert went and fetched him in, and he sat and had his breakfast between Alice and Sam. They were all delighted with him; such a child, and yet so bold and self-helpful, making himself quietly at home, and answering such questions as were put to him modestly and well. Would that all midshipmen were like him!

But it became time to go on board, and Captain Blockstrop, coming by where Alice sat, said, laughing:

"I hope you are not giving my officer too much marmalade, Miss Brentwood? He is over-young to be trusted with a jam-pot —eh, Tacks?"

"Too young to go to sea, I should say," said Alice.

"Not too young to be a brave-hearted boy, however!" said the Captain. "The other day, in Sydney harbour, one of my marines who couldn't swim went overboard, and this boy soused in after him, and carried the life-buoy to him, in spite of sharks. What do you think of that for a ten-year-old?"

The boy's face flushed scarlet as the Captain passed on, and he held out his hand to Alice to say good-bye. She took it, looked at him, hesitated, and then bent down and kissed his cheek—a tender, sisterly kiss—something, as Jim said, to carry on board with him!

Poor little Tacks! He was a great friend of mine; so I have been tempted to dwell on him. He came to me with letters of introduction, and stayed at my place six weeks or more. He served brilliantly, and rose rapidly, and last year only I heard that Lieutenant Tacks had fallen in the dust, and never risen again, just at the moment that the gates of Delhi were burst down, and our fellows went swarming in to vengeance.

CHAPTER XXXVI

AN EARTHQUAKE, A COLLIERY EXPLOSION, AND AN ADVENTURE

So the Captain, the Colonial Secretary, and the small midshipman left the station and went on board again, disappearing from this history for evermore. The others all went home and grew warlike, arming themselves against the threatened danger; but still weeks, nay months, rolled on, and winter was turning into spring, and yet the country-side remained so profoundly tranquil that every one began to believe that the convicts must after all have been drowned, and that the boat found by sagacious Blockstrop had been capsized and thrown bottom upwards on the beach. So that, before the brown flocks began to be spotted with white lambs, all alarm had gone by.

Only four persons, besides Mary Hawker herself, were conversant of the fact that the bushranger and George Hawker were the same man. Of these only three, the Doctor, Major Buckley, and Captain Brentwood, knew of his more recent appearance on the shore, and they, after due consultation, took honest Tom Troubridge into their confidence.

But, as I said, all things went so quietly for two months, that at the end of that time no one thought any more of bushrangers than they would of tigers. And just about this time, I, Geoffry Hamlyn, having finished my last consignment of novels from England, and having nothing to do, determined to ride over, and spend a day or two with Major Buckley.

But when I rode up to the door of Baroona, having pulled my

shirt collar up, and rapped at the door with my whip, out came the housekeeper to inform me there was not a soul at home. This was deeply provoking, for I had got on a new pair of riding trousers, which had cost money, and a new white hat with a blue net veil (rather a neat thing too), and I had ridden up to the house under the idea that fourteen or fifteen persons were looking at me out of the window. I had also tickled my old horse, Chanticleer, to make him caper and show the excellency of my seat. But when I came to remember that the old horse had nearly bucked me over his head instead of capering, and to find that my hat was garnished with a large cobweb of what is called by courtesy native silk, with half a dozen dead leaves sticking in it, I felt consoled that no one had seen me approach, and asked the housekeeper with tolerable equanimity where they were all gone.

They were all gone, she said, over to Captain Brentwood's, and goodness gracious knew when they would be back again. Mrs. Hawker and Mr. Charles were gone with them. For her part, she should not be sorry when Mr. Sam brought Miss Brentwood over for good and all. The house was terrible lonesome when they were all away.

I remarked, " Oho! " and asked whether she knew if Mr. Troubridge was at Toonarbin.

No, she said; he was away again at Port Phillip with store-cattle; making a deal of money, she understood, and laying out a deal for the Major in land. She wished he would marry Mrs. Hawker and settle down, for he was a pleasant gentleman, and fine company in a house. Wouldn't I get off and have a bit of cold wild duck and a glass of sherry?

Certainly I would. So I gave my horse to the groom and went in. I had hardly cut the first rich red slice from the breast of a fat teal, when I heard a light step in the passage, and in walked my man Dick. You remember him, reader. The man we saw five-and-twenty years ago on Dartmoor, combining with William Lee to urge the unhappy George Hawker on to ruin and forgery, which circumstance, remember, I knew nothing of at this time. The same man I had picked up footsore and penniless in the bush sixteen years ago, and who had since lived with me, a most excellent and clever servant—the best I ever had. This man now came into Major Buckley's parlour, hat in hand, looking a little foolish, and when I saw him my knife and fork were paralysed with astonishment.

" Why, what the Dickens " (I used that strong expression) " brings you here, my lad ? "

" I went to Hipsley's about the colt," he said, " and when I got home I found you were gone off unexpectedly; so I thought it better to come after you and tell you all about it. He won't take less than thirty-five."

" Man! man ! " I said, " do you mean to say that you have ridden fifty miles to tell me the price of a leggy beast like that, after I told you that twenty-four was my highest offer ? "

He looked very silly, and I saw very well that he had some other reason for coming than that. But with a good servant I never ask too many questions, and when I went out a short time after, and found him leaning against a fence, and talking earnestly to our old acquaintance William Lee, I thought, " He wanted an excuse to come up and see his old friend Lee. That is quite just and proper, and fully accounts for it."

Lee always paid me the high compliment of touching his hat to me, for old Devon's sake I suppose. " How's all at Toonarbin, Lee ? " I asked.

" Well and hearty, sir. How is yourself, sir ? "

" Getting older, Lee. Nothing worse than that. Dick, I am going on to Captain Brentwood's. If you like to go back to Toonarbin and stay a day or two with Lee, you can do so."

" I would rather come on with you, sir," he said eagerly.

" Are you sure ? " I said.

" Quite sure, sir." And Lee said, " You go on with Mr. Hamlyn, Dick, and do your duty, mind."

I thought this odd; but knowing it useless to ask questions of an old hand, or try to get any information which was not volunteered, I held my tongue and departed, taking Dick with me.

I arrived at Captain Brentwood's about three o'clock in the afternoon. I flatter myself that I made a very successful approach, and created rather a sensation among the fourteen or fifteen people who were sitting in the veranda. They took me for a distinguished stranger. But when they saw who it was they all began calling out to me at once to know how I was, and to come in (as if I wasn't coming in), and when at last I got among them, I nearly had my hand shaken off; and the Doctor, putting on his spectacles and looking at me for a minute, asked what I had given for my hat ?

Let me see, who was there that day ? There was Mary Hawker, looking rather older, and a little worn; and there was her son Charles sitting beside pretty Ellen Mayford, and carrying on a terrible flirtation with that young lady, in spite of her fat jolly-looking mother, who sat with folded hands beside her. Next to her sat her handsome brother Cecil, looking, poor lad! as miserable as he well could look, although I did not know the cause. Then came Sam, beside his mother, whose noble happy face was still worth riding fifty miles to see; and then, standing beside her chair, was Alice Brentwood.

I had never seen this exquisite creature before, and I immediately fell desperately and hopelessly in love with her, and told her so that same evening, in the presence of Sam. Finding that my affection was not likely to be returned, I enrolled myself as one of her knights, and remain so to this present time.

The Major sat beside his wife, and the Doctor and Captain Brentwood walked up and down, talking politics. There were also present, certain Hawbucks, leggy youths with brown faces and limp hair, in appearance and dress not unlike English steeplechase-riders who had been treated, on the face and hands, with walnut-juice. They never spoke, and the number of them present I am uncertain about, but one of them I recollect could spit a good deal farther than any of his brothers, and proved it beyond controversy about twice in every three minutes.

I missed my old friend Jim Brentwood, and was informed that he had gone to Sydney, " on the spree," as Sam expressed it, along with a certain Lieutenant Halbert, who was staying on a visit with Major Buckley.

First I sat down by Mary Hawker, and had a long talk with her about old times. She was in one of her gay moods, and laughed and joked continuously. Then I moved up by invitation, to a chair between the Major and his wife, and had a long private and confidential conversation with them.

" How," I began, " is Tom Troubridge ? "

" Tom is perfectly well," said the Major. " He still carries on his old chronic flirtation with Mary; and she is as ready to be flirted with as ever."

" Why don't they marry ? " I asked peevishly. " Why on earth don't they marry one another ? What is the good of carrying on that old folly so long ? They surely must have made up their minds by now. She knows she is a widow, and has known it for years."

" Good God! Hamlyn, are you so ignorant ? " said the Major. And then he struck me dumb by telling me of all that had happened latterly: of George Hawker's reappearance, of his identity with the great bushranger, and, lastly, of his second appearance, not two months before.

" I tell you this in strict confidence, Hamlyn, as one of my oldest and best friends. I know how deeply your happiness is affected by all this."

I remained silent and thunderstruck for a time, and then I tried to turn the conversation:

" Have you had any alarm from bushrangers lately? I heard a report of some convicts having landed on the coast."

" All a false alarm! " said the Major. " They were drowned, and the boat washed ashore, bottom upwards."

Here the Doctor broke in: "Hamlyn, is not this very queer weather?"

When he called my attention to it, I remarked that the weather was really different from any I had seen before, and said so.

The sky was grey and dull, the distances were clear, and to the eye it appeared merely a soft grey autumnal day. But there was something very strange and odd in the deadly stillness of all nature. Not a leaf moved, not a bird sang, and the air seemed like lead. At once Mrs. Buckley remarked:

" I can't work, and I can't talk. I am so wretchedly nervous that I don't know what to do with myself, and you know, my dear," she said, appealing to her husband, " that I am not given to that sort of thing."

Each man looked at his neighbour, for there was a sound in the air now—a weird and awful sound like nothing else in nature. To the south arose upon the ear a hollow quivering hum, which swelled rapidly into a roar beneath our feet; then there was a sickening shake, a thump, a crash, and away went the Earthquake, groaning off to the northward.

The women behaved very well, though some of them began to cry; and hearing a fearful row in the kitchen I dashed off there, followed by the Doctor. The interior was a chaos of pots and kettles, in the centre of which sat the cook, Eleanor, holding on by the floor. Every now and then she would give a scream which took all the breath out of her; so she had to stop and fetch breath before she could give another. The Doctor stepped through the saucepans and camp-ovens, and trying to raise her, said:

" Come, get up, my good woman, and give over screaming. All danger is over, and you will frighten the ladies."

At this moment she got her " second wind," and as he tried to get her up she gave such a yell that he dropped her again, and bolted, stopping his ears; bolted over a tea-kettle which had been thrown down, and fell prostrate, resounding, like an Homeric hero, on to a heap of kitchen utensils, at the feet of Alice, who had come in to see what the noise was about.

"Good Lord!" said he, picking himself up, "what lungs she has got. I shall have a singing in my ears to my dying day. Yar! it went through my head like a knife."

Sam picked up the cook, and she, after a time, picked up her pots, giving, however, an occasional squall, and holding on by the dresser, under the impression that another earthquake was coming. We left her, however, getting dinner under way, and went back to the others, whom we soon set laughing by telling poor Eleanor's misadventures.

We were all in good spirits now. A brisk cool wind had come up from the south, following the earthquake, making a pleasant rustle as it swept across the plain or tossed the forest boughs. The sky had got clear, and the nimble air was so inviting that we rose as one body to stroll in groups about the garden and wander down to the river.

The brave old river was rushing hoarsely along, clear and full between his ruined temple-columns of basalt, as of old. "What a grand salmon river this would be, Major!" said I; "what pools and stickles are here! Ah! if we only could get the salmon-spawn through the tropics without its germinating.—Can you tell me, Doctor, why these rocks should take the form of columns? Is there any particular reason for it that you know?"

"You have asked a very puzzling question," he replied, "and I hardly know how to answer it. Nine geologists out of ten will tell you that basalt is lava cooled under pressure. But I have seen it in places where that solution was quite inapplicable. However, I can tell you that the same cause which set these pillars here, to wall the river, piled up yon Organ-hill, produced the caves of Widderin, the great crater-hollow of Mirngish, and accommodated us with that brisk little earthquake which we felt just now. For you know that we mortals stand only on a thin crust of cooled matter, but beneath our feet is all molten metal."

"I wish you could give us a lecture on these things, Doctor," I said.

"To-morrow," said he, "let us ride forth to Mirngish and have a picnic. There I will give you a little sketch of the origin of that hill."

In front of the Brentwoods' house the plains stretched away for a dozen miles or so, a bare sheet of grass with no timber, grey in summer, green in winter. About five miles off it began to roll into great waves, and then heaved up into a high bald hill, a lofty down, capped with black rocks, bearing in its side a vast round hollow, at the bottom of which was a little swamp, perfectly circular, fringed with a ring of white gum-trees, standing in such an exact circle that it was hard to persuade oneself that they were not planted by the hand of man. This was the crater of the old volcano. Had you stood in it you would have remarked that one side was a shelving steep bank of short grass, while the other reared up some five hundred feet, a precipice of fire-eaten rock. At one end the lip had broken down, pouring a torrent of lava, now fertile grass-land, over the surrounding country, which little gap gave one a delicious bit of blue distance. All else, as I said, was a circular wall of grass, rock, and tumbled slag.

This was Mirngish. And the day after the earthquake there was a fresh eruption in the crater. An eruption of horsemen and horsewomen. An eruption of talk, laughter, pink-bonnets, knives and forks, and champagne. Many a pleasant echo came ringing back from the old volcano-walls overhead, only used for so many ages to hear the wild rattle of the thunder and the scream of the hungry eagle.

Was ever a poor old worn-out grass-grown volcano used so badly? Here into the very pit of Tophet had the audacious Captain that very morning sent on a spring-cart of all eatables and drinkables, and then had followed himself with a dozen of his friends, to eat and drink, and talk and laugh, just in the very spot where of old roared and seethed the fire and brimstone of Erebus.

Yet the good old mountain was civil, for we were not blown into the air, to be a warning to all people picknicking in high places; but when we had eaten and drunk, and all the ladies had separately and collectively declared that they were *so* fond of the smell of tobacco in the open air, we followed the Doctor, who led the way to the summit of the hill.

I arrived last, having dragged dear fat old Mrs. Mayford up the slippery steep. The Doctor had perched himself on the highest flame-worn crag, and when we all had grouped ourselves below him, and while the wind swept pleasantly through the grass, and rushed humming through the ancient rocks, he in a clear melodious voice thus began:

" Of old the great sea heaved and foamed above the ground on which we stand; ay, above this, and above yon farthest snowy peak, which the westering sun begins to tinge with crimson.

"But in the lapse of ten thousand changing centuries, the lower deeps, acted on by some Plutonic agency, began to grow shallow; and the imprisoned tides began to foam and roar as they struggled to follow the moon, their leader, angry to find that the stillness of their ancient domain was year by year invaded by the ever-rising land.

"At that time, had man been on the earth to see it, those towering Alps were a cluster of lofty islands, each mountain pass which divides them was a tide-swept fiord, in and out of which, twice in the day, age after age, rushed the sea, bringing down those vast piles of water-worn gravel which you see accumulated, and now covered with dense vegetation, at the mouth of each great valley.

"So twenty thousand years went on, and all this fair champagne country which we overlook became, first a sand-bank, then a dreary stretch of salt-saturated desert, and then, as the roar of the retiring ocean grew fainter and fainter, began to sustain such vegetation as the Lord thought fit.

"A thousand years are but as yesterday to Him, and I can give you no notion as to how many hundred thousand years it took to do all this; or what productions covered the face of the country. It must have been a miserably poor region: nothing but the debris of granite, sandstone, and slate; perhaps here and there partially fertilised by rotting seaweed, dead fish and shells; things which would, we may assume, have appeared and flourished as the water grew shallower.

"New elements were wanting to make the country available for man, so soon to appear in his majesty; and new elements were forthcoming. The internal fires so long imprisoned beneath the weight of the incumbent earth, having done their duty in raising the continent, began to find vent in every weak spot caused by its elevation.

"Here, where we stand, in this great crack between the granite and the sandstone, they broke out with all their wildest fury; hurling stones high in the air, making midday dark with clouds of ashes, and pouring streams of lava far and wide.

"So the country was desolated by volcanoes, but only desolated that it might grow greener and richer than ever, with a new and hitherto unknown fertility; for, as the surface of the lava disintegrated, a new soil was found, containing all the elements of the old one, and many more. These are your black clay, and your red burnt soil, which, I take it, are some of the richest in the world.

"Then our old volcano, our familiar Mirngish, in whose crater we have been feasting, grew still for a time, for many ages probably; but after that I see the traces of another eruption; the worst, perhaps, that he ever accomplished.

"He had exhausted himself, and gradually subsided, leaving a perfect cup or crater, the accumulation of the ashes of a hundred eruptions; nay, even this may have been filled with water, as is Mount Gambier, which you have not seen, forming a lake without a visible outlet; the water draining off at that level where the looser scoriæ begin.

"But he burst out again, filling this great hollow with lava, till the accumulation of the molten matter broke through the weaker part of the wall, and rolled away there, out of that gap to the northward, and forming what you now call the 'stony rises'—turning yon creek into steam, which by its explosive force formed that fantastic cap of rocks, and, swelling into great bubbles under the hot lava, made those long underground hollows which we now know as the caves of Bar-ca-nah.

"Is he asleep for ever? I know not. He may arise again in his wrath and fill the land with desolation; for that earthquake we felt yesterday was but a wild throe of the giant struggling to be free.

"Let us hope that he may not break his chains, for as I stand here gazing on those crimson Alps, the spirit of prophecy is upon me, and I can see far into the future, and all the desolate landscape becomes peopled with busy figures.

"I see the sunny slopes below me yellow with trellised vines. They have gathered the vintage, and I hear them singing at the wine-press. They sing that the exhausted vineyards of the old world yield no wine so rare, so rich, as the fresh volcanic slopes of the southern continent, and that the princes of the earth send their wealth that their hearts may get glad from the juice of the Australian grapes.

"Beyond I see fat black ridges grow yellow with a thousand corn-fields. I see a hundred happy homesteads, half-hidden by clustering wheat-stacks. What do they want with all that corn? say you; where is their market?

"There is their market! Away there on the barren forest ranges. See, the timber is gone, and a city stands there instead. What is that on the crest of the hill? A steam-engine: nay, see, there are five of them, working night and day, fast and busy. Their cranks gleam and flash under the same moon that grew red and lurid when old Mirngish vomited fire and smoke twenty thousand years ago. As I listen I can hear the grinding of the busy quartz-mill. What are they doing? you ask. They are gold-mining.

"They have found gold here, and gold in abundance, and hither have come, by ship and steamship, all the unfortunate of the earth. The English factory labourer and the farmer-ridden peasant; the Irish pauper; the starved Scotch Highlander. I hear a grand swelling chorus rising above the murmur of the evening breeze; that is sung by German peasants revelling in such plenty as they never knew before, yet still regretting fatherland, and then I hear a burst of Italian melody replying. Hungarians are not wanting, for all the oppressed of the earth have taken refuge here, glorying to live under the free government of Britain; for she, warned by American experience, has granted to all her colonies such rights as the British boast of possessing."

I did not understand him then. But, since I have seen the living wonder of Ballarat, I understand him well enough.

He ceased. But the Major cried out, "Go on, Doctor, go on. Look farther yet, and tell us what you see. Give us a bit more poetry while your hand is in."

He faced round, and I fancied I could detect a latent smile about his mouth.

"I see," said he, "a vision of a nation, the colony of the greatest race on the earth, who began their career with more advantages than ever fell to the lot of a young nation yet. War never looked on them. Not theirs was the lot to fight, like the Americans, through bankruptcy and inexperience towards freedom and honour. No. Freedom came to them, heaven-sent, red-tape bound, straight from Downing Street. Millions of fertile acres, gold in bushels were theirs, and yet——"

"Go on," said the Major.

"I see a vision of broken railway-arches and ruined farms. I see a vision of a people surfeited with prosperity and freedom grown factious, so that now one party must command a strong majority ere they can pass a law the goodness of which no one denies. I see a bankrupt exchequer, a drunken Governor, an Irish ministry, a——"

"Come down out of that," roared the Major, "before I pull you down. You're a pretty fellow to come out for a day's pleasure! Jeremiah was a saint to him," he added, turning appealingly to the rest of us. "Hear my opinion, *per contra,* Doctor. I'll be as near right as you."

"Go on, then," said the Doctor.

"I see," began the Major, "the Anglo-Saxon race——"

"Don't forget the Irish, Jews, Germans, Chinese, and other barbarians," interrupted the Doctor.

"Asserting," continued the Major scornfully, "as they always do, their right to all the unoccupied territories of the earth——"

("Blackfellows' claims being ignored," interpolated the Doctor.)

"And filling all the harbours of this magnificent country——"

("Want to see them.")

"With their steamships and their sailing vessels. Say there be gold here, as I believe there is, the time must come when the mines will be exhausted. What then? With our coals we shall supply——"

("Newcastle," said the Doctor again.)

"The British fleets in the East Indies——"

"And compete with Borneo," said the Doctor quietly, "which contains more coal than ever India will burn, at one-tenth the distance from her that we are. If that is a specimen of your prophecies, Major, you are but a Micaiah after all."

"Well," said the Major, laughing, "I cannot reel it off quite so quick as you; but think we shall hardly have time for any more prophesying; the sun is getting very low."

We turned and looked to westward. The lofty rolling snow-downs had changed to dull lead-colour, as the sun went down in a red haze behind them; only here and there some little elevated pinnacle would catch the light. Below the mountain lay vast black sheets of woodland, and nearer still was the river, marked distinctly by a dense and rapidly-rising line of fog.

"We are going to have a fog and a frost," said the Major. "We had better hurry home."

Behind all the others rode Alice, Sam, and myself. I was fearful of being *de trop,* but when I tried to get forward to the laughing, chattering crowd in front, these two young lovers raised such an outcry that I was fain to stay with them, which I was well pleased to do.

Behind us, however, rode three mounted servants, two of Captain Brentwood's, and my man Dick.

We were almost in sight of the river, nearly home in fact, when there arose a loud lamentation from Alice.

"Oh, my bracelet! my dear bracelet! I have lost it."

"Have you any idea where you dropped it?" I inquired.

"Oh, yes," she said. "I am sure it must have been when I fell down, scrambling up the rocks, just before the Doctor began his lecture. Just as I reached the top, you know, I fell down, and I must have lost it there."

"I will ride back and find it, then, in no time," I said.

"No, indeed, Uncle Jeff," said Sam. "I will go back."

"I use an uncle's authority," I replied, "and I forbid you. That miserable old pony of yours, which you have chosen to bring out to-day, has had quite work enough, without ten miles extra. I condescend to no argument; here I go."

I turned, with a kind look from both of them, but ere I had gone ten yards, my servant Dick was alongside of me.

"Where are you going, sir?" said he.

"I am going back to Mirngish," I replied. "Miss Alice has dropped her bracelet, and I am going back for it."

"I will come with you, sir," he said.

"Indeed no, Dick; there is no need. Go back to your supper, lad, I shan't be long away."

"I am coming with you, sir," he replied. "Company is a good thing sometimes."

"Well, boy," I said, "if you will come, I shall be glad of your company; so come along."

I had noticed lately that Dick never let me go far alone, but would always be with me. It gave rise to no suspicion in my mind. He had been tried too often for that. But still, I thought it strange.

On this occasion, we had not ridden far before he asked me a question which rather surprised me. He said:

"Mr. Hamlyn; do you carry pistols?"

"Why, Dick, boy?" I said, "why should I?"

"Look you here, Mr. Hamlyn," said he. "Have you tried me?"

"I have tried you for twenty years, Dick, and have not found you wanting."

"Ah!" said he, "that's good hearing. You're a magistrate, sir, though only just made. But you know that coves like me, that have been in trouble, get hold of information which you beaks can't. And I tell you, sir, there's bad times coming for this country-side. You carry your pistols, sir, and what's more, *you use 'em.* See here."

He opened his shirt, and showed me a long sharp knife inside.

"That's what I carries, sir, in these times, and you ought to carry ditto, and a brace of barkers besides. We shan't get back to the Captain's to-night."

We were rising on the first shoulder of Mirngish, and daylight was rapidly departing. I looked back. Nothing but a vast sea of fog, one snow peak rising from it like an iceberg from a frozen sea, piercing the clear frosty air like a crystal of lead and silver.

"We must hurry on," I said, "or we shall never have daylight to find the bracelet. We shall never find our way home through that fog, without a breath of wind to guide us. What shall we do?"

"I noticed to-day, sir," said Dick, "a track that crossed the hill to the east; if we can get on that, and keep on it, we are sure to get somewhere. It would be better to follow that than go blundering across the plain through such a mist as that."

As he was speaking, we had dismounted and commenced our search. In five minutes, so well did our recollection serve us, Dick had got the bracelet, and, having mounted our horses, we deliberated what was next to be done.

A thick fog covered the whole country, and was rapidly creeping up to the elevation on which we stood. To get home over the plains without a compass seemed a hopeless matter. So we determined to strike for the track which Dick had noticed in the morning, and get on it before it was dark.

We plunged down into the sea of fog, and, by carefully keeping the same direction, we found our road. The moon was nearly full, which enabled us to distinguish it, though we could never see above five yards in front of us.

We followed the road above an hour; then we began to see ghostly tree-stems through the mist. They grew thicker and more frequent. Then we saw a light, and at last rode up to a hut door, cheered by the warm light, emanating from a roaring fire within, which poured through every crack in the house-side, and made the very fog look warm.

I held Dick's horse while he knocked. The door was opened by a wee feeble old man, about sixty, with a sharp clever face, and an iron-grey rough head of hair.

"Night, daddy," said Dick. "Can me and my master stay here to-night? We're all abroad in this fog. The governor will leave something handsome behind in the morning, old party, I know." (This latter was in a whisper.)

"Canst thou stay here, say'st thou?" replied the old fellow. "In course thou canst. But thy master's money may bide in a's pouch.

Get thy saddles off, lad, and come in; 'tis a smittle night for rheumatics."

I helped Dick to take off the saddles, and, having hobbled our horses with stirrup-leathers, we went in.

Our little old friend was the hut-keeper, as I saw at a glance. The shepherd was sitting on a block before the fire, in his shirt, smoking his pipe and warming his legs preparatory to turning in.

I understood him in a moment, as I then thought (though I was much deceived). A short, wiry, black-headed man, with a cunning face—convict all over. He rose as we came in, and gave us good evening. I begged he would not disturb himself; so he moved his block into the corner, and smoked away with that lazy indifference that only a shepherd is master of.

But the old man began bustling about. He made us sit down before the fire, and make ourselves comfortable. He never ceased talking.

" I'll get ye lads some supper just now," said he. " There's na but twa bunks i' the hut; so master and man must lie o' the floor, 'less indeed the boss lies in my bed, which he's welcome to. We've aplenty blankets, though, and sheepskins. We'll mak ye comfortable, boys. There's a mickle back log o' the fire, and ye'll lie warm, I'se warrant ye. There's cowd beef, sir (to me), and good breed, no' to mind boggins o' tea. Ye'll be comfortable, will ye. What's yer name?"

" Hamlyn," I said.

" Oh, ay! Ye're Hamlyn and Stockbridge! I ken ye well; I kenned yer partner: a good man—a very good man, a man o' ten thousand. He was put down up north. A bad job—a very bad job! Ye gat terrible vengeance, though. Ye hewed Agag in pieces! T' Governor up there to Sydney was wild angry at what ye did, but he darena say much. He knew that every free man's heart went with ye. It were the sword of the Lord and of Gideon that ye fought with! Ye saved many good lives by that raid of yours after Stockbridge was killed. The devils wanted a lesson, and ye gar'd them read one wi' a vengeance!"

During this speech, which was uttered in a series of interjections, we had made our supper, and drawn back to the fire. The shepherd had tumbled into his blankets, and was snoring. The old man, having cleared away the things, came and sat down beside us. The present of a fig of tobacco won his heart utterly, and he, having cut up a pipeful, began talking again.

" Why," said he, " it's the real Barret's twist—the very real article! Eh, master, ye're book-learned: do you ken where this grows? It must be a fine country to bring up such backer as this; some o' they Palm Isles, I reckon."

"Virginia," I told him, " or Carolina, one of the finest countries in the world, where they hold slaves."

"Ah," said he, " they couldn't get white men to mess with backer and such in a hot country, and in course, everyone knows that blacks won't work till they're made. That's why they bothers themselves with 'em, I reckon. But, Lord! they are useless trash. White convicts is useless enough; think what black niggers must be!"

How about the gentleman in bed? I thought; but he was snoring comfortably.

"I am a free man, myself," continued the old man. "I never did aught, say, or thought o' doing aught, that an honest man should not do. But I've lived among convicts twenty odd year, and do you know, sir, sometimes I hardly know richt fra wrang. Sometimes I see things that whiles I think I should inform of, and then the devil comes and tells me it would be dishonourable. And then I believe him till the time's gone by, and after that I am miserable in my conscience. So I haven't an easy time of it, though I have good times, and money to spare."

I was getting fond of the honest, talkative old fellow; so when Dick asked him if he wanted to turn in, and he answered no, I was well pleased.

"Can't you pitch us a yarn, daddy?" said Dick. "Tell us something about the old country. I should like well to hear what you were at home."

"I'll pitch ye a yarn, lad," he replied, " if the master don't want to turn in. I'm fond of talking. All old men are, I think," he said, appealing to me. "The time's coming, ye see, when the gift o' speech will be gone from me. It's a great gift. But happen we won't lose it after all."

I said, "No, that I thought not; that I thought on the other side of the grave we should both speak and hear of higher things than we did in the flesh."

"Happen so," said he; "I think so too, sometime. I'll give ye my yarn; I have told it often. Howsoever, neither o' ye have heard it, so ye're the luckier that I tell it better by frequent repetition. Here it is:

"I was a collier lad, always lean, and not well favoured, though I was active and strong. I was small too, and that set my father's heart agin me somewhat, for he was a gran' man, and a mighty fighter.

"But my elder brother Jack, he was a mighty fellow, God bless him; and when he was eighteen he weighed twelve stone, and was earning man's wages, tho' that I was hurrying still. I saw that father loved him better than me, and whiles that vexed me, but most times it didn't, for I cared about the lad as well as father did, and he liked me the same. He never went far without me; and whether he fought, or whether he drunk, I must be wi' him and help.

"Well, so we went on till, as I said, I was seventeen, and he eighteen. We never had a word till then; we were as brothers should be. But at this time we had a quarrel, the first we ever had; ay, and the last, for we got something to mind this one by.

"We both worked in the same pit. It was the Southstone Pit; happen you've heard of it. No? Well, these things get soon forgot. Father had been an overman there, but was doing better now above ground. He and mother kept a bit shop, and made money.

"There was a fair in our village, a poor thing enough; but when we boys were children we used to look forward to it eleven months out o' twelve, and the day it came round we used to go to father, and get sixpence, or happen a shilling apiece to spend.

"Well, time went on till we came to earn money; but still we kept up the custom, and went to the old man reg'lar for our fairin', and he used to laugh and chaff us as he'd give us a fourpenny or such, and we liked the joke as well as he.

"Well this time—it was in '12, just after the comet, just the worst times of the war, the fair came round 24th of May, I well remember, and we went in to the old man to get summut to spend —just for a joke, like.

"He'd lost money, and been vexed; so when Jack asked him for his fairin' he gi'ed him five shillin', and said, 'I'll go to gaol but what my handsome boy shan't have summut to treat his friends to beer.' But when I axed him, he said, 'Earn a man's wages, and thee'll get a man's fairin',' and heaved a penny at me.

"That made me wild mad, I tell you. I wasn't only angry wi' the old man, but I was mad wi' Jack, poor lad! The devil of jealousy had got into me, and, instead of kicking him out I nursed him. I ran out o' the house, and away into the fair, and drunk, and fought, and swore like a mad one.

"I was in one of the dancing booths, half drunk, when a young fellow came to me, and said, 'Where has thee been? Do thee know thy brother has foughten Jim Perry, and beaten him?'

" I felt like crying, to think my brother had fought, and I not there to set him up. But I swore, and said, 'I wish Jim Perry had killed un;' and then I sneaked off home to bed, and cried like a lass.

" And next morning I was up before him, and down the pit. He worked a good piece from me, so I did not see him, and it came on nigh nine o'clock before I began to wonder why the viewer had not been round, for I had heard say there was a foul place cut into by some of them, and at such times the viewer generally looks into every corner.

" Well, about nine, the viewer and underviewer came up with the overman, and stood talking alongside of me, when there came a something sudden and sharp, as tho' one had boxed your ears, and then a ' whiz, whiz,' and the viewer stumbled a one side, and cried out, ' God save us!'

" I hardly knew what had happened till I heard him singing out clear and firm, ' Come here to me, you lads; come here. Keep steady, and we'll be all right yet.' Then I knew it was a fire, and a sharp one, and began crying out for Jack.

" I heard him calling for me, and then he ran up and got hold of me; and so ended the only quarrel we ever had, and that was a one-sided one.

" ' Are you all here?' said the viewer. ' Now follow me, and if we meet the afterdamp, hold your breath and run. I am afraid it's a bad job, but we may get through yet.'

" We had not gone fifty yards before we came on the afterdamp, filling the headway like smoke. Jack and I took hold of each other's collars and ran, but before we were half-way through, he fell. I kept good hold of his shirt, and dragged him on on the ground. I felt as strong as a horse; and in ten seconds, which seemed to me like ten hours, I dragged him out under the shaft into clear air. At first I thought he was dead, but he was still alive, and very little of that. His heart beat very slow, and I thought he'd die; but I knew if he got clear air that he might come round.

" When we had gotten to the shaft bottom we found it all full of smoke; the waft had gone straight up, and they on the top told us after that all the earth round was shook, and the black smoke and coal-dust flew up as though from a gun-barrel. Anyway it was strong enough to carry away the machine, so we waited there ten minutes and wondered the basket did not come down; but they above, meanwhile, were rigging a rope to an old horse-whim, and as they could not get horses, the men run the poles round themselves.

"But we at the bottom knew nothing of all this. There were thirty or so in the shaft bottom, standing there, dripping wet wi' water, and shouting for the others, who never came; now the smoke began to show in the west drive, and we knew the mine was fired, and yet we heard nought from those above.

"But what I minded most of all was, that Jack was getting better. I knew we could not well be lost right under the shaft, so I did not swear and go on like some of them, because they did not mind us above. When the basket came down at last, I and Jack went up among the first, and there I saw such a sight, lad, as ye'll never see till ye see a colliery explosion. There were hundreds and hundreds there. Most had got friends or kin in the pit, and as each man came up, his wife or his mother would seize hold of him and carry on terrible.

"But the worst were they whose husbands and sons never came up again, and they were many; for out of one hundred and thirty-one men in the pit, only thirty-nine came up alive. Directly we came to bank, I saw father; he was first among them that were helping, working like a horse, and directing everything. When he saw us, he said, 'Thank the Lord, there's my two boys. I am not a loser to-day!' and came running to us, and helped me to carry Jack down the bank. He was very weak and sick, but the air freshened him up wonderful.

"I told father all about it, and he said, 'I've been wrong and thou'st been wrong. Don't thou get angry for nothing; thou hast done a man's work to-day, at all events. Now come and bear a hand. T'owd 'ooman will mind the lad.'

"We went back to the pit's mouth; the men were tearing round the whim faster than horses would a' done it. And first amongst 'em all was old Mrs. Cobley, wi' her long grey hair down her back, doing the work o' three men; for her two boys were down still, and I knew for one that they were not with us at the bottom; but when the basket came up with the last, and her two boys missing, she went across to the master, and asked him what he was going to do, as quiet as possible.

"He said he was going to ask some men to go down, and my father volunteered to go at once, and eight more went with him. They were soon up again, and reported that all the mine was full of smoke, and no one had dared to leave the shaft bottom fifty yards.

" ' It's clear enough, the mine's fired, sir,' said my father to the owner. ' They that's down are dead. Better close it, sir.'

" ' What! ' screamed old Mrs. Cobley, ' close the pit, ye dog, and my boys down there? Ye wouldn't do such a thing, master dear?' she continued; ' ye couldn't do it.' Many others were wild when they heard the thing proposed; but while they raved and argued, the pit began to send up a reek of smoke like the mouth of hell, and then the master gave orders to close the shaft, and a hundred women knew they were widows, and went weeping home.

" And Jack got well. And after the old man died, we came out here. Jack has gotten a public-house in Yass, and next year I shall go home and live with him.

" And that's the yarn about the fire at the Southstone Pit."

We applauded it highly, and after a time began to talk about lying down, when on a sudden we heard a noise of horses' feet outside; then the door was opened, and in came a stranger.

He was a stranger to me, but not to my servant, who I could see recognised him, though he gave no sign of it in words. I also stared at him, for he was the handsomest young man I had ever seen.

Handsome as an Apollo, beautiful as a leopard, but with such a peculiar style of beauty, that when you looked at him you instinctively felt at your side for a weapon of defence, for a more reckless, dangerous-looking man I never yet set eyes on. And while I looked at him I recognised him. I had seen his face, or one like it, before, often, often. And it seemed as though I had known him just as he stood there, years and years ago, on the other side of the world. I was almost certain it was so, and yet he seemed barely twenty. It was an impossibility, and yet as I looked I grew every moment more certain.

He dashed in in an insolent way. " I am going to quarter here to-night and chance it," he said. " Hallo! Dick, my prince! You here? And what may your name be, old cock? " he added, turning to me, now seeing me indistinctly for the first time, for I was sitting back in the shadow.

" My name is Geoffry Hamlyn. I am a Justice of the Peace, and I am at your service," I said. " Now perhaps you will favour me with *your* name? "

The young gentleman did not seem to like coming so suddenly into close proximity with a " beak," and answered defiantly:

" Charles Sutton is my name, and I don't know as there's anything against me at present."

" Sutton," I said; " Sutton? I don't know the name. No, I have
nothing against you, except that you don't appear very civil."

Soon after I rolled myself in a blanket and lay down. Dick lay
at right angles to me, his feet nearly touching mine. He began
snoring heavily almost immediately, and just when I was going
to give him a kick, and tell him not to make such a row, I felt
him give me a good sharp shove with the heel of his boot, by which
I understood that he was awake, and meant to keep awake, as he
did not approve of the strangers.

I was anxious about our horses, yet in a short time I could keep
awake no longer. I slept, and when I next awoke, I heard
voices whispering eagerly together. I silently turned, so that I
could see whence the voices came, and perceived the hut-keeper
sitting up in bed, in close confabulation with the stranger.

" Those two rascals are plotting some villainy," I said to myself;
" somebody will be minus a horse shortly, I expect." And then
I fell asleep again; and when I awoke it was broad day.

I found the young man was gone, and, what pleased me better
still, had not taken either of our horses with him. So, when we had
taken some breakfast, we started, and I left the kind little old man
something to remember me by.

We had not ridden a hundred yards, before I turned to Dick and
said :

" Now mind; I don't want you to tell me anything you don't
like, but pray relieve my mind on one point. Who was that young
man? Have I ever seen him before?"

" I think not, sir; but I can explain how you come to think you
have. You remember, sir, that I knew all about Mrs. Hawker's
history?"

" Yes! yes! Go on."

" That young fellow is George Hawker's son."

It came upon me like a thunderbolt. This, then, was the illegitimate son that he had by his cousin Ellen. O miserable child of sin
and shame! to what end, I wondered, had he been saved till now?

We shall see soon. Meanwhile I turned to my companion and
said, " Tell me how he came to be here."

" Why you see, sir, he went on in his father's ways, and got
lagged. He found his father out as soon as he was free, which
wasn't long first, for he is mortal cunning, and since then they two

have stuck together. Most times they quarrel, and sometimes they fight, but they are never far apart. Hawker ain't far off now."

"Now, sir," he continued, "I am going to tell you something which, if it ever leaks out of your lips again, in such a way as to show where it came from, will end my life as sure as if I was hung. You remember three months ago that a boatful of men were supposed to have landed from Cockatoo?"

"Yes," I said, "I heard it from Major Buckley. But the police have been scouring in all directions, and can find nothing of them. My opinion is that the boat was capsized, and they were all drowned, and that the surf piled the boat over with seaweed. Depend on it they did not land."

"Depend on it they did, sir; those men are safe and well, and ready for any mischief. Hawker was on the lookout for them, and they all stowed away till the police cleared off, which they did last week. There will be mischief soon. There; I have told you enough to cut my throat, and I'll tell you more, and convince you that I am right. That shepherd at whose hut we stayed last night was one of them; that fellow was the celebrated Captain Mike. What do you think of that?"

I shuddered as I heard the name of that fell ruffian, and thought that I had slept in the hut with him. But when I remembered how he was whispering with the stranger in the middle of the night, I came to the conclusion that serious mischief was brewing, and pushed on through the fog, which still continued as dense as ever, and, guided by some directions from the old hut-keeper, I got to Captain Brentwood's about ten o'clock, and told him and the Major the night's adventures.

We three armed ourselves secretly and quietly, and went back to the hut with the determination of getting possession of the person of the shepherd Mike, who, were he the man Dick accused him of being, would have been a prize indeed, being one of the leading Van Diemen's Land rangers, and one of the men reported as missing by Captain Blockstrop.

"Suppose," said Captain Brentwood, "that we seize the fellow, and it isn't him after all?"

"Then," said the Major, "an action for false imprisonment would lie, sir, decidedly. But we will chance it."

And when we got there we saw the old hut-keeper, he of the colliery explosion experiences, shepherding the sheep himself, and found that the man we were in search of had left the hut that morning, apparently to take the sheep out. But that going out about eleven the old man had found them still in the yard, whereby he concluded that the shepherd was gone, which proved to be the case. And making further inquiries we found that the shepherd had only been hired a month previously, and no man knew whence he came: all of which seemed to confirm Dick's story wonderfully, and made us excessively uneasy. And in the end the Major asked me to prolong my visit for a time and keep my servant with me, as every hand was of use; and so it fell out that I happened to be present at, and chronicle all which follows.

CHAPTER XXXVII

IN WHICH GEORGE HAWKER SETTLES AN OLD SCORE WITH WILLIAM
LEE, MOST HANDSOMELY, LEAVING, IN FACT, A LARGE BALANCE
IN HIS OWN FAVOUR

I PAUSE here—I rather dread to go on. The events of the next month are seldom alluded to by any of those persons mentioned in the preceding pages; they are too painful. I remark that the Lucknow and Cawnpore men don't much like talking about the affairs of that terrible six weeks; much for the same reason, I suspect, as we, going over our old recollections, always omit the occurrences of this lamentable spring.

The facts contained in the latter end of this chapter I got from the Gaol Chaplain at Sydney.

The Major, the Captain, and I, got home to dinner, confirmed in our suspicions that mischief was abroad, and very vexed at having missed the man we went in search of. Both Mrs. Buckley and Alice noticed that something was wrong, but neither spoke a word on the subject. Mrs. Buckley now and then looked anxiously at her husband, and Alice cast furtive glances at her father. The rest took no notice of our silence and uneasiness, little dreaming of the awful cloud that was hanging above our heads, to burst, alas! so soon.

I was sitting next to Mary Hawker that evening, talking over old Devon days and Devon people, when she said:

" I think I am going to have some more quiet peaceful times. I am happier than I have been for many years. Do you know why? Look there."

I shuddered to hear her say so, knowing what I knew, but looked where she pointed. Her son sat opposite to us, next to the pretty Ellen Mayford. She had dropped the lids over her eyes and was smiling. He, with his face turned toward her, was whispering in his eager impulsive way, and tearing to pieces a slip of paper which he held in his hand. As the firelight fell on his face, I felt a chill come over me. The likeness was so fearful!—not to the father (that I had long been accustomed to), but to the son, to the half-brother —to the poor lost young soul I had seen last night, the companion of desperate men. As it struck me I could not avoid a start, and a moment after I would have given a hundred pounds not to have done so, for I felt Mary's hand on my arm, and heard her say, in a low voice:

" Cruel! cruel! Will you never forget? "

I felt guilty and confused. As usual, on such occasions, Satan was at my elbow, ready with a lie, more or less clumsy, and I said, " You do me injustice, Mrs. Hawker, I was not thinking of old times. I was astonished at what I see there. Do you think there is anything in it? "

" I sincerely hope so," she said.

" Indeed, and so do I. It will be excellent on every account. Now," said I, " Mrs. Hawker, will you tell me what has become of your old servant, Lee? I have reasons for asking."

" He is in my service still," she said; " as useful and faithful as ever. At present he is away at a little hut in the ranges, looking after our ewes."

" Who is with him? " I asked.

" Well, he has got a new hand with him, a man who came about a month or so ago, and stayed about splitting wood. I fancy I heard Lee remark that he had known him before. However, when Lee had to go to the ranges, he wanted a hut-keeper; so this man went up with him."

" What sort of a looking man was he? "

" Oh, a rather large man, red-haired, much pitted with the small-pox."

All this made me uneasy. I had asked these questions by the advice of Dick, and, from Mrs. Hawker's description tallying so well with his, I had little doubt that another of the escaped gang was living actually in her service, alone, too, in the hut with Lee.

The day that we went to Mirngish, the circumstances I am about to relate took place in Lee's hut, a lonely spot, eight miles from the home station, towards the mountain, and situated in a dense dark

stringy-bark forest—a wild desolate spot, even as it was that afternoon, with the parrots chattering and whistling around it, and the
bright winter's sun lighting up the green tree-tops.

Lee was away, and the hut-keeper was the only living soul about
the place. He had just made some bread, and, having carried out
his camp-oven to cool, was sitting on the bench in the sun, lazily,
thinking what he would do next.

He was a long, rather powerfully-built man, and seemed at first
sight, merely a sleepy half-witted fellow, but at a second glance you
might perceive that there was a good deal of cunning, and some
ferocity in his face. He sat for some time, and beginning to think
that he would like a smoke, he got out his knife preparatory to
cutting tobacco.

The hut stood at the top of a lone gully, stretching away in a
vista, nearly bare of trees for a width of about ten yards or so,
all the way down, which gave it the appearance of a grass-ride,
walled on each side by tall dark forest. Looking down this, our
hut-keeper saw, about a quarter of a mile off, a horseman cross from
one side to the other.

He only caught a momentary glimpse of him, but that was enough
to show him that it was a stranger. He neither knew horse nor
man, at least judging by his dress; and while he was still puzzling
his brains as to what stranger would be coming to such an out-of-
the-way place, he heard the " Chuck, kuk, kuk, kuk," of an opossum
close behind the hut, and started to his feet.

It would of course have startled any bushman to hear an opossum
cry in broad day, but he knew what this meant well. It was the
arranged signal of his gang, and he ran to the place from whence
the sound came.

George Hawker was there—well dressed, sitting on a noble
chestnut horse. They greeted one another with a friendly curse.

As is my custom, when recording the conversations of this class
of worthies, I suppress the expletives, thereby shortening them by
nearly one half, and depriving the public of much valuable information.

" Well, old man," began Hawker, " is the coast clear? "

" No one here but myself," replied the other. " I'm hut-keeping
here for one Bill Lee, but he is away. He was one of the right sort
once himself, I have heard; but he's been on the square for twenty
years, so I don't like to trust him."

" You are about right there, Moody, my lad," said Hawker. " I've just looked up to talk to you about him, and other matters—I'll come in. When will he be back?"

"Not before night, I expect," said the other.

"Well," said Hawker, "we shall have the more time to talk; I've got a good deal to tell you. Our chaps are all safe and snug, and the traps are off. Only two, that's you and Mike, stayed this side of the hill; the rest crossed the ranges and stowed away in an old lair of mine in one of the upper Murray gullies. They've had pretty hard times, and if it hadn't been for the cash they brought away, they'd have had worse. Now the coast is clear, they're coming back by ones and twos, and next week we shall be ready for business. I'm going to be head man this bout, because I know the country better than any; and the most noble Michael has consented, for this time only, to act as lieutenant. We haven't decided on any plans yet, but some think of beginning from the coast, because that part will be clearest of traps, they having satisfied themselves that we ain't there. In fact, the wiseacres have fully determined that we are all drowned. There's one devil of a foreign doctor knows I'm round though: he saw me the night before you came ashore, and I am nigh sure he knew me. I have been watching him, and I could have knocked him over last week as clean as a whistle, only, thinks I, it'll make a stir before the time. Never mind, I'll have him yet. This Lee is a black sheep, lad. I'm glad you are here; you must watch him, and if you see him flinch, put a knife in him. He raised the country on me once before. I tell you, Jerry, that I'd be hung, and willing, to-morrow, to have that chap's life, and I'd have had it before now, only I had to keep still for the sake of the others. That man served me the meanest, dirtiest trick, twenty years ago, in the old country, that ever you or any other man heard of, and if he catches sight of me the game is up. Mind, if you see cause, you deal with him, or else——" (with an awful oath) "you answer to the others."

"If he's got to go, he'll go," replied the other doggedly. "Don't you fear me; Moody the cannibal ain't a man to flinch."

"What, is that tale true, then?" asked Hawker, looking at his companion with a new sort of interest.

"Why, in course it is," replied Moody; "I thought no one doubted that."

Hawker bent and whispered in his ear; the other listened for a time, and then said:

"Make it twenty."

Hawker after a little consideration nodded—then the other

nodded—then they whispered together again. Something out of the common this must be, that they, not very particular in their confidences, should whisper about it.

They looked up suddenly, and Lee was standing in the doorway.

Hawker and he started when they saw one another, but Lee recovered himself first, and said—

" George Hawker, it's many years since we met, and I'm not so young as I was. I should like to make peace before I go, as I well know that I'm the chief one to blame for you getting into trouble. I'm not humbugging you, when I say that I have been often sorry for it of late years. But sorrow won't do any good. If you'll forgive and forget, I'll do the same. You tried my life once, and that's worse than ever I did for you. And now I'll tell you, that if you want money to get out of the country and set up anywhere else, and leave your poor wife in peace, I'll find it for you out of my own pocket."

" I don't bear any malice," said Hawker; " but I don't want to leave the country just yet. I suppose you won't peach about having seen me here? "

" I shan't say a word, George, if you keep clear of the home station; but I won't have you come about there. So I warn you."

Lee held out his hand, and George took it. Then he asked him if he would stay there that night, and George consented.

Day was fast sinking behind the trees, and making golden boughs overhead. Lee stood at the hut door watching the sun set, and thinking, perhaps, of old Devon. He seemed sad, and let us hope he was regretting his old crimes while time was left him. Night was closing in on him, and having looked once more on the darkening sky, and the fog coldly creeping up the gully, he turned with a sigh and a shudder into the hut, and shut the door.

Near midnight, and all was still. Then arose a cry upon the night so hideous, so wild, and so terrible, that the roosting birds dashed off affrighted, and the dense mist, as though in sympathising fear, prolonged the echoes a hundredfold. One articulate cry, " Oh! you treacherous dog! " given with the fierce energy of a dying man, and then night returned to her stillness, and the listeners heard nothing but the weeping of the moisture from the wintry trees.

The two perpetrators of the atrocity stood silent a minute or more, recovering themselves. Then Hawker said in a fierce whisper:

" You clumsy hound; why did you let him make that noise? I shall never get it out of my head again, if I live till a hundred.

Let's get out of this place before I go mad; I could not stay in the house with it for salvation. Get his horse, and come along."

They got the two horses, and rode away into the night; but Hawker, in his nervous anxiety to get away, dropped a handsome cavalry pistol—a circumstance which nearly cost Dr. Mulhaus his life.

They rode till after daylight, taking a course toward the sea, and had gone nearly twelve miles before George discovered his loss, and broke out into petulant imprecations.

" I wouldn't have lost that pistol for five pounds," he said; " no nor more. I shall never have one like it again. I've put over a parrot at twenty yards with it."

" Go back and get it then," said Moody, " if it's so valuable. I'll camp and wait for you. We want all the arms we can get."

" Not I," said George; " I would not go back into that cursed hut alone for all the sheep in the country."

" You coward," replied the other; " afraid of a dead man! Well, if you won't, I will: and, mind, I shall keep it for my own use."

" You're welcome to it, if you like to get it," said George. And so Moody rode back.

CHAPTER XXXVIII

HOW DR. MULHAUS GOT BUSHED IN THE RANGES, AND WHAT BEFELL HIM THERE

I MUST recur to the same eventful night again, and relate another circumstance that occurred on it. As events thicken, time gets more precious; so that, whereas at first I thought nothing of giving you the events of twenty years or so in a chapter, we are now compelled to concentrate time so much that it takes three chapters to twenty-four hours. I read a long novel once, the incidents of which did not extend over thirty-six hours, and yet it was not so profoundly stupid as you would suppose.

All the party got safe home from the picnic, and were glad enough to get housed out of the frosty air. The Doctor, above all others, was rampant at the thoughts of dinner, and a good chat over a warm fire, and burst out, in a noble bass voice, with an old German student's song about wine and Gretchen, and what not.

His music was soon turned into mourning; for, as they rode into the courtyard, a man came up to Captain Brentwood, and began talking eagerly to him.

It was one of his shepherds, who lived alone with his wife towards the mountain. The poor woman, his wife, he said, was taken in labour that morning, and was very bad. Hearing there was a doctor staying at the home station, he had come down to see if he could come to their assistance.

"I'll go, of course," said the Doctor; "but let me get something to eat first. Is anybody with her?"

"Yes, a woman was with her; had been staying with them some days."

"I hope you can find the way in the dark," said the Doctor, "for I can tell you I can't."

"No fear, sir," said the man; "there's a track all the way, and the moon's full. If it wasn't for the fog it would be as bright as day."

He took a hasty meal, and started. They went at a foot's pace, for the shepherd was on foot. The track was easily seen, and although it was exceedingly cold, the Doctor, being well wrapped up, contrived, with incessant smoking, to be moderately comfortable. All external objects being a blank, he soon turned to his companion to see what he could get out of him.

"What part of the country are you from, my friend?"

"Fra' the Isle of Skye," the man answered. "I'm one of the Macdonalds of Skye."

"That's a very ancient family, is it not?" said the Doctor at a venture, knowing he could not go wrong with a Highlander.

"Very ancient, and weel respeckit," the man answered.

"And whom is your sheik, rajah, chieftain, or what you call him?"

"My lord Macdonald. I am cousin to my lord."

"Indeed! He owns the whole island, I suppose?"

"There's Mackinnons live there. But they are interlopers; they are worthless trash," and he spat in disgust.

"I suppose," said the Doctor, "a Mackinnon would return the compliment, if speaking of a Macdonald."

The man laughed, and said, he supposed "Yes," then added, "See! wat's yon?"

"A white stump burnt black at one side—what did you think it was?"

"I jaloused it might be a ghaist. There's a many ghaists and bogles about here."

" I should have thought the country was too young for those gentry," said the Doctor.

" It's a young country, but there's been muckle wickedness done in it. And what are those blacks do you think?—next thing to devils —at all events they're no' exactly human."

" Impish, decidedly," said the Doctor. " Have you ever seen any ghosts, friend?"

" Ay! many. A fortnight agone, come to-morrow, I saw the ghost of my wife's brother in broad day. It was the time of the high wind ye mind of; and the rain drove so thick I could no' see all my sheep at once. And a man on a white horse came fleeing before the wind close past me; I knew him in a minute; it was my wife's brother, as I tell ye, that was hung fifteen years agone for sheep-stealing, and he wasn't so much altered as ye'd think."

" Someone else like him! " suggested the Doctor.

" Deil a fear," replied the man, " for when I cried out and said, ' What, Col, lad! Gang hame, and lie in yer grave, and dinna trouble honest folk,' he turned and rode away through the rain, straight from me."

" Well! " said the Doctor, " I partly agree with you that the land's bewitched. I saw a man not two months ago who ought to have been dead five or six years at least. But are you quite sure the man you saw was hung?"

" Well-nigh about," he replied. " When we sailed from Skye he was under sentence, and they weren't overmuch given to reprieve for sheep-stealing in those days. It was in consequence o' that that I came here."

" That's a very tolerable ghost story," said the Doctor. " Have you got another? If you have, I shouldn't mind hearing it, as it will beguile the way."

" Did ye ever hear how Faithful's lot were murdered by the blacks up on the Merrimerangbong?"

" No, but I should like to; is it a ghost story?"

" Deed ay, and is it. This is how it happened: When Faithful came to take up his country across the mountains yonder, they were a strong party, enough to have been safe in any country, but whether it was food was scarce, or whether it was on account of getting water, I don't know, but they separated, and fifteen of them got into the Yackandandah country before the others.

" Well, you see, they were pretty confident, being still a strong mob, and didn't set any watch or take any care. There was one among them (Cranky Jim they used to call him—he has told me this yarn—he used to be about Reid's mill last year) who always was going on at them to take more care, but they never heeded him at all.

" They found a fine creek, with plenty of feed and water, and camped at it to wait till the others came up. They saw no blacks, nor heard of any, and three days were past, and they began to wonder why the others had not overtaken them.

" The third night they were all sitting round the fire, laughing and smoking, when they heard a loud cooee on the opposite side of the scrub, and half a dozen of them started up and sang out, 'There they are!'

" Well, they all began cooeeing again, and they heard the others in reply, apparently all about in the scrub. So off they starts, one by one, into the scrub, answering and halloing, for it seemed to them that their mates were scattered about, and didn't know where they were. Well, as I said, fourteen of them started into the scrub, to collect the party and bring them up to the fire; only old Cranky Jim sat still in the camp. He believed, with the others, that it was the rest of their party coming up, but he soon began to wonder how it was that they were so scattered. Then he heard one of them scream, and then it struck him all at once that this was a dodge of the blacks to draw the men from the camp, and, when they were abroad, cut them off one by one, plunder the drays, and drive off the sheep.

" So he dropped, and crawled away in the dark. He heard the cooees grow fewer and fewer as the men were speared one by one, and at last everything was quiet, and then he knew he was right, and he rose up and fled away.

" In two days he found the other party, and told them what had happened. They came up, and there was some sharp fighting, but they got a good many of their sheep back.

" They found the men lying about singly in the scrub, all speared. They buried them just where they found each one, for it was hot weather. They buried them four foot deep, but they wouldn't lie still.

" Every night, about nine o'clock, they get up again, and begin cooeeing for an hour or more. At first there's a regular coronach of them, then by degrees the shouts get fewer and fewer, and, just when you think it's all over, one will break out loud and clear close to you, and after that all's still again."

"You don't believe that story, I suppose?"

"If you press me very hard," said the Doctor, "I must confess, with all humility, that I don't!"

"No more did I," said Macdonald, "till I heard 'em!"

"Heard them!" said the Doctor.

"Ay, *and seen them!*" said the man, stopping and turning round.

"You most agreeable of men! pray, tell me how."

"Why, you see, last year I was coming down with some wool-drays from Parson Dorken's, and this Cranky Jim was with us, and told us the same yarn, and when he had finished, he said, 'You'll know whether I speak the truth or not to-night, *for we're going to camp at the place where it happened.*'

"Well, and so we did, and as well as we could reckon, it was a little past nine when a curlew got up and began crying. That was the signal for the ghosts, and in a minute they were cooeeing like mad all round. As Jim had told us, one by one ceased until all was quiet, and I thought it was over, when I looked, and saw, about a hundred yards off, a tall man in grey crossing a belt of open ground. He put his hand to his mouth, gave a wild shout, and disappeared!"

"Thank you," said the Doctor. "I think you mentioned that your wife's confinement was somewhat sudden."

"Yes, rather," replied the man.

"Pray, had you been relating any of the charming little tales to her lately—just, we will suppose, to wile away the time of the evening?"

"Well, I may have done so," said Macdonald, "but I don't exactly mind."

"Ah, so I thought. The next time your good lady happens to be in a similar situation, I think I would refrain from ghost stories. I should not like to commit myself to a decided opinion, but I should be inclined to say that the tales you have been telling me were rather horrible. Is that the light of your hut?"

Two noble collie dogs bounded to welcome them, and a beautiful barelegged girl, about sixteen, ran forth to tell her father, in Gaelic, that the trouble was over, and that a boy was born.

On going in, they found the mother asleep, while her gossip held the baby on her knee; so the Doctor saw that he was not needed, and sat down, to wait until the woman should wake, having first, however, produced from his saddle two bottles of port wine, a present from Alice.

The woman soon awoke and the Doctor, having felt her pulse, and left some medicine, started to ride home again, carrying with him an incense of good wishes from the warm-hearted Highlanders.

Instead of looking carefully for the road, the good Doctor was soon nine fathoms deep into the reasons why the mountaineers and coast folk of all northern countries should be more blindly superstitious than the dwellers in plains and in towns; and so it happened that, coming to a fork in the track, he disregarded the advice of his horse, and, instead of taking the right hand, as he should have done, he held straight on, and, about two o'clock in the morning, found that not only had he lost his road, but that the track had died out altogether, and that he was completely abroad in the bush.

He was in a very disagreeable predicament. The fog was thicker than ever, without a breath of air; and he knew that it was as likely as not that it might last for a day or two. He was in a very wild part of the mountain, quite on the borders of all the country used by white men.

After some reflection, he determined to follow the fall of the land, thinking that he was still on the watershed of the Snowy River, and hoping, by following down some creek, to find some place he knew.

Gradually day broke, cold and cheerless. He was wet and miserable, and could merely give a guess at the east, for the sun was quite invisible; but, about eight o'clock, he came on a track, running at right angles to the way he had been going, and marked with the hoofs of two horses, whose riders had apparently passed not many hours before.

Which way should he go? He could not determine. The horsemen, it seemed to him, as far as he could guess, had been going west, while his route lay east. And, after a time, having registered a vow never to stir out of sight of the station again without a compass, he determined to take a contrary direction from them, and to find out where they had come from.

The road crossed gully after gully, each one like the other. The timber was heavy stringy-bark, and, in the lower part of the shallow gullies, the tall white stems of the blue gums stood up in the mist like ghosts. All nature was dripping and dull, and he was chilled and wretched.

At length, at the bottom of a gully, rather more dreary looking, if possible, than all the others, he came on a black reedy waterhole, the first he had seen in his ride, and perceived that the track turned short to the left. Casting his eye along it, he made out the dark indistinct outline of a hut, standing about forty yards off.

He rode up to it. All was as still as death. No man came out to welcome him, no dog jumped, barking forth, no smoke went up from the chimney; and, looking round, he saw that the track ended here, and that he had ridden all these miles only to find a deserted hut.

But was it deserted? Not very long so, for those two horsemen, whose tracks he had been on so long, had started from here. Here, on this bare spot in front of the door, they had mounted. One of their horses had been capering; nay, here were their footsteps on the threshold. And, while he looked, there was a light fall inside, and the chimney began smoking. "At all events," said the Doctor, "the fire's in, and here's the camp-oven, too. Somebody will be here soon. I will go in and light my pipe."

He lifted the latch, and went in. Nobody there. Stay—yes, there is a man asleep in the bed-place. "The watchman, probably," thought the Doctor, "he's been up all night with the sheep, and is taking his rest by day. Well, I won't wake him; I'll hang up my horse a bit, and take a pipe. Perhaps I may as well turn the horse out. Well, no. I shan't wait long; he may stand a little without hurting himself."

So soliloquised the Doctor, and lit his pipe. A quarter of an hour passed, and the man still lay there without moving. The Doctor rose and went close to him. He could not even hear him breathe.

His flesh began to creep, but his brows contracted, and his face grew firm. He went boldly up, and pulled down the blanket, and then, to his horror and amazement, recognised the distorted countenance of the unfortunate William Lee.

He covered the face over again, and stood thinking of his situation, and how this had come to pass. How came Lee here, and how had he met his death? At this moment something bright, half hidden by a blue shirt lying on the floor, caught his eye, and, going to pick it up, he found it was a beautiful pistol, mounted in silver, and richly chased.

He turned it over and over, till in a lozenge behind the hammer, he found, apparently scratched with a knife, the name, "G. Hawker."

Here was light with a vengeance! But he had little time to think of his discovery, ere he was startled by the sound of horses' feet rapidly approaching the hut.

Instinctively he thrust the pistol into his pocket, and stooped down, pretending to light his pipe. He heard some one ride up to the door, dismount, and enter the hut. He at once turned round, pipe in mouth, and confronted him.

He was a tall, ill-looking, red-haired man, and to the Doctor's pleasant good-morning, he replied by sulkily asking what he wanted.

"Only a light for my pipe, friend," said the Doctor; "having got one, I will bid you good morning. Our friend here sleeps well."

The new-comer was between him and the door, but the Doctor advanced boldly. When the two men were opposite their eyes met, and they understood one another.

Moody (for it was he) threw himself upon the Doctor with an oath, trying to bear him down; but, although the taller man, he had met his match. He was held in a grasp of iron; the Doctor's hand was on his collar, and his elbow against his face, and thus his head was pressed slowly backwards till he fell to avoid a broken neck, and fell, too, with such force that he lay for an instant stunned and motionless, and before he came to himself the Doctor was on horseback, and some way along the track, glad to have made so good an escape from such an awkward customer.

"If he had been armed," said the Doctor, as he rode along, "I should have been killed: he evidently came back after that pistol. Now, I wonder where I am? I shall know soon at this pace. The little horse keeps up well, seeing he has been out all night."

In about two hours he heard a dog bark to the left of the track, and, turning off in that direction, he soon found himself in a courtyard, and before a door which he thought he recognised: the door opened at the sound of his horse, and out walked Tom Troubridge.

"Good Lord!" said the Doctor, "a friend's face at last; tell me where I am, for I can't see the end of the house."

"Why, at our place, Toonarbin, Doctor."

"Well, take me in, and give me some food; I have terrible tidings for you. When did you last see Lee?"

"The day before yesterday; he is up at an outlying hut of ours in the ranges."

"He is lying murdered in his bed there, for I saw him so not three hours past."

He then told Troubridge all that had happened.

"What sort of a man was it that attacked you?" said Troubridge. The Doctor described Moody.

"That's his hut-keeper that he took from here with him; a man he said he knew, and you say he was on horseback. What sort of a horse had he?"

" A good-looking roan, with a new bridle on him."

" Lee's horse," said Troubridge; " he must have murdered him for it. Poor William! "

But when Tom saw the pistol and read the name on it, he said:

" Things are coming to a crisis, Doctor; the net seems closing round my unfortunate partner. God grant the storm may come and clear the air! Anything is better than these continual alarms."

" It will be very terrible when it does come, my dear friend," said the Doctor.

" It cannot be much more terrible than this," said Tom, " when our servants are assassinated in their beds, and travellers in lonely huts have to wrestle for their lives. Doctor, did you ever nourish a passion for revenge? "

" Yes, once," said the Doctor, " and had it gratified in fair and open duel; but when I saw him lying white on the grass before me, and thought that he was dead, I was like one demented, and prayed that my life might be taken instead of his. Be sure, Tom, that revenge is of the devil, and, like everything else you get from him, is not worth having."

" I do not in the least doubt it, Doctor," said Tom; " but oh, if I could only have five minutes with him on the turf yonder, with no one to interfere between us! I want no weapons; let us meet in our shirts and trousers, like Devon lads."

" And what would you do to him? "

" If you weren't there to see, *he'd* never tell you."

" Why nourish this feeling, Tom, my old friend? you do not know what pain it gives me to see a noble open character like yours distorted like this. Leave him to Desborough—why should you feel so deadly towards the man? He has injured others more than you."

" He stands between me and the hopes of a happy old age. He stands between me and the light, and he must stand on one side."

That night they brought poor Lee's body down in a dray, and buried him in the family burying-ground close beside old Miss Thornton. Then the next morning he rode back home to the Buckleys', where he found that family with myself, just arrived from the Brentwoods'. I of course was brimful of intelligence, but when the Doctor arrived I was thrown into the shade at once. However, no time was to be lost, and we despatched a messenger, post haste, to fetch back Captain Desborough and his troopers, who had now been moved off about a week, but had not been as yet very far withdrawn, and were examining into some " black " outrages to the northward.

Mary Hawker was warned, as delicately as possible, that her husband was in the neighbourhood. She remained buried in thought for a time, and then, rousing herself, said suddenly:

" There must be an end to all this. Get my horse, and let me go home."

In spite of all persuasions to the contrary, she still said the same.

" Mrs. Buckley, I will go home, and see if I can meet him alone. All I ask of you is to keep Charles with you. Don't let the father and son meet, in God's name."

" But what can you do? " urged Mrs. Buckley.

" Something, at all events. Find out what he wants. Buy him off, perhaps. Pray don't argue with me. I am quite determined."

Then it became necessary to tell her of Lee's death, though the fact of his having been murdered was concealed; but it deeply affected her to hear of the loss of her old faithful servant, faithful to her at all events, whatever his faults may have been. Nevertheless, she went off alone, and took up her abode with Troubridge, and there they two sat watching in the lonely station, for him who was to come.

Though they watched together, there was no sympathy or confidence between them. She never guessed what purpose was in Tom's heart; she never guessed what made him so pale and gloomy, or why he never stirred from the house, but slept half the day on the sofa. But ere she had been a week at home, she found out. Thus:

They would sit, those two, silent and thoughtful, beside that unhappy hearth, watching the fire, and brooding over the past. Each had that in their hearts which made them silent to one another, and each felt the horror of some overflowing formless calamity, which any instant might take form, and overwhelm them. Mary would sit late, dreading the weary night, when her overstrained senses caught every sound in the distant forest; but, however late she sat, she always left Tom behind, over the fire, not taking his comfortable glass, but gloomily musing—as much changed from his old self as man could be.

She now lay always in her clothes, ready for any emergency; and one night, about a week after Lee's murder, she dreamt that her husband was in the hall, bidding her in a whisper which thrilled her heart, to come forth. The fancy was so strong upon her, that saying aloud to herself, " The end is come! " she arose in a state little short of delirium, and went into the hall. There was no one there, but she went to the front door, and, looking out into the profoundly black gloom of the night, said in a low voice:

"George, George, come to me! Let me speak to you, George. It will be better for both of us to speak."

No answer: but she heard a slight noise in the sitting-room behind her, and, opening the door gently, saw a light there, and Tom sitting with parted lips watching the door, holding in his hand a cocked pistol.

She was not in the least astonished or alarmed. She was too much *tête montée* to be surprised at anything. She said only, with a laugh:

"What! are you watching, too, old mastiff?—Would you grip the wolf, old dog, if he came?"

"Was he there, Mary? Did you speak to him?"

"No! no!" she said. "A dream, a wandering dream. What would you do if he came—eh, cousin?"

"Nothing! nothing!" said Tom. "Go to bed."

"Bed, eh?" she answered. "Cousin; shooting is an easier death than hanging—eh?"

Tom felt a creeping at the roots of his hair, as he answered, "Yes, I believe so."

"Can you shoot straight, old man? Could you shoot straight and true if he stood there before you? Ah, you think you could now, but your hand would shake when you saw him."

"Go to bed, Mary," said Tom. "Don't talk like that. Let the future lie, cousin."

She turned and went to her room again.

All this was told me long after by Tom himself. Tom believed, or said he believed, that she was only sounding him, to see what his intentions were in case of a meeting with George Hawker. I would not for the world have had him suppose I disagreed with him; but I myself take another and darker interpretation of her strange words that night. I think, that she, never a very strong-minded person, and now grown quite desperate from terror, actually contemplated her husband's death with complacency, nay, hoped, in her secret heart, that one mad struggle between him and Tom might end the matter for ever, and leave her a free woman. I may do her injustice, but I think I do not. One never knows what a woman of this kind, with strong passions and a not over-strong intellect, may be driven to. I knew her for forty years, and loved her for twenty. I knew in spite of all her selfishness and violence that there were many good, nay, noble points in her character; but I cannot disguise from myself that that night's conversation with Tom showed me a darker point in her character than I knew of before. Let us forget it. I would wish to have none but kindly recollections of the woman I loved so truly and so long.

For the secret must be told sooner or later—I loved her before any of them. Before James Stockbridge, before George Hawker, before Thomas Troubridge, and I loved her more deeply and more truly than any of them. But the last remnant of that love departed from my heart twenty years ago, and that is why I can write of her so calmly now, and that is the reason, too, why I remain an old bachelor to this day.

CHAPTER XXXIX

THE LAST GLEAM BEFORE THE STORM

But with us, who were staying down at Major Buckley's, a fortnight passed on so pleasantly that the horror of poor Lee's murder had begun to wear off, and we were getting once more as merry and careless as though we were living in the old times of profound peace. Sometimes we would think of poor Mary Hawker, at her lonely watch up at the forest station; but that or any other unpleasant subject was soon driven out of our heads by Captain Desborough, who had come back with six troopers, declared the country in a state of siege, proclaimed martial law, and kept us all laughing and amused from daylight to dark.

Captain Brentwood and his daughter Alice (the transcendently beautiful!) had come up, and were staying there. Jim and his friend Halbert were still away, but were daily expected. I never passed a pleasanter time in my life than during that fortnight's lull between the storms.

"Begorra (that's a Scotch expression, Miss Brentwood, but very forcible)," said Captain Desborough. "I owe you more than I can ever repay for buying out the Donovans. That girl Lesbia Burke would have forcibly abducted me, and married me against my will, if she hadn't had to follow the rest of the family to Port Phillip."

"A fine woman, too," said Captain Brentwood.

"I'd have called her a little coarse, myself," said Desborough.

"One of the finest, strangest sights I ever saw in my life," resumed Captain Brentwood, "was on the morning I came to take possession. None of the family were left but Murtagh Donovan and Miss Burke. I rode over from Buckley's, and when I came to the door, Donovan took me by the arm, and saying 'whist,' led me into the sitting-room. There, in front of the empty fireplace, crouched down on the floor, bareheaded, with her beautiful hair hanging about her shoulders, sat Miss Burke. Every now and then she would utter the strangest low wailing cry you ever heard: a cry, by Jove, sir, that went straight to your heart. I turned to Donovan, and whispered, 'Is she ill?' and he whispered again, 'Her heart's broke at leaving the old place where she's lived so long. *She's raising the keen over the cold hearthstone.* It's the way of the Burkes.' I don't know when I was so affected in my life. Somehow, that exquisite line came to my remembrance—

'And the hare shall kindle on the cold hearthstone.'

and when I went back quietly with Donovan; and, by Jove, sir, when we came out the great ass had the tears running down his cheeks. I have always felt kindly to that man since."

"Ah, Captain," said Desborough, "with all our vanity and absurdity, we Irish have good warm hearts under our waistcoats. We are the first nation in the world, sir, saving the Jews."

This was late in the afternoon of a temperate spring day. We were watching Desborough as he was giving the finishing touches to a beautiful water-colour drawing.

"Doctor," he said, "come and pass your opinion."

"I think you have done admirably, Captain," said the Doctor; "you have given one a splendid idea of distance in the way you have toned down the plain, from the grey appearance it has ten miles off to the rich, delicate green it shows close to us. And your mountain, too, is most aerial. You would make an artist."

"I am not altogether displeased with my work, Doctor, if you, who never flatter, can praise it with the original before you. How exceedingly beautiful the evening tones are becoming!"

We looked across the plain; the stretch of grass I have described was lying before one like a waveless sea, from the horizon of which rose the square abrupt-sided mass of basalt which years ago we had named the Organ hill, from the regular fluted columns of which it was composed. On most occasions, as seen from Major Buckley's, it appeared a dim mass of pearly grey, but to-night, in the clear, frosty air, it was of a rich purple, shining on the most prominent angles with a dull golden light.

" The more I look at that noble fire-temple, the more I admire it," said the Doctor. " It is one of the most majestic objects I ever beheld."

" It is not unlike Staffa," said Desborough. " There come two travellers."

Two dots appeared crawling over the plain, and making for the river. For a few minutes Alice could not be brought to see them, but when she did, she declared that it was Jim and Halbert.

" You have good eyes, my love," said her father, " to see what does not exist. Jim's horse is black, and Halbert's roan, and those two men are both on grey horses."

" The wish was parent to the thought, father," she replied, laughing. " I wonder what is keeping him away from us so long? If he is to go to India, I should like to see him as much as possible."

" My dear," said her father, " when he went off with Halbert to see the Markhams, I told him that if he liked to go on to Sydney, he could go if Halbert went with him, and draw on the agent for what money he wanted. By his being so long away, I conclude he has done so, and that he is probably at this moment getting a lesson at billiards from Halbert before going to dinner. I shall have a nice little account from the agent just now, of ' Cash advanced to J. Brentwood, Esq.' "

" I don't think Jim's extravagant, papa," said Alice.

" My dear," said Captain Brentwood, " you do him injustice. He hasn't had the chance. I must say, considering his limited opportunities, he has spent as much money on horses, saddlery, etc., as any young gentleman on this country-side. Eh, Sam? "

" Well, sir," said Sam, " Jim spends his money, but he generally makes pretty good investments in the horse line."

" Such as that sweet-tempered useful animal Stampedo," replied the Captain, laughing, " who nearly killed a groom, and staked himself trying to leap out of the stockyard the second day he had him. Well, never mind; Jim's a good boy, and I am proud of him. I am in some hopes that this Sydney journey will satisfy his wandering propensities for the present, and that we may keep him at home. I wish he would fall in love with somebody, providing she wasn't old enough to be his grandmother.—Couldn't you send him a letter of introduction to some of your old schoolfellows, Miss Puss? There was one of them, I remember, I fell in love with myself one time when I came to see you; Miss Green, I think it was. She was very nearly being your mamma-in-law, my dear."

" Why, she is a year younger than me," said Alice, " and, oh goodness, such a temper! She threw the selections from Beethoven at Signor Smitherini, and had bread and water-melon for two days for it. Serve her right!"

"I have had a narrow escape, then," replied the father. "But we shall see who these two people are immediately, for they are crossing the river."

When the two travellers rose again in sight on the near bank of the river, one of them was seen galloping forward, waving his hat.

"I *knew* it was Jim," said Alice, "and on a new grey horse. I thought he would not go to Sydney." And in a minute more she had run to meet him, and Jim was off his horse, kissing his sister, laughing, shouting, and dancing around her.

"Well, father," he said, "here I am back again. Went to Sydney and stayed a week, when we met the two Marstons, and went right up to the Clarence with them. That was a pretty journey, eh? Sold the old horse, and bought this one. I've got heaps to tell you, sister, about what I've seen. I went home, and only stayed ten minutes; when I heard you were here, I came right on."

"I am glad to see you back, Mr. Halbert," said Major Buckley; "I hope you have had a pleasant journey. You have met Captain Desborough?"

"Captain Desborough, how are you?" says Jim. "I am very glad to see you. But, between you and I, you're always a bird of ill omen. Whose pig's dead now? What brings *you* back? I thought we should be rid of you by this time."

"But you are not rid of me, Jackanapes," said Desborough, laughing. "But I'll tell you what, Jim; there is really something wrong, my boy, and I'm glad to see you back." And he told him all the news.

Jim grew very serious. "Well," said he, "I'm glad to be home again; and I'm glad, too, to see you here. One feels safer when you're in the way. We must put a cheerful face on the matter, and not frighten the women. I have bought such a beautiful brace of pistols in Sydney. I hope I may never have the chance to use them in this country. Why, there's Cecil Mayford and Mrs. Buckley coming down the garden, and Charley Hawker, too. Why, Major, you've got all the world here to welcome us."

The young men were soon busy discussing the merits of Jim's new horse, and examining with great admiration his splendid new pistols. Charley Hawker, poor boy! made a mental resolution to go to Sydney, and also come back with a new grey horse, and a pair of pistols more resplendent than Jim's. And then they went in to get ready for dinner.

When Jim unpacked his valise, he produced a pretty bracelet for his sister, and a stock-whip for Sam. On the latter article he was very eloquent.

" Sam, my boy," said he, " there is not such another in the country. It was made by the celebrated Bill Mossman, of the Upper Hunter, the greatest swearer at bullocks, and the most accomplished whipmaker on the Sydney side. He makes only one in six months, and he makes it a favour to let you have it for five pounds. You can take a piece of bark off a blue gum, big enough for a canoe, with one cut of it. There's a fine of two pounds for cracking one within a mile of Government House, they make such a row. A man the other day cracked one of them on the South Head, and broke the windows in Pitt Street."

" You're improving, master Jim," said Charles Hawker. " You'll soon be as good a hand at a yarn as Hamlyn's Dick." At the same time he wrote down a stock-whip, similar to this one, on the tablets of his memory, to be procured on his projected visit to Sydney.

That evening we all sat listening to Jim's adventures; and pleasantly enough he told them, with not a little humorous exaggeration. It is always pleasant to hear a young fellow telling his first impressions of new things and scenes, which have been so long familiar to ourselves; but Jim had really a very good power of narration, and he kept us laughing and amused till long after the usual hour for going to bed.

Next day we had a pleasant ride, all of us, down the banks of the river. The weather was slightly frosty, and the air clear and elastic. As we followed the windings of the noble rushing stream, at a height of seldom less than three hundred feet above his bed, the Doctor was busy pointing out the alternations of primitive sandstone and slate, and the great streams of volcanic bluestone which had poured from various points towards the deep glen in which the river flowed. Here, he would tell us, was formerly a lofty cascade, and a lake above it, but the river had worn through the sandstone bar, drained the lake, leaving nothing of the waterfall but two lofty cliffs, and a rapid. There again had come down a lava stream from Mirngish, which, cooled by the waters of the river, had stopped, and, accumulating, formed the lofty overhanging cliff on which we stood. He showed us how the fern-trees grew only in the still sheltered elbows facing northward, where the sun raised a warm steam from the river, and the cold south wind could not penetrate. He gathered for Mrs. Buckley a bouquet of the tender sweet-scented yellow oxalis, the winter flower of Australia, and showed us the copper-lizard basking on the red rocks, so like the stone on which he lay, that one could scarce see him till a metallic gleam betrayed him, as he slipped to his lair. And we, the elder of the party, who followed the Doctor's handsome little brown mare, kept our ears open, and spoke little—but gave ourselves fully up to the enjoyment of his learning and eloquence.

But the Doctor did not absorb the whole party; far from it. He had a rival. All the young men, and Miss Alice besides, were grouped round Captain Desborough. Frequently we elders, deep in some Old World history of the Doctor's, would be disturbed by a ringing peal of laughter from the other party, and then the Doctor would laugh, and we would all join; not that we had heard the joke, but from sheer sympathy with the hilarity of the young folks. Desborough was making himself agreeable, and who could do it better? He was telling the most outrageous of Irish stories, and making, on purpose, the most outrageous of Irish bulls. After a shout of laughter louder than the rest, the Doctor remarked:

"That's better for them than geology—eh, Mrs. Buckley?"

"And so my grandmother," we heard Desborough say, "waxed mighty wrath, and she up with her gold-headed walking-stick in the middle of Sackville Street, and says she, 'Ye villain, do ye think I don't know my own Blenheim spannel when I see him?' 'Indeed, my lady,' says Mike, ''twas himself tould me he belanged to Barney.' 'Who tould you?' says she. 'The dog himself tould me, my lady.' 'Ye thief of the world,' says my aunt, 'and ye'd believe a dog before a dowager countess? Give him up, ye villain, this minute, or I'll hit ye!'"

These were the sort of stories Desborough delighted in, making them up, he often confessed, as he went on. On this occasion, when he had done his story, they all rode up and joined us, and we stood admiring the river, stretching westward in pools of gold between black cliffs, towards the setting sun; then we turned homeward.

That evening Alice said, "Now do tell me, Captain Desborough, was that a true story about Lady Covetown's dog?"

"True!" said he. "What story worth hearing ever was true? The old lady lost her dog certainly, and claimed him of a dog-stealer in Sackville Street; but all the rest, my dear young lady, is historic romance."

" Mr. Hamlyn knows a good story," said Charley Hawker, " about Bougong Jack. Do tell it to us, Uncle Jeff."

" I don't think," I said, " that it has so much foundation in fact as Captain Desborough's. But there must be some sort of truth in it, for it comes from the old hands, and shows a little more sign of imagination than you would expect from them. It is a very stupid story too."

" Do tell it," they all said. So I complied, much in the same language as I tell it now:

" You know that these great snow-ranges which tower up to the west of us are, farther south, of great breadth, and that none have yet forced their way from the country of the Ovens and the Mitta Mitta through here to Gippsland.

" The settlers who have just taken up that country trying to penetrate to the eastward here towards us, find themselves stopped by a mighty granite wall. Any adventurous men, who may top that barrier, see nothing before them but range beyond range of snow Alps, intersected by precipitous cliffs, and frightful chasms.

" This westward range is called the Bougongs. The blacks during summer are in the habit of coming thus far to collect and feed on the great grey moths (Bougongs) which are found on the rocks. They used to report that a fine available country lies to the east embosomed in mountains, rendered fertile by perpetual snow-fed streams. This is the more credible, as it is evident that between the Bougong range on the west and the Warragong range on the extreme east, towards us, there is a breadth of at least eighty miles.

" There lived a few years ago, not very far from the Ovens River, a curious character, by name John Sampson. He had been educated at one of the great English universities, and was a good scholar, though he had been forced to leave the university, and, as report went, England too, for some great irregularity.

" He had money, and a share in his brother-in-law's station, although he never stayed there many months in the year. He was always away at some mischief or another. No horse-race or prize-fight could go on without him, and he himself never left one of these last-mentioned gatherings without finding someone to try conclusions with him. Beside this, he was a great writer and singer of comic songs, and a consummate horseman.

" One fine day he came back to his brother's station in serious trouble. Whether he had mistaken another man's horse for his own or not, I cannot say; but, at all events, he announced that a warrant was out against him for horse-stealing, and that he must go into hiding. So he took up his quarters at a little hut of his brother-in-law's, on the ranges, inhabited only by a stock-keeper and a black boy, and kept a young lubra in pay to watch down the glen for the police.

"One morning she came running into the hut, breathless, to say that a lieutenant and three troopers were riding towards the hut. Jack had just time to saddle and mount his horse before the police caught sight of him, and started after him at full speed.

"They hunted him into a narrow glen; a single cattle-track, not a foot broad, led on between a swollen rocky creek, utterly impassable by horse or man, and a lofty precipice of loose broken slate, on which one would have thought a goat could not have found a footing. The young police lieutenant had done his work well, and sent a trooper round to head him, so that Jack found himself between the devil and the deep sea. A tall armed trooper stood in front of him, behind was the lieutenant, on the right the creek, and on the left the precipice.

"They called out to him to surrender; but, giving one look before and behind, and seeing escape was hopeless, he hesitated not a moment, but put his horse at the cliff, and clambered up, rolling down tons of loose slate in his course. The lieutenant shut his eyes, expecting to see horse and man roll down into the creek, and only opened them in time to see Jack stand for a moment on the summit against the sky, and then disappear.

"He disappeared over the top of the cliff, and so he was lost to the ken of white men for the space of four years. His sister and brother-in-law mourned for him as dead, and mourned sincerely, for they and all who knew him liked him well. But at the end of that time, on a wild winter's night, he came back to them, dressed in opossum skins, with scarce a vestige of European clothing about him. His beard had grown down over his chest, and he had nearly forgotten his mother tongue, but, when speech came to him again, he told them a strange story.

"It was winter time when he rode away. All the tablelands were deep with snow; and, when he had escaped the policemen, he had crossed the first of the great ridges on the same night. He camped in the valley he found on the other side; and, having his gun and some ammunition with him, he fared well.

"He was beyond the country which had ever been trodden by white men, and now, for the mere sake of adventure, he determined to go farther still, and see if he could cross the great White

Mountains, which had hitherto been considered an insurmountable barrier.

"For two days he rode over a high tableland, deep in snow. Here and there, in a shallow sheltered valley, he would find just grass enough to keep his horse alive, but nothing for himself. On the third night he saw before him another snow-ridge, too far off to reach without rest, and, tethering his horse in a little crevice between the rocks, he prepared to walk to and fro all night, to keep off the deadly snow sleepiness that he felt coming over him. 'Let me but see what is beyond that next ridge,' he said, 'and I will lie down and die.'

"And now, as the stillness of the night came on, and the Southern Cross began to twinkle brilliantly above the blinding snow, he was startled once more by a sound which had fallen on his ear several times during his toilsome afternoon journey: a sound as of a sudden explosion, mingled, strangely too, with the splintering of broken glass. At first he thought it was merely the booming in his ears, or the rupture of some vessel in his bursting head. Or was it fancy? No; there it was again, clearer than before. That was no noise in his head, for the patient horse turned and looked towards the place where the sound came from. Thunder? The air was clear and frosty, and not a cloud stained the sky. There was some mystery beyond that snow-ridge worth living to see.

"He lived to see it. For, an hour after daybreak next morning, he, leading his horse, stumbled over the snow-covered rocks that bounded his view, and, when he reached the top, there burst on his sight a scene that made him throw up his arms and shout aloud.

"Before him, pinnacle after pinnacle, towered up a mighty Alp, blazing in the morning sun. Down through a black rift on its side, wound a gleaming glacier, which hurled its shattered ice crystals over a dark cliff, into the deep profound blue of a lake, which stretched north and south, studded with green woody islets, almost as far as the eye could see. Toward the mountain the lake looked deep and gloomy, but, on the other side, showed many a pleasant yellow shallow, and sandy bay, while between him and the lake lay a mile or so of park-like meadow-land, in the full verdure of winter. As he looked, a vast dislocated mass of ice fell crashing from the glacier into the lake, and solved at once the mystery of the noises he had heard the night before.

"He descended into the happy valley, and found a small tribe of friendly blacks, who had never before seen the face of white man, and who supposed him to be one of their own tribe, dead long ago, who had come back to them, renovated and beautified, from the other world. With these he lived a pleasant slothful life, while four years went on, forgetting all the outside world, till his horse was dead, his gun rusted and thrown aside, and his European clothes long since replaced by the skin of the opossum and the koala. He had forgotten his own tongue, and had given up all thoughts of crossing again the desolate barriers of snow which divided him from civilisation, when a slight incident brought back old associations to his mind, and roused him from sleep.

"In some hunting excursion he got a slight scratch, and, searching for some linen to tie it up, found in his mi-mi an old waistcoat, which he had worn when he came into the valley. In the lining, while tearing it up, he found a crumpled paper, a note from his sister, written years before, full of sisterly kindness and tenderness. He read it again and again before he lay down, and the next morning, collecting such small stock of provisions as he could, he started on the homeward track, and after incredible hardships reached his station.

"His brother-in-law tried in vain with a strong party to reach the lake, but never succeeded. What mountain it was he discovered, or what river is fed by the lake he lived on, no man knows to this day. Some say he went mad, and lived in the ranges all the time, and that this was all a mere madman's fancy. But, whether he was mad or not then, he is sane enough now, and has married a wife, and settled down to be one of the most thriving men in that part of the country.

"Well," said the Doctor, thrusting his fists deep into his breeches pockets, "I don't believe that story."

"Nor I either, Doctor," I replied. "But it has amused you all for half an hour; so let it pass."

"Oh!" said the Doctor, rather peevishly, "if you put it on those grounds, I am bound, of course, to withhold a few little criticisms I was inclined to make on its probability. I hope you won't go and pass it off as authentic, you know, because if we once begin to entertain these sort of legends as meaning anything, the whole history of the country becomes one great fog-bank, through which the devil himself could not find his way."

"Now, for my part," said mischievous Alice, "I think it a very pretty story. And I have no doubt that it is every word of it true."

"Oh, dear me, then," said the Doctor, "let us vote it true. And, while we are about it, let us believe that the Sydney ghost actually did sit on a three-rail fence, smoking its pipe, and directing an anxious crowd of relatives where to find its body. By all means let us believe everything we hear."

The next morning our pleasant party suffered a loss. Captain Brentwood and Alice went off home. He was wanted there, and all things seemed so tranquil that he thought it was foolish to stay away any longer. Cecil Mayford, too, departed, carrying with him the affectionate farewells of the whole party. His pleasant even temper, and his handsome face, had won every one who knew him, and, though he never talked much, yet, when he was gone, we all missed his merry laugh, after one of Desborough's good stories. Charley Hawker went off with him, too, and spent a few hours with Ellen Mayford, much to his satisfaction, but came in again at night, as his mother had prayed of him not to leave the Major's till he had seen her again.

That night, the Major proposed punch, and, after Mrs. Buckley had gone to bed, Sam sang a song, and Desborough told a story, about a gamekeeper of his uncle's, whom the old gentleman desired to start in an independent way of business. So he built him a new house, and gave him a keg of whisky, to start in the spirit-selling line. "But the first night," said Desborough, "the villain finished the whisky himself, broke the keg, and burnt the house down; so my uncle had to take him back into service again after all." And after this came other stories, equally preposterous, and we went rather late to bed.

And the next morning, too, I am afraid, we were rather late for breakfast. Just as we were sitting down, in came Captain Brentwood.

"Hallo," said the Major; "what brings you back so soon, old friend. Nothing the matter, I hope?"

"Nothing but business," he replied. "I am going on to Dickson's, and I shall be back home to-night, I hope. I am glad to find you so late, as I have had no breakfast, and have ridden ten miles."

He took breakfast with us and went on. The morning passed somewhat heavily, as a morning is apt to do, after sitting up late and drinking punch. Towards noon Desborough said:

"Now, if anybody will confess that he drank just three drops too much punch last night, I will do the same. Mrs. Buckley, my dear lady, I hope you will order plenty of pale ale for lunch."

Lunch passed pleasantly enough, and afterwards the Major, telling Sam to move a table outside into the veranda, disappeared, and soon came back with a very "curious" bottle of Madeira. We sat then in the veranda smoking for about a quarter of an hour.

I remember every word that was spoken, and every trivial circumstance that happened during that quarter of an hour; they are burnt into my memory as if by fire. The Doctor was raving about English poetry, as usual, saying, however, that the modern English poets, good as they were, had lost the power of melody a good deal. This the Major denied, quoting.

"By torch and trumpet fast array'd."

"Fifty such lines, sir, are not worth one of Milton's," said the Doctor.   "The trumpet spake not to the armed throng."

There's melody for you; there's a blare and a clang; there's a——"

I heard no more. Mrs. Buckley's French clock, in the house behind, chimed three quarters past one, and I heard a sound of two persons coming quickly through the house.

Can you tell the step of him who brings evil tidings? I think I can. At all events, I felt my heart grow cold when I heard those footsteps. I heard them coming through the house, across the boarded floor. The one was a rapid, firm, military footstep, accompanied with the clicking of a spur, and the other was unmistakably the "pad, pad" of a blackfellow.

We all turned round and looked at the door. There stood the sergeant of Desborough's troopers, pale and silent, and close behind him, clinging to him as if for protection, was the lithe naked figure of a black lad, looking from behind the sergeant, with terrified visage, first at one and then at another of us.

I saw disaster in their faces, and would have held up my hand to warn him not to speak before Mrs. Buckley. But I was too late, for he had spoken. And then we sat for a minute, looking at one another, each man seeing the reflection of his own horror in his neighbour's eyes.

CHAPTER XL

THE STORM BURSTS

POOR little Cecil Mayford had left us about nine o'clock in the morning of the day before this, and, accompanied by Charles Hawker, reached his mother's station about eleven o'clock in the day.

All the way Charles had talked incessantly of Ellen, and Cecil joined in Charles's praises of his sister, and joked with him for being " awfully spooney " about her.

" You're worse about my sister, Charley," said he, " than old Sam is about Miss Brentwood. He takes things quiet enough, but if you go on in this style till you are old enough to marry, by Jove, there'll be nothing of you left! "

" I wonder if she would have me? " said Charles, not heeding him.

" The best thing you can do is to ask her," said Cecil. " I think I know what she would say, though."

They reached Mrs. Mayford's, and spent a few pleasant hours together. Charles started home again about three o'clock, and having gone a little way turned to look back. The brother and sister stood at the house door still. He waved his hand in farewell to them, and they replied. Then he rode on and saw them no more.

Cecil and Ellen went into the house to their mother. The women worked, and Cecil read aloud to them. The book was *Waverley;* I saw it afterwards, and when supper was over he took it up to begin reading again.

" Not that book to-night, my boy," said his mother. " Read us a chapter out of the Bible. I am very low in my mind, and at such times I like to hear the Word."

He read the Good Book to them till quite late. Both he and Ellen thought it strange that their mother should insist on that book on a week-night; they never usually read it, save on Sunday evenings.

The morning broke bright and frosty. Cecil was abroad betimes, and went down the paddock to fetch the horses. He put them in the stock-yard, and stood for a time close to the stable, talking to a tame black lad, that they employed about the place.

His attention was attracted by a noise of horses' feet. He looked up and saw about a dozen men riding swiftly and silently across the paddock towards the house.

For an instant he seems to have idly wondered who they were, and have had time to notice a thick-set gaudily dressed man, who rode in front of the others, when the kitchen door was thrown suddenly open, and the old hut-keeper, with his grey hair waving in the wind, run out, crying, " Save yourself, in God's name, Master Cecil. The bushrangers! "

Cecil raised his clenched hands in wild despair. They were caught like birds in a trap. No hope!—no escape! Nothing left for it now, but to die red-handed. He dashed into the house with the old hut-keeper and shut the door.

The black lad ran up to a little rocky knoll within two hundred yards of the house, and, hiding himself, watched what went on. He saw the bushrangers ride up to the door and dismount. Then they began to beat the door and demand admittance. Then the door was burst down, and one of them fell dead by pistol-shot. Then they rushed in tumultuously, leaving one outside to mind the horses. Then the terrified boy heard the dull sound of shots fired rapidly inside the building, and then all was comparatively still for a time.

Then there began to arise a wild sound of brutal riot within, and after a time they poured out again, and mounting, rode away.

Then the black boy slipped down from his lair like a snake, and stole towards the house. All was still as death. The door was open, but, poor little savage as he was, he dared not enter. Once he thought he heard a movement within, and listened intently with all his faculties, as only a savage can listen, but all was still again. And then gathering courage, he went in.

In the entrance, stepping over the body of the dead bushranger, he found the poor old white-headed hut-keeper knocked down and killed in the first rush. He went on into the parlour; and there— oh, lamentable sight!—was Cecil; clever, handsome little Cecil, our old favourite, lying across the sofa, shot through the heart, dead.

But not alone. No; prone along the floor, covering six feet or more of ground, lay the hideous corpse of Moody, the cannibal. The red-headed miscreant, who had murdered poor Lee, under George Hawker's directions.

I think the poor black boy would have felt in his dumb, darkened heart some sorrow at seeing his kind old master so cruelly murdered. Perhaps he would have raised the death-cry of his tribe over him, and burnt himself with fire, as their custom is; but he was too terrified at seeing so many of the lordly white race prostrated by one another's hands. He stood and trembled, and then, almost in a whisper, began to call for Mrs. Mayford.

"Missis," he said, "Miss Ellen! All pull away, bushranger chaps. Make a light, good Missis. Plenty frightened this fellow."

No answer. No sign of Mrs. Mayford or Ellen. They must have escaped then. We will try to hope so. The black boy peered into one chamber after another, but saw no signs of them, only the stillness of death over all.

Let us leave this accursed house, lest prying too closely, we may find crouching in some dark corner a Gorgon, who will freeze us into stone.

The black lad stripped himself naked as he was born, and running like a deer, sped to Major Buckley's before the south wind, across the plain. There he found the Sergeant, and told him his tale, and the Sergeant and he broke in on us with the terrible news as we were sitting merrily over our wine.

CHAPTER XLI

WIDDERIN SHOWS CLEARLY THAT HE IS WORTH ALL THE MONEY SAM GAVE FOR HIM

THE Sergeant, as I said, broke in upon us with the fearful news as we sat at wine. For a minute no man spoke, but all sat silent and horror-struck. Only the Doctor rose quietly, and slipped out of the room unnoticed.

Desborough spoke first. He rose up with deadly wrath in his face, and swore a fearful oath, an oath so fearful, that he who endorsed every word of it then, will not write it down now. To the effect, " That he would take neither meat, nor drink, nor pleasure, nor rest, beyond what was necessary to keep body and soul together, before he had purged the land of these treacherous villains! "

Charles Hawker went up to the Sergeant, with a livid face and shaking hands: " Will you tell me again, Robinson, *are they all dead?* "

The Sergeant looked at him compassionately. " Well, sir," he said, " the boy seemed to think Mrs. and Miss Mayford had escaped. But you mustn't trust what he says, sir."

" You are deceiving me," said Charles. " There is something you are hiding from me. I shall go down there this minute, and see."

" You will do nothing of the kind, sir," said Mrs. Buckley, coming into the doorway and confronting him; " your place is with Captain Desborough. I am going down to look after Ellen."

During these few moments, Sam had stood stupefied. He stepped up to the Sergeant, and said:

" Would you tell me which way they went from the Mayfords'? "

" Down the river, sir."

" Ah! " said Sam; " towards Captain Brentwood's, and Alice at home, and alone!—There may be time yet."

He ran out of the room and I after him. " His first trouble," I thought,—" his first trial. How will our boy behave now? "

Let me mention again that the distance from the Mayfords' to Captain Brentwood's, following the windings of the river on its right bank, was nearly twenty miles. From Major Buckley's to the same point, across the plains, was barely ten; so that there was still a chance that a brave man on a good horse, might reach Captain Brentwood's before the bushrangers, in spite of the start they had got.

Sam's noble horse, Widderin, a horse with a pedigree a hundred years old, stood in the stable. The buying of that horse had been Sam's only extravagance, for which he had often reproached himself, and now this day, he would see whether he would get his money's worth out of that horse, or no.

I followed him up to the stable, and found him putting the bridle on Widderin's beautiful little head. Neither of us spoke, only when I handed him the saddle, and helped him with the girths, he said, "God bless you."

I ran out and got down the slip-rails for him. As he rode by he said, "Good-bye, Uncle Jeff, perhaps you won't see me again;" and I cried out, "Remember your God and your mother, Sam, and don't do anything foolish."

Then he was gone; and looking across the plains the way he should go, I saw another horseman toiling far away, and recognised Dr. Mulhaus. Good Doctor! he had seen the danger in a moment, and by his ready wit had got a start of everyone else by ten minutes.

The Doctor, on his handsome long-bodied Arabian mare, was making good work of it across the plains, when he heard the rush of horse's feet behind him, and turning, he saw tall Widderin bestridden by Sam, springing over the turf, gaining on him stride after stride. In a few minutes they were alongside of one another.

"Good lad!" cried the Doctor; "on, forwards; catch her, and away to the woods with her. Bloodhound Desborough will be on their trail in half an hour. Save her, and we will have noble vengeance."

Sam only waved his hand in good-bye, and sped on across the plain like a solitary ship at sea. He steered for a single tree, now becoming dimly visible, at the foot of Organ hill.

The good horse, with elastic and easy motion, fled on his course like a bird; lifting his feet clearly and rapidly through the grass. The brisk south wind filled his wide nostrils as he turned his graceful neck from side to side, till, finding that work was meant, and not play, he began to hold his head straight before him, and rush steadily forward.

And Sam, poor Sam! All his hopes for life are now brought down to this: to depend on the wind and pluck of an unconscious horse. One stumble now, and it were better to lie down on the plain and die. He was in the hands of God, and he felt it. He said one short prayer, but that towards the end was interrupted by the wild current of his thoughts.

Was there any hope? They, the devils, would have been drinking at the Mayfords', and perhaps would go slow; or would they ride fast and wild? After thinking a short time, he feared the latter. They had tasted blood, and knew that the country would be roused on them shortly. On, on, good horse!

The lonely shepherd on the plains, sleepily watching his feeding sheep, looked up as Sam went speeding by, and thought how fine a thing it would be to be dressed like that, and have nothing to do but ride blood-horses to death. Mind your sheep, good shepherd; perhaps it were better for you to do that and nothing more all your life, than to carry in your breast for one short hour such a volcano of rage, indignation, and terror, as he does who hurries unheeding through your scattered flock.

Here are a brace of good pistols, and they, with care, shall give account, if need be, of two men. After that, nothing. It were better, so much better, not to live if one were only ten minutes too late. The Doctor would be up soon; not much matter if he were, though, only another life gone.

The Organ hill, a cloud of misty blue when he started, now hung in aerial fluted cliffs above his head. As he raced across the long glacis which lay below the hill, he could see a solitary eagle wheeling round the topmost pinnacles, against the clear blue sky; then the hill was behind him, and before him another stretch of plain, bounded by timber, which marked the course of the river.

Brave Widderin had his ears back now, and was throwing his breath regularly through his nostrils in deep sighs. Good horse, only a little longer; bear thyself bravely this day, and then pleasant pastures for thee till thou shalt go the way of all horses. Many a time has she patted, with kind words, thy rainbow neck, my horse; help us to save her now.

Alas! good willing brute, he cannot understand; only he knows that his kind master is on his back, and so he will run till he drops. Good Widderin! think of the time when thy sire rushed triumphant through the shouting thousands at Epsom, and all England heard that Arcturus had won the Derby. Think of the time when thy grandam, carrying Sheik Abdullah, bore down in a whirlwind of sand on the toiling affrighted caravan. Ah! thou knowest not of these things, but yet thy speed flags not. We are not far off now, good horse, we shall know all soon.

Now he was in the forest again, and now, as he rode quickly down the steep sandy road among the bracken, he heard the hoarse rush of the river in his ears, and knew the end was well-nigh come.

No drink now, good Widderin! a bucket of champagne in an hour's time, if thou wilt only stay not now to bend thy neck down to the clear gleaming water; flounder through the ford, and just twenty yards up the bank by the cherry-tree, we shall catch sight of the house, and know our fate.

Now the house was in sight, and now he cried aloud some wild inarticulate sound of thankfulness and joy. All was as peaceful as ever, and Alice, unconscious, stood white-robed in the veranda, feeding her birds.

As he rode up he shouted out to her and beckoned. She came running through the house, and met him breathless at the doorway. "The bushrangers! Alice, my love," he said. "We must fly this instant, they are close to us now."

She had been prepared for this. She knew her duty well, for her father had often told her what to do. No tears! no hysterics! She took Sam's hand without a word, and placing her fairy foot upon his boot, vaulted up into the saddle before him, crying, "Eleanor, Eleanor!"

Eleanor, the cook, came running out. "Fly!" said Alice. "Get away into the bush. The gang are coming; close by." She, an old Vandemonian, needed no second warning, and as the two young people rode away, they saw her clearing the paddock rapidly, and making for a dense clump of wattles, which grew just beyond the fence.

"Whither now, Sam?" said Alice, the moment they were started.

"I should feel safer across the river," he replied; "that little wooded knoll would be a fine hiding-place, and they will come down this side of the river from Mayfords'."

"From Mayfords'! why, have they been there?"

"They have, indeed. Alas! poor Cecil."

"What has happened to him? nothing serious?"

"Dead; my love, dead."

"Oh! poor little Cecil," she cried, "that we were all so fond of. And Mrs. Mayford and Ellen?"

"They have escaped!—they are not to be found—they have hidden away somewhere."

They crossed the river, and dismounting, they led the tired horse up the steep slope of turf that surrounded a little castellated tor of bluestone. Here they would hide till the storm was gone by, for from here they could see the windings of the river, and all the broad plain stretched out beneath their feet.

"I do not see them anywhere, Alice," said Sam presently. "I see no one coming across the plains. They must be either very near us in the hollow of the river-valley, or else a long way off. I have very little doubt they will come here, though, sooner or later."

"There they are!" said Alice. "Surely there are a large party of horsemen on the plain, but they are seven or eight miles off."

"Ay, ten," said Sam. "I am not sure they are horsemen." Then he said suddenly in a whisper, "Lie down, my love, in God's name! Here they are, close to us!"

There burst on his ear a confused sound of talking and laughing, and out of one of the rocky gullies leading towards the river, came the men they had been flying from, in number about fourteen. They had crossed the river, for some unknown reason, and to the fear-struck hiders it seemed as though they were making straight towards their lair.

He had got Widderin's head in his breast, blindfolding him with his coat, for should he neigh now, they were undone, indeed! As the bushrangers approached, the horse began to get uneasy, and paw the ground, putting Sam in such an agony of terror that the sweat rolled down his face. In the midst of this he felt a hand on his arm, and Alice's voice, which he scarcely recognised, said, in a fierce whisper:

"Give me one of your pistols, sir!"

"Leave that to me!" he replied in the same tone.

"As you please," she said; "but I must not fall alive into their hands. Never look your mother in the face again if I do."

He gave one more glance round, and saw that the enemy would come within a hundred yards of their hiding-place. Then he held the horse faster than ever, and shut his eyes.

Was it a minute only, or an hour, till they heard the sound of the voices dying away in the roar of the river; and, opening their eyes once more, looked into one another's faces?

Faces, they thought, that they had never seen before—so each told the other afterwards—so wild, so haggard, and so strange! And now that they were safe and free again—free to arise and leave their dreadful rock prison, and wander away where they would, they could scarcely believe that the danger was past.

They came out silently from among the crags, and took up another station, where they could see all that went on. They saw the miscreants swarming about the house, and heard a pistol-shot—only one.

"Who can they be firing at?" said Alice, in a subdued tone. They were both so utterly appalled by their late danger, that they spoke in whispers, though the enemy were a quarter of a mile off.

"Mere mischief, I should fancy," said Sam; "there is no one there. Oh! Alice, my love, can you realise that we are safe?"

"Hardly yet, Sam! But who could those men be we saw at such a distance on the plain? Could they have been cattle? I am seldom deceived, you know; I can see an immense distance."

"Why," said Sam, "I had forgotten them! They must be our friends, on these fellows' tracks. Desborough would not be long starting, I know."

"I hope my father," said Alice, "will hear nothing till he sees me. Poor father! what a state he will be in. See, there is a horseman close to us. It is the Doctor!"

They saw Dr. Mulhaus ride up to one of the heights overlooking the river, and reconnoitre. Seeing the men in the house, he began riding down towards them.

"He will be lost!" said Alice. "He thinks we are there. Cooee Sam, at all risks."

Sam did so, and they saw the Doctor turn. Alice showed herself for a moment, and then he turned back, and rode the way he had come. In a few minutes he joined them from the rear, and, taking Alice in his arms, kissed her heartily.

"So our jewel is safe, then—praise be to God! Thanks due also to a brave man and a good horse. This is the last station those devils will ruin, for our friends are barely four miles off. I saw them just now."

"I wish, I only wish," said Sam, "that they may delay long enough to be caught. I would give a good deal for that."

There was but little chance of that though; their measures were too well taken. Almost as Sam spoke, the three listeners heard a shrill whistle, and immediately the enemy began mounting. Some of them were evidently drunk, and could hardly get on their horses, but were assisted by the others. But very shortly they were all clear off, heading to the north-west.

"Now we may go down, and see what destruction has been done," said Alice. "Who would have thought to see such times as these!"

"Stay a little," said the Doctor, "and let us watch these gentlemen's motions. Where can they be going nor'-west—straight on to the mountains?"

"I am of the opinion," said Sam, "that they are going to lie up in one of the gullies this evening. They are full of drink and madness, and they don't know what they are about. If they get into the main system of gullies, we shall have them like rats in a trap, for they can never get out by the lower end. Do you see, Doctor, a little patch of white road among the trees over there? That leads to the Limestone Gates, as we call it. If they pass those walls upwards, they are confined as in a pound. Watch the white road, and we shall see."

The piece of road alluded to was about two miles off, and winding round a steep hill among trees. Only one turn in it was visible, and over this, as they watched, they saw a dark spot pass, followed by a crowd of others.

"There they go," said Sam. "The madmen are safe now. See, there comes Desborough, and all of them; let us go down."

They turned to go, and saw Jim coming towards them, by the route that Sam had come, all bespattered with clay, limping and leading his new grey horse, dead lame.

He threw up his hat when he saw them, and gave a feeble hurrah! but even then a twinge of pain shot across his face, and, when he was close, they saw he was badly hurt.

"God save you, my dear sister," he said; "I have been in such a state of mind; God forgive me, I have been cursing the day I was born. Sam, I started about three minutes after you, and had very nearly succeeded in overhauling the Doctor, about two miles from here, when this brute put his foot in a crab hole, and came down, rolling on my leg. I was so bruised I couldn't mount again, and so I have walked. I see you are all right though, and that is enough for me. Oh, my sister—my darling Alice! Think what we have escaped!"

So they went towards the house. And when Major Buckley caught sight of Alice, riding between Dr. Mulhaus and Sam, he gave such a stentorian cheer that the retreating bushrangers must have heard it.

"Well ridden, gentlemen," he said. "And who won the race? Was it Widderin, or the Arabian, or the nondescript Sydney importation?"

"The Sydney importation, sir, would have beaten the Arabian, barring accident," said Jim. "But, seriously speaking, I should have been far too late to be of any service."

"And I," said the Doctor, "also. Sam won the race, and has got the prize. Now, let us look forward, and not backward."

They communicated to Desborough all particulars, and told him of the way they had seen the bushrangers go. Everyone was struck with the change in him. No merry stories now. The laughing Irishman was gone, and a stern, gloomy man, more like an Englishman, stood in his place. I heard after, that he deeply blamed himself (though no one else thought of doing so), and thought he had not taken full precautions. On the present occasion he said:

"Well, gentlemen, night is closing in. Major Buckley, I think you will agree with me that we should act more effectually if we waited till daylight, and refresh both horses and men. More particularly as the enemy in the drunken madness have hampered themselves in the mountains. Major, Dr. Mulhaus, and Mr. Halbert, you are military men—what do you say?"

They agreed that there was no doubt. It would be much the best plan.

"I would sooner he'd have gone to-night and got it over," said Charles Hawker, taking Sam's arm. "Oh! Sam, Sam! Think of poor Cecil! Think of poor Ellen, when she hears what has happened. She must know by now!"

"Poor Charley," said Sam, "I am so sorry for you! Lie down, and get to sleep; the sun is going down."

He lay down as he was bid, somewhere out of the way. He was crushed and stunned. He hardly seemed to know at present what he was doing. After a time, Sam went in and found him sleeping uneasily.

But Alice was in sad tribulation at the mischief done. All her pretty little womanly ornaments overturned and broken, her piano battered to pieces, and, worst of all, her poor kangaroo shot dead, lying in the veranda. "Oh!" said she to Major Buckley, "you must think me very wicked to think of such things at a time like this, but I cannot help it. There is something so shocking to me in such a sudden *bouleversement* of old order. Yet, if it shocks me to see my piano broken, how terrible must a visitation like the Mayfords' be! These are not the times for moralising, however. I must see about entertaining the garrison."

Eleanor, the cook, had come back from her lair quite unconcerned. She informed the company, in a nonchalant sort of way, that this was the third adventure of the kind she had been engaged in, and, that although they seemed to make a great fuss about it, on the other side (Van Diemen's Land), it was considered a mere necessary nuisance; and so proceeded to prepare such supper as she could. In the same off-hand way she remarked to Sam, when he went into the kitchen to get a light for his pipe, that, if it was true that Mike Howe had crossed and was among them, they had better look out for squalls; for that he was a devil, and no mistake.

Desborough determined to set a watch out on the road towards the mouth of the gully, where they were supposed to be. "We shall have them in the morning," said he. "Let everyone get to sleep who can sleep, for I expect everyone to follow me to-morrow."

Charles Hawker had lain down in an inner room and was sleeping uneasily, when he was awakened by some one, and, looking up, saw Major Buckley, with a light in his hand, bending over him. He started up.

"What is the matter, sir?" he asked. "Why do you look at me so strangely? Is there any new misfortune?"

"Charles," said the Major, "you have no older friend than me."

"I know it, sir. What do you want me to do?"

"I want you to stay at home to-morrow."

"Anything but that, sir. They will call me a coward."

"No one shall do so. I swear that he who calls you a coward shall feel the weight of my arm."

"Why am I not to go with them? Why am I to be separated from the others?"

"You must not ask," said the Major; "perhaps you will know some day, but not yet. All I say to you is, go home to your mother to-morrow, and stay there. Should you fire a shot, or strike a blow against those men we are going to hunt down, you may do a deed which would separate you from the rest of mankind, and leave you to drag on a miserable guilty life. Do you promise?"

"I will promise," said Charles; "but I wonder——"

"Never mind wondering. Good night."

The troopers lay in the hall, and in the middle of the night there was a sound of a horse outside, and he who was nearest the door got up and went out.

"Who is there?" said the voice of Captain Brentwood.

"Jackson, sir."

"My house has been stuck up, has it not?"

"Yes, sir."

" And my daughter ? "

" Safe, sir. Young Mr. Buckley rode over and caught her up out of it ten minutes before they got here."

" Long life to him, and glory to God. Who is here ? "

The trooper enumerated them.

" And what has become of the gang ? " asked the Captain.

" Gone into the limestone gully, sir. Safe for to-morrow."

" Ah, well, I shall come in and lie in the hall. Don't make a noise. What is that ? "

They both started. Some one of the many sleepers, with that strange hoarse voice peculiar to those who talk in their dreams, said, with singular energy and distinctness:

" I will go, sir; they will call me coward."

" That's young Mr. Hawker, sir," said the trooper. " His sweetheart's brother, Mr. Mayford, was killed by them yesterday. The head of this very gang, sir, that villain Touan—his name is Hawker. An odd coincidence, sir."

" Very odd," said the Captain. " At the same time, Jackson, if I were you, I wouldn't talk about it. There are many things one had best not talk about, Jackson. Pull out the corner of that blanket, will you ? So we shall have some fun to-morrow, up in the pass, I'm thinking."

" They'll fight, sir," said the trooper. " If we can bail them up, they'll fight, believe me. Better so; I think we shall save the hangman some trouble. Good night, sir."

So Captain Brentwood lay down beside the trooper, and slept the sleep of the just among his broken chairs and tables. The others slept too, sound and quiet, as though there were no fight on the morrow.

But ere the moon grew pale they were awakened by Desborough, tramping about with clicking spurs among the sleepers, and giving orders in a loud voice. At the first movement, while the rest were yawning and stretching themselves, and thinking that battle was not altogether so desirable on a cold morning as it was overnight, Major Buckley was by Charles Hawker's bedside, and, reminding him of his promise, got him out unperceived, helped him to saddle his horse, and started him off to his mother with a note.

The lad, overawed by the Major's serious manner, went without debate, putting the note in his pocket. I have seen that note; Sam showed it to me the next day, and so I can give you the contents. It was from Major Buckley to Mary Hawker, and ran thus:

I have sent your boy to you, dear old friend, bearing this. You will have heard by now what has happened, and you will give me credit for preventing what might come to be a terrible catastrophe. The boy is utterly unconscious that his own father is the man whose life is sought this day above all others. He is at the head of this gang, Mary. My own son saw him yesterday. My hand shall not be raised against him; but further than that I will not interfere. Your troubles have come now to the final and most terrible pass; and all the advice I have to give you is to pray, and pray continually, till this awful storm is gone by. Remember, that come what may, you have two friends entirely devoted to you —my wife and myself.

Hurriedly written, scrawled rather as this note was, it showed me again plainer than ever, what a noble, clear-hearted man he was who had written it. But this is not to the purpose. Charles Hawker departed, carrying this, before the others were stirring, and held his way through the forest-road towards his mother's station.

This same two days' business was the best stroke of work that the Devil did in that part of the country for many years. With his usual sagacity he had busied himself in drawing the threads of mischief so parallel, that it seemed they must end in one and only one lamentable issue; namely, that Charles Hawker and his father should meet, pistol in hand, as deadly enemies. But at this last period of the game, our good, honest Major completely checkmated him, by sending Charles Hawker home to his mother. In this terrible pass, after this unexpected move of the Major's, he (the Devil, no other) began casting about for a scoundrel, by whose assistance he might turn the Major's flank. But no great rogue being forthcoming he had to look round for the next best substitute, a great fool—and one of these he found immediately, riding exactly the way he wished. Him he subpœnaed immediately, and found to do his work better even than a good rogue would have done. We shall see how poor Charles Hawker, pricking along through the forest, getting every moment farther from danger and mischief, met a man charging along the road, full speed, who instantly pulled up and spoke to him.

This was the consummate fool, sent of the Devil, whom I have mentioned above. We have seen him before. He was the longest, brownest, stupidest of the Hawbuck family. The one who could spit farther than any of his brothers.

"Well, Charley," he said, "is this all true about the bush-rangers?"

Charles said it was. And they were bailed up in the limestone gully, and all the party were away after them.

"Where are you going then?" asked the unfortunate young idiot.

"Home to my mother," blurted out poor Charles.

"Well!" said the other, speaking unconsciously exactly the words which the enemy of mankind desired. "Well, I couldn't have believed that. If a chap had said that of you in my hearing, I'd have fought him if he'd been as big as a house. I never thought that of you, Charley."

Charles cursed aloud. "What have I done to be talked to like this? Major Buckley has no right to send me away like this, to be branded as coward through the countryside. Ten times over better to be shot than have such words as these said to me. I shall go back with you."

"That's the talk," said the poor fool. "I thought I wasn't wrong in you, Charley." And so Charles galloped back with him.

We, in the meantime, had started from the station, ere day was well broke. Foremost of the company rode Desborough, calm and serene, and on either side of him Captain Brentwood and Major Buckley. Then came the Doctor, Sam, Jim, Halbert, and myself; behind us again, five troopers and the Sergeant. Each man of us all was armed with a sword; and every man in that company, as it happened, knew the use of that weapon well. The troopers carried carbines, and all of us carried pistols.

The glare in the east changing from pearly green to golden yellow, gave notice of the coming sun. One snow peak, Tambo I think, began to catch the light, and blaze like another morning star. The day had begun in earnest, and, as we entered the mouth of the glen to which we were bound, slanting gleams of light were already piercing the misty gloom, and lighting up the loftier crags.

A deep, rock-walled glen it was, open and level; though, in the centre, ran a tangled waving line of evergreen shrubs, marking the course of a pretty bright creek, which, half-hidden by luxuriant vegetation, ran beside the faint track leading to one of Captain Brentwood's mountain huts. Along this track we could plainly see the hoof marks of the men we were after.

It was one of the most beautiful gullies I had ever seen, and I turned to say so to some one who rode beside me. Conceive my horror at finding it was Charles Hawker! I turned to him fiercely, and said:

" Get back, Charles. Go home. You don't know what you are doing, lad."

He defied me. And I was speaking roughly to him again, when there came a puff of smoke from among the rocks overhead, and down I went, head over heels. A bullet had grazed my thigh, and killed my horse, who, throwing me on my head, rendered me *hors de combat*. So that during the fight which followed, I was sitting on a rock, very sick and very stupid, a mile from the scene of action.

My catastrophe caused only a temporary stoppage; and, during the confusion, Charles Hawker was unnoticed. The man who had fired at me (why at me I cannot divine), was evidently a solitary guard perched among the rocks. The others held on for about a quarter of an hour, till the valley narrowed up again, just leaving room for the track, between the brawling creek and the tall limestone cliff. But after this it opened out into a broader amphitheatre, walled on all sides by inaccessible rock, save in two places. Sam, from whom I got this account of affairs, had just time to notice this, when he saw Captain Brentwood draw a pistol and fire it, and, at the same instant, a man dashed out of some scrub on the other side of the creek, and galloped away up the valley.

" They have had the precaution to set two watches for us, which I hardly expected," said Captain Desborough. " They will fight us now, they can't help it, thank God. They have had a sharp turn and a merry one, but they are dead men, and they know it. The Devil is but a poor paymaster, Buckley. After all this hide-and-seek work, they have only got two days' liberty."

The troopers now went to the front with Halbert and the other military men, while Sam, Jim, and Charles, the last all unperceived by the Major in his excitement, rode in the rear.

" We are going to have a regular battle," said Jim. " They are bailed up, and must fight: some of us will go home feet foremost to-day."

So they rode on through the open forest, till they began to see one or two horsemen through the tree stems, reconnoitring. The ground began to rise towards a lofty cliff that towered before them, and all could see that the end was coming. Then they caught sight of the whole gang, scattered about among the low shrubs, and a few shots were fired on both sides, before the enemy turned and retreated towards the wall of rock, now plainly visible through the timber. Our party continued to advance steadily in open order.

Then under the beetling crags, where the fern-trees began to feather up among the fallen boulders, the bushrangers turned like hunted wolves, and stood at bay.

CHAPTER XLII

THE FIGHT AMONG THE FERN-TREES

THEN Captain Desborough cried aloud to ride at them, and spare no man. And, as he spoke, every golden fern-bough, and every coign of vantage among the rocks, began to blaze and crackle with gun and pistol shot. Jim's horse sprung aloft and fell, hurling him forcibly to the ground, and a tall young trooper, dropping his carbine, rolled heavily off his saddle, and lay on the grass face downward, quite still, as if asleep.

"There's the first man killed," said the Major very quietly. "Sam, my boy, don't get excited, but close on the first fellow you see a chance at." And Sam, looking in his father's face as he spoke, saw a light in his eyes, that he had never seen there before—the light of battle. The Major caught a carbine from the hands of a trooper who rode beside him, and took a snap-shot, quick as lightning, at a man whom they saw running from one cover to another. The poor wretch staggered and put his hands to his head, then stumbled and fell heavily down.

Now the fight became general and confused. All about among the fern and the flowers, among the lemon-shrubs, and the tangled vines, men fought, and fired, and struck, and cursed; while the little brown bandicoots scudded swiftly away, and the deadly snake hid himself in his darkest lair, affrighted. Shots were cracking on all sides, two riderless horses, confused in the mêlée, were galloping about neighing and a third lay squealing on the ground in the agonies of death.

Sam saw a man fire at his father, whose horse went down, while the Major arose unhurt. He rode at the ruffian, who was dismounted, and cut him so deep between the shoulder and the neck, that he fell and never spoke again. Then seeing Halbert and the Doctor on the right, fiercely engaged with four men who were fighting with clubbed muskets and knives, he turned to help them, but ere he reached them, a tall, handsome young fellow dashed out of the shrub, and pulling his horse short up, took deliberate aim at him, and fired.

Sam heard the bullet go hissing past his ear, and got mad. "That young dog shall go down," said he. "I know him. He is one of the two who rode first yesterday." And as this passed through his mind, he rode straight at him, with his sword hand upon his left shoulder. He came full against him in a moment, and as the man held up his gun to guard himself, his cut descended, so full and hard, that it shore through the gun-barrel as through a stick, and ere he could bring his hand to his cheek, his opponent had grappled him, and the two rolled off their horses together, locked in a deadly embrace.

Then began an awful and deadly fight between these two young fellows. Sam's sword had gone from his hand in the fall, and he was defenceless, save by such splendid physical powers as he had by nature. But his adversary, though perhaps a little lighter, was a terrible enemy, and fought with the strength and litheness of a leopard. He had his hand at Sam's throat, and was trying to choke him. Sam saw that one great effort was necessary, and with a heave of his whole body, threw the other beneath him, and struck downwards, three quick blows, with the whole strength of his ponderous fist, on the face of the man, as he lay beneath him. The hold on his throat loosened, and seeing that they had rolled within reach of his sword, in a moment he had clutched it, and drawing back his elbow, prepared to plunge it into his adversary's chest.

But he hesitated. He could not do it. Maddened as he was with fighting, the sight of that bloody face, bruised beyond recognition by his terrible blows, and the wild fierce eyes, full of rage and terror, looking into his own, stayed his hand, and while he paused the man spoke, thick and indistinct, for his jaw was broken.

"If you will spare me," he said, "I will be King's evidence."

"Then turn on your face," said Sam; "and I will tie you up."

And as he spoke a trooper ran up, and secured the prisoner, who appealed to Sam for his handkerchief. "I fought you fair," he said; "and you're a man worth fighting. But you have broken something in my face with your fist. Give me something to tie it up with."

"God save us all!" said Sam, giving him his handkerchief. "This is miserable work! I hope it is all over."

It seemed so. All he heard were the fearful screams of a wounded man lying somewhere among the fern.

" Where are they all, Jackson? " said he.

" All away to the right, sir," said the trooper. " One of my comrades is killed, your father has had his horse shot, the Doctor is hit in the arm, and Mr. James Brentwood has got his leg broke with the fall of his horse. They are minding him now. We've got all the gang, alive or dead, except two. Captain Desborough is up the valley now after the head man, and young Mr. Hawker is with him. Damn it all! hark to that."

Two shots were fired in quick succession in the direction indicated; and Sam, having caught his horse, galloped off to see what was going on.

Desborough fought neither against small nor great, but only against one man, and he was George Hawker. Him he had sworn he would bring home, dead or alive. When he and his party had first broken through the fern, he had caught sight of his quarry, and had instantly made towards him, as quick as the broken scrub-tangled ground would allow.

They knew one another; and, as soon as Hawker saw that he was recognised, he made to the left, away from the rest of his gang, trying to reach, as Desborough could plainly see, the only practicable way that led from the amphitheatre in which they were back into the mountains.

They fired at one another without effect at the first. Hawker was now pushing in full flight, though the scrub was so dense that neither made much way. Now the ground got more open and easier travelled, when Desborough was aware of one who came charging recklessly up alongside of him, and, looking round, he recognised Charles Hawker.

" Good lad," he said; " come on. I must have that fellow before us there. He is the arch-devil of the lot. If we follow him to hell, we must have him! "

" We'll have him safe enough! " said Charles. " Push to the left, Captain, and we shall get him against those fallen rocks."

Desborough saw the excellence of this advice. This was the last piece of broken ground there was. On the right the cliff rose precipitous, and from its side had tumbled a confused heap of broken rock, running out into the glen. Once past this, the man they were pursuing would have the advantage, for he was splendidly mounted, and beyond was clear galloping ground. As it was, he was in a recess, and Desborough and Charles pushing forward, succeeded in bringing him to bay. Alas, too well!

George Hawker reigned up his horse when he saw escape was impossible, and awaited their coming with a double-barrelled pistol in his hand. As the other two came on, calling on him to surrender, Desborough's horse received a bullet in his chest, and down went horse and man together. But Charles pushed on till he was within ten yards of the bushranger, and levelled his pistol to fire.

So met father and son, the second time in their lives, all unconsciously. For an instant they glared on one another with wild threatening eyes, as the father made his aim more certain and deadly. Was there no lightning in heaven to strike him dead, and save him from this last horrid crime? Was there no warning voice to tell him that this was his son?

None. The bullet sped, and the poor boy tumbled from his saddle, clutching wildly, with crooked, convulsive fingers, at the grass and flowers—shot through the chest.

Then, ere Desborough had disentangled himself from his fallen horse, George Hawker rode off laughing—out through the upper rock walls into the presence of the broad bald snow-line that rolled above his head in endless lofty tiers towards the sky.

Desborough arose, swearing and stamping; but, ere he could pick up his cap, Sam was alongside of him, breathless, and with him another common-looking man—my man, Dick, no other—and they both cried out together, "What has happened?"

"Look there!" said Desborough, pointing to something dark among the grass—"that's what has happened. What lies there was Charles Hawker, and the villain is off."

"Who shot Charles Hawker?" said Dick.

"His namesake," said Desborough.

"His own father!" said Dick; "that's terrible."

"What do you mean?" they both asked aghast.

"Never mind now," he answered. "Captain Desborough, what are you going to do? Do you know where he's gone?"

"Up into the mountain, to lie by, I suppose," said Desborough.

"Not at all, sir! He is going to cross the snow, and get to the old hut, near the Murray Gate."

"What! Merryman's hut?" said the Captain. "Impossible! He could not get through that way."

"I tell you he can. That is where they came from at first; that is where they went to when they landed; and this is the gully they came through."

"Are you deceiving me?" said Desborough. "It will be worse

for you if you are! I ain't in a humour for that sort of thing. Who are you?"

"I am Mr. Hamlyn's groom—Dick. Strike me dead if I ain't telling the truth!"

"Do you know this man, Buckley?" said Desborough, calling out to Sam, who was sitting beside poor Charles Hawker, holding his head up.

"Know him! of course I do," he replied; "ever since I was a child."

"Then, look here," said Desborough to Dick, "I shall trust you. Now, you say he will cross the snow. If I were to go round by the Parson's I shouldn't get much snow."

"That's just it, don't you see? You can be round at the huts before him. That's what I mean," said Dick. "Take Mr. Buckley's horse, and ride him till he drops, and you'll get another at the Parson's. If you have any snow, it will be on Broadsaddle; but it won't signify. You go round the low side of Tambo, and sight the lake, and you'll be there before him."

"How far?"

"Sixty miles, or thereabouts, plain sailing. It ain't eleven o'clock yet."

"Good; I'll remember you for this. Buckley, I want your horse. Is the lad dead?"

"No; but he is very bad. I'll try to get him home. Take the horse; he is not so good a one as Widderin, but he'll carry you to the Parson's. God speed you."

They watched him ride away almost south, skirting the ridges of the mountain as long as he could; then they saw him scrambling up a lofty wooded ridge, and there he disappeared.

They raised poor Charles Hawker up, and Sam, mounting Dick's horse, took the wounded man up before him, and started to go slowly home. After a time, he said, "Do you feel worse, Charles?" and the other replied, "No; but I am very cold." After that, he stayed quite still, with his arm round Sam Buckley's neck, until they reached the Brentwoods' door.

Some came out to the door to meet them, and, among others, Alice. "Take him from me," said Sam to one of the men. "Be very gentle; he is asleep." And so they took the dead man's arm from off the living man's shoulder, and carried him in; for Charles Hawker was asleep indeed—in the sleep that knows no waking.

That was one of the fiercest and firmest stands that was ever made by bushrangers against the authorities. Of the former five were shot down, three wounded, and the rest captured, save two. The gang was destroyed at once, and life and property once more secure, though at a sad sacrifice.

One trooper was shot dead at the first onset—a fine young fellow, just picked from his regiment for good conduct to join the police. Another was desperately wounded, who died the next day. On the part of the independent men assisting, there were Charles Hawker killed, Dr. Mulhaus shot in the left arm, and Jim with his leg broke; so that, on that evening, Captain Brentwood's house was like a hospital.

Captain Brentwood set his son's leg, under Dr. Mulhaus's directions, the Doctor keeping mighty brave, though once or twice his face twisted with pain, and he was nearly fainting. Alice was everywhere, pale and calm, helping everyone who needed it, and saying nothing. Eleanor, the cook, pervaded the house, doing the work of seven women, and having the sympathies of fourteen. She told them that this was as bad a job as she'd ever seen; worse, in fact. That the nearest thing she'd ever seen to it was when Mat Steedman's mob were broke up by the squatters; "But then," she added, "there were none but prisoners killed."

But when Alice had done all she could, and the house was quiet, she went up to her father, and said:

"Now, father, comes the worst part of the matter for me. Who is to tell Mrs. Hawker?"

"Mrs. Buckley, my dear, would be the best person. But she is at the Mayfords', I am afraid."

"Mrs. Hawker must be told at once, father, by some of us. I do so dread her hearing of it by some accident, when none of her friends are with her. Oh, dear; oh, dear; I never thought to have had such times as these."

"Alice, my darling," said her father, "do you think that you have strength to carry the news to her? If Major Buckley went with you, he could tell her, you know; and it would be much better for her to have him, an old friend, beside her. It would be such a delay to go round and fetch his wife. Have you courage?"

"I will make courage," she said. "Speak to Major Buckley, father, and I will get ready."

She went to Sam. "I am going on a terrible errand," she said; "I am going to tell Mrs. Hawker about this dreadful, dreadful business. Now, what I want to say is, that you mustn't come; your father is going with me, and I'll get through it alone, Sam. Now please," she added, seeing Sam was going to speak, "don't argue about it; I am very much upset as it is, and I want you to stay here. You won't follow us, will you?"

"Whatever you order, Alice, is law," said Sam. "I won't come if you don't wish it; but I can't see——"

"There now. Will you get me my horse? And please stay by poor Jim, for my sake."

Sam complied; and Alice, getting on her riding-habit, came back trembling, and trying not to cry, to tell Major Buckley that she was ready.

He took her in his arms, and kissed her. "You are a brave, noble girl," he said; "I thank God for such a daughter-in-law. Now, my dear, let us hurry off, and not think of what is to come."

It was about five o'clock when they went off. Sam and Halbert, having let them out of the paddock, went indoors to comfort poor Jim's heart, and to get something to eat, if it were procurable. Jim lay on his bed tossing about, and the Doctor sat beside him, talking to him, pale and grim, waiting for the doctor who had been sent for; no other than his drunken old enemy.

"This is about as nice a kettle of fish," said Jim, when they came and sat beside him, "as a man could possibly wish to eat. Poor Cecil and Charley; both gone, eh? Well, I know it ain't decent for a fellow with a broken leg to feel wicked; but I do, nevertheless. I wish now that I had had a chance at some of them before that stupid brute of a horse got shot."

"If you don't lie still, you Jim," said Sam, "your leg will never set; and then you must have it taken off, you know. How is your arm, Doctor?"

"Shooting a little," said the Doctor; "nothing to signify, I believe. At least, nothing in the midst of such a tragedy as this. Poor Mary Hawker; the pretty little village-maid we all loved so well. To come to such an end as this!"

"Is it true, then, Doctor, that Hawker, the bushranger, is her husband?"

"Quite true, alas! Everyone must know it now. But I pray you, Sam, to keep the darkest part of it all from her; don't let her know that the boy fell by the hand of his father."

"I could almost swear," said Sam, "that one among the gang is his son too. When they rode past Alice and myself yesterday morning. one was beside him so wonderfully like him, that even at that time I set them down for father and son."

"If Hamlyn's strange tale be true, it is so," said the Doctor.

" Is the young man you speak of among the prisoners, do you know ? "

" Yes; I helped to capture him myself," said Sam. " What do you mean by Hamlyn's story ? "

" Oh, a long one. He met him in a hut the night after we picnicked at Mirngish, and found out who he was. The secret not being ours, your father and I never told any of you young people of the fact of this bushranger being poor Mrs. Hawker's husband. I wish we had; all this might have been avoided. But the poor soul always desired that the secret of his birth might be kept from Charles, and you see the consequence. I'll never keep a secret again. Come here with me; let us see both of them."

They followed him, and he turned into a little side room at the back of the house. It was a room used for chance visitors or strangers, containing two small beds, which now bore an unaccustomed burden, for beneath the snow-white coverlets lay two figures, indistinct indeed, but unmistakable.

" Which is he ? " whispered the Doctor.

Sam raised the counterpane from the nearest one, but it was not Charles. It was a young, handsome face that he saw, lying so quietly and peacefully on the white pillow, that he exclaimed:

" Surely this man is not dead ! "

The Doctor shook his head. " I have often seen them like that," he said. " He is shot through the heart."

Then they went to the other bed, where poor Charles lay. Sam gently raised the black curls from his face, but none of them spoke a word for a few minutes, till the Doctor said, " Now let us come and see his brother."

They crossed the yard, to a slab outbuilding, before which one of the troopers was keeping guard, with a loaded carbine; and, the Sergeant coming across, admitted them.

Seven or eight fearfully ill-looking ruffians lay about on the floor, handcuffed. They were most of them of the usual convict stamp; dark, saturnine-looking fellows, though one offered a strange contrast by being an albino, and another they could not see plainly, for he was huddled up in a dark corner, bending down over a basin of water, and dabbing his face. The greater part of them cursed and blasphemed desperately, as is the manner of such men when their blood is up, and they are reckless; while the wounded ones lay in a fierce sullen silence, more terrible almost than the foul language of the others.

"He is not here," said Sam. "Stay, that must be him wiping his face."

He went towards him, and saw he was right. The young man he had taken looked wildly up like a trapped animal into his face, and the Doctor could not suppress an exclamation when he saw the likeness to his father.

"Is your face very bad?" said Sam quietly.

The other turned away in silence.

"I'll tie it up for you, if you like," said Sam.

"It don't want no tying up."

He turned his face to the wall, and remained obstinately silent. They perceived that nothing more was to be got from him, and departed. But, turning at the door, they still saw him crouched in the corner like a wild beast, wiping his bruised face every now and then with Sam's handkerchief, apparently thinking of nothing, hoping for nothing. Such a pitiful sight—such an example of one who was gone beyond feeling hope, or sorrow, or aught else, save physical pain, that the Doctor's gorge rose, and he said, stamping on the gravel:

"A man, who says that that is not the saddest, saddest sight he ever saw, is a disgrace to the mother that bore him. To see a young fellow like that with such a physique—and God only knows what undeveloped qualities in him—only ripe for the gallows at five-and-twenty, is enough to make the angels weep. He knows no evil but physical pain, and that he considers but a temporary one. He knows no good save, perhaps, to be faithful to his confederates. He has been brought up from his cradle to look on every man as his enemy. He never knew what it was to love a human being in his life. Why, what does such a man regard this world as? As the antechamber of hell, if he ever heard of such a place. I want to know what either of us three would have been if we had his training. I want to know that now. We might have been as much worse than he is as a wolf is worse than an evil-tempered dog."

A beautiful collie came up to the Doctor and fawned on him, looking into his face with her deep, expressive, hazel eyes.

"We must do something for that fellow, Sam. If it's only for his name's sake," said the Doctor.

That poor boy, sitting crouched there in the corner, with a broken jaw, and just so much of human feeling as one may suppose a pole-cat to have, caught in a gin, is that same baby that we saw Ellen

Lee nursing on the door-step in the rain, when our poor Mary came upon her on one wild night in Exeter.

Base-born, workhouse-bred! Tossed from workhouse to prison, from prison to hulk—every man's hand against him—an Arab of society. As hopeless a case, my lord judge, as you ever had to deal with; and yet I think, my lord, that your big heart grows a little pitiful, when you see that handsome face before you, blank and careless, and you try, fruitlessly, to raise some blush or shame, or even anger in it, by your eloquence.

Gone beyond that, my lord. Your thunderbolts fall harmless here, and the man you say is lost, and naturally. Yet, give that same man room to breathe and act; keep temptation from him, and let his good qualities, should he have any, have fair play, and, even yet, he may convert you to the belief that hardened criminals may be reformed, to the extent of one in a dozen; beyond that no reasonable man will go.

Let us see the end of this man. For now the end of my tale draws near, and I must begin gathering up the threads of the story, to tie them in a knot, and release my readers from duty. Here is all I can gather about him:

Sam and the Doctor moved heaven, earth, and the Colonial Secretary, to get his sentence commuted, and with success. So when his companions were led out to execution, he was held back; reserved for penal servitude for life.

He proved himself quiet and docile; so much so that when our greatest, boldest explorer was starting for his last hopeless journey to the interior, this man was selected as one of the twelve convicts who were to accompany him. What follows is an extract which I have been favoured with from his private journal. You will not find it in the published history of the expedition:

Date—lat.—long.—Morning. It is getting hopeless now, and to-morrow I turn. Sand, and nothing but sand. The salsolaceous plants, so long the only vegetation we have seen, are gone; and the little sienite peak, the last symptom of a water-bearing country, has disappeared behind us. The sandhills still roll away towards the setting sun, but get less and less elevated. The wild fowl are still holding their mysterious flight to the north-west, but I have not wings to follow them. Oh, my God! if I only knew what those silly birds know. It is hopeless to go on, and, I begin to fear, hopeless to go back. Will it never rain again?

Afternoon—My servant Hawker, one of the convicts assigned

to me by Government, died to-day at noon. I had got fond of this man, as the most patient and the bravest, where all have been so patient and so brave. He was a very silent and reserved man, and had never complained, so that I was deeply shocked, on his sending for me at dinner-time, to find that he was dying.

He asked me not to deceive him, but to tell him if there was any truth in what the gaol-chaplain had said, about there being another life after death. I told him earnestly that I knew it as surely as I knew that the earth was under my feet; and went on comforting him as one comforts a dying man. But he never spoke again; and we buried him in the hot sand at sundown. The first wind will obliterate the little mound we raised over him, and none will ever cross this hideous desert again. So that he will have as quiet a grave as he could wish.

Eleven o'clock at night.—God be praised. Heavy clouds and thunder to the north.—

So this poor workhouse-bred lad lies out among the sands of the middle desert.

CHAPTER XLIII

ACROSS THE SNOW

HAWKER the elder, as I said, casting one glance at the body of his son, whom he knew not, and another at Captain Desborough, who was just rising from the ground after his fall, set spurs to his noble chestnut horse, and pushing through the contracted barriers of slate which closed up the southern end of the amphitheatre where they had been surprised, made for the broader and rapidly rising valley which stretched beyond.

He soon reached the rocky gate, where the vast ridge of limestone alternating with the schist, and running north and south in high serrated ridges, was cut through by a deep fissure, formed by the never idle waters of a little creek, that in the course of ages had mined away the softer portions of the rock, and made a practicable pass towards the mountains.

He picked his way with difficulty through the tumbled boulders that lay in the chasm; and then there was a cool brisk wind on his forehead, and a glare in his eyes. The chill breath of the west wind from the mountain—the glare of the snow that filled up the upper end of the valley, rising in level ridges towards the sky-line.

He had been this path before; and if he had gone it a hundred times again, he would only have cursed it for a rough desperate road, the only hope of a desperate man. Not for him to notice the thousand lessons that the Lord had spread before him in the wilderness! not for him to notice how the vegetation changed when the limestone was passed, and the white quartz reefs began to seam the slaty sides of the valley like rivers of silver! Not for him to see how as he went up and on, the hardy Dicksonia still nestled in stunted tufts among the more sheltered side gullies, long after her tenderer sister, the queenly Alsophylla, had been left behind. He only knew that he was a hunted wild beast, and that his lair was beyond the snow.

The creek flashed pleasantly among the broken slate, full and turbid under the midday sun. After midnight, when its fountains are sealed again by the frosty breath of night, that creek would be reduced to a trickling rill. His horse's feet brushed through the delicate asplenium, the Venus'-hair of Australia; the sarsaparilla still hung in scant purple tufts on the golden wattle, and the scarlet correa lurked among the broken quartz.

Upwards and onwards. In front, endless cycles agone, a lava stream from some crater we know not of, had burst over the slate, with fearful clang and fierce explosion, forming a broad roadway of broken basalt up to a plateau twelve hundred feet or more above us, and not so steep but that a horse might be led up it. Let us go up with him, not cursing heaven and earth, as he did, but noticing how, as we ascend, the scarlet wreaths of the Kennedia and the crimson Grevillea give place to the golden Grevillea and the red Epacris; then comes the white Epacris, and then the grass-trees, getting smaller and scantier as we go, till the little blue Gentian, blossoming boldly among the slippery crags, tells us that we have nearly reached the limits of vegetation.

He turned when he reached this spot, and looked around him. To the west a broad rolling down of snow, rising gradually; to the east, a noble prospect of forest and plain, hill and gully, with old Snowy winding on in broad bright curves to the sea. He looked over all the beauty and undeveloped wealth of Gippsland, which shall yet, please God, in fullness of time, be one of the brightest jewels in the King of England's crown, but with eyes that saw not. He turned towards the snow, and mounting his horse, which he had led up the cliff, held steadily westward.

His plans were well laid. Across the mountain, north of Lake Omeo, not far from the mighty cleft in which the infant Murray spends his youth, were two huts, erected years before by some settler, and abandoned. They had been used by a gang of bush-rangers, who had been attacked by the police, and dispersed. Never-theless, they had been since inhabited by the men we know of, who landed in the boat from Van Diemen's Land, in consequence of Hawker himself having found a pass through the ranges, open for nine months in the year. So that, when the police were searching Gippsland for these men, they, with the exception of two or three, were snugly ensconced on the other water-shed, waiting till the storm should blow over. In these huts Hawker intended to lie by for a short time, living on such provisions as were left, until he could make his way northward on the outskirts of the settlements, and escape.

There was no pursuit, he thought: how could there be? Who knew of this route but himself and his mates? hardly likely any of them would betray him. No creature was moving in the valley he had just ascended, but the sun was beginning to slope towards the west, and he must onwards.

Onwards, across the slippery snow. At first a few tree-stems, blighted and withered, were visible right and left, proving that at some time during their existence, these bald downs had either a less elevation or a warmer climate than now. Then these even disappeared, and all around was one white blinding glare. To the right, the snow-fields rolled up into the shapeless lofty mass called Mount Tambo, behind which the hill they now call Kosciusko— as some say, the highest ground in the country—began to take a crimson tint from the declining sun. Far to the south, black and gaunt among the whitened hills, towered the rounded hump of Buffalo, while the peaks of Buller and Aberdeen showed like dim blue clouds on the farthest horizon.

Snow, and nothing but snow. Sometimes plunging shoulder-deep into some treacherous hollow, sometimes guiding the tired horse across the surface frozen over unknown depths. He had been drinking hard for some days, and, now the excitement of action had gone off, was fearfully nervous. The snow-glint had dizzied his head, too, and he began to see strange shapes forming them-selves in the shade of each hollow, and start at each stumble of his horse.

A swift-flying shadow upon the snow, and a rush of wings over-head. An eagle. The lordly scavenger is following him, impatient for him to drop and become a prey. Soar up, old bird, and bide thy time; on yonder precipice thou shalt have good chance of a meal.

Twilight, and then night, and yet the snow but half past. There is a rock in a hollow, where grow a few scanty tufts of grass, which the poor horse may eat. Here he will camp, fireless, foodless, and walk up and down the livelong night, for sleep might be death. Though he is not in thoroughly Alpine regions, yet still, at this time of the year, the snow is deep and the frost is keen. It were as well to keep awake.

As he paced up and down beneath the sheltering rock, when night had closed in, and the frosty stars were twinkling in the cold blue firmament, strange ghosts and fancies came crowding on him thick and fast. Down the long vista of a misspent, ruined life, he saw people long since forgotten trooping up towards him. His father tottered sternly on, as with a fixed purpose before him; his gipsy-mother, Madge, strode forward pitiless; and poor ruined Ellen, holding her child to her heart, joined the others and held up her withered hand as if in mockery. But then there came a face between him and all the other figures which his distempered brain had summoned, and blotted them out; the face of a young man, bearing a strange likeness to himself; the face of the last human creature he had seen; the face of the boy that he had shot down among the fern.

Why should this face grow before him wherever he turned, so that he could not look on rock or sky without seeing it? Why should it glare at him through a blood-red haze when he shut his eyes to keep it out, not in sorrow, not in anger, but even as he had seen it last, expressing only terror and pain, as the lad rolled off his horse, and lay a black heap among the flowers? Up and away! anything is better than this. Let us stumble away across the snow, through the mirk night once more, rather than be driven mad by this pale boy's face.

Morning, and the pale ghosts have departed. Long shadows of horse and man are thrown before him now, as the slope dips away to the westward, and he knows that his journey is well-nigh over.

It was late in the afternoon before, having left the snow some hours, he began to lead his horse down a wooded precipice, through vegetation which grew more luxuriant every yard he descended. The glen, whose bottom he was trying to reach, was a black profound gulf, with perpendicular, or rather, overhanging walls, on every side, save where he was scrambling down. Here indeed it was possible for a horse to keep his footing among the belts of trees, that, alternating with a precipitous granite cliff, formed the upper end of one of the most tremendous glens in the world—the Gates of the Murray.

He was barely one-third of the way down this mountain wall, when the poor tired horse lost his footing and fell over the edge, touching neither tree nor stone for five hundred feet, while George Hawker was left terrified, hardly daring to peer into the dim abyss, where the poor beast was gone.

But it was little matter. The hut he was making for was barely four miles off now, and there was meat, drink, and safety. Perhaps there might be company, he hoped there might—some of the gang might have escaped. A dog would be some sort of friend. Anything sooner than such another night as last night.

His pistols were gone with the saddle, and he was unarmed. He reached the base of the cliff in safety, and forced his way through the tangled scrub that fringed the infant river, towards the lower end of the pass. Here the granite walls, overhanging, bend forward above to meet one another, almost forming an arch, the height of which, from the river-bed, is computed to be nearly, if not quite, three thousand feet. Through this awful gate he forced his way, overawed and utterly dispirited, and reached the gully where his refuge lay, just as the sun was setting.

There was a slight track, partly formed by stray cattle, which led up to it; and casting his eyes upon this, he saw the marks of a horse's feet. "Some one of the gang got home before me," he said. " I'm right glad of that, anything better than such another night."

He turned a sharp angle in the path, just where it ran round an abrupt cliff. He saw a horseman within ten yards of him with his face towards him. Captain Desborough, holding a pistol at his head.

"Surrender, George Hawker!" said Desborough. "Or, by the living Lord! you are a dead man."

Hungry, cold, desperate, unarmed; he saw that he was undone, and that hope was dead. The Captain had an easier prey than he had anticipated. Hawker threw up his arms, and ere he could fully appreciate his situation, he was chained fast to Desborough's saddle, only to be loosed, he knew, by the gallows.

Without a further word on either side, they began their terrible journey. Desborough riding, and Hawker manacled by his right wrist to the saddle. Fully a mile was passed before the latter asked sullenly:

" Where are you going to take me to-night ? "

" To Dickenson's," replied Desborough. " You must step out, you know. It will be for your own good, for I must get there to-night."

Two or three miles further were got over, when Hawker said abruptly:

" Look here, Captain, I want to talk to you."

" You had better not," said Desborough. " I don't want to have any communication with you, and every word you say will go against you."

" Bah!" said Hawker. " I must swing. I know that. I shan't make any defence. Why, the devils out of hell would come into court against me if I did. But I want to ask you a question or two. You haven't got the character of being a brutal fellow, like O——. It can't hurt you to answer me one or two things, and ease my mind a bit."

" God help you, unhappy man; " said Desborough. " I will answer any questions you ask."

" Well, then, see here," said Hawker, hesitating. " I want to know—I want to know first, how you got round before me ? "

" Is that all ? " said Desborough. " Well, I came round over Broadsaddle, and got a fresh horse at the Parson's."

" Ah!" said Hawker. " That young fellow I shot down when you were after me, is he dead ? "

" By this time," said Desborough. " He was just dying when I came away."

" Would you mind stopping for a moment, Captain ? Now tell me, who was he ? "

" Mr. Charles Hawker, son of Mrs. Hawker, of Toonarbin."

He gave such a yell that Desborough shrunk from him appalled —a cry as of a wounded tiger, and struggled so wildly with his handcuff that the blood poured from his wrist. Let us close this scene. Desborough told me afterwards, that that wild, fierce, despairing cry, rang in his ears for many years afterwards, and would never be forgotten till those ears were closed with the dust of the grave.

CHAPTER XLIV

HOW MARY HAWKER HEARD THE NEWS

TROUBRIDGE'S Station, Toonarbin, lay so far back from the river, and so entirely on the road to nowhere, that Tom used to remark, that he would back it for being the worst station for news in the country. So it happened while these terrible scenes were enacting within ten miles of them, down, in fact, to about one o'clock in the day when the bushrangers were overtaken and punished, Mary and her cousin sat totally unconscious of what was going on.

But about eleven o'clock that day, Burnside, the cattle-dealer, mentioned once before in these pages, arrived at Major Buckley's, from somewhere up country, and found the house apparently deserted.

But having cooeed for some time, a door opened in one of the huts, and a sleepy groom came forth, yawning.

" Where are they all?" asked Burnside.

" Mrs. Buckley and the women were down at Mrs. Mayford's, streaking the bodies out," he believed. " The rest were gone away after the gang."

This was the first that Burnside had heard about the matter. And now, bit by bit, he extracted everything from the sleepy groom.

I got him afterwards to confess to me, that when he heard of this terrible affair, his natural feeling of horror was considerably alloyed with pleasure. He saw here at one glance a fund of small talk for six months. He saw himself a welcome visitor at every station, even up to farthest lonely Condamine, retailing the news of these occurrences with all the authenticity of an eye-witness, improving his narrative by each repetition. Here was the basis of a new tale, ode, epic, saga, or what you may please to call it, which he Burnside, the bard, should sing at each fireside throughout the land.

" And how are Mrs. and Miss Mayford, poor souls?" he asked.

" They're as well," answered the groom, " as you'd expect folks to be after such a mishap. They ran out at the back way and down the garden towards the river before the chaps could burst the door down. I am sorry for that little chap Cecil; I am, by Jove! A straightforward, manly little chap as ever crossed a horse. Last week he says to me, says he, ' Benjy, my boy,' says he, ' come and be groom to me. I'll give you thirty pound a year.' And I says, ' If

Mr. Sam——' Hallo, there they are at it, hammer and tongs! Sharp work, that!"

They both listened intently. They could hear, borne on the west wind, a distant dropping fire and a shouting. The groom's eye began to kindle a bit, but Burnside, sitting yet upon his horse, grasped the lad's shoulder and cried, " God save us, suppose our men should be beaten!"

" Suppose," said the groom, contemptuously shaking him off; " why then you and I should get our throats cut."

At this moment the noise of the distant fight breezed up louder than ever.

" They're beat back," said Burnside. " I shall be off to Toonarbin, and give them warning. I advise you to save yourself."

" I was set to mind these here things," said Benjy, " and I'm a-going to mind 'em. And they as meddles with 'em had better look out."

Burnside started off for Toonarbin, and when half-way there he paused and listened. The firing had ceased. When he came to reflect, now that his panic was over, he had very little doubt that Desborough's party had gained the day. It was impossible, he thought, that it could be otherwise.

Nevertheless, being half-way to Toonarbin, he determined to ride on, and, having called in a moment, to follow a road which took a way past Lee's old hut towards the scene of action. He very soon pulled up at the door, and Tom Troubridge came slowly out to meet him.

" Hallo, Burnside!" said Tom. " Get off, and come in."

" Not I, indeed. I am going off to see the fight."

" What fight?" said Mary Hawker, looking over Tom's shoulder.

" Do you mean to say you have not heard the news?"

" Not a word of any news for a fortnight."

For once in his life, Burnside was laconic, and told them all that had happened. Tom spoke not a word, but ran up to the stable and had a horse out, and, saddled in a minute, he was dashing into the house again for his hat and pistols when he came against Mary in the passage, leaning against the wall.

" Tom," she whispered hoarsely. " Bring that boy back to me safe, or never look me in the face again!"

He never answered her, he was thinking of someone beside the boy. He pushed past her, and the next moment she saw him gallop away with Burnside, followed by two men, and now she was left alone indeed, and helpless.

There was not a soul about the place but herself; not a soul within ten miles. She stood looking out of the door fixedly, at nothing, for a time; but then, as hour by hour went on, and the afternoon stillness fell upon the forest, and the shadows began to slant, a terror began to grow upon her which at length became unbearable, and well-nigh drove her mad.

At the first she understood that all these years of anxiety had come to a point at last, and a strange feeling of excitement, almost joy, came over her. She was one of those impetuous characters who stand suspense worse than anything, and now, although terror was in her, she felt as though relief was nigh. Then she began to think again of her son, but only for an instant. He was under Major Buckley's care, and must be safe; so that she dismissed that fear from her mind for a time, but only for a time. It came back to her again. Why did he not come to her? Why had not the Major sent him off to her at once? Could the Major have been killed? even if so, there was Dr. Mulhaus. Her terrors were absurd.

But not the less terrors, that grew in strength hour by hour, as she waited there, looking at the pleasant spring forest, and no one came. Terrors that grew at last so strong, that they took the place of certainties. Some hitch must have taken place, and her boy must be gone out with the rest.

Having got as far as this, to go further was no difficulty. He was killed, she felt sure of it, and none had courage to come and tell her of it. She suddenly determined to verify her thoughts at once, and went indoors to get her hat.

She had fully made up her mind that he must be killed at this time. The hope of his having escaped was gone. We, who knew the real state of the case, should tremble for her reason, when she finds her fears so terribly true. We shall see.

She determined to start away to the Brentwoods', and end her present state of terror one way or another. Tom had taken the only horse in the stable, but her own brown pony was running in the paddock with some others; and she sallied forth, worn out, feverish, half-mad, to try to catch him.

The obstinate brute would not be caught. Then she spent a weary hour trying to drive them all into the stockyard, but in vain. Three times, she, with infinite labour, drove them up to the sliprail, and each time the same mare and foal broke away, leading off the others. The third time, when she saw them all run whinnying down to the further end of the paddock, after half an hour or so of weary work driving them up, when she had run herself off her poor tottering legs, and saw that all her toil was in vain, then she sank down on the cold hard gravel in the yard, with her long black hair streaming loose along the ground, and prayed that she might die. Down at full length, in front of her own door, like a dead woman, moaning and crying, from time to time, " Oh, my boy, my boy."

How long she lay there she knew not. She heard a horse's feet, but only stopped her ears from the news she thought was coming. Then she heard a steady heavy footstep close to her, and someone touched her, and tried to raise her.

She sat up, shook the hair from her eyes, and looked at the man who stood beside her. At first she thought it was a phantom of her own brain, but then looking wildly at the calm, solemn features, and the kindly grey eyes which were gazing at her so inquiringly, she pronounced his name—" Frank Maberly."

" God save you, madam," he said. " What is the matter ? "

" Misery, wrath, madness, despair! " she cried wildly, raising her hand. " The retribution of a lifetime fallen on a luckless head in one unhappy moment."

Frank Maberly looked at her in real pity, but a thought went through his head. " What a magnificent actress this woman would make." It merely passed through his brain and was gone, and then he felt ashamed of himself for entertaining it a moment; and yet it was not altogether an unnatural one for him who knew her character so well. She was lying on the ground in an attitude which would have driven Siddons to despair; one white arm, down which her sleeve had fallen, pressed against her forehead, while the other clutched the ground; and her splendid black hair fallen down across her shoulders. Yet how could he say how much of all this wild despair was real, and how much hysterical ?

" But what is the matter, Mary Hawker ? " he asked. " Tell me, or how can I help you ? "

" Matter ? " she said. " Listen. The bushrangers are come down from the mountains, spreading ruin, murder, and destruction far and wide. My husband is captain of the gang: and my son, my only son, whom I have loved better than my God, is gone with the rest to hunt them down—to seek, unknowing, his own father's life. There is mischief beyond your mending, priest! "

Beyond his mending, indeed. He saw it. " Rise up," he said, " and act. Tell me all the circumstances. Is it too late ? "

She told him how it had come to pass, and then he showed her that all her terrors were but anticipations, and might be false. He got her pony for her, and, as night was falling, rode away with her along the mountain road that led to Captain Brentwood's.

The sun was down, and ere they had gone far, the moon was bright overhead. Frank, having fully persuaded himself that all her terrors were the effect of an overwrought imagination, grew cheerful, and tried to laugh her out of them. She, too, with the exercise of riding through the night air, and the company of a handsome, agreeable, well-bred man, began to have a lurking idea that she had been making a fool of herself; when they came suddenly on a hut, dark, cheerless, deserted, standing above a black, stagnant, reed-grown water-hole.

The hut where Frank had gone to preach to the stockmen. The hut where Lee had been murdered—an ill-omened place; and as they came opposite to it, they saw two others approaching them in the moonlight—Major Buckley and Alice Brentwood.

Then Alice, pushing forward, bravely met her, and told her all —all, from beginning to end; and when she had finished, having borne up nobly, fell to weeping as though her heart would break. But Mary did not weep, or cry, or fall down. She only said, " Let me see him," and went on with them, silent and steady.

They got to Garoopna late at night, none having spoken all the way. Then they showed her into the room where poor Charles lay, cold and stiff, and there she stayed hour after hour through the weary night. Alice looked in once or twice, and saw her sitting on the bed which bore the corpse of her son, with her face buried in her hands; and at last, summoning courage, took her by the arm and led her gently to bed.

Then she went into the drawing-room, where, besides her father, were Major Buckley, Dr. Mulhaus, Frank Maberly, and the drunken doctor before spoken of, who had had the sublime pleasure of cutting a bullet from his old adversary's arm, and was now in a fair way to justify the sobriquet I have so often applied to him. I myself also was sitting next the fire, alongside of Frank Maberly.

" My brave girl," said the Major, " how is she? "

" I hardly can tell you, sir," said Alice; " she is so very quiet. If she would cry now, I should be very glad. It would not frighten me so much as seeing her like that. I fear she will die! "

" If her reason holds," said the Doctor, " she will get over it. She had, from all accounts, gone through every phase of passion down to utter despair, before she knew the blow had fallen. Poor Mary! "

There, we have done. All this misery has come on her from one act of folly and selfishness years ago. How many lives are ruined, how many families broken up, by one false step! If ever a poor soul has expiated her own offence, she has. Let us hope that brighter times are in store for her. Let us have done with moral reflections; I am no hand at that work. One more dark scene, reader, and then—

It was one wild dreary day in the spring; a day of furious wind and cutting rain; a day when few passengers were abroad, and when the boatmen were gathered in knots among the sheltered spots upon the quays, waiting to hear of disasters at sea; when the ships creaked and groaned at the wharves, and the harbour was a sheet of wind-driven foam, and the domain was strewed with broken boughs. On such a day as this, Major Buckley and myself, after a sharp walk, found ourselves in front of the principal gaol in Sydney.

We were admitted, for we had orders; and a small, wiry, clever-looking man, about fifty, bowed to us as we entered the white-washed corridor, which led from the entrance hall. We had a few words with him, and then followed him.

To the darkest passage in the darkest end of that dreary place; to the condemned cells. And my heart sunk as the heavy bolt shot back, and we went into the first one on the right.

Before us was a kind of bedplace. And on that bedplace lay the figure of a man. Though it is twenty years ago since I saw it, I can remember that scene as though it were yesterday.

He lay upon a heap of tumbled blankets, with his face buried in a pillow. One leg touched the ground, and round it was a ring, connecting the limb to a long iron bar, which ran along beneath the bed. One arm also hung listlessly on the cold stone floor, and the other was thrown around his head. A head covered with short black curls, worthy of an Antinous, above a bare muscular neck, worthy of a Farnese Hercules. I advanced towards him.

The governor held me back. "My God, sir," he said, "take care. Don't, as you value your life, go within length of his chain." But at that moment the handsome head was raised from the pillow, and my eyes met George Hawker's. Oh, Lord! such a piteous wild look. I could not see the fierce desperate villain who had kept our country-side in terror so long. No, thank God, I could only see the handsome curly-headed boy who used to play with James Stockbridge and myself among the gravestones in Drumston churchyard.

I saw again the merry lad who used to bathe with us in Hatherleigh water, and whom, with all his faults, I had once loved well. And seeing him, and him only, before me, in spite of a terrified gesture from the governor, I walked up to the bed, and, sitting down beside him, put my arm round his neck.

"George! George! Dear old friend!" I said. "Oh, George, my boy, has it come to this?"

I don't want to be instructed in my duty. I know what my duty was on that occasion as well as any man. My duty as a citizen and a magistrate was to stand at the further end of the cell, and give this hardened criminal a moral lecture, showing how honesty and virtue, as in my case, had led to wealth and honour, and how yielding to one's passions had led to disgrace and infamy, as in his. That was my duty, I allow. But then, you see, I didn't do my duty. I had a certain tender feeling about my stomach which prevented me from doing it. So I only hung there, with my arm round his neck, and said, from time to time, "O George, George!" like a fool.

He put his two hands upon my shoulders, so that his fetters hung across my breast, and he looked me in the face. Then he said, after a time, "What! Hamlyn? Old Jeff Hamlyn! The only man I ever knew that I didn't quarrel with! Come to see me now, eh? Jeff, old boy, I'm to be hung to-morrow."

"I know it," I said. "And I came to ask you if I could do anything for you. For the sake of dear old Devon, George."

"Anything you like, old Jeff," he said, with a laugh, "so long as you don't get me reprieved. If I get loose again, lad, I'd do worse than I ever did yet, believe me. I've piled up a tolerable heap of wickedness as it is, though. I've murdered my own son, Jeff. Do you know that?"

I answered—"Yes; I know that, George; but that was an accident. You did not know who he was."

"He came at me to take my life," said Hawker. "And I tell you, as a man who goes out to be hung to-morrow, that, if I had guessed who he was, I'd have blown my own brains out to save him from the crime of killing me. Who is that man?"

"Don't you remember him?" I said. "Major Buckley."

The Major came forward, and held out his hand to George Hawker. "You are now," he said, "like a dead man to me. You die to-morrow; and you know it; and face it like a man. I come to ask you to forgive me anything you may have to forgive. I have been your enemy since I first saw you: but I have been an honest and open enemy; and now I am your enemy no longer. I ask you to shake hands with me. I have been warned not to come within arm's length of you, chained as you are. But I am not afraid of you."

The Major came and sat on the bed-place beside him.

"As for that little animal," said George Hawker, pointing to the governor, as he stood at the further end of the cell, "if he comes within reach of me, I'll beat his useless little brains out against the wall, and he knows it. He was right to caution you not to come too near me. I nearly killed a man yesterday; and to-morrow, when they come to lead me out——. But, with regard to you, Major Buckley, the case is different. Do you know I should be rather sorry to tackle you; I'm afraid you would be too heavy for me. As to my having anything to forgive, Major, I don't know that there is anything. If there is, let me tell you that I feel more kind and hearty towards you and Hamlyn for coming to me like this to-day, than I've felt toward any man this twenty year. By the by, let no man go to the gallows without clearing himself as far as he may. Do you know that I set on that red-haired villain, Moody, to throttle Bill Lee, because I hadn't the pluck to do it myself."

"Poor Lee," said the Major.

"Poor devil," said Hawker. "Why, that man had gone through every sort of villainy, from " (so-and-so up to so-and-so, he said; I shall not particularise) " before my beard was grown. Why that man laid such plots and snares for me when I was a lad, that a bishop could not have escaped. He egged me on to forge my own father's name. He drove me on to ruin. And now, because it suited his purpose to turn honest, and act faithful domestic to my wife for twenty years, he is mourned for as an exemplary character, and I go to the gallows. He was a meaner villain than ever I was."

"George," I asked, "have you any message for your wife?"

"Only this," he said; "tell her I always liked her pretty face, and I'm sorry I brought disgrace upon her. Through all my rascalities, old Jeff, I swear to you that I respected and liked her to the last. I tried to see her last year, only to tell her that she needn't be afraid of me, and should treat me as a dead man; but she and her blessed pig-headed lover, Tom Troubridge, made such knife and pistol work of it, that I never got the chance of saying the word I wanted. She'd have saved herself much trouble if she hadn't acted so much like a frightened fool. I never meant her any harm. You may tell her all this if you judge right, but I leave it to you.

Time's up, I see. I ain't so much of a coward, am I, Jeff? Good-bye, old lad, good-bye."

That was the last we saw of him; the next morning he was executed with four of his comrades. But now the Major and I, leaving him, went off again into the street, into the rain and the furious wind, to beat up against it for our hotel. Neither spoke a word till we came to a corner in George Street, nearest the wharf: and then the Major turned back upon me suddenly and I thought he had been unable to face the terrible gust which came sweeping up from the harbour: but it was not so. He had turned on purpose, and putting his hands upon my shoulders, he said:

"Hamlyn, Hamlyn, you have taught me a lesson."

"I suppose so," I said. "I have shown you what a fool a tender-hearted soft-headed fellow may make of himself by yielding to his impulses. But I have a defence to offer, my dear sir, the best of excuses, the only real excuse existing in this world. I couldn't help it."

"I don't mean that, Hamlyn," he answered. "The lesson you have taught me is a very different one. You have taught me that there are bright points in the worst man's character, a train of good feeling which no tact can bring out, but yet which some human spark of feeling may light. Here is this man Hawker, of whom we heard that he was dangerous to approach, and whom the good chaplain was forced to pray for and exhort from a safe distance. The man for whose death, till ten minutes ago, I was rejoicing. The man I thought lost, and beyond hope. Yet you, by one burst of unpremeditated folly, by one piece of silly sentimentality, by ignoring the man's later life, and carrying him back in imagination· to his old schoolboy days, have done more than our good old friend the chaplain could have done without your assistance. There is a spark of the Divine in the worst of men, if you can only find it."

In spite of the Major's parliamentary and didactic way of speaking, I saw there was truth at the bottom of what he said, and that he meant kindly to me, and to the poor fellow who was even now among the dead; so instead of arguing with him, I took his arm, and we fought homewards together through the driving rain.

Imagine three months to have passed. That stormy spring had changed into a placid, burning summer. The busy shearing-time was past; the noisy shearers were dispersed, heaven only knows where (most of them probably suffering from a shortness of cash, complicated with delirium tremens). The grass in the plains had

changed from green to dull grey; the river had changed his hoarse
roar for a sleepy murmur, as though too lazy to quarrel with his
boulders in such weather. A hot dull haze was over forest and
mountain. The snow had perspired till it showed long black streaks
on the highest eminences. In short, summer had come with a
vengeance; every one felt hot, idle, and thirsty, and "there was
nothing doing."

Now that broad cool veranda of Captain Brentwood's, with its
deep recesses of shadow, was a place not to be lightly spoken of.
Any man once getting footing there, and leaving it, except on
compulsion, would show himself of weak mind. Any man once
comfortably settled there in an easy-chair, who fetched anything
for himself when he could get any one else to fetch it for him,
would show himself, in my opinion, a man of weak mind. One
thing only was wanted to make it perfect, and that was niggers.
To the winds with *Uncle Tom's Cabin*, and *Dred* after it, in a
hot wind! What can an active-minded, self-helpful lady like Mrs.
Stowe, freezing up there in Connecticut, obliged to do something
to keep herself warm—what can she, I ask, know about the require-
ments of a southern gentleman when the thermometer stands at 125°
in the shade? Pish! Does she know the exertion required for
cutting up a pipe of tobacco in a hot north wind? No! Does she
know the amount of perspiration and anger superinduced by knocking the head off a bottle of Bass in January? Does she know the
physical prostration which is caused by breaking up two lumps
of hard white sugar in a pawnee before a thunderstorm? No, she
doesn't, or she would cry out for niggers with the best of us! When
the thermometer gets over 100° in the shade, all men would have
slaves if they were allowed. An Anglo-Saxon conscience will not,
save in rare instances, bear a higher average heat than 95°.

But about this veranda. It was the model and type of all
verandas. It was made originally by the Irish family, the Donovans,
before spoken of; and, like all Irish-made things, was nobly
conceived, beautifully carried out, and then left to take care of
itself, so that when Alice came into possession, she found it a
neglected mine of rare creepers run wild. Here, for the first time,
I saw the exquisite crimson passion-flower, then a great rarity.
Here, too, the native passion-flower, scarlet and orange, was tangled
up with the common purple sarsaparilla and the English honeysuckle and jessamine.

In this veranda, one blazing morning, sat Mrs. Buckley and Alice making believe to work. Mrs. Buckley really was doing something. Alice sat with her hands fallen on her lap, so still and so beautiful, that she might then and there have been photographed by some enterprising artist, and exhibited in the print shops as " Argia, Goddess of Laziness."

They were not alone, however. Across the very coolest, darkest corner was swung a hammock, looking at which you might perceive two hands elevating a green paper-covered pamphlet, as though the owner were reading—the aforesaid owner, however, being entirely invisible, only proving his existence by certain bulges and angles in the canvas of the hammock.

Now having made a nice little mystery as to who it was lying there, I will proceed to solve it. A burst of laughter came from the hidden man, so uproarious and violent, that the hammock strings strained and shook, and the magpie, waking up from a sound sleep, cursed and swore in a manner fearful to hear.

" My dearest Jim! " said Alice, rousing herself, " what is the matter with you? "

Jim read aloud the immortal battle of the two editors, with the carpet bag and the fire shovel, in *Pickwick*, and, ere he had half done, Alice and Mrs. Buckley had mingled their laughter with his, quite as heartily, if not so loudly.

" Hallo! " said Jim; " here's a nuisance! There's no more of it. Alice, have you got any more? "

" That is all, Jim. The other numbers will come by the next mail."

" How tiresome! I suppose the governor is pretty sure to be home to-night. He can't be away much longer."

" Don't be impatient, my dear," said Alice. " How is your leg? "

Please remember that Jim's leg was broken in the late wars, and, as yet, hardly well.

" Oh, it's a good deal better. Heigho! This is very dull."

" Thank you, James! " said Mrs. Buckley. " Dear me! the heat gets greater every day. If they are on the road, I hope they won't hurry themselves."

Our old friends were just now disposed in the following manner: The Major was at home. Mary Hawker was staying with him. Dr. Mulhaus and Halbert were staying at Major Buckley's, while Captain Brentwood was away with Sam and Tom Troubridge to Sydney; and, having been absent some weeks, had been expected home now for a day or two. This was the day they came home, riding slowly up to the porch about five o'clock.

When all greetings were done, and they were sat down beside the others, Jim opened the ball by asking, " What news, father？ "

" What a particularly foolish question! " said the Captain. " Why, you'll get it all in time—none the quicker for being impatient. May be, also, when you hear some of the news, you won't like it! "

" Oh, indeed! " said Jim.

" I have a letter for you here, from the Commander-in-Chief. You are appointed to the 3—th Regiment, at present quartered in India."

Alice looked at him quickly as she heard this, and, as a natural consequence, Sam looked too. They had expected that he would have hurrahed aloud, or thrown up his hat, or danced about when he heard of it. But no; he only sat bolt upright in his hammock, though his face flushed scarlet, and his eyes glistened strangely.

His father looked at him an instant, and then continued:

" Six months' leave of absence procured at the same time, which will give you about three months more at home. So you see you now possess the inestimable privilege of wearing a red coat; and what is still better, of getting a hole made in it; for there is great trouble threatening with the Afghans and Beloochs, and the chances are that you will smell powder before you are up in your regimental duties. Under which circumstances I shall take the liberty of requesting that you inform yourself on these points under my direction, for I don't want you to join your regiment in the position of any other·booby. Have the goodness to lie down again and not excite yourself. You have anticipated this some time. Surely it is not necessary for you to cry about it like a great girl."

But that night, after dark, when Sam and Alice were taking one of those agreeable nocturnal walks, which all young lovers are prone to, they came smoothly gliding over the lawn close up to the house, and then, unseen and unheard, they saw Captain Brentwood with his arm round Jim's neck, and heard him say:

" Oh, James! James! Why did you want to leave me？ "

And Jim answered, " Father, I didn't know. I didn't know my own mind. But I can't call back now."

Sam and Alice slipped back again, and continued their walk. Let us hear what conversation they had been holding together before this little interruption.

" Alice, my darling, my love, you are more beautiful than ever! "

" Thanks to your absence, my dear Sam. You see how well I thrive without you."

"Then when we are——"

"Well?" said Alice. For this was eight o'clock in the evening, you know, and the moon being four days past the full, it was pitch dark. "Well?" says she.

"When we are married," says Sam audaciously, "I suppose you will pine away to nothing."

"Good gracious me!" she answered. "Married? Why surely we are well enough as we are."

"Most excellently well, my darling," said Sam. "I wish it could last for ever."

"Oh, indeed!" said Alice, almost inaudibly though.

"Alice, my love," said Sam, "have you thought of one thing? Have you thought that I must make a start in life for myself?"

No, she hadn't thought of that. Didn't see why Baroona wasn't good enough for him.

"My dear!" he said. "Baroona is a fine property, but it is not mine. I want money for a set purpose. For a glorious purpose, my love! I will not tell you yet, not for years perhaps, what that purpose is. But I want fifty thousand pounds of my own. And fifty thousand pounds I will have."

Good gracious! What an avaricious creature. Such a quantity of money. And so she wasn't to hear what he was going to do with it, for ever so many years. Wouldn't he tell her now? She would so like to know. Would nothing induce him?

Yes, there was something. Nay, what harm! Only an honest lover's kiss, among the ripening grapes. In the dark, you say. My dear madam, you would not have them kiss one another in broad daylight, with the cook watching them out of the kitchen window?

"Alice," he said, "I have had one object before me from my boyhood, and since you told me that I was to be your husband, that object has grown from a vague intention to a fixed purpose. Alice, I want to buy back the acres of my forefathers; I wish, I intend, that another Buckley shall be the master of Clere, and that you shall be his wife."

"Sam, my love!" she said, turning on him suddenly. "What a magnificent idea. Is it possible?"

"Easy," said Sam. "My father could do it, but will not. He and my mother have severed every tie with the old country, and it would be at their time of life only painful to go back to the old scenes and interests. But with me it is different. Think of you and I taking the place we are entitled to by birth and education, in the splendid society of that noble island. Don't let me hear all that balderdash about the founding of new empires. Empires take too long in growing for me. What honours, what society, has this little colony to give, compared to those open to a fourth-rate gentleman in England? I want to be a real Englishman, not half a one. I want to throw in my lot heart and hand with the greatest nation in the world. I don't want to be young Sam Buckley of Baroona. I want to be the Buckley of Clere. Is not that a noble ambition?"

"My whole soul goes with you, Sam," said Alice. "My whole heart and soul. Let us consult, and see how this is to be done."

"This is the way the thing stands," said Sam. "The house and park at Clere were sold by my father for £12,000 to a brewer. Since then, this brewer, a most excellent fellow by all accounts, has bought back, acre by acre, nearly half the old original property as it existed in my great-grandfather's time, so that now Clere must be worth fifty thousand pounds at least. This man's children are all dead; and as far as Captain Brentwood has been able to find out for me, no one knows exactly how the property is going. The present owner is the same age as my father; and at his death, should an advantageous offer be made, there would be a good chance of getting the heirs to sell the property. We should have to pay very highly for it, but consider what a position we should buy with it. The county would receive us with open arms. That is all I know at present."

"A noble idea," said Alice, "and well considered. Now what are you going to do?"

"Have you heard tell yet," said Sam, "of the new country to the north, they call the Darling Downs?"

"I have heard of it from Burnside the cattle-dealer. He describes it as a paradise of wealth."

"He is right. When you get through the Cypress, the plains are endless. It is undoubtedly the finest piece of country found yet. Now do you know Tom Troubridge?"

"Slightly enough," said Alice, laughing.

"Well," said Sam. "You know he went to Sydney with us, and before he had been three days there he came to me full of this Darling Down country. Quite mad about it in fact. And in the end he said: 'Sam, what money have you got?' I said that my father had promised me seven thousand pounds for a certain purpose, and that I had come to town partly to look for an investment. He said, 'Be my partner;' and I said, 'What for?'

' Darling Downs,' he said. And I said I was only too highly honoured by such a mark of confidence from such a man, and that I closed with his offer at once. To make a long matter short, he is off to the new country to take up ground under the name of Troubridge and Buckley. There! "

" But oughtn't you to have gone up with him, Sam? "

" I proposed to do so, as a matter of course," said Sam. " But what do you think he said? "

" I don't know."

" He gave me a great slap on the back," said Sam; " and, said he, ' Go home, my old lad, marry your wife, and fetch her up to keep house.' That's what he said. And now, my own love, my darling, will you tell me, am I to go up alone, and wait for you; or will you come up, and make a happy home for me in that dreary desert? Will you leave your home, and come away with me into the grey hot plains of the west? "

" I have no home in future, Sam," she said, " but where you are, and I will gladly go with you to the world's end."

And so that matter was settled.

And now Sam disclosed to her that a visitor was expected at the station in about a fortnight or three weeks; and he was no less a person than our old friend the dean, Frank Maberly. And then he went on to ask, did she think that she could manage by that time to——, eh? Such an excellent opportunity, you know; seemed almost as if his visit had been arranged; which, between you and I, it had.

She thought it wildly possible, if there was any real necessity for it. And after this they went in; and Alice went into her bedroom.

" And what have you been doing out there with Alice all this time, eh? " asked the Captain.

" I've been asking a question, sir."

" You must have put it in a pretty long form. What sort of an answer did you get? "

" I got ' yes ' for an answer, sir."

" Ah, well! Mrs. Buckley, can you lend Baroona to a new-married couple for a few weeks, do you think? There is plenty of room for you here."

And then into Mrs. Buckley's astonished ear all the new plans were poured. She heard that Sam and Alice were to be married in a fortnight, and that Sam had gone into partnership with Tom Troubridge.

"Stop there," she said; "not too much at once. What becomes of Mary Hawker?"

"She is left at Toonarbin, with an overseer, for the present."

"And when," she asked, "shall you leave us, Sam?"

"Oh, in a couple of months, I suppose. I must give Tom time to get a house up before I go and join him. What a convenient thing a partner like that is, eh?"

"Oh, by the by, Mrs. Buckley," said Captain Brentwood, "what do you make of this letter?"

He produced a broad thick letter, directed in a bold running hand:

> Major Buckley,
> Baroona, Combermere County,
> Gippsland.

If absent, to be left with the nearest magistrate, and a receipt taken for it.

"How very strange," said Mrs. Buckley, turning it over. "Where did you get it?"

"Sergeant Jackson asked me, as nearest magistrate, to take charge of it; and so I did. It has been forwarded by orderly from Sydney."

"And the Governor's private seal, too," said Mrs. Buckley. "I don't know when my curiosity has been so painfully excited. Put it on the chimney-piece, Sam; let us gaze on the outside, even if we are denied to see the inside. I wonder if your father will come to-night?"

"No; getting too late," said Sam. "Evidently Halbert and the Doctor have found themselves there during their ride, and are keeping him and Mrs. Hawker company. They will all three be over to-morrow morning, depend on it."

"What a really good fellow that Halbert is," said Captain Brentwood. "One of the best companions I ever met. I wish his spirits would improve with his health. A sensitive fellow like him is apt not to recover from a blow like his."

"What blow?" said Mrs. Buckley.

"Did you never hear?" said the Captain. "The girl he was going to be married to, got drowned coming out to him in the *Assam*."

CHAPTER XLV

IN WHICH THERE ARE SOME ASTONISHING REVELATIONS WITH REGARD
TO DR. MULHAUS AND CAPTAIN DESBOROUGH

AT ten o'clock the next morning arrived the Major, the Doctor, and Halbert; and the first notice they had of it was the Doctor's voice in the passage, evidently in a great state of excitement.

"No more the common bower-bird than you, sir; a new species. His eyes are red instead of blue, and the whole plumage is lighter. I will call it after you, my dear Major."

"You have got to shoot him first," said the Major.

"I'll soon do that," said the Doctor, bursting into the room door. "How do you do, all of you? Sam, glad to see you back again. Brentwood, you are welcome to your own house. Get me your gun —where is it?"

"In my bedroom," said the Captain.

The Doctor went off after it. He reappeared again to complain that the caps would not fit; but, being satisfied on that score, he disappeared down the garden, on murder intent.

Sam got his father away into the veranda, and told him all his plans. I need hardly say that they met with the Major's entire approval. All his plans, I said; no, not all. Sam never hinted at the end and object of all his endeavours; he never said a word about his repurchase of Clere. The Major had no more idea that Sam had ever thought of such a thing, or had been making inquiries, than had the owner of Clere himself.

"Sam, my dear boy," said he, "I am very sorry to lose you, and we shall have but a dull time of it henceforth; but I am sure it is good for a man to go out into the world by himself" (and all that sort of thing). "When you are gone, Brentwood and I mean to live together to console one another."

"My dear, are you coming in?" said Mrs. Buckley. "Here is a letter for you, which I ought to have given you before."

The Major went in and received the mysterious epistle which the Captain had brought the night before. When he saw it he whistled.

They sat waiting to know the contents. He was provokingly long in opening it, and when he did, he said nothing, but read it over twice, with a lengthening visage. Now also it became apparent that there was another letter inside, at the superscription of which the Major having looked, put it in his pocket, and turning round to the mantel-piece, with his back to the others, began drumming against the fender with his foot, musingly.

A more aggravating course or proceeding he could not have resorted to. Here they were all dying of curiosity, and not a word did he seem inclined to answer. At last, Mrs. Buckley, not able to hold out any longer, said:

"From the Governor, was it not, my love?"

"Yes," he said, "from the Governor. And very important too," and then relapsed into silence.

Matters were worse than ever. But after a few minutes he turned round to them suddenly, and said:

"You have heard of Baron Landstein?"

"What," said Sam, "the man that the Doctor's always abusing so? Yes, I know all about him, of course."

"The noble Landstein," said Alice. "In spite of the Doctor's abuse he is a great favourite of mine. How well he seems to have behaved at Jena with those two Landwehr regiments."

"Landsturm, my love," said the Major.

"Yes, Landsturm, I mean. I wonder if he is still alive, or whether he died of his wounds."

"The Doctor," said Sam, "always speaks of him as dead."

"He is not only alive," said the Major, "but he is coming here. He will be here to-day. He may come any minute."

"What! the great Landstein?" said Sam.

"The same man," said the Major.

"The Doctor will have a quarrel with him, father. He is always abusing him. He says he lost the battle of Jena, or something."

"Be quiet, Sam, and don't talk. Watch what follows."

The Doctor was seen hurrying up the garden-walk. He put down his gun outside, and bursting open the glass door, stepped into the room, holding aloft a black bird, freshly killed, and looking around him for applause.

"There!" he said; "I told you so."

The Major walked across the room, and put a letter in his hand, the one which was enclosed in the mysterious epistle before mentioned. "Baron," he said, "here is a letter for you."

The Doctor looked round as one would who had received a blow, and knew not who smote him. He took the letter, and went into the window to read it.

No one spoke a word. "This, then, my good old tutor," thought Sam, "turns out to be the great Landstein. Save us, what a piece of romance." But, though he thought this, he never said anything, and catching Alice's eye, followed it to the window. There, leaning against the glass, his face buried in his hands, and his broad back shaking with emotion, stood Dr. Mulhaus. Alas! no. Our kindly, good, hearty, learned, irritable, but dearly-beloved friend, is no more. There never was such a man in reality: but in his place stands Baron von Landstein of the Niederwald.

What the contents of the Doctor's (I must still call him so) letter, I cannot tell you. But I have seen the letter which Major Buckley received enclosing it, and I can give it you word for word. It is from the Governor himself, and runs thus:

MY DEAR MAJOR,—

I am informed that the famous Baron von Landstein has been living in your house for some years, under the name of Dr. Mulhaus. In fact, I believe he is a partner of yours. I therefore send the enclosed under cover to you, and when I tell you that it has been forwarded to me through the Foreign Office, and the Colonial Office, and is, in point of fact, an autograph letter from the King of P—— to the Baron, I am sure that you will ensure its safe delivery.

The Secretary is completely "fixed" with his estimates. The salaries for the Supreme Court Office are thrown out. He must resign. Do next election send us a couple of moderates.—Yours, etc.,

G.G.

This was the Major's letter. But the Doctor stood still there, moved more deeply than any had seen him before, while Alice and Sam looked at one another in blank astonishment.

At length he turned and spoke, but not to them, to the empty air. Spoke as one aroused from a trance. Things hard to understand, yet having some thread of sense in them too.

" So he has sent for me," he said, " when it seems that he may have some use for me. So the old man is likely to go at last, and we are to have the golden age again. If talking could do it, assuredly we should. He has noble instincts, this young fellow, and some sense. He has sent for me. If H——, and B——, and Von U——, and myself can but get his ear!

" Oh, Rhineland! my own beloved Rhineland, shall I see you again? Shall I sit once more in my own grey castle, among the vineyards, above the broad gleaming river, and hear the noises from the town come floating softly up the hillside! I wonder are there any left who will remember——"

He took two short turns through the room, and then he turned and spoke to them again, looking all the time at Sam.

" I am the Baron von Landstein. The very man we have so often talked of, and whose character we have so freely discussed. When the French attacked us, I threw myself into the foremost ranks of my countrymen, and followed the Queen with two regiments which I had raised almost entirely myself.

" I fled away from the blood-red sun of Jena, wounded and desperate. ' That sun,' I thought, ' has set on the ruins of Great Frederick's kingdom. Prussia is a province of France: what can happen worse than this? I will crawl home to my castle and die.'

" I had no castle to crawl to. My brother, he who hung upon the same breast with me, he who learnt his first prayer beside me, he whom I loved and trusted above all other men, had turned traitor, had sold himself to the French, and deceived my bride that was to be, and seized my castle.

" I fled to England, to Drumston, Major. I had some knowledge of physic, and called myself a doctor. I threw myself into the happy English domestic life which I found there, and soon got around me men and women whom I loved full well.

" Old John Thornton and his sister knew my secret, as did Lord Crediton; but they kept it well, and by degrees I began to hope that I would begin a new life as a useful village apothecary, and forget for ever the turmoils of politics.

" Then you know what happened. There was an Exodus. All those I had got to love, arose, in the manner of their nation, and went to the other end of the earth, so that one night I was left alone on the cliff at Plymouth, watching a ship which was bearing away all that was left me to love in the world.

" I went to Prussia. I found my brother had made good use of his prosperity, and slandered me to the King. His old treachery seemed forgotten, and he was high in power. The King, for whom I had suffered so much, received me coldly, and leaving the palace, I spoke to my brother, and said, ' Send me so much yearly, and keep the rest for a time.' And then I followed you, Major, out here.

" Shall I tell you any more, Sam ? "

" No! " said Sam, smiting his fist upon the table. " I can tell the rest, Baron, to those who want to know it. I can tell of ten years' patient kindness towards myself. I can tell—I can tell——"

Sam was the worst orator in the world. He broke down, sir. He knew what he meant very well; and so I hope do you, reader, but he couldn't say it. He had done what many of us do, tried to make a fine speech when his heart was full, and so he failed.

But Alice didn't fail—not she, though she never spoke a word. She folded up her work; and going up to the good old man, took both his hands in hers and kissed him on both his cheeks. A fine piece of rhetorical action, wasn't it? And then they all crowded round him, and shook hands with him, and kissed him, and God-blessed him, for their kind, true, old friend; and prayed that every blessing might light upon his noble head, till he passed through them speechless and wandered away to his old friend, the river.

About the middle of this week, there arrived two of our former friends—Frank Maberly and Captain Desborough, riding side by side. The elders, with the Doctor, were outside, and detained the Dean, talking to him and bidding him welcome. But Captain Desborough, passing in, came into the room where were assembled Alice, Sam, and Jim, who gave him a most vociferous greeting.

They saw in a moment that there was some fun in the wind. They knew, by experience, that when Desborough's eyes twinkled like that, some absurdity was preparing, though they were quite unprepared for the mixture of reality and nonsense which followed.

"Pace," said Desborough, in his affected Irish accent, "be on this house, and all in it. The top of the morning to ye all."

"Now," said Alice, "we are going to have some fun; Captain Desborough has got his brogue on."

"Ye'll have some fun directly, Miss Brentwood," he said. "But there's some serious, sober earnest to come first. My cousin, Slieve-donad, is dead."

"Lord Slievedonad?"

"The same. That small Viscount is at this moment in pur——. God forgive me, and him too."

"Poor fellow!"

"That's just half. My uncle Lord Covetown was taken with a fit when he heard of it, and is gone after him, and the Lord forgive him too. He turned me, his own brother's son, out into the world with half an education, to sink or swim; and never a kind word did he or his son ever give me in their lives. It must have broken the old man's heart to think how the estate would go. But as I said before, God forgive him."

"You must feel his loss, Captain Desborough," said Alice. "I am very sorry for you."

"Ahem! my dear young lady, you don't seem to know how this ends."

"Why, no," said Alice, looking up wonderingly; "I do not."

"Why, it ends in this," said Desborough; "that I myself am Earl of Covetown, Viscount Slievedonad, and Baron Avoca, with twenty thousand a year, me darlin', the laste penny; see to there now!"

"Brogue again," said Alice. "Are you joking?"

"True enough," said Desborough. "I had a letter from my grandmother, the Dowager (she that lost the dog), only this very day. And there's a thousand pounds paid into the Bank of New South Wales to my account. Pretty good proof that last, eh?"

"My dear lord," said Alice, "I congratulate you most heartily. All the world are turning out to be noblemen. I should not be surprised to find that I am a duchess myself."

"It rests with you, Miss Brentwood," said Desborough, with a wicked glance at Sam, "to be a countess. I now formally make you an offer of me hand and heart. Oh! tell me, Miss Brentwood, will ye be Mrs. Mars—— I beg pardon, Countess of Covetown?"

"No, I thank you, my lord," said Alice, laughing and blushing. "I am afraid I must decline."

"I was afraid ye would," said Lord Covetown. "I had heard that a great six-foot villain had been trifling with your affections, so I came prepared for a refusal. Came prepared with this, Miss Brentwood, which I pray you to accept; shall I be too bold if I say, as a wedding present, from one of your most sincere admirers."

He produced a jewel-case, and took from it a bracelet, at the sight of which Alice gave an honest womanly cry of delight. And well she might, for the bauble cost £150. It was a bracelet of gold, representing a snake. Half-way up the reptile's back began a row of sapphires, getting larger towards the neck, each of which was surrounded by small emeralds. The back of the head contained a noble brilliant, and the eyes were two rubies. Altogether, a thorough specimen of Irish extravagance and good taste.

"Can you clasp it on for her, Sam?" said Lord Covetown.

"Oh, my lord, I ought not to accept such a princely present!" said Alice.

"Look here, Miss Brentwood," said Covetown, laying his hand on Sam's shoulder. "I find that the noblest and best fellow I know is going to marry the handsomest woman, saving your presence, that I ever saw. I myself have just come into an earldom, and twenty thousand a year; and if, under these circumstances, I mayn't make that woman a handsome present, why then the deuce is in it, you know. Sam, my boy, your hand. Jim, your hand, my lad. May you be as good a soldier as your father."

"Ah!" said Jim. "So you're an earl, are you? What does it feel like, eh? Do you feel the blue blood of a hundred sires coursing in your veins? Do you feel the hereditary class prejudices of the Norman aristocracy cutting you off from the sympathies of the inferior classes, and raising you above the hopes and fears of the masses? How very comical it must be! So you are going to sit among the bigwigs in the House of Lords. I hope you won't forget yourself, and cry 'Faug a Ballagh' when one of the bishops rises to speak. And whatever you do, don't sing, 'Gama crem'ah cruiskeen' in the lobby."

"My dear fellow," said he, "I am not in the House of Lords at all. Only an Irish peer. I intend to get into the Commons though, and produce a sensation by introducing the Australian 'Cooee' into the seat of British Legislature."

How long these four would have gone on talking unutterable nonsense, no man can say. But Frank Maberly coming in, greeted them courteously, and changed the conversation.

Poor Frank! Hard and incessant work was beginning to tell on that noble frame, and the hard marked features were getting more hard and marked year by year. Yet, in spite of the deep lines that now furrowed that kindly face, those who knew it best, said that it grew more beautiful than it had ever been before. As that magnificent physique began to fail, the noble soul within began to show clearer through its earthly tenement. That noble soul was getting purified and ready for what happened but a few years after this in Patagonia. When we heard that that man had earned the crown of glory, and had been thought worthy to sit beside Stephen and Paul in the Kingdom; none of us wept for him, or mourned. It seemed such a fitting reward for such a pure and noble life. But even now, when I wake in the night, I see him before me as he was described in the last scene by the only survivor. Felled down upon the sand, with his arms before his eyes, crying out, as the spears struck him one after another, "Lord, forgive them, they know not what they do!"

CHAPTER XLVI

IN WHICH SAM MEETS WITH A SERIOUS ACCIDENT, AND GETS CRIPPLED FOR LIFE

WHAT morning is this, when Sam, waking from silver dreams to a golden reality, turns over in his bed and looks out of the open glass door; at dog Rover, propped up against the lintel, chopping at the early flies; at the flower-garden, dark and dewy; at the black wall of forest beyond, in which the magpies were beginning to pipe cheerily; at the blessed dawn which was behind and above it, shooting long rays of primrose and crimson half-way up the zenith; hearing the sleepy ceaseless crawling of the river over the shingle bars; hearing the booming of the cattle-herds far over the plain; hearing the chirrup of the grasshopper among the raspberries, the chirr of the cicada among the wattles—what happy morning is this? Is it the Sabbath?

Ah, no! The Sabbath was yesterday. This is his wedding morn.

My dear brother bachelor, do you remember those old first-love sensations, or have you got too old, and too fat? Do you remember the night when you parted from her on the bridge by the lock, the night before her father wrote to you and forbade you the house? Have you got the rose she gave you there? Is it in your Bible, brother? Do you remember the months that followed—months of mad grief and wild yearning, till the yearning grew less—less wild —and the grief less desperate; and then, worst of all, the degrading consciousness that you were, in spite of yourself, getting rid of your love, and that she was not to you as she had been? Do you remember all this? When you come across the rose in your Bible, do you feel that you would give all the honour and wealth of the world to feel again those happy, wretched old sensations? Do you not say that this world has nothing to give in comparison to that?

Not this world, I believe. You and I can never feel that again. So let us make up our minds to it—it is dead. In God's name don't let us try to galvanise an old corpse, which may rise upon us hideous, and scare us to the lower pit. Let us be content as we are. Let us read that Book we spoke of just now with the rose in it, and imitate the Perfect Man there spoken of, who was crucified 1800 years ago, believing, like Him, that all men are our brothers, and acting up to it. And then, Lord knows what may be in store for us.

Here's a digression. If I had a good wife to keep me in order, I never should have gone so far out of the road. Here is Sam in bed, sitting up, with his happy head upon his hands, trying to believe that this dream of love is going to be realised—trying to believe that it is really his wedding morn.

It evidently is; so he gets out of bed and says his prayers like an honest gentleman—he very often forgot to do this same, but he did it this morning carefully—much I am afraid as a kind of charm or incantation, till he came to the Lord's Prayer itself, and then his whole happy soul wedded itself to the eternal words, and he arose calm and happy, and went down to bathe.

Happy, I said. Was he really happy? He ought to have been; for every wish he had in this life was fulfilled. And yet, when Jim, and he, and Halbert, were walking, towel in hand, down the garden, they held this conversation:

" Sam, my dear old brother, at last," said Jim, " are you happy? "

" I ought to be, Jim," said Sam; " but I'm in the most confounded fright, sir."—They generally are in a fright, when they are going to be married, those Benedicts, What the deuce are they afraid of?

Our dear Jim was in anything but an enviable frame of mind. He had found out several things which did not at all conduce to his happiness; he had found out that it was one thing to propose going to India, or No-man's-land, and cutting off every tie and association which he had in the world; and that it was quite another thing to leave his sister in the keeping of his friend Sam, and another to part from her probably for ever; and, last of all, he had found out, ever since his father had put his arm round his neck and kissed him that night we know of, that he loved that father beyond all men in this world. It was a new discovery; he had never known it till he found he had got to part with him. And now, when he woke in the night, our old merry-hearted Jim sat up in bed, and wept; ay, and no shame to him for it, when he thought of that handsome, calm, bronzed face, tearless and quiet there, over the fortifications and the mathematics, when he was far away.

" He will never say a word, Sam," said Jim, as they were walking down to bathe this very morning of the wedding; " but he'll think the more. Sam, I am afraid I have done a selfish thing in going; but if I were to draw back now, I should never be the same to him again. He couldn't stand that. But I am sorry I ever thought of it."

" I don't know, Jim," said Halbert, pulling off his trousers, " I really don't know of any act of parliament passed in favour of the Brentwood family, exempting them from the ordinary evils of humanity. Do you think now, that when John Nokes, aged nineteen, goes into market at Cambridge, or elsewhere, and 'lists, and never goes home again; do you think, I say, that that lad don't feel a very strange emptiness about the epigastric region when he thinks of the grey-headed old man that is sitting waiting for him at the cottage door? And," added Halbert, standing on the plunging-stage Adamically, without a rag upon him, pointing at Jim with his finger in an oratorical manner, " do you think that the old man who sits there, year after year, waiting for him who never comes, and telling the neighbours that his lad who is gone for a sodger, was the finest lad in the village, do you think that old man feels nothing? Give up fine feelings, Jim. You don't know what trouble is yet."

And so he went souse into the water.

And after the bathe all came up and dressed—white trousers and brilliant ties being the order of the day. Then we all, from the bachelor side of the house, assembled in the veranda, for the ceremony was not to be performed till eight, and it was not more than half-past seven. There was the promise of a very awkward half-hour, so I was glad of a diversion caused by my appearing in a blue coat with gilt buttons, and pockets in the tails—a coat I had not brought out for twenty years, but as good as new, I give you my honour. Jim was very funny about that coat, and I encouraged him by defending it, and so we got through ten minutes, and kept Sam amused. Then one of the grooms, a lad I mentioned before as bringing a note to Baroona on one occasion, a long brown-faced lad, born of London parents in the colony, made a diversion by coming round to look at us. He admired us very much, but my gilt buttons took his attention principally. He guessed they must have cost a matter of twenty pound, but on my telling him that the whole affair was bought for three pounds, he asked, I remember:

" What are they made on, then? "

Brass, I supposed, and gilt. So he left me in disgust, and took up with Jim's trousers, wanting to know " if they was canvas."

" Satin velvet," Jim said; and then the Major came out and beckoned us into the drawing-room.

And there she was, between Mrs. Buckley and Mary Hawker, dressed all in white, looking at beautiful as morning. Frank Maberly stood beside a little table, which the women had made into an altar, with the big Prayer-book in his hand. And we all stood around, and the servants thronged in, and Sam, taking Alice's hand, went up and stood before Frank Maberly.

Captain Brentwood, of the artillery, would give this woman to be married to this man, with ten thousand blessings on her head; and Samuel Buckley, of Baroona, would take this woman as his wedded wife, in sickness and health, for richer, for poorer, till death did them part. And, " Yes, by George, he will," says Jim to himself—but I heard him, for we were reading out of the same Prayer-book.

And so it was all over. And the Doctor, who had all the morning been invisible, and had only slipped into the room just as the ceremony had begun, wearing on his coat a great star, a prodigy, which had drawn many eyes from their Prayer-books, the Doctor, I say, came up, star and all, and taking Alice's hand, kissed her forehead, and then clasped a splendid necklace round her throat.

Then followed all the usual kissings and congratulations, and then came the breakfast. I hope Alice and Sam were happy, as happy as young folks can be in such a state of flutter and excitement; but all I know is, that the rest of the party were thoroughly and utterly miserable. The certainty that this was the break-up of our happy old society, that all that was young, and merry, and graceful among us was about to take wing and leave us old folks sitting there lonely and dull. The thought, that neither Baroona nor Garoopna could ever be again what they had once been, and that never again we should hear those merry voices, wakening us in the morning, or ringing pleasant by the river on the soft summer's evening; these thoughts, I say, made us but a dull party, although Covetown and the Doctor made talking enough for the rest of us.

There was something I could not understand about the Doctor. He talked loud and nervously all breakfast-time, and afterwards, when Alice retired to change her dress, and we were all standing about talking, he came up to me in a quiet corner where I was, and took me by the hand. " My dear old friend," he said, " you will never forget me, will you?"

" Forget you, Baron! never," I said. I would have asked him more, but there was Alice in the room, in her pretty blue riding-habit and hat, ready for a start, and Sam beside her, whip in hand; so we all crowded out to say good-bye.

That was the worst time of all. Mrs. Buckley had said farewell and departed. Jim was walking about, tearless, but quite unable to answer me when I asked him a question. Those two grim old warriors, the Captain and the Major, were taking things very quietly, but did not seem inclined to talk much, while the Doctor was conducting himself like an amiable lunatic, getting in everybody's way as he followed Sam about.

"Sam," he said, after Alice had been lifted on her horse, "my dear Sam, my good pupil, you will never forget your old tutor, will you?"

"Never, never!" said Sam; "not likely, if I lived to be a hundred. I shall see you to-morrow."

"Oh yes, surely," said the Baron; "we shall meet to-morrow for certain. But good-bye, my boy; good-bye."

And then the young couple rode away to Baroona, which was empty, swept, and garnished, ready for their reception. And the servants cheered them as they went away, and tall Eleanor sent one of her husband's boots after them for luck, with such force and dexterity that it fell close to the heels of Widderin, setting him capering—then Sam turned round and waved his hat, and they were gone.

And we turned round to look at one another, and lo! another horse, the Doctor's, was being led up and down by a groom, saddled; and, while we wondered, out came the Doctor himself and began strapping his valise on to the saddle.

"And where are you going to-day, Baron?" asked the Major.

"I am going," said he, "to Sydney. I sail for Europe in a week."

Our astonishment was too great for ejaculations; we kept an awful silence; this was the first hint he had given us of his intention.

"Yes," said he, "I sail from Sydney this day week. I could not embitter my boy's wedding-day by letting him know that he was to lose me; better that he should come back and find me gone. I must go, and I foresaw it when the letter came; but I would not tell you, because I knew you would be so sorry to part. I have been inside and said farewell to Mrs. Buckley. And now, my friends, shorten this scene for me. Night and day, for a month, I have been dreading it, and now let us spare one another. Why should we tear our hearts asunder by a long leave-taking? Oh, Buckley, Buckley! after so many years——"

Only a hurried shaking of hands, and he was gone. Down by the paddock to the river, and when he reached the height beyond, he turned and waved his hand. Then he went on his way across the old plains, and we saw him lessening in the distance until he disappeared altogether, and we saw him no more. No more!

In two months from that time Jim and Halbert were gone to India, Sam and Alice were away to the Darling Downs, Desborough and the Doctor had sailed for Europe, and we old folks, taking up our residence at Baroona, had agreed to make common house of it. Of course we were very dull at first, when we missed half of

the faces which had been used to smile upon us; but this soon
wore off. During the succeeding winter I remember many pleasant
evenings, when the Captain, the Major, Mrs. Buckley, and myself
played whist, shilling points and the rigour of the game, and while
Mary Hawker, in her widow's weeds, sat sewing by the fireside,
contentedly enough.

CHAPTER XLVII

HOW MARY HAWKER SAID "YES"

IT was one evening during the next spring, and the game of whist
was over for the night. The servant had just brought in tumblers
with a view to whisky-and-water before bed. I was preparing to
pay fourteen shillings to Mrs. Buckley, and was rather nervous
about meeting my partner, the Major's eye, when he, tapping the
table with his hand, spoke:

"The most childish play, Hamlyn; the most childish play."

"I don't defend the last game," I said. "I thought you were
short of diamonds—at least I calculated on the chance of your
being so, having seven myself. But please to remember, Major,
that you yourself lost two tricks in hearts, in the first game of the
second rubber."

"And why, sir?" said the Major. "Tell me that, sir. Because
you confused me by leading queen, when you had ace, king, queen.
The most utterly schoolboy play. I wouldn't have done such a
thing at Eton."

"I had a flush of them," I said eagerly. "And I meant to lead
ace, and then get trumps out. But I put down queen by mistake."

"You can make what excuses you like, Hamlyn," said the Major.
"But the fact remains the same. There is one great fault in your
character, the greatest fault I know of, and which you ought to
study to correct. I tell you of it boldly as an old friend. You are
too confoundedly chary in leading out your trumps, and you can't
deny it."

"Hallo!" said Captain Brentwood, "who comes so late?"

Mary Hawker rose from her chair, and looked eagerly towards
the door. "I know who it is," she said, blushing. "I heard him
laugh."

In another moment the door was thrown open, and in stalked
Tom Troubridge.

" By George! " he said. " Don't all speak to me at once. I feel
the queerest wambling in my innards, as we used to say in Devon,
at the sight of so many old faces. Somehow, a man can't make a
new home in a hurry. It's the people make the home, not the
house and furniture. My dear old cousin, and how are you? "

" I am very quiet, Tom. I am much happier than I thought to
have been. And I am deeply thankful to see you again."

" And how is my boy, Tom? " said the Major.

" And how is my girl, Tom? " said the Captain.

" Sam," said Tom, " is a sight worth a guinea, and Mrs. Samuel
looks charming, but—— In point of fact, you know, I believe she
expects——"

" No! " said the Captain. " You don't say so."

" Fact, my dear sir."

" Dear me." said the Major, drumming on the table. " I hope it
will be a b——. By the by, how go the sheep? "

" You never saw such a country, sir! " said Tom. " We have got
nearly five thousand on each run, and there is no one crowding
up yet. If we can hold that ground with our produce, and such
store-sheep as we can pick up, we shall do wonders."

By this time Tom was at supper, and between the business of
satisfying a hunger of fifteen hours, began asking after old friends.

" How are the Mayfords? " he asked.

" Poor Mrs. Mayford is better," said Mrs. Buckley. " She and
Ellen are just starting for Europe. They have sold their station,
and we have bought it."

" What are they going to do in England? " asked Tom.

" Going to live with their relations in Hampshire."

" Ellen will be a fine match for some young English squire," said
Tom. " She will have twenty thousand pounds some day, I suppose."

And then we went on talking about other matters.

A little scene took place in the garden next morning, which may
astonish some of my readers, but which did not surprise me in the
least. I knew it would happen, sooner or later, and when I saw
Tom's air, on his arrival the night before, I said to myself, " It is
coming," and so sure enough it did. And I got all the circumstances
out of Tom only a few days afterwards.

Mary Hawker was now a very handsome woman, about one-and-
forty. There may have been a grey hair here and there among
her long black tresses, but they were few and far between. I used
to watch her sometimes of an evening, and wonder to myself how
she had come through such troubles, and lived; and yet there she

was on the night Tom arrived, for instance, sitting quite calm and cheerful beside the fire in her half-mourning (she had soon dropped her weeds, perhaps, considering who her husband had been, a piece of good taste), with quite a placid, contented look in her fine black eyes. I think no one was capable of feeling deeper for a time, but her power of resilience was marvellous. I have noticed that before. It may, God forgive me, have given me some slight feeling of contempt for her, because, forsooth, she did not brood over and nurse an old grief as I did myself. I am not the man to judge her. When I look back on my own wasted life; when I see how for one boyish fancy I cut myself off from all the ties of domestic life, to hold my selfish way alone, I sometimes think that she has shown herself a better woman than I have a man. Ah! well, old sweetheart, not much to boast of either of us. Let us get on.

She was walking in the garden next morning, and Tom came and walked beside her; and after a little he said:

" So you are pretty well contented, cousin ? "

" I am as well content," she said, " as a poor, desolate, old childless widow could hope to be. There is no happiness left for me in this life! "

" Who told you that? " said Tom. " Who told you that the next twenty years of your life might not be happier than any that have gone before? "

" How could that be? " she asked. " What is left for me now, but to go quietly to my grave? "

" Grave! " said Tom. " Who talks of graves for twenty years to come! Mary, my darling, I have waited for you so long and faithfully, you will not disappoint me at last? "

" What do you mean? What can you mean? "

" Mean! " said he; " why, I mean this, cousin: I mean you to be my wife—to come and live with me as my honoured wife, for the next thirty years, please God! "

" You are mad! " she said. " Do you know what you say? Do you know who you are speaking to? "

" To my old sweetheart, Polly Thornton! " he said, with a laugh —" to no one else in the world."

" You are wrong," she said; " you may try to forget now, but you will remember afterwards. I am not Mary Thornton. I am an old broken woman, whose husband was transported for coining. and hung for murder, and worse! "

" Peace be with him! " said Tom. " I am not asking who your husband was; I have had twenty years to think about that, and at the end of twenty years, I say, my dear old sweetheart, you are free at last: will you marry me?"

"Impossible!" said Mary. "All the countryside knows who I am. Think of the eternal disgrace that clings to me. Oh, never, never!"

"Then you have no objection to me? eh, cousin?"

"To you, my kind, noble old partner? Ah, I love and honour you above all men!"

"Then," said Tom, putting his arm round her waist, "to the devil with all the nonsense you have just been talking, about eternal disgraces and so forth! I am an honest man, and you're an honest woman, and, therefore, what cause or impediment can there be? Come, Mary, it's no use resisting; my mind is made up, and you *must*!"

"Oh, think!" she said; "oh, think only once, before it is too late for ever!"

"I have thought," said Tom, "as I told you before, for twenty years; and I ain't likely to alter my opinion in ten minutes. Come, Mary. Say, yes!"

And so she said yes.

"Mrs. Buckley," said Tom, as they came up arm-in-arm to the house; "it will be a good thing if somebody was to go up to our place, and nurse Mrs. Sam in her confinement."

"I shall go up myself," said Mrs. Buckley, "though how I am to get there I hardly know. It must be nearly eight hundred miles, I am afraid."

"I don't think you need, my dear madam," said he. "My wife will make an excellent nurse!"

"Your wife!"

Tom looked at Mary, who blushed, and Mrs. Buckley came up and kissed her.

"I am so glad, so very glad, my love!" she said. "The very happiest and wisest thing that could be! I have been hoping for it, my love, and I felt sure it would be so, sooner or later. How glad your dear aunt would be if she were alive!"

And, in short, he took her off with him, and they were married, and went up to join Sam and his wife in New England—reducing our party to four. Not very long after they were gone, we heard that there was a new Sam Buckley born, who promised, said the wise woman, to be as big a man as his father. Then, at an interval of very little more than two years, Mrs. Buckley got a long letter from Alice, announcing the birth of a little girl to the Troubridges.

This letter is still extant, and in my possession, having been lent me, among other family papers, by Agnes Buckley, as soon as she heard that I was bent upon correcting these memoirs to fit them for the press. I will give you some extracts from it:

   . . . Dear Mary Troubridge has got a little girl, a sweet, quiet, bright-eyed little thing, taking, I imagine, after old Miss Thornton. They are going to call it Agnes Alice, after you and I, my dearest mother.

You cannot imagine how different Mary is grown from what she used to be! Stout, merry, and matronly, quite! She keeps the house alive, and I think I never saw a couple more sincerely attached than are she and her husband. He is a most excellent companion for my Sam. Not to make matters too long, we are just about as happy as four people can be. Some day we may all come to live together again, and then our delight will be perfect.

I got Jim's letter which you sent me. . . . Sam and his partner are embarking every sixpence they can spare in buying town and suburban lots at Melbourne. I know every street and alley in that wonderful city (containing near a hundred houses) on the map, but I am not very likely to go there ever. Let us hope that Sam's speculations will turn out profitable.

Best love to Mr. Hamlyn. . . .

I must make a note to this letter. Alice refers to a letter received from Jim, which, as near as I can make the dates agree, must be the one I hold in my hand at this moment. I am not sure, but I think so. This one runs:

Dear Dad, . . . I have been down among the dead men, and since then up into the seventh heaven, in consequence of being not only gazetted, but promoted. The beggars very nearly did for us. All our fortifications, the prettiest things ever done under the circumstances, executed under Bobby's own eye, were thrown down by—what do you think?—an earthquake! Perhaps we didn't swear—Lord forgive us! Akbar had a shy at us immediately, but got a most immortal licking!

Is not this a most wonderful thing about Halbert? The girl that he was to be married to was supposed to be lost, coming out in the *Assam*. And now it appears that she wasn't lost at all (the girl, I mean, not the ship), but that she was wrecked on the east coast of Madagascar, and saved, with five-and-twenty more.

She came on to Calcutta, and they were married the week after he got his troop. She is uncommonly handsome and ladylike, but looks rather brown and lean from living on birds' nests and seaweed for above six months of her life.

[Allow me to remark that this must be romance on Jim's part; birds' nests and trepang are not found in Madagascar.]

My wound is nearly all right again. It was only a prick with a spear in my thigh——

It is the very deuce editing these old letters without anything to guide me. As far as I can make out by myself (Jim being now down at Melton, hunting, and not having answered my letter of inquiries), this letter must have come accompanied by an Indian newspaper containing the account of some battle or campaign in which he was engaged. Putting this and that together, I am inclined to believe that it refers to the defence of Jellalabad by Sir Robert Sale, in which I know he was engaged. I form this opinion from the fact of his mentioning that the fortifications were destroyed by an earthquake. And I very much fear that the individual so disrespectfully mentioned above as "Bobby," was no other than the great hero himself.

After this time there was a long dull time with no news from him or from anyone. Then Sam came down from New England, and paid us a visit, which freshened us up a little. But in spite of this and other episodes, there was little change or excitement for us four. We made common house of it, and never parted from one another more than a day. Always of an evening came the old friendly rubber, I playing with the Major, and Captain Brentwood with Mrs. Buckley. The most remarkable event I have to chronicle during the long period which followed, is, that one day a bushfire came right up to the garden rails, and was beaten out with difficulty; and that same evening I held nine trumps, ace, queen, knave, nine of hearts, and the rest small. I cannot for the life of me remember what year it was in, somewhere between forty-two and forty-five, I believe, because within a year or two of that time we heard that a large comet had appeared in England, and that Sir Robert Peel was distrusted on the subject of Protection. After all, it is no great consequence, though it is rather provoking, because I never before or since held more than eight trumps. Burnside, the cattle-dealer, claims to have had eleven, but I may state, once for all, that I doubt that man's statements on this and every other subject on which he speaks.—He knows where I am to be found.

My man Dick, too, somehow or another constituted himself my groom and valet. And the Major was well contented with the arrangement. So we four, Major and Mrs. Buckley, Captain Brentwood and I, sat there in the old station night after night, playing our whist, till even my head, the youngest of the four, began to be streaked with grey, and sixteen years were past.

CHAPTER XLVIII

THE LATEST INTELLIGENCE

IT is March, 1856. The short autumn day is rapidly giving place to night; and darkness, and the horror of a great tempest, is settling down upon the desolate grey sea, which heaves and seethes for ever round Cape Horn.

A great clipper ship, the noblest and swiftest of her class, is hurling along her vast length before the terrible west wind. Hour by hour through the short and gloomy day, sail after sail has gone fluttering in; till now, at nightfall, she reels and rolls before the storm under a single, close-reefed, main-topsail.

There is a humming, and a roaring, and a rushing of great waters, so that they who are clinging to the bulwarks, and watching, awe-struck, this great work of the Lord's, cannot hear one another though they shout. Now there is a grey mountain which chases the ship, overtakes her, pours cataracts of water over her rounded stern, and goes hissing and booming past her. And now a roll more frantic than usual, nigh dips her mainyard, and sends the water spouting wildly over her bulwarks.

(" Oh, you very miserable ass," said Captain Brentwood; " to sit down and try to describe the indescribable. Do you think that because you can see all the scene before you now, because your flesh creeps, and your blood moves, as you call it to mind, do you think, I say, that you can describe it? Do you think that you can give a man, in black and white, with ink, and on paper, any real notion of that most tremendous spectacle, a sharp-bowed ship running before a gale of wind through the ice in the great South Sea, where every wave rolls round the world? Go to—read Tom Cringle, who has given up his whole soul to descriptions, and see how many pictures dwell in your mind's eye, after reading his books. Two, or at most three, and they, probably, quite different from what he intended you to see, lovely as they are;—leave describing things, man, and give us some more facts."

Said Major Buckley, " Go on, Hamlyn, and do the best you can. Don't mind him." And so I go on accordingly.)

61° 30" South. The Horn, storm-beaten, desolate, four hundred miles to the North, and barely forty miles to the South, that cruel, gleaming ice barrier, which we saw to-day when the weather lifted at noon, and which we know is there yet, though we dare not think about it. There comes to us, though, in spite of ourselves, a vision of what may happen at any hour. A wild cry from the foretop. A mass, grey, indistinct, horrible, rising from the wild waters, scarce a hundred yards from her bowsprit. A mad hurrying to and fro. A crash. A great ruin of masts and spars, and then utter, hopeless destruction. That is the way the poor old *Madagascar* must have gone. The Lord send us safe through the ice.

Stunned, drenched to the skin, half-frightened, but wildly excited and determined to see out, what a landsman has but seldom a chance of seeing, a great gale of wind at sea, I clung tight to the starboard bulwarks of Mr. Richard Green's new clipper, *Sultan*, Captain Sneezer, about an hour after dark, as she was rounding the Horn, watching much such a scene as I have attempted to give you a notion of above. And as I held on there, wishing that the directors of my insurance office could see me at that moment, the first mate, coming from forward, warping himself from one belaying-pin to another, roared in my ear, " that he thought it was going to blow."

" Man! man! " I said, " do you mean to tell me it is not blowing now ? "

" A bit of a breeze," he roared; but his roar came to me like a whisper. However, I pretty soon found out that this was something quite out of the common; for, crawling up along the gangway which runs between the poop-house and the bulwarks, I came with great difficulty to the stern; and there I saw the two best men in the larboard watch (let us immortalise them, they were Deaf Bob, and Harry the Digger), lashed to the wheel, and the skipper himself, steadfast and anxious, alongside of them, lashed to a cleat on the afterpart of the deck-house. So thinks I, if these men are made fast, this is no place for me to be loose in, and crawled down to my old place in the waist, at the after end of the spare topsail-yard, which was made fast to the starboard bulwarks, and which extended a little abaft of the main shrouds.

If any gentleman can detect a nautical error in that last sentence, I shall feel obliged by his mentioning it.

Somebody who came forth from the confusion, and was gone again, informed me that " He was going to lay her to, and that I'd better hold on." I comforted myself with the reflection that I was doing exactly the right thing, holding on like grim death.

Then something happened, and I am sorry to say I don't exactly know what. I find in my notes, taken shortly afterwards, from the dictation of an intelligent midshipman, " that the fore-royal yárd got jammed with the spanker-boom, and carried away the larboard quarter-boat." Nautical friends have since pointed out to me that this involves an impossibility. I dare say it does. I know it involved an impossibility of turning in without subjecting yourself to a hydropathic remedy of violent nature, by going to bed in wet blankets, and of getting anything for breakfast besides wet biscuit and cold tea. Let it go; something went wrong, and the consequences were these.

A wall of water, looming high above her mainyard, came rushing and booming along, dark, terrible, opaque. For a moment I saw it curling overhead, and would have cried out, I believe, had there been time; but a midshipman, a mere child, slipped up before me, and caught hold of my legs, while I tried to catch his collar. Then I heard the skipper roar out, in that hoarse throaty voice that seamen use when excited, " Hold on, the sea's aboard," and then a stunning, blinding rush of water buried us altogether. The *Sultan* was on her beam-ends, and what was more, seemed inclined to stay there, so that I, holding on by the bulwarks, saw the sea seething and boiling almost beneath my feet, which were swinging clear of the deck.

But the midshipman sung out that she was righting again, which she did rather quicker than was desirable, bringing every loose article on deck down to our side again with a rush. A useless, thundering, four-pounder gun, of which terrible implements of war we carried six, came plunging across from the other side of the deck, and went crashing through the bulwarks, out into the sea, within two feet of my legs.

" I think," I said, trying to persuade myself that I was not frightened, " I think I shall go into the cuddy."

That was not very easy to do. I reached the door, and got hold of the handle, and, watching my opportunity, slipped dexterously in, and making a plunge, came against the surgeon, who, seated on a camp-stool, was playing piquette, and overthrew him into a corner.

" Repique, by jingo," shouted Sam Buckley, who was the surgeon's opponent. "See what a capital thing it is to have an old friend like Hamlyn, to come in and knock your opponent down just at the right moment."

"And papa was losing, too, Uncle Jeff," added a handsome lad, about fifteen, who was leaning over Sam's shoulder.

"What are they doing to you, Doctor?" said Alice Buckley, _née_ Brentwood, coming out of a cabin, and supporting herself to a seat by her husband and son.

"Why," replied the surgeon, "Hamlyn knocked me down just in a moment of victory, but his nefarious project has failed, for I have kept possession of my cards. Play, Buckley."

Let us give a glance at the group which is assembled beneath the swing lamp in the reeling cabin. The wife and son are both leaning over the father's shoulder, and the three faces are together. Sam is about forty. There is not a wrinkle in that honest forehead, and the eyes beam upon you as kindly and pleasantly as ever they did; and when, after playing to the surgeon, he looks up and laughs, one sees that he is just the same old Sam that used to lie, as a lad, dreaming in the veranda at Garoopna. No trouble has left its shadow there. Alice, whose face is pressed against his, is now a calm young matron of three or four-and-thirty, if it were possible, more beautiful than ever, only she has grown from a Hebe into a Juno. The boy, the son and heir, is much such a stripling as I can remember his father at the same age, but handsomer. And while we look, another face comes peering over his shoulder; the laughing face of a lovely girl, with bright sunny hair, and soft blue eyes; the face of Maud Buckley, Sam's daughter.

They are going home to England. Sam—what between his New England runs, where there are now, under Tom Troubridge's care, 118,000 sheep, and his land speculations at Melbourne, which have turned him out somewhere about 1000 per cent. since the gold discovery—Sam, I say, is one of the richest of her Majesty's subjects in the Southern hemisphere. I would give £200,000 for Sam, and make a large fortune in the surplus. "And so," I suppose you say, "he is going home to buy Clere." Not at all, my dear sir. Clere is bought, and Sam is going home to take possession. "Marry, how?" Thus:

Does any one of my readers remember that our dear old friend Agnes Buckley's maiden name was Talbot, and that her father owned the property adjoining Clere? "We do not remember," you say; "or at least, if we do, we are not bound to; you have not mentioned the circumstance since the very beginning of this exces-

sively wearisome book, forty years ago." Allow me to say, that
I have purposely avoided mentioning them all along, in order that,
at this very point, I might come down on you like a thunderbolt
with this piece of information; namely: That Talbot of Beaulieu
Castle, the towers of which were visible from Clere Terrace, had
died without male issue. That Marian and Gertrude Talbot, the
two pretty girls, Agnes Buckley's eldest sisters, who used to come
in and see old Marmaduke when James was campaigning, had
never married. That Marian was dead. That Gertrude, a broken
old maid, was sole owner of Beaulieu Castle, with eight thousand
a year; and that Agnes Buckley, her sister, and consequently, Sam
as next in succession, was her heir.

All the negotiations for the purchase of Clere had been carried
on through Miss Gertrude and her steward. The brewer died, the
property was sold, and Sam, by his agents, bought old Clere back,
eight months before this, for £48,000.

"Then, why on earth," says Mrs. Councillor Wattlegum (our
Colonial Mrs. Grundy), "didn't they go home overland? How
could people with such wealth as you describe, demean themselves
by going home round the Horn, like a parcel of diggers?"

"Because, my dear Madam, the young folks were very anxious
to see an iceberg. Come, let us get on."

The gale has lasted three days, and in that time we have run
before it on our course 970 miles. The fourth morning breaks
gloriously bright, with the shadows of a few fleecy clouds flying
across the bright blue heaving sea. The ship, with all canvas
crowded on her, alow and aloft, is racing on, fifteen knots an hour,
with a brisk cold wind full on her quarter, heeling over till the
water comes rushing and spouting through her leeward ports, and
no man can stand without holding on, but all are merry and happy
to see the water fly past like blue champagne, and to watch the
seething wake that the good ship leaves behind her. Ah! what is
this, that all are crowding down to leeward to look at? Is this the
Crystal Palace, of which we have read, come out to sea to meet us?
No! the young folks are going to be gratified. It is a great iceberg,
and we shall pass about a mile to windward.

Certainly worth seeing. Much more tremendous than I had
expected, though my imagination had rather run riot in expectation.
Just a great floating cluster of shining splintered crystals, about
a mile long and 300 feet high, with the cold hungry sea leaping and
gnawing at its base—that is all. Send up those German musicians
here, and let us hear the echo of one of Strauss's waltzes come

ringing back from the chill green caverns. Then away; her head is northward again now, we may sight the Falklands the day after to-morrow.

Hardly worth telling you much more about that happy voyage, I think, and really I remember but few things more of note. A great American ship in 45°, steaming in the teeth of the wind, heaving her long gleaming sides through the roll of the South Atlantic. The *Royal Charter* passing us like a phantom ship through the hot haze, when we were becalmed on the line, waking the silence of the heaving glassy sea with her throbbing propeller. A valiant vainglorious little gunboat going out all the way to China by herself, giving herself the airs of a seventy-four, requiring boats to be sent on board her, as if we couldn't have stowed her, guns and all, on our poop, and never crowded ourselves! A noble transport, with 53 painted on her bows, swarming with soldiers for India, to whom we gave three times three. All these things have faded from my recollection in favour of a bright spring morning in April.

A morning which, beyond all others in my life, stands out clear and distinct, as the most memorable. Jim Buckley shoved aside my cabin door when I was dressing, and says he—" Uncle Jeff, my Dad wants you immediately; he is standing by the davits of the larboard quarter-boat."

And so I ran up to Sam, and he took my arm and pointed northward. Over the gleaming morning sea rose a purple mountain, shadowed here and there by travelling clouds; and a little red-sailed boat was diving and plunging towards us, with a red flag fluttering on her mast.

" What! " I said—but I could say no more.

" The *Lizard*! "

But I could not see it now for a blinding haze, and I bent down my head upon the bulwarks—Bah! I am but a fool after all. What could there have been to cry at in a Cornish moor, and a Falmouth pilot boat? I am not quite so young as I was, and my nerves are probably failing. That must have been it. " When I saw the steeple," says M. Tapley, " I thought it would have choked me." Let me say the same of Eddystone Lighthouse, which we saw that afternoon; and have done with sentiment for good. If my memory serves me rightly, we have had a good deal of that sort of thing in the preceding pages.

I left the ship at Plymouth, and Sam went on in her to London. I satisfied my soul with amazement at the men-of-war, and the breakwater; and, having bought a horse, I struck boldly across the moor for Drumston, revisiting on my way many a well-known snipe-ground, and old trout-haunt; and so, on the third morning, I reached Drumston once more, and stabled my horse at a little public-house near the church.

It was about eight o'clock on a Tuesday morning; nevertheless, the church bell was going, and the door was open as if for prayer. I was a little surprised at this, but having visited the grave where my father and mother lay, and then passed on to the simple head-stone which marked the resting place of John Thornton and his wife, I brushed through the docks and nettles, towards the lych-gate, in the shadow of which stood the clergyman, a gentlemanly-looking young man, talking to a very aged woman in a red cloak.

He saluted me courteously, and passed on, talking earnestly and kindly to his aged companion, and so the remarkable couple went into the church, and the bell stopped.

I looked around. Close to me, leaning against the gate, was a coarse-looking woman about fifty, who had just set down a red earthen pitcher to rest herself, and seemed not disinclined for a gossip. And at the same moment I saw a fat man, about my own age, with breeches unbuttoned at the knee, grey worsted stockings and slippers, and looking altogether as if he was just out of bed, having had too much to drink the night before; such a man, I say, I saw coming across the road, towards us, with his hands in his pockets.

"Good morning," I said to the woman. "Pray what is the clergyman's name?"

"Mr. Montague," she answered with a curtsey.

"Does he have prayers every morning?"

"Every marnin' of his life," she said. "He's a Papister."

"You'm a fool, Cis Jewell," said the man, who had by this time arrived. "You'm leading the gentleman wrong, he's a Pussyite."

"And there bain't much difference, I'm thinking, James Gosford," said Cis Jewell.

I started. James Gosford had been one of my favourite old comrades in times gone by, and here he was. Could it be he? Could this fat red-faced man of sixty-one be the handsome hard-riding young dandy of forty years ago? It was he, doubtless, and in another moment I should have declared myself, but a new interruption occurred.

The bell began again, and service was over. The old woman came out of the porch and slowly down the path towards us.

"Is that all his congregation?" I asked.

"That's all, sir," said Gosford. "Sometimes some of they young villains of boys gets in, and our old clerk, Jerry, hunts 'em round and round all prayer-time; but there's none goes regular except the old 'ooman."

"And she had need to pray a little more than other folks," said Cis Jewell, folding her arms, and balancing herself in a conversational attitude. "My poor old grandfather——"

Further conversation was stopped by the near approach of the old woman herself, and I looked up at her with some little curiosity. A very old woman she was surely; and while I seemed struggling with some sort of recollection, she fixed her eyes upon me, and we knew one another.

"Geoffry Hamlyn," she said, without a sign of surprise. "You are welcome back to your native village. When your old comrade did not know you, I, whose eyes are dim with the sorrow of eighty years, recognised you at once. They may well call me the wise woman."

"Good God!" was all I could say. "Can this be Madge?"

"This is Madge," she said, "who has lived long enough to see and to bless the man who saw and comforted her poor lost boy in prison, when all beside fell off from him. The Lord reward you for it."

"How did you know that, Madge?"

"Ask a witch where she gets her information!" laughed she. "God forgive me. I'll tell you how it was. One of the turnkeys in that very prison was a Cooper, a Hampshire gipsy, and he, knowing my boy to be half-blooded, passed all the facts on through the tribes to me, who am a mother among them! Did you see him die?" she added, eagerly putting her great bony hand upon my arm, and looking up in my face.

"No! no! mother," I answered; "I hadn't courage for that."

"I heard he died game," she continued, half to herself. "He should a done. There was a deal of wild blood in him from both sides. Are you going up to the woodlands, to see the old place? 'Tis all in ruins now; and the choughs and stares are building and brooding in the chimney-nook where I nursed him. I shall not have much longer to wait; I only stayed for this. Good-bye."

And she was gone; and Gosford, relieved by her departure, was affectionately lugging me off to his house. Oh, the mixture of wealth and discomfort that house exhibited! Oh, the warm-hearted jollity of every one there! Oh, to see those three pretty, well-educated girls taking their father off by force, and making him clean himself in honour of my arrival! Oh, the merry evening we had! What, though the cider disagreed with me? What, though I knew it would disagree with me at the time I drank it? That noisy, jolly night in the old Devonshire grange was one of the pleasantest of my life.

And, to my great surprise, the Vicar came in in the middle of it, and made himself very agreeable to me. He told me that old Madge, as far as he could see, was a thoroughly converted and orderly person, having thrown aside all pretence of witchcraft. That she lived on some trifle of hoarded money of her own, and a small parish allowance that she had; and that she had only come back to the parish some six years since, after wandering about as a gipsy in almost every part of England. He was so good as to undertake the delivery of a small sum to her weekly from me, quite sufficient to enable her to refuse the parish allowance, and live comfortably (he wrote to me a few months afterwards, and told me that it was required no longer, for that Madge was gone to rest at last); and a good deal more news he gave me, very little of which is interesting here.

He told me that Lord C——, John Thornton's friend, was dead; that he never thoroughly got over the great Reform debate, in which he over-exerted himself; and that, after the passing of that Bill, he had walked joyfully home and had a fit, which prevented his ever taking any part in politics afterwards, though he lived above ten years. That his son was not so popular as his father, in consequence of his politics, which were too conservative for the new class of tenants his father had brought in; and his religious opinions, which, said the clergyman, were those of a sound Churchman; by which he meant, I rather suspect, that he was a pretty smart Tractarian. I was getting won with this young gentleman, in spite of religious difference, when he chose to say that the parish had never been right since Maberly had it, and that the Dissenters always raved about him to this day; whereby, he concluded, that Frank Maberly was far from orthodox. I took occasion to say that Frank was the man of all others in this world whom I admired most, and that, considering he had sealed his faith with his life, I thought that he ought to be very reverently spoken of. After this there arose a little coolness, and he went home.

I went up to town by the Great Western, and, for the first time, knew what was meant by railway travelling. True, I had seen and travelled on that monument of human industry, the Hobson's Bay

Railroad, but that stupendous work hardly prepared me for the Great Western. And on this journey I began to understand, for the first time in my life, what a marvellous country this England of ours was. I wondered at the wealth and traffic I saw, even in comparatively unimportant towns. I wondered at the beauty and solidity of the railway works; at the vast crowds of people which I saw at every station; at the manly, independent bearing of the men of the working classes, which combined so well with their civility and intelligence; and I thought, with a laugh, of the fate of any eighty thousand men who might shove their noses into this beehive, while there was such material to draw upon. Such were the thoughts of an Englishman landing in England, from whom the evils produced by dense population were as yet hidden.

But when I got into the whirl of London, I was completely overwhelmed and stupefied. I did not enjoy anything. The eternal roar was so different to what I had been used to; and I had stayed there a couple of months before I had got a distinct impression of anything, save and except the Crystal Palace at Sydenham.

It was during this visit to London that I heard of the fall of Von Landstein's (Dr. Mulhaus's) Ministry, which had happened a year or two before. And now, also, I read the speech he made on his resignation, which, for biting sarcasm and bitter truth rudely told, is unequalled by any speech I ever read. A more witty, more insolent, more audacious tirade, was never hurled at a successful opposition by a fallen minister. The K—— party sat furious, as one by one were seized on by our ruthless friend, held up to ridicule, and thrown aside. They, however, meditated vengeance.

Our friend, in the heat of debate, used the word, " Drummer-kopf," which answers, I believe, to our " wooden head." He applied it to no one in particular; but a certain young nobleman (Bow-wow Von Azelsberg was his name) found the epithet so applicable to his own case, that he took umbrage at it; and, being egged on by his comrades, challenged Von Landstein to mortal combat. Von Landstein received his fire without suffering, adjusted his spectacles, and shot the young gentleman in the knee, stopping *his* waltzing for ever and a day. He then departed for his castle, where he is at this present speaking (having just gone there after a visit to Clere)—busy at his great book, *The History of Fanatics and Fanaticism, from Mahomet to Joe Smith*. Beloved by all who come in contact with him; happy, honoured, and prosperous, as he so well deserves to be.

But I used to go and see everything that was to be seen, though, having no companion (for Sam was down at Clere, putting his house in order), it was very wretched work. I *did,* in fact, all the public amusements in London, and, as a matter of course, found myself one night, about eleven o'clock, at Evans's in Covent Garden.

The place was crowded to suffocation, but I got a place at a table about half-way up, opposite an old gentleman who had been drinking a good deal of brandy-and-water, and was wanting some more. Next me was an honest-looking young fellow enough, and opposite him his friend. These two looked like shop-lads, out for a " spree."

A tall old gentleman made me buy some cigars, with such an air of condescending goodwill, that I was encouraged to stop a waiter and humbly ask for a glass of whisky-and-water. He was kind enough to bring it for me; so I felt more at ease, and prepared to enjoy myself.

A very gentlemanly-looking man sang us a song, so unutterably funny that we were dissolved in inextinguishable laughter; and then, from behind a curtain, began to come boys in black, one after another, as the imps in a pantomime come from a place I dare not mention, to chase the clown to his destruction. I counted twelve of them and grew dizzy. They ranged themselves in a row, with their hands behind them, and began screeching Tennyson's *Miller's Daughter* with such a maximum of shrillness, and such a minimum of expression, that I began to think that tailing wild cattle on the mountains, at midnight, in a thunderstorm, with my boots full of water, was a far preferable situation to my present one.

They finished. Thank goodness. Ah! delusive hope. The drunken old miscreant opposite me got up an encore with the bottom of his tumbler, and we had it all over again. Who can tell my delight when he broke his glass applauding, and the waiter came down on him sharp, and made him pay for it. I gave that waiter sixpence on the spot.

Then came some capital singing, which I really enjoyed; and then came a remarkable adventure; "an adventure!" you say; "and at Evans's!" My dear sir, do you suppose that, at a moment like this, when I am pressed for space, and just coming to the end of my story—do you suppose that, at a moment like this, I would waste your time at a singing-house for nothing?

A tall, upright-looking man passed up the lane between the tables, and almost touched me as he passed. I did not catch his face, but there was something so *distingué* about him that I watched him. He had his hat off, and was smoothing down his close-cropped hair, and appeared to be looking for a seat. As he was just opposite to us, one of the young clerks leant over to the other, and said:

"That is ———." I did not catch what he said.

"By George," said the other lad. "Is it now?"

"That's *him,* sir," said the first one, with a slight disregard of grammar.

The new-comer was walking slowly up the room, and there began to arise a little breeze of applause, and then someone called out, "Three cheers for the Inkerman pet," and then there was a stamping of feet, and a little laughter and cheering, in various parts of the room; but the new-comer made one bow and walked on.

"Pray, sir," said I, bending over to one of those who had spoken before, "who is that gentleman?"

He had no need to tell me. The man we spoke of reached the orchestra and turned round. It was Jim Brentwood!

There was a great white seam down his face, and he wore a pair of light curling moustachios, but I knew him in a moment; and, when he faced round to the company, I noticed that his person seemed known to the public, for there was not a little applause with the bottom of tumblers, not unlike what one remembers at certain banquets I have been at, with certain brethren, Sons of Apollo.

In one moment we were standing face to face, shaking one another by both hands; in another, we were arm-in-arm, walking through the quiet streets towards Jim's lodgings. He had been in Ireland with his regiment, as I knew, which accounted for my not having seen him. And that night, Major Brentwood recounted to me all his part in the last great campaign, from the first fierce rush up the hill at the Alma, down to the time when our Lady pinned a certain bit of gun metal on to his coat in St. James's Park.

A few days after this, Jim and I were standing together on the platform of the Wildmoor station, on the South-Western Railway, and a couple of porters were carrying our portmanteaus towards a pair-horse phaeton, in which stood Sam Buckley, shouting to us to come on, for the horses wouldn't stand. So, in a moment, I was alongside of Sam in the front seat, with Jim standing up behind, between the grooms, and leaning over between us, to see after Sam's driving; and away we went along a splendid road, across a heath, at what seemed to me a rather dangerous pace.

"Let them go, my child," said Jim to Sam, "you've got a fair mile before you. You sit at your work in capital style. Give me time and I'll teach you to drive, Sam. How do you like this, Uncle Jeff?"

I said, "That's more than I can tell you, Master Jim. I know so little of your wheeled vehicles that I am rather alarmed."

"Ah!" said Jim, "you should have been in Calcutta when the O'Rourke and little Charley Badminton tried to drive a pair of fresh imported Australians tandem through the town. Red Maclean and I looked out of the billiard-room, and we saw the two horses go by with a bit of a shaft banging about the wheeler's hocks. So we ran and found Charley, with his head broke, standing in the middle of the street, mopping the blood off his forehead. 'Charley,' says I, 'how the deuce did this happen?' 'We met an elephant,' says he, in a faint voice."

"Have you heard anything of the Mayfords lately?" said Jim.

"You know Ellen is married?" said Sam.

"No! Is she?" I said. "And pray to whom?"

"The Squire of Monkspool," he answered. "A very fine young fellow, and clever withal."

"Did old Mrs. Mayford," asked Jim, "ever recover her reason before she died?"

"Never, poor soul," said Sam. "To the last she refused to see my mother, believing that the rivalry between Cecil and myself in some way led to his death. She was never sane after that dreadful morning."

And so with much pleasant talk we beguiled the way, till I saw, across a deep valley on our right, a line of noble heights, well timbered, but broken into open grassy glades, and smooth sheets of bright green lawn. Between us and these hills flowed a gleaming river, from which a broad avenue led up to the eye of the picture, a noble grey stone mansion, a mass of turrets, gables, and chimneys, which the afternoon sun was lighting up right pleasantly.

"That is the finest seat I have seen yet, Sam," I said. "Whose is that?"

"That," said Sam, "is Clere. My house and your home, old friend."

Swiftly up under the shadow of the elm avenue, past the herds of dappled deer, up to the broad, gravelled terrace which ran along in front of the brave old house. And there beneath the dark wild porch, above the group of servants that stood upon the steps to receive their master, was Alice, with her son and daughter beside her, waiting to welcome us, with the happy sunlight on her face.

I bought a sweet cottage, barely a mile from Clere, with forty acres of grass-land round it, and every convenience suited for an old bachelor of my moderate though comfortable means.

I took to fishing, and to the breeding of horses on a small scale, and finding that I could make myself enormously busy with these occupations, and as much hunting as I wanted, I became very comfortable, and considered myself settled.

I had plenty of society, the best in the land. Above all men I was the honoured guest at Clere, and as the county had rallied round Sam with acclamation, I saw and enjoyed to the fullest extent that charming English country life, the like of which, I take it, no other country can show.

I was a great favourite, too, with old Miss Gertrude Talbot at the castle. Her admiration and love for Sam and his wife was almost equal to mine. So we never bored one another, and so, by degrees, gaining the old lady's entire confidence, I got entrusted with a special mission of a somewhat peculiar character.

The leading desire of this good old woman's life was, that her sister, Agnes, should come back with her husband, the Major, and take possession of the castle. Again, Alice could not be content, unless her father could be induced to come back and take up his residence at Clere. And letters having failed to produce the desired effect in both instances, the Major saying that he was quite comfortable where he was, and the Captain urging that the English winters would be too rigorous for his constitution; under these circumstances, I say, I, the confidant of the family, within fifteen months of landing at Plymouth, found myself in a hot omnibus with a Mahomedan driver, jolting and bumping over the desert of Suez on my way back to Australia, charged to bring the old folks home, or never show my face again.

And it was after this journey that the scene described in the first chapter of this book took place; when I read aloud to them from the roll of manuscript mentioned there, my recollections of all that had happened to us during so many years. But since I have come back to England, these *Recollections* have been very much enlarged and improved by the assistance of Major Buckley, Agnes, and Captain Brentwood.

For I succeeded in my object, and brought them back in triumph through the Red Sea, across the Isthmus of Suez, and so by way of the Mediterranean, the Bay of Biscay, the English Channel, Southampton Water, the South-Western Railway, and Alice's new dark-blue barouche, safe and sound to Clere and the castle, where they all are at present speaking, unless some of them are gone out a-walking.

As for Tom Troubridge and Mary, they are so exceedingly happy and prosperous, that they are not worth talking about. They will come either by the *Swiftsure* or the *Norfolk,* and we have got their rooms ready for them. They say that their second child, the boy, is one of the finest riders in the colony.

" You have forgotten someone after all," says the reader after due examination. " A man we took some little interest in. It is not much matter though, we shall be glad when you have done."

Is this the man you mean?

I am sitting in Sam's " den " at Clere. He is engaged in receiving the " afterdavy " of a man who got his head broke by a tinker at the cricket match in the park (for Sam is in the commission, and sits on the bench once a month " a perfect Midas," as Mrs. Wattlegum would say). I am busy rigging up one of these wonderful new Yankee spoons with a view to killing a villainous pike, who has got into the trout-water. I have just tied on the thirty-ninth hook, and have got the fortieth ready in my fingers, when a footman opens the door, and says to me:

" If you please, sir, your stud groom would be glad to see you."

I keep two horses of all work and a grey pony, so that the word " stud " before the word " groom " in the last sentence must be taken to refer to my little farm, on which I rear a few colts annually.

" May he come in, Sam? " I ask.

" Of course! Uncle Jeff," says he.

And so there comes a little old man, dressed in the extreme of that peculiar dandyism which is affected by retired jockeys and trainers, and which I have seen since attempted, with indifferent success, by a few young gentlemen at our great Universities. He stands in the door and says:

" Mr. Plowden has offered forty pound for the dark chestnut colt, sir."

" Dick," I say (mark that if you please), " Dick, I think he may have the brute."

And so, my dear reader, I must at last bid you heartily farewell. I am not entirely without hope that we may meet again.